SINNERS
&
ROCK STAR

JACKIE COLLINS

Jackie Collins brings the wild and sexy world of superstardom alive. Her phenomenally successful novels have made her as famous as the movers and shakers, power-brokers and superstars she writes about with an insider's knowledge. With 200 million copies of her books sold in more than forty countries, Jackie Collins is one of the world's top-selling writers. In a series of sensational bestsellers, she has blown the lid off Hollywood life and loves. 'It's all true,' she says. 'I write about real people in disguise. If anything, my characters are toned down – the real thing is much more bizarre.'

There have been many imitators, but only Jackie Collins can tell you what *really* goes on in the fastest lane of all. From Beverly Hills bedrooms to a raunchy prowl along the streets of Hollywood. From glittering rock parties and concerts to stretch limos and the mansions of the power-brokers – Jackie Collins chronicles the *real* truth.

JACKIE COLLINS

SINNERS
&
ROCK STAR

PAN BOOKS

Rock Star first published 1988 by William Heinemann
Sinners first published as *Sunday Simmons and Charlie Brick* 1972
by W. H. Allen & Co. Ltd

This omnibus edition published 2002 by Pan Books
an imprint of Pan Macmillan Ltd
Pan Macmillan, 20 New Wharf Road, London N1 9RR
Basingstoke and Oxford
Associated companies throughout the world
www.panmacmillan.com

ISBN 0 330 41505 0

Copyright © Jackie Collins 1972, 1984

The right of Jackie Collins to be identified as the
author of this work has been asserted by her in accordance
with the Copyright, Designs and Patents Act 1988.

I Fall in Love Too Easily © 1944 (renewed 1972) Metro-Goldwyn-Mayer Inc.
Used by permission of Columbia Pictures Publications/international Music Publications

Yesterday © 1965 Northern Songs under licence to SBK Songs Ltd,
3/5 Rathbone Place, London W1P 1DA

1 3 5 7 9 8 6 4 2

A CIP catalogue record for this book is available from
the British Library.

Printed and bound in Great Britain by
Mackays of Chatham plc, Chatham, Kent

SINNERS

For my brother,
Bill Collins,
who has always
been there for me

Herbert Lincoln Jefferson stared disgustedly at his wife Marge. She sprawled on a couch in front of the television, legs apart, displaying fat white thighs, eating an orange so that the juice dribbled down her chin, and holding a beer can from which she took occasional swigs. She was wearing a blue cotton dress which was so tight that it had split under one arm. Her huge bosom hung in a dirty white bra which peeked through the split. A stranger seeing her would have found it hard to judge her age, and perhaps assessed her as ten years older than she was. Actually she was thirty-five.

'I'm going,' Herbert announced.

Marge didn't shift her eyes from the TV set. She crammed some more orange into her mouth and mumbled, 'O.K., hon.'

Herbert left the faded pink house, one in a row of many faded houses. He kicked viciously at Marge's cat which wandered under his feet, and started the walk to the bus stop. It was early evening and particularly hot. Herbert felt enraged that he had no car. Everyone had a car in Los Angeles. Last week he had had a beautiful shiny grey Chevrolet, but they had taken it away as he hadn't kept up the payments.

Herbert was of medium height, a thin man, with brown hair and sharp features. He wasn't good-looking, he wasn't ugly, he was just perfectly ordinary-looking. He was the sort of man you never remembered, that is unless he stared at you with his oblique brown eyes, and then suddenly you would get an odd sort of shudder. His eyes were mean and cruel and grabbing.

There was a young Mexican girl at the bus stop in front of him, and he appraised her quickly. Too skinny and too young, but a virgin, he was sure of that. He pressed up against her as they boarded the bus, and she turned round and gave him a startled look. He ignored her and took a seat next to a plump matron, probably some rich movie star's housekeeper. No, if she was, she would have her own car.

There was a musty smell of dried sweat in the bus, and Herbert wrinkled up his nose in disgust. He had taken a shower before coming out. Sometimes he showered four or five times a day. The man he really admired was Tiny Tim, because he had read somewhere that he showered every time he took a leak. Herbert really admired such cleanliness.

The plump matron shifted in her seat. She didn't like the pressure of Herbert's leg beside her. But he stared straight ahead with his ordinary face, and she was sure he couldn't be doing it purposely.

The old bag's wearing suspenders, Herbert thought. One of them was digging into him. He moved his arm so that it nudged against the side of her bosom. She squashed nearer to the window, and Herbert stared impassively forward.

At the next stop the woman got out, and Herbert shifted his knees so that she had to squeeze past him. He felt the outline of her big buttocks against his knees, and he laughed silently. Old cow, give her a thrill. They all loved a thrill, even the old ones.

He thought lovingly about the letter he had sent to sexy red-headed film star, Angela Carter. He had mailed it the previous evening, and she had probably read it by now. He had managed to get her home address; that was an advantage of doing the job he was in now. They had a file in the office of most of the film stars' addresses. He was working for a chauffeur service employed by Radiant Productions. It was most important when writing to people that you were sure they would open the letter themselves. That was the whole point.

To Angela he had written lovingly in glowing and explicit terms about what he would like to do to her. No detail had been spared and he enclosed a small plastic bag into which he had proudly masturbated.

It was one of his better literary efforts, and he hoped that Miss Angela Carter appreciated it.

The bus arrived at his stop and he walked the short distance to the Supreme Chauffeur Company.

2

The woman caressed the man beneath her, and in return his hands stroked her arched naked back.

She was beautiful in no conventional sense. Long wild hair, framing a tanned, almost animalistic face. Eyes a mixture of brown and yellow. Mouth wide and sensual.

They lay on a bed with black silk sheets, one sheet covering the woman just below her waist. She had a marvellous body, a combination of long limbs, curves and fine muscles.

She sighed and bent to kiss the man. He was also naked. A brown hard body with hairs on his chest and a fine display of muscles.

As they kissed she reached down to the floor, and from under the bed produced a small gun which she stealthily brought up to his head.

Ending the kiss she whispered, 'Goodbye, Mr Fountain.'

In one quick movement he threw her off him and twisted the gun from her hand.

Furious, she crouched on the floor glaring at him.

He laughed. 'Better luck next time, baby, you're not dealing with a Boy Scout.'

She brought up her arm to try to strike him, and a voice shouted 'Cut.'

Sunday Simmons's hands flew to cover herself. Quickly a wardrobe lady appeared and threw a robe around her.

Abe Stein, the director, strolled over. He was fat, and chewing on an ancient, stinking cigar. He spoke to the man lying on the bed. 'Sorry, Jack, too much tit.'

Jack Milan grinned. He was a well-preserved forty-nine, with jet black hair and a smile that had kept him hot at the box-office for twenty years. 'There's never too much tit for me, Abe old boy.'

Everyone within earshot laughed, except Sunday who huddled miserably on the floor, clutching the robe around her.

Why had she ever agreed to do this film? In Italy, in fact in most European countries, she was regarded as almost a star; and here in Hollywood, she was treated as a nothing.

Abe addressed himself to her. 'Look, honey, I know you got a gorgeous pair of boobs there, but just keep them pointed at Mr Milan, huh?'

'I'm sorry,' she said stiffly. 'When he throws me to the floor it is very difficult. Perhaps if you let me wear some sort of covering, as I wanted to . . .'

'No, those things look worse than nothing.' He was referring to 'patsies' which some female stars insisted on wearing in any kind of nude scenes. They were round flesh-coloured pads which stuck over the nipples. Sunday had asked to wear them, but her contract for the film stipulated she had to do what the film company wanted, and they wanted no patsies. So here she was, exposed, except for a brief pair of panties, to the entire unit, which seemed to have doubled itself on this day.

She dreaded having to remove the robe again.

As if reading her thoughts, Abe said, 'Get on the bed, let me show you what I mean. Do you mind, Jack? Shall I get your stand-in?'

'Do I mind? Just get me a Scotch and a cigarette, and I'll shoot this scene all day!'

More laughter, and Sunday reluctantly took off her robe. She tried not to care, tried to blank out the grinning faces watching her.

She got on the bed, partly under the sheets, and half lying across Jack Milan.

'Now let's take it in slow motion,' Abe said. 'Show me how you throw her off you.'

Jack's strong arms lifted her slowly and edged her sideways. Abe's fat arms brushed across her until both men were holding her.

'Try and keep her towards you like this,' Abe said. 'That's it, marvellous. Now on the floor, dear, when you go to hit him, just make sure your back is to the camera. Like this.'

Once more he handled her body, and this time she was sure his fat hands didn't slide across her breasts by accident.

'We'll break for lunch now.' He turned to Jack Milan who climbed out of the bed, wearing orange jockey shorts and matching socks. 'Everyone back by two p.m. sharp. Come on, Jack, I'll buy you that Scotch.'

Sunday walked slowly to her dressing room. She was close to tears. It was so humiliating to be treated like this. She had thought a Jack Milan film would be a good thing to do, but it had turned out to be just another girl in a multi-girl spy film. She had been so anxious to leave Rome that she had hardly even looked at the script. And she had wanted to see Hollywood; the nearest she had been before was Rio, where she was born.

Sunday had had a happy childhood. Her father was South American and her mother French, and the two nationalities were very compatible.

By the time she was sixteen she had decided to be an actress, and she persuaded her parents to send her to a dramatic academy in London. It was the best, and arrangements were made for Sunday to stay in London with her mother's elder sister, Aunt Jasmin. Of course, she was to return to Rio for all vacations, and immediately if she didn't care for England.

It didn't make any difference whether she cared or not. Her parents were killed in a car crash two days after she left.

Sunday was heartbroken. She blamed herself, reasoning that if she had been there it might not have happened.

Her father left hardly any money at all. Generous, he had lived big, spending and lending in every direction.

After the funeral, Sunday decided to stay in London and continue her studies. She had a few thousand pounds left to her by her mother.

It was a far different life for her to adjust to. A small apartment in Kensington, the cold weather, and Aunt Jasmin, who thought it a sin to show any affection.

Sunday found this strange and worrying. She *needed* love and affection, and it seemed there was no-one she could turn to.

She threw herself into her work at the academy.

One day after she had been there a year and a half, she met Raf Souza.

Raf was a dynamic young man, currently the most in-demand fashion photographer and very aware of it. He turned up at the school with three thin model girls, a hairdresser, a battery of equipment, and three huge dogs. He had permission to use the

9

interior of the academy for a *Vogue* lay-out with students in the background.

At that time, Sunday wore her hair flattened down and scraped back. She dressed for the cold, wearing at least three sweaters and baggy trousers. She wore no makeup.

Raf picked her out immediately, made her loosen her hair, and had her kneeling with the dogs looking up at the three model girls.

She was secretly delighted, but to the other students she pretended it was an awful bore.

When Raf left he handed her his card and said, 'If you want to see the pictures, drop around tomorrow about six.'

Raf's studio was the wrong end of Fulham Road, and it took her ages to find it. He hardly gave her a glance when she arrived, just threw the contact sheets at her.

She studied them intently. How blank her face looked beside the models. How lumpy she appeared in her loads of sweaters.

'How old are you?' Raf asked casually.

'Nearly seventeen. Why?'

'Just wondered. I had an idea you might be good for. You want to try some test shots?'

'Yes, I'd like to.'

'If they're any good it will mean a week abroad plus all expenses paid and a hundred quid.'

Raf was no fool. He was getting paid a thousand for the job, and if he took a really good professional model it would dig deeper than a hundred. Anyway, he saw great potential in this girl. That fabulous skin would photograph a million dollars in colour, and with the right makeup and hairstyle she would be a knock-out. He was fed up with the usual faces. They all looked the same. This girl could be quite a diversion.

Raf, in his short career, had been to bed with many of the top photographic models, lady editors of magazines, and generally any female who could do him some good. He was stocky, untidy, with a little-boy smile that turned women on.

He tried it now on Sunday. 'What do you think? Could you make it with no family problems?'

She thought how nice he was. 'Yes, I'm sure I could Term ends tomorrow and I didn't have any definite plans.'

'Great! Let's get started. You'd better get out of your clothes. I'll give you a shirt to put on. Oh, and take your hair down, it looks terrible scruffed back like that.'

She had second thoughts. What sort of pictures did he want to take anyway? She hesitated when he threw her a shirt.

He noticed her hesitation. 'They're going to be fashion shots, darling, beach jazz and harem gear, I've got to see if you've got a body underneath all that. Get changed upstairs if you like.' He busied himself with a camera.

She took the shirt, went upstairs, and put it on over her bra and pants. It looked quite decent. Then she loosened her hair and padded quietly downstairs.

Christ! Raf thought, he'd picked a winner this time. The girl was magnificent. She had the most incredible long legs, and he imagined the wild shots he could do with her. Her breasts jutted through the shirt, and she had a special kind of walk. Very, very sexy.

He spent an hour taking photographs. She fell into poses naturally. He couldn't wait to get her out of that shirt. Apart from fancying her, she was going to make this assignment really good.

Arrangements were made, and they went to Morocco.

Raf, who used women purely as a convenience, found himself completely fascinated by Sunday.

Because of the situation with her aunt, Sunday found herself spending more and more time with him. On her seventeenth birthday he made love to her, and shortly afterwards she moved into his studio.

Aunt Jasmin accepted the move as she accepted everything else in life, tight-lipped and silent.

'I'll keep in touch,' Sunday promised.

Aunt Jasmin just shrugged her disapproval.

Raf was the first person Sunday had been really close to since her parents died. They lived together for several months, Sunday finishing her last term at the academy, and Raf getting on with his work. Then the pictures of Sunday in Morocco appeared, and the magazine was inundated with calls wanting to know who she was. There were offers for her to do a hair commercial, a toothpaste commercial, and a film company wanted to test her.

Raf withdrew into a black mood. Sunday was thrilled.

The magazine wanted Raf to arrange another session with her immediately. He talked her out of doing the commercials, although the money was excellent. But she insisted that she wanted to do the film test.

Raf took her to Rome, and while they were taking the photographs she fell in love with the city. It reminded her of Rio.

When they got back she did the part in the film she had tested for.

Raf brooded, extremely jealous about having to share her. For the first time since she came to live with him he had other women, got drunk before she came home, and took to insulting and ridiculing her in front of their friends.

She couldn't understand why Raf had become so bitter towards her. What had she done?

But he couldn't explain how he felt about her success, that he was terrified of losing her.

She did a couple of other small parts, and then the first movie appeared and she received an offer to do a film in Rome.

'Take it,' Raf said bitterly, 'we're about through anyway.' And to settle the matter he told her he had found someone else.

Sunday was quite successful in Rome, appearing in a string of movies that usually showed off her more physical charms.

All thoughts of becoming a 'serious actress' were pushed to the back of her mind. She enjoyed the excitement and attention she seemed to create wherever she went.

The Italian men chased after her in full force, but her thoughts remained with Raf. He had been her first man and she had loved him. She had *thought* he loved her.

Then Paulo appeared on the scene. Count Paulo Gennerra Rizzo. He was to bring nothing but trouble.

'Miss Simmons.' There was a knock on her dressing-room door. 'Miss Simmons, you're wanted on the set please.'

Automatically she checked herself in the mirror and vaguely realised she hadn't had any lunch. Oh well, back to the charming Abe Stein and delightful Jack Milan, who hadn't addressed one word to her. What a way to start one's first day's work in Hollywood.

12

On the set there was much activity. Word had spread about the nude scene, and little groups of men whom she hadn't noticed before were dotted around the sidelines. She also noticed several men with cameras who hadn't been there before. Neither Jack Milan nor Abe Stein was present.

A makeup man with whom she had argued that morning approached her. It had been a silly argument as far as Sunday was concerned. She had asked to do her own eye makeup, as she always did, and the man had refused. That annoyed her, as she knew her face a lot better than someone who had merely glanced at her for five minutes. She insisted, and the man stamped out of the room in a fury, muttering about 'Dirty foreign starlets.'

Now he approached her with a cake of makeup and a sponge. He said, 'Take your robe off. I've got to check your body makeup.'

She glared at the man who had gathered a bunch of mates to watch the fun. 'Where is the woman who did it this morning?' she asked.

'On another set. Don't be bashful, everybody's seen your big tits already!'

She felt her face blaze, and turned to leave the set, bumping into Jack Milan and Abe.

'Where are you rushing off to, honey?' Abe asked, gripping her arm with his fleshy hand. 'Let's get this scene in the can, come on.' He pulled her back to the set.

She had a sudden feeling that she wasn't going to be able to take her robe off in front of this whole group. She said to Abe: 'In Italy when we shoot such a scene, the set is cleared until only the essential technicians remain. I would like that done here please.'

'Oh, would you?' Abe coughed and spat. 'This isn't Italy, honey, and all these guys are needed around here.'

Sunday, who rarely lost her temper, was burning now. 'In that case you can shoot the scene without me. I am not an animal to be stared at. I am an actress.'

'Ha!' Abe snorted. 'An actress, huh? One that can't even keep her tits out of the camera. Don't get high-hat with me, baby, you've got a contract, remember?'

'Yes, I am well aware of that. However, I cannot work under these condition. I'm so sorry.'

And with that, she walked off the set.

It was the first time anyone had walked off a Jack Milan movie.

3

Charlie Brick and the girl sat side by side in the dimly-lit restaurant overlooking Park Lane. Several waiters hovered nearby, ready to spring forward at the slightest sign from the man.

They sipped coffee, the girl eagerly, bright eyes darting all over the place. She was pretty and young. Charlie was much older, nearing forty. He had a long sad face, and wore heavy horn-rimmed glasses.

'I wish my mum could see me now!' the girl said suddenly.

'What, my darling?' Charlie leaned closer towards her, groping for her hand under the tablecloth.

'My mum,' the girl continued brightly. 'She just wouldn't believe it, me sitting here in a place like this with you.'

'Why not?' He gave her hand a tight squeeze.

'Well, y'know,' she giggled. 'They could hardly believe it when I won that beauty competition and came to London; they're a bit square where I come from. So you can imagine what they would think if they knew I was sitting in some posh old restaurant with a real live film star!'

'You're such a pretty little thing.'

She looked pleased. 'Do you think so?' She covered his hand with her own. 'My mum always said I should be on the movies.' She looked at him hopefully. 'What do *you* think?'

He let go of her hand and summoned one of the nearby waiters. 'I think it's time we were going. I have a very early call in the morning.'

'Oh,' she looked disappointed. 'I thought you were going to show me your new stills back at the hotel.'

'Some other time.' His attitude had changed; it was distant, hurried.

The head waiter came rushing over. 'Everything all right, Mr Brick?'

Charlie stood up. 'Thank you, Luigi, it was fine.'

'I saw your latest film last week, Mr Brick, sir. It was funny, very funny indeed. It's a pleasure to have you here tonight.'

'Thank you, Luigi.'

They moved out into the cold London night; it was spitting with rain. The doorman sprang to attention. 'Evening, Mr Brick, sir, your car's just coming.'

A long black Bentley rolled into sight. They climbed in.

'Thank you, sir, thank you very much,' the doorman said as he was handed a large tip.

The car slid silently off.

'Where to?' the chauffeur asked.

'Drop me back at the hotel, George, and then take Miss Marymont home.'

'Yes, sir.' George allowed himself a fleeting smile. Another choked bird to deliver home!

They drove to the hotel in silence. The girl too nonplussed by his sudden change of mood to know what to say.

'Are you sure you don't want me to come up?' she asked upon arrival.

'That's very sweet of you, love, but you know, it's the old five a.m.-up bit. I'll call you some time next week.' He got quickly out of the car. 'Bye.'

He stood and watched the car thread its way slowly back among the traffic. Foolish little girl, he thought. Was that really the only reason they went out with him. Did they honestly believe that he could be used to get them into the movies?

How many times had he heard it now? How many different ways? The direct approach: *Do you think you could get me a screen test?* The oblique hint: *I've always wanted to act.* The actress's approach: *My agent says I'm perfect for the girl's part in your next film.*

Lorna had warned him, laughed at him. 'Oh yes, sure,' she

had said, 'you'll have tons of little girls just lining up to jump into bed with you. But ask yourself, my darling, is it *you* they want? Or is it Charlie Brick?'

The divorce had been final just one month now. Twelve years of marriage shattered. Lorna with another man. The children shuttled back and forth between them. And a terrible loneliness that couldn't be filled, however many people he was with.

He walked into the hotel. The desk clerk immediately sent a bellboy rushing over to him. 'There is a call coming through from Hollywood for you, Mr Brick, sir.'

'I'll take it in my suite,' he said.

The liftman was pleased to see him. 'My little girl was thrilled to bits with the photo, Mr Brick. She's seen your last film four times now.'

Charlie smiled, always pleased to hear praise.

The phone was ringing as he entered his suite. It was his agent, Marshall K. Marshall, calling from Hollywood to check certain details about his arrival the following week. He was due to start work on his next film.

They had a short chat about things, and Marshall concluded by saying, 'Charlie, we'll be looking forward to seeing you on the twenty-eighth. Everyone will be at the reception.' There was a slight pause, then: 'Do you want me to line up any broads for you?' He named a couple of well-known bit players. 'No? All right then, I'm sure you can manage on your own.'

They said their goodbyes and Charlie hung up.

He paced around the room restlessly. There seemed to be a conspiracy on everyone's part to annoy him with sly little digs. He could hardly imagine Robert Redford or Michael Caine being asked if they needed to be fixed up with a date. Why him? Oh yes, he knew he wasn't exactly a matinée idol, but he had his own teeth and hair, and a pleasant enough face, rather distinguished-looking really. And since he had lost all that weight for his last picture he was in rather good shape. After all, he was still quite young, and he never had any trouble getting girls to go to bed with him. As a matter of fact it was a job to get rid of them later. A quick look at the watch, 'My God! Is that really the time? I had no idea!'—and eventually they would take the hint and go.

The penthouse suite was cold and impersonal in spite of the wealth of possessions strewn around. Cameras, books, scripts, an elaborate stereo set and stacks of records.

He wouldn't be sorry to leave it: A hotel room never gave one any feeling of permanence.

The phone rang again. He picked it up.

'I dropped the lady home,' said his chauffeur. 'She didn't seem too pleased. Do you need anything else tonight?'

'No.' he yawned. 'Think I'll get into bed. Make it about eight in the morning. Night, George.' He hung up. Almost immediately the phone rang again.

The voice on the other end was female and heavily accented. It said reproachfully, 'Darling, you didn't call, what happened?'

Kristen Sweetzer, a large-bosomed would-be actress he had met at a party the night before and had a scene with. He had been quite smashed, and only vaguely remembered her.

'Oh, hello, love,' he said. 'Sorry, did I say I'd call today?'

'Yes, darling, but I'll forgive you just this once.' There was a short pause, and then, 'Well, darling, when am I going to see you again?'

He suddenly remembered that he couldn't stand her. She reminded him of a bossy gym mistress, always talking in her unattractive guttural accent. 'We'll go back to my place,' she had stated the night before. Not would you like to? Or shall we? And he had gone.

'Listen, love,' he said, 'let's go out to dinner later in the week. I'm a bit tied up these next few days, but I'll call you soon, all right?'

She sighed, 'I was looking forward to seeing you more quickly.'

He stood his ground, 'Thursday or Friday, I'll speak to you then.'

'Very well, but I think you're a naughty man!'

He shuddered at her choice of adjective. 'Yes, love, you're probably right.' He put the receiver down quickly, before she could continue the conversation.

Women never failed to disappoint him. For as long as he could remember they had always managed to let him down.

Even his ex-wife Lorna, after all the years they had been together, had finally proved herself to be like all the rest.

The bitter memories of the last few months came rushing back. The accusations on both sides, the days of long silences followed by interminable rows. And worst of all, the utter hate and lack of interest Lorna seemed to project towards him.

He bought her presents, jewelry, furs, a new car. She accepted them all in a cold unthrilled way, the way she accepted him in bed. She had never been of a very passionate nature, but in the last months, before the end, forget it. His very touch seemed to make her shrivel away from him. One memorable night he had been lying on top of her, trying to do what he had to as quickly as possible, when she had started to cry, long stifled sobs. He had withdrawn quickly, and felt there could be no greater distance between them than this.

When he thought of Lorna he imagined that perhaps she was all the things a woman should be. But had he really behaved so badly that she couldn't find it in herself to forgive him?

In the end it had been *she* who had ended it, *not* he.

He stopped thinking about the past, and put his mind to the future.

Charlie Brick, a name well-known to millions. He had made a lot of films. A lot of money. Not bad after starting his career touring the variety halls as a comedian for fifteen pounds a week. If he didn't want to, he need not work for the rest of his life. It was a comforting thought.

His mother lived in a handsome house in Richmond with two servants, a car and chauffeur. His two children had money in trust for them. He had insisted. Lorna had not wanted a penny from him, but he had seen that the children were well looked after. On the material side, things couldn't be better.

The new picture should be interesting. The director was an old friend of his. His co-star, Michelle Lomas, was also an old friend, although in a different way. Michelle was a big star, a big voluptuous woman. Discovered in the south of France wearing a bikini at the age of nineteen, now, ten years later, she had an international reputation, both as an actress and a woman. Charlie had first met her five years previously, when his career

18

as a film actor was jogging along nicely and hers beginning to smoulder.

For the first time in a film, instead of being just a comedy actor, he had been given the romantic interest as well. Women everywhere took to him immediately in his new role as lover. If he was good enough to make love to Michelle Lomas, then he was good enough for them.

The letters started to pour in, and his career started to zoom.

It was the beginning of the end as far as Lorna and he were concerned.

The start of his affair with Michelle had changed his life a great deal. In the beginning he just couldn't believe that a famous sex symbol, probably *the* most famous European sex symbol of that time, could possibly fancy him. But fancy him she had. Most of the arrangements had been manoeuvred by her. She had a husband who conveniently stayed in Paris and appeared only occasionally.

'You are a wonderful man,' she used to purr at him. 'A wonderful lover, the best.'

No-one had ever said anything like that to him before. He had always felt inadequate, or, at the very most, average in bed. But Michelle had changed all that: She made him feel like a king.

Of course his marriage suffered. He would return home from the studio later and later. At weekends, he would always say he had to work. In the end he hardly ever saw Lorna; they just happened to live in the same house.

Occasionally they saw each other long enough for a brief exchange of insults.

Lorna: 'I know you're screwing that big French cow.'

Charlie: 'I don't understand you, how can you say that?'

Lorna: 'You're like a dog after a bitch in heat. What a fool you're making of yourself.'

And so it went on, fight after fight, insult after insult, until one day things really came to a head. Charlie was planning to follow Michelle back to France. She had been gone two weeks following the completion of their film, and they spoke on the phone every day.

'My husband will be away in the south for ten days,' she told him at last. 'He will be leaving tomorrow, you can come then.'

It was unfortunate that this should have coincided with his daughter's birthday, and Lorna had arranged a party. He told her he had to leave immediately for discussions about a film.

She stared at him very long and very hard. 'If you go to her,' she said very slowly, 'then hold yourself responsible for the consequences.'

When he returned things were different. There were no more fights, because Lorna was very rarely there to argue with. She seemed to manage to be just going out whenever he came in. She stayed away from home at night, not even bothering to say where she was.

He didn't question her. He was too involved with planning to see Michelle as often as possible.

His career continued to progress in the best possible way. He found himself in the enviable position of being able to pick and choose what films he would do. His notices were always the best: 'CHARLIE BRICK SHINES AGAIN'; 'BRICK SAVES THE FILM'; 'THE COMIC GENIUS OF CHARLIE BRICK'.

Lorna and he decided to move from their country home to a penthouse in Knightsbridge. The affair with Michelle had more or less finished, due to the fact that they were both working in different countries, and meetings became impossible to arrange.

Of course he realised he had been a fool. It had all been his fault. But the actual thing of making it with Michelle Lomas had been too much for him to miss. He felt in a funny sort of way that maybe he and Lorna would be closer because of it.

She didn't feel the same. She was cold and unfriendly in spite of his attentiveness.

He decided to buy the penthouse in the hope that new surroundings would bring them together again.

Lorna did not become enthusiastic about it. She insisted they hire an interior decorator, and left the whole thing to him.

Two weeks after they moved in, Charlie had to go to Spain. When he returned, Lorna had moved out. She had left the children, and a short note saying: *This is all your fault, don't ever blame me.*

She had vanished, and it took Charlie two weeks to find her.

A private detective discovered her in a hotel room in Bayswater, in bed with an out-of-work stuntman. The detective took photos, and that was that. One divorce coming up.

At first Charlie couldn't believe that Lorna would leave him for a 'nothing', a 'nobody'. Why, the man wasn't even good-looking.

But Lorna didn't seem to care about anything. 'Go ahead and divorce me,' was all she said, 'it will be a pleasure.'

He was left with the children, a nanny, his chauffeur, and a huge penthouse.

He could hardly believe it. He had finished with Michelle. He wanted Lorna. She was his wife. Couldn't she understand that? He was prepared to forgive her for the stuntman. Surely she should forgive him? For the children alone she should be prepared to try again.

But she didn't want to know.

She moved in with her boyfriend, and shortly afterwards her lawyer demanded the children. The law being what it was, she got them, but Charlie had ample access.

He sold the penthouse and moved into a hotel suite. He spent long evenings alone, sometimes just staring blankly at a wall, sometimes getting stoned on pot.

There were many girls. One night he would be with a stripper, the next with a married woman whose husband just happened to be out of town.

And they all let him down. One by one they tried to use him in some way or other.

With all of them he told his story: how unhappy he was: how his wife had left him for another man: how life and success only meant something if shared.

The women he saw more than once all half-expected him to propose. He hinted at it all the time. He made them each feel as if she were the only woman he wanted. But he treated them badly, stood them up, never called when he said he would, contacted them only when he felt like it, sometimes at two in the morning. He felt, in a way, he was getting his own back on Lorna. A different woman every night. But none of them meant anything.

It was a big change from the days when he had gone after

Lorna. *He* had been the chaser then, and she had certainly given him a hard time.

They had met at a party in Manchester. He could remember his first impression of her very clearly as she was so unlike any other girls he had met. Her hair was pale yellow, pulled severely back into a bun, and she wore huge National Health glasses, which made her face look strangely small and pathetic. She wore no makeup, and was a bit on the short side. No raving beauty by any means, but to Charlie she was lovely.

Within a year they were married and spent their wedding night in the best hotel in Manchester, an extravagance they could hardly afford but which Charlie decided would be worth it. It wasn't.

Although he had been seeing her for nearly a year, it hadn't been an every night thing. Most of the time he was travelling round the country, and their time together had been limited. She lived with her family and had told him firmly and clearly, early on in the relationship, that there would be 'none of that' until she got married.

It was one of the reasons he decided to marry her. He was getting plenty of 'that' elsewhere, and the thought of a 'nice' girl he could marry and have children with was appealing. Besides, she really seemed to care about him. And he certainly cared about her.

At twenty-one Lorna was still a virgin, and from the way she carried on, it seemed she planned to stay that way.

She had undressed in the bathroom, and then refused to come out until all the lights were out. She then made a quick dive into bed, and by the time Charlie had washed and cleaned his teeth, she appeared to be asleep, bundled up beneath the covers with her dressing-gown still on. He slid into bed beside her.

After ten months of seeing each other as often as possible, they were still complete strangers as far as their bodies were concerned.

'Are you asleep?' he whispered, trying to work his hands beneath her tightly-tied dressing-gown.

No reply.

After a struggle he reached her breasts. He played with them gently. She lay as if still asleep, eyes tightly shut.

It was very exciting for him to fondle this strange motionless body. After a short while he became so excited that he pulled all the bedclothes away and roughly yanked her nightdress above her waist.

She opened her eyes rapidly and started to protest.

She was the only virgin he had ever been with, and he became so carried away that he forgot about the fact that it was her first time. He bore down, harder and harder, until at last he came to a shuddering, shattering halt, and fell off her exhausted.

She lay there sobbing until gradually the sound of her crying got through to him. He lazily reached out and put his arm around her. 'It's all right,' he said tenderly. 'Nothing to worry about.'

'It's not all right.' Her voice was harsh between her sobs.

'What are you talking about?' He was genuinely surprised. 'I love you. I know it's not good for you the first time, but it's best to do it quickly, get it over with. Next time you'll love it, you'll see.'

But the next time didn't happen for months, and when she finally did consent, it was only under protest.

On the few occasions they made love she lay beneath him as stiff and as still as a board. Perhaps if she had liked it better Michelle would never have happened . . .

Things improved when Charlie got a job in London. It was only in a run-down nightclub, but it was better than trudging from town to town week after week.

Lorna was pleased. They rented a small flat in Old Compton Street. It was no more than one large room, but it was somewhere permanent, more or less. Apart from their unsatisfactory sex life things were fine.

Charlie stayed at the nightclub for three years. He was sort of M.C. and comedian rolled into one, and although it was a clip-joint, it was a good steady living.

He was seen there one night by an American producer, who arrived backstage. 'I want you to come to my office tomorrow and read for the part of Bernie the Pimp in my new show. It's a small cameo, but important, very showy.'

Charlie started to protest that he wasn't an actor, but the

producer thrust his card at him and said it didn't matter, he was just right.

The next day he read for the part and got it.

After six weeks of touring, the show finally came to London, and Charlie with his 'small cameo' part walked off with all the reviews. The show was panned, but he came out of it glowing.

He got himself an agent, and slowly but surely things started to happen. Another show, in which he again stole all the reviews. A small part in a film. A television appearance which turned into a highly successful series. A play. Several more films, and then the big break—a major British comedy film in which he was the star. From there he never looked back.

After his success in the first show, Lorna became pregnant and they had a son—Sean. Then two years later, a little girl—Cindy. They moved into a big house in Wimbledon, and everything was fine until the film with Michelle.

Charlie wondered how Michelle would greet him. It had been nearly two years since they had last met. He was so fed up with the endless procession of girls who were only too willing to jump into bed with him at the mention of his name or the thought of being seen *out* with him. A woman like Michelle was different. Thank God.

He reached for one of the many scripts stacked on a table. He liked to read everything sent to him. That way there was no chance of missing out on anything good that might go to another actor.

He started to read. Thinking about Lorna had depressed him, but he soon became immersed in the script, and fell asleep while reading.

4

Carey St Martin was a tall attractive black girl of twenty-eight. She wore her hair in a sleek Vidal Sassoon bob, and her clothes were smart and gave the impression of being expensive. She smoked twenty cigarettes a day, drove a pale beige year-old Thunderbird, and lived in an elegant three-room apartment high above the Strip.

Carey had done very well for herself.

It was a hot June day and the smog hung like cobwebs over Hollywood.

Carey yawned. What a drag for the agency to pick *her* to go and persuade Sunday Simmons to get her ass back on the picture. These starlets were all the same. Cute, dumb, bits of fluff, who had finally laid enough guys to get on film. Carey was proud to think that she had never laid anybody in *her* career to get where she was today.

She stopped at a red light, and a man in a Lincoln tried to catch her eye. She ignored him, and turned the air-conditioning higher. Wow—it was *hot!*

Carey worked for Marshall K. Marshall, one of the biggest agents in town. She had started as a secretary seven years ago, and now she was, and had been for two years, a personal representative, looking after some of the clients he handled. Actually for some time now Carey had been seriously thinking of branching out on her own. What she really wanted to do was personal management. *Carey St Martin, Public Relations & Management.* Incredible!

She parked her car near the Château Marmont where Sunday was staying, and picked up the contract lying on the seat beside her. It stipulated that Sunday Simmons was contracted to work three weeks for Milan Productions from June 3rd to the 24th. Clause three mentioned a nude scene from the waist up, as written in the script.

Carey wondered what Sunday's problem was. She must have read the contract before signing it.

Marshall had told her, 'Get the silly little broad back to the studio—and fast. If she's not back by four she's off the picture, and they'll probably sue. Anyway she won't be able to work anywhere else—stupid bitch!'

Carey put on green-tinted sunglasses and walked into the Château. She was wearing a green linen two-piece dress purchased at Orbach's, a Paris copy.

'Yes?' the little old lady at the desk glanced up.

She asked for Sunday's room. It was funny how the lobby of the Château always seemed like a piece of Hollywood long gone. Shades of *Sunset Boulevard*.

Sunday had a suite on the fifth floor and Carey took the newly decorated elevator. Her mind was dwelling on an office building nearby where she had looked at space the previous week. She really meant to break with Marshall soon.

Sunday answered the door. She was dressed in a short orange muu-muu, her feet were bare, and she still had on her film makeup.

Carey felt a jolt at the sheer magnetism of the girl's face. She held out her hand and said, 'Hi, I'm Carey St Martin. Marshall K. Marshall sent me over to see if we can get things sorted out.'

'I suppose you had better come in.' Sunday's big eyes were cloudy.

She led Carey into the living room, which was strewn with clothes and half-opened suitcases. Carey couldn't decide if she was packing or unpacking.

'Would you like a Coca-Cola? I'm afraid there's no ice.'

'Lovely. Can I get it?'

'No, that's all right.' Sunday padded into the kitchen.

Carey sat down and opened up the contract. She wondered if Marshall had seen this girl.

Sunday came back in and handed her a glass. 'I'm sorry about all this,' she said quickly. 'I know it makes me look like I'm being difficult, but really, I must explain it to you.'

'Yes, sure,' Carey replied, slightly taken aback. She hadn't expected the apologetic bit, rather the ranting and raving scene. 'By the way, if we can get you back on the set by four, all will be well.'

'I'm sorry, I can't go back. Not unless things are different.'

'You signed a contract, you know.'

26

'I do know. Everyone keeps on pointing it out to me. But I have certain principles, and one of them is to be treated like a human being—not a piece of prize meat. Let me tell you about it. I'm sure, as a woman you will understand.'

Carey was fascinated by Sunday's low husky voice, and the way she seemed to pick her words so precisely. She sat back and listened as Sunday related the whole story.

At the end she felt quite sorry for her. What a bunch of rat finks most guys were. However, it didn't really merit the walking off the film bit. After all, she wasn't a star, and only stars could get away with action like that. Besides which, there was still the contract to consider.

'Look, honey, I know it's tough. But the guys don't mean any harm, and you did agree to take your clothes off. Now how about if I take you back to the studio, have a word with Abe Stein, and stay there with you?'

Sunday shook her head stubbornly. 'No, I am definitely not going back. Not unless I get a formal apology from Mr Stein and a closed set.'

Carey sighed. 'You're asking the impossible.'

The phone rang and Sunday picked it up. The operator said, 'The "Hollywood Reporter" is on the line, dear, and three other calls from papers holding on.'

She covered the mouthpiece: 'The newspapers. What shall I tell them?'

Carey took the phone: 'Let me deal with it.' How the hell had they picked it up so quickly? She answered questions smoothly. No, Miss Simmons wasn't available for comment. Yes, it would all be sorted out. No, she had not had a fight with Jack Milan. Yes, Miss Simmons would be back on the set later on today.

'Why didn't you tell them the truth?' Sunday questioned after Carey had dealt with all the calls.

'Because, sweetheart, if you're smart we'll take off for the studio right now. You don't want a lawsuit on your hands, do you? And I gather you have plans for working in this town again. After all, everyone takes off their clothes today, there's nothing wrong with it.'

Sunday suddenly laughed. 'Carey, you're a nice girl, very

helpful, but we obviously are not going to see eye to eye on this, so I don't think I should waste any more of your time.'

Carey looked at her in surprise. Was she being dismissed? What a laugh! She had expected to walk in here, deal with some hysterical attention-grabbing actress, dump her back at the studios and that would have been that. Instead she was faced with a girl who seemed to know exactly what she was doing and went about it in a cool and calm fashion.

The phone rang again, and this time Sunday picked it up and kept it.

'Yes, this is she. Yes, that is correct. No, I will not be returning unless I get a formal apology from the director and Mr Milan. I feel that as a woman I have every right to be treated with respect and that . . .'

Carey listened in amazement. She had a funny feeling that Sunday Simmons was going to be a big star. She just felt it.

The interview was perfect. Carey could see it in print now. Abe Stein and Jack Milan were going to appear as the villains, and Sunday a put-upon innocent.

Oh boy, she had done her duty for Marshall K. Marshall; now how about looking at it from Sunday's point of view, and becoming her personal manager?

This girl was a natural.

5

London was going through a once-in-a-blue-moon heatwave, and Charlie was delighted that he had insisted on having a swimming pool built in his mother's Richmond garden.

It was the weekend, and he had arrived to spend the day with his children, who were staying with their grandmother for a few days. It seemed to him that Lorna was only too anxious to get rid of Cindy and Sean whenever she could. It was a bloody shame that the judge hadn't given *him* custody of them. Sean at eight, was sturdy and tough, and Cindy, two years younger, was a prettier version of her mother.

Charlie lay on a beach-chair next to his mother, watching them splash in the pool. She was a bird-like woman, clad in a two-piece swimsuit that showed off gnarled flesh and drooping bosom. She wore a vivid makeup, heavy rouge, green eye-shadow, and a splash of carmine for her mouth. Her hair was mostly hidden beneath a cyclamen scarf, and a cigarette drooped permanently from her mouth.

'I look wonderful for nearly sixty,' she would often proudly announce. And indeed there was always a 'gentleman friend' around.

Charlie adored his mother. Such a character, always happy, living life to its full potential. Serafina Brick, exile from the variety palaces of England.

Charlie had brought a girl with him. Her name was Polly Quinn. At least she didn't talk too much.

She emerged from the house wearing a polka-dot bikini. Bouncy breasts and baby rolls of fat around the middle. She settled herself on the grass, next to Charlie. 'Isn't this weather super?' she stated, and lying on her stomach she unhooked her bra strap. Not another word was heard out of her until lunch.

Natalie and Clay Allen and their three-year-old child arrived at twelve. Clay was one of Charlie's best friends, an ex-actor, now a successful screenwriter. They had known each other from the days of Charlie's first film. Natalie Allen was thin and attractive. She and Charlie had a sort of unspoken 'thing' going. He knew she fancied him, but she being Clay's wife and everything, nothing had actually been done about it. Once at a party when they had both been drunk, they had necked, but Charlie was rather ashamed of this one lapse.

'Hello, my darling,' Natalie said, 'What a divine day. I've simply got to strip off and collapse in the pool.' She kissed him on the cheek and set off for the house to change.

Clay squatted on the grass and indicated the lifeless body of Polly.

'Asleep,' Charlie explained.

Clay winked. 'Hard night, I expect,' he said with a chuckle.

29

Serafina cackled knowingly, as Cindy and Sean came running over to say hello.

Lunch was served in the garden.

'Who needs Hollywood?' Natalie said, spooning in mouthfuls of strawberries and cream. 'This is heavenly. Clay, darling, why can't we build a pool?'

'Because, my sweet, for the two weeks of summer we get a year it's just not worth it.'

'Charlie thought it was worth it. If he can do it, why can't we?'

There were times, Clay reflected, when Natalie was a pain in the bum.

'I wish you would sit down,' Charlie said to his mother, 'The maid will clear away.'

Serafina gave him one of her girlish smiles, revealing rotten teeth. 'I have too much nervous energy,' she trilled. 'I must keep on the go. That is my secret.'

'What secret?' asked Natalie.

'Eternal youth, my dear. Joy and vitality.'

Natalie looked at Clay, who quickly looked away. He knew she wanted to send the poor old lady up.

'Can we swim, daddy?' asked Cindy.

'Yes, come on. Want a dip, Poll?'

Polly had finished her lunch. She jumped up and obediently joined Charlie and the children as they raced for the pool.

'What a fat tub of lard,' Natalie remarked. 'Charlie really goes through all the scrubbers.'

Clay had just been admiring Polly's retreating bottom. 'Do you think so?' he asked mildly.

Natalie snorted: 'I suppose you fancy her. *You* would. Just your type, big breasts and fat ass.'

Yes, not bits of skin and bone like you, Clay thought. Since the birth of their baby, Natalie had dieted away to nothing.

In the pool Cindy sat on Charlie's shoulders, squeaking with joy. He dropped her into the water and she squealed for more. Polly leisurely swam the length of the pool and back again. Then she got out and flopped on the grass.

Charlie joined her. 'Where do you want to eat tonight?' he asked.

'I'm easy,' she spread her arms to the sun.

I know that, he thought. 'Well, let's have a bite at my hotel then. I'll get them to arrange something on the terrace.'

'Fine.' Her eyes were closed.

Actually he had already arranged everything before leaving. Champagne on ice. Caviar and sour cream, steak and asparagus.

Natalie came walking over. 'What day are you leaving?'

'Wednesday.'

'Only two weeks and we'll be there with you. It seems a shame to leave England with this wonderful weather.'

Charlie grimaced. 'I'll be glad to get away.'

Natalie put a sympathetic hand on his shoulder. 'I know. It's been rough for you.'

His eyes misted over. God, it was good to have friends. 'Yes, you do understand, don't you, love?'

'Of course I do. And anytime you want to talk about it, just don't hesitate to phone me. Clay is always so busy. I have lots of free time. If you want to have lunch or something before you go, call me. Really, Charlie, it would do you good to get it all off your chest. Actually I'm free tomorrow. I'll tell you what, I'll come by the hotel about twelve and we'll have a good old heart to heart.'

'I'm having lunch with my agent. It's awfully sweet of you but—'

'You know,' Natalie stared thoughtfully into space, 'I think I'm one of the few people who actually knew Lorna. We talked quite a bit, she confided a lot in me.'

'Did she?' Charlie was at once interested. 'What about tea tomorrow? I could be back at the hotel by three.'

'I think I could manage that.' Natalie glanced at Polly who was breathing evenly and seemed asleep. 'Only don't mention it to Clay. I'm supposed to be visiting his parents and he'll go all stuffy on me if I get out of it.'

The weather stayed hot for the whole day, and it was past seven by the time Charlie and Polly left.

At the hotel Polly collapsed in a chair and announced, 'I'm absolutely exhausted!'

Charlie looked at her in surprise. As far as he had seen she had spent the day flaked out on the grass, not moving a muscle.

He put on a new Sergio Mendes tape and rang the desk for his messages. His mind was half-occupied wondering if Polly would indulge in a little pot-smoking. He needed something to relax him.

The switchboard told him Mrs Lorna Brick had telephoned twice, and would he please return her call.

Charlie sat quite still by the telephone. Lorna had phoned him. Lorna, who hadn't even spoken to him, except through lawyers, for months. All thoughts of Polly, getting high, and dinner were forgotten.

Perhaps Lorna wanted to come back.

Perhaps he would take her back.

They had been through a lot together, and there were the children to consider. He had known all along that Lorna would see sense. She could fly to Hollywood with him, a sort of second honeymoon.

He glanced over at Polly, sprawled in a chair with her eyes closed.

'Listen, love, I'm rather done in myself. All that sun. Let's take a raincheck on dinner tonight. I'll call you a cab.'

Her eyes flicked open. 'I'm not *that* tired, Charlie.'

But he was already on the phone ordering her a taxi.

With Polly gone, he paced the room, wondering how to play it.

Should he be hard and unforgiving, softening as the conversation progressed? Or should he acquiesce immediately and say something like, 'We've both made our mistakes. Let's just forget about it and start afresh.'

He had a moment of doubt as to why Lorna was calling him, but the moment passed and he was sure it could only be for one thing. He dialled her number, feeling elated. It was almost like calling a girl you fancied for the first time.

A man's voice answered, which threw him. Hadn't the berk left yet?

Lorna got on the line, her familiar flat accent cool and impersonal. 'Hello, Charlie, thank you for phoning back.'

'That's all right.' He paused awkwardly, waiting for her to say something.

'How's everything?'

'Well, y'know, fine, I suppose. I just left Cindy and Sean.'

'Oh. Listen, Charlie, I want to ask you a favour.'

Here it came. He breathed deeply. 'Yes?'

'I would have asked your mother but she hardly talks to me any more. The thing is I'm getting married.'

'You're *what?*'

Her voice went very cold. 'Getting married, and I wondered if the children could stay with you in America on July 15th instead of the 29th. You see, I'm going to Africa on location with Jim, and I won't be here when they break up from school. I thought it would be better for them to be with you.'

Charlie was stunned. 'You're not actually marrying that—that stupid prick!'

'Let's not resort to childish insults, please, I can't stand it. Now that we're no longer connected with each other, can't we at least be civil? Can you take the children on that date or not?'

'Yes, I bloody well can. I can take them for good and all, get them out of your clutches.'

Lorna sighed. 'They'll be returning the end of August as arranged. I shall be back by then.'

'You silly cow. What are you marrying that layabout for? Is he a good screw? You don't even like to do that—so what for?'

'Goodbye, Charlie. My lawyer will take care of the details.' She hung up.

He stared blankly at the receiver. Rotten bitch! How could she possibly marry a lousy stuntman? It just wasn't logical, not when he was prepared to forgive and forget and have her back. Christ Almighty, why had he sent Polly home? Her body was just what he needed now.

It was great being a movie star, wasn't it? Just great. Sitting in a hotel suite all alone and no-one anywhere who gave a fuck. Charming! Perhaps it would have been better if he had stayed plain Charlie—not *the* Charlie Brick.

The phone rang and he wondered abruptly if it was Lorna ringing back to apologise.

It wasn't. It was Kristen Sweetzer.

'I thought you was going to call me?' she said reproachfully. 'We had such a good time together. When shall I see you?'

'Soon, love, soon. But this week's been impossible. I'm going away tomorrow. I'll call you when I get back.'

He wondered why he found it necessary to lie, to try to be nice. He had no intention of ever seeing the big horse again.

'Charlie, you are a *very* bad boy. But I shall forgive you. How long will you be away?'

'Not long. I must rush now. See you soon. Bye.' He replaced the receiver. He hated these women who chased him. They either gurgled with the thrill of being with a film star, or they tried to put him down, insulting him and his films in the hope that this would make them more interesting.

Damn Lorna and her stupid stuntman!

He wondered what Natalie would have to tell him tomorrow, something of interest he hoped. Determined not to spend the evening alone, he phoned his chauffeur and told him to get hold of a good movie they could run.

George, who was enjoying his day off, relaxing in bed with a plump secretary, reluctantly sent her home and did as his boss asked. He had a great job, more a sort of friend than an employee. He had been with Charlie six years, and he prided himself on always being available. With Charlie Brick you never knew what he would want, and whatever it was, George did his best.

6

Sunday liked Carey immediately, so when Carey asked if she might become her manager and press representative, Sunday was only too pleased.

She *didn't* want to stay off the movie, and she certainly *didn't* want to go back to Rome, but she was determined that Abe Stein and Jack Milan should apologise.

Once Carey realised that this was something about which Sunday was serious, she suddenly switched sides and came around to her way of thinking.

And it worked. Oh, how it worked.

The next day, Sunday was headlines. Nothing much else was happening. The papers were short of stories, so they played it up. Sunday was the hard-done-by heroine, and Abe and Jack were the big bad villains.

Carey arranged everything. She gave out brief ladylike press releases, arranged the right TV talk-shows, and by the end of the week Sunday was back on the film.

Abe Stein had sent her a short stilted letter, expressing his concern for her feelings and asking her forgiveness. He was furious about having to do it, but realised it was for the best.

Jack Milan threw a huge press party and was exceedingly charming to Sunday. Privately he said to his wife, 'The little bitch could really screw up my reputation.' He had read some of the letters from his fans who were shocked at his treatment of her.

Meanwhile Sunday's part in the film was enlarged, and the nude scene took place on a closed set, with Carey nearby. Abe ordered it printed after one take.

In spite of the fact that Carey had been telling Marshall for some time that she was going to leave, he was nevertheless upset. 'At least give a couple of weeks' notice,' he said. 'What am I supposed to do with Charlie Brick coming in any day, and the deal you were arranging for Salamanda Smith? I'm up to my ears with the TV package.'

'You're the one that taught me to be tough in this business and grab all the chances when they come,' Carey said, perching on his desk and swinging her long legs. 'Sorry, Marsh, but I'm grabbing. Send me Charlie Brick as a client if you like.'

'Listen, baby. Who are you kidding? You can't buck the big outfits here, they've got everyone tied up. You'll flop right on your nice round ass.'

'We'll see.' she smiled. 'By the way, now that I'm Sunday Simmons' manager, how would you like her as your exclusive client?'

'Forget it. I have enough to handle. She's just another broad. You'll learn your lesson and come wiggling back for your job.'

'Oh yeah? Don't be so sure. Well, I have lots to do, so I'll be on my way.'

Marshall got up and put his arm around her waist. He was a

wide-faced man in his early fifties and he wore the best that Cy Devore had to offer. Nothing could hide the fact that one leg was shorter than the other and that he dragged a heavy club foot.

'You know I wish you luck, sweetheart,' he said. 'And believe me, you're going to need it.'

When the film was finished, Jack Milan decided to throw a party at his Bel Air mansion. Sunday was invited.

She hated parties. She didn't really enjoy drinking, social small talk, and sly passes from drunk old men whose wives stood not five feet away.

The Hollywood wolf-pack would be present. Following her publicity, she had been approached by various well-known actors for a date, but had turned them all down.

'Who needs it?' she said to Carey. 'I don't enjoy going out unless it's with someone I really want to be with.'

Carey shrugged. 'Your personal life is your own. Do what you like.'

So Sunday did just that. She bought herself a Yorkshire terrier and a stack of books, and each evening she stayed home reading. She remembered her last experience with a man, her husband, and she didn't feel able to cope with any new relationships—however casual. That was why she had fled from Rome.

It all seemed like yesterday, not three years ago, when she was first introduced to Count Paulo Gennerra Rizzo. She had been in Italy seven months, and still thought often of Raf. But Paulo had finally made her forget.

He was a romantic, an expert in the art of making a woman feel completely beautiful. He flattered her constantly, showered her with flowers, looked only into *her* eyes adoringly. When they walked into a restaurant, people stared. What a couple they made! How the press loved them, and how Paulo adored the publicity. They were married three months later.

A few weeks afterwards Sunday discovered the truth about Paulo. She found him in the bathroom one day, his leather belt tied tightly around his arm, his eyes bulging, just about to stick a syringe in a waiting vein.

She cried out in horror. His eyes bulged even further,

distorting his arrogant Roman features, then the needle was safely in, and he sucked his breath quickly and turned his back to her.

She rushed from the room.

When he emerged his face was perfectly composed.

'Don't be frightened, my little one,' he said. 'It is correct for me to inject myself daily under my doctor's orders. I did not wish to tell you before, however now . . .' He shrugged, perfectly at ease.

'But why?' Sunday asked, still horrified by the sight she had seen.

'Oh, depression you know, nothing very serious.'

'I've never seen you depressed.'

'That is because of my good doctor. You see? There is nothing to worry about.'

'Yes,' she said uneasily, 'But why do you have to inject yourself? It's horrible.'

'I could not bother the doctor every day, could I now? So he showed me what to do, and I just do it. See, it is simple. Come, let me take you to the beach for lunch. Make yourself even more *bellisimo*.'

Later they left their apartment and drove in Paulo's Lamborghini to the beach, where they lunched with friends, and then played miniature golf and lay on the sand at Freggenni. Paulo had put her mind at rest. After all, if his doctor had told him to do it, then it must be all right.

She enjoyed the afternoon. She was due to begin work on a film the next day, and it was good to relax.

The new movie started, and this time her voice was not dubbed. She spoke her part in Italian, which took up all her time and attention. Paulo fetched her in the evenings, and they dined with friends. Once home she would collapse into bed, exhausted. It only occurred to her after the film was finished that Paulo no longer made love to her. She also noticed that at night, when he thought she was asleep, he would creep from their bed and prowl around the apartment.

The first night she realised this she fell asleep soon after. But the next night she forced herself to stay awake, and an hour later crept out of bed to look for him.

The apartment door was wide open, and Paulo was nowhere to be seen. She knew he couldn't have dressed without her seeing him, and he couldn't have gone very far with just his pyjamas on, so she waited by the door and surprised him when he came back. He was carrying a package, which he dropped when he saw her, spilling the contents—box after box of glass ampoules, three syringes and two bottles of large green pills.

They stared at each other. 'Why are you up? Why are you spying on me?' he asked coldly, as he bent to pick up the things.

'The door was open,' she stammered. 'Where have you been? What do you need all that for?'

He slammed the door in a fury. Then, eyes narrow and mean, he hit her across the face and screamed, 'Spying bitch!' With that he marched off to the bathroom, locking the door.

She was stunned. Her face blazed red where he had hit her. She bent to the bathroom keyhole and peered in. He was giving himself an injection. Frightened, she ran to bed.

The next morning he appeared charming and gay as if nothing had happened.

Sunday found out who his doctor was and went to see him. The doctor was as shocked as she was. Paulo had never been under orders to administer drugs to himself.

Together they planned to catch him. The next afternoon Sunday went out, only to return immediately with the doctor, who had been waiting downstairs by arrangement. They caught Paulo in the bathroom, the door open, injecting himself in the leg.

In a way he seemed relieved to have been caught. He was giving himself up to five intravenous injections a day, plus massive doses of sleeping pills to calm himself down.

The drug he was taking was methadrine, which after a time could become as addictive as heroin.

The doctor ordered him straight into a private nursing home, and there for the first time Sunday met the man she had married. He lay in bed day after day, his eyes glassy and blank, hardly talking, completely passive.

She visited him every day, and after a few weeks he begged her to get him out, to let him come home. He assured her he was completely cured.

The doctor said no, it was too soon. But she felt so sorry for him just lying there. She felt sure that at home he would become his old self.

She persuaded the doctor to release him, and within two days at home he had made a miraculous recovery. He was his old charming assured self.

Of course he was back on the drug.

The next two years were a nightmare. She became his nurse, enemy, spy, welfare visitor, and jailer. And he went from doctor to doctor, hospital to nursing home, with intervals in between at home—supposedly cured. But she would always discover the truth, and back to another doctor he would go.

Her life became an existence of visiting him, or if he was home, watching him. She also had to work as much as she could, for suddenly there was no money, and his family didn't care to be involved.

The end came one morning when she awoke uneasily. Paulo had been home a week, off the drug, just lying in bed staring at the ceiling, his once-handsome face unshaven and drawn. Now he was not beside her.

She ran first to the bathroom. The door was locked. She knocked and called his name, but there was no reply. She looked through the keyhole, he was lying on the floor quite still.

Panic stricken she called the doctor, and together they broke the door down.

Paulo was dead. Killed by a massive overdose.

At the inquest they called it accidental death. In her own mind Sunday wasn't sure.

She endured the gossip for a few weeks, and then the opportunity to go to Hollywood arose and she leaped at the chance.

Rome no longer held the same magic for her.

'Look, I really think you should go to this party of Jack's,' Carey said for the second time.

Sunday was staring out of the window cuddling her little dog. 'Did you know my husband killed himself?' she asked.

'What?' Carey looked at her in amazement. They had never discussed Sunday's former life although Carey knew all about it from newspaper clippings.

'Yes,' Sunday nodded dreamily. 'How will that fit into my big publicity build-up?'

'Look, honey,' Carey put a hand lightly on her shoulder, 'I know about your past and that's what it is—past. It's not normal for you to shut yourself up here. You're a beautiful girl, you've got to get out and enjoy yourself. Apart from which, it will be good for your image to be seen. Just Jack's party to start off with, huh?'

'I suppose you're right,' Sunday said. 'O.K., I'll go.'

'Great! There's a good girl. Now what are you going to wear that will knock 'em all cold?'

7

Herbert Lincoln Jefferson polished the faded crinkled leather of his best brown shoes. He had had them eight years but they still gave good service.

Marge shuffled into the kitchen to fetch herself a beer from the fridge. She was chewing on a chicken leg.

'You want me to do that?' she asked mouth full of chicken.

Herbert shook his head. She asked him every night, and every night he said no.

Marge pulled the ring on the beer can and some of the liquid sprayed out over Herbert's shoes, which he was cleaning on the table.

'Gee, I'm sorry, Herbie,' she said nervously, grabbing at a corner of her dress and attempting to rub the shoes.

He gave her a shove.

She looked at him with hurt eyes. 'I'm sorry, Herbie, I said I'm sorry . . .' She took her can of beer and left the kitchen.

Muttering under his breath Herbert finished polishing the shoes. He put them on and admired them, one foot at a time. Then he put on his jacket, patted the letter in the inside pocket, and left the house on his way to the bus stop.

He liked working nights for the Supreme Chauffeur Company. He hated the daytime jobs, boring trips to the airport and back.

He wondered who he would be driving tonight. The previous week had been very dull, just old married couples. He liked to get single actors with their dates. They were the interesting ones. They were the ones that kept you waiting outside the girl's house or apartment at the end of the evening while they screwed her. Once he had managed to watch. The girl lived on a deserted hill in a big glass house, and she and her date had gone inside and started right at it in the middle of the floor. Herbert had crawled to the bottom of a glass pane and seen the whole thing. He wrote to that girl regularly once a week.

The bus arrived and he climbed aboard. It was a hot sweaty ride and he was pleased to get off. He hurried to his place of work, posting the letter on the way.

'Hello, Jefferson,' the man behind the desk nodded to him. 'Tonight you're driving Sunday Simmons. She's to be picked up at the Château Marmont at eight and taken to a party at Jack Milan's. You know his house in Bel Air?'

Herbert nodded.

'You're to wait. Take the number-four black Caddy. It needs gas and a wash.'

He nodded again, pleased with his assignment. He had read about Sunday Simmons. She was the one who wouldn't show her tits or something. Now he would have a chance to look her over and see if she was worth writing to.

8

Charlie got back to his hotel just after three. Natalie Allen was waiting in the lobby.

'Sorry, love,' he said. 'You know the Elephant at lunchtime, it's like a meeting of Equity. Come on up.'

Natalie had been to the hairdressers, and her short dark hair hugged her head like a cap. She was wearing a yellow linen suit, and Charlie couldn't help thinking how attractive she was. Clay was a lucky fellow.

'You must have heaps to do before you go,' she remarked.

'Not really. I'm all set. George will pack everything.'

'Oh yes, the trusty George. Are you taking him with you?'

'Of course. I don't know what I'd do without him.'

'Lorna didn't like him, you know.'

'Didn't she?' He looked surprised. What was there not to like about George? And Lorna had never said anything to him about disliking George.

'Yes, she was jealous. I mean he's more like your closest friend than a servant.'

He winced at the word servant. He didn't like it. As far as he was concerned George worked for him because he wanted to, not because he had to.

'Do you want some tea or a drink or what?'

They were in the suite, and Natalie took off her jacket and sat on the couch. 'A drink, I think. A pernod with masses of ice.' She leaned back. 'Do you know this is the first time we've been alone together since that party?'

He had not been aware of that fact, but was embarrassed thinking about it. Clay and Natalie had had a fight, and Clay had gone off in a fury. Then Charlie had tried to console her, and ended up kissing her. Fortunately, Clay had come back, but Charlie felt badly about the whole thing. You didn't go around grabbing other people's wives, especially your best friend's.

'I'm sorry about that night,' he said, 'let's just forget about it. I was drunk, and so were you.'

She smiled thinly. 'But I don't want to forget it. I enjoyed it, didn't you?'

'Of course I did. But you know, love, it's a bit tricky, Clay's my friend, and I want it to stay that way.' Charlie was disturbed at the direction the conversation was taking. He had thought Natalie was going to talk about Lorna.

'Clay's a shit,' Natalie said firmly. 'A lousy, egotistical shit! I know all about the little girls he bangs. Why shouldn't *I* have some fun? You do fancy me, don't you, Charlie? Well, of course, I know you do.' She got up slowly and came towards him.

He backed away warily.

She wound her arms around his neck and started to kiss him.

How the hell did he get out of this?

'I've always liked you,' she whispered. 'Lorna was never any good for you. I always felt something between us—something special, didn't you?'

The phone rang, and with relief he untangled himself and went to answer it.

It was George, phoning from the lobby. 'I thought if you didn't need me for an hour I'd pop round to Hayward's and pick up your suits.'

'What, *now*?' Charlie said loudly in an annoyed voice.

'I don't have to, I just thought—'

'Oh, God. All right. I suppose I'll have to. I'll be right down.'

He hung up on an amazed George.

'What's the matter?' Natalie asked.

'Business. Some bloody appointment I clean forgot about. Sorry, love, what a drag.'

'Shall I wait?'

'God knows how long it will take, you'd better not.'

She sighed. 'Whoever invented phones should be shot.'

'You're right.' He helped her on with her jacket and hustled her to the door.

'About us,' Natalie said. 'What's going to happen?'

'We'll figure something out,' he replied, making a mental note never to be caught with Natalie Allen alone again.

'Goodbye, darling.' She kissed him. 'Don't forget, we'll be in Hollywood two weeks after you. Wait for me.'

He nodded. Charming! Clay wasn't so lucky after all.

At the airport Charlie was stoned. He was petrified of flying and could only board a plane completely out of his mind. Before leaving for the airport he had smoked two joints, and the plane now looked like a beautiful big bird ready to receive him. He smiled benignly at the photographers, pantomiming funny faces for them, and waving his horn-rimmed glasses in the air.

George hissed at him: 'You know you don't like photos without your glasses on.'

'Oh, yes, very very factual,' Charlie replied in his best Indian imitation.

'Bye Charlie—good luck,' one of the photographers called.

A pretty air hostess arrived to escort them to the V.I.P. lounge.

'The flight will be boarding in ten minutes,' she said, 'Can I get you a drink?'

He nodded. 'A double scotch, my dear.' He needed it.

Once airborne he fell into a deep sleep.

9

Jack Milan's house stood in acres of grounds, surrounded by electrified fences. At the entrance there was a small guardhouse. Nobody had access to the main house unless the guard said so. This was due to the fact that Jack had five children, and in the past there had been several kidnapping threats. Although the kids were all grown up now, he was taking no chances.

Sunday sat nervously in her car while the chauffeur thrust her invitation at the guard. Then the car swept up a long drive to a big white Colonial mansion.

Sunday felt nervous. First she had decided Carey was right, and she should have brought an escort. Second she was sure she wouldn't know anyone. And third, since Paulo's death, she hated to be among lots of people. In fact, she dreaded the whole evening.

She looked quite fantastic in a long black sequin outfit that she had had made for a film in Italy. She wore nothing underneath, and her body was shown off to great advantage.

A butler greeted her, and led her through the house and out onto the sloping floodlit terraces at the back.

'Miss Sunday Simmons,' he announced through a loudspeaker system, and left her standing there.

The many people drinking on the terraces all turned to stare. Her name was already known.

A plump fortyish woman came over extending her hand. 'Hi, Sunday dear, I'm Jack's wife, Ellie. It's lovely to see you. Come along, and I'll introduce you around.'

Sunday immediately liked the warm plump Ellie. She followed her to a group of people and soon found herself mingling easily into the small talk.

It wasn't going to be too bad. After dinner she could slip quietly away. She would have done her duty.

She was chatting to a bleached-blond actor, a well-known queen and an elderly red-headed woman who kept one protective hand on the queen's arm in case he should flit off, when a girl said, 'Sunday. How great to see you. How *are* you?'

She looked at the girl. Very trampy with long blonde hair, and a busty figure crammed into a shiny red dress. Sunday knew she had seen her somewhere before, but she couldn't for the life of her think where.

'Hello,' she said.

The girl laughed. 'Don't you remember me? Dindi Sydne—Prince Benno's friend. We all used to go to the beach together in Rome. You and Paulo—gee, I'm sorry, I guess I shouldn't mention him. It was so awful what happened. Benno was heartbroken. Anyway, you remember me, don't you?'

'Yes, of course.' Vaguely she remembered her.

'Well, here I am. Back in my home town,' Dindi continued. 'It just didn't work out with Benno. Anyway, I was offered a movie, so here I am again. Would you believe I had to go all the way to Rome to get a job *here*? Ain't life funny? *You* look great. Are you having a good time? Your publicity's wonderful. Hey, did you see Steve Magnum yet? I'd love to meet him. Do you know him?'

Sunday shook her head. She knew who he was, of course. A film star, swinger, four-times married (all to famous ladies) millionaire. At least that's what one read about him.

'He's a great friend of Jack Milan's,' Dindi said, 'so I guess *you'll* meet him. I haven't even met Jack yet. My date is a real creep cameraman. Doesn't know anyone. I don't know how the hell he got invited in the first place. By the way, where are you staying? Let's get together.'

'The Château Marmont. But I really don't go out much and—'

'We'll soon change that. I can fix you up with some *live* ones. Things can get a little dull around here if you just mix with the importants. Agreed, that's a good scene, but a little action on the side doesn't hurt. I'll call you, must rush now, there's a director over there I've had my eye on for weeks.'

Dindi wriggled off in her tight dress, and Sunday found herself standing alone. She looked around. The party was in full swing. Soon, she hoped, they would serve dinner and then her ordeal would be over.

She felt very much alone, but that had been a constant feeling ever since Paulo's death. In the few months before hand, she had watched him degrade himself. Would she ever forget the lengths he had gone to in hiding the drugs from her? Burrowing beneath the tiles in the bathroom like a dog, hiding little stores under the mattress, in the light fixtures, even on the narrow ledges outside the windows of their apartment. In the end she had been thinking about divorce, and the week before he died had threatened him with it. He had cried like a baby, making her fervent promises of how good he would be, how this time he was cured.

'Sunday, dear,' Ellie Milan bore down on her, 'I'm putting you at a table with Jack. Table number two, you'll see a place card for yourself. I'm trying to get everyone seated.'

She smiled. 'Thank you.' She followed the groups of people drifting towards the tables.

Dindi was sitting earnestly at a table, her hand laid casually on top of a fat man's arm. His eyes were glued firmly down her neckline.

'Hi there, Sunday.' Jack Milan waved at her from table two.

She went over, returning his smile and shaking hands with the people already sitting there, to whom he introduced her. Abe Stein was among them, with a horse-faced wife who glared.

She was seated next to Jack on one side, with two vacant chairs on the other.

'You look wonderful,' he said, 'And great in the dailies too. I understand Radiant are giving you a contract.'

'Well, they *have* offered me one, but I'm not taking it. I don't believe in long-term contracts, they're too restricting.'

There was a short shocked silence from everyone.

Abe said, 'I'd take it if I were you.'

'*I* haven't done too badly,' Jack said mildly. 'I've been with Radiant seventeen years.'

'No, the kid's right.' Steve Magnum had appeared, accompanied by his latest steady, Angela Carter. He sat down next to Sunday. 'Forget it. Long contracts are a thing of the past. Radiant's about the only studio left who sign people, and they don't know their ass from a hole in the ground. Don't let them talk you into anything, kid.'

'I won't,' she replied, trying to stop herself from staring at him. His face was so familiar. Back in Rio, when she was still at school, he had been her favourite film star.

Steve Magnum had aged well. At fifty he wore his years with style. He barely made five foot eleven and he was very thin—his unkinder critics described him as scrawny—but his face still had the same boney hungry quality that had made him a huge star some twenty-five years before. Steve Magnum was a legend in his own time. Women were mad about him. Even his four ex-wives never tired of saying they would always have him back. He had been single eight years now, and the newspapers and columns were always speculating about who would be the next Mrs Magnum. There were many candidates, but most people in the know bet there wouldn't be another Mrs Magnum at all. Some said he might even go back to his first wife, by whom he had three children.

'Hey now,' he looked Sunday over with his famous pale blue eyes, 'You've handled yourself pretty well so far. Came into town and caused quite a stir. Even told old Abe and Jack where to get off.'

Jack laughed, but Abe scowled and tried to ignore his wife who was nudging him to say something.

'Carey St Martin is looking after me. She's terrific. I'm sure I have her to thank for all the offers I'm getting. If it wasn't for her I'd probably have been out of here on the next plane to Rome.'

Angela laughed prettily. 'How sweet. All because of some itsy-bitsy nude scene. Darling, they're all the rage now. If you want to get on in this business, you have to learn to take your clothes off.' She snaked an arm around Steve and gazed at him adoringly.

'Yeah, honey,' Steve said, 'and you *certainly* know how to do that. On *and* off the screen.'

During the meal Steve kept on talking to Sunday. She was well aware of Angela on his other side, listening to every word and trying to join in.

Angela had been his steady girlfriend for three months and she had high hopes of continuing the role, perhaps even making it permanent. She was infuriated by Steve's interest in Sunday. What idiot had sat him next to her, and what the hell was all that slop she was coming out with about principles and good scripts?

She could hardly believe her ears when she heard Steve say to Sunday, 'You know you'd be great as the rich sexy broad in my new movie. Want to test?'

Angela had hoped that Steve was going to let *her* do that part. It wasn't a star role, but it was good. She had hinted that she would like to do it, but Steve had brushed her off. And now he was practically offering the part to this unknown bitch! And the unknown bitch was replying: 'I'm sorry. I don't test. There are quite a few Italian films I am in that you could run. I don't believe in testing.'

Steve looked at Jack, and they both burst out laughing.

'Sonofabitch!' Steve said. 'You were right. This broad *is* different.'

10

Marshall K. Marshall left his custom-built white Rolls Royce with the doorman at the Beverly Hills Hotel, and limped into the lobby.

Actors—lousy actors. They were becoming so damn demanding. They seemed to want to have a say in everything. He remembered the days when all they did was sign their contracts and get on with it.

Marshall had arrived at the hotel to be present at a meeting between Cy Hamilton, Jnr.—producer of Roundabout—and Charlie Brick, star of said picture. The meeting was due to the fact that they could stall Charlie no longer. He certainly wasn't a fool, and it was becoming increasingly obvious that Michelle Lomas was not going to appear.

Already they were shooting around her, and the previous day Charlie had stalked off the set, leaving a message for Cy that unless Michelle was there he wasn't doing another day's work. So the time had come to tell him that Michelle Lomas was pregnant, a fact confirmed yesterday. She was confined to her house by Lake Lugano and wouldn't be budging, on doctor's orders, for nine months.

Marshall carried a small briefcase in which were photographs and brief biographies of his ideas for replacements.

The main thing was to convince Charlie that it was worthwhile to go ahead with the picture without Michelle. He had every contractual right to walk out if he wanted to. It was up to Marshall as his agent to persuade him not to.

In his tastefully decorated pale beige suite with two colour-televisions going full blast, Charlie paced the floor wearing a white towelling bathrobe and brown Gucci slippers.

George hovered respectfully in a corner, one eye on the television and one on Charlie. A rented secretary sat at a table, day-dreaming about being discovered. And another table held a spread of eggs, toast, fruit and coffee, all untouched.

'You should eat something,' George said mildly.

Charlie grunted, still pacing. His work was more important than anything else, and he was incensed that they should have done this to him. Without Michelle the film wouldn't be the same. Where the hell was she? Why had she backed out?

He wasn't going to do it. He would go back to London and screw 'em. They weren't going to fob him off with some replacement.

Six boring days he had been waiting for Michelle, and apart from a press party, where he was asked a string of inane questions, he hadn't been anywhere except to the studio.

Of course, he had had a stack of invitations. Hollywood was always delighted to see a new face in town. Any excuse to throw a party. Several well-known hostesses vied with each other to be the first to have a dinner party for him. This time they were out of luck. He said no to everything. He didn't believe in a social life until the film was under way.

There was a knock at the door and Marshall K. Marshall limped in. In spite of the air-conditioning he was sweating profusely. He rarely left his office during the day, only in emergencies.

'You look great,' Marshall said. 'Even thinner than last week.'

'Yes, I am managing to keep the old weight down,' Charlie smiled. He knew it was only supreme willpower that kept him looking as good as he did. Four weeks of normal eating and he would be back to the fatty he once was.

'You're not going to like this,' Marshall said, 'Cy's not exactly ecstatic about it. But Michelle is expecting a baby. She's got us by the balls.'

Charlie slumped into a chair. That was the last thing he expected.

'We got a doctor's written confirmation yesterday—so that's why there's been all the shillyshallying. Who would imagine Michelle would get herself knocked up? Not only knocked up, but thrilled about it. Cy wanted her to go ahead and do the movie anyway—after all, it won't notice for another four or five months—but no, she ain't taking no risks. Sorry, Charlie, that's it. Look Cy's in a bind, if you walk out it will be bad, and I know you *can* walk out, and personally I wouldn't blame you. But listen, baby, if we can find a replacement—someone you O.K., and you stay, then I reckon it will be another ten per cent of the gross, and that ain't chicken feed. What do you think?'

The rented secretary sat straight in her chair, trying to listen over the noise of the television. George still lingered in the corner.

Charlie closed his eyes and tried to think. Another ten per cent. Not bad. But who could replace Michelle?

As if reading his thoughts Marshall said, 'We could have a re-write. Instead of the parts being equal, build yours up and cut hers down. It would be your movie, all the way. Can we turn that goddam television off?'

'George, turn it off,' Charlie said, his mind racing. 'And I don't need you, dear,'—to the secretary—'come back tomorrow, same time.'

The rented secretary got up, smoothed down her mini, and wriggled past Marshall. Perhaps he would discover her. He didn't even give her a glance.

At the door she paused, trying to decide whether to tell them she was an actress, but George blocked her path and ushered her out.

She wriggled off, angry at not having been discovered.

Charlie said slowly, 'It sounds good. What about Cy? Has he agreed?'

Marshall felt relief. 'He will.'

By the time Cy Hamilton, Jnr. arrived, fresh from an argument with his recent third wife, Charlie and Marshall had sorted everything out.

Cy was a likeable man, but he had a steely temper that appeared on occasion.

'You bastards—you're holding me to ransom,' he said. But eventually he agreed.

All that remained to be settled was a new actress for the role, and they all had different ideas.

'Magda Seal,' Charlie said.

'Forget it, she's booked solid.'

'Mirielle Montane' from Cy.

'No tits—skinny, useless.'

'Anna Karl.'

'Too old.'

They discussed the possibilities, eventually running out of foreign actresses and deciding that the girl could be any nationality.

'How about a new girl?' Marshall suggested, opening his brief-case and bringing out pictures. 'Sunday Simmons.'

'Sunday what?' asked Charlie.

'Simmons. You've seen her, Cy, haven't you? Great body, big boobs, good publicity potential.'

Cy nodded. 'Not a bad idea. Can she act?'

Marshall shrugged. 'Who knows? We could run some film of her—she's in the new Jack Milan.'

'I don't want an unknown,' Charlie said.

'Take a look at her pictures,' Marshall replied. 'She's a wild-looking broad.'

Charlie thumbed through the stills, lingering on one that showed Sunday in the nude scene with Jack Milan. He felt suddenly aroused. My God, he realized it was at least two weeks since he'd had a woman. Have to do something about *that*.

'She's gorgeous,' he said. 'What's her phone number?'

'Yeah, what *is* her phone number?' Cy asked, smiling slowly.

Marshall laughed. 'Shall we run film on her?'

They both nodded.

'Now another idea I had,' Marshall said, 'and don't blow your stacks—is Angela Carter.'

'Angela Carter,' Cy exlaimed.

'Yeah, Angela. She's a name. I think I can get her to test.'

Charlie nodded. 'O.K. with me. It sounds like a good idea.'

They decided on another three possibles, and since time was at a premium, they arranged to meet eight o'clock at Cy's house, where he would have film on all five girls to show in his private screening room.

As Marshall was leaving, Charlie called him to the side and said something he hadn't wanted to: 'Can you fix me a girl for later?'

'Sure. Any preferences?'

Charlie shook his head, already regretting asking Marshall. But after all, he didn't know anyone in town and he didn't want someone from the studio sending him a hooker.

'Leave it to me,' Marshall said, limping off, relieved to be on his way back to the office.

11

'I love drive-ins!' Sunday exclaimed, examining the menu on a stand by the car window. 'I want two hamburgers and a chocolate malt.'

Carey laughed. 'You'll get fat.'

'I don't care. I think I'm beginning to like it here.'

'I'm not surprised.' Carey pressed the buzzer on the car-side speaker and gave their order. 'If I was in your position I'd be crazy about it. I mean, let's just consider things. You get into town with a small part in a Jack Milan movie. You march out of that like a star, grab all the headlines—march back in again, plus apologies all round. Meet Steve Magnum at a party. He showers you with roses and invitations all week long. You refuse to even date him—Mr Number-One Hollywood Catch. And now today a firm offer for you to be in his new movie. Six glorious weeks in Acapulco. Wow—no wonder you're beginning to like it.'

Sunday smiled. 'Thanks to you. If it wasn't for you I would have gone back to Rome.' .

'Thanks to *you*, kiddo, I got myself out of that agency job, and now things are really swinging for me. I'm picking up new clients every day. Do you know Angela Carter called me yesterday and wants to know if I'd be interested in handling her. She must hate you.'

Sunday frowned. 'I don't know why. Life is too short to go around hating people.'

A waiter in tight white jeans came bearing two trays with their order. 'Aren't you Sunday Simmons?' he asked in a feminine voice, peering through the window.

She nodded.

53

'Lots of luck, dear, my friend and I think you're lovely. We saw you on TV the other night.'

'Thank you.'

Carey waited until the boy had gone, then said, 'Fame, baby, that's fame.'

Sunday munched on her hamburger. 'Delicious!' she exclaimed.

Carey picked daintily at her cottage cheese and fruit salad. 'You really are an unusual girl. I ask you out for a celebration lunch, thinking maybe the Polo Lounge or Bistro and where do you want to go? A drive-in! I shall be glad to pack you off to Acapulco.'

'When am I supposed to leave? And when do I get a copy of the script? And don't forget the clause about no nude scenes.'

'I'm hardly likely to forget that. They're sending a script to your hotel today. You start costume fittings, hair and makeup tests next week. They want you to leave July tenth. What are you going to do about Steve Magnum?'

Sunday smiled sweetly. 'Nothing.'

'Oh God, you're too much. Why not go out with him? He's not going to eat you—and even if he was—wowee baby, I hear he's the greatest!'

'I don't want everyone saying the only reason I'm in his movie is because I'm having an affair with him. If he's that anxious to go out with me he'll just have to wait until Acapulco, and then we'll see.'

She spoke calmly, but she had given a lot of thought to Steve Magnum. She *was* attracted to him, but she knew his reputation with women, and instinct told her that the only way to hold his interest beyond a few dates was to play it very cool indeed. Also she was frightened of what a relationship with Steve Magnum would involve. There had only been two men in her life—Raf and Paulo—and she wasn't yet sure if she were ready to cope with a third.

'I think Stevie the lady-killer has met his match,' Carey said with a laugh, 'Only don't under estimate him—he's been playing the boy-meets-girl game for a long long time. Whatever you do, don't *ever* take him seriously—there are more hearts broken by Magnum than convertible cars in Southern California!'

54

'I've got the message, thank you.'

They called for the check and Carey drove her car down La Cienega to Sunset, dropping Sunday at the Château.

'When you get back from Mexico we should really find you a house or apartment, and you've got to get a car.'

'I think I'd like a little place at the beach.'

Carey shrugged. 'You're impossible. That's just not chic. However, knowing how definite you are, I'll ask around and see what's available. Talk to you later. Oh, by the way, we'll break this to the press about the movie tomorrow, so stay available.' She waved and drove off.

Sunday walked slowly inside. She had decided to spend the afternoon by the pool. It was so hot that her thin cotton trousers and shirt were sticking to her body.

The old lady at the desk beckoned her over. 'There's more flowers for you, Miss Simmons. And a letter from England. I wonder if I might have the stamp? My grandson collects them, you know. And there's a young woman here for you, she's sitting over there.'

Sunday looked over in surprise and saw a girl, flopped out in a chair, sunglasses shielding her eyes. 'Who is she?'

The old lady reached for a message pad. 'Dindi Sydne.'

'Oh!' Sunday remembered her from Jack Milan's party. The girl who had known Paulo. What on earth was she doing here?

Sunday took the flowers and letter, carefully peeling off the stamp and handing it to the old lady. It was from her aunt; She would read it later.

The note with the two dozen roses read: *'When are you going to change your mind? S.M.'*

She walked over to the girl in the chair and nudged her gently.

The girl sat up like a startled rabbit. 'Shit!' she exclaimed loudly. 'Sunday! Oh, and you've brought me flowers—how nice!' She stood up. She was wearing tight hipster orange pants, and a brief sweater. Her exposed midriff was very tanned. 'Guess what happened to *me*? I was driving along Sunset in my beautiful T-Bird and the frigging little monster goes and blows up! Fortunately it happened not two blocks from here, right by a gas station, and this adorable mechanic with muscles like Superman is fixing it for me. I remembered you lived here, so I figured I'd

55

while away the afternoon with you. He's going to drop it back here when it's fixed. You should see him—a real sex machine!'

Excuses leapt to Sunday's lips, but she hated to lie, and anyway, the girl was only trying to be friendly.

'That's fine. I thought I might sit by the pool, you're welcome to join me.'

'Yeah, great. I'll borrow a bikini. My tan could do with a booster.' She examined her stomach.

'I'm just going upstairs, I'll bring you down a bikini.'

Dindi linked arms with her. 'I'll come with you.'

Upstairs, Limbo, Sunday's little dog, came bounding to greet them. The rooms were stuffy and Sunday turned up the air conditioning.

Dindi wandered around, picking up everything to inspect. 'Who are all these flowers from?' she asked.

'Just a friend,' Sunday replied shortly.

'A very *good* friend,' Dindi said with a chuckle. 'I adore good friends. I once made it with a guy on top of six dozen red roses. It was the end, very sexy. Only he couldn't come, said the smell put him off. Some guys are so weird.'

'Here,' Sunday handed her a green and white bikini. Dindi stepped out of her pants and sweater, revealing that she wore nothing underneath. She put on the bikini. 'Man, you've got big boobs—give me some cotton wool to pad this thing out. I wish I had a big pair, guys really dig that.'

Dindi was not exactly flat-chested, Sunday had observed.

They rode down in the elevator and walked the short distance to the pool. It was nearly deserted except for an aged woman in a huge flowered hat, and a muscle-bound man stretched out and covered with oil.

'Not much happening here,' Dindi said, a note of disappointment in her voice. 'You should move to the Beverly Hills, the pool there is always full of action.'

'Listen, Dindi. Let's get one thing clear. I *am not* looking for any action. I enjoy peace and quiet.'

Dindi lifted orange tinted sunglasses and stared in disbelief. 'Sorry, I didn't realise I was with such queenly company. For someone who doesn't want to swing, you certainly look the part.

Do you want me to go? Buzz away and leave you to your peace and quiet?'

'No, of course not. I just wanted you to know, that's all.'

'So I know. Hey, I'm going to ask that guy to lend me some of his oil.' And she was off.

Sunday decided she quite liked her. She was loudmouthed, nosey, and obviously a pushover with men, but she had a certain honest charm.

She came back after ten minutes, triumphantly bearing a bottle of sun oil. 'That's Branch Strong,' she announced, 'He's in from New York to do a test. He swings both ways.'

'How do you know?' Sunday asked curiously.

'I have a feeling for these things. Anyway he was brought in by Sam Plum, who is *the* faggot agent.'

Sunday rubbed some oil on her body and lay back. It was good to get to know people. Carey had said she was strange because she stayed alone all the time. Well, Carey didn't know the full story about Paulo. About the hurt he had left behind, and the lingering guilt—which she knew she had no reason to feel, but couldn't help.

Soon Branch Strong (formerly Sydney Blumcor from the Bronx) came lumbering over. He had a smooth good-looking face without a trace of character.

'Hello there, little ladies,' he said. 'Hot enough for you?'

'Yeah,' Dindi grinned. 'Hey, Branch, this is Sunday Simmons.'

'Pleased to meet you,' he said, rubbing oily hands over his muscle-bound stomach. He thought he had never seen such a beautiful girl as Sunday, and the body on her—wowee—what a couple they would make!

'When do you test?' Dindi asked.

'Tomorrow,' he replied nervously. 'Keep your fingers crossed.'

'You bet,' she giggled. 'I'd cross my legs too but that would be *too* boring.'

Sunday stood up. 'I think I'll swim.' She walked to the deep end of the pool and dived off the low board. Then she swam a length under water.

Branch watched admiringly. 'She's really something,' he said with a note of awe.

'Yeah,' Dindi agreed. 'But a bit uptight—no action—you understand?'

'Huh?'

'Forget it.' She decided Branch Strong was a big good-looking hunk of blond idiot. He was still watching Sunday in the pool, his mouth hanging slackly open, his tongue nervously jumping up and down. Dindi had to admit that Sunday certainly was a fantastic-looking girl, but she didn't seem to have much personality, a bit of a drag really. Dindi wondered what she would say if she told her about the scene she and her Roman boyfriend, old Prince Benno, had had with her faggy husband, the one who had knocked himself off. Three days locked up in a Rome hotel room. What a time that had been. Only a few weeks before he killed himself.

Sunday emerged from the pool and lay down. 'It's absolutely lovely, you must go in.' She draped her wet hair over the back of the chair and closed her eyes. The sun was hot, and as it dried the tiny rivulets of water on her body, she fell into a light sleep.

Branch didn't take his eyes off her.

12

Herbert Lincoln Jefferson smiled contentedly, displaying one black tooth amongst a row of off-white ones. For someone so obsessed with bodily cleanliness, he held the inside of his mouth in complete disregard, cleaning his teeth only when he remembered, which wasn't often.

He stood under the rusty shower, soaping his thin hairless body and grinning all the while.

It had taken him two weeks but at last he had done it. He had written a letter to Sunday Simmons of such poetic obscenity that the mere thought of it excited him—in spite of the fact that he had only five minutes previously ejaculated into a plastic bag to be enclosed with the precious letter.

He stroked his fine upstanding member with soap and felt very proud of himself. What a man he was! What joy and thrills he could give to any woman!

The wait had been worth it. As soon as he saw Sunday he had realised that this was the girl for him. To hell with Angela Carter and all the other past recipients of his letters. This was the woman he dreamed about. Perfect, from her tawny mane of hair to her rounded sensual body. Even her feet, peeking at him through gold sandals, were sexy.

On the drive to the Milan house he watched her in the rear-view mirror. Once her big browny yellow eyes met his, and he coughed unobtrusively, making some remark about the weather.

Since that night he had hoped to be assigned to drive her again, but no such luck. So he had started to compose a letter. His early efforts did not meet with his approval. The first letter had to be something special, something that would intrigue and excite her so much that she would want to meet the man who could write with such explicit passion and know-how.

And now, at last, he had written such a letter. A masterpiece. The crowning touch being instructions as to what she should do with his plastic-bag offering. Tomorrow he would sit and imagine her reading it and following his instructions. He would fill another plastic bag and write another wonderful letter, explaining how the second bag was filled as he thought of her lovingly dealing with the first.

'Herbie.' The whiney voice of his wife was accompanied by a knock on the bathroom door and a rattling of the handle. 'Herbie, I wanna go to the john. Can I go to the john, please? You've been in there an hour.'

The big fat cow *would* have to spoil these few pleasant moments for him.

'Just a minute, dear,' he called back mildly. He wrapped a towel around himself and unlocked the door.

'I don't know why you have to always lock the door,' she complained. 'Makes me feel like an intruder.' She lifted her skirt to sit on the toilet and Herbert rapidly left the room.

Heavy thighs, Marge had thick heavy thighs. She forgot to shave her legs for weeks on end and they were covered in an unpleasant ginger stubble. They had been married ten years, and glancing at the photo on the dressing table, Herbert could hardly believe that the pretty red-head with the slim figure and big breasts was now the slovenly, fat, Marge, squatting on the john. Did he know he was marrying an eating maniac? A woman to whom six eggs and a loaf of bread for breakfast were not unusual?

She had been so lovely. Their first meeting near Los Angeles airport, in a bar at lunchtime, had been so romantic. He had gone with a friend for a beer and a sandwich—at that time he was driving trucks—and Marge had come forward to serve them, looking girlish in a short fringed cowboy skirt, white boots, and a stetson hat. It was a topless bar, and her large bosoms had bobbed tantalizingly at him, a sheriff's star cheekily covering each nipple.

'What'll you have?' she had asked, standing by his table, a pad in her hand, and a sheriff's star nearly in his mouth.

Herbert would never forget that first meeting. They married a few months later, Marge already pregnant. But she had lost the baby, and then another. Shortly afterwards she started to eat, and Herbert started to write his letters.

'Hon,' Marge came shuffling into the bedroom, 'what do you think I should wear?'

'Wear?' He looked at her in surprise. 'For what?' This was about the time she always settled in front of the television.

She was wriggling her fat body out of her shabby house-dress. 'I told you, hon, I'm gonna go to a movie with our new neighbour. She asked me two days ago. I told you.'

'Oh, yes.' He remembered now. A married couple had moved into the yellow house next door, and Marge, on her daily trip to the supermarket, had met the wife. The two women had arranged to go to a film. Marge was thrilled. She had no friends and Herbert never took her anywhere, so to go to a movie was a rare treat.

Marge was trying to struggle into a blue sailor dress that no longer fitted. She grew larger every year.

'We're gonna see a movie,' she repeated, 'it's supposed to be a real weird movie—y'know, weirdy weird, and dirty too.' She abandoned the struggle with the sailor dress and chose instead a loose polka-dot shift that she had bought for her sister's wedding the previous year. She managed to squeeze into that, although it was no longer a loose shift.

Herbert said, 'What time are you going?' He wasn't sure that he liked the idea of his wife roaming around enjoying herself at dirty movies whilst he was out working.

'Louella's calling for me at seven. She's got a car.' She pouted at herself in the mirror, applied a jammy red lipstick and touched her cheeks with it, wiping the residue on her dress. 'It's so hot,' she sighed, running a comb through her scraggy red hair.

'Yes,' Herbert agreed, but his mind was no longer on Marge. His mind was on the letter waiting to be posted.

After Marge went downstairs he would pocket his prize and set off lovingly to post it.

She splashed cheap cologne over her fat freckled arms and put on a pair of white scuffed shoes. 'There. How do I look?'

She looked like a ginger elephant in a polka-dot dress. 'Very nice,' he said, noticing that the back of her hem was hanging loose. 'Don't you two girls do any flirting.'

She cackled. 'Herbie!' She lumbered off downstairs and he quickly pocketed the letter.

Oh, Miss Sunday Simmons, what a treat you have in store for you!

13

Charlie was pleased at the way things worked out. He stood to make a great deal more money, he would be the main star of 'Roundabout', and they would pick a leading lady of his choice. After all, were he truthful with himself, the main reason he had wanted Michelle was personal. His ego had taken a bad beating with the divorce, and he had needed the reassurance that a sex-symbol, a woman most red-blooded men would give their right arm to possess, desired him—and not as a star, but as a man.

Michelle's defection was a great personal disappointment. But he had to admit that professionally it was probably better.

He dressed prior to leaving for Cy's house. His clothes reflected the new Charlie Brick, the free divorced Charlie Brick, the *thin* Charlie Brick.

He wore brown slacks, and a loose Indian-type shirt. He adjusted his horn-rimmed glasses, and peering at himself in the mirror decided that maybe he should try some tinted lenses, something a bit newer.

George was waiting in the red Maserati at the front of the hotel.

'I think I'll drive myself tonight,' Charlie said. He felt good. So good in fact that he had sent Michelle a telegram of congratulation.

'Are you sure?' George asked doubtfully. The car was always in terrible shape after Charlie drove it.

'Of course I'm sure. You take the Mercedes and go and have some fun. I'll see you in the morning.'

'All right.' George was quite pleased at the prospect of an evening off. He was bored with sitting around the hotel each night trying to keep Charlie cheerful. He stepped out of the car. Charlie climbed in and revved the engine, loving the sound of unleashed power.

A pretty girl, leaving the hotel with a small poodle, turned to stare at him. He winked, she winked back. Why the hell had he told Marshall to fix a girl for him? He could manage very nicely on his own.

Cy Hamilton Jnr.'s wife, Emerald, was a lush. She was attractive, with long straight black hair parted in the middle. She wore gold patio pyjamas, and drank straight scotch on the rocks while directing bitchy put-downs at her husband's every other sentence. She clung onto Charlie's arm, swaying slightly and breathing lethal alcohol fumes in his face.

Marshall caught Charlie by the arm as they were going into the Venetian dining-room. 'Take no notice of Emerald,' he whispered, 'She's always smashed. She'll probably try to grab your cock under the table. Just pretend not to notice.'

'What?' Charlie found the thought of Emerald making a grab for him highly amusing, and also improbable with her husband sitting right there.

'I should have warned you before,' Marshall muttered, 'only Cy gets very steamed up if you say anything. She makes a play for everyone, it's her way of getting at him.'

'Why?'

'It's a long story. To put it in a nutshell, once he marries them he can't get it up any more. He's in analysis about it.'

'Yes, I should think he would be.'

Charlie felt an immediate rapport with Cy. What an awful position to be in. He had always harboured a secret fear that one day it might happen to him.

The four of them sat down to dinner served by two Mexican maids wearing starched black and white uniforms.

Emerald immediately knocked over a glass of wine and accused Cy of having pushed her elbow. They squabbled like two children, ignoring the melon and Parma ham put before them.

Marshall and Charlie ate, trying to ignore the bickering.

Marshall said quietly, 'There'll be a young lady coming to your hotel at eleven. She's a nice kid, a big fan of yours. As a matter of fact, she's quite an up and coming actress. She doesn't usually go on blind dates, but as I said, she's a fan of yours. You'll like her, her name's Dindi Sydne.'

'Great.' Charlie raised his eyebrows. 'Does this go on all through dinner?' He indicated the battling couple.

'No. She'll throw something at him in a minute and walk out. She'll be back for dessert.'

Sure enough, Emerald suddenly got up, called Cy a string of four-letter names, threw the bread basket at him and stalked out.

'Broads!' Cy exclaimed.

True to Marshall's prediction she re-appeared at the strawberry-shortcake stage. She had changed into a silk jersey floorlength dress which clung to her like a second skin, and was split from the neck to the navel, showing off lightly-tanned skin and an almost·flat bosom.

She smiled at everyone and sat down, sipping at a large glass of Scotch she had brought with her.

Cy continued talking about a recent production of his.

Is that a hand creeping up my leg? Charlie thought. My Goo, it is! Light fingers were stalking past his knee and fiddling with his fly. He was thankful that these new trousers had buttons instead of the usual zipper. Marshall certainly knew the order of events!

Emerald was making no progress with the buttons, and her fingers started to rub impatiently. To his embarrassment he started to get an erection.

Emerald smiled and sipped her drink. Cy droned on. Charlie uncomfortably spooned a mouthful of strawberry shortcake and tried to think of other things.

At last dinner was over, and Charlie excused himself quickly and went to the bathroom. What an unbelievable scene! And Marshall said she did it to everyone. The woman must be insane, and Cy even more insane to put up with it.

He cleaned his teeth with a gold Asprey's toothpick, washed his hands, and returned to the others.

'I thought we'd have coffee in the screening room,' Cy said. 'Are you going to come and watch, darling?'

Emerald shook her head and made some crack about having better things to do than watch a load of dumb starlets—only she didn't use the word starlets.

Cy's viewing room was done entirely in red leather. Even the screen was fitted into a red leather surround, studded with gold horseshoes.

Charlie admired it, and thought to himself that when he was finished on this film, he must buy a home for himself somewhere. It was important to get out of hotels. Now that he knew he was staying to do the movie, he would send George out to rent a house tomorrow. The children would be joining him soon, and they deserved the best.

The first girl came on the screen. She was blonde and curvaceous, but she lacked a certain something. All three of them said no. The second clip was Angela Carter. She was tall, with a particular gamine quality that appealed to Charlie. The scene was backstage at a theatre and she was wearing a leotard that made her legs appear six feet long.

'Y'know, I don't think she'd be bad at all,' Charlie mused.

'Yeah,' Marshall agreed. Angela was bugging the life out of him to get her a part. 'After all, it's a comedy—no big dramatics. I think it would be a clever bit of casting.'

'She looks like a pekinese,' Cy said.

'But a sexy one,' Marshall continued, 'and there's talk around that she and Steve Magnum might even get married. What a publicity natural that would be!'

'Let's see the others before we get carried away.'

The next girl was a new English discovery who had just starred in her first film. Rumour had it that she had screwed everyone on it from the star to the clapper boy.

'No,' Charlie shook his head, 'she speaks like she's got a plum in her mouth.'

'Maybe somebody left their prick there!' Marshall said with a dirty laugh.

Girl number four was Sunday Simmons, in the bedroom scene with Jack Milan.

'Now *that's* what I call sensational,' Cy said, sitting up very straight, 'I don't know about using her for the movie, but I have to meet her. Fix it up, Marsh. That is *all* woman.'

Charlie agreed. She *was* gorgeous. But who had ever heard of her? Angela Carter was certainly the best bet as far as he was concerned.

It was the first time Marshall had seen Sunday on the screen, and he suddenly understood what Carey was so excited about. This girl had it. He must phone Carey first thing and sign her up. His bad leg tingled, a sure sign that he was on to something good. 'It wouldn't be such a bad idea to use an unknown,' he said slowly, 'She's done a lot of Italian films.'

'No,' Charlie shook his head. 'She's not right.'

'She's got a wild pair of tits!' Cy said, running the scene again.

'You don't judge an actress by the size of her tits,' Charlie replied coldly. He refused to be fobbed off with an unknown just because Cy wanted to lay her.

'Let's run the last girl,' Cy said.

The last girl was a young television actress. She was appealing and nice. Not sexy enough, all three men agreed.

'I'm happy to decide on Angela Carter,' Charlie declared.

Cy nodded. 'I guess she's the best choice. Is she free right away, Marsh?'

'Free as a bird. What about Sunday Simmons for the other girl, the small part?'

'Not a bad idea. What do you think, Charlie?'

'Yes—fine with me.' He glanced at his watch. It was ten-thirty, time to be getting back to the hotel and preparing for his date. He got up and stretched. 'Thank your—er—um—wife for a lovely dinner.'

'Pleasure.' Cy stood too. 'I hope we didn't disturb you with our little tiff. Emeràld's alone all day and she gets very bored. Our fights are just her way of letting off steam.'

'Of course. Well, I'll leave you two to discuss details.'

'Charlie—the re-write was started today. All being well we can start shooting again next week.'

Back at his hotel Charlie changed into a black track suit. He then decided he didn't like it, and was just struggling back into his original outfit when Dindi arrived.

She had dressed carefully for the occasion. Nothing too far out, she didn't want to frighten him off with some wild outfit. After all, each star was a golden opportunity, and one of these days she was going to strike it rich.

Of course she had heard of Charlie Brick—who hadn't? And when Marshall had called her about entertaining him, she had jumped at the chance. Marshall had promised to see she got a small part in 'Roundabout'. They had a good working arrangement.

She remembered with amusement her first encounter with Marshall. Seeing he was such a big important agent and all, she had thought she had better put out for him. But he hadn't wanted to know, practically fell under his desk with embarrassment when she unzipped her dress and wriggled her bare ass at him.

In moments of idleness, which were few in Dindi's life, she

tried to figure out what the agent's sexual hang-up was. He didn't swing with girls. Boys? She didn't think so. Anyway, she entertained his more important clients, and he got her a small contract and plenty of walk-on speaking parts, so as far as she was concerned it was a good arrangement.

Charlie Brick was thinner and more attractive than on the screen. Not her type at all though. She liked them big, young, and good-looking. Maybe he was sensational in bed. The English were pretty wild in that department.

She played it sweet and friendly.

'Hi, I'm Dindi Sydne. What a fabulous suite. I'd *love* a frozen banana daquiri.'

Charlie thought her a charming girl, obviously not a hooker—exceedingly pretty, with silky blond hair pulled back and tied with a big blue bow that matched the sleeveless dress she was wearing. The dress clung in all the right places and had diamond patterns cut around the midriff which showed off her glowing tan.

'Marshall tells me you're an actress,' he said, wondering why on earth he had brought up *that* subject.

'Trying to be, but I'm not terribly ambitious.' She smiled disarmingly.

He ordered drinks from room service, put on a Jose Feliciano tape, showed Dindi a book of stills from his latest film, and reminded himself to thank Marshall for sending him such a delightful girl.

Dindi admired pictures of his children, sipped her drink like a lady, enthused over his stills, and carefully and unobtrusively saw to it that her skirt hitched its way up, showing lots of naked tanned thigh.

Several frozen banana daquiris later she pretended to be ever so slightly drunk. Actually they didn't affect her at all, but she was smart enough to know when to play it tough, and when to play it Baby Girl. Charlie was definitely Baby Girl. Already he was telling her about his wife, the divorce, and how lonely he was.

She made sympathetic clucking noises, and secretly thought here was a goose good and ready to be plucked.

After he had complained bitterly about all women being after his money, fame, or both, she said, 'How awful. I guess people just use you, and girls hope you can get them in your movies.'

'That's right, love, that's absolutely right.' What an intelligent girl, he thought, hardly aware of the fact that he had been doing all the talking. 'Y'know, if I ever get married again, one thing I'll be sure to do, and that is see my wife has a separate bedroom. I understand that she wouldn't want to be with me all the time.'

This guy is a nut, Dindi thought, an out and out nut. 'I understand how you feel,' she said softly, 'although if I was your wife, that would be the last thing I'd want.'

Charlie suddenly grabbed her and kissed her. What a wonderful understanding girl. He moved his hands over her breasts and she gave a little gasp.

'Listen, love,' he said quietly, letting her go and moving over to the desk drawer. 'There's something I want you to try with me.'

Oh goody—action at last, Dindi thought.

'Yes?' she said, her voice barely a whisper as he lowered the lights and turned up the music.

'I want you to smoke a little grass with me. It will make you feel good, you'll enjoy it. Here.' He lit the joint and passed it to her. 'Just drag deeply and inhale very very slowly.'

She choked back a laugh. She had been smoking pot on and off since she was fourteen. Gingerly she took the brown cigarette and puffed, manufacturing a small frightened cough. It was weak stuff, had no kick to it.

'There's a clever girl.' Charlie was pleased. He took the joint from her and dragged long and hard. It was the only thing in the world that really relaxed him.

They lay back on the couch and shared the rest. Dindi despaired of him ever making a move. But at last he began to kiss her again and run his hands over her body. She sighed and moved and moaned and said, 'I feel so wonderful, you make me feel so wonderful.'

Then he was gently pulling her dress off, and manipulating her bosom over the top of her bra (a Fredericks special—black lace and pink ruffles), and kissing her nipples until they stood up firm and hard. She suppressed a desire to scream at him what to do next. He was so slow. After five minutes of playing with her breasts she wanted him to shove it into her good and hard, but he was making no move in that direction. Shit! she thought—shit! shit! shit! And she squirmed uncomfortably until at last she came to an unsatisfactory climax.

Unaware of this, Charlie continued to play with her nipples. By this time she was a mass of raw nerve-edges silently screaming at him to stop.

Could a Baby Girl reach for his prick?

Why not, if she were a stoned Baby Girl?

She deftly moved out of his grasp and felt for his fly. What the hell were all these buttons?

'Can I touch you?' she asked shyly.

'Of course, darling—of course.'

He got up quickly, feeling a bit guilty at having made her turn on, and struggled out of his pants.

Before he could sit down, she fastened her mouth on him like a limpet, forcing him to a quick climax.

He gave a long and anguished moan.

She let him free, and fell back on the couch murmuring, 'Oh Charlie, I've never done that before. You're so sexy. So great.'

He smiled. Yes, he could give women a good time. Movie star or dustman, he was a good lover. Hadn't this sweet girl just said so?

The phone started to ring and he padded to answer it, feeling stupid in just his shirt, socks, and horn-rimmed glasses.

Dindi lay back, feeling pleased with herself. She was definitely playing all her cards right. With any luck she would get a good cameo part in 'Roundabout', plus maybe a spell as Charlie Brick's girlfriend. It was always good to go with a star, got you around to all the right parties and premières, where important people noticed you. He obviously liked her. She could see his big bag was flattery, and man, she was the best at that. The main thing with any guy was sweet-talking him about what a stud he was.

Charlie was surprised to hear Clay Allen on the phone. It was early morning in London, and since Clay was arriving in Hollywood the following week, he wondered what he wanted. He hoped to God that Natalie hadn't said anything. Not that there was anything for her to say, but you never knew with women. They had a way of fabricating things.

They exchanged pleasantries, then Clay said: 'Look, old boy, I think there's something I had better tell you before some smart reporter blurts it at you. It's about Lorna. As you know, she's marrying that berk, and what is more, my friend, she's pregnant—five months.'

'Is it his?' Charlie blurted foolishly, in a state of shock.

'Well, it certainly isn't yours. Anyway, Natalie found out and we thought you should know.'

'Yes, yes, thanks, Clay.' He replaced the receiver.

Lorna had really gone and done it. Now there was no hope of them getting back together, no hope at all. His Lorna. Pregnant with another man's child.

He gazed blankly at Dindi lying on the couch. Blond hair spread around her pretty face, bosoms peeking at him over the top of her bra, long brown legs. She was at least ten years younger than Lorna, a real little beauty. One whom all his mates back in London would really fancy.

'Hey,' Charlie said. 'Let's get in the Maserati and drive somewhere—anywhere. How about Las Vegas? I've never been there. Let's get married.'

14

'Smile,' Carey whispered to Sunday, 'you look like a girl who's just had bad news.'

Sunday obediently manufactured a smile for the photographers buzzing round her and Steve Magnum. Actually the last thing in the world she felt like doing was smiling. She had had a terrible morning.

First, the pornographic letter with its sickening contents. Then, in her confusion, her little dog Limbo had somehow or other got lost. She had visions of it being trapped on Sunset Boulevard, and couldn't wait for the press conference to end, so that she could get back to the search.

'You've done a pretty good job of avoiding me,' Steve said, putting his arm around her for the photographers.

'Thank you for the flowers,' she replied dutifully.

'Is that all you've got to say on the subject? Why don't we discuss it over dinner tonight?'

'I'm sorry, I'm busy.'

He looked at her quizzically. It was such a change to meet a girl who played hard to get. He had a reputation as a lady-killer and most of the ladies couldn't wait to get killed.

In the whole of Steve's life there had only been two women who had actually turned down the opportunity of going to bed with him. One was a girl in high school who had called him skinny, and the other his mother's best friend. He bet they were sorry now. They were shrivelled-up old bags by this time anyway.

Still, it was refreshing to meet a girl like Sunday. She was so unlike the usual Hollywood actresses, and really great looking, not your hairpieces and false-eyelashes type of beauty. Jack Milan had been right when he said, 'There's a broad you've got to meet. I'm sitting you next to her.' Angela was getting to be a habit. Sunday had appeared at just the right time.

'What's the matter, am I too old for you?' he said with a smile. He knew that at fifty he was not too old for anyone. Not with the fame, the millions, the various homes around the world, the private plane, and the reputation—especially the reputation.

'How old *are* you?' Sunday asked sweetly, wondering if maybe Limbo had got shut in a closet somewhere.

Carey, watching on the sidelines as the photographers jostled for good shots, wished that Sunday would ease up just a little. She was really uptight. The best thing in the world for her would be an affair with someone like Steve Magnum—although those movie stars were such unpredictable bastards.

'That's enough, fellows,' Steve said, 'you'll be seeing a lot more of Sunday in our new movie.' He turned to her, fixing her with his famous pale-blue eyes. 'The dinner invitation is open any night you care to pick it up. Otherwise I'll see you in Acapulco.'

'O.K.' She did find him attractive, or was it that his face was so very familiar?

It was quite an achievement for Steve Magnum to appear at a press reception to introduce his latest leading lady. It made the whole thing more important.

Carey was delighted. 'You looked great, honey. It will make every front page tomorrow.'

'I must get back to the Château. Can we leave now?'

'Sure. Don't worry, Limbo's probably safely asleep under the bed.'

But he wasn't. Sunday searched her suite again, and wandered around the hotel, looking everywhere. She hired a taxi and cruised up and down Sunset. She called the police. By six o'clock she gave up hope and went home.

It took some time for the knocking on the door to get through to her. It was past seven, and her eyes were red-rimmed, her cheeks streaked.

Branch Strong stood there, Limbo barking cheekily under his arm.

'Er—Miss—er, I guess this is your dog, huh? Found him jigging about outside, down by the pool. I think he must have fallen in a few times 'cos he's wet through.' He handed the tiny dog to Sunday and it immediately covered her face with wet licks.

'Oh yes, yes. Come in.' Her face lit up as she muttered to the dog half scoldingly, half lovingly.

Branch walked in, swaggering unconsciously in his very tight blue jeans and thin white tee shirt. He was really quite knocked out with Sunday.

'I can't tell you how grateful I am. I've been going mad with worry. I was imagining the most awful things.'

'Yeah.' Branch stood awkwardly, his hands dangling beside him. 'I guess it was a good thing I found him.'

'You bet it was. Honestly, I am so relieved. If there's anything I can ever do for you—just name it.'

'I'll name it,' he hesitated. 'That is—er—I thought maybe you might like to have a bite to eat with me tonight.'

He paused hopefully, then quickly added, 'Nothing fancy—there's this great health-food place I found. What do you think?'

'Can we take Limbo?'

'Sure, yeah sure. You mean you'll come?' His big boyish face beamed. 'That's great. I guess I'd better go and wash up, and I'll fetch you in half-an-hour. Is that all right with you?'

'That's fine.'

She took Limbo in the kitchen and gave him a dish of meat and some water, then watched as he wolfed the lot down. Then she changed into a pair of white slacks and a sweater, brushed her hair and cleaned her face. Branch seemed nice; there could be no harm in having a quiet dinner with him.

In the bedroom she noticed the revolting letter she had received that morning, still lying in fragments in the wastepaper basket. She shuddered. It was so vile, so obscene. Carey had laughed when she told her about it. 'You'll be inundated with pieces of garbage like that. Don't even bother to read them; it gives some poor sick guy somewhere his jollies. Forget it, they never do anything else but write.'

Didn't they? In spite of the fact that they seemed convinced that they *would* do the things described?

Of course they didn't. Only it gave Sunday a bad feeling to know that somewhere, someone, knew where she was and had such thoughts about her.

15

Charlie tried to get hold of George but couldn't locate him. George, taking advantage of his night of freedom was sitting in a strip club admiring the scenery.

Charlie was very stoned, and completely carried away with the idea of running off to Las Vegas with Dindi.

She was sceptical. Could this nut really be serious about getting married? But if it came off, what a break!

Charlie thought: *Screw you, Lorna. Screw you, Michelle. Screw you, Natalie. I'm going to show the lot of you.* They would all see how much he cared when they read their papers tomorrow.

He told Dindi they wouldn't bother picking up any of her things, she would have everything new in Las Vegas. Then, throwing a few clothes in an overnight bag, they headed for the Maserati and took off.

It was an easy ride, freeway all the way, and Charlie really put his foot down, revelling in the sound of the powerful engine. He played his new stereo tape equipment and they shared another joint.

Dindi hoped to hell they wouldn't get stopped for speeding or anything. If they got booked for smoking pot it would ruin a beautiful scene.

She contemplated giving him a little going over while he was driving, but at the speed they were travelling it was probably unwise. Anyway, she didn't want to appear too forward—yet. Maybe it was her supposed innocence that he went for. She lay back in her seat and listened to the music.

It was around four a.m. when Vegas loomed ahead. It was a mass of blazing neon signs as they drove through the downtown section. In spite of the hour the streets and gambling halls were crowded. It was a waste of time to go to bed in Vegas—unless of course that was the business you were in. Charlie had never been there before, but he had had the desk clerk at the Beverly Hills phone through to the Forum hotel to alert them of his arrival. It was the latest hotel to be built on the main strip.

Dindi had fallen asleep. Charlie woke her. 'Which way to the strip?' he asked.

She had already told him she had been there before, although not in what circumstances. She had been dating a small-time hood at the time who had dumped her there without a cent, after three glorious days together. She had hung around and worked as a cocktail waitress and made it with a few fantastic swimming coaches, and had then got a ride back to L.A. with an up-and-coming actor—the only trouble was he was up and coming practically the whole trip! That was before Rome.

'Just keep on this street and take a right at the top.' She

thought a minute, then added, 'Hey, there's a fabulous new hotel—the Forum. I'd love to go there, it's supposed to be wild, TV in the john and fruit machines in the elevators.' She had decided it was better to go somewhere she might not be known. It wouldn't be cool to have half the croupiers greeting her by name.

'That's just where we're going.'

The Forum was approached through a driveway of marble Roman soldiers—very impressive. Several bleached-blond boys in short togas surrounded the Maserati as it arrived at the entrance. They opened the doors, took the one bag, and escorted Charlie and Dindi inside.

Charlie asked for the Manager, who appeared almost immediately—a dead ringer for a young George Raft. He appraised Dindi with a flick of his eyes, greeted Charlie profusely, and organised the biggest suite in the hotel. He was no slouch at recognising celebrities, and was used to dealing with all their peculiar requests. However, it did shake him a bit when Charlie said they wanted to get married right then and there. 'Give me an hour,' he said.

Charlie nodded. It seemed quite reasonable in his present state of mind that a marriage could be arranged at four a.m. in Las Vegas.

Dindi was starting to feel shaky. The sonofabitch was actually serious.

Charlie indicated the arcade of shops around the lobby. 'Miss Sydne would like to buy a dress, and I'd like to get in the jewellers.'

'Certainly.' By this time the Manager was unflappable. Charlie had slipped him a large tip, and as far as he was concerned he could have what he liked. 'I'll send a selection of dresses to your suite: Size ten, Miss Sydne?'

She nodded. The Manager was just the type of good-looking, smooth bastard she could fall for.

'OK, Mr Brick, as soon as I've located the jeweller I'll put him in touch with you. Meanwhile, leave everything to me. Will there be any guests?'

Charlie shook his head.

'Do you have any objection to publicity?'

'None at all.' The whole point as far as Charlie was concerned was to have large photos of himself and gorgeous blond Dindi spread all over the newspapers for everyone to see.

The preacher was a southern cracker. Hurriedly dressed in a shiny blue suit, he peered at the couple before him and drawled out his version of the wedding ceremony.

Dindi noticed that his fly was undone and tried to stifle a giggle. She was wearing a pink frilled dress, and her blond hair fell loosely around her shoulders. She looked like a lovely innocent doll. On her finger she wore a huge cluster diamond ring, a present from Charlie.

He had also noticed the preacher's undone fly, and couldn't help his eyes from straying there. The funny old chap had probably been fast asleep. What an accent! He listened intently. This would be a great voice to use in some future film.

The Manager had arranged the wedding in the penthouse, with the hotel photographer, press-man and two representatives of the local newspaper, with their photographer, present. The Manager and his girlfriend were the two witnesses.

The preacher pronounced them man and wife, belched unobtrusively, and shook Charlie's hand. Then there was champagne, photographs, and congratulations all round.

The preacher sidled up to Charlie—'Here's my card if you need me again.'

Charming—Charlie thought—only just married and he's asking me if I need him again!

It was seven a.m. by the time they got back to their suite. Charlie was beginning to feel the strain. His eyes hurt behind his glasses, and the beautiful high he had achieved was beginning to wear off. For the first time he thought about the sanity of what he had just done. He had married a girl he didn't even know. It was the most ridiculous insane thing. She was very pretty, but he didn't even *know* her.

It was all Lorna's fault. He had done it to spite her. What would Serafina say?

Dindi was dazed, but for different reasons. So suddenly and unexpectedly she was someone. *She* had married a movie star!

She took off her dress and caught Charlie staring at her with a puzzled expression.

She giggled. 'Hey, lover, now we can do it legal!'

16

Sunday was as amazed as the rest of Hollywood when Dindi and Charlie Brick appeared on the front of all the newspapers—married in Las Vegas. She couldn't understand why Dindi hadn't mentioned it to her, as she wasn't exactly the sort of girl to keep a secret.

Carey was laughing. 'I tell you, honey, Marsh is fit to be tied, but beside himself! Seems he fixed her up for Charlie to get himself laid, and the schmuck ups and marries her. Can you imagine? That chick had really been around—but I mean *really*.'

'Maybe it was love at first sight,' Sunday replied, always a believer in romance.

'Maybe, my ass. She must have cast one hell of a mean spell on him.'

'She's very pretty, and she certainly has lots of personality. Why couldn't it be love at first sight?'

'Oh, Sunday, baby. Sometimes you are *so* naïve. It's times like this I realize you're only twenty, and not the cool forty-five-year-old you usually come across as. By the way, they pushed you and Steve right off the front pages, but there's still good coverage inside.'

'Anyway, I think it's wonderful for Dindi, I really do. I'm going to send her a telegram.'

'Save your money. I don't give it two weeks. When Charlie comes to his senses and finds out what a hooker she is—then—like—the party's over.'

'Carey, you're much to cynical.'

Carey hooted with laughter.

'By the way, I just turned down a part for you in 'Roundabout'. The timing was wrong. Marshall suddenly accepted the fact that you exist and flipped. He saw a clip from the Milan movie.'

The two girls were talking over an ice cream. Sunday spooned peppermint into her mouth and said, 'I wonder how Branch will do with his test.'

She had told Carey about her date with him the previous evening and how pleasant it had been.

'Listen, kid, I know you think I'm always putting people down, but I checked up on Mr Branch Strong, and he is purely fag time. It's not a good scene for you to go out with him.'

'According to you, everyone is either a hooker or gay. I don't intend to go to bed with him. He's just very simple and straightforward, and I like him, purely as a friend.'

'Simple is the right word. All right, as long as you're not planning a grand love affair, although while we are on the subject, about your sex life—'

'Look, I appreciate everything you're doing and have done for me, but my sex life is my own business, and if I don't care to have one, that's also my own business.'

Carey smoothed her hands over her sleek cap of black hair. Sometimes Sunday could be very cold.

They finished their ice-creams in silence, then Carey said, 'I'll drop you off for your fittings.' She noticed that everyone in the place turned to stare at Sunday as they left. When this girl was really exposed to the public, when her films came out, she wouldn't be able to travel around alone. She was destined to be a Monroe-Sinatra type of celebrity, the kind they wanted to mob and touch. Marshall's reaction to seeing her on film had been an indication. He never got excited about anything.

Carey thought of Marshall fondly for a few moments. She missed being with him, missed his sudden bouts of temper, and his gammy footsteps as he stamped about his office. He was a real character. Although she had worked with him for seven years, she knew practically nothing about his personal life, nor apparently did anyone else. There was a wife, long ago divorced and now living in Pasadena. The only reason she knew about her was because of the alimony cheques that were sent every month.

'You want to go to a movie tonight?' Carey asked, when she dropped Sunday at the costumiers.

'Thanks, but I think I'll study my script.'

'Talk to you tomorrow then.'

The fittings were perfect: a white leather micro dress with matching bikini; a startling fall of white jersey folds to the floor, plunging to expose most of her bosom; a white linen suit with huge cowboy hat.

Steve Magnum had decided her wardrobe should be all white to complement her golden skin and tawny mass of hair.

'You'll adore Acapulco,' Hanna said. Hanna, a gaunt English lady wearing a mannish suit and unappealing flat brogue shoes, was doing the fittings.

'I'm sure I will.' Sunday shivered slightly as Hanna's stubby fingers delved across her bosom, adjusting a button.

'There,' Hanna stood back and surveyed her work. 'You look quite ravishing.'

'I love the clothes,' Sunday said. 'Who should I talk to about buying them for myself after the film?'

Hanna looked at her strangely. 'I would think you'd have no difficulty with Steve Magnum. He's very generous, especially to *close* friends.' She allowed herself a fleeting private smile, which Sunday understood only too well.

'Thanks. But I don't think I shall be asking Mr Magnum for favours like that.'

'Really?' Hanna's arch smile said: Who are you kidding?

So that's what they all thought. Sunday was furious, and furthermore she resolved to keep her relationship with Steve Magnum absolutely and utterly professional.

Let them all see just how wrong they were.

17

Herbert pissed a perfect arch, which landed delicately in Cy Hamilton's horseshoe-shaped swimming pool. He zipped up his fly with pleasure. One more Hollywood pool had the addition of his wine. What a blow he was striking for the poorer classes!

Herbert had been in the habit of relieving himself in the best pools in Hollywood during the two years he had been working for the Supreme Chauffeur Company. The opportunities were not to be ignored, and as long as there were no nosey servants hanging around, he usually managed it while waiting to pick up his parties. He was always kept waiting, and it gave him a thrill when his passengers finally climbed in the car, all dressed up, to think of them the next day swimming around in his piss.

He had driven the Hamiltons before and he loathed them. The drunken woman with her steely eyes and skinny body, purposely giving him a good flash of her intimate parts as she got in the car: And the man, so obviously rich and powerful, sitting and listening to the woman nag and whine and bitch her way to wherever they were going.

Tonight it was a party. The woman was wearing skin-tight leopard-printed chiffon trousers and hardly any top.

Herbert thought it disgusting the way some men let their wives go around. As a matter of fact, he was rather concerned about Marge—dear fat old Marge, who for so many years had been simply content to squat in front of the television and eat. Since her first outing with Louella Crisp—the new neighbour—she had changed. She was always popping over to visit the house next door, and her dresses actually looked clean. She made up her face, and had even gone to the beauty parlour to have her scraggy hair styled.

Herbert was amazed, and not pleased at all.

The final straw had come that evening, before he left for work.

'Louella's having a little party next week,' Marge announced. 'She wants to know if you can come. It will be awful good fun, games and things. Her husband's gonna be there too. *Will* you be able to come, hon? I'm gonna get myself a pretty new dress, *and* go on a diet.'

Herbert regarded his wife's elephantine form coldly. 'I don't want you going to no party.'

Marge's eyes brimmed full of tears, which, mixing with her mascara, dribbled down her cheeks. 'But Herbie, hon, she's my friend, my only friend . . .'

'She's a bad influence on you. I don't want you seeing her no more. Look at yourself—made up like a whore.'

She chewed on her lower lip, the tears ceased, and a crafty expression passed across her fat face.

'If you don't let me go, I'm gonna tell about you writing those dirty letters. I'm gonna tell the police and they'll put you in jail for being . . .'

She trailed off as Herbert fixed her with his eyes. They were the meanest eyes she had ever seen.

'What letters?' His voice was very controlled, but inside he was shaking with fury. *Nobody* knew about his letters. He wrote them upstairs, locked away in the little box-room. Marge was always busy watching television. 'What letters?' he repeated, taking her fleshy arm in a tight grip.

She was frightened. Herbert got so strange at times. She wished she hadn't mentioned the letters, after all she had only found two, and she certainly didn't mind if he wanted to write to those fancy movie stars.

'Angela Carter,' she gulped, 'it was torn up, and I stuck it together. It's all right, Herbie, I was only joking. Herbie, you're hurting my arm—Herbie . . .' She screamed as his nails raked into her soft skin and drew blood, then she sniffled quietly as he paced up and down the room, beside himself with anger.

How could he have been so careless? He usually tore up, and flushed down the toilet, any unfinished efforts.

'Get them,' he demanded.

She scurried off immediately and fetched the two letters, hidden carefully under the mattress. She was reluctant to part with them. They had kept her company many a long and lonely night. She handed them over.

'I wish you'd do some of those things you write about to me,' she whined, 'You never do anything to me any more.'

She rubbed her vast bosom up against him. 'I'd like to do all those things again, Herbie. Can we start doing them again?'

He pushed her away. 'You're too fat,' he muttered. How could he ever consider touching that gross body again when he had someone like Sunday Simmons?

'But, Herbie.' In desperation Marge was unbuttoning her blouse and releasing a mammoth bosom from the confines of a dirty white bra. 'Look what I've got. I've got beautiful titties, you used to love my titties.'

He glanced at her with disgust. Big fat floppy bosom. He turned his back. 'Get dressed, you whore. And see you stay in tonight.'

Then he grabbed his jacket and marched out.

Yes, the whole episode with Marge was most disturbing. Especially the sexual part, the exhibiting of herself to him. Didn't she realise that that part of their life was over? It made him feel unclean and disgusted just thinking about it.

'Hey, driver,' the woman was leaning drunkenly forward from the back seat, a cigarette dangling from her painted scarlet lips. 'Got a light?'

'Emerald, sit down please. I'll light your cigarette.' Cy's voice was tense.

'I wouldn't dream of bothering you, my sweet. *You* don't want me to smoke. *You* don't think it's the done thing for a lady to arrive at a party smoking. Well, fuck *you*.'

'Emerald, please.'

She waved the cigarette at Herbert. 'Light me up, Sam.'

Furious with the man in the back for letting this woman get away with such foul talk, he silently handed her the automatic lighter.

She threw it down on the front seat when she was finished, and Herbert burnt his fingers returning it to the dashboard. Then the man in the back pressed a button, and the glass partition slid up, cutting off the rest of their conversation.

Herbert resolved to pee in their swimming pool again on the return journey. He would drink plenty of beer and piss another perfect arch . . .

18

Charlie wasn't sure when he first realised he had made a terrible mistake. Was it the day after his Las Vegas wedding—or the day after that?

Viewing things in the cold light of reality, he couldn't imagine how he could have done it.

Dindi was just as pretty as ever, but an idiot, a pretty little unintelligent idiot. Every time she opened her pouty lips it was to ask for something.

Even after two days it was beginning to drive him mad.

'Baby, can I have some money for roulette?' 'Sweetie, can I have those *marvellous* diamond and turquoise earrings?' 'Pussycat, what about a little mink to keep off the cold night air?'

He gave her everything she wanted. After all, it was their honeymoon.

Public reaction to their wedding was mixed. The newspapers made the most of it: 'Beautiful starlet marries Charlie Brick', and similar headlines all over the world.

Personal acquaintances were another matter. George arrived by plane, and he and Dindi seemed to become instant enemies. Marshall on the phone was positively rude; he talked business and ignored the marriage until the end of the conversation, when he mumbled something about lots of luck, you're going to need it.

From England came a long telegram from his mother. 'Son, what have you done? Couldn't you have waited? Will arrive soon. Serafina, your loving mother.'

It irked Charlie that everyone wasn't going around saying how lucky he was to have married such a gorgeous young girl. He was infuriated that there had been no word from Lorna.

Serafina was merely upset because she had not been present. She hated to miss anything, and was looking forward to her forthcoming trip to Hollywood. A new daughter-in-law wasn't exactly what she had been anticipating.

Dindi was immediately jealous of George. He arrived,

summoned by Charlie after the wedding, and as usual, stayed near Charlie, available for all his requests.

'Is he going to come everywhere with us?' she questioned, a little put out because George had hovered near them at the swimming pool all day, and was now back in their suite setting up stereo equipment.

'He doesn't bother you, does he, darling?' Charlie asked mildly.

'Oh no,' she shrugged, 'I guess I'll go downstairs and have a looksee through the shops. Can I have some bread?'

Charlie was beginning to be irritated by Dindi's constant use of what she considered to be hip phraseology.

He gave her yet another stack of dollars, she seemed to go through money like confetti. She left and he went to watch George at work on the stereo.

'How long will we stay here?' George asked. He had already summed up the marriage as a dead loss, and couldn't understand how Charlie had been so foolish.

'A few days, maybe longer. I was thinking of having you drive the Maserati back and coming to fetch us in the Mercedes. There's a couple of houses you can look at for me. I've got to get something settled before the children arrive.'

Downstairs, Dindi bought three new bikinis, and a big straw sunhat. The rest of the money she took over to the roulette table and covered number twenty. She bit her lip with excitement as she watched the wheel spin, and hey presto—twenty came up. She gave a little squeak of joy, and then the Manager was beside her and muttered, 'Let it ride.'

She looked up at him. He smelt of a very funky after-shave. She let the money ride, and twenty came up again. She had won a bundle.

Laughing, he took her arm. 'Take it all off.'

She smiled at him. 'The money?'

'For now.'

They understood each other.

Dindi felt a tingle of excitement. Charlie didn't excite her: She didn't feel free to be herself. With him she was still playing Baby Girl.

'Listen, if you want to count your money, I have an apartment on the eighteenth floor, apartment E.' He winked at her and walked off.

Well, the sonofabitch was certainly sure of himself, but so what, she had nothing to lose. She was a married lady now, and fun was fun. She scooped up her chips and went off to change them. Then she took the elevator to the eighteenth floor.

They stayed in Vegas five days, at the end of which Charlie was bored stiff and couldn't wait to get to work. Angela Carter had been signed for 'Roundabout' and the new script was completed. They were still looking for another girl, as Sunday Simmons was unavailable. It was only a small part and presented no major problem.

Unbeknown to Charlie, Dindi had plans to grab the role for herself: A little chat with Marshall, a few hints to Charlie, and the whole thing should be a cinch.

George had chosen a house in Bel Air which he thought would meet with Charlie's approval. It was a two-storey ranch with indoor and outdoor swimming pools, tennis courts, a guest house, and numerous bedrooms and entertaining rooms. It had been a choice between that house or a glass and steel modernistic effort up in the Hollywood Hills. George had instinctively known Dindi would prefer the modern house, so he had picked the other one.

Charlie was delighted with it. There was more than enough room to assemble all his stereo equipment, records, tapes, cameras and other toys that took his fancy. He was a great collector, getting a bug about something for months on end, then abandoning it and going on to something else. At the moment it was stereo and cars, but he was just starting a photography phase.

Dindi was impressed with the house. She had had a great time in Las Vegas, and had returned to Hollywood loaded with clothes, jewellery and a movie-star husband. What more could a girl want? She didn't even bother to collect her things from her old apartment, just instructed the landlady by phone to find her passport and mail it on to her. Who needed old things when she could have everything new?

She opened charges everywhere, and, the first day back, went on a wild spending spree.

Clay and Natalie Allen arrived in town.

'Why don't we have a little dinner party, a sort of celebration?' Charlie asked Dindi. 'You can ask some of your friends, as many as you like. We'll have it catered by Trader Vic's.' He had decided to make the most of his mistake. After all, Dindi was very young, and surely it would be a fairly simple matter to make her into the kind of girl he had thought he had married. She was bound to be willing to improve herself.

'Yeah,' Dindi nodded thoughtfully. Who of her so-called friends could she possibly invite? All the guys she had screwed. And as for her girlfriends—well, who needed those big mouths? The only person she could think of was Sunday Simmons.

'Really, I don't have many friends here,' she said; 'Most of my close friends and all my family are in Philadelphia.' Dindi had never been to Philadelphia in her life, but she figured it sounded like a pretty respectable town to come from. Actually she had been born in Arizona and hadn't been back since she zoomed out of town with a travelling salesman at the age of fifteen.

'It doesn't have to be a big party,' Charlie said. He didn't want to present his new wife to the Allens on her own; she seemed more intelligent among people. 'We'll make it small—just Marshall, Cy and Emerald Hamilton, Clay and Natalie and a few others.'

'My best friend is Sunday Simmons, I'd like to invite her.'

'Fine. Make out a list, and we'll try and arrange it for the weekend.'

He went off to study his new script. Everything was going to work out. At least now he wouldn't have to go running after little ding-a-lings. He could concentrate on his work, and Dindi would soon have the children arriving to keep her occupied. Maybe she and Natalie would become friends. Natalie could teach her a lot. He just had to remember she was seventeen years younger than himself and hadn't been around. It would all work out.

19

Sunday found herself spending a lot of time with Branch. He was easy-going, and pleasant. She didn't fancy him sexually; she thought of him as a big brother, and hoped that he regarded her with the same feelings. She hadn't forgotten that both Dindi and Carey had said he was gay and since he hadn't made a pass at her, she was prepared to believe he was.

He was a strange boy in many ways. He hated to talk about himself or his past, was very nervous about the outcome of his test, and dreaded the thought of having to return to New York if it was unsuccessful.

It was good for Sunday to have a male companion. With Carey, when they had gone out together at night, they had been constantly bothered by men: Now, with Branch by her side she was never pestered.

Carey was most put out by the whole situation.

'If your name has to be linked with someone, at least let it be Steve Magnum, not some little unknown schnook.'

Sunday just laughed, and she and Branch were soon regarded as an item.

Steve Magnum was unamused. It was not often he was turned down for some muscle-bound nothing. Just wait until he got Miss Sunday Simmons in Acapulco!

Branch's test was successful. He was signed for a cowboy movie that was to start shooting in Mexico almost immediately. He was delighted.

The night before he left, Sunday took him to Dindi and Charlie's party. She was looking forward to seeing Dindi again, and hearing about the wedding. She was also excited about meeting Charlie Brick. She was a fan, and considered him to be a brilliant comedy actor. It was a shame she hadn't been available to do the part in 'Roundabout', but Carey had said it was a small part anyway, and 'Cash' was more important.

Dindi was playing Hollywood Hostess to the hilt. Her blond hair was joined by a long fall of ringlets cascading down her back, and she wore a full-length green chiffon dress that laced Roman-style down the front to her waist. Around her person she wore every bit of jewellery that Charlie had bought her.

'Darling!' she greeted Sunday, her voice high and strained. 'How wonderful to see you.' She flashed her diamond ring and leant forward to exchange kisses, whispering in her normal voice, 'Thank Christ you're here. This is the draggiest crowd ever!'

'What a marvellous house,' Sunday said. She looked around the huge living room, the walls covered with interesting paintings. There were about twelve people standing about drinking and talking. 'You remember Branch Strong, don't you?'

'Of course,' Dindi smiled brightly at him. 'I read where your test was fantastic.'

He looked embarrassed.

'Come and have a drink. Sunday, you look great. When do you start the movie with Steve Magnum? I'm green with envy. I understand he's one of *the* great Hollywood lays.'

Dindi hasn't changed, Sunday thought, looking around for Charlie. She was intrigued to see what kind of man he was. Branch was dragged off by Emerald Hamilton, who trapped him in a corner.

Marshall arrived accompanied by Carey, and Sunday spent all her time chatting to them. She was surprised to see Carey, who hadn't mentioned coming to the party.

'It was a last-minute thing,' Carey told her. 'Marsh called and said he had some important things to discuss with me, so I blew out my date and came here. Business before pleasure, you know. Anyway I wanted to catch this scene.'

Sunday thought how chic and attractive she looked, her dark skin setting off the white lace dress she was wearing perfectly.

Charlie came over then. Thinner than Sunday expected. A long sad face with heavy horn-rimmed glasses. Black hair. He smiled at Sunday, a slightly crooked smile, almost boyish. His voice was very warm. She liked him at once, and wondered why his eyes behind the glasses were sad.

'Dindi's spoken a lot about you,' he said, struck at once by her strange browny-yellow eyes and wide sensual mouth. She was far more beautiful than she had seemed in that short piece of film.

'Has she?' Sunday smiled.

Marshall said, 'Charlie, you never met Carey, did you? My ex-right-hand. Took a powder to make it on her own.'

'Very wise too.' Charlie appraised her. 'Anyone who sets up on their own has the right idea. Especially if it means escaping from old Marsh. He must be a bastard to work for.'

Carey grinned. 'He is.'

Charlie found his eyes wandering back to Sunday's and she met his stare. He wondered if the gossip about her and Steve Magnum were true. Probably—most actresses were the same; just mention a part in a movie and they would sell their mother.

Sunday thought: He's not a happy man.

'I love your house,' she said, to break the stare.

'Do you? Thank you. It's only rented, but I'm quite pleased with it.'

Dindi appeared then and pushed her arm through his. 'Baby, the head waiter's getting all uptight about serving dinner. You want to tell him it's O.K.?'

'All right, love' He gave her an absent-minded kiss and went off to organise things.

Dindi winked at Marshall. 'It's something, huh? Little old me finally made it. Hey, girls, would you mind if I grabbed Marshall for a private tête-à-tête?'

'Be my guest,' Carey said, picking up her martini and sipping it slowly.

Dindi took Marshall off.

'Well?' Carey said. 'What do you think?'

'About what?' Sunday replied.

'This whole scene. Do you still think it's love at first sight?'

'I don't know, how can anybody know? Dindi seems happy enough.'

'And Charlie?'

'I don't know Charlie.'

'No, but he'd like to know you.'

'What do you mean?'

'You *know* what I mean. The two of you had your own private electricity-line buzzing between you.'

'Sometimes I think you're nuts.' But Sunday knew exactly what she meant.

'Hi, Carey.' Cy came strolling over. 'How about introducing me to your client?'

'Sure. Sunday, this is Cy Hamilton, my favourite producer.'

'Hello.'

'Hello, there.' Cy took her hand in a clammy grip and didn't release it. His eyes probed beneath her silk jersey top, and lingered on her naked bosom.

She pulled her hand free.

'I'm disappointed you're not available to do "Roundabout", for me,' he said, 'but I'm sure we'll fix something together soon.' He glanced at Carey. 'I think Sunday and I should have a meeting to discuss future projects. Maybe lunch on Monday?'

Sunday said, 'Carey arranges everything for me, I just follow her advice. She's the one you should have lunch with. Carey, Branch is trapped in a corner by some woman. Who is she?'

'Cy's wife.'

'Oh!'

Cy laughed. 'Jealous?'

'Of course not. I just wondered who she was.'

'And for your information your muscle-bound boyfriend is the one that has my wife trapped. You know something, you're a snotty broad.'

With that he walked off.

'Honestly!' Sunday exclaimed.

'Take no notice,' Carey replied, 'he's just annoyed 'cos you turned down his lunch invitation. It's not often he gets a no. He's banged practically every actress that ever set foot on a movie of his. His wife's a boozer and screws everything in sight. They're a beautiful couple.'

20

Natalie and Clay were suitably impressed with Charlie's house. They were also renting, but on a more modest scale. They arrived an hour before the party was due to start, and Charlie sat with them in the study and heard all the London gossip.

He hadn't seen Natalie since that day in his hotel, and it was to her credit that her attitude towards him was exactly the same as before. He felt relieved, and hoped that now he was married again she would just forget all about it.

'Where's your wife?' she asked. 'I can't wait to meet her. Did Clay tell you he knows her?'

'Knows her?' Charlie was incredulous.

'Only vaguely,' Clay said quickly, shooting Natalie a glance that said, Why don't you keep your big mouth shut? 'I met her in Rome a year or so ago. I'm sure she won't remember me.'

Clay was banking on the fact that Dindi would definitely prefer not to remember him. They had met at a party, and he and some Italian producer had both screwed her one after the other, while she had shrieked with laughter and said, 'I hope this gets me the part!'

Of course Clay hadn't told Natalie the whole story, in fact he wished he hadn't mentioned it at all. But he had been so surprised when he had picked up his morning paper and found a large picture of Dindi and Charlie on the front page, that he had exclaimed, 'My God! Where did he ever dig up *that* one?'

'Yes, Dindi spent some time in Rome with her parents,' Charlie said. 'She's finishing dressing, she'll be down in a minute.'

'I hope you didn't mind my inviting Max Thorpe,' Clay said quickly to change the subject. 'His television show is a big hit here.'

'Not at all,' Charlie replied. Actually he couldn't stand Max Thorpe, a half-assed clairvoyant palm-reader who had got lucky by foretelling a couple of world events that any fool knew were bound to happen, and had ended up with his own show from Hollywood called 'I Predict'. Charlie knew him from his struggling days when they had both been performing in Soho. One drunken evening he had read Charlie's palm at a party and had said a lot of things Charlie didn't like.

'You know it must be three years since I've seen Max,' Clay remarked: 'He told me then I'd be doing a lot of travelling.'

'Have you seen Lorna?' Charlie tried to sound casual, although even now it was difficult to say her name without feeling she was still his wife.

'Yes, as a matter of fact we bumped into her at a little restaurant in Hampstead,' Natalie said: 'She's absolutely huge, although she claims she's only six months. Frankly she looks like she's going to pop at any minute. I think they're getting married this week.'

'That's ñice,' He tried to keep his voice emotionless. 'Did she mention me?'

Natalie and Clay both spoke at once, Natalie said yes, and Clay no.

Charlie laughed nervously. 'It's all right, I'm immune to any of her comments now.' He poured himself another Scotch, with a shaky hand.

'She said she was glad you had married again so soon.' Natalie smiled slightly, savouring the next remark. 'She said it would serve you right marrying a girl so much younger than yourself.'

'Why the hell did she say that?'

'Oh, you know Lorna. Always full of cryptic remarks.'

Dindi walked in, kissed Charlie, and smiled brightly at the Allens. The smile froze on her face when she recognised Clay. Dindi had screwed two hundred and twenty-three men, and remembered the faces—though not the names—of all of them.

Clay bridged the gap quickly, but not before Natalie had noticed the girl's look of shock.

'We met in Rome,' Clay said, 'Remember? At Claudio Finca's party. I was teasing you because you were with your mother.'

'Oh, yes.' Dindi's smile unfroze. This was one smart guy. 'Mummy's back in Philadelphia now.'

Charlie said, 'This is Natalie, darling. Clay and Natalie are two of my oldest friends.'

'Now, now,' Natalie chided gently, 'be careful when you say

oldest, I'm very sensitive. How are you, Dindi? I've been so looking forward to meeting you.'

The two women took stock of each other.

Natalie saw a pretty blonde girl with too much hair and too much bosom on show. She noted that the blue eyes were sharp and bright, and she didn't underestimate her.

Dindi saw an attractive thin dark woman in her late twenties, very sure of herself, and very possessive of Charlie. It was possible that she might have screwed him.

'Charlie's talked lots about you,' Dindi said, 'I feel I know all about you.'

'Oh, good,' Natalie smiled thinly. The girl thought she and Charlie had had an affair.

'You look lovely,' Charlie said, patting Dindi on the bottom. 'Isn't she a little darling?'

'Adorable,' Natalie said.

'Yes,' Clay agreed, remembering what a little darling she had been with her pants down. It occurred to him that maybe he should have been truthful with Charlie. After all, they had been close friends for many years. But he had married the girl, so what was the point?

Later in the evening Marshall K. Marshall felt the same way. He had fixed Charlie up with Dindi in the first place. How was he supposed to know that the idiot was going to blow his mind and marry the girl? Now that he *was* married to her, it certainly wouldn't be the time to tell him that she was a semi-hooker, accepting film parts instead of money—although Marshall could remember the one occasion when he paid her five hundred dollars to spend a weekend in Palm Springs with a German midget who was up for a Best Supporting Actor award. Anyway, it certainly shouldn't take long for Charlie to see the truth.

Dindi approached him during the evening and told him she wanted the other girl's part in 'Roundabout'.

'You can convince Charlie,' she said. 'It will be great publicity for the movie, and I know I'll be good in it: All I need is a decent chance.'

'Ask Charlie yourself,' Marshall replied. 'You got him to marry you, you shouldn't have any problem getting in the film.'

'Oh, Marsh it's got to come from you. I don't want him

thinking I married him to get in his movie. Please, just give me a chance. Now I'm Mrs Brick I'm a changed girl, I really would be just right for the part.'

In spite of everything he liked Dindi, and it would be a natural publicity break to put her in the film, and she *was* right for the part. It was a simple role that would just require her to look pretty and sexy, and that she could certainly do.

'I'll talk to Charlie.'

She gave him a kiss on the cheek. 'You're a doll. You won't be sorry. I'll become a big star and you'll make a fortune off of me. And Marsh, anytime I can return the favour,' she winked, 'just give me the word.'

Max Thorpe was a plumpish man of Charlie's age. He had a bright red suntan, and had recently bleached his mousy brown hair with vivid yellow streaks. He wore a black and white striped cotton suit with matching shirt and tie.

'All he needs is a straw hat with "Kiss me quick" on it, and he would fit straight into a Brighton day trip,' Charlie remarked to Natalie.

However, Max Thorpe was the hit of the party. Nobody could resist knowing what good things the future had in store for them, and it was Max's policy only to predict good things. He was soon surrounded by anxious outstretched palms, but the hand that really interested him was that of Branch Strong.

Max, like Charlie, had come a long way from the Soho joints where he had first appeared. And along the way his tastes had changed from flat-chested long-legged girls to muscle-bound beautiful young men. Branch was a perfect specimen.

Max felt his heart pounding as it hadn't done since he had met a fake Indian at Disneyland. He recognised a kindred spirit in Branch immediately, and holding his hand tightly, he foresaw great fortune and success, and that someone with the initial 'M' would become most prominent in his life. He advised the young man to follow his natural inclinations, and asked whether he would like to appear on an 'I Predict' television show?

Branch listened intently, a wide grin on his perfect features. Fame, fortune and success were just what he wanted, and then perhaps he could get rid of all the perverts who swarmed around him. 'M' must stand for Mother. He had been too ashamed to go home and see her for two years. Follow your natural inclinations must mean tell all the queer boys to stay away from him. As soon as he achieved the fame, fortune and success, he could do just that, including getting rid of his agent, whose demands were the most demeaning of all. Then perhaps he could have a real relationship with Sunday. He didn't feel it would be proper to touch her until all his past associations were finished.

'How about appearing on my show?' Max persisted.

'Yeah, well, I'm off to Mexico tomorrow. Got me a great little part in a cowboy movie, but when I come back, I'd sure love to.'

Max asked anxiously, 'When will that be?'

'They reckon I should be there six or seven weeks.' Branch pushed a lock of fallen blond hair off his forehead.

'We could pay in advance.' Max lowered his voice and said this quickly. 'In fact I could pay you tonight if you could come back to my house and collect. Fifteen hundred dollars.'

'Yeah?' It slowly dawned on Branch what Max Thorpe had in mind. If he had fame, fortune and success he would punch him right on his burnt-up red nose. But he didn't have any of those things yet, and fifteen hundred dollars was an awful lot of money. 'Is that so? Well, I guess I could meander by later. First, I have to take a little lady home.'

'Fine, fine. Any time will do.' Max felt his whole body slump with relief. 'I'll let you have my address.'

Later in the evening Charlie found himself the object of Max's interest. 'Remember what I told you, old boy. You didn't like it at the time, but it's all come true.'

'Some of it,' Charlie admitted reluctantly.

'Pretty accurate I was.' Max chuckled at his own cleverness, and also because he knew he was annoying Charlie, whom he disliked. 'Broken marriage. New marriage across water. The initials "R" and "S". Well, "S" is your wife's second initial, isn't it? Two more children.'

'Yes, yes' Charlie interrupted, 'but what about all the things that didn't happen? An accident or illness. A scandal. The initials "H.S." What about them?'

'Oh, don't worry about them,' Max said tartly, 'there's plenty of time for them. As far as I remember you have rather a good lifeline. Shall we have another reading?'

'No, thanks.'

After dinner Carey said, 'What was the business you wanted to talk about, Marsh?'

He was smoking a short fat cigar and didn't answer.

'Hey listen, I gave up a hot date for tonight, don't brush me off with your agent's stare.'

He took the cigar out of his mouth and studied it. Then he suddenly said, 'I'm fifty-six years old, a cripple—and don't give me any bullshit about a club-foot not making me a cripple—*you* try dragging it around for a few days. I've been married once and made a mess of it. On the good side I'm rich, powerful in my own little way. I don't gamble, drink too much or screw any good-looking piece of ass that comes my way. I'm kind, generous and clean. I don't give a shit about the black so-called problems and I want you to marry me.'

Carey looked at him in amazement. 'What?'

'You heard me right. I want to marry you. You're a very sharp broad, you should jump at the chance.' He was trying to play it funny, but the way he was shredding the leaves of tobacco on his cigar with nervous fingers made it quite plain he was serious.

Carey recovered her composure. She had never even considered Marshall in a romantic sense. He had been the boss figure in her life for seven years, and during that time she had watched and learnt from him, and pulled herself right up from being a dumb little secretary to where she was today.

'You don't have to answer me at once,' he said. 'Take time to think about it. I know it's a shock for you, but *I've* been thinking about it for the last year. We'd be good for each other. If you like, I'll romance you a bit, take you out to dinner, send you flowers, although Christ knows I'm a bit too old for all that. But if it's what you want I'll do it.'

She put her slim hand over his. 'I'm very flattered, Marsh. I'm sort of speechless though. I never thought, well, I mean, what I want to say, well, Oh God, I told you I was sort of speechless.'

He stood up. 'Think it over. We'll talk about it later, or not at all. See how you feel.'

He limped off to join the crowd gathered around Max Thorpe.

'I predict,' Max was saying to Natalie Allen, 'two more beautiful babies, could be twins, and plenty of travelling; it seems you're always on the move. It looks like you and Clay are going to have a long and happy life together.'

Natalie pulled her hand away and covered her irritation with a charming smile. It wasn't what she had wanted to hear at all.

'Who's next?' Max enquired, enjoying himself immensely. 'How about you?' He addressed himself to Sunday. She started to protest, but found herself propelled towards Max by an enthusiastic Dindi.

'You have very delicate hands,' Max remarked. 'You are not married but perhaps you have been. Yes, I see a definite indication that you have been. It was not a happy marriage. I see signs of great stress—very great stress. Your parents are dead—a crash—perhaps an aeroplane? You are on your own, you are very quiet. I see many lovers, another marriage.'

Sunday sat quite still, listening intently. This man was uncanny. He knew everything. She forgot about the other people listening too.

'You're right,' she whispered. 'What else do you see? Will I be happy?'

A strange question, Max thought. Usually they asked, Will I be rich, famous, successful?

He said, 'I would have to do a proper chart to tell you that. I see an extremely strong career line, fantastic success. I see—a letter, a letter. You must not ignore the letter. Your lifeline broken—no, no, no, I mean marriage.' He stopped abruptly. 'I can't see any more.'

'Oh, please!' She wondered if Paulo had left a letter she had somehow or other missed. She pushed her hand back at Max. 'Please tell me more.'

His eyes clouded over and his head ached. Sometimes this

happened and he got carried away and went too far. He had gone too far with this girl. He should never have mentioned a broken lifeline. It was so strange, this power he had. 'I'm sorry, dear. There is no more. I can see nothing else.'

Charlie noticed how upset she was and he broke up the gathering around Max to tell a funny story. Then when everyone was drinking again, he went to find her. He had noticed her slip out onto the patio.

She was standing beside the pool, but as he went to join her, Branch appeared and from the shadows he watched them chat for a while and then turn and walk to the house. Charlie went quickly back inside.

Once home, Max Thorpe changed into a silk dressing gown, hand-embroidered with the signs of the Zodiac. First he washed and liberally splashed his round pink body with a musky-smelling perfume. He put on some Japanese music—so soothing—and opened a bottle of Champagne in preparation for Branch's arrival.

Then he sat on a pile of cushions and let his mind drift back over the evening. It had been another triumph for him. Practically every party he went to now came under his spell. The Great Max Thorpe held court, and all the most important people gathered around him. He made it a firm rule never to tell them anything bad; they were only interested in hearing the good things. Sometimes it was difficult though. Sometimes, when their faces became mere shadows and words poured forth from his mouth, words he found hard to control. He remembered the year before when a very famous actor had sat beside him, and in the man's palm he had only seen emptiness. He had talked fast about new deals and triumphs and successes. The man was pleased. Two days later he died in a 'plane crash en route to Spain. Such was life. Max would certainly have made him no happier by telling him he had no future. With the girl tonight he had seen strange things, not necessarily death, but something strange.

The doorbell chimed and he hurriedly got up. What a marvellous physique Branch Strong had. What a wonderful night lay ahead.

He turned the Japanese music louder and answered the door. Branch shuffled from one foot to the other, making no attempt to enter. 'Hi,' he muttered.

'Come in, dear boy, come in.'

They went together into the living room and Max gestured for Branch to sit on the cushions. Then he poured him a glass of Champagne and waggled a short pink finger at him. 'Tonight, I predict, *you* are going to get fucked!'

21

The next two weeks passed quickly for Sunday. She was busy with fittings, interviews and publicity photos. She heard from Steve Magnum only once. He telephoned to know if she would like to use his private plane to fly to Acapulco. She politely refused.

Carey had lined up some houses for her to look at, and she rented a car so that she could get around without having to depend on Carey or cabs.

The houses were not what she wanted—either too big and ornate, or not near enough to the sea. Finally she found a beach house at Malibu which was available for a year.

It was situated on a private road right by the beach, and although small, was just what she wanted. She loved the small patio at the back, with wooden steps leading practically into the sea. The house would be vacant by the time she returned from Acapulco, and she rented it at once.

Branch had written her one long scrawly letter. She missed him and their dinners at his favourite health restaurant.

Since the party at Dindi's, she had tried in vain to see Max Thorpe. It seemed imperative to her that she talk to this man. Perhaps he could tell her more. Anyway it became an obsession that she have a meeting with him.

He was impossible to get hold of. His secretary said on the

phone that he no longer gave private readings. She tried to contact him at his television studio, but he was unobtainable. She wrote and received no reply. Finally, she asked Carey's advice. Carey said, 'Forget it, he's an old faggot quack. But if you really want to see him, get your boyfriend Branch to arrange you an appointment—*he'll* have *no* problem.'

She called Branch in Mexico. It took three days to locate him, and although unenthusiastic, he promised to see what he could do.

The next day Max Thorpe's secretary phoned and said an appointment had been made for her on Saturday at 12 o'clock. It would cost her a thousand dollars and please bring cash. In the meantime, what were her time and date of birth?

Max Thorpe rarely did personal charts any more. It was too time-consuming and he had other things to occupy him. His television show took up most of his time, and then he wrote a weekly column of horoscopes which was syndicated to one hundred and forty newspapers. He had various other forms of activity also. 'I Predict' tee shirts and badges and posters. In fact, he was involved in negotiations to open a chain of 'I Predict' shops throughout the country.

Max Thorpe was doing very well indeed.

He only agreed to see Sunday because of Branch's phone call. For days he had been trying to reach the boy. He had sent cables and letters and tried to get through on the phone, but all to no avail. After the one night at his house, Branch had collected his fifteen hundred dollars and taken off for Mexico. He hadn't even acknowledged the cables. Then suddenly out of the blue he had telephoned. Max was delighted and asked if he could come up to see him for a weekend.

'Sure,' Branch drawled, 'only we'll have to meet away from the location, and I want you to do me a favour.'

'Anything,' Max declared. Branch had far surpassed the fake Indian from Disneyland.

So that was how Sunday got her appointment.

She appeared at Max's house promptly at twelve. The thousand dollars cash had come as a bit of a shock, but she wanted to see him, and if that was what it cost—well, that's what she would have to pay.

He kept her waiting twenty minutes in a strange dark room with the sunlight curtained firmly out.

He swept in finally, wearing a Zodiac shirt and black leather trousers that emphasised his plumpness. He then talked for half-an-hour about himself, his show, and his talent.

Sunday was beginning to despair about him ever getting around to her.

At last he said, 'I think we shall start with the cards. I have a chart for you, but perhaps you would care to take notes.' He handed her a notepad embossed at the top of each page with 'Max Thorpe—I Predict'.

He started to speak very rapidly in short unfinished sentences, things about her that she knew no-one could have told him. It was incredible.

He covered her past briefly until he came to the time of her marriage. Then he talked for quite some time about how she should not blame herself for what had happened, that it would have come to pass anyway.

He stared at her with watery eyes. 'You must forget all about it. It is a closed period of your life. You are not to blame. You must close it from your mind and think no more of it. Look to the future with a light heart, for I see much success.'

He told her initials of people important to her future. Of contracts, of advice from an older man to which she must listen. Then he stopped. He could go no further. There was something strange, something he couldn't fathom—not death, just something.

He stood up. 'Sunday, you are a very lucky girl. Yours will be no mediocre fame. Take great care of yourself and always behave with caution. But believe me, you must forget the past.'

He had been talking to her for over an hour.

'Thank you, Mr Thorpe. I really appreciate your seeing me.' She felt lightheaded and relieved. He had been right about everything else, so perhaps he was right that the whole thing with Paulo wasn't her fault. She fumbled in her white shoulder-bag. 'I have the money, the cash.'

He held up his hand. 'No. I have changed my mind. I don't

want your money. Feel free to see me again. We shall be friends.' He had decided payment was a petty gesture, and perhaps it would disturb Branch. After all, he certainly didn't need money, and anyhow, he liked the girl, they *would* be friends. And if he were right about her future, she would be a friend worth having.

Sunday flew to Acapulco, feeling much better. Somehow the session with Max Thorpe had relieved her immensely. The fact that he had told her she must forget the past seemed to change things. She *would* forget. She would forget about Rome and Paulo and start afresh. She would go out and mix and date and do all the things that Carey had been nagging her to do. Acapulco and the new film would be a starting-point, and then she had the beach house to look forward to on her return.

Carey was delighted with the change in her. 'That Maxie boy must be one hell of an analyst,' she said. 'Maybe I should see him myself.' Since the party and Marshall's proposal, she was confused. She had never thought of Marshall as a potential boyfriend, let alone a lover. Her life was very well organised—several boyfriends at a time, one of whom she would be sleeping with. Then, when it looked even vaguely serious, on to the next. She had worked too long and too hard to put her job second to anything or anyone.

However, Marshall was different. She had always looked up to him, admired him, copied him, even been a little bit in awe of him. His proposal had come as a great shock. She had decided to fly to Acapulco with Sunday and stay a few days, think things out.

They sat in the black Cadillac sent to meet them at the airport, the air conditioning going full blast and a glass partition separating them from the young Mexican driver allocated to Sunday.

'What am I going to do?' Carey asked for the fifteenth time.

'It's simple,' Sunday replied patiently, 'if you love him, marry him, and if you don't love him, don't marry him.'

'Oh honey, what the hell has *love* got to do with it? It's far more complex than that. I might hate him in bed, he might hate me if we should have black children, I might—'

'That's a healthy sign, at least you're considering children.'

'I'd love children,' Carey's eyes clouded over, 'only they might be little black cripples.'

'Carey, shut up. Is that your problem? Are you worried because of his leg?'

'Not really. I don't know. I'm frightened. I've never been involved with a man like him before.'

'Sleep with him then. Maybe that will help you decide how you feel.'

'Listen to you—Miss Anti-Sex!'

Sunday laughed. 'I never said I was anti-sex, Just anti-everything.'

'Hmmm, it's going to be interesting to see the new you with Steve Magnum. He'll eat you for breakfast in your present frame of mind.'

'I'm not going to leap into Steve's bed. I may have changed, but not that much.'

Carey grinned. 'They say he's the best.'

The driver pressed a button and the glass slid open. 'Your hotel, Miss Simmons. Very beautiful, yes?'

'Yes.' It reminded her of Rio. Pale pink bungalows perched on a hillside, each with their own pool. 'I'm going to love it here,' she said to Carey.

Carey nodded. 'Who wouldn't?'

22

Not one decent job. Not one good screw to watch. No action at all. And Marge shuffling around at home, nagging and watchful.

Herbert felt well and truly frustrated. He hadn't even been able to follow up his first and glorious letter to Sunday Simmons. Was she wondering what had become of him?

He had finished his job for the evening, driving an old-time horror star on a personal appearance at a supermarket opening. No-one had turned up, so Herbert was finished three hours before he expected to be. He decided to use those three hours to his advantage—the Supreme Chauffeur Company would never know.

It was nine o'clock when he left the Beverly Hills area. He drove slowly along the Strip, the big black Cadillac easy beneath his touch.

The hippies were gathered outside their usual haunts, sitting huddled on the sidewalk or wandering aimlessly about.

Herbert spat out of his window. Let the little long-haired morons get some discipline. The girls were all whores, fourteen-and fifteen-year-old whores with flowing hair and weird outfits. One of them sidled up to the car as it waited at a light.

'I'll screw for ten bucks,' she mumbled.

Herbert looked her up and down. She was about eighteen, skinny, with a pointed ugly face and freaked-out hair. She wore a shabby multi-coloured robe to the ground, and many rows of black beads.

He started to sweat. It had been a long time. 'Get in,' he said harshly.

The girl ran round the car and jumped in. She began to bite her nails, and surveyed Herbert with blank red eyes. 'Don't go too far,' she said, 'just drive up in the hills a couple of blocks. For a straight screw it's fifteen—anything special it's more.'

He didn't say anything, just swung the big Cadillac up Miller Drive and kept going.

'Not too far,' the girl said sharply.

He remained silent.

'Christ! What are you—deaf and dumb?'

He had found a suitable side-turning and pulled the car to a halt. It was dark and all that could be heard was the chirping of crickets.

The girl started to pull off her robe.

He watched her. She had a flat chest like a boy.

'O.K. Hand over the bread and let's get it done.'

They were all whores. They all wanted money and sex in that order. Sometimes in the other order. All of them. 'Come on,' she whined, 'I haven't got all night.' She reached for his fly and started to unzip it. 'You can pay me after. I'll give you a special for twenty. You look like a nice john.'

All the while she was manipulating him out of his trousers. He sat behind the steering wheel, staring staight ahead. She smelt. He could smell various body odours as she leant down and tried to push his limp member in her mouth.

'Stop it,' he cried, bringing his hand down and smashing it on her head. 'Get your filthy mouth off me. Stop it—stop it—stop it.'

He didn't cease hitting her until she crumpled to the floor of the car and lay there very still.

He was sobbing with rage. The bitch. Why had she picked on him?

He struggled and kicked her out of the car, throwing her robe after her.

He adjusted his clothing and calmed down. Then he thought of Sunday Simmons, and miraculously he was hard and virile, a real man. If only he could write to her now and enclose his precious offering. There was no other way for him, not with Marge, not with anyone. The ultimate delight was only possible with pen in hand.

He left the girl lying there and drove off. To hell with Marge poking and nosing around. He was going home to lock himself in and write a masterpiece. Then he would have a long, cleansing shower. Later he would take the car back and mail the letter.

Marge was out.

'Bitch!' Herbert muttered. He had told her quite clearly that she wasn't to go out at night. He supposed she was with their neighbour. Well, he would soon put a stop to *that*. After he'd written his letter he would go next door and drag her home, *and* tell the cow neighbour what he thought of her.

He went in the kitchen and poured himself a glass of milk. A large moth fluttered around the light. Quietly he caught it, and tore off both its wings before throwing it in the garbage can.

Then he went upstairs into the box-room. He picked up his pen . . .

It was a wonderful letter. So full and explicit, and there was a plastic bag to go with it.

He was satisfied. Perhaps one day Sunday and he would read

through his letters together and do everything that he had written about. She was sure to save them, perhaps bound with pink ribbon. After all, they *were* love letters.

He sang in the shower, in a flat toneless voice that he liked to think sounded like Perry Como's.

Then he dressed and carefully put his letter in the glove-compartment of the Cadillac, locking it up before setting off to find Marge.

The front yard was a mass of overgrown grass and weeds. The Crisps had not touched it since moving in.

Herbert could imagine what kind of people they were—slobs, like Marge. Uneducated coarse slobs. Well, they weren't getting their dirty hands on *his* wife.

They were obviously home, as lights peeped from every room, although the drapes were closed.

He edged up to the house, intending to surprise them. Round the side there was a small gap in one of the drapes. He bent down and peered in. It was difficult to see as the gap was so small he could only focus with one eye.

Marge was spreadeagled on a sofa, stark naked, and around her 'stood ten nude men and women, who appeared to be singing, Marge was joining in, and she was smiling. There was some sort of paint—or was it blood?—all over her breasts.

Herbert froze. One of the men, fat and balding, stepped towards Marge. He was wearing a black mask. One of the women handed round black candles, and when they were lit, the lights were turned out, and the fat man fell onto Marge, heaving back and forth, while the others knelt down and watched.

Herbert could not believe what he was witnessing. It was disgusting. But it was exciting him and he stayed quietly where he was.

One by one the men in the group stepped forward and fell upon Marge, and only when they had all had their turn were the candles extinguished and the lights turned on.

Marge got up, quite happy, and accepted a glass of something and an affectionate pat on the back from a tall woman with straggly white hair and stringy breasts.

Herbert remained frozen to the spot. His eye hurt and his mouth was dry.

Finally he made his way home. He eradicated any sign of having been there earlier. Then he got in the Cadillac and sped silently away.

23

Serafina adored Hollywood. She arrived dressed from head to toe in crimson, with a slinky silver-fox fur, complete with crafty face, draped around her shoulders.

Charlie was proud of her. She was one hell of a mother who acted like a woman half her age.

His two children were solemn and respectful, almost as if Lorna had told them to be on their best behaviour.

'Daddy, we don't have to call your new wife Mummy, do we?' Sean asked in the car from the airport.

'No, you can call her what you like,' Charlie replied. There were a few names he would like to call Dindi himself. She had refused to come to the airport, claiming a headache. A headache indeed. More like a bellyache because he had turned down the idea of her being in 'Roundabout'. He realized that if Serafina and the kids were going to have any sort of decent holiday, he would have to relent and let her be in the picture, although the last thing he wanted as a wife was an aspiring actress.

'It's wonderful here, wonderful, Charlie. Where's your wife?' Serafina asked, bright bird eyes staring him down.

'She thought it would be better to meet you at the house.'

'Did she now, did she? Pretty little thing. Sharp, I bet. Smart as a button. I don't know why you wanted to go tying yourself up again so soon. You can take your pick now, have a bit of fun. Is she—you know?'

He laughed. Trust Serafina to think the worst. 'No, she's not pregnant. You'll like her.'

'I hope so.' Serafina rescued several straggles of bright red hair escaping from her crimson beret. 'I'd like to have been here for the wedding. I love weddings. I'd like to have seen that Lost Vega.'

'Las Vegas,' Charlie corrected. 'We'll go there, maybe next weekend. Natalie and Clay might come.'

'Can we go to Disneyland, Daddy?' Cindy enquired. She looked exactly like Lorna, much to Charlie's annoyance.

'We can go wherever you want.'

Sean supported his sister. 'Mummy said we should go to Disneyland. She said it's super.'

'Mummy's never been there,' Charlie retaliated.

'No, but Uncle Jim has, and *he* says it's terrific, with real Indians and cowboys and a showboat and wagons and—'

'We'll go, I said,' Charlie was furious at the reference to Uncle Jim.

Back at the house Dindi was nowhere to be seen. George was sent off to find her.

Serafina said, 'A nice cup of tea, that's what I'd like. There's nothing as good as a nice cup of tea. Show me where the kitchen is. I brought six packets of Lyons Quick Brew with me.' She fumbled in her handbag and produced a packet.

'You can't start messing around in the kitchen, the maid will do it.' When on earth would his mother realise that he was a big star and had people to do everything?

'I wouldn't trust an American to make *my* tea,' Serafina huffed. 'Show me the kitchen.'

Dindi was shopping. She had so far spent two and a half thousand dollars and was still going strong. She was trying on a skimpy orange silk jersey dress and preening in the mirror. 'What do you think of this?' she asked the salesgirl.

The salesgirl, wearing a similar dress, stifled a yawn and said, 'Great.' She was bored with watching Mrs Charlie Brick buy everything in sight.

'O.K. I'll take it. What other colours does it come in?'

'White, black and a sort of plum.'

'I'll have it in all colours.'

'Dindi?'

108

'Yeah. Oh—hi, Natalie.'

'Hello, I was told this was *the* place to buy clothes. What a terrific dress.'

'Yeah.' Dindi wished she had stayed in the fitting room instead of coming out to inspect herself in the main room.

'I thought Charlie's mother and the children were arriving today.'

'Yeah,·well I guess they are. I figured they'd want to be alone.'

'Oh.' Natalie smiled. 'Very thoughtful of you. You haven't met Serafina yet, have you?'

'Nope.' Dindi shook her head, edging back to the fitting room.

Natalie followed. 'She's quite a character, idolizes Charlie of course, and he adores her. I do hope the two of you get along.'

'Why shouldn't we?' Dindi shrugged off the dress, revealing red bikini pants—and that was all.

Natalie felt her eyes drawn jealously to the girls pointy young breasts. 'No reason really, but she *is* difficult. She's quite old and yet she still wants to have men . . .'

Dindi giggled. 'She sounds like a swinger. I expect I'll still want to have men when I'm quite old, won't you?'

Natalie flushed. 'I just thought I'd warn you about her.' Oh God, Charlie had married a real little bitch. She would have to move swiftly to get rid of her.

'Yeah—well, thanks for the warning. I'll fix Charlie's mom up with a live one! Oh, by the way, how's Clay?'

'He's fine,' Natalie replied stiffly. 'Did you know him long in Rome?'

Dindi winked. 'Long enough.' She giggled as Natalie opened her mouth to reply. 'I'm kidding. Are you jealous?'

'Not at all. In fact I'm quite used to the fact that Clay will go to bed with any silly little tart that gives him the green light.'

Dindi's eyes narrowed.

'Well, bye bye, dear. I do hope we'll all get together soon.'

'Bye bye, Natalie dear.' Furious, Dindi put on her clothes and called to the salesgirl. 'For Christ sake hurry up with my things, I haven't got all day.'

*

'Where have you been?' Charlie didn't relish playing the jealous husband, but having made excuses to Serafina all day about Dindi's absence, he was in a mild fury.

'Shopping. I get so bored just sitting around.'

'But you knew my mother was arriving today. You knew I'd only gone to the airport.'

She looked sulky. 'I guess I forgot.'

'I guess you did.' Angrily he marched to the window and stared out. Cindy and Sean were splashing in the pool. Serafina was upstairs, taking a nap. 'Look, if you want the part so badly, it's yours,' he blurted.

Her face lit up. 'Honestly baby? That's marvie. I'll be terrific in it, you won't be sorry.' She rushed over to him and hugged him from behind, rubbing herself against him.

He turned round and she slid her hands under his shirt.

'I didn't want to marry an actress,' he remarked.

Her hands wriggled their way under the waistband of his trousers and grabbed hold of him. She felt him harden and sank to her knees.

'Not here, Dindi,' he muttered.

'Why not? We're married, aren't we?'

'The secret of eternal youth, my dear, is keeping busy,' Serafina announced at dinner. 'I myself have never been idle.'

'I can believe that,' Dindi replied, quite exhausted at just watching Serafina darting off to the kitchen every five minutes.

'When I was in the theatre, I was known affectionately back-stage as Miss Vitality.'

'Really?' Dindi looked interested. Since Charlie had told her she had the part in 'Roundabout' she had gone out of her way to charm Serafina and his rotten kids.

'Yes, Miss Vitality. Oh dear me, those were the days. I can remember the line of gentlemen friends waiting at the stage door, all well to do and handsome, and then I met Charlie's father—God rest his soul—a fine man. We had a wonderful life together.'

Charlie looked at his mother in surprise. She must be getting old. His old man had been a right bastard and walked out on her. A fine life indeed.

'Has Charlie told you of his early days?'

'Nope,' Dindi shook her head. 'I guess he was figuring you would.' She stifled a yawn and smiled brightly. How she longed to say 'Has anyone ever told you you're an old bore?'

The phone rang and Charlie reached for the dining table extension. When he hung up he said, 'Clay and Natalie are going to drop by for coffee.'

'That's nice,' Serafina said. 'Anyone else?'

Charlie knew she was wondering if he had picked out any potential 'friends' for her. When he had first asked her to come to Hollywood with the children she had wanted to bring Archie, her current beau. But Charlie couldn't stand Archie, so he had said that Serafina would meet plenty of more interesting men if she came on her own. It was a problem fixing up one's mother. Not that she liked young men, she preferred them older than herself, but in Hollywood finding an older man prepared to take on a nearly seventy-year old woman was impossible. Hollywood was full of young available women. It was a problem Charlie had decided to ignore, and when Serafina got too fidgety he would send for Archie.

'Er, I don't think so. By the way, I thought perhaps next weekend we might fly up to Las Vegas. Would you like that?'

Serafina nodded. She didn't plan to spend her holiday closeted up in Charlie's house. She was still an attractive woman, she must get out and be seen. Just because Charlie was jealous of introducing her to men, fancy, her own son jealous. Well it was understandable really.

'I am sixty-three years of age,' she announced to Dindi, cleverly deducting six years, 'and I feel like a girl.'

'You look wonderful,' Dindi murmured, thinking she might look a bit better if she cleaned off all that terrible theatrical make-up and false eyelashes at her age! Really!

'Yes, people find it hard to believe, but it's the truth. And you my dear, how old are you?' Serafina fixed her with a penetrating stare as if daring her to lie.

'Twenty,' replied Dindi, smiling sweetly and knocking off three years. If the old bitch could lie about her age so could she.

'Oh, twenty,' Serafina fluttered. 'Twenty. In my day girls of twenty—'

'Did I ever show you the pictures I have of Serafina when she was twenty?' Charlie interrupted.

'No,' replied Dindi, thinking, so this is how one spends one's evening when married to a movie star.

'I'll have to show you. She was a real knockout, weren't you, love?' He put his arm around his mother.

She smiled, and Charlie thought—I must get her to a good dentist while she's here.

'Do you remember the good old days, Charlie son?'

Yes, he remembered. The fading old theatres, stale smells and Serafina's boyfriends.

'Those were the days.' A tear sprang to her eyes. 'Those were the good times. Just your father, you and me.'

What good times? Charlie thought. Stuck outside a pub in some asshole of a town with a packet of crisps and a lemonade while Serafina and her latest 'beau' lived it up. Anyway—so what. No good looking back. He loved Serafina. She was his mother. She had kept him with her when he was a boy, and that was the main thing.

'I always knew Charlie would be a star,' Serafina said sharply. 'I encouraged him in everything he wanted to do. He's got my vitality and drive. I could have been a star myself, but I gave it all up to look after him.'

Dindi yawned openly. People's pasts were a bore. As far as she was concerned, Charlie was a big movie star, and before that she didn't want to know.

'Tired?' Serafina questioned.

'Yes,' Dindi replied, 'I had a job to do this afternoon that tired me out.' She shot a secret smile at Charlie.

He smiled back. She looked so pretty and innocent. He could hardly believe that she was the same girl who had made love to him earlier.

'You pop on up to bed love if you like,' he said, 'Serafina won't mind, and I'll explain to the Allens.'

'Are you sure, darling? I *would* like to.' She wanted to go upstairs and try on her new clothes and read the script of 'Roundabout' now that she had the part.

'You go ahead love, see you later.' He watched her say good-night to Serafina, then peck him on the cheek. She had such a compact sexy body. It made him feel good to think that she was all his. It might not be such a bad idea having her in the movie after all. Other men could look but not touch. Let the world see what Charlie Brick had.

24

Acapulco was hot. After the first day's shooting in the mountains, Sunday was a wreck, the heat was impossible.

She had been working hard, surrounded by a mostly Mexican crew, and three Americans—the director, Woody, the cameraman, Mike, and the continuity girl, Marisa.

Woody and Marisa were having an affair. He was a pleasant, thirtyish man who Steve Magnum had picked personally. He had not directed a movie before, only television. Marisa was 24 and pretty.

Sunday liked them both. As a director Woody was quiet, considerate and extremely encouraging. There was a great difference between him and Abe Stein. Abe represented the old style Hollywood. Woody the new.

Upon arrival, she had received a huge basket of flowers from Steve, with a note saying 'Welcome'. Apart from that, no word from him at all.

'You had your chance and blew it,' Carey said. 'He's probably shacked up in that mansion of his with a beautiful Mexican virgin.'

'I hope he is,' Sunday replied. She was secretly glad. Now that she had reached the stage of deciding to get involved, there was no need to.

For a week she and Carey had done nothing but loaf around, sunbathing and swimming.

The day before she started work, Carey left, saying, 'Well, I guess it's decision time.'

She found it lonely with Carey gone. The Las Brisas Hilton

Hotel was very beautiful, but somehow Sunday felt it was the sort of place one should be with a man.

She spent a quiet evening on her own, sending out for food, and studying her script. The next day Steve was due to appear for a scene in the mountains where he was supposed to rescue her. In the script she had escaped after being kidnapped. It was also a love scene, and she looked forward to it with a mixture of anticipation and uncertainty.

'Ha!' Marisa exclaimed. 'How about that bundle of goodies?' She nudged Sunday, who was sitting in the canvas chair next to her, reading a book.

Steve Magnum was approaching accompanied by a young curvy Mexican girl, with long black hair flowing to her waist and green hungry eyes.

'Hello, ladies.' Steve waved casually from a distance, and patting the young girl on the bottom, shoved her towards them. 'Keep an eye on Enchilada for me, Marisa baby.' He then went off in a huddle with Woody.

'That man!' Marisa said, shaking her head and laughing. 'He's too much!'

The girl, nicknamed Enchilada, came over with sulky suspicious eyes.

'Hi,' Marisa said, 'grab a chair and make yourself at home, it's going to be a long hard day. I'm Marisa and this is Sunday Simmons.'

The girl nodded briefly and sat in a chair several yards away. She then turned to stare at Steve, and Woody.

'Friendly,' Marisa remarked. 'Sunday, I think they're going to be ready soon. You want to get dressed, I'll send wardrobe in to you.'

'Good idea.' It was eleven in the morning and Sunday was becoming bored just sitting around. The Mexicans seemed to take much longer to get started than the Americans. She had arrived at eight, spent two hours in makeup and hairdressing, and then the long wait. Steve had now disappeared into the makeup caravan, so perhaps they would start soon.

In the scene she was wearing white trousers and a skimpy

white top. A matching jacket was around her shoulders. She was supposed to appear dishevelled and distraught.

'You look great,' Steve said, when they were in front of the camera. 'How do you like Acapulco?'

'It's nice.' She smiled at him with her eyes. 'Thank you for the flowers.'

'You're always thanking me for flowers. How about sending some?'

They both laughed while Enchilada glowered from the sidelines.

'Took myself a little insurance,' he said.

'Insurance?'

'Against you, baby—against you. My little Mexican tomato is only sixteen, so I guess that should keep my greedy hands from grabbing you. That's the way you want it, isn't it?'

She just smiled. She wasn't sure at all that that was the way she wanted it. Steve was magnetically attractive, and it had been a long time between men.

Woody came over and chatted to them about the scene.

The rest of the morning passed quickly. Steve and Sunday worked well together and they finished three short scenes with hardly any retakes.

When the lunch break came, Steve grabbed Enchilada and took off in his helicopter. Sunday had her lunch with the rest of the crew from a mobile canteen. She sat with Woody and Marisa. She was beginning to be a little piqued by Steve's apparent uninterest.

The first scene after lunch was the love scene. It started with Steve pulling off her jacket, laying it on the ground and pushing her down on it. In the film she was supposed to fight him, struggle, and then submit.

'Look,' Woody explained, 'when you're on the ground I want him to pull your top down. That's when I want you to lie very still and just stare at him with those eyes of yours.'

'How far down?' Sunday asked suspiciously.

'Well, off, sweetheart. The camera won't see anything, Steve will be covering you.'

'In that case my top won't have to come right off.'

Woody laughed. 'I'm not looking for a free show, but sure the top will have to come off. When I say the camera won't see anything, I mean we're not going to pan in for a great close-up on your bosom. But it's quite obvious that you can't have the top down a little; it will look messy and awkward. He's got to get it off and throw it out of shot. Then you'll be in an embrace with him, so all we're going to see is arms and sides and things.'

'Woody, I have a clause in my contract that says no nude scenes. Didn't you know?'

'No, I didn't,' he snapped. 'Christ, you make me feel like a dirty-minded little schoolboy trying to glimpse a lady's boobs. I'm a director and I hope a good one, and in these days of truth and realism you're going to look mighty silly clutching a top around you to preserve a little old-fashioned modesty.' His tone changed, becoming persuasive and soft. 'Trust me, honey. I know what's going to look right.'

She sighed. 'I don't understand what difference there is whether I keep the top on or not.'

'There, you see,' he was triumphant, '*You* don't understand the difference, but *I* do. So please believe I'm right.'

'I had a horrible experience with Abe Stein on—'

'I am *not* Abe Stein. We'll send everyone who's not needed home. O.K., sweetheart, O.K.?'

'If you really think it's necessary.'

'I really think.'

She wished that Carey were still there. Why was there this obsession with nudity? Why didn't she have the strength to stick to her decision? Was it because she liked and trusted Woody? Or did she know in her own mind that the scene would be more realistic the way he wanted it.

Steve returned in his helicopter, Enchilada sulky by his side.

Woody was getting rid of crew members whose presence was not strictly necessary.

Marisa entered Sunday's caravan and offered her a stick of gum. 'Believe me,' she said, 'I'd be the first one to yell if it wasn't right for the scene. Do you think I want my boyfriend getting an eyeful of what I'm sure are a beautiful pair?'

*

They rehearsed the scene first.

Steve grabbed her from behind, snatched the jacket off her shoulders and forced her down, pinning her arms to her side. Then he kissed her.

'The mechanics are fine,' Woody said when they had got that far.

'Yeah!' Steve agreed. He was lying on top of Sunday and she could feel his thin hard body, and shivered in spite of herself. His lips had been insistent and demanding.

'Now,' Woody said, 'I want you to keep holding her with one hand and edge the top down with the other. We'll take it from the beginning and shoot.'

Steve smiled at her as he got up. 'One take, huh?'

She smiled back at him. 'I'll try.' She felt elated and excited in spite of herself. She knew Steve would be impressed with her body. She became unaware of the crew, Woody, everybody, and immersed herself in thinking only of Steve.

The scene started smoothly, but then Steve fluffed a line and Woody shouted 'Cut.'

They began again, the small Mexican clapper boy saying in his fractured English—' "Cash", Scene 31. Take two.'

Everything went well. Steve started to kiss her and pull off her top. 'Mamma mia!' he muttered under his breath as he looked at her briefly, and then embraced her tightly.

His shirt was open and she felt a cool film of sweat between them. Her fingernails raked his back.

'Cut,' shouted Woody. 'Cut,' he repeated as they made no move to separate.

Steve drew slowly off her. She was breathing heavily and staring at him.

'I think I just blew my insurance,' he said.

25

'Roundabout' was going well. The new script favoured Charlie, and even Angela Carter's part had become minor in comparison.

He threw himself into his role completely, enjoying himself. He knew he was giving a good performance—the dailies told him that, and the way the crew laughed after certain scenes. It was notoriously hard to get any reaction from a crew. They were there to do their job and nothing ever moved them.

Angela and he were casually friendly. Since her break-up with Steve Magnum, she had started an affair with Cy: It occurred to her that professionally Cy was a much better bet. So she concentrated on playing her part effectively, and getting Cy to dump Emerald.

A rush of publicity resulted from Dindi joining the cast. The newspapers started to refer to her as film star Dindi Sydne or Mrs Charlie Brick. She posed for countless stills and enjoyed it all thoroughly.

On the screen she came over as surprisingly fresh and appealing, and Angela started complaining to Cy that her part was too big.

In a way Charlie was pleased, but it didn't please him when reporters visited the set and took more interest in her than in him. After all, he was the star of the family.

Eventually he insisted that all reporters be banned, and a feud between him and the publicity department began. Dindi was on the publicity department's side, and she and Charlie had a series of fights about his attitude. They also had fights about the money she was spending. And about Serafina and the children, who had been with them nearly a month.

Charlie complained that Dindi spent no time with them at all. *He* was busy at the studio every day, but *she* was only needed a couple of days a week, so she had plenty of time to spend with his family if she wanted to.

She *didn't* want to. She loathed Serafina and thought the children a couple of brats.

Charlie was furious, especially because he had only agreed to her appearance in 'Roundabout' so that she would be polite to his family. Secretly he tried to get her taken off the film, but that was one request he wasn't granted. It was too late.

He fully realized now that he had married a tough, money-grabbing, ambitious female. Just the sort he had been running from.

One lunchtime he confessed his mistake to Clay.

'I don't know what to do, love, I don't know what came over me. I must have been bloody mad. I don't even fancy her any more.'

He didn't tell Clay that the reason he no longer fancied her was because in a recent argument she had yelled at him, 'You might be a good actor, but you're a lousy lay.' The remark had stayed with him. He was extremely sensitive about his sexual prowess.

Was he a lousy lay? Michelle Lomas hadn't thought so.

He brooded on it and finally went to bed with a pretty extra, who assured him that he was 'fantastic.'

Clay was embarrassed. He was in two minds whether to tell Charlie about Rome. He decided not. The marriage was floundering anyway and Charlie might be choked that he hadn't mentioned it before.

Serafina had fortunately found herself a boyfriend. He was a gardener on the estate, a former character actor, about the same age as she was, and very charming. They made a colourful pair.

Charlie suggested that they went on the trip to Las Vegas which he had promised Serafina. She would be returning to London with the children in two weeks, and he wanted to be sure she enjoyed herself. He hired a private jet for the short journey.

Dindi was unenthusiastic about going, but it was either that or staying in Los Angeles with the children, so she agreed to go. It would only be a two-day trip, and perhaps she could fit in a little session with the George Raft type manager.

Clay and Natalie came along, and Serafina's friend, whose name was Morton, and whom Dindi had cruelly nicknamed Mortuary. She was especially furious that he was accompanying them. 'A fuckin' gardener, only your mother would pick a gardener!' she moaned.

They stayed at the Forum, arriving early on Saturday morning.

Clay, Natalie and Charlie relaxed round the pool, while Serafina and Morton, armed with six hundred dollars given to them by Charlie, set off to try their luck at the tables.

Dindi complained she was tired and left to take a nap.

'This is the life!' Clay exclaimed, as a toga-clad redhead served him a giant Planters Punch beside the pool. 'What a great place!'

'Any place would be great for you where they have girls sticking their bottoms in your face,' Natalie said tartly. She smiled at Charlie. 'Coming for a swim?'

'No, love, I'm just going to relax.'

Two women in multi-coloured flowered bathing-caps were arguing nearby. 'It is him, Ethel, I *know* it is.' 'No, it's not, he's much *fatter* than that.' 'Ethel, I'm telling you it's him.' They stared pointedly at Charlie until the one called Ethel suddenly approached and said loudly, 'Are you Charlie Brick?'

He lapsed into his Indian voice, 'I'm very sorry, madam, but you are quite mistaken.'

Clay joined in and said, 'This is the very famous Swahili poet, Señor Charles Bleakworth.'

'Oh!' The woman's mouth dropped open. 'I told my friend you weren't anyone.'

The woman departed, leaving Charlie and Clay in fits of laughter. It was a game they had been playing for years, making up names, characters, confusing people. For a movie star, Charlie was very infrequently recognised—a fact that both disturbed and delighted him. He became so immersed in each role he played that he became that character on the screen and as each role was different, the real Charlie Brick became very hard to spot.

By lunchtime Charlie wondered if he should phone the room and wake Dindi.

'I'll get her,' Natalie said, 'I have to go upstairs anyway.'

'We'll find Serafina and meet you in the Orgy Room,' Charlie said.

'The *what?*'

'It's a restaurant, great food and near-naked waitresses.'

'Oh, Clay will *love* that. I'll see you there in about twenty mintues.'

'She's a great girl,' Charlie remarked, watching Natalie's slim figure out of sight. 'You're a lucky man.'

Clay laughed. 'I suppose I am. You know it's going to be seven years this month. Seven years!'

'Lorna and I would have been married thirteen years this year. December's our anniversary. December the fifth,' he sighed. 'You know, with all I've got now, the money, the fame, everything, all I really want is Lorna back.'

'Oh come on, Charlie, it's over, finished. She's married to someone else now, and so are you. For Christ sake don't keep thinking about her. You've got a world of cooze at your feet.'

'Is that all you ever think about?'

Clay laughed. 'Give me something better to think of. I've knocked off two beautiful little pieces since I've been here.'

It irritated Charlie when Clay talked about his sex life. It was a known fact that he was well hung, and the thought made Charlie extremely jealous. He always made a careful point of never going to bed with a girl with whom Clay had slept.

'Doesn't Natalie mind?' he asked, thinking of the embarrassing scene he had had with her in London.

'She doesn't know,' Clay protested, 'just suspects sometimes. In fact, she only ever caught me once, and that was with the German au pair. Terrible fight. I told you about it, didn't I? When she chased me bollock-naked into the garden and I fell in the pond?'

'Yes,' Charlie laughed, remembering the story well.

'That German bit had the biggest pair of knockers I ever saw. It was Natalie's fault for hiring her. She knows what I'm like about tits. By the way, while we're on the subject, that friend of Dindi's—Sunday Simmons—what wouldn't I give for a piece of that!'

'Hmm . . .' Charlie thought about Sunday reflectively. He had thought about her several times since the party and decided that she was one of the most beautiful women he had ever seen. He remembered her eyes, strange browny yellow tiger eyes.

'I wonder if she fucks,' Clay said.

'They all do,' Charlie replied shortly. 'You offer them a job and they all do.'

Natalie went upstairs and changed into pants and a shirt. After lunch she thought she would try the hairdressers, she wanted to look particularly attractive for that evening. She knocked on Dindi's door, they had adjoining suites. There was no reply.

Blast the little tart! She wasn't about to go searching the hotel for her. The bitch would just have to miss lunch.

Natalie walked slowly to the elevator. Things were going well between her and Charlie. She had noticed the small intimate looks he kept giving her. She smiled to herself. It wouldn't be long.

The elevator arrived and she stepped in. It was going up. A tall brunette in a short toga said, 'You musta pressed the wrong button, people are always doing that. It's a drag, you'll have to come right to the top, and then it'll stop at every floor down.'

The elevator zoomed silently up, finally stopping at the eighteenth floor. The girl in the toga got out, and two girls got in, pressing the hold button for another girl hurrying to join them.

Natalie, standing at the back of the elevator, saw Dindi emerge from a room with a good-looking dark-haired man. Then the elevator doors closed and she saw no more.

The girls were talking. 'Well, he grabbed my thigh and I said, "Knock it off, jerk".'

'Honestly, some guys have such nerve.'

'You can get black and blue just walking around here!'

'Excuse me,' Natalie said. 'What's on the eighteenth floor. Is it part of the hotel?'

The three girls all stared at her. 'Offices,' said one.

'Steam room, staff rooms, management suites. Are you English?' said another.

'Yes.'

'Charlie Brick's staying here, you know,' the third girl confided, 'and Tom Jones came in here one night when he was playing Caesar's. Hey, I've a cousin in a place called Leeds, maybe you know her? Her name's Myrtle Long, she's a model.'

'No, I don't know her,' Natalie shook her head.

'I *looove* English actors,' the first girl said, 'Roger Moore, Peter Sellers, Omar Sharif. Oh, boy!'

'Omar Sharif's not English,' said the girl with the cousin, 'He's an Arab.'

'Well, I dig Arabs too.'

Natalie smiled. Steam rooms, offices, staff rooms, management suites was definitely where Dindi must have been. She wondered with whom. But whoever it was, she planned to find out.

'I think Dindi's still sleeping,' Natalie remarked, arriving for lunch.

Serafina scowled, furious at having been dragged away from the roulette wheel to eat. 'That girl will sleep her life away. A truly fit person needs no more than six hours a night.'

Morton yawned, as if to confirm the fact that Serafina needed only six hours a night.

Clay was grinning at a statuesque lady, poised with pencil and pad, ready to take their order.

Charlie wished he were back at the house in Los Angeles quietly getting stoned. He didn't feel social. It wasn't right for him to be forced to spend an active weekend when he was working. He should be resting, studying his script. He wished he had brought George, instead of leaving him with the children.

'What's on for this afternoon?' Clay asked.

'I'm going to the hairdressers,' Natalie announced.

'Morton and I shall be returning to the tables,' said Serafina. 'The sun saps your vital energy and ruins your skin.'

'I think I may sleep.' Charlie said.

At that moment Dindi appeared, flushed and pretty. 'Hi there. I thought this is where I'd find you. Charlie, sweetie, I'm doing stills this afternoon. Can I have some bread? I've seen some things I want to buy.'

'Stills for what?' Charlie asked, unaware that the Studio had arranged anything for Dindi that weekend.

She pouted. 'For a magazine.'

'What magazine?'

'Just some magazine, I don't know.'

'Well you had better know, otherwise just forget it.'

'Forget it?' Her blue eyes narrowed. 'What do you mean, forget it?'

Charlie realized the whole table was listening—Clay embarrassed, Serafina spiteful, Natalie sympathetic, Morton uninterested.

He smiled coldly. 'Dindi love, be a good girl and run along and find out what magazine it is. Now that you're such an aspiring actress it wouldn't do for you to appear in the wrong sort of publication.'

His voice was mild, but Dindi realised she had pushed too far. 'O.K., honeybunch,' she said, tossing blond curls. 'See you later, gang.' And she wriggled off in tight jersey slacks and cut-off sweater.

Charlie sighed. He didn't want it and he didn't need it. After the movie Dindi was out.

He went upstairs after lunch and phoned George.

'Send me a cable immediately,' he said, 'Say—meeting imperative on "Roundabout", urgent. Return at once. Sign it Cy Hamilton.'

An hour or so later the cable arrived, and full of apologies, Charlie showed it to Serafina, now playing Black-jack.

She looked dismayed. 'Does that mean we have to go too?'

'No love, not at all. I'll leave you credit, and you can stay as long as we planned. Dindi will stay too, and Clay and Natalie. You'll be fine.'

Serafina didn't argue.

Next, he located Clay by the pool, chatting up a showgirl. He showed him the cable. 'Sorry, love, it's a real drag. You'll keep an eye on Serafina for me, won't you? I've left her plenty of credit but if she needs any money, give it to her.'

Clay nodded. 'What about Dindi?'

'She's staying too. I don't know where she is, but I've left her a note. Just make *sure* she stays, and see she's nice to Serafina.'

'Yes, boss!'

'I don't know what I'd do without you and Nat.'

Clay grinned. 'You'd manage.'

Charlie was on a plane half-an-hour later on his way back to Los Angeles.

26

The item read: *'Steve Magnum and ravishing eye-stopping Sunday Simmons seem to have found each other on the sunny shores of Acapulco where they are filming "Cash" together. Do we hear wedding bells?'*

The item read: *'Sexsational Sunday Simmons and much-married Steve Magnum constant companions on location for "Cash".'*

The item read: *'Steve Magnum seems to have bewitched lovely newcomer Sunday Simmons. Friends say they are inseparable. They are working on "Cash" together.'*

For once the Hollywood gossip columns read correctly. Sunday and Steve were constantly together.

She found him charming, easygoing, and very attractive. He was so unlike anyone she had ever met before. Always in command of any situation, always laughing and joking. She wasn't sure if she was in love, so she refused to sleep with him.

He couldn't believe it. 'Honey, it's not like you're a *virgin*. How long has it been for Chrissake?'

She smiled in reply. 'Long enough. I don't want to be another Steve Magnum conquest. Let me be sure.'

So she waited.

'I'm in shock,' he confessed to friends. 'This broad's put me in shock!' But he laughed when he said it, and he respected her and didn't push her into bed. What he did was install Enchilada in a nearby hotel, and she visited him when Sunday returned at night to Las Brisas. It seemed like a fair arrangement. What Sunday didn't know wouldn't hurt her, and as soon as she overcame her doubts, Enchilada would be sent packing, with a couple of thousand dollars to soothe her ruffled pride. Actually, it rather pleased Steve that Sunday wasn't prepared to leap straight into the sack; at least it suggested that there hadn't been a long line of guys in front of him. She told him, and he believed her, that there had been no-one since her husband. What a change it made from the usual Hollywood scene which was like a bizarre game of Change Partners.

'Cash' was nearing completion. The film Sunday had made with Jack Milan was released, and although her part was only small, she was mentioned favourably in the reviews and started to receive an avalanche of fan mail.

Carey phoned her every day to report the offers she was getting. There was a movie in Europe. A 'Bonnie and Clyde'-type film in Texas. A comedy in Hollywood.

Steve advised her not to accept anything. 'Keep 'em waiting and your price will rocket. When they see you in our movie you'll be able to name any terms you want.'

Sunday wasn't sure. It would be months before 'Cash' came out and she didn't want to wait that long. It was too much of a risk with the industry in its present state.

Carey was persuaded. 'O.K., let's strike while you're hot.'

So Sunday signed for the comedy.

Steve sulked. 'Wouldn't listen to me, huh?' he complained. 'Five minutes in the business and you know it all.'

'I haven't been five minutes in the business. Anyway it's a very good script.'

They were sitting by the pool at his house. It was early evening and they had just finished the day's shooting.

'I'm going for a swim,' she announced, and went to a cubicle and changed into a white bikini.

'Hey, listen, do an old man one favour at least and swim in the raw.'

'What?' she asked laughing. 'You're as bad as all the directors I work with.'

'Listen, baby, it's enough not having you yet. If anyone knew my reputation would be shot to hell. So give me a cheap thrill, huh? Just for kicks.'

'Steve, I can't. You've got a house full of servants. Anyway, I don't think—'

'O.K.,' he shrugged. 'O.K., if you don't even care that much about me. You know we're completely secluded from the house.' He turned away, staring at the pink uneven walls surrounding the pool area and wondering what it was about her that had him so hooked.

There was a splash, and then she called him.

She was floating in the pool, her hair wet and streaming out behind her, and her naked breasts outlined clearly in the opalescent blue water. She wore only the bottom half of her bikini.

He was pleased. 'Hey, baby, that's really something.'

She waited for him to dive in, but he just smiled his famous smile and said, 'Baby, *you are beautiful*.' So conditioned was he to not having her that it didn't occur to him that she might be ready. Besides, he had had a three hour session with Enchilada the previous evening, and at his age it was exhausting.

She swam slowly around the pool. Soon the film would be finished and she had to decide about herself and Steve.

'Listen, baby,' he said, 'I promised we'd go to a party tonight. O.K. with you?'

She climbed out of the pool, covering her breasts with her hands. 'Fine.'

The Acapulco Film Festival was in full swing, and Sunday and Steve had already attended several parties together.

Sunday enjoyed them. It was interesting meeting the foreign contingent, and she had run into two or three people she had worked with in Rome.

'You're quite a celebrity,' Steve said with a mixture of jealousy and pride when an important Italian director greeted her with a stream of praise about a film they had made together.

'I did exist before Hollywood,' she said with a smile.

'You bet your ass you did, and I don't want to hear about it.'

Claude Hussan, the French director, was brought over to be introduced by an anxious publicity girl. Claude was a tall angular man with dark emaciated features, black eyes and long straight hair. He was the current rage in French film circles, and married to a French actress who had starred in his latest film. The film was collecting a series of awards, and his wife was being acclaimed as a young Garbo.

Sunday was excited at meeting him, but he greeted her with

bored eyes and a great lack of interest, talking only to Steve. It upset her. She couldn't understand why he was so rude. She had seen his new film and admired it greatly. Secretly she harboured the wish to work for him. She knew that he was in the process of preparing his first American film, although no-one seemed to know much about it.

On the way home Steve said, 'What did you think of Claude?'

She shrugged. 'Full of his own importance.'

'Yeah, he's a cold fish. I hear he's a bastard with the ladies.'

'Yes, well you're not exactly Little Boy Blue.'

He told the chauffeur to pull over and stop. 'Listen kid, you have no complaints. I'll tell you what I was thinking. You want to try the marriage bit?'

'What are you talking about?'

'Marriage baby. Let's get MARRIED. Then maybe I can score a little sex around here.' Memories of Sunday swimming half-naked gave him his first hard-on of the day.

'You're not serious, are you?'

'I'm serious. When do you want to do it? Jesus, I thought the days of a broad holding out until after the ring was on her finger were over, but I guess they're not. When, baby? You name the day.'

'I—I don't know.' A proposal of marriage was the last thing she expected. She certainly hadn't been holding out for that reason. 'I mean are we compatible? Do we like the same things?'

'Take off your clothes, sugar, and we'll soon find out.'

'Steve, don't joke. I'll have to think about it.'

His voice echoed disbelief. 'You'll have to think about it. What is there to think about? My God, I've met difficult broads but you beat the band.'

'I can't just rush into a decision. It's a little more complicated than that.'

'Jesus, Sunday. Do you think now that we're practically married I can get on with my sex life? I feel like a *goddamn* monk, it's been so long.'

'Is that why you want to marry me, just for sex?'

'Don't talk like an idiot.'

'I'll tell you what. We'll go to bed together and then we'll see.'

128

'We'll see what?'

'We'll see if we want to get married.'

He shook his head. 'You know, you're a nutty broad.'

'I'm not a broad.'

'No, I guess you're not.' He lit a cigarette. 'So when do I get lucky?'

She smiled. 'Soon, I promise.'

The next day, without asking her, Steve announced their forthcoming marriage. Journalists started to flow into Acapulco from all over the world. 'Cash' received a million dollars worth of free publicity. Sunday Simmons became a household name.

She was angry. 'You should have waited. This isn't fair.'

He grinned his famous grin and presented her with a flawless square-cut diamond ring. It was difficult to stay angry with him, he was so pleased.

She phoned Carey, who was delighted about the whole thing. Then she phoned Max Thorpe. He hadn't predicted an immediate marriage.

'I'd like to see you,' she pleaded. 'We're having an engagement party tomorrow night. Can you possibly come?'

'I'd love to,' Max said. 'Will Branch be there?'

'I hope so.'

'So do I, my dear, so do I.' Max chuckled and envisaged himself in his pink frilled evening shirt.

It seemed all of Acapulco turned out, plus a certain section of Hollywood, and most of the wandering jet-setters.

Sunday was amazed at Steve's wide range of friends.

Her guests were few—Carey, with Marshall, smiling all over her face and whispering, 'I want to hear the whole story.' Branch, strangely quiet and morose. Max Thorpe, telling fortunes, in particular that of an eighteen-year-old rock idol. And Dindi, alone and pretty in the skimpiest dress, which showed off every one of her assets.

'Where's Charlie?' Sunday asked, slightly disappointed by his absence.

'That man is such a drag,' Dindi said. 'All he has on his mind is work. I'm seriously thinking of trading him for a newer model

129

now that I'm making it on my own. Did you know I'm starring in "All the World Loves a Stripper"? It's a fabulous part. Lots of nude scenes, but it's very artistic, and absolutely imperative to the story.'

'That's terrific, I'm sorry that things aren't too good with you and Charlie.'

'Good, schnood, who cares.' Dindi peered closely at Sunday. 'Say, is it all true or what?'

'Is what true?'

'The sexy Mr Magnum. Is he where it's at or not? I mean does he swing like they say? Is he *that* good?'

'Er, Dindi, I'll see you in a minute, there are some people I must talk to.' Sunday hurried off.

'For a great-looking girl she sure is dull,' Dindi muttered. 'Bet she wouldn't know a good screw if it was staring her in the face.'

Dindi was particularly disturbed by the engagement. She had got herself lumbered with a moody English actor, and Sunday had picked the plum, Steve Magnum himself.

Steve was talking to a well-known senator when Dindi zeroed in. 'Hi,' she said, 'I'm Dindi Sydne, Mrs Charlie Brick. I'm Sunday's best-friend. I guess she told you about me.'

'If you give yourself any more billing, you'll own the studio!' Steve said with a laugh.

Dindi laughed too, as did the senator, who said, 'My wife is a big fan of your husband's.'

'You don't say,' Dindi replied. 'How nice. I'll tell Charlie. Great house you have here, Steve.'

'Thank you.' Where had Sunday found this ding-a-ling? If indeed she was a friend, for Sunday had never mentioned her.

'I may get Charlie to buy a house here. How would you like us as neighbours?' She gazed at Steve wide-eyed.

He looked her up and down. 'It sure as hell would improve the scenery.'

Carey dislodged herself from the senator's wife and found Sunday.

'I know we can't get involved in long talks now, but tell me, are you happy?'

'Happy?' Sunday replied. 'Does one ever really know at the time? I think I'm happy. I *know* Steve is.'

'You certainly surprised us all. I mean everyone thought he was much too slippery to get caught again.'

'I didn't *catch* him. I didn't set any traps. He *wants* to marry me.'

'Of course he does. All I'm saying is that you were clever the way you played it. Like very smart.'

'Carey, I haven't been playing any games. I haven't even slept with him yet.'

'*What?*'

'Oh, don't worry, tomorrow's the big day. I'm not fool enough to marry a man I don't know sexually.'

'You've been going together two whole months and you haven't slept with him and *that's* not playing games! Wowee you've got to be made of stone.' She started to laugh. 'I've really got to hand it to you.'

'Don't you dare say a word to anyone. Not anyone. Steve would kill me if he thought I had mentioned it.'

'You know you can trust me. What's he been doing for action?'

'You're beginning to sound like Dindi. Nothing. That's one of the things I like about him, he's been prepared to wait.'

'*Come on.* Steve Magnum?'

'Yes. Steve Magnum.'

'If you say so.' But Carey wasn't really prepared to believe that. He must have had *something* going for him.

'Anyway, what about you?' Sunday asked. 'Have you decided about Marshall yet?'

Carey looked sheepish. 'Gee, I just don't know, it's so *difficult.* He's sweet and nice when you get to know him, but marriage . . . we've got a lot of problems going for us that other people just don't have.'

'I hope you work it out. I think the only place one can really be safe is in a good marriage, and one that's not based entirely on sex.'

Later, Max took Sunday into a corner and studied her hand. 'It's all here, you know,' he said, 'a very strong man, a powerful influence. I just didn't see it as marriage. But of course, it is so.'

'Do you see children?' she asked anxiously.

'Perhaps, after a while.' Sunday's hand perplexed him; there was this strange break, something . . . 'Yes, I see children eventually. Two.'

She smiled. 'You know Max, since I came to visit you that day I've felt like a new person.'

He nodded. He knew he had the power to reassure people, relax them. It pleased him. 'Tell me, my dear, do you know the Senator? I'd very much like to meet him.'

Max felt he *should* meet the senator. He adored to acquire people and watch them fall under his spell as he told them about themselves. The Senator could be an important acquisition. Max was rather upset at the way Branch was treating him. He had attempted to make a rendezvous but Branch had brushed him off edgily. The fact that he had done this only made him more interesting. 'Such a sexy boy,' Max muttered under his breath, 'what muscles!'

It was a shame, he reflected, that he couldn't predict his own future.

Branch was steering well clear of Max Thorpe. It seemed every way he turned there was a fag lying in wait. Even the director of the film he was doing was one, with a wife and three children tucked away somewhere.

It disgusted Branch. He only did it for his career and to get on. When he was a Star, they had better not come sniffing around.

He watched Sunday with lovesick eyes.

Why hadn't she waited for him?

Dindi followed Steve carefully, stationing herself in nearby groups and keeping her eye on him. When he went upstairs she was a discreet distance behind. He went into a room and shut the door.

After a few minutes she followed. The room was a study which led into a black marble bathroom.

He was in the bathroom taking a leak.

'Oops, excuse me,' said Dindi, 'I was looking for the powder room.'

He finished what he was doing, and then casually zipped himself out of sight. 'Yeah?'

'Well, really,' she giggled, 'I was following you.'

Ignoring her, he peered at himself in the mirror, combing his hair and deciding whether to take a quick eye-bath as his eyes were bloodshot from all the booze he had put away.

'I was following you because I like you, and I thought, well, you're not going to be a bachelor much longer, and well, y'know, you have the *wildest* reputation, and I thought maybe it would be fun—for you as well as me—if we had a little sort of goodbye-Steve Magnum fuck!'

He started to laugh. 'You're a hell of a friend.'

'I'm not *really* Sunday's friend. In fact, I don't even know her. I came here with a guy. She'd *never* find out.'

'Forget it, baby.' He turned back to the mirror.

Dindi walked out of the bathroom and locked the door in the study. She took off her clothes, leaving only the long chains she was wearing around her neck. Then she went back into the bathroom and said, 'I hear you *adore* being whipped. Maybe one last time. . . .?'

27

It took Herbert Lincoln Jefferson time to adjust. The fact that his wife Marge was involved in some kind of sexual black magic was bad enough, but before he had made up his mind to do anything about it, he was stunned by the news that a young girl had been murdered on Miller Drive. Her description fitted the girl he had picked up the previous evening.

He was shocked. He couldn't have killed her: It was impossible. He had only knocked her around a little, given her the sort of treatment she deserved. She wasn't the first woman he had hit, and with the others it had always been all right. Some-one else had probably come across her after he had driven off.

There was a picture in the paper of two policemen standing at the spot where she was found. The report said she was about eighteen or nineteen, a heroin addict, victim of a brutal beating, naked but with no signs of sexual assault. She was unidentified. The police claimed to be working on several leads.

Herbert went cold with fear when he read about it. If the police got him he couldn't stand it. It would mean prison and filth. He had heard about what went on in the prisons, with men raping other men.

Was there anything to connect him with the girl? Had anyone seen her get in his car? Had they noted the number?

He had left the car in the Supreme Chauffeur garage. Her fingerprints must be inside it. What if the police went there and found them? He must clean them off at once.

Shaking with fear, he hurried upstairs and dressed. Marge was still asleep, snoring and seeming to smile.

He shook her awake. 'If anyone comes here asking where I was last night, I was here with you from nine o'clock until twelve when I took the car back. Understand?'

'Wassamatter?' Her sleepy eyes opened.

'I was with you,' he shouted, 'all night.'

'But you was working last night,' she whined.

Controlling an impulse to drag her out of bed and shake her, he said, 'I was here with you. That's what you tell them. No matter what. O.K.?'

'Are you in trouble?' she asked suspiciously.

'Maybe,' he muttered. 'But you'd better say what I told you to say, otherwise you'll be good and sorry.'

'All right. Where are you going?'

'I have to go to the garage. They have an early job for me.'

'But you're on night shift.'

'Now remember, I came home nine o'clock because I finished early. Then I took the car back at twelve and came straight home again.'

'O.K.' She shifted her bulky body out of bed and reached for a bar of chocolate on the dressing table.

When he was gone she got up. Herbert *was* in trouble, she knew that. But how could she be his alibi when she had been next door all evening? She would have to talk it over with Louella Crisp. What a wonderful neighbour she was, so kind and understanding. Thank goodness she had come to live next door and rescued Marge from a life that consisted merely of eating, watching T.V., and Herbie.

She shuffled downstairs to make her usual breakfast of eggs, toasted muffins and low-calorie chocolate malt. She was trying to cut down, she had promised Louella she would. It was so wonderful of Louella to let her join her 'circle of friends', as she called them. The previous evening had been her initiation, and it had involved sex with each of the five men present. But Marge didn't mind. Louella had explained to her that she had to submit to become part of the group; every new member did the same thing.

'It's a great honour,' Louella had told her. 'We select very few people. The men who will be with you are very respected members of the community.'

Thrilled, Marge had looked covertly at their faces, hoping to recognise a movie star at least. She was a little disappointed for they hadn't *looked* very important, mostly ageing and nondescript. But all the same it had been so long since Herbert had touched her that it didn't really matter *what* they looked like.

She picked the paper off the kitchen floor where Herbie had left it, and glanced at an advertisement for a fake mink hat. Then she read about the murder of a hippie girl, sinking her teeth into a fat fuzzy peach as she did so.

Herbert arrived at the Supreme Chauffeur Company in record time.

'What are you doing here, Jefferson?' the man at the desk asked him. 'You're not on nights *and* days, are you?'

Herbert shook his head, his eyes shifting uneasily. 'No. Lost me cigarette lighter. It's valuable. Thought I'd better look for it right away. Is the Caddy I had last night still in the garage?'

The man consulted a book. 'Nope. Went in for a service this morning. Be back at six.'

Herbert felt sweat form on his body. 'Where's it gone?'

135

'Usual place on La Cienega.'

Herbert turned and walked out. If it was being serviced it would finish up with a thorough clean inside and out. But he didn't dare take a chance. He would have to go to the garage, and examine it. Maybe the girl had dropped something in the car.

He quickened his step to the bus stop and cursed the fact that he still had no car. You were dead without one in Los Angeles, the public transport system stank.

It was a hot smoggy morning and he felt in desperate need of a shower. How he hated to feel dirty. When his mother was alive she used to beat him if he tried to skip his nightly bath. 'You dirty little bastard,' she would scream, 'you're filthy, like your father.'

How pleased she would be if she could see him now, showering two or three times a day.

On the bus he took care to sit alone, scowling out of the window at the passing people.

He thought about the letter he had posted to Sunday Simmons. It made him feel good.

He thought about her supposed engagement to Steve Magnum. Of course it wasn't true—just publicity because they were acting in a film together. Herbert imagined himself wise in the ways of Hollywood.

He thought about Marge and the strange scene he had witnessed next door. He hated the whole idea of it. God, when this business of the murder was off his mind he was going to do something about it. He wasn't having his wife mixing with a bunch of perverts. Meanwhile he would leave Marge in ignorance, let her think he knew nothing.

The car was up on a block, a workman poking about underneath.

'I have to get in there,' Herbert said abruptly.

'Yeah?' The man looked him over.

'I'm from the Supreme Chauffeur Company. A customer lost something inside the car, and I have to look for it.'

The workman's eyes narrowed. 'I didn't take anything.'

Herbert nodded impatiently. 'I know you didn't, I just have to look. It might not be there, but I have to look—now.'

Complaining, the man lowered the car and Herbert got inside. He sat behind the wheel, gripping it tightly, and forced his eyes to look slowly around. Having done that, he got out and tipped the seats forward, bending down to study the thick pile rugs, first the driver's side, then the other.

He searched carefully, his mean brown eyes covering every inch. Satisfied, he was about to stand up when his eye caught the glint of something stuck down the side of the carpet. He picked it up. It was a fine gold chain with a small disc attached. On the disc were three tiny diamonds with the word 'DAD' engraved.

He pocketed it quickly and strolled away from the car.

The workman was busy talking to another mechanic as he left.

Louella Crisp, a sharp bird-like woman, stared piercingly at Marge Lincoln Jefferson. 'You've got to find out what he's done,' she said for the third time.

'I don't know how I can,' Marge whined in reply. 'He never tells me nothin' unless he feels like it.'

'I'm telling you that you *must* find out. Don't you understand that he *has* to tell you if he wants *you* to tell people he was with you.'

'I'll try,' Marge said reluctantly.

'See that you do,' Louella clapped her hands together. 'There's to be another gathering next Saturday. There will be other men that will initiate you. Soon you will be one of us absolutely. I'm afraid that I must ask you again for the five hundred dollars membership token. Do you have it?'

Marge fidgeted uncomfortably. 'Gee I'll give it to you soon. I have it, but Herbert's got my bank book. I'll get it from him by Saturday.'

'I hope so, otherwise it will be impossible for you to continue to come to our little parties.' Louella put a thin hand on her shoulder. 'I like you very much, Marge dear, but if the other members find you haven't paid, well—whatever I say, I'm afraid they won't want you.'

'I'll get it, I swear I'll get it,' Marge said quickly. Now that she had found Louella and her circle of friends, she was terrified of losing them. There was fifteen hundred dollars in her bank book, money she had saved before she even met Herbie. He had tried many times to get her to take the money out, but she had refused. It was all she had. Furious on one occasion, he had grabbed the book and said that if he couldn't have it, neither could she. He had hidden it, but she knew that she must find it and get the money for Louella.

28

'Roundabout' was finished.

Serafina and the children had returned to London.

In the big house there were only Charlie, Dindi, George and the servants.

In the garage there was a new white Lamborghini Muira.

In the study the latest camera equipment piled high, some boxes containing Leicas and Rolleiflexes unopened.

Charlie was depressed. The completing of a film always left him strangely melancholy and alone. It took him days, sometimes weeks to adjust, get rid of the character he had been playing and become himself. Fortunately the character in 'Roundabout' had not been too complex. Mr Everyman. Ordinary Schmuck caught in extraordinary situations. Charlie had captured him to a T. The man-in-the-street was one of his most masterly comic exercises. Everyone at the studio agreed it was probably one of his best performances. The film was destined to be a huge moneymaker.

Angela Carter was adequate, but it was Dindi on whom everyone commented. She came over pretty and appealing, the Baby Girl she had played for Charlie on their first date. She was lucky to have Marshall as her agent.

'I'm amazed,' Marshall confided to Carey. 'She really comes

across cute on the screen. Even the women like her. Cy wants her for another picture at once.'

Since Las Vegas relations between Dindi and Charlie had been strained. They lived together, hostility cutting the air like a knife. One of Dindi's most constant moans was how could he have left her with the Allens, his mother and a gardener!

'You can look after yourself,' Charlie had said when she telephoned in a rage from Las Vegas.

'You bet your ass I can, and just you watch me!'

Reports of her liaisons with the hotel manager came back with both Serafina and Natalie.

'It was disgusting and humiliating,' Serafina wailed. 'You're wife, Charlie, *my son's* wife, going everywhere with another man.'

Natalie was more subtle. 'I think I should tell you, Charlie, as a friend. I know she's very young, but really, she was practically having an affair with this third-rate gangster-type in public.' Natalie gazed at him sympathetically and laid an understanding hand on his arm. 'You need a more mature woman, Charlie, a woman who appreciates you.'

'You're right, love. I made a horrible mistake,' he admitted.

Natalie smiled. Soon it would be right for her to step in.

She was dismayed to find herself pregnant shortly afterwards. Clay had ruined her plans. Why did she have to be the one woman in God knows how many whom the pill had let down?

Clay was delighted and refused to let her do anything about it. 'Old Max Thorpe, the bum, was right,' he whooped. 'Don't you remember he told us at that party of Charlie's you were going to get knocked up again?'

Thin-lipped, Natalie considered how long it would be before the whole thing would be over and she was back in shape. At least a year. Would Charlie wait that long?

She sighed. What an infuriating twist of fate! Just when Dindi was on her way out too.

Shortly after returning to London, Serafina was taken ill.

Charlie was unsure what to do.

'How bad is she?' he demanded of her boyfriend, Archie, who had phoned to tell him.

'Pretty bad,' Archie replied glumly. 'They took her to the hospital today. She was asking for you.'

'What hospital? What's her doctor's number? Is she in a private room?'

Charlie telephoned the doctor and established that she had suffered a mild heart attack. 'Should I fly in?' he asked.

'I don't think that's necessary,' her doctor replied. 'Although, of course, she's getting on in years a bit, and you never know.'

Charlie hung up, despondent. If he were not so scared of flying he would get on a plane without hesitation. But the thought of sitting captive on an aeroplane, a piece of machinery that to his mind could disintegrate at any moment, was just too terrifying. He had already decided that when he did return to London it was going to be by train and ship.

The doctor's words hung in his ears—'She's getting on a bit.' 'You never know,' He was in an agony of indecision.

Later that day Dindi returned from Acapulco. She burst into the house, laughing and chattering. 'Acapulco was absolutely great, you should have come. The party was lovely, I met all sorts of people—'

'Serafina's very sick,' he said gravely.

'Oh, is she? By the way, what do you think of this idea. In "All the World Loves a Stripper", you doing a sort of guest appearance, like a one-day shot as a gag? The publicity would be great. Jerry suggested it. I think he's the greatest publicity guy ever, he really knows where it's at. Do you know—'

'Dindi, didn't you hear me? I said Serafina is very sick.' He stared at her in a white-faced rage.

'I heard you. She's sick. So what do you want me to do—a chorus of "Dixie"? Too much screwing at her age, that's what—'

He slapped her hard across the face. Her hat fell off and the imprint of his hand blazed across her skin.

'You bastard,' she sobbed. 'You lousy English bastard. What did you do that for?'

'That's my mother you're talking about.' He started to shout. 'My mother is a fine woman and I don't even want to hear her name coming out of your mouth. You are a tramp, Dindi, a tramp. Don't think I don't know what went on in Las Vegas after I left. Serafina was ashamed of you, ashamed—'

'That old bat was ashamed of *me*. Why, I was embarrassed to be in the same company as that over-made-up old crow! How dare you talk about *me*, when she was screwing a fuckin' gardener! That's a hell of a mother you've got there, a real old—'

'Out of my house. Pack your bags and *get out*.'

'You're kidding, aren't you? This is California, baby, and you can get the hell out of *my* house.'

In disgust he turned his back to walk away.

Grabbing a silver-framed picture of Serafina from the piano, Dindi hurled it at him. 'That's what I think about your old mother,' she yelled.

The photo frame shattered on the floor, Charlie bent to extract his mother's picture. In a fury Dindi snatched it from him and ripped it in half. He slapped her again, and she spat at him, tears rolling down her cheeks. 'I know you tried to get me cut out of the film. I know you're jealous of my success. You're an old has-been with no friends. *No* friends, you hear me. Everyone on 'Roundabout' hated you.'

Slowly he picked up the torn picture of his mother. 'You know I'm very lucky.' He forced his voice to be calm. 'Very lucky that it didn't take me too long to find out what a *cunt* I married.' With that he walked out of the room, out of the house, got into the Lamborghini Muira, and drove off.

Dindi followed him, yelling insults until the car disappeared from sight. 'Bastard! Prick!' she muttered, until gradually the tears stopped and the mind started to work. It wasn't too bad, it wasn't too bad at all. And the publicity would be great. She could picture herself in court, blue eyes wide and innocent, demure little powder-pink dress. 'Yes, he beat me, I know it was because he was jealous of my success. I put up with it as long as I could.' The statement could be interrupted with a choked sob at that point.

'I'll fix that limey sonofabitch!' she muttered. 'I'll fix him good!'

Charlie drove to the Beverly Hills Hotel. His mind was very clear, very calm. He phoned George at the house and told him to pack a bag for London. Then he made a reservation on the evening jet over the pole. Next he called Marshall K. Marshall and obtained the name of the best lawyer in L.A.

He was able to see him before he left.

'I want a divorce,' he stated. 'I don't care what it costs, but I want to settle a lump sum and I want her off my back.'

Knowing Dindi's love of money, he was sure her natural greed would persuade her to accept an outright payment and he wanted nothing more to do with her. The thought of paying alimony every month disgusted him.

'It's going to be mighty expensive,' the lawyer said.

'I know,' Charlie replied. 'Do it.'

Serafina's face was worth the long hours of terror while strapped into his seat above the Atlantic.

'You're a good boy,' she crooned.

He was shocked to see her without makeup. Ever since he could remember her face had been ornamented with blue eye-shadows, thick creamy pan-stiks, bright vermilion lipsticks.

Now she lay in the hospital bed, her skin a deathly mottled green, her eyes sunken and lifeless. For the first time he realised just how old his mother was.

'I'm going to be all right, son,' she said, 'Archie's looking after me.'

Archie, a shabby little man hunched in the corner, nodded eagerly. 'I'm looking after her, Charlie boy, not to worry.'

Charlie knew she was going to die. Her tired, beaten face told him that. But he smiled and said, 'Where's all that life and vitality I was always hearing about? I thought you'd be dashing around making some tea.'

She managed to show her cracked, decayed teeth. 'Soon, Charlie, soon.' Then she appeared to fall into a sleep, and later that night she passed away.

Charlie went to the big house in Richmond and wandered around.

Downstairs it was in beautiful order, with the smart modern furniture put there by the decorator he had commissioned.

Upstairs the only two rooms that seemed to have been used

were Serafina's bedroom, and an adjoining dressing-room where Archie slept.

Her room was flooded with pieces of her life. There were photos of Charlie everywhere. Pictures of him as a boy. Smiling blandly beneath a mask of pancake on his first stage appearance. Growing up to be a fat young man. Marrying Lorna, two blank un-lived-in faces setting off on life. A rare photo of his father, stern-faced. Serafina at the age of sixteen, a thin lively girl with luxuriant red ringlets.

Then came the photos of Charlie Brick—star. Meeting the Queen. Receiving an award. Going to a première—They were all there, a pictorial record of his life.

In her wardrobe hung her old stage dresses, musty and faded with age, but still smelling of the old days, the theatres, and greasepaint.

Charlie buried his nose in them and was assailed by so many memories that a lump formed and stayed in his throat.

It was hard to believe that Serafina was dead. His Serafina. His mother.

He slept that night in her big fourposter bed, and the next day he arranged the funeral and comforted Archie, who had broken down completely.

Charlie regretted not having brought him to Hollywood with Serafina. He had had no idea how much the funny little man cared.

Lorna phoned at once when she heard.

'Do you want me to bring the children over?' she asked.

'No, I don't think so. I'd like them at the funeral. It's tomorrow. If you came to the house at ten perhaps we could all go together.'

'Yes, of course. And Charlie, I'm really sorry. Serafina and I were never the best of friends, but she was a wonderful old lady, the children adored her.'

'Thank you.' He hung up, near to tears.

Lorna arrived the next day on time. It had been such a long time since he had seen her and she had changed. Her hair was longer, fluffier, and she had put on weight, but of course she had just had a baby.

She kissed him on the cheek, and the smell of her old familiar perfume made him think for a moment that nothing had changed between them.

'My goodness, you're thin,' she exclaimed.

He hugged the children. Little Cindy was crying. 'I want Serry, Daddy,' she said.

Serafina had insisted that they never called her Grandma. 'Do I *look* like a grandmother?' she was always demanding of people.

George arrived in time for the funeral. He had been left behind to transfer Charlie's personal belongs from the house in Bel Air to the Beverly Hills Hotel, and had then caught the next plane over. He decided not to mention that Dindi had thrown a huge party for what seemed like every deadbeat in L.A. the evening Charlie had left. He was merely relieved that his boss had caught on to her fairly quickly.

'How long are you going to stay?' Lorna asked Charlie as they drove to the cemetery.

He shrugged. 'I suppose I'll go straight back. I'm starting another film on the thirtieth. Besides, there's nothing for me here.' He looked at her pointedly.

'I—I was talking to Jim, and he said it would be fine if you could come to our house for dinner before you go.'

He bit back a sharp retort. After all, she *was* trying to be nice. 'No, love, sorry, I don't think that would work out.'

'If you change your mind we have an old place in Islington. We've got lots to do to it, but it will be lovely when we finish.' She squeezed his arm impulsively. His cold, unaffectionate Lorna actually squeezed his arm. 'I'm glad we can be friends, Charlie. I want to be friends. Jim and I are very happy, and I'm glad you remarried. Natalie wrote and told me she's very pretty.' Lorna laughed with no bitterness. 'I was never pretty enough for you, Charlie.' He went to interrupt but she continuated, 'No, don't start telling me lies. As soon as you became a film star I could see all the new people we met thinking. "Huh, not so hot, he could do better than that".'

'Not true,' he objected.

'Oh yes, it is. *You* know how bitchy everyone is in show business. We were at a party once and there were two girls discussing you in the loo. "Charlie Brick's quite sexy," one of them said—of course they didn't know who I was—"Yes," replied the other one, "and available too, with that wife he's got tucked away somewhere. I've never seen her but I hear she's a dog".'

'I don't believe you.'

'Don't. It doesn't really matter, not now anyway, but it *is* true.'

They sat in silence the rest of the way to the cemetery, the children strangely quiet in the front seat.

It was probably true, Charlie reflected. People *were* bitchy if your wife wasn't some kind of raving beauty. With regret he could even remember doing it himself, meeting a star and thinking—Well, the wife's not much.

Why did people rest so much importance on physical attributes? He did so himself. That was why he dieted so strenuously, and only took out dozey starlets and models, and finally married one. The lovely Dindi, who had absolutely nothing to offer except her looks.

Perhaps that was why he still wanted Lorna, because she was an ordinary person who had known him when he was a nobody. He didn't fancy her, there was nothing sexual left, but he still wanted her.

The burial was depressing. It seemed that relatives whom he never knew existed appeared from all over the country.

Serafina's elder sister, Lily, fell upon him, crying and moaning. He knew for a fact that they never got along, and had not even seen each other for five years.

'They're all jealous,' Serafina had once said, 'jealous of my youth and vitality and my famous son. I was always the queen in our family.'

Serafina had seven sisters and three brothers, and they all appeared with their respective sons, daughters, son-in-laws, daughter-in-laws, and grandchildren. Charlie hardly knew any of them.

The service was brief. Serafina had never been a religious

woman. Then everyone walked across to the cemetery to see the coffin lowered into the ground.

Charlie gritted his teeth. He decided funerals were unnecessary. People should be allowed the dignity of dying in private and peace. He made a decision to write in his will that he was to be cremated immediately and that there was to be no funeral.

Lorna stayed by his side, both in the church and at the grave. They held on to a child each. She squeezed his arm once, and he squeezed her back. He had never felt so close to anyone in his life.

After the funeral there was the disturbing business of entertaining all the relatives back at the house.

They came in their Morris Oxfords, and Mini Minors and battered old Fords.

They descended on the table of refreshments like locusts.

They oohed and they aahed. Three children fell into the swimming pool. One of Serafina's brothers started telling dirty jokes. Lily asked Charlie what was going to happen to all Serafina's things. Family gossip was rife. Serafina was forgotten.

The last Mini Minor was finally on its way at five o'clock.

'What a joke!' Charlie exclaimed. 'What a bloody horrible joke. Serafina would have had a fit if she'd been here.'

'What are you going to do now?' Lorna asked with concern, as she found the children's coats and prepared to go.

'Don't worry about me, love. Archie and I will have a bite together.'

'Are you *sure* you wouldn't like to come to dinner?' Shyly she added, 'I'd like you to see the baby. She's sweet. We call her Gemma.'

'I'm sorry. I haven't even asked about your baby.'

'There's nothing to ask really. A baby is a baby, and everyone thinks theirs is the most beautiful. Actually she looks a little like Cindy.'

Charlie debated whether this was a dig at him, but decided it wasn't. Then because he wanted to please her he said, 'I've decided to fly back to Hollywood tomorrow. Maybe next time I'm here I will come over.'

'My goodness, flying everywhere without a second thought nowadays.'

'I suppose you get over everything in time, love.'

George cooked bacon and eggs for Charlie and Archie. They sat in the kitchen and Charlie noticed how shrivelled Archie had become since Serafina's death.

There but for the grace of success go I, Charlie thought—a shabby little stand-up knock-down comic, who Charlie saw now had really cared for Serafina.

'I'll be out of here tomorrow before you leave,' Archie said, his eyes red-rimmed and sad.

'Where will you go?'

'I don't know. I'll travel around a bit. There's a club up in Manchester wants me back.'

'Look, Archie,' Charlie said impulsively, 'you don't have to go, you were good to my mother. I want you to have this house. *She* would have wanted you to have it.'

'No, Charlie, no,' Archie shook his head slowly. 'You don't have to give me a house because I looked after Serafina. Besides, I couldn't live here without her.'

'But I want you to have it. Sell it, do what you like with it, it's yours.'

Archie rose from the kitchen table with dignity, 'No. I said no and I mean no. I'll be going to bed now, see you in the morning.'

The little man departed, leaving Charlie alone. Depressed, he too went up to bed, Serafina's bed. He slept badly dreaming of plane crashes. He awoke in a cold sweat at 4 a.m. and was unable to get back to sleep.

In the morning Archie was gone. No forwarding address, nothing—he had packed his one suitcase and left quietly.

Charlie was upset. He had wanted to give him some money at least.

George helped him pack all of Serafina's personal things, which were sent off to storage.

Agents were instructed to put the house on the market.

By 4 p.m., fortified with Mexican Gold, and protected from prying reporters by George, Charlie was on a plane back to L.A.

29

The morning after the engagement party. Sunday awoke to the sound of the telephone. It was Carey 'phoning from the airport.

'I'm sorry I have to dash off like this, but you and Steve don't need me around anyway and I'm expecting some important contracts.'

'Couldn't you stay at least a couple of days? I've hardly seen you.'

'I know, but work calls. Now, when are you naming the big day? Don't forget, *I* want to be the first to know.'

'Don't worry. I'll call you at once if we decide before we come back. By the way, if things work out tonight I expect I'll move into his house.'

Carey chuckled. 'With Steve Magnum at the wheel and you in the driver's seat, I'd like to take a little bet that things will *definitely* work out.'

Sunday smiled. She hoped so. She needed a man so badly now. She needed Steve.

It was a beautiful morning. A clear hot balmy day. Steve had promised to telephone her when he woke up. That probably wouldn't be until late, for the party had still been going strong when she had left at 4 a.m. with Marisa and Woody.

There had been so many people. Steve had many friends. She had found him playing craps with a bunch of men. Quietly she kissed him and whispered, 'I want to have dinner in tomorrow night, just the two of us.'

He was drunk. He laughed and shouted, 'Say goodnight to my Princess.' Then he fished in his pocket and pulled out a small package. 'Open this when you're in bed.'

She had done as he said. The package contained the figures of a man and woman their hands joined. They were about two inches high, exquisitely made in solid gold. The female figure had two bright round diamonds for breasts and another pear-shaped diamond strategically placed. The male figure was practically all diamond.

A note was enclosed. All it said was, 'I don't want to boast but . . . '

Sunday laughed. It was the most vulgar gift she had ever received.

Breakfast was a mango and some peaches by her small private pool. Then she swam, cleaning away the slight hangover. Next she did her daily exercises underwater.

'My God, aren't we the energetic one!' It was Dindi, hidden from the world by a huge cowboy hat, tinted sun-glasses, and a yellow pant suit. 'I was sure you'd be up, so I thought I'd drop by before leaving.'

Sunday climbed out of the pool, shaking water out of her hair and hitching up the bottom of her bikini. 'Are you going too? What a pity. Carey just called me from the airport. I suppose you have to get back to Charlie.'

Dindi hooted with laughter. 'You're kidding, aren't you? *I* have to get back for work, darling, hard work. Did I tell you I'm starring in "All the World Loves a Stripper"? My reviews for "Roundabout" say I steal the whole film.'

'That's great. Can't wait to see it.'

'I'll have it run for you,' she said airily. 'When are you coming back?'

Sunday shrugged. 'I don't know. Whatever Steve wants.'

Dindi took off her hat and threw her face back to catch the sun. 'I think I should tell you, after all we *are* friends and I'm not one for keeping secrets. Anyway if it was me *I* would want to know.'

'Know what?'

'Well, I guess it was my fault too,' she admitted, 'but I *was* sort of stoned, and you know what I'm like when a guy comes on strong, and I *was* curious.'

'What *are* you talking about?'

'Sunday, I don't want to hurt you. I know how uptight you are about sex, and Gods knows you had a bad enough time with that freaked-out first husband of yours. But I must be honest, and I do think you would be better off knowing.'

Coldly Sunday said, 'Please don't call my first husband names. He was sick, that's all, sick. Why, you hardly even knew him.'

Dindi sighed. 'I suppose I should have told you before. I knew him very well. As a matter of fact, Benno used to make me have scenes with the two of them. I was mad about Benno. I rather fancied myself as a Roman Princess. He was, like all men though, a first-class shit, and after Paulo died he was so miserable he kicked me out. You know, of course, that Benno and Paulo were making it?'

White-faced, Sunday said, 'You must be out of your mind.'

Dindi shrugged. 'Believe me or don't believe me, it doesn't make any difference. Fly to beautiful Roma and ask Benno yourself. I thought you must have known, everybody else did. All those tall blond Roman Counts and Princes swing both ways, it's in their blood. Listen, the three of us were holed up in a hotel for three days a week before he died.'

Very quietly Sunday said, 'I think you had better go.'

'Oh shit,' Dindi exclaimed. 'I'm doing you a *favour*, telling you the truth. I think you live in a little ivory tower or something. Anyway, that's not even what I came to say. I thought you knew all that. What I *wanted* to tell you was about your new boyfriend, Mister Magnum.'

'I don't want to hear anything else you have to say, Dindi. Can't you understand that I—'

'Yeah—I can understand that you're trying to shut yourself off from life. Well, whether you like hearing it or not, the fact is I screwed your big movie-star boyfriend last night. They're all bastards, baby, and Steve Magnum ain't no different. He screwed me at *your* party while you were chatting politely to *his* guests.' She sighed. 'In this life you have to look out for number one, you're always alone in the end. You may think I'm a bitch, but I like you, and I figure you're better off knowing what kind of guy you're marrying.' She stood up. 'Well, there it is, I'm sorry if you're upset, but that's show biz.' She put on her hat. 'By the way, he's a fantastic lay!'

For a while Sunday sat in silence. Instinctively she knew that Dindi had spoken the truth. She pushed the information about Paulo to the back of her mind to be dealt with later.

Steve Magnum.

Goodbye.

She didn't want to listen to his lies.

150

Quickly she hurried into the bungalow, packed, and ordered a limousine. Then she called Carey's secretary in Los Angeles and dictated a brief statement to be given to the press.

'I'm going away for a week or so,' she told the girl.

'Tell Miss St Martin that I'm fine. I don't want to be disturbed, and I'll call her in a couple of days.'

She took the two gold figures Steve had given her and replaced them in their box. Then she wrote a short note saying, 'I understand you're fantastic.' Next she enclosed her large diamond engagement ring.

The Mexican driver arrived and began to load her suitcases into the car. She handed him the package and note. 'After you have taken me to the airport please deliver this to Señor Magnum.'

The driver nodded, his eyes fixed firmly on her bosom.

30

'You're a real friend. With friends like you I have no need of enemies.' Charlie sat in his Beverly Hills hotel bungalow and stared Clay down. 'I mean what the hell was all that bit about you met her with her mother? You laid her, didn't you? Her mother—what a load of crap. And the horrible thing is I'm sitting here like a right schmuck, believing you!' He shook his head. 'Thanks a lot, *friend*.'

Clay gulped his scotch down quickly. 'What did you want me to say, for Christ's sake? Oh yes, I *have* met your wife, I fucked her with a drunken Italian in Rome. After all by the time I saw her again you were *married* to her.'

'Bullshit! We've been friends long enough. You could have told me.'

'What good would telling you have done? I thought maybe she had reformed. After all, if I'd told you then, you might have ended up hating *me*!'

'That's great, you weren't concerned about me having made a right berk of myself marrying some ding-dong, you were just concerned about yourself. You're a selfish bastard.'

Clay helped himself to another scotch from the bottle on the table. 'Come on, Charlie. Let's forget about it. Everyone's allowed one mistake in life. Why did you marry her anyway?'

'Who knows? I was stoned, getting over Lorna. She looked like some pretty innocent little angel, and she gave great head.'

'So do half the hookers in Hollywood,' Clay remarked wisely.

It was 10 p.m. Charlie had been back in Los Angeles a week, and he and Clay had just been to see a special rough cut of 'Roundabout'. Natalie was at home.

'She has a bad attack of morning sickness all day and all night,' Clay remarked with a laugh. 'It's going to be a boy this time, I can feel it in my balls!'

After viewing the film, they returned to Charlie's bungalow, chatting and drinking. It was the first time Charlie had been out since getting back. He had holed up in the hotel, working on a script, and playing with his tape-recorders and cameras.

Dindi had derived the maximum amount of publicity out of their forthcoming divorce, giving forth with several conflicting statements and posing for innumerable pictures until her lawyer had forced her to be silent.

Charlie merely produced that well-worn quote: 'No comment.'

Along with the Sunday Simmons/Steve Magnum engagement breaking up, Dindi and Charlie were the show-business talk of the week.

'What do you say we go out and have some fun?' Clay suggested. 'It's not often I get a night off.'

'Where do you want to go?'

'Cruising. We could cruise a bit and pull two lovely little darlings.'

Charlie laughed. 'You haven't changed much, have you? Remember the first time we ever met?'

'Could I ever forget!' Clay exclaimed. 'Vietary Studios. I was banging a real hot one in the dressing-room and you barged in. She pulled up her knickers so quick, I thought she had taken my cock with her!'

152

'You always were a randy old bastard,' Charlie said with an admiring chuckle.

'You came in calm as you like and said in that camp faggot accent you were using then—"Oh, did I come at the wrong time?" I could have killed you! The bird scampered off, and I ended up with nothing!'

'The start of a beautiful friendship.'

'Yes. Well, we've both come a long way from those days, haven't we? Of course, you're in the best position. Famous film star. You can pull more or less anyone you want. When you were having that fling with Michelle Lomas, I don't mind telling you I was goddam jealous.'

'Were you?'

'Sure I was. Any fellow worth his balls would have been.'

Charlie laughed modestly. 'Michelle was a fabulous woman.'

'Come on, let's have another drink for Serafina, she was always fond of a drop of Scotch. I'm going to miss that grand old lady.'

Solemnly they re-filled their glasses and toasted Serafina.

Clay said, 'Fancy dropping into a disco?'

Charlie shook his head. 'You go.'

'Come on, it will do you good. Anyhow, I fancy having a ride in that flash car of yours.'

The discotheque was jammed as usual. Charlie had only ever been there once with Dindi. The place made him uncomfortable. It was jammed with starlets and beach-boys and actors and young celebrities and a few old celebrities who figured they were still young, and hookers of both sexes.

Clay pushed his way through and found them a place at the bar. He immediately started to chat to a blonde in a gold cat-suit who looked completely stoned.

Charlie wished he hadn't come. Clay meant well, but this really wasn't his scene.

'You're Charlie Brick, aren't you?' a smaller, not so pretty version of Dindi asked him. She had the same flaxen hair and big blue eyes. 'I'm here with my boyfriend, but I wanted to tell you that you really turn me on.' She fidgeted in her see-through

153

mini and abstractedly stroked her small breasts. 'Your glasses are *so* sexy. What star are you?'

'Virgo,' Charlie replied, fascinated as he watched her nipples harden under her own touch.

'Hmm,' she cast her eyes heavenwards, 'I thought so. I'm Aquarius. I'm an actress.'

As if I didn't know, he thought.

'Well, I guess I'd better get on back to my boyfriend. Shall I call you?'

'Don't call me, I'll call you.'

'Huh?'

'Nothing. It's a joke. Yes, do call me. I'm at the Hilton.'

She flitted away, and Charlie turned to see how Clay was getting on. He was doing nicely, whispering in the blonde's ear.

'Er, I think I've had enough of this place,' Charlie commented. 'Shall we move on?'

Reluctantly Clay agreed, scribbling the blonde's 'phone number in a small notebook.

Then he suggested they cruise down the Strip to inspect the action there. 'If I'm lucky, I might find myself a fourteen-year-old drop-out,' he joked.

Charlie had lost all enthusiasm for the trip. They might just as well have 'phoned for a couple of hookers, because whoever they found wandering about at this time of night was bound to be one anyway. He wasn't sure if he even felt like getting laid.

'Slow down, get over to the side,' Clay said excitedly.

Two girls were walking towards them, both dressed in tight chinos and clinging sweaters, both swinging fringed suede handbags and chewing gum. They edged towards the car as it stopped, first having a good look around for any cops.

'Looking for a little action?' the first girl asked, leaning down to the open window and peering in at Clay. 'We're available for any trips you care to take.'

He started to reply, but Charlie suddenly jammed his foot down on the accelerator, sending the car racing away.

'Hey, what's the matter?' Clay asked indignantly.

'For God's sake, the pair of them stank. Hopped up to the eyeballs on top of the stink!'

'I didn't realise we were on the look-out for Miss Clean America.'

'Fuck you.'

They rode in silence.

'What do you want then?' Clay finally asked.

Charlie shrugged. He was tired. What he really wanted was to go home to bed. They were passing by a strip joint. 'Let's go in here,' he said, swerving the Lamborghini into an adjoining parking lot. It was certainly better than cruising up and down like a couple of hicks.

'Good idea.' Clay's face brightened.

Charlie thought, 'What's this all about? What the hell are we looking for? A quick flash of tit like a couple of high school boys?' He was annoyed with himself and annoyed with Clay.

The place was sleazy, with plain wooden tables arranged around an L-shaped stage. A waitress, wearing black tights and a tired red bra, took their order.

A girl was up on the stage, going through her routine. She was wearing a bathing suit and a sash saying 'Miss Hot California'. She had flaming red hair and an enormous bosom. California packed in more enormous bosoms, thanks to all the doctors using silicone injections, than any other State.

She moved energetically, wriggling out of the bathing suit before you knew it, wearing just the sash and a red-white-and-blue G-string.

'Get a load of that!' Clay exclaimed happily.

Charlie sighed. The girl looked unreal. Two great globes of upstanding flesh. He ordered a bottle of Scotch, which he proceeded to empty fast.

The next performer had piles of raven hair and a low-cut purple beaded evening dress. She was introduced as Crazy Harold, and the music blared 'Big Spender'. She bumped and grinded her way automatically around the stage.

Charlie found the whole thing completely asexual. Clay was as excited as a schoolboy getting laid for the first time.

Between strippers, a comedian told weak blue jokes in a straight-out-of-Brooklyn accent. Charlie studied the voice. He found it much more interesting than the girls. It had a particular nasal twang that he wished to capture exactly for the character he was playing in his next film.

'Now I give you a coupla wild mustangs! Little Skinny Sackcloth and Fantastic Fat Fanny!' the comedian said.

The way he said 'Mustang' knocked Charlie out. He muttered it under his breath, trying to get the intonation right.

Clay was roaring with laughter, along with the rest of the room, as the two new strippers appeared.

Little Skinny Sackcloth was a Twiggy-type girl, extremely pretty and wearing a pink mini shift.

Fantastic Fat Fanny was also pretty, but a mountainous balloon of a girl from her wobbling double chins to her jelly-like legs. She too was wearing a pink mini dress.

They paraded the stage to the strains of 'Hello, Dolly'.

'Christ!' Clay muttered. 'I always fancied having a fat girl.'

Charlie was getting through the Scotch and feeling no pain, but even in the most stoned of conditions he could never have fancied the fat one. The little skinny one was a different proposition. She was rather appealing, with her wispy yellow hair and fawn-like eyes.

The girls removed their clothes in unison. First the skimpy mini shifts, under which they were wearing bras, panties and stockings clipped to old-fashioned suspenders.

Fat Fanny was grotesque, rolls upon rolls of uncontrollable flesh, quivering and shaking in time to the music. In comparison, Skinny Sackcloth was a skeleton, with ribs sticking out of an emaciated ribcage.

The combination of the two female forms was almost obscene. Their bras unclipped down the front, and now rolling their hips in time to a honky-tonk arrangement of 'Hard-Hearted Hannah', they undid the clips.

'I've got to have the fat one,' Clay groaned.

If Natalie could only see him now, Charlie thought, amused at Clay's enthusiasm. Fat Fanny looked like some sort of gross animal. Big boobs flopping and falling, nipples the size of the skinny one's entire little buds.

They ended the show. The comedian leaped up on the stage, cracked a couple of stale jokes, and promised everyone a brilliant new show in exactly one hour's time.

Clay grabbed the man on his way to the bar. Charlie called for the check and paid it. He was going to drop Clay off at his car ànd go to bed. Any more cruising Clay could do on his own.

Clay fumbled in his pocket and handed the comedian money.

Charlie got up. He had taken off his glasses, as no-one ever recognised him without them, and who needed to be recognised in such a dump? 'Come on,' he said patiently.

'It's all arranged,' Clay said excitedly. 'All fixed.'

'What's all fixed?'

'Fantastic Fat Fanny and the Skinny bit. I gave the fellow two hundred dollars and we're to go across the street to their apartment. They've only got an hour. How about *that* for organisation?'

'Two hundred dollars for those two freaks. I think you're going soft.'

'Soft I'm not. Let's go.'

Reluctantly Charlie trailed behind. Natalie had always said that Clay would screw anything, but this was ridiculous.

Little Skinny Sackcloth opened the door of the apartment. She was wearing a black chiffon ostrich-feather-trimmed dressing-gown and a vacuous smile.

The apartment was one room, and reminded Charlie of his first sexual encounter so long ago in a dingy dressing-room with a sister act. It had the same smells: cheap perfume and stale sweat.

Clay pushed eagerly forward. 'Got any booze?' he asked.

Skinny looked at him blankly. 'Jake didn't say nothin' 'bout booze bein' part of the deal.'

A toilet flushed and Fat Fanny emerged from the bathroom. She was wearing the same style dressing-gown as the skinny one. Immediately she took control. 'You want scotch, it's ten bucks a piece. Take your pants off and make yourselves at home, not too at home, we've only got an hour. Any rough stuff is extra, you read me—extra. And if you both want to make it with me at the same time, that's also extra.' She spoke very quickly in a fluffy light voice that didn't match up to her size.

Clay looked at Charlie and Charlie looked at Clay and they both burst out laughing.

'Well, *you* might be able to get it up but I certainly can't,' Charlie said.

'For two hundred dollars I'm going to try,' Clay replied, unzipping his pants and stepping out of them.

'I think I'll just watch,' Charlie said politely as the skinny girl approached him.

The fat one shook off her dressing-gown and lay on a couch. Clay mounted her, a foolish grin on his face.

'Tell my friend I'll wait in the car,' Charlie said to the skinny one, and quietly slipped out.

31

Sunday caught the first plane out of Acapulco airport. Destination—Mexico City.

She wore her hair scraped back, dark glasses, and bought her ticket in the name of Miss Sands. She hadn't decided where she was going, but she had to move fast before the barrage of publicity broke.

Getting engaged to Steve Magnum had catapulted her into the public eye. And now she had to get away—especially from Steve. She knew if he found her there would be excuses and apologies and finally insults. She didn't want to go through that.

Once in Mexico City she scanned the next flights out. She didn't want to travel too far. Then the idea of Rio occurred to her. Why not Rio? She had not been back since her parents died, and this was the perfect opportunity. There was a plane leaving within the hour.

The small boy stood wide-eyed by the boarding-gate. Sunday noticed him immediately, because for one thing he seemed much too young to be travelling alone—about five or six—and secondly, he was the most beautiful child she had ever seen. He had long dark hair framing his face like a halo, and huge black eyes set in an olive-skinned oval face. If I ever have a child, she thought, I would like him to look just like this.

The boy stood very still, occasionally darting his huge eyes anxiously around, obviously expecting someone.

When the flight was called he started to cry, not in a whining, snivelling way; tears just seemed to form in his big black eyes and trickle down his cheeks.

She went over to him. 'Are you waiting for your mother?'

He shook his head.

'Is someone coming for you?'

The child nodded. 'Oui, Papa.'

'Are you French?'

'Yes, he is French,' a bored masculine voice said behind her. 'And he is quite all right, thank you, so you may now leave him alone.'

The man took the boy firmly by the hand and they set off for the plane, leaving Sunday standing there.

She followed them, catching up as they entered the aircraft.

'I'm sorry,' she said, 'I thought he was alone. I was only trying to see if he needed any help. He was crying.'

'Crying?' the man's voice was amused. 'Jean-Pierre never cries.'

'Oh, you're Claude Hussan, aren't you?' She could have bitten off her tongue, she sounded like some cloying fan.

He ignored her, just took his seats without giving her another glance.

She realised that he obviously didn't remember her. She had been all dressed up and at her most glamorous when they had met in Acapulco. Now she was hidden behind glasses and her hair was a mess. Still, he *was* a rude man, and the child *had* been crying. 'Jean-Pierre never cries.' What a ridiculous and typically masculine statement to make about a five-year-old boy.

The plane taxied down the runway and was suddenly airborne. Sunday loved flying. It was so exhilarating, so powerful.

She felt relaxed and in a way relieved. Steve Magnum had not been the right man for her. She had accepted him for all the wrong reasons. Down the aisle Claude Hussan was chatting to a stewardess who was smiling and flashing even white teeth. He wasn't being rude to *her*.

The journey went fast. At the stopover Sunday bought the newspapers, but there was no report yet about her and Steve Magnum. She had a coffee, went to the Ladies room, and again noticed the little boy standing alone. She smiled at him, and he grinned back. His two front teeth were missing and he looked like a little urchin.

She wondered where his father was—probably in a bar somewhere, getting drunk.

She re-boarded the plane, and shortly before take-off Claude appeared with Jean-Pierre. She turned her head away as they went past.

Carey arrived at her office direct from the airport. She was tired and hot, and the copy of a Saint Laurent suit she was wearing had crumpled from the journey.

Marshall—who had flown in with her—had spent the entire journey trying to convince her they should get married immediately. He had suddenly—for some unknown reason—blown his entire cool after she had slept with him for the first time following Sunday and Steve's party. Instead of saying 'Think about it', 'Take your time', 'I know I'm much older than you', he was now saying, 'Name the day, Carey, and make it soon; in fact next week would be perfect.'

She sat behind her desk and chewed on a pencil. There was a stack of messages which she didn't even bother to look at.

Marshall had been great in bed. Surprisingly so for a fifty-six-year-old man. In fact, better than the twenty-three-year-old actor who had been her last encounter.

It was funny going to bed with Marshall. Old Marshall with whom she had worked for seven years. It had seemed almost incestuous at the time, and she had had to get well and truly drunk before they went back to their hotel.

There was definitely a lot to be said for the older man's technique in bed, which certainly beat stamina any day.

She giggled quietly to herself. What was to stop her getting married now? She was twenty-eight years old, she had been around, she was ready to settle with one man, and Marshall had told her that she could keep on her business.

160

Of course, her mother, who lived in a nice house in Pasadena with her married brother and his wife, would have a fit. Whenever Carey visited them they were always trying to fix her up with nice up-and-coming lawyers or accountants. She would be the disgrace of the family if she married a white man. But so what? She wasn't prejudiced.

She buzzed her secretary. What the hell? If she didn't take the plunge now, she never would.

'Sue, get me Sunday Simmons in Acapulco.' She decided Sunday should be the first to know.

'She won't be there, will she?' Sue said. 'I've got Steve Magnum for you.'

'Put him through.'

There was a pause and then Steve's voice crackled urgently across the line. 'Where is she, Carey?'

'Where is who?'

'Don't be smartass. Where is she?'

'Steve, I just got in. I had a lousy trip and I don't feel too great, so please stop shouting. If you're looking for Sunday I spoke to her just before I left, and she was in bed. Why don't you two move in together and then you won't be so anxious every time she pops out to go shopping or something.'

'Cut the shit,' he said coldly.

Sue, who had a habit of listening in on all Carey's calls, suddenly came dashing into the office and picked up the top message on Carey's pad. She waved it under her nose. Carey read it quickly.

'What the fuck is going on?' Steve demanded. 'Are you going to tell me where she is or not?'

'What happened?' Carey said. 'Everything was fine when I left, but my dumb secretary's just shown me a message from Sunday.'

'What message?'

'It seems she called in a press release I'm supposed to give out, and she said she was fine and would call me in a couple of days.'

'What's the press release?'

'It just says "Sunday Simmons and Steve Magnum have decided to call off their engagement by mutual agreement".'

'Mutual agreement, shit,' he snapped. 'Have you given it out?'

'I told you, I just this second saw it.'

'I don't want you to give that announcement out.'

'*You're* not my client, Steve.'

'I am now, honey, I'm sending you over a large retainer.'

'I'm sorry. If Sunday wants me to give out that statement, I'm going to have to do it.'

'If there's one thing I can't stand it's a spade with integrity.'

There was a short silence, during which she contemplated hanging up.

'Aw—I'm sorry,' Steve said. 'I'll tell you what, I'm going to hire you anyway.'

'What happened between Sunday and you?' she snapped.

'What happened—who knows. Sunday is a funny lady. I was bombed last night and I guess I did something I shouldn't have—according to her mixed-up standards.'

'What did you do?'

'It was nothing much.' He hesitated. 'Anyone else would have laughed it off.'

'What was it, for God's sake? It must have been *something* for Sunday to call everything off.'

'I had a scene with some nothing broad—a five-minute fuck.'

'And you *told* Sunday?'

'Are you crazy? Of course I didn't tell her. But somehow or other she must have found out. She sent back the ring with a note and just took off. By the time I got up today she was gone.'

'Dindi?'

'Huh?'

'It was Dindi Sydne, wasn't it?'

'I don't know who it was. Those broads all look the same to me. Some little blonde who's married to the English actor—whatshisname—Charlie Brick. A real freak-out.'

'Yes, that's Dindi. I bet she couldn't wait to tell Sunday all about it. Honestly, Steve, what made you do it?'

'A hard-on, honey, a plain old-fashioned hard-on. Do me one big favour—don't release that statement for twenty-four hours. Once I find her I'll talk her round.'

'I don't know, Steve, I should really—'

'Twenty-four hours, for Crissake, I'm not asking for ten million bucks. I really love the girl. Give me a break.'

'All right. But only twenty-four hours, and then, if I haven't heard anything, I'm going to have to give it out.'

'You won't regret it when you're flower-girl at our wedding. Just keep this quiet. I've got a detective flying in from L.A. and he'll track her fast.'

'Well, of course *I'll* keep quiet, but I can't say the same for Dindi Sydne.'

'Don't worry, I'll take care of her. Keep in touch if you hear anything.'

He hung up.

Great, thought Carey, a great situation. Knowing Sunday, Steve Magnum had lost already.

She sighed. Looking at it from a purely business point of view, the publicity was invaluable.

32

Marge Lincoln Jefferson sat nervously in the bank manager's office. Her palms were wringing wet. She wiped them surreptitiously on the cotton skirt of her dress.

Louella had been over time and time again how she was to behave, what she was to say. But still she was nervous as she waited for the man to respond to her speech. 'So, Mrs Lincoln Jefferson, you've lost your bankbook, I see. You should be more careful, you know; bankbooks must be looked after, put away, then we can just add all that nice fat juicy interest on without any trouble.'

When he said fat and juicy, his eyes considered her large floppy breasts sagging beneath the cotton dress in an old dirty bra. She was saving her only good one for the gathering on Saturday.

'Yeah, I know,' she said, gathering courage. 'But I gotta have five hundred dollars quickly, I gotta have it today.'

'Today? Hmm, I certainly don't think you can get anything today. We do have a seven-day withdrawal period, you know. However, I'll take specimens of your signature and details, and then if you come back in a week everything should be fine.'

What would Louella think of that? She might not even let her go to the gathering on Saturday night.

Marge squeezed out two fat tears. 'I *gotta* have it today. A week's time might be too late. I gotta go into the hospital, woman's problems, y'know?'

The bank manager flushed. He didn't want to hear about this gross woman's intimate problems.

Marge remembered what Louella had said, 'Any sign of trouble, and you sweet-talk the guy.'

She got up and leaned over his desk, resting her vast bosom on the desk top. 'You gotta give me a break,' she said, remembering the line from an old Mae West movie she had seen six times on television, 'er—you be good to me and I'll—er—be good to you—you know what I mean?'

The bank manager knew only too well what she meant. He cleared his throat and coughed nervously. 'I'll see if we can make an exception, Mrs Lincoln Jefferson. Would you please wait a minute?' Anything to get this awful woman out of his office.

Marge sat down and waited. If Herbie knew what she was doing he would kill her, but Louella had said it was all right. Louella had told her she had to do it, otherwise there would be no more circle of friends, no more meetings, no more parties and fun.

A secretary came in and smiled at Marge. 'Would you sign these forms please?' she requested. 'Mr Marvin has had to slip out, but he has authorized me to hand over five hundred dollars from your account.'

Two days passed and nothing happened. Herbert went about his business as normal. He scanned the papers every day, looking for more news about the murder, but there was nothing after the initial item. Murders were everyday occurrences in Los

Angeles, and nothing to get excited about unless there was some additional news potential, such as the victim being famous or the crime particularly horrendous.

Marge kept asking in her whiney nasal voice: 'Whadid you *do*, Herbie? Why do you want me to tell the police you was here?'

He ignored her. He took more showers than usual, and thought in a dreamy way what he would have done if it had been Sunday Simmons instead of that stinking dirty hippie—Sunday Simmons taking her dress off and offering herself to him.

He took the bus to work as usual, trying to find a seat on his own, and deciding that as soon as he got paid he would put a deposit on a car. He couldn't stand travelling on the bus, what with the smell and the people. He needed to pay the rent on his house which was two months overdue. He also had to meet the monthly payments on the television and refrigerater, but a car was more important. A car was a basic necessity.

It was a pity Marge didn't go back to work, although she could no longer get a job as a topless waitress.

Herbert coughed in disgust. He didn't want her any more. She had been useful to cook his meals and wash his clothes, but he could get a day maid to do that. No, after what he had witnessed the other evening, he didn't want the dirty bitch around.

Divorce was an expensive business. He thought carefully of other ways to dispose of her . . .

'I got the money,' Marge announced triumphantly.

Louella, sitting tight-lipped in her old green Chevvy, took it from Marge's outstretched hand and counted it. Then she put it in her purse and smiled, 'What a clever girl. Now you are *really* one of us.'

They drove back to Louella's house. She made some herb tea, then she went through the last two days papers with Marge, showing her all the items she had underlined.

There were forty burglaries, twelve muggings, a bank hold-up, thirty-three rapes, and two murders.

'It must be one of these,' Louella said. 'I want you to read everything carefully until you are familiar with them all.'

'Do I have to, Louey? My readin ain't the greatest.'

'If we want to know what your husband has been up to, you have to. If we find out for instance that it was him that raped that woman alone in her house, then he can never boss you around again. *We* will be in control.'

Marge giggled. 'I guess you're right, but Herbie would never rape anyone.'

'How do you know? What you must do is familiarize yourself with these cases and mention them to Herbert. When you hit on the right one you will know at once by his reaction.'

'But what if it's not any of these?'

Louella shrugged. 'Then we think of another way to find out what he did.'

'O.K., Louey. Gee, I don't know what I'd have done if you hadn't of come and lived next door. You're so nice to me, letting me join your "circle of friends" and everything.' She gripped Louella's arm with a warm, pudgy hand. 'You've changed my whole life, I really mean that.'

Louella smiled, the smile never reaching her small violet eyes. She regarded Marge in the same way that Herbert did, as a lumbering, brainless idiot. But it was stupid women like Marge who enabled her to make a living.

What would Marge do if she knew that the 'circle of friends' consisted of a lot of kinky business men who could only make it by pretending they were at some sort of black-magic orgy? Lonely women were so easy to find in Los Angeles—widows, divorcees, actresses who had never got further than the studio gates. Without exception, once Louella found them and befriended them, they were only too happy to join the circle of friends, and none objected to the so-called sexual initiations. It boiled down to the fact that they all wanted to have sex, and putting a respectable name to it and charging *them* five hundred dollars made everything all right.

Louella found the women. Her husband collected together the male misfits, who paid fifty dollars each and attended only once. Had Marge been offered to them as a prostitute for fifty dollars, they would probably all have baulked, but the very bizarreness of the situation made everyone happy.

After two months, by which time Marge would have been

initiated by over fifty men, Louella and her husband would quietly vanish with the best part of five thousand dollars, leaving Marge bewildered and suddenly friendless again.

In four years they had treated nearly forty women in this fashion, and the future looked bright, for they hadn't even half covered the State of California. None of the women ever complained. What could they say? It was as simple as that.

A lucrative sideline, Louella had discovered, was getting something on the victims, something in their past they wished to hide. This could often produce a few hundred dollars more.

Louella sensed that if she could pin something on Marge's husband, she could pry the rest of their savings away from them. Herbert Lincoln Jefferson looked like a shifty character. A rapist at least.

When Herbert reported for work at the Supreme Chauffeur Company on Saturday night, the man at the desk said, 'Jefferson, you're wanted down at the main office.'

'Me?' questioned Herbert stupidly.

'Yeah, you, there's been a complaint or something.'

Herbert's body broke out in a cold sweat. A complaint?

He tried to decide what to do. It must be the police. They must have found out about the girl. Should he run? Where to? He had only a few dollars on him and without a car he wouldn't get very far.

No, the best thing to do was to stay and deny everything. Marge would back him up with his alibi. At least he hoped she would.

The only thing that could possibly connect him with the case was the girl's neck-chain he had found on the floor of the car, but he had carefully hidden that under the mattress of his bed. Marge hardly ever made the bed, so there was little likelihood of her ever finding it. It was quite safe where it was. He wasn't even sure that it had belonged to the girl; any of his passengers could have dropped it.

In the main office Mr Snake, the manager, lolled in a black leather chair, his feet up on the desk in front of him. He was on the 'phone and ignored Herbert when he was ushered into the office by a secretary.

Herbert stood ill at ease in front of the desk and thought about sitting down. Mr Snake hadn't indicated that he should, and in the face of employers Herbert always liked to do the right thing. At least the police weren't present, which was something to be thankful for.

Mr Snake finished his conversation, banged the receiver down, fumbled for a cigarette, and snapped, 'Have you been taking a leak in our customers' swimming pools, Jefferson?'

'What?' Herbert questioned, his sallow skin reddening.

'You heard me. Right or wrong?'

'Wrong,' he said quickly. That was something they couldn't prove.

'You're fired. I gave you a chance to tell the truth and you blew it. Some kid was taking a film of his mother before she went out, and through the glass doors there's you taking a piss in their pool, calm as you like. I saw the film myself this afternoon. Pick up your things and get out of here. The cashier's got your check made up until today.'

Mr Snake picked up the 'phone again, and by the time Herbert turned to leave he was deep in conversation.

33

After the incident with Clay and the two strippers, Charlie went into a deep depression. He shut himself in his hotel bungalow with the ever-faithful George, and refused to see anyone except on business about the film he was due to start. The film, a comedy, was called 'Fred'.

The main girl's part was to be played by Laurel Jones, an ugly-pretty girl who had been nominated, but had not won, the previous year's Oscar for best-supporting actress. She came to dinner with Charlie at his hotel, bringing her husband of two months, a long-haired member of a currently successful pop group called 'Sons'.

Charlie liked them both. They were full of talk about politics, drop-outs, world air pollution, world starvation. To Charlie it made a refreshing change from conversation consisting of either the film industry or who was laying whom.

Laurel and her husband, Floss, were vegetarians and planning six months off work to become involved with a World Starvation project in India.

'That's where it's at, man,' Floss said, 'helping people who can't help themselves.'

Laurel nodded, her eyes shining with agreement.

'Yes, but what about your careers?' Charlie asked. 'You're both sort of at the start. I mean I know you're doing very well, but if you just throw it up right now—'

'We worked it all out,' Floss said.

'Yes,' Laurel joined in, 'Floss and the boys are going to record enough stuff and tape appearances to keep them going, and I've got another movie to do after "Fred".'

'Man, if you can't spare six months of your time to help other human beings I just don't know.' Floss shook his head sadly.

Charlie tried to recall what *he* had done to help other people. He always gave George his old clothes, and he had given over fifty thousand dollars to various charity organisations in the last few years. That was tax deductible, of course. He had been approached some months back to make a public appeal for the homeless, but had declined to do so, not because he didn't believe in the cause, but because it embarrassed him to appear in public unless he was acting. He had signed a petition along with many other prominent people to legalise pot. Laurel and Floss, both nineteen, made him feel very old.

After dinner he suggested maybe they could all turn on and listen to some sounds.

Laurel and Floss exchanged smiles. 'We gave it up,' Laurel said.

'Yeah, either you need it or you don't, and we figured we had reached a point where we just didn't need it any more.' Floss ran his hand through his long blond hair. 'You go ahead,' he added.

Sheepishly Charlie put away the joint he had taken out. 'No, I don't need it,' he said, 'I just thought you er . . .'

'Everybody thinks all we do is fly on drugs and trial marriages and all that stuff. Laurel and I want to show people that our main concern is for the future of the world we live in. Every day we both meditate for an hour. That's the greatest. Throw off your clothes, man, and meditate, it's better than getting high.'

After they left, Charlie took off his black-ribbed turtle-neck sweater and pants. How did one meditate?

He sat cross-legged in the middle of the floor, contemplating. Then after five minutes he said, 'Fuck it!', lit a joint, put on some sounds, and went to bed.

Apart from Laurel Jones there was supposed to be six gorgeous girls in 'Fred'. Charlie, who had casting approval, told Cy Hamilton Junior to hire whomever he wanted. They were only small parts, and Charlie simply couldn't be bothered to audition a load of starlets.

Cy said on the 'phone, 'Come on down to the office, shmuck, I've got more delicious cooze passing through here than you've ever seen.'

Charlie wondered what kick it gave men like Cy and Clay to be on the continual look-out for available girls. They were married, so what was the point? How many girls could you screw at once? When he had been married to Lorna he had never bothered to look around; there had only been Michelle. But on thinking it over, he had to admit that before Dindi he had been exactly the same—searching for the prettiest face, the biggest breasts, the longest legs. It didn't matter if they were all raving idiots, he had been concerned only with outward appearances. Underneath all the lions' manes of hair and false eyelashes had there lurked one reasonable brain?

'I have definitely learnt my lesson,' Charlie confided to George, who was used to receiving intimate revelations from his boss. 'No more dumb starlets.'

George nodded wisely. He wouldn't have minded a few of Charlie's cast-offs.

The first day on the set Charlie was working with a six-foot-two-inch redhead named Thames Mason.

She smiled and widened her large hazel eyes. 'Mr Brick, it's such a delight to work with you. I've simply adored all of your movies. You don't know what a thrill it is for me today.' She spoke a heavy Southern drawl.

Charlie drew under cover of the character he was playing and became Fred. Although the accent was fascinating, he had no plans to become friendly with anyone on the film. They would know him as Fred, and that was all—except for Laurel. She and Floss began to see a lot of Charlie, who enjoyed listening to them.

He visited their house and met their friends. They were a different group from the film crowd—young record producers, singers, musicians. Most of them favoured hippy-style dress and they accepted Charlie quite easily. What he liked was that nobody seemed impressed by who he was; in fact he wasn't at all sure if anybody knew or cared. He was just another friend of Laurel's and Floss's.

He took to going to see them almost every night after work. They held open house for their friends.

A Mexican couple took care of the house and there was always plenty of food.

Charlie took his own supply of pot, because although Laurel and Floss didn't turn on, they didn't object to their friends doing so, and most of their friends did.

It was a good scene as far as Charlie was concerned. He got himself some long flowing tops, baggy trousers, and love beads. He stopped wearing his thick horn-rimmed spectacles and switched to granny glasses. He couldn't grow his hair because of the movie, but he planned to as soon as it was finished.

'You look great, man,' Floss told him. 'You're really part of the seventies scene.'

Charlie smiled. He was sitting on the floor in their living room watching slides of butterflies projected onto the wall, and listening to a new album. He passed the joint he was holding to the fair-haired boy beside him, who in turn passed it along to a girl.

'You really should get on to the meditating kick,' Floss remarked. 'Laurel was a mess until I put her on to it.'

Charlie nodded. 'Yes, I will try it.' He had been coming to

their house for ten days now, and Floss was always on at him to meditate. About eleven o'clock every night Laurel and Floss, and whoever else wanted to, solemnly stripped off and sat cross-legged and silent in the middle of the room for at least half-an-hour.

Charlie couldn't really see the point of it. He had never been enthusiastic at the idea of mass nudity.

Laurel had a perfect body. Everything was very small and compact. Floss was muscled and rangey.

Sex in Laurel and Floss's house appeared to be a very casual event. There were two bedrooms for their friends to use, and often a couple would stroll off to one, spend an hour or so and then re-emerge.

Charlie had his eye on a girl. She was English, and he had only seen her at the house once before. She wasn't pretty. She had a ratty, sulky face with suspicious eyes, but in any discussions she always spoke intelligently. She was young, very skinny, with long coarse light brown hair.

Charlie had not actually spoken to her, but she accepted a joint from him, and caught him staring when she took off her clothes to meditate. She was so thin that her ribcage stuck out, and she had tiny upturned breasts with crushed nipples.

When she dressed he sought her out. 'You're English,' he remarked.

'I would have thought that was obvious,' she replied, eyeing him with suspicious eyes.

'Yes, well of course it is. London with a touch of the north.'

'That's right. Why didn't you meditate? And why were you staring at my body? I'm not beautiful.'

'Er—well, love—well—er—you're certainly not ugly.'

She laughed suddenly. She had little-girl teeth. 'I'd love something sweet. Do you think there's any chocolate cake around?'

'Let's go and get some.'

'O.K.'

They left silently. She made no comment on his car, just acted as if she'd been climbing into Lamborghini Muiras all her life.

'Go to the market on Doheny,' she instructed.

He drove there and they picked out chocolate cakes, cookies, pecan nuts, different flavoured ice-creams, and some candy bars.

172

'What a feast!' she exclaimed.

Poor kid, he thought, she probably hasn't eaten. More than likely she was eking out an existence in some crash pad on the Strip. 'Shall we take it back to Laurel and Floss?' he suggested.

'Whatever you like.'

I'd like to get laid, he thought. There had been no one since Dindi. But the hell with it, he wanted more than a quick lay, he wanted some sort of relationship with a girl to whom he could actually talk.

The following night he learnt from Laurel that the girl was Lady Phillipa Longmead, and that she was visiting her mother and stepfather who had a house on Beverly Drive.

Whilst he was talking to Laurel, having caught her just before the hour of meditation, Phillipa was sitting on the floor, shovelling handfuls of chocolate cake into an effeminate boy's mouth.

Charlie went over and said, 'Are you going to meditate tonight?'

She shrugged. 'I might, if there's nothing else going on. Are you going to?'

He quickly shook his head.

'Ashamed of your body?' she asked casually.

'Certainly not.'

'Let it all hang out,' the effeminate boy sang.

'I could take you home,' Charlie ventured.

'Who, me?' the boy asked.

Phillipa shoved the last of the chocolate cake into the boy's mouth. 'I don't usually go home this early, but if you've got any grass I'll come to your place.'

During the drive to the hotel she discussed the latest student riots. 'It's just sad the way those kids get beaten on the head.' Then she talked about a big open-air rock festival being held near San Francisco the following weekend. 'Laurel and Floss are going. I may go with them.'

At the hotel she flicked through his record albums with an air of dismissal. 'Don't you have any new sounds? No, I suppose you don't.' She finally selected a Rolling Stones album of which she approved. Then she put her dirty feet on a table and smoked the joint he gave her. She took very strong, deep pulls, closing her eyes and letting the smoke snake slowly out of her nostrils.

Charlie sat opposite her. He felt a very strong need to have this girl approve of him. He wanted her to realise that he might be over thirty but that he wasn't one of the dreaded older generation; he was still young, still hip.

They listened to the Stones in silence. When the album was finished she said, 'If you want some sex, just ask me. I don't particularly care for it myself, but I don't mind.'

He was immediately excited. 'No, no,' he said, 'Don't worry, it's the last thing I was thinking of.'

'I suppose you don't find me very desirable after all those beautiful big-busted freaks you mix with. Personally I think sex is all a mental thing.'

He nodded. 'I agree.'

'Do you?' She was surprised. 'Do you really?'

'Yes, well I could never really fancy a girl—go to bed with her I mean—unless I could talk to her. Sex for sex's sake is just . . .' he trailed off, searching for words. Oh, if Clay could only hear me now, he thought.

'I think that's so commendable of you, I really do. Most old men think quite differently. My stepfather's friends are always trying to touch me, it makes me sick.'

Most *old* men!! Charlie was choked. Did she think he was old? He was only 39, thin as a rake, in perfect condition, dressed in the latest style. How could she possibly think he was old?

'How old do you think I am?' he asked.

She shrugged, her favourite gesture. 'I don't know, how old are you?'

'No, come on, seriously, take a guess. How old would you say I was?'

'If I guess too old you'll only be angry, and if I guess too young I'll be flattering you.'

'How old?'

She studied him through narrowed eyes. 'Thirty-nine,' she said at last.

'You're kidding?'

'No, why? Younger or older?'

'Spot on, you're spot on. How did you know?'

She shrugged. 'You look thirty-nine.'

'I look thirty-nine?'

She smiled a peculiarly evil smile. 'I told you you'd be angry.'

'I'm not angry,' he said quickly. 'Why should I be?'

She stood up and bit her nails silently for a few moments. 'I'm eighteen and I feel old, so I can understand it must be pretty dreadful to be your age.'

'I'll drive you home,' he said abruptly. The girl was an idiot.

'You don't have to bother, I'm not going home yet anyway, I have to meet some friends on the Strip.'

She was worse than the fawning starlets with her offhand manner.

'Fine,' he said coldly. 'The desk will call you a cab.'

'See you,' she said. 'Thanks for the pot.'

Charlie then 'phoned Thames Mason, whose number he had taken just in case.

She was with him in less than half-an-hour, her six-foot-two body clad in floral lounging pyjamas. She plugged her career for ten minutes, suggested that maybe her part could be built up in 'Fred', and then stripped off to reveal an amazon body.

Charlie made love to her quickly and inefficiently and sent her home with a promise of another scene to be written in for her.

When she left he felt more alone than ever. If he had not been who he was, she wouldn't have come running over.

So-called actresses, they weren't worth shit!

34

Sunday checked into the hotel directly from the airport. She was tired and angry. What a fool she must have been to trust a man like Steve Magnum! It worried her that she had even been planning to marry him. What kind of relationship could a girl expect with a much-married movie star?

The trouble was she had not been leading a normal life. She

had arrived in Hollywood depressed and withdrawn, done two films in quick succession, and Steve Magnum had made a play for her at the right time.

She undressed and ordered a hamburger and a milk shake in her room. She also had the newspapers sent up, but there was still nothing in them about her and Steve. If it didn't appear the following day she would just have to 'phone Carey and find out what was going on.

She brushed her hair at the window, admiring the view. Was it worth flying to Rome to find out the truth from Benno? No, of course not, because Dindi had been speaking the truth, and somehow, now that she knew it, everything fell into place. Paulo had never really seemed to enjoy making love to her; he had always seemed a little distracted, sometimes bored. The only times he was genuinely passionate were when he could persuade her to go down on her knees in front of him while he admired his long blond beautiful body in the mirror.

The two men in her life—Raf and Paulo—had never given her any real satisfaction.

Thinking about it, she felt her body become warm. Angrily she got into bed. She knew only too well what frustration meant. When the Steve Magnum affair was over she would go out like other girls, and have an affair with the first man she liked well enough.

She couldn't sleep. Thoughts kept crowding in on her. After an hour of tossing and turning she took two of the sleeping pills that had been given to her in Rome after Paulo's death. This was the first time since then that she had had cause to take them. She disliked taking medicines after seeing what drugs had done to Paulo, but she needed sleep desperately.

At last she slept, a deep heavy sleep, because the pills were strong and she was unused to them. She dreamt of Steve. He was in bed with her, pulling her nightdress off and moulding her breasts with rough hands. She moaned in her sleep. He was pinning her arms down and entering her roughly, and she was gasping and curling her legs around him, and raking her nails down his back. Then she was on a roller-coaster of sensation, her whole body taut, nerve-ends ready to explode in a fantastic climax. Nothing mattered any more except reaching the top of the mountain, and as she hit the peak she started to laugh, and the relief and the joy of it was incredible.

Then she opened her eyes in time to watch Claude Hussan roll off her.

She lay there for a moment, her mind in a fog.

Calmly, he was lighting a cigarette. Puffing on it once, he handed it to her.

She brushed it away, the truth of what had just happened dawning on her. He had somehow or other *got into her room and raped her,* and she hadn't even woken up—or had she?

'What are you doing here?' she asked in a low voice, realising how ridiculous the question was even as she asked it. 'How did you get in?'

'I have my ways. I was merely answering your invitation on the plane.'

'What invitation?'

He laughed. 'My dear lady, I knew what you wanted, even if you may not have known yourself.'

She was ashamed. Had it been so obvious that she needed a man?

Her body was in a soft state of abandon and fulfilment.

His hands started to use her again. 'If I was wrong I'll go,' he said.

She sat up quickly. 'Get out of here!'

He wound his hand in her hair and pulled her back beside him. Then he kissed her long and hard. 'It's better this way,' he said. 'Now we can have an honest relationship without going through all the *mérde* of dating, and juvenile things like that.'

She moaned, responding to his body. What did she have to lose? It was too late for outrage and cries of rape, and since their first meeting in Acapulco she had been attracted to him. 'All right,' she muttered, surprising herself.

'You're a clever woman, Sunday,' Claude said, only a trace of a French accent in his voice. 'Now I shall make love to you while you're awake, and tomorrow we will get to know each other.'

By the time Steve Magnum's detectives tracked Sunday down, she and Claude Hussan were inseparable. Steve was furious. He was sure that the reason Sunday had run out of him in Acapulco was because of the French director. He snarled at Carey to release the statement to the press, which she did at once, sparking off much speculation and gossip.

Steve immediately started dating every available girl in town. He even stopped blaming Dindi, and saw her too. She attached herself like a leech, gradually getting rid of rivals and moving in on him as his constant companion.

Carey shuddered at Sunday's latest choice in men. Claude Hussan had the reputation of being a mean, cynical, bastard, who enoyed great success with the ladies. His wife was a lesbian, and he had two mistresses in Paris who had both borne him children. He was a brilliant director, but apparently murderous to work with, and completely ruthless when it came to other people's feelings. Rumour also had it that he was prepared to indulge in any sexual deviation, especially orgies.

Carey shook her head. He didn't sound like Sunday's sort of man at all. She wished that Sunday would at least telephone her. She hadn't heard one word and although she left messages at the hotel in Rio her calls were not returned.

Marshall said, 'Don't worry. As long as she's back in time for her next movie it's not your business. She's your client, that's all.'

'She's also my friend,' Carey replied, and continued to worry.

Claude Hussan was in Rio to interview two actors he wanted for his film. As it was to be his first American film he wanted every part perfectly cast.

He gave Sunday the script to read. She was excited about it. If only he would consider her for the woman's role; it was a wonderful part.

'Who do you have in mind for Stefanie?' she asked casually one night.

'An actress of great strength,' Claude replied. 'A woman like Bancroft or Woodward. An American Moreau.'

She was silent. He would obviously never consider her, although she was sure she could play the part. Stefanie, a rich Beverly Hills wife who lives in a mansion with her husband, an ageing voyeuristic banker. One day their house is broken into by two boys, who make love to Stefanie, forcing her husband to watch. They stay, keeping the couple prisoners, until gradually Stefanie's loyalties switch from her husband to the boys and she becomes like them.

'I have to get back to L.A. soon,' she remarked later that evening, 'I really should let Carey know I'm on my way.'

'I'm not stopping you,' he said brusquely. 'Our arrangement is to do what we want when we want to.'

'But I don't *want* to go. You know I signed for a film.'

'A film? Is that what you call those flimsy pieces of garbage you make?'

They had been together only two weeks. She knew she must be in love because it didn't seem to matter what he did, she just wanted to be with him. He was incredibly rude to everyone—waiters, maids, the hotel receptionists, he treated them all like dirt. He had a contemptuous attitude towards everyone.

One day she asked him, 'How can you talk to people that way?'

'If they have no more ambition in life than being a servant, they deserve whatever treatment they get,' he snapped.

She was embarrassed by his behaviour. She smiled at the waiter he had recently screamed at, tipped the maid he threw out of the room, chatted amiably to the temporary nurse he had hired to take care of his son.

Jean-Pierre was a lovable little boy, although rather quiet for a five-year-old. Claude hardly seemed to notice his existence, but Sunday spent a lot of time with him. She took him to play on the beach, for walks, and started to teach him English.

'Why is he with you?' she asked Claude one day, 'You never give him any attention. Where is his mother?'

He ignored her, a habit he had when he did not wish to answer a question.

She sighed. He was an impossible, difficult, spoilt man. But when he made love to her every night it was so thrilling and beautiful that she chose to ignore his faults.

She knew she couldn't put off contacting Carey any longer. She had been reluctant to 'phone her, knowing she would criticise, but it had to be done as she had to get back to Los

Angeles. It wouldn't be *so* bad. Claude was flying to Paris for a week and then he too would be in L.A.

'Are you bringing Jean-Pierre back with you,' she asked. 'Or will he stay in Paris with his mother?'

'His mother does not want him with her,' Claude replied shortly. 'Usually he stays with his grandmother, but she is sick, so I suppose I shall have to keep him with me.'

'It makes me very sad the way you treat him,' she said. 'You take no notice of him. Don't you care?'

'He is with me, isn't he? That should mean that I care, shouldn't it?' He was angry. 'I could have arranged to leave him, but I bring him with me.'

'Shall I take him back to L.A. with me tomorrow?' she asked on impulse. 'We get along very well. I think he likes me, and after all, you will be with us in a week.'

He turned away from her. They were lying in bed, resting before a dinner engagement.

She touched his back gently. 'Please let him come with me, Claude, it would be like having a little piece of you near me. I'm going to miss you so much. We could 'phone the nurse now and tell her to prepare his things. I don't leave until the afternoon, there's plenty of time.'

He kicked the covers off and lay on his back. 'Make love to me the way I like it, and if it's good, we'll see.'

35

Charlie's lawyer telephoned him on the set. 'She's agreed to an outright payment,' he announced. 'Her lawyers advised her to stick out for alimony, but she decided to accept your offer.'

'Natural greed got the better of her,' Charlie said, relieved. 'I knew it would. Finalise the whole thing as soon as possible.'

He hung up, delighted. The money he would have to pay was worth it—anything to cut Dindi Sydne completely out of his life.

Dindi was also delighted. Charlie Brick had served her purpose, and to get rid of him *plus* receiving a large cash settlement was more than she had hoped for.

Everything was going her way. 'All the World Loves a Stripper' was well into production. She was receiving a great deal of publicity, and not only from the film. In the columns her name was constantly mentioned as the girl who was consoling Steve Magnum after his broken engagement. And it was true, she *was* consoling him; nothing consoled him more than a long raunchy session with the whip. She didn't mind that, though. In fact, she really quite enjoyed it, and on the side she was banging a beautiful pale blond pool boy who came to her house three mornings a week, serviced her, and then serviced the pool.

It was really very convenient the way everything had worked out—Sunday getting hooked up with Claude Hussan, and Steve blaming *him* for Sunday's behaviour. Of course Dindi was smart enough to know that Steve was carrying one big torch, but that was only because he hadn't had an affair with Sunday, a fact he had admitted to Dindi one drunken night.

Secretly Dindi admired Sunday. Miss Simmons certainly knew how to grab a guy by the balls.

She wondered how she was making out with darling Claude. Once, in Rome, Dindi had had a scene with his wife while he sat fully dressed on a couch, watching. He had never spoken to her, just paid her the money she had been promised by the agent who had taken her there. Sunday certainly believed in getting mixed up with weirdos!

When her film was finished Dindi planned to visit Las Vegas with Steve on his once-a-year gambling stint. At the same time she could get the quick divorce from Charlie. She was just as anxious to be rid of him as he was of her, and if she played her cards right, maybe—hopefully—there might be a chance that Dindi Brick—née Sydne—might just possibly become Mrs Steve Magnum.

'I hear you're all going up to that rock festival,' Charlie said to Laurel casually.

'Yes,' she agreed, 'it's going to be so great, we've hired a bus

181

to take us, and we're going to sleep out in tents. Floss says it's going to be a beautiful experience. Hey, why don't you come?'

'No, you don't want me along, it's going to be all you kids—'

'Charlie, *please* come. You know we'd love to have you with us. Floss will be knocked out if I tell him you're coming.'

'Perhaps I could drive there, maybe follow your bus in my car.'

She grimaced. 'That would look sort of funny. Can't you come in the bus with us? Mick's coming, and Tina, Rex and Janie, Phillipa—'

'Well, if you're sure there's room.'

'I'm sure. We'll have a great time. We'll leave Friday straight after shooting.'

He nodded. Why shouldn't he go? He was one of the crowd, they had accepted him. Besides which, he wanted to see Philippa again, to prove to her that he wasn't as old as she seemed to think.

When they finished work that night he had George drive him to the latest psychedelic shop, where he browsed among the ponchos, army jackets and T-shirts, emblazoned with 'Don't go to pot—take it'. He finally chose a white canvas Indian style shirt and a fringed suede jacket, similar to one Floss was always wearing.

Outside in the Mercedes, George wondered how long *this* phase would last.

Charlie decided against going to Laurel and Floss's house that night. He had George drive him straight back to his hotel. There were several scripts he wanted to read. He just felt like relaxing and being on his own.

There were a lot of messages from people who wanted him to contact them. Natalie Allen had left her name several times over the past week, and Marshall K. Marshall requested that he telephone him at home as soon as possible. They were the only two calls Charlie felt obliged to make.

He 'phoned Natalie first, feeling guilty because he hadn't spoken to either of them since his night out with Clay.

'Well, well, stranger,' she said, 'what *have* you been doing with yourself? I've been trying to ring you for days.'

'I'm sorry, love,' he replied warmly. 'Been so busy on the film, just haven't had a minute.'

'You certainly had a minute for Clay the other night. He came staggering home at 4 a.m., smelling like a brewery. What *were* the two of you up to?'

He changed the subject. 'Why don't you visit the set one day, have a spot of lunch? I'll send George to fetch you.'

'I'd love to, but I'm absolutely exhausted, I just can't be bothered to leave the house. Why don't *you* fix up a night, *now* while I've got you on the 'phone, to come over to dinner. How about tomorrow?'

The next night was Thursday and he wanted to prepare himself for the weekend trip. 'Can't make that.'

'Friday then, or better still come for the day Saturday and stay for dinner.'

'No, I can't love, I'm off for the weekend.'

'Oh! Off where?'

'I'm going to that—er—big rock festival thing.'

Natalie laughed. 'You're doing what?'

Defensively Charlie said, 'The rock festival out in the open. Should be great.'

'Who on earth got you to go to that? It will be full of freaks. I saw the television show on the last one and it was unbelievable. All those filthy-looking kids, you'll hate it, Charlie.'

How did she know what he would hate and what he would not hate? The trouble with Natalie was that she didn't move with the times.

'Is Clay around?' he asked.

Still laughing, she said, 'Just a minute, I'll get him.' Then he heard muffled conversation and more laughter as she explained to Clay where he was going.

'Off to the flower people, I hear,' Clay said, joining in the fun. 'Find me a little thirteen-year-old darling.'

'Yes, and don't you wish you were going with me?'

'I do. Natalie wants to know about dinner Monday.'

'Fine.'

'Have a good time, see you then.'

Next Charlie 'phoned Marshall K. Marshall.

'I'd like to have a meeting with you,' Marshall said. 'Bad news, I'm afraid.'

'Bad news? What?'

'I'd sooner meet with you, Charlie, have a proper discussion.'

'What is it, for Chrissakes? If there's one thing I can't stand it's suspense.'

'Look, if you're going to be free for lunch tomorrow I'll come to the studio.'

'What about now? Can't you come over now?'

'No, I can't,' Marshall snapped, 'I've put in a heavy day and I'm in bed.'

'Can I come over to see you? I mean if it's *that* important.'

'It's not a matter of life and death, it's just a business discussion I think we should have, and the sooner the better.'

Like all actors Charlie couldn't wait. When it came to his career he was supersensitive. 'If you don't mind, I'll be with you in half-an-hour.'

'All right, you're the client.'

Marshall hung up and studied the sleeping Carey, lying beside him. She had the most beautiful skin he had ever seen, a rich warm milk chocolate. He shook her awake. They had fallen into bed at five o'clock and it was now nearly eight.

She awoke smiling. 'You're never satisfied, are you? You're worse than a nineteen-year-old high-school boy. If I marry you, you're going to wear me out in no time flat, and—'

He brushed his chubby cigar-stained hands across her hard taut breasts. 'Relax, I've got Charlie Brick coming over, so shift your sexy ass and go home and decide what day next week it's going to be, and I *mean* next *week*. No more stalling.'

She smiled. 'The thing I love about you is you still talk to me like I'm the little secretary you hired way back.'

It was his turn to smile. 'What's so different about you now?'

'I'm making it with the boss—sorry—ex-boss.' She dressed in the copy of a pink Cardin suit she had worn to the office that day. 'I'm meeting Sunday at the airport in the morning, so I'll call you when I'm back in the office.'

Downstairs the maid was just admitting Charlie Brick as Carey was about to leave.

Marshall came downstairs in a plain maroon dressing gown.

Carey blew him an affectionate kiss and left. '*That* is one hell of a girl,' he remarked.

'She's very attractive,' Charlie agreed. He had heard rumours that Marshall was planning to marry her.

They went into the living-room and Charlie accepted a brandy. 'Well, come on,' he said, hardly able to contain his annoyance. 'What's all this bad news then?'

'I didn't want to talk on the 'phone,' Marshall said. 'You never know who may be listening in, and in this town news travels fast enough without giving it a boot up the ass. The fact is, Charlie, your next picture has been cancelled.'

'What?'

'Yes, I know, it's screwy as hell. "Roundabout" is going to make a lot of money and I hear that "Fred" couldn't be going better, but you know what the industry's like now, everyone's running scared. Money is very, very tight. They can't get the deal together, and frankly I never was impressed with that script.'

'But it doesn't make sense. My films make money, I haven't had a flop yet. I'm still one of the top ten box-office stars. It's ridiculous.'

'Sure it's ridiculous, and they're going to realize it. Listen, it's not going to affect you too badly. Your working schedule in Europe is crammed anyway; I should think you would be glad of some time off.'

'I don't like not working,' Charlie said stiffly, 'I don't enjoy sitting around on my backside while newer, younger, actors push themselves forward. Find me something else to do—an independent, a low-budget art film. I wouldn't mind a change of pace. I'll drop my price if it's something I really like. Take a piece of the action.'

'O.K., Charlie.'

'I might even be prepared to finance something myself.'

Marshall shook his head in disbelief. 'You actors—you're all the same, you'll even pay to see yourself on the screen!'

36

'What's with the kid?' Carey asked, her mouth open in astonishment.

Sunday, looking incredibly beautiful in a yellow dress, her hair wild around her suntanned face, smiled. 'Jean-Pierre, meet Carey. Carey, this is Jean-Pierre Hussan.'

The small boy stared up at Carey solemnly and extended his hand.

'Wow,' Carey sighed, 'if the father looks anything like the son, I can understand your hang-up.'

'The father is just as beautiful,' Sunday laughed. 'Oh, Carey, I'm so happy!'

'You look like you are, in fact you look great. I want to hear all about it, but first let's get to the car before some wandering photographer spots you and pounces. By the way, why did you tell me no press at the airport?'

Sunday nodded at the boy. 'Claude insisted. Anyway, they would only be asking me stupid questions about Steve Magnum.'

'We have to go straight for fittings. You were needed two weeks ago.'

'I'm sorry, but everything's been so marvellous, I couldn't come before.'

'I understand.'

After the fittings they drove to the Château Marmont where Sunday collected the rest of her luggage. There was a lot of mail that she had told them to hold for her.

'I don't know why you didn't have it all forwarded on to you in Acapulco,' Carey said. 'It's ridiculous, there might be something important.'

Sunday shook her head. 'The only letter that could even be remotely important will be from my aunt in England, and she only writes twice a year. In fact I can't imagine who all these letters are from.'

'You'd be surprised who you get letters from when you're famous. Probably other agents trying to steal you away!'

Sunday laughed. 'I'll open them at the house. I'm so excited about it. Jean-Pierre's going to love it with the ocean right there, aren't you, sweetheart?'

She gave the little boy a hug and he smiled, something he had only just started to do.

Carey said, 'I checked the house out yesterday, it's all in order. I got in some groceries. I really can't understand why you want to be stuck down in Malibu.'

'I'm not stuck down in Malibu. I'm going to be in a great little house overlooking the sea, away from all the smog and phoney social bit. I think Claude will love it.'

'Is Claude going to be moving in with you?'

'I hope so. Carey, I *know* you'll like him, I can't wait for the two of you to meet. I want to have a little barbecue dinner when he arrives, just maybe you and Marshall, Branch, if he's back, and perhaps Max Thorpe.'

'Sounds like a fun group. Why not ask Dindi and Steve to make it *really* fun?'

'Are they going together?'

'Rumour and Joyce Haber has it. I hear that he's so tanked up that it's an effort for him to get it up any more!'

'You're really disgusting!' But she was laughing, and once more Carey marvelled at the change in her. Good, bad or indifferent, Claude Hussan had certainly brought out a new Sunday.

They stopped off at Carey's apartment to fetch Limbo. Then they drove straight down to the house.

'It's so great,' Sunday exclaimed. 'Much better than I remember. Why don't you borrow a suit and we'll have a swim? Come on, Jean-Pierre, get changed.'

She opened his suitcase and threw him a small pair of bathing shorts. Limbo was running around, going mad with excitement.

'I can't stay,' Carey said wistfully, 'I'd like to, but I've been out of the office all day and there's things to be done. Now tomorrow your press conference is at 2 p.m. I'll have a car pick you up at one. I do think it would be a good idea not to bring the child. The maid comes in tomorrow at ten; have her look after him. There are several interesting offers I'd like to discuss with you, so I thought maybe dinner tomorrow night at Marshall's house.'

'I want to hear all about that. Is there going to be a wedding?'

'Listen, kid, I must rush, I'll call you later. There's a list of local services in the kitchen in case you need anything, and I'm always available on the 'phone.'

'We won't need anything. We're going to have a swim, something to eat, and an early night.'

The ocean was warm, throwing up big waves that knocked Jean-Pierre flat and sent Limbo scurrying in mad circles on the shore. Sunday set the little boy firmly on her shoulders and waded in.

Later, after the child was in bed she unpacked a few things, fed Limbo and wandered around, exploring the house. Carey telephoned and they had a short chat. Claude didn't, although he had promised.

She wondered how he would like the house. It would be peaceful for him, a place where he could really relax. He was so involved in his work, always planning and thinking about it, having discussions and meetings.

That was a good thing she decided. A man *should* be dedicated to his work. She didn't care if she ever worked again. If things worked out with Claude, perhaps she wouldn't: it would be enough just to be with him, look after him and have his children, lots and lots of them, all looking like Jean-Pierre.

She sighed. It was a dream. He was still married, and even if he were single, she knew he wasn't the marrying kind. Well, she didn't mind that. They could just live together, and still have children. She wouldn't tie him down.

What was her career all about anyway? Nobody cared about her as an actress, a person. All they cared about was the maximum exposure of breasts, legs, and anything else that was going. Even if she became a star, that was still all they would care about.

She sat down and started opening her mail.

Carey was right. Two letters from agents, offering her their services; circulars about cars, televisions and household equipment; a short letter from Aunt enclosing an English press clipping and complaining about Sunday's lack of clothes in the photograph.

There were three bulky envelopes, all addressed in the same

scrawly hand. She inspected the postmarks and opened the oldest one first. A plastic bag fell out. *'Sunday—when will you—'*

'Oh God!' she groaned. It was full of obscenities about what the writer wanted to do to her, imagined doing, and said they would soon be doing.

She read it briefly in fascinated horror.

'I promise not to keep you waiting too long, we will be together soon, so keep your lovely—'

She tore it up.

The other two were the same, the ravings of a sick mind.

It was very depressing, and because the man seemed so certain they would be together, a little frightening. She was glad the writer didn't know where she was now; at least he only knew the hotel where she had been.

She telephoned the Château in a panic, and told them not to give out her address.

It was nothing to worry about. Carey said that all actresses got these kind of letters.

She went to bed feeling sick, and looked forward to the brightness of the morning.

37

It was Herbert's third shower of the day. The water trickled lukewarm down his thin hairless body.

His eyes were clenched shut, as he thought about what he had caught his fat whore of a wife doing. Legs spread, she had been next door taking on all comers. Of course from the window where he had crouched watching, he didn't have the best vantage point, but he certainly knew what was going on, oh yes, he certainly knew.

It was good he had not told Marge about getting fired from the Supreme Chauffeur Company. Now he was free to spy on her. In fact he was free to do what he wanted all day and all night.

As he had been working night shifts, he left the house at the usual time. Then he would either spend the evening at the movie theatre where the Jack Milan film with Sunday Simmons was playing, or he would go to a topless bar and watch the scenery with his cold hard eyes.

He knew when Marge was planning to go out. She became jumpy and nervous, fussing around him, trying to hurry him out of the house. He obliged by leaving quickly, but then he would return and watch her disgusting behaviour through his neighbour's window.

Money was running short. He would have to get another job soon. He wasn't worried, because long before being fired he had been prudent enough to steal some Supreme Chauffeur notepaper, and had written himself several glowing references.

When he found a job he would leave Marge—just walk out and leave her. Why should he work hard to put food in the mouth of such a filthy woman?

First he decided he would draw out her savings and buy himself a car. He would trick her into signing something, giving him access to her money, or he would forge her signature. That shouldn't be too difficult.

'Are you gonna be in there all day, Herbie?' Marge whined outside the door.

She was always whining about something, asking him stupid questions about bank raids and women getting raped. Only that very morning she had said to him, 'Herbie, isn't it kinda difficult to rape a woman unless she wants it?'

'You think of nothing but sex,' he had replied in disgust.

'There's nothing wrong with that, is there? I can remember when your tongue used to hang out when I worked in that place with my titties all bare. You loved it.'

'I don't love it now, you're a fat cow. Aren't you ashamed of your body?'

Marge banged loudly on the bathroom door. 'I'm gonna pee in my pants if you don't let me in.'

Reluctantly he climbed out of the shower and, covering himself with a towel, opened the door.

190

She bounced in, and with a flash of fat thighs plonked herself on the toilet.

'Hey, Herbie, remember that murder up on er—Miller Drive—just off the Strip? Remember it? Some young girl.' She paused. 'What's the matter?'

He had turned white. The towel had fallen from his hands and he stared at her in horror. She *knew*. The bitch knew!

With a sense of triumph Marge realized that she had hit on something at last. Louella had been right! Her plan had worked! All the studying of newspapers and remembering names of streets, banks and victims had paid off.

'What do you know?' He demanded harshly.

'Enough,' she replied, remembering Louella's advice to stay quiet. 'Enough to put you behind bars for life.' She added the last line on impulse; it sounded good. Lana Turner had said it on the late movie two nights before, and the guy she said it to had crumbled, buried his head in his hands and begged for mercy.

Herbert did neither of those things. He just stood there in his hairless nakedness, chewing on his bottom lip and narrowing his small mean eyes.

Marge felt good. In all their years of marriage Herbert had treated her like a piece of furniture, bossed her around, and even beaten her up. No wonder she had let herself get fat. For years before meeting Louella, she had hardly been out of the house except to go to the market. And there had been no sex at all after she lost the baby. Not that Herbert had been any great shakes at it—in and out like a rabbit and straight into the shower—but it had been better than nothing. Later Marge had harboured a grumbling resentment against him, especially when she found the filthy letters he was writing to all those fancy movie stars. The letters had helped, though; instead of Herbert, she took the letters to bed and imagined he was talking to her.

Herbert's mind was racing. How had the bitch found out? Did he talk in his sleep? How did she know? And more important, what did she want from him?

'What are you going to do?' he asked, picking up the towel and wrapping it around himself, trying to stay calm and cool and not beat the fat bitch in case perhaps she had told someone else. Maybe she had told that crabby neighbour, or one of the men she had been with at those disgusting sex orgies.

'Don't worry.' Marge shifted herself off the toilet. 'Why should I do anything? You're my husband, aren't you? And husband and wife should stick together.' On impulse she put her arms around him and did a little wriggle against his body.

With horror he knew what she wanted.

'Yeah, you're my husband and I'm your wife, so even if I *wanted* to go to the cops it wouldn't seem right, would it?'

She suddenly pulled off her cheap cotton dress, dragging it impatiently over her head. Then she released her mammoth bosom from a pink bra and shook it at him. 'I guess we should do some of those things married people like to do together, huh? I guess that would be a lot of fun.'

She tugged at the towel round his waist. He stood quite still. If he did *that* with her he could catch something. He had seen her with all those other men; she must be *crawling* with germs.

But she didn't want him to do *that*. She wanted him to do something to her much more intimate, something she had tried to get him to do when they were first married but he had refused.

He couldn't refuse now. Bile rose in his throat and he went to work.

Later when Marge had gone out, smiling, triumphant and unwashed, Herbert wrote to Sunday Simmons, pouring out all his desires and needs, and charged his frustration into a clean plastic bag. She was all he had in life, the only beautiful thing.

He went out, posted the letter, and then went to see her in the Jack Milan movie, where he spent the rest of the day, watching it four times. He left after slipping his hand up the leg of an unsuspecting woman. Before she could complain he was gone.

He bought a newspaper and sat in a coffee shop studying the jobs vacant. He circled several possibilities. Tomorrow he had to get a job. There was no money, and with Marge knowing what he had done he could hardly walk out and leave her; she'd have the cops after him in no time.

The only answer, he realized, was to get rid of Marge—get rid of her once and for all.

It needed planning, but it could be done.

38

'I wouldn't have thought this would be your scene at all,' Lady Phillipa said. She was sitting next to Charlie on the bus, her long hair wispy around her unmade-up face. She was wearing a purple patterned flowing dress and no shoes.

'Why ever not?' Charlie asked, feeling very much part of the group in his new outfit.

'Well, you're part of the whole film star bit, aren't you? Big cars and houses. Surrounded by possessions. Possessions are your hang-up, aren't they? You probably use women as possessions too. Tell me this, a woman is a sexual object to you, is she not?'

'No, she's not,' he replied sharply. This ratty girl had a great knack of making him angry. 'And possessions are not my hang-up, as you put it. I don't even have a house of my own.'

'Tough shit.' She started to laugh. 'Don't even have one little house of your own, that's *really* bad.'

'Is there something you don't like about me?' he asked tightly.

'Nothing about you personally. Just you generally. I mean you're part of the so-called establishment, you're one of them, not one of us. Why are you hanging around with us?'

'I'm not hanging around with you—I'm taking a trip with friends, Laurel and Floss and the others. Why does that upset you?'

'Because you belong to a different generation. You're my mother's whole scene. You don't belong here.'

The different-generation crack hurt Charlie. He stared out of the window and wished he hadn't come.

After a while Phillipa said, 'I could do with getting high. Got anything?'

'Oh, I'm all right for supplying you with pot, am I?'

'Yes. If you like I'll pay you by sleeping with you.'

'That's the second time you've offered me sex. Haven't you got any money?'

She flushed. 'I told you I don't like sex much, money's more important to me, so I offered you the least important.'

'Bully for you!' Maybe one was better off with a big-breasted dumb girl. 'By the way, I don't even know your mother.'

'You don't *have* to know her. You're part of the great show biz world, aren't you?'

'So are Laurel and Floss,' he pointed out mildly.

'They're different.'

He produced a joint and wondered if it was all right to smoke it on the bus. He didn't feel like it, but he wanted to keep Phillipa company, so he lit up and in two minutes Floss was by his side, hissing, 'Are you crazy? If the cops should stop us there'd be no trip of any kind.'

'Sorry,' said Charlie, quickly stubbing out the cigarette.

Phillipa laughed. 'Everyone's so uptight. Get pleasantly happy on a little hash and that's bad.'

'I'm with you,' he agreed.

'Yes, but the rest of your neurotic age-group aren't.'

There she went again, another dig about his age.

'They don't want to see the young enjoying all the things they never had. They hate to think of us doing what we want, wearing what we want, turning on and having sex without feeling guilty about it.'

'You feel guilty about sex.'

'I do not.'

'Yes, you do—otherwise you'd enjoy it.'

Patiently she explained. 'I do not enjoy sex because I cannot achieve any type of orgasm. I'm built that way.'

'How do you know?'

'I just know. Now go on and tell me that you're the one and only man who can bring me to a full and beautiful climax.'

'Maybe I could.' He started to feel a bit horny. Maybe he could.

She laughed mirthlessly. 'Do you know how many old men have told me that?'

'How many *old* men have you *had*?'

'Four—well, five, if you want to count my stepfather, and he was lousy. It's an interesting fact that he told me my mother doesn't achieve orgasm either. How about that? And she's been married twice and had countless boy-friends.'

'And I thought you were a modern girl! But you're really

charmingly old-fashioned, even down to knocking off your stepfather. Couldn't you have least made it your father?'

She shrugged. 'I really don't care whether you believe me or not. I'm way past the stage of bothering about what people think of me.'

He wondered how long it would take George to drive up and collect him. Lady Phillipa Longmead was a screwed-up adolescent, and that was not what he needed in his life.

Laurel came down the aisle. 'Isn't this fun' she enthused, her face alert and flushed. 'Only three more hours to go, and then a beautiful night under the stars. Charlie, I'm so glad you came with us. Did you remember your sleeping bag?'

'You didn't tell me to bring a sleeping bag.'

'Didn't I? Sometimes I'm so forgetful. Philly, can Charlie squeeze in with you?'

'I think that's what he had in mind anyway.'

Laurel smiled. 'I love you both. You know that, I truly love you.' She touched them both on the shoulder as if she were a faith-healer, and carried on up the aisle.

'We were at school together in Switzerland,' Phillipa remarked. 'We learnt French, cooking and masturbation.'

'What do you do now?' Charlie asked.

'I bum around. I'm supposed to be studying modern design, but right now I'm taking a holiday to get over my abortion. I don't have to do anything really; I've got plenty of money—trust funds and things. When I get back to London I'm buying a house somewhere in Hampstead or maybe the country, and turning it into a commune. People will be free to come and go and do their own thing. No rules, just a lovely uncomplicated life.'

'And you footing all the bills?'

'Why not? I've got the money. Why shouldn't I use it on other people. What do you do with all your money?'

'I pay taxes, look after my children, and pay bills. Sometimes I buy myself a car or a camera or anything I fancy.'

'Including a woman, a sexual object.'

'For someone who's not interested in sex it does seem to be your only subject.'

'My mother doesn't know where it's at. She's like you, always trying to be smart. She's sending me to an analyst here. You go in to see this man and he makes you take off all your clothes and lie on a couch. Everything has to come off. He says he can see the tension points on the body that way. How about *that*? He got a bit of a shock when he first saw me; he's used to all those Beverly Hills rich ladies with big boobs and flat stomachs and sexy thighs. I think he was choked when he got me. Nothing to feast his greedy little eyes on.'

Charlie laughed. He could imagine the scene. 'Why do you go?'

'My mother's a trustee. I don't get my money until I'm twenty-one, so meanwhile she doles out what she thinks I should get. Actually she can't stand me, it's mutual. Would you care to meet her? She'd *love* to meet you.'

'Are you inviting me?'

She yawned. 'Aren't you bored with me yet? I usually bore people quite early on in a relationship.'

Well, she *was* different.

The festival was being held in the grounds of a large old farm-house. Acres and acres of greenland, swarming with the thous-ands of young visitors who were steadily appearing by the hour.

It was quite a sight. They were arriving on foot, by car, motor-cycle, bus, and train. A colourful procession, some of the girls carried babies, and a few toddlers moved along with the crowd. Nearly everyone had long hair and flowing clothes. Ordinarily dressed people were regarded as suspect.

A few policemen were to be seen, travelling in pairs, looking grim and tough in their dark uniforms.

It was just beginning to get dark. Laurel and Floss with their whole group moved steadily through the crowds to find a good vantage point to spend the night.

Hot-dog, hamburger, and icecream stands were dotted around. Tents were being erected for the night. Some people just had blankets to lie on.

Phillipa walked silently beside Charlie, who carried her heavy sleeping bag. This wasn't quite the way he had imagined it. Laurel had quite definitely mentioned tents, and he thought they had the whole matter arranged. He had imagined luxurious tents set up on a hill overlooking the crowd, certainly not sleeping bags down among the herd.

He was tired from the day's work at the studio, the hot dusty bus-ride, and now this long trek. He was also starving hungry, and anxious to take a leak.

A dreamy-looking girl was sitting on the grass, breast-feeding a rather large baby. Two teeny boppers recognised Floss and giggled around him. A group of leather-jacketed boys swaggered past, all greasy hair and sneery faces. Over everything there hung the acrid bitter-sweet aroma of marijuana.

Laurel and Floss finally found a place to settle, and Laurel went around asking all their friends sweetly, 'Is this O.K. for you? Are you *sure*?'

Phillipa said to Charlie, 'I have to go to the loo.'

At last, a common interest! They went off together to find the convenience tents that Floss assured them couldn't be far away. In fact, they walked for ten minutes before they found them, by which time it was dark and Charlie wondered how they were going to find their way back.

'Wait for me right outside,' he commanded Phillipa.

She smiled a rare smile. 'You know you're not all bad. I can't see my mother doing this.'

Great, he thought. I should have gone after the mother!

In the badly smelling men's convenience a bearded boy was giving himself a shot, an old belt tied tightly around his arm, the vein bulging. Two characters sporting beards lounged around, watching. Charlie got out as fast as he could.

Phillipa took her time and then emerged ruffled. 'You wouldn't believe the scene in there,' she remarked. 'There's a couple of lady fuzz searching everyone for acid or pot or something ridiculous. What a nerve!'

Charlie was glad they hadn't been where he was. He could see the headline now. 'Actor caught with marijuana at pop festival.'

'We're never going to find our way back,' she complained.

He took her hand and led her through the crowds. He had always had a good sense of direction.

What would she say if he suggested they get the hell out of this and go home?

It started to spit rain, fine warm rain, that was hardly noticeable.

'I'm hungry,' she moaned.

How would a sleeping bag be in the rain, Charlie wondered. He stopped and bought two hot-dogs—ruinous for his diet—and they kept looking for their group.

'There they are,' Phillipa yelled at last. 'There's Janie and Rex. Hey, where's everyone else?'

Out of the busload only a few were left.

Janie, a fat girl dressed like a gypsy, said, 'Everyone's chickened off. They didn't like the scene. The cops are patrolling round with great big dogs and it's just not cool. You can't even get high in peace.'

'Where have they gone?' Charlie asked, furious at having been left behind.

'Some party one of the groups is having. They'll all be back tomorrow for the show. We're supposed to keep the pitch. How about a bite of your hot-dog?'

'Didn't Laurel or Floss leave a message for us?' Charlie demanded furiously.

Janie shook her head. 'Guess not.'

'Come on.' He tossed the remains of his hot-dog at the fat girl, and gripped Phillipa's arm. 'Let's get out of here.'

39

Sunday's press conference went smoothly. She countered questions about herself and Steve Magnum with charm and tact.

Carey had decided that the best way to present Sunday to the press was at a cocktail party where she could circulate freely among the reporters.

She was a hot property. On the strength of the Jack Milan movie alone, she was receiving a huge amount of fan mail.

Carey had several firm offers to discuss with her. It had been a good move to hold off signing anything while the word spread. Sunday could now pick and choose.

'What about you and Claude Hussan?' an alert girl columnist asked.

Sunday smiled. She wanted to say 'We're in love and I hope we will always be together', but Carey had warned her to say nothing about him beyond the old worn-out quote that they were merely good friends.

'We're just friends,' she said lamely.

'But you were in South America with him and his son?' the girl persisted.

'Well, yes.' She was surprised, no-one was supposed to know about that.

'Is it true he's divorcing his wife?'

'I don't know. Is he?'

'I thought if anyone would know it would be *you*.' The girl's voice was sarcastic. She didn't like actresses. She had been one herself and failed miserably.

'Excuse me,' Sunday said politely. 'They need me for a photo.'

'Just one more question before you go. Could you love a man like Claude Hussan? Isn't he just another Steve Magnum with a French accent?'

Sunday blinked. 'You'll have to excuse me,' and she edged away.

Later there was dinner at Marshall's house, just the three of them, and they discussed the various offers.

'I don't want to make any decisions until I talk it over with Claude,' Sunday stated.

Carey shrugged. 'Fine. But my personal opinion is that we should accept the new Milan film. After all, it's an equal part and a marvellous script. Then we could follow it up with the Constable movie, he's such a great director.'

Sunday nodded. None of the propositions particularly excited her. They all called upon her to look fantastic, and the money was good, but was it too much to expect that her parts should require some acting ability?

'You know the industry is in a crazy state,' Marshall said. 'Hardly anyone's working, it's tough all round. You seem to be the golden girl of the moment. Enjoy it, sweetheart—while you can.'

Sunday got up to leave.

'Don't forget fittings and makeup tests at ten tomorrow,' Carey reminded her. 'A car will collect you at nine. By the way, when is Claude arriving?'

'The end of the week. He was supposed to call me but I guess he's been too busy. He works so hard, sometimes he forgets to eat.'

Carey and Marshall exchanged glances.

The next day Alert Girl Reporter wrote in her widely syndicated gossip column: '*Sunday Simmons is the beautiful new Sex Goddess of our ever-searching tinsel city. I met her last night and she told me confidentially—batting foot-long false eyelashes and tossing her fall of auburn hair—that as far as she is concerned, rumoured new love of her life, notorious French film director Claude Hussan, is merely another Steve Magnum with a French accent. Our Steve, as you may recall, is a recent fiancé of the up-and-coming Miss Simmons. This lovely girl with the Raquel Welch-type body and Mickey Mouse quotes should go far.*'

Sunday was dismayed. What if Claude should see it? It made her look such an empty-headed little idiot.

She raged at Carey. 'No more press parties. I don't care if my name never appears in a gossip column again. I won't talk to any more of these bitchy, frustrated women!'

'Fine,' Carey soothed. 'But they're not all like that. It's not so terrible. People just remember they saw your name, not what it said about you.'

'That's what you think,' Sunday replied shortly. 'I always remember what I read, and anyway, how do you think Claude's going to feel?'

'Claude's not even going to see it unless you show it to him.'

That evening Sunday had dinner with Branch. He took her to their favourite health restaurant. Over coffee Max Thorpe appeared, plump and red-faced with his streaky bleached-blond hair. He greeted Sunday warmly and joined them. 'I told you we'd come by the house later,' Branch said peevishly.

'I know, I know, but I couldn't wait to see the beautiful Sunday Simmons,' Max enthused. His watery eyes darted all over the place and came to settle on Branch. 'You don't mind, do you?'

Surly-mouthed, Branch shook his head.

'He's doing so well,' Max said, patting Sunday's hand.

'Yes, I know,' she smiled. 'I think the television series will be wonderful for him.'

'Did he tell you he's moving in with me? So stupid for him to pay all that money to a hotel when I have such a big house.' Max shifted his hand from Sunday's to Branch's, where it lingered. 'It gets quite lonely there at times; it will be nice to have some company.'

Branch looked miserably at Sunday. She felt the tension between the two men and feigned a yawn. 'Sorry, everyone, but I think it's time I was off. Early call tomorrow.'

'I don't like you driving back to the beach alone,' Branch mumbled. 'This town is full of nuts.'

'Don't be silly. I have a perfectly reliable rented Ford, full up with gas, and I'll close all the windows and lock all the doors.'

Branch grunted and called for the check which Max paid. They all strolled to the parking lot where Branch left with Max in his white Rolls Royce and Sunday set off for the beach in her pale blue Ford.

She drove fast, keeping to the middle lane and not glancing around when she was held up at traffic lights. If you so much as peeked left or right, it was odds on that you would catch a man's eye and he would take that as an immediate invitation. Los Angeles was the sort of city where women, especially women who looked like Sunday, rarely drove alone at night.

Claude hadn't 'phoned, and she was worried about him. She didn't even know for certain what day to expect his arrival.

She thought about Branch and Max. Carey and Marshall.

She did not notice the old grey Buick following her. Its licence plate obscured by mud. Its driver hidden behind heavy dark glasses.

She was too busy thinking, so she noticed nothing. Not even

when she turned off along the lonely beach road and the old grey Buick was right behind her.

40

'How long have you been here?' Natalie asked, her polite phrasing hardly hiding the distaste she felt towards the skinny barefoot girl whom Charlie had brought to dinner.

Phillipa yawned openly, not concealing her gaping mouth with her hand, but treating all to a full view of her tonsils. 'Long enough,' she said in her flat, slightly Northern voice. She had made Charlie promise that he wouldn't tell them who she was until after dinner. She wanted to prove to him the change in people's reactions when they found out she had a title.

Natalie choked down some prawn cocktail. Who did the little bitch think she was? Some pick-up from that awful hippy freak-out Charlie had gone to!

'I like your outfit,' Clay remarked. 'Very lovely, very unusual.'

'Thanks,' Phillipa flashed a rare smile, 'I picked it up off a junk stall in Portobello Road.'

She was wearing a rather tatty, nearly see-through, dress. It was embroidered with lace in places, and hung open to her waist. Her small bosom stayed hidden, only emerging when she stretched for her wine. Clay watched, fascinated.

'How was the concert?' Natalie asked. 'I saw on the news that a girl had a baby there.' She patted her own small bulge protectively. 'It must have been terrible for her.'

'Worse for the onlookers, I should think,' Phillipa said, removing a prawn from her mouth and examining it before abandoning it on the side of her plate.

'Something wrong?' Natalie asked when the ratty girl did the same thing with a second prawn.

'I think they're off,' Phillipa replied offhandedly.

Everyone stopped eating and Natalie glared. If there was one thing she couldn't stand it was to see food wasted. 'They can't be off,' she said quickly, 'I got them from the market myself this morning.'

Clay pushed his plate away. 'Let's not risk it, darling.'

Natalie's eyes filled with angry tears.

'What's next?' Clay asked.

'Roast lamb,' Natalie replied tightly.

'Ah, folks,' Clay said, 'the Allens will now treat you to some rancid roast lamb.' He roared with laughter.

'You're not funny,' Natalie said coldly, and banging the dishes together, she stamped out of the room.

'I don't know what's the matter with her,' Clay said glumly, 'she's so bloody sensitive lately.'

'She's pregnant,' Charlie said quietly. 'Women are always touchy when they're pregnant.' For a brief moment he remembered Lorna when she was carrying his two children. It had been the happiest time of his life. She had been soft and warm and affectionate. Women were beautiful when they were pregnant. He followed Natalie out to the kitchen.

Phillipa picked on a hang nail and Clay filled her glass with wine.

'Where did you and old Charlie meet up?' he asked.

'At an orgy,' Phillipa replied, and concentrated on her nail.

After dinner they went out to the patio for coffee. Natalie was calm and happy. Charlie was being especially sweet to her. His unbelievable girlfriend had lapsed into an hour-long silence.

There seemed no point in telling the Allens that plain Phillipa was actually Lady Phillipa Longmead. Charlie was sure it would make no difference to them.

'I hired a chauffeur today,' Clay remarked. 'A nice quiet chap. He can take Natalie around. The doctor said she's got to give up driving—her back or something.'

'I wish you had let *me* interview him,' Natalie said. 'After all, it will be I who is with him most of the time.'

'You were asleep, darling. Anyway I was lucky to get him. *They* interview you. He'll be here at ten in the morning, so you'll see him soon enough. His name is Herbert Lincoln Jefferson. Are you ready for that name?'

*

They sat in the Lamborghini in front of Phillipa's parents' house.

'Your friends didn't like me and I don't care,' she said.

'Well, you weren't exactly charm personified were you? Telling Natalie the prawns were off. You should have just kept quiet about it.'

'Why?'

'Because it would have been the polite thing to do.'

'Oh Charlie, don't be so uptight and antiquated. That's the trouble with your stupid generation, you're all so busy being polite that you don't even see what's going on under your nose. Wars and violence, people starving, young kids being sent off to get their brains blown out, and worse—if it's an arm or a leg they lose, they just get dumped in some lousy army hospital and left to rot like garbage.'

'I don't want any of your lectures. I know what's going on. I don't like it any more than you do, but it's life, you have to accept it.'

'Accept it?' Her lip curled sarcastically. 'That's just what we're *not* going to do.' She got out of the car and walked into the house without a backward glance.

Charlie sat glumly, watching her disappear. She was a strange girl. She made him feel guilty. She made him feel that his life was small and useless and that he wasn't *doing* anything. However, at least she could open her mouth and talk. She was aware, and that was a commendable quality.

He gunned the car into action, and feeling depressed, drove back to his hotel.

Charlie and Laurel were hardly talking. He could not conceal his anger at the way she and Floss had just taken off at the rock festival. Neither of them mentioned it, but there was a cold barrier between them which everyone noticed. He stopped going to their house. He was busy reading properties anyway, looking for something he could do in the gap left by the cancelled movie. He had no reason to return to England before the end of the year.

He saw Phillipa. She came to his hotel most evenings and sat around while he read. Sometimes she read scripts for him. She

204

had surprisingly bright criticisms, and as he got to know her she relaxed and was a much more pleasant person to be with. It remained a purely platonic relationship. He didn't really fancy her sexually, so he didn't push it. Of course everyone thought they were at it day and night. Apart from the fact that Clay dropped by occasionally, they saw hardly anyone.

One day Phillipa said, 'My mother is having one of her parties. She wants me to bring you.'

Charlie looked at her in surprise. 'I thought you hated parties.'

'I do. But she's been on and on about you, so in a weak moment I said yes.'

'I didn't know *you* had weak moments.'

She flushed. 'It's tomorrow night at eight. Will you come?'

'If you want me to.'

Phillipa's mother, Jane, was in her early forties. She was slim, tall, perfectly groomed, with a typically English prettiness. She looked nothing like her daughter. She wore a long red dress, and two thin diamond bracelets on each wrist. Her hair was swept back into a chignon, and in contrast to her husband she was the blueprint of good taste.

Husband Sol, short and paunchy, with a giant cigar shoved obscenely between his lips, made no concession to the fact that they were having a party. He wore a gaudy Palm Beach shirt and baggy brown trousers.

Jane extended an elegant hand and said, 'I'm so delighted to meet you, Mr Brick. Phillipa talks of you all the time.'

Sol shifted the cigar to the side of his mouth and rasped in pure Brooklynese, 'Hey, Charlie, baby, good t'see ya. Name your poison.'

Phillipa was nowhere in sight.

Charlie made himself comfortable at the bar and chatted to Angela Carter and her escort.

It was an hour before Phillipa appeared. Charlie hardly recognised her. Her normally long flowing hair was arranged in the semblance of a style, and instead of shaggy robes, she wore a white Victorian dress and *shoes!* Her face, with the small amount of makeup she had applied, was less interesting but more attractive.

'You look great,' he said, smiling.

'Do I?' Suddenly she seemed like a rather shy eighteen-year-old and not the tough independent hippie he was used to.

Her mother descended and threw up her hands in horror. 'Phillipa, what *are* you wearing? Honestly, Mr Brick, I just don't know what to do about this girl, she always looks such a frightful mess.'

A look of pain flitted quickly across Phillipa's face and was just as quickly gone. She stepped out of her shoes defiantly. 'Sorry, Jane, I know you hate the smell of my feet, but it's so much more *healthy*!'

Jane smiled. 'Such a *young* girl, she'll learn won't she, Mr Brick. Or shall I call you Charlie? After all, when *we* were her age we had to go through this silly Bohemian phase too, I suppose, but it's so *boring* while it lasts. Don't you agree?'

They stood on either side of him: Phillipa, eyes sulky and defiant; Jane, confident and poised. They waited to see whose side he would take.

He sidestepped the issue and said, 'This is a really lovely house. Have you lived here long?'

When Jane went off to talk to other guests, Phillipa whispered, 'Let's go. This is really awful. I can't stand all these phoney people.'

Charlie was just about to agree when he spotted Dindi at the door. She was in a white satin pyjama-suit slashed to the waist, her suntanned bosom barely concealed, her blond hair fluffy around her pouty face. She was with Steve Magnum and his entourage.

Charlie felt a jolt of outrage at the sight of her. He would never forget the way she had spoken of Serafina the day before his dear mother died. He loathed her, and it also galled him that she was becoming so successful. She had used him, a fact he would always remember.

Abruptly he downed the rest of his drink and said to Phillipa, who was absently picking at her long hair, 'One more drink and we'll be on our way. OK, love?' He wasn't about to slink out the moment Dindi appeared.

Across the room she had noticed him, and in a loud voice she said to Steve, 'Who on earth is Charlie with?'

'Charlie who?' Steve asked, swaying slightly.

'You'd think he could do better than that,' Dindi giggled, 'I guess times are bad. I heard that they cancelled his next movie.'

Steve wasn't listening. He was hugging Jane, with whom he had once had an affair.

Dindi headed across the room towards Charlie. 'Hello,' she said loudly.

He wanted to ignore her, but sensed that that would give her more satisfaction than a cool greeting. He nodded at her coldly, 'Dindi.'

'Putting on a little weight, I see,' she giggled in her customary manner.

He smiled tightly. She had hit him where it hurt—his ego.

Jane joined them at that point, kissing Dindi on both cheeks and gushing, 'But of course you two know each other, don't you? Really it's quite difficult to keep up with who was married to whom in this town.'

'You manage,' Phillipa muttered under her breath.

'What dear? Oh Dindi, darling, have you met my little girl? She makes me feel quite ancient. Phillipa, this is Dindi Synde.' She smiled prettily at Charlie. 'Mr Brick's ex-wife, or *are* you divorced yet, one never knows?'

Silently Charlie surveyed the three women: Jane, so sure of herself, a hint of bitchery gleaming in her flat grey eyes: Dindi, bursting out of her top, all blond hair and nasty curled lips. Phillipa, flushed and a little panicky.

He gripped Phillipa by her boney arm, saying, 'I just remembered a very urgent appointment, thanks so much,' and steered her across the room, through the hall, and out of the front door.

'Thank God you did that,' she exclaimed. 'I don't think I could have stood it in there one more minute. Were you really married to *her*?'

'It's a short story,' he mumbled quickly. 'Let's go back to the hotel and light up a nice big fat relaxing joint. I need to get the smell of that cow out of my nose.'

'Who—Jane or Dindi?'

'Both of them—they go together beautifully.'

Later, when they were both pleasantly high, and the voice of Nina Simone filled the room, Charlie undressed her.

It was time. They had been together weeks without really being together.

She was painfully thin, and stiffened in his arms, although she never spoke a word of objection. She was rigid with distaste, tight, dry, unwelcoming.

He produced a jar of Vaseline and she shied away in disgust. The whole thing was a mistake. It was wrong.

Charlie felt all the desire drain away from him and he told her to get dressed.

She muttered 'I'm sorry. I *told* you I didn't like it. I *warned* you.'

He shut himself in the bathroom and stared at his reflection in the mirror. Slowly he took off the trendy glasses he was wearing and snapped them in half. What was he trying to prove? That he was a young swinger? She would have liked it well enough if he had been some young stud.

When he came out she was gone.

41

Claude Hussan arrived in town and checked into the Beverly Hills Hotel.

Sunday found out about it by reading the 'Hollywood Reporter'.

She was furious, and immediately called Carey from the set. 'Can you have lunch?' she asked. 'I need your advice.'

'Sure, I'll be there at twelve.' Carey hung up thoughtfully. She too had read the trades.

The director was patient with Sunday that morning. She fluffed lines, dried up, and several times cut in on other actors. It was very unlike her.

Carey was first in the studio restaurant. She smoked a cigarette and thought about what she would say.

Sunday rushed in fifteen minutes late. She was wrapped in

a pink silk housecoat, her long tan legs attracting everyone's attention. She flopped down, ordered an orange juice and an egg salad, then said, 'I just don't understand it, it's quite ridiculous. I've called the hotel but they say he left orders not to be disturbed. Carey—I don't even care about me, but I've got his *child*! He hasn't even called me *once* since I left Rio. That's *two* weeks ago.'

'Calm down.' It was the first time Carey had seen Sunday blow her cool. 'Just take it easy and I'll give you the facts.'

'What facts?'

'He arrived yesterday morning with his wife. He's apparently busy casting and interviewing all day long. Marshall has three clients seeing him today. As you know, his movie should start in three weeks and he still hasn't gotten a star.'

Sunday bit her lip. 'His wife? But I thought they were separated, getting a divorce—'

'Did he tell you that?'

'No, but I just assumed. He never spoke of her except to say that she didn't want Jean-Pierre. I just can't believe they're together. Why doesn't he phone me—explain?'

'I didn't want to burst your bubble before, you seemed so happy. But this is a real mean guy. He has a horrible reputation, and frankly I was amazed at you getting caught up with him.'

'You *always* think the worst of people. Claude is a beautiful sensitive man.' But even as she said it the words rang false. It wasn't true. Claude was a surly, difficult bastard—but she loved him.

'Then why hasn't he phoned you?'

'There must be a reason. I'm sure there's some perfectly logical explanation. Why, I'll probably get home and find him playing with Jean-Pierre on the beach.'

She picked at her egg salad.

'How's the movie going?' Carey asked. 'I thought I might spend some time on the set tomorrow morning.'

'OK. By the way I've been getting more of those sick letters I told you about. Three this week—and whoever it is has my address.'

'I've told you, tear them up and take no notice. It's probably

209

your friendly milkman. Those nuts never do anything. You get a stack of dirties at the office too.'

'But this is the same person who was writing to me at the Château, I think I should—'

'Hello, Carey.' Charlie Brick stopped by the table. 'Where's Marshall?'

'We're not always together, you know. I expect he's slaving away at the office. Charlie, do you know Sunday Simmons?'

'Er, yes,' he smiled at her; then remembering she was a friend of Dindi, his smile froze.

'I sneaked onto your set the other day,' Sunday said. 'You were marvellous. When I was a kid I was a tremendous fan—in fact I still am.' Why did it always sound so stupid when you were admiring someone?

Christ Almighty! Was his life to be fraught with oblique references to his age? When she was a kid indeed! He had only been making films for ten years. 'Thank you. Come over again, I'll buy you a coffee.'

'I'd love to. Next time I have a break I'll be there.'

'He's very attractive in that funky English way,' Carey remarked after he left. 'When he's playing himself, that is. I really dig that kind of subtle appeal. Marshall has it. I think we may actually get married any day now. He's finally persuaded me.'

'That's wonderful. You never told me.'

'Why should I? You've got enough problems. Anyway, I have made the fateful decision and now all I have to do is name the day. My mother will kill me!'

Sunday finished shooting early. The director cautioned her to go home and get a good night's sleep. She drove twice past the Beverly Hills Hotel, trying to decide whether to go in. She knew it was the wrong way to approach Claude, yet she desperately wanted everything to be all right. Frustratedly she drove to Malibu.

Jean-Pierre was playing on the beach with Katia, the young Mexican girl she had hired to look after him. Mr Hussan had not called.

*

Jack Milan arrived at six, for a drink, his youngest child Victoria with him. He owned a neighbouring beach house and had telephoned Sunday to ask if he could talk to her.

'Good to see you. I was only saying to Ellie the other day how we should call you up and ask you over for dinner,' he said.

She smiled. 'Drink?'

'Fine. I'll take scotch on the rocks.' He prowled around the tiny house. 'Nice place you've got here, very cosy.'

'I like it.'

'Yeah, you know I just found out you have a kid. You certainly know how to keep a secret.'

'He's not mine. I wish he was. I'm just looking after him for a friend.'

'Sure,' Jack said disbelievingly. 'It's a shame about you and Steve, you would have been great together. I was congratulating myself on playing Cupid.'

She smiled again and wondered what he wanted. She was sure this was not a social call. The 'phone rang and automatically she picked it up.

'I want to fuck you,' a voice whispered. 'I want to—'

She quickly slammed down the receiver. 'Oh God!' The day had become too much for her and she burst into tears.

'Hey, honey, what's the matter?' Jack was embarrassed.

'Jack, please go. I'm just tired, everything's getting on top of me. Please understand.'

The child was watching her with unconcealed interest.

Jack got up reluctantly. 'Are you sure there's nothing I can do?'

'Nothing. I'm really sorry. Forgive me.'

'If you promise to have dinner with us next week. Ellie will call you.'

'That would be nice.'

He left and she called the Beverly Hills Hotel, but Mr Hussan was unobtainable, so she left her name and number and went to bed.

Outside an old grey Buick cruised slowly past her house.

42

Getting the job with Clay Allen was easy. Herbert answered the advertisement in the paper, went along wearing his one and only suit, showed the glowing references he had written himself, and he was in.

It was an easy job. He spent most of the day lolling around the Allen's kitchen, for neither of them seemed to go out much. As often as not, Clay spent most of the day writing in the poolhouse, and Natalie made only an occasional trip to Saks or Magnum's. She sent the maid to the market, and sometimes he had to take the nanny and their child over to someone's house. He kept himself to himself, communicating with neither the maid nor the nanny.

Clay paid him an advance and he purchased an old grey Buick.

If it were not for Marge, he would have been reasonably happy. She had become unbearable, bossy and demanding, nagging and shrill. Worst of all, she required his services sexually. This amazed him, after what he continually observed going on next door.

Now that he had a car he made careful plans about how to do away with her. The first thing was to move away from those stinking neighbours, to somewhere where they were unknown. It would be no easy move, and Marge would be furious, but he had a plan, and now with a job and a car things were looking up.

He found time to track down Sunday Simmons. He had read about her arriving back from Rio, and it was a simple matter to wait outside Carey St Martin's office and follow her until she led him to Sunday and the house at the beach. After that, he followed her whenever he was free. He knew what time she usually left the studio, and if possible he was there. Sometimes he spent the night sleeping in his car near her house and he would follow her again at seven in the morning when she drove to the studio.

She even looked beautiful at that hour with her hair pulled back, and big tinted sunglasses.

One day he watched Sunday leave, and then waited for the Mexican girl to take the child shopping. It was easy for him to break into the house through the patio. He wandered around, sniffing anxiously through her belongings. He wrote down her 'phone number and took some pictures from a large stack lying on a table. In her bedroom he pocketed a lacy bra and panties; then he left as stealthily as he had arrived.

In his mind he knew that with Marge out of the way he and Sunday would be together. It never occurred to him that she would refuse him once he revealed himself to her.

He wrote her many letters, each one better than the last. On two occasions he even risked telephoning her, but she had cut off instantly both times, so he decided it was better to wait until he was in a position to present himself personally.

Marge waited two weeks before she told Louella of her discovery. She was having a good time. Herbert was doing what she wanted and she didn't need it spoiled in any way.

Why *should* she tell Louella anyway? It was none of her business. Sometimes Louella was almost as mean as Herbert, especially last Saturday night when she had made her accept one of the 'circle of friends' in a most unspeakable manner.

'I don't like to do it like that,' Marge had protested. 'It hurts!'

'Do you want to leave the circle?' Louella demanded coldly. 'There are plenty of other women who would be happy to be in your position.'

Marge agreed, hated it, and was reduced to tears.

Louella had laughed in front of everyone. 'You're behaving like a sixteen-year-old virgin,' she had jeered.

Later she had been sorry and made Marge hot milk and chatted sweetly to her.

It was only pride of accomplishment that made her finally reveal to Louella what Herbert had done. *Her* accomplishment at being clever enough to find out. As she was telling Louella, the enormity of it struck her for the first time. Herbert had *killed* a girl, *murdered* her. It was unthinkable.

She started to blubber and cry and panic. Perhaps by even knowing about it she was an accomplice.

Louella confirmed her worst fears. 'Of course you're part of it,' she remarked. 'Just by not going to the police makes you as guilty as him.'

Marge jumped with fright. '*You* know too,' she blurted out.

'Yes, but *I* might go to the police.'

Marge's face crumpled in horror. 'But—but you wouldn't do that.'

'Perhaps I should. I didn't realise how serious this would turn out to be.'

Marge started to cry loudly. Why had she ever interfered? Why had she ever become friendly with Louella Crisp? She had been happy watching her television and eating.

'However,' Louella continued, 'maybe as your friend I can help you. Of course it will take money. How much do you have?'

'A thousand dollars,' Marge stammered. 'It's *all* I've got, though, kind of my savings for my old age.' She gave a sickly grin. 'What do you need money for?'

Louella clucked her tongue. 'If you're going to ask stupid questions I don't think I can help you. We need professional advice and of course there's my friend at police headquarters. A thousand dollars won't be enough if we're to get this matter dropped, the investigation quashed.'

'What investigation?' Marge squealed in alarm.

'I didn't want to worry you before, but I suspected what Herbert had done, so I made some discreet enquiries and I found that they are pursuing this case very strongly.'

'Oh!' Marge went white and her mouth hung open in a strange disjointed way.

'Of course, with, say, three thousand dollars I think we can settle everything.'

Marge started to cry again. 'I don't *have* three thousand dollars.'

'What about Herbert?' Louella's mind was racing. Was three thousand dollars too much to ask for? Marge, the silly bitch, believed her story, but would Herbert see it for the black-mail it was? He was probably smarter than Marge, but how much smarter could he be, having married her in the first place?

'Herbie doesn't have any money,' Marge whined. 'We're always behind, catchin' up on payin' for somethin' or other.'

'You had better talk to him.' Louella said coldly.

'I can't do that! He'd kill me.'

'Then there is nothing I can do to help you. I shall have to go straight to the police, otherwise I'll find myself in the same position as you, and *I* don't want to spend the rest of my life in jail.'

Marge shuddered. 'I'll get you my thousand dollars,' she said quickly, 'and I'll talk to Herbie, he'll think of something. Is that O.K.? Will that help us?'

Louella nodded. 'I should think so. Only I don't expect my friend can wait too long for the rest of the money.'

Herbert didn't go home that night. He had found a way to get onto the patio on the beach side of Sunday's house. By crawling along on his hands and knees, then resting on his stomach, he could peer through a chink in the curtains into her bedroom.

He waited two hours after the lights went off, to be sure everyone was asleep. He was especially nervous that the little dog would wake up, start yapping, and give him away.

He inched himself slowly and silently towards her window, then raised himself to look inside.

His luck was in. She hadn't bothered to pull the drapes at all, and he had a clear view of her sprawled across the bed, covered only by a thin sheet. One long brown leg was thrown over the sheet, and a bare arm.

It occurred to him that she was naked beneath the sheet, and that if he waited patiently she would throw it off altogether. His mouth went dry at the thought, and his breathing became laboured and heavy.

It would be so easy, he thought, to force the safety-catch on her window and let himself in. He was confident that once he identified himself as the writer of the letters, she would welcome him with open arms. But it was too soon. He wasn't ready. He had to be free.

Chewing on his lower lip, he crouched uncomfortably,

watching her until dawn. Then he made his way back to his car and dozed until she emerged at seven o'clock and set off for the studios.

He followed her. Only when she was safely inside the studio gates did he go home to Marge.

43

Charlie was in a depression. His birthday came and went and he celebrated it alone at his hotel.

He had not telephoned Phillipa since the night she had walked out on him. He had given up the struggle as far as she was concerned.

He took out Thames Mason, who bored him with talk about the number of magazine covers she had appeared on that year. He took out a mousey studio secretary, who bored him, period. He took out a pseudo-intellectual magazine writer, who wanted to be tied up and raped. He took out a blonde pretty ding-a-ling, who unfortunately reminded him of Dindi. He took out a different woman every night.

One evening, sitting in the back of the Mercedes with a Swedish starlet, he complained to George. 'You drive this car like a bus, can't you get a move on?'

George glanced in the rear-view mirror. It was very unlike Charlie to be picky with him, when in any case he was already exceeding the speed limit.

Charlie leaned back in the car, trying to avoid the onslaught of words from the Swede. She hadn't stopped all night. After five minutes of her company he had been ready to slit her throat, and now they had been together for two long hours.

'So the producer said to me, "You are a beautiful girl, Lena, and the star refuses to have you in the same scene with her. Can you blame her?" he said. So they cut me out. Of course I *can* understand it, Clara is ten years older than me and—'

Charlie tuned out. Enough was enough. He would 'phone Phillipa the next day.

'Come on, George, I've got a seven o'clock call tomorrow,' he said irritably.

George put his foot down and the big car surged forward. They were approaching a changing light and, sensing his boss's impatience, George pressed his foot down even harder. They could just make it across the light.

That was the last George remembered before the accident. He never even saw the Cadillac coming the other way.

In the split second before the cars hit, Charlie knew what was happening, and he grabbed the girl, covering her with his body.

He woke up two days later in the Cedars of Lebanon Hospital.

It was the strangest feeling to open your eyes and not know where you were or what was happening. There was a tube attached to his arm, but apart from that he couldn't feel or see any sign of injury.

He was in a plain white room. A nurse sat next to the bed, knitting, her head bent in concentration.

'Nurse,' he tried to say. His voice came out as a dried-up croak, just enough to attract her attention.

She dropped the knitting and jumped up. 'Mr Brick,' she fluttered, 'you're awake, that's wonderful. Please don't move, I'll call for the doctor.'

'Must have some water,' he gasped. His throat felt swollen and intolerably dry.

She lifted his head and allowed him a few sips, although he could have drunk the whole pitcher twice over. Then she departed, returning with a doctor and two more nurses.

Slowly, he pieced together the story. The two cars, travelling in opposite directions, had both been trying to jump the light. The passenger in the front seat of the Cadillac died. The driver and George were both suffering from multiple injuries. Charlie, by protecting the girl in the back, had smashed his head on the side and been unconscious for two days. The girl—Lena—had escaped with a few bruises.

Charlie had a bump on his head the size of an egg, and a nasty cut across his forehead. He felt relieved to be alive. It had been a close call, and the doctors had been unable to predict how long he would stay unconscious. It could have been weeks or even months.

'I never realised so many people cared,' Charlie told Clay a few days later. 'You should see some of the letters I've had, it's bloody marvellous.' He was thinking in particular of a letter from Lorna, a letter full of all the love and affection she had never given him in their marriage. God, she had changed. But then so had he.

'There were a lot of people thought you might not pull through,' Clay remarked. 'Those head injuries are very dodgy things.'

'I've seen the papers. Christ, the English ones are almost obituaries. But I feel good. In fact I never really felt anything except a diabolical headache when I woke up. It's poor old George I'm worried about. He's broken about everything there is to break. They say he'll be O.K. although it will take some time. I don't know what I'll do without him.'

'I wanted to talk to you about that. We've got this great chauffeur who we never seem to use. Natalie is too tired to go shopping now, and I prefer to drive myself anyway, so he's all yours.'

'Wait a minute, I don't want to—'

'No argument, Charlie. You don't need all the drag of interviewing and finding someone, this guy will do you fine. His name is Herbert. I'll have him meet you tomorrow. In fact I'll come with him.'

Charlie was anxious to leave the hospital. The doctors had insisted that he stay there for at least a week's observation, but he was bored and jumpy and felt he didn't need to. Besides there was the film he was shooting; the delay was costing a lot of money. He knew that while he had been unconscious there had been talk of a replacement. The director and producer had both been to see him, and he had reassured them that he would be back within a week.

He had received a stream of visitors.

Laurel and Floss came, friendly and anxious, bearing a gift of chocolate cake heavily impregnated with pot which Charlie, unknowingly, had given to the nurses, who had never been quite the same since.

He was glad to see Phillipa, serious and apologetic about the last evening they had spent together. After all, there were more things to a relationship than sex.

The Swedish starlet who had been in the car wreck with him was basking in all the publicity. She came to visit him with two photographers. He saw her, but banned the photographers. She was furious.

At his age, and in his position, he knew it was ridiculous to run around with little starlets just so people would think what a swinger he was. Why should he care what people thought?

True to his word, Clay arrived with his chauffeur to take Charlie home.

Home was his suite at the Beverly Hills Hotel, which seemed depressingly quiet and empty without George pottering about.

Clay had invited him to stay a few days with Natalie and himself, but Charlie declined. He wanted to finish the movie and then take a holiday. In a way things had worked out for the best. Now he was not committed until the end of the year and could do what he wanted.

He fell once more into the routine of working at the studio all day, and seeing Phillipa in the evenings.

He made good use of Clay's chauffeur, but found him cold and withdrawn and could not establish any contact with him. This disturbed Charlie, who needed some sort of rapport with the people who worked for him.

Phillipa complained that Herbert was always staring at her in a strange way. Charlie replied that it was because most of her long hippy clothes were transparent.

'I've seen him somewhere before,' she said, 'I wish I could remember where. I don't like him. I hope you get rid of him soon.'

The next day Charlie gave Herbert a hundred-dollar bonus, and sent him back to Clay.

Clay, who really no longer needed him, gave him a month's salary and dismissed him.

It was nearly a week later when Phillipa remembered where she had seen him. 'It was on the Strip one night, several months ago. He was cruising along in a big black car and he picked up this girl. I didn't know her but we had all been chatting—she was in a bad way—needed money. Anyway this creep in the car picked her up and the next day she was found murdered in the hills.'

Charlie laughed incredulously. 'That's ridiculous.'

'Why?' Her face was tight and serious. 'It was him, I'm sure of it.'

'Oh, come on, you sound like a bad movie, love. Anyway, if it had been *that* important, you would have remembered him before.'

'I think we should do something.'

Charlie laughed. 'What did you have in mind? 'Phone up Clay and say, "Hey, about your chauffeur—Phillipa just remembered she saw him pick up a girl several months ago who was later found murdered"?'

'I can't stand you when you're flippant, you remind me of my mother.'

She knew how to put the boot in.

'All right, if it will make you happy we'll call the police, and you'll find out the case was solved the next day, and Herbert what's-his-name will sue you for a fortune.'

'Forget it, Charlie, let's just forget it.'

44

A week after Claude's return he telephoned Sunday. She could hardly keep the hurt and anger out of her voice.

'I've been so busy,' he complained.

'Didn't you get my messages?' she asked.

'Come up to my hotel this evening. We'll have dinner, I'll explain.'

'Don't you want to come to my house and see Jean-Pierre?'

'He's fine, isn't he?'

'Yes, of course.' She bit her lip, hating and loving at the same time. 'But I thought you'd want to see him.'

'Another time,' he said brusquely. 'Tonight I want to talk to you. Be here at eight.'

He hung up, leaving her angry and confused. She knew that if she were smart, she would give him back his child and walk away from the relationship. And she planned to be smart.

Claude opened the door of his suite. He was wearing an all-black outfit and tinted glasses. He smoked a short black cigarette.

Sunday couldn't help thinking how much he looked like a French movie star. The compelling, almost ugly face, the long rangey body. She felt her reserves start to crumble.

The attraction, she reminded herself, was purely physical. He had come at her with his body-first, and that was all he had ever given.

'Hello.' He kissed her briefly on the cheek.

She brushed her hand in her hair nervously, determined to stay unaffected. 'Hello, Claude, you're looking well.' Everything she wanted to say sounded like an accusation, so she remained silent. What she wanted was a drink, an exchange of small talk, and then a discussion about when Jean-Pierre should be delivered back—nothing dramatic, no hysterics.

'Your breasts are getting smaller,' he remarked, rubbing his hands familiarly across them.

She backed away angrily. With a sudden sickness, she realised that merely his touch made her desire him, and she knew that he knew it too.

Would it matter if she went to bed with him one last time? Men behaved like that continually. After all, she was a grown woman, and there was nothing wrong in wanting sex.

As if reading her thoughts, Claude said, 'Let's screw first and talk after.' He was already peeling off his black silk turtle-neck sweater.

She hesitated. She wanted very much to be able to say no.

'Come on.' He stood naked in front of her and roughly fiddled with the thin snake-skin belt on her brown trousers.

She stood still while he stripped her item by item, until her clothes rested in a small pile beside them.

Then he was on her, knocking her on the floor, his hands and mouth rough.

She was silent, listening to the stream of obscenities uttered in French and English. It reminded her in a frightening way of the letters she had been getting.

Her body responded to his, but her mind remained above them, a detached onlooker.

Afterwards, when Claude went into the bathroom, she huddled on the floor, feeling the bites and scratches he had given her. *Why did she still love him so much*?

He emerged in good spirits. 'You've changed,' he said. 'You're better at it now. Who's been teaching you?'

It insulted her that he did not care if she had been with other men.

'I want you to do my film,' he said abruptly. 'You're probably a terrible actress, but I'm a director who can do something for you. I don't believe in false modesty. If you do it, it will make you as an actress. But you have to put yourself in my hands entirely. You have to *live, eat* and *breathe* Stefanie.'

She had read the script. She knew she could do the part, but she hadn't thought in a million years he would ever think of her.

She stared at him for a long thoughtful moment, then she nodded. 'Thank you, Claude, I know you won't be sorry.'

Carey was not excited at the prospect of meeting Claude Hussan. She regarded as a no-good bastard any man who could treat Sunday the way he had done. She was also sceptical about Sunday doing his film. Was it the right vehicle for her? She read the script, and wasn't sure. Sunday was too young and beautiful to fit the part. More important, was she a good enough actress? It was heavy stuff, and, Carey wasn't sure if Sunday could manage it. There were also explicit sex scenes. In the hands of an American director they would cause no embarrassment, but who knew what Hussan would expect his leading actress to do?

Sunday had 'phoned that morning, bubbling over with delight. As far as she was concerned, there were no uncertainties. She would make the picture, and that was that. Carey had to insist on having the script sent over at once, since Claude wanted to settle contracts and money that very afternoon.

'Accept anything,' Sunday had said. 'I *have* to do it.'

Carey would have been a lot happier for her to do the film with Jack Milan. Now came this bombshell, Claude Hussan's first American film.

He had insisted on meeting Carey in his suite, although she would have preferred to see him at her office.

A secretary answered the door, a girl typical of the many out-of-work actresses who also typed. She asked Carey to take a seat, then disappeared into the bedroom.

Carey leafed through a copy of 'Films and Filming'.

The secretary re-emerged shortly, now clad in a polka-dot bikini. She collected some papers from the desk, said 'Mr Hussan will be right with you,' and wiggled out the door.

Carey's first impression was of Hussan's eyes. They were the eyes of a man who had made it, but done many things along the way to get there. Then she took in the rest of him, and suddenly Sunday's hang-up became clear.

'You want a drink?' he offered.

She said no, annoyed at the fact that he neither bothered to introduce himself or even acknowledge the fact that he knew who she was. But she was being silly. Of course he knew who she was.

He lounged in a chair opposite her and stared.

She tried to establish control. 'I'm not sure if this is the right part for my client,' she began.

He interrupted her. 'Neither am I. She's probably a terrible actress, but in my hands that doesn't matter. I know what I want and I am prepared to take a chance. This film will make her.'

'She's already made. I could sign contracts for her tomorrow that would keep her working solidly. She's very much in demand.'

'Crap, that's all she's done, commercial crap. *I* will develop this girl, and as an actress, not as a big-breasted wonder.'

'I can't argue,' Carey said stiffly. 'Sunday has made up her mind, as you well know. Her price will be high, the usual stipulations that she approves all publicity stills and material about her, no nude scenes, no—'

'Don't waste your breath. We will pay her fifty thousand dollars, plus she signs a personal contract with me. If I want her naked hanging from a light fixture, I'll have her that way. Don't you worry about it, just tell Sunday, she'll agree.' He went to the desk and picked up some papers. 'Here's the contract. I want it signed and back here tomorrow.'

Carey, shaking with anger, drove straight to the studio.

'You can't do it,' she told Sunday when she came off the set. 'He won't pay your money, nor allow you any special clauses. You'll be completely in his hands. He could ruin you.'

'Relax, he won't ruin me. Have you seen any of his films? He's brilliant.'

'But your money, if you drop your price now it will be bad. I *know* I can get you good money on the Milan film, and maybe even a piece of the action. I—'

'Don't knock yourself out, Carey. I love you and appreciate everything you've done for me, but whether you like it or not I just *have* to do Claude's film.'

Carey sighed. 'This man has some hold over you, and I bet I know where it is. Right between the legs.'

'You're wrong, it's not that. Just be patient and go along with me. I *know* this film is right for me, and if it's not,' she smiled softly, 'then I'll get out of this business.'

45

Lena, the Swedish starlet, was suing Charlie for three million dollars.

'All she had was a couple of bruises,' he told his lawyer incredulously.

'She's suing for back injury, permanent headaches, a scar on her leg and blurred vision.'

'Why doesn't she throw in a broken neck while she's at it? Christ, these money-grabbing little hookers are unbelievable!'

'Of course you're not responsible. Insurance will cover you. I'll keep you informed.'

'Thanks a lot.'

He had finished shooting the movie, and was staying in a rented house in Palm Springs with Phillipa.

Under doctor's orders he had to relax and take things easy for a few months. He didn't know how he was going to do *that*, for after only a week of inactivity he was going mad.

Phillipa was no great help. She was there and that's about all there was to the relationship—no sex, just companionship, and a strange companionship at that. She rarely spoke except to comment on some disaster somewhere in the world.

He often wondered why, if she were so concerned, she was not out doing something? She seemed quite content to exist with him in the very luxury she was always criticizing . . .

His day was routine. Up at nine, a work-out, a sauna, a swim. Then he read the papers by the pool until lunch was served by the maid. After lunch he had a sleep upstairs and then from four until dinner at seven he would potter about with his stereo sets or cameras.

Phillipa was a reluctant model for his photography. He had to shift her, complaining, out of her chair, and move her around almost by force. It made him laugh. It clearly showed the difference between actresses and other girls. Actresses were only too delighted to pose for innumerable photos, changing their clothes, their expressions, their hairstyles, anything just to continue their love-affair with a camera lens.

He remembered one day he had started taking pictures of Dindi early in the morning and she had posed happily until eight o'clock at night. She had changed her outfit forty times!

After dinner they watched television, usually smoking a little grass.

Charlie wished he could do something creative, perhaps write or paint, but his talent lay strictly in performing.

225

He had never looked so good in his life—thin, suntanned, in great shape.

He spent a great deal of time on the 'phone, talking to his children, or chatting to George in hospital to cheer him up. He spoke to Lorna, who was obviously embarrassed about the letter she had sent him when she thought he might not recover. Their conversation was short and flustered.

Was she happy? he wondered. Or did she miss him and the excitement of their life together? Although what excitement had she really had? It was always *he* who was doing everything. *She* was usually stuck at home with the kids.

She was certainly making more of a go with her second marriage than he had done with his. Maybe he should have knocked Dindi up, that might have kept her quiet and at home. But how did you knock up a girl who used a diaphragm *and* took the pill?

There were a lot of invitations—parties, dinners, barbecues—but Charlie was content to go nowhere, and Phillipa was certainly no social butterfly.

He felt, unconsciously, that their relationship was doing neither of them any good. She seemed to have opted out of everything, and while his day was full of minor activity of sorts, Phillipa just appeared in the morning, flopped out in a lounging chair in the shade, and slept the day away.

Then there was sex. She didn't want to try again, and he didn't want to force himself on her, but things were getting a bit desperate. His physical fitness seemed to increase his sexual appetite.

It was a tricky problem. He didn't want to upset Phillipa, of whom he was very fond in a brotherly way, but his need was becoming more demanding every day.

He finally decided to have people to stay for the weekend. Natalie and Clay; Marshall and Carey; and Thames Mason, with a butch-looking queen called Marvin Mariboo who had worked in publicity on the last film. That should solve everything for the benefit of Phillipa, and with the promise of a part, Thames could be relied on to be discreet.

The weekend got off to a bad start. Carey turned up on Friday morning without Marshall. She said he was working and would arrive the next day. Clay arrived in the afternoon without Natalie, who felt queasy and had decided to stay at home. To make matters complete, Thames drove in on Friday night with the news that Marvin had been beaten up by a sailor and wouldn't be coming at all!

Dinner on Friday night consisted of Clay chatting up first Carey and then Thames. He obviously fancied them both strongly.

Phillipa sat silently at one end of the table, making faces at Charlie, her way of telling him that she didn't approve of any of his guests.

Carey put Clay down at every turn. She made it quite clear that he was going to get exactly nowhere with her.

Thames, however, found his line of chat particularly fascinating, especially when he said what a wonderful idea it would be to write a television series for her.

'I'm surprised no-one has suggested it before,' he said, leaning closer to her across the asparagus. 'Any idiot can see that you have great comic potential. You could be a young beautiful Lucille Ball.'

Thames visibly preened.

'That's you, Clay, old love, any idiot!' Charlie said, furious at the sure-fire conclusion that Thames was going to be sharing Clay's bed that evening, not his.

'I'm going for a walk,' Phillipa announced, suddenly getting up.

'But dinner's not finished,' Charlie protested.

'I'm not hungry. I'll see you in the morning.'

He realised she was miserable. She knew why he had organized this weekend, and she obviously didn't want to sit around and watch Clay and him bicker over Thames. He laughed out loud. The situation suddenly struck him as terribly funny.

'What's the matter?' Carey asked.

He noticed what a fantastic coffee-cream colour her skin was. 'Nothing, love, just thinking.' She was very womanly. He had never had a . . . He stamped on his thoughts quickly. She was Marshall's.

After dinner he went to the study to select some tapes.

Clay followed him, drunk and happy. 'You don't mind, old boy, do you?' he asked. 'She's ripe and ready. Where on earth did you find her? Thank Christ Natalie didn't come.'

Like everyone else, Clay imagined that Charlie and Phillipa were having an affair. It didn't occur to him that Charlie had invited Thames for himself.

'Go right ahead,' Charlie said. 'Do what the fuck you like.' He was disgusted with Clay. Somehow it didn't seem quite fair when your wife was lying at home, pregnant.

'Of course, I really fancy the spade,' Clay continued, 'but there's no free pussy being handed out in *that* direction.'

'Tough,' Charlie said, putting on Miles Davis good and loud.

The four of them sat in the living-room, drinking, talking and listening to the sounds.

Charlie got out some pot and they all turned on, including Carey. She really wanted to go to bed, but she hadn't smoked in a long time as it wasn't quite Marshall's scene. She felt like it. Having made the decision to marry Marshall didn't mean that she had to stop living.

Thames was a mass of giggles. She would have let Clay strip her and have her in front of everyone if he had been so inclined, but he dragged all six feet of her off to his bedroom with a sheepish goodnight.

'Where's Phillipa?' Carey asked.

'I don't know.' Charlie was irritable. 'She's a funny girl. Probably walking around the desert.'

'Do you know Claude Hussan? He's a sonofabitch, a real mean bum.' Carey's thoughts became disjointed when she was stoned, and she switched from one subject to the next, never even waiting for an answer.

Charlie on the other hand, if he wasn't involved in sexual activity, became rather melancholy and morbid. 'What's it all about, love' he suddenly asked. 'Where are we all running to?'

'Marshall likes you,' Carey remarked. 'Put on Aretha Franklin.'

He changed tapes to Carey's request. He felt a very strong urge to make love to her. She was lying back in a chair, her eyes closed.

'Didn't you ever want to be an actress?' he asked. 'Most beautiful women, especially in this town, see it as their life's ambition.'

She shook her head. 'Hell, no. Who needs that shit? I could never have handled myself like Sunday. She really knows where it's at, or at least I thought she did until Claude.'

'What's she like?' he asked, with only vague interest. After all, he was thinking, Marshall isn't *that* close a friend, and if we had a scene who would know?

'Sunday is a marvellous girl. Very young in some ways, yet old in others. Sometimes she—*Charlie, what are you doing*?'

He had approached her from behind and now he bent over, plunging his hands inside the neckline of her dress. She was wearing no bra and he was able to pop her small bosom out of the material before she could object.

She stood up quickly. 'You bastard! I'm not some little Holly-wood hooker, you know. How dare you!'

He hadn't expected such a reaction. Being a movie star meant that most ladies were ready and willing.

'Sorry,' he mumbled sheepishly, and moved quickly away from her. 'I, er, just thought . . .'

'Well, think again.' Her anger was caused by the fact that she fancied him and was furious with herself. She had made up her mind that when she married Marshall, she would be faithful; there would be no screwing around on the side as was the case with *all* the unhappy married couples she knew.

He buried his head in his hands. 'I have always found,' he said sadly, 'that the women I want in life are usually the ones I can't have. I want a woman I can come home to and say "Fuck you", and she just says "Yes, darling, that's right, let's go to bed". Sometimes I think it's better to go with a hooker, at least you know where you are. All they want from you is your money.'

Adjusting her dress, Carey listened quietly. 'You're wrong, Charlie,' she said. 'There are plenty of girls who don't just like you for who you are. You're a very attractive man.'

'Do you mean that?' His face brightened.

'Yes, I mean it. The trouble with you is you mix with the wrong people. I bet all your friends are show biz. That way you only meet people looking to be with a star. What about you and Phillipa?'

'Platonic. Purely friendship. She's a nice girl, but very young.'

Carey kissed him on the cheek. 'I'm going to bed.'

He held her lightly around the waist. 'No hard feelings?'

'It's forgotten. Let's be friends, Charlie.'

'All right, love, I'd like that, I really would.'

46

It bothered Sunday that Carey didn't approve of Claude. She knew that he wasn't the most likeable of people at first acquaintance, but she was sure that if they met socially, the atmosphere between them would become less strained.

Of Carey, Claude said, 'She's just mad because she won't be making much commission out of you. Only *you* would have the only black agent in town. She starts off with a chip on her shoulder.'

'Carey doesn't care about the money,' Sunday defended. 'She's honestly not sure the part is for me.'

It was the weekend, and they were lying on Sunday's patio. She had finally succeeded in getting him to come to her house, and he seemed to be enjoying himself lazing around and doing nothing. At first Jean-Pierre had been shy with him. Now he had gone off to swim with Katia.

'The boy likes you,' Claude remarked, 'better than his mother.'

Sunday wanted to ask, 'Was it true she was here with you?' But instead she bit her lip, and said, 'Don't you think he should go back with you? The Nanny is very good, she'll stay.'

'Fed up with him?' he chided.

'Don't be silly, of course not. I would love him to stay here; I was just thinking of you.'

'Think of the boy, he's happier with you.'

'What about the Palm Springs location? Shall he come with me or you?'

'We'll leave him here with the Nanny. You are going to be working, creating a character. I don't want you to have a child hanging around. It's not going to be another easy piece of shit with the crew admiring you and you just showing your tits and looking beautiful. By the way, we'll live at the house'.

'What house?'

'The house in Palm Springs I'm shooting the film in,' he yawned. 'It will be good for you, you'll see.'

Later she reflected on their conversation. She wasn't sure how she felt any more. Did she love him, or was it just a very physical attraction? He was spoilt, arrogant, rude, a bastard. How could she love a man like that?

She resigned herself to the fact that their relationship was transient and would probably only last as long as the movie.

I'm getting hard, she thought, I'm thinking only of what's good for me. In a way I'm using Claude, but then he's using me, so I suppose that makes us even.

The weather in Palm Springs was unbearably hot. The idea that Claude had of living and shooting in the same house was bizarre.

The house, surrounded on all sides by acres of desert, was nice enough. It had a swimming pool, tennis court, sauna, billiard room, all the usual extras that Los Angeles executives expected in their cosy desert retreats. However, Sunday found that Claude wanted them to sleep in the actual bedroom in which he was filming. It was horrible to sleep in a bed with a camera looming across the room, arc lights, cables, sound equipment everywhere.

'I can't stand this,' she announced the first night. 'We have no privacy: It's like being in a shop window.'

He stared at her. 'You want to be an actress for once, try and live the part without bitching.'

He was tough to work with, demanding, critical, rude.

Every detail had to be just so, every take perfect.

There were only three other actors on the location—the man who was playing her husband, and the two young men who broke into the house and raped her.

Claude's eye for casting was uncanny. The three men fitted their roles perfectly. The husband was pot bellied, weak and greedy-eyed. The first boy, thin blond, Southern, with a slow evil smile, had green eyes. The second boy, the actor Claude had gone after in Rio, was dark, about twenty. He had long-lashed black eyes, a panther-like walk, and was intent, beautiful. His name was Carlos Lo.

Claude allowed Sunday no contact with them except when they were doing a scene together.

It was a clever move that worked beautifully.

The four actors became the characters in the film, and Claude merely manipulated them as he wanted.

47

Herbert read that Sunday Simmons was going to Palm Springs. Maybe he would follow her. Marge could be fobbed off with the excuse that the Allens were going, she was under the misguided impression that he still worked for them.

Perhaps this would be the answer to all his problems. He would find an opportunity to present himself to Sunday, who, with her money and influence, would be able to help him, perhaps take him to Europe, far away from Marge and her accusations.

The idea appealed to him.

That evening he trailed Sunday to Malibu. To his disgust she had a guest. Sitting in his parked car, he watched with annoyance as a long black Cadillac pulled up at her house and a man emerged. This meant she would not be going to bed early as she usually did, and he would have to wait for the man to leave before he could crawl along the side of the house and watch her while she slept.

He settled back in the driving seat, aware, with a slight sniff of distaste, that he needed a shower. It would have been good to have gone home earlier and taken one, but he was avoiding Marge as much as possible now that he was expected to perform disgusting sexual acts as soon as he entered the house.

The blowsy hag had become insatiable. Bile entered his throat at the very thought of her.

'I've gotta talk t'ya, Herbie,' she had whined that very morning. 'Try and get home early.'

He was no fool. He knew why she wanted him home early.

He must have dozed, for when he looked at his watch it was one o'clock, and the Cadillac was still there, although the house was now in darkness.

His body was stiff and cramped. He slid out of the car and edged towards the house. It was silent. He crawled along the side, and crouched in his usual position at Sunday's window.

She was asleep, lying on her back, naked. Beside her, one dark hairy arm thrown casually across her belly, was a man.

Herbert's first reaction was pain—a pain so deep that he was forced to belch to get rid of it. He didn't move, he just stared, his eyes taking in the contours of her rounded perfect breasts, her long tanned legs, and the thin white space where her bikini had covered her.

The pain convulsed him and he stayed very still and quiet until it gradually subsided and turned into a deep vicious hate.

Bitch! Why hadn't she waited for him?

How he would love to see her face if he confronted her now. She would squirm, apologize, beg his forgiveness. It would all be too late.

He was suddenly seized with a great excitement, a feeling too difficult to hold back. With a convulsive jerk he relieved himself in his trousers. Then stealthily, silently, he crawled away, back to his car, back to Marge.

Marge was propped in bed watching the late movie and determinedly eating her way through four Hershey bars, a giant-size bag of popcorn, three packets of nuts, and two bananas.

She needed it all. It presented some sort of defence against the barrage of fury that would come from Herbert when she told him that Louella knew everything.

She couldn't postpone telling him any longer. Although she

had given Louella the thousand dollars, Louella was pressing for the rest.

Eventually she fell asleep, the television still on, a half-peeled orange in her hand, the juice oozing slowly on to the bedspread.

Herbert, arriving home much later, was annoyed to see the lights still on. He had wanted to creep in unseen, dispose of his ruined trousers, and take a good hot shower. Now Marge would start fussing and grabbing him.

He was pleased to see she was asleep, and he crept about stealthily, hoping not to wake her.

It was very hard for him to believe that he had seen Sunday Simmons lying in the arms of another man. He knew that occasionally women—even respectable women—needed sex. But Sunday surely needed nothing more than the letters he had been sending her. *She should have been prepared to wait.* He had told her quite clearly that they would eventually be together. She deserved to be punished.

As soon as he switched off the television Marge awoke. Her mouth and eyes clogged with sleep, she immediately started to tell him the truth.

'Herbie, I done a stupid thing, well, aw, it really ain't all that stupid, I mean it was you that was stupid in the first place. Y'see . . .'

He listened in grim silence, his anger only slightly abated by the fact that at least he would no longer have to have sex with her, that he was once more in charge of the marriage. *She* was as frightened of Louella as *he* should have been. But he would find a way to deal with the blackmailing bitch next door.

Marge was blubbering and crying. He asked her very coldly, very matter-of-factly, who were all the men with whom she had been fornicating next door. She told him, between sobs, about Louella's circle of friends.

He started to hit her, heavy, hate-filled slaps across her face and body.

She cowed under him, frightened to scream, and he continued to beat her until he felt better. Then he sat on the end of the bed and inspected his hands, thin white hands with carefully clipped nails.

Slowly ideas were forming in his head. Ideas that would take care of everyone. He could punish Sunday and at the same time pay Louella the two thousand dollars, get her off his back.

It was a bizarre idea, but one that could quite possibly work.

48

Inactivity did not agree with Charlie. He became uneasy and unsure. He needed the reassuring eye of the camera on him.

As far as he was concerned the doctors were full of crap, and after two tedious weeks of Palm Springs sunshine, he phoned Marshall to tell him so.

Marshall was unsympathetic. 'You're supposed to rest,' he reminded him. 'Anyhow, there's nothing for you to do now.'

'I'll do a guest appearance,' Charlie insisted. 'A few days on something for a gag. How about a TV Special?'

Marshall was quiet for a moment. 'You wouldn't enjoy it.'

'For Christ's sake, love, there must be *something*.'

It had taken Phillipa two days to return after walking out of the dinner. She waited until the house guests left and then she came back.

'Where were you?' Charlie stormed.

She looked dirty and unkempt. 'I stayed with some friends. We tripped out for two days non-stop, it was a beautiful experience. I got you some great hash.'

Her eyes were wide and starey and he knew she had been tripping on acid. He didn't approve. Smoking pot was one thing, but anything else was playing with fire.

'I've made a very interesting discovery,' she said. 'If I mix pot and speed I think I can make it.'

'Make what?' he asked sharply.

'Fuck, of course. Have sex. You know what I mean—the thing you had that great fucking beanpole down here for.'

'I think it's time you went back to Mother. If you think I'm flattered by you telling me that you can only make it with me by being stoned out of your head, then think again.'

'Well, you were so bloody desperate to get laid, and that horrible friend of yours, Clay what's-it, and that Carey woman, I *hate* your friends, they're all phoney shit!'

'And so are you, Phillipa, sweetheart, so are you. In·fact, you're a lot phonier than they are because you pretend to be something you're absolutely not. You're really screwed-up, you know that, don't you?'

'You *old* man,' she jeered. 'You *stupid old man*. How about you, then? Dieting, and growing your hair, wearing freaky clothes, and *only* being accepted because you're a movie star. People laugh at you. You're ridiculous, so think about *that*.'

The call to Marshall was desperate. Being alone in the Palm Springs house was murder. If Marshall didn't come up with something within the next few days, he thought seriously of going home to London.

It saddened him that every time a relationship ended he seemed to get snowed under with abuse. Even Phillipa had thrown in the crack about him only being accepted because he was Charlie Brick, film star. He had somehow never thought she regarded him in that way.

Dozy starlets or otherwise, they were all sisters under the skin, and it was a hell of a lot more fun with the starlets as far as sex was concerned.

Carey was in town and Charlie took her out to dinner.

She was seething. 'That French superstar sonofabitch director is going to ruin Sunday's career. He has her locked up in that house, and won't even let me *talk* to her for more than ten minutes. He thinks he's God.'

'Carey, love, you've got to speak to Marsh, I'm going spare down here. I've worked all my life and this doing nothing bores the shit out of me. I'm fit as a fiddle. Tell him to fix up *something* for me.'

'But the doctors said you were to rest.'

'Fuck the bloody doctors, love, I *have* to work.'

'I'll talk to Marshall. I know he thinks you should take it easy

236

for now: After all, you have two movies to do at the end of the year. Now you *are* coming to our wedding?'

'Wouldn't miss it. Hey, love, I've got a *marvellous* idea. How many people are you inviting?'

'Fifty. We're going to insult most of Hollywood, but I just can't stand a gang war. It's strictly family and close friends.'

'Why not have it here?'

'Where?'

'In my house here. In this highly expensive rented shack. The garden would be marvellous. We'll hire a preacher. Bring everyone in on a special plane. It's a *great* idea. My wedding present to you and Marsh.'

She laughed. 'It's a wild idea. Why not? We haven't arranged anything.' She leaned forward and kissed him on the cheek. 'I think it will be wonderful. Can we get it all together by Saturday?'

'Leave it to me, it will give me something to do.'

Charlie wanted the wedding to be special. He had known Marshall for years and was very fond of him—and he liked Carey a lot.

He hired a secretary called Maggi to handle all the details, and issued instructions about what he wanted. She was a pugfaced redhead, covered in freckles. She stayed, keeping him company. She was a good listener and didn't talk too much. Charlie had decided conversations were *out*.

49

'Take these pills.'

'I've told you I don't take pills. They make me sick, and anyhow I don't *need* sleeping pills.'

Sunday was lying in bed with Claude, the camera looming

over them like a third person. It was three in the morning and she was tired enough to close her eyes and fall into a deep sleep.

Claude had been in a strange mood all evening, talking to her about the film, the characters, what it all meant. Then at one o'clock he had wanted to make love, and she had never known him better, so controlled, so commanding. He kept on bringing them both to the brink, and then stopping, lighting a cigarette or prowling round the room for a few moments. Finally it was breathtaking. Now she felt very relaxed, and he was nagging her to take sleeping pills.

'I want you to take them,' he insisted. 'There is a very important reason.'

'What reason?'

'Look, I have told you if you work well tomorrow morning, you can go to your friend's wedding. O.K. I do something for you—you do something for me. Now take them, and stop arguing like a baby.' He thrust the two turquoise capsules at her.

'No, Claude, I will not take pills. That's it. Besides, if we're to start shooting at seven I'll still be asleep.'

He sighed. 'Clever girl, *half* asleep, that's how I want you, half asleep and groggy. I was going to surprise you, but since you're being difficult . . . We are shooting the rape scene tomorrow, first thing. I don't want you to get out of bed.'

'Oh, come on!' She didn't believe him. 'With unwashed face and dirty teeth?'

'How the hell do you think Stefanie *was* when the boys broke in? She was in bed, wasn't she? Asleep, wasn't she? And she took sleeping pills, didn't she? And that, my dear, is how we are going to shoot it. If you want to be an actress, then do it my way.'

Reluctantly she swallowed the pills and closed her eyes. There was no dialogue to the scene, just a lot of struggling. She wondered vaguely how Claude would shoot it. Close-ups, that would be his way, close-ups of her face, that's why he wanted her to look real.

She fell asleep unworried. He was a brilliant director. She trusted him.

The first sensation was one of the covers being pulled off, and then weight, something heavy crawling on top of her.

She tried to move. Then tearing, her nightdress coming off.

She tried to open her eyes, but her eyelids felt stuck together. Hands were covering her breasts, clumsy hands, rough hands. She heard a loud whirring noise, the camera. Where was Claude?

She managed to open her eyes but the blinding lights forced her to shut them quickly. She said, 'Get *off* me,' and in a haze opened her eyes again and stared bewildered at Carlos Lo's face. He sat astride her, his hands on her bosom, his breath coming in short excited gasps.

Beside him the other actor crouched over her, laughing softly.

'What is this?' she protested. She felt weak, without strength, half asleep.

'Oh, the bastard,' she muttered, 'the lousy bastard. He's shooting this for real. He's actually going to let these two punks rape me.'

She started to struggle but there was no strength to her movements.

One of the actors pinned her arms down, while the other forced her legs apart, and at the moment of entry Claude was above her with a hand-held camera, the lens as close to her face as was possible.

'You bastards!' she screamed weakly.

Then it was the thin one's turn, evil green eyes smiling at her. She lay back. There was no point in struggling. She was no match for two of them.

He licked her face while he did it. Then he climbed off and the camera wandered over her like another lover.

She lay very still, very quiet, spreadeagled on the bed, the way they had left her.

'I'll never forgive you for this, Claude,' she said, '*never*.'

'Maybe when you read your glowing notices you might.' He casually put his camera down and she noticed that the big camera was still going. The two actors had left.

'By the way,' Claude said, 'I want you to meet my wife.'

A woman stepped out from behind the big camera, a thin pale blonde in her early thirties. She smiled good-naturedly.

'Don't worry about this, dear. It is Claude's way. The end-result is all that matters, I'm sure you agree.'

Sunday sat up, hugging her knees to her, rocking back and forth in disbelief.

'We always knew you were right for Stefanie. You have a beautiful body. Claude is a very lucky man to have had the pleasure of that. But now, alas, things are different. I am sure you understand. Perhaps while we finish the film we can come to some new arrangement. Three can be—how you say?—très compatible. I am sure I would be able to show you a few things that even Claude couldn't manage.'

'You don't honestly think I'm going to stay and *finish* this film?' Sunday asked, trying to control her voice.

'You would be a very silly girl if you didn't. You would have nothing to gain and everything to lose.'

She laughed incredulously. The whole thing was like a bad dream, and she still felt groggy and half asleep, too tired to argue.

'You really have no choice *but* to finish the film,' Claude's wife continued. 'Firstly, we have a contract. Secondly, if you refuse, the film that we just shot will be used—you know what I mean—not in connection with this production, just Sunday Simmons off the set. That sort of thing has a big market.'

Sunday stared at Claude. 'Why?' she cried.

His wife replied for him. 'Because Claude is an artist, a genius, everything must be perfect. In the stuff he shot this morning he will just use your eyes, your face. It will be perfect. You will be acclaimed as a great actress. You wait, my dear, when this film comes out you will be *thanking* us.'

Shakily she got out of bed. She felt dirty and used. She just wanted to get away from these two sick people. She just wanted to get out of the house.

She pulled on jeans and a sweater.

'Where are you going?' Claude asked, as she walked unsteadily to the door.

'A wedding.'

'Fine. But we work tomorrow as usual. I'm sure when you think about it, you'll see how right everything is.'

She picked up her big bag and left without another word.

Fortunately her car was outside. She leaned her head on the steering-wheel and tried to think where to go. It was too far to attempt to drive to Los Angeles, at least in the state she was in. Yet she had nowhere else to go. It was seven o'clock in the morning. A hotel?

Suddenly she thought of Charlie Brick. He had a house. Carey was getting married there that afternoon. She fished in her bag and found the address, then drove to the nearest filling station and asked directions.

50

Charlie always woke up early. He liked to swim before it got too hot. This morning in particular he was anxious to check everything out, to inspect the patio and the archway of flowers specially erected for the wedding, to test out the platform where the couple would stand to be married.

Long white trestle-tables stood ready to be laden with food. Striped awnings, hung with flowers, protected them from the sun.

He put his two movie cameras, the Japanese Argus and the Bolex, carefully on a special table. Next to them went the stills cameras, the Leica, Rolleiflex, and Pentax, and a neat pile of film.

Carey was arriving at eleven, the caterers at twelve, the preacher at one, the guests at two.

The wedding was planned to take place at two-thirty. There was plenty of time.

He glanced at his watch, it was just past seven. There was not much left for him to do. He had decided what to wear. Perhaps he should give old Marsh a call, wake him up and tell him to come over for coffee. Marshall was staying with friends nearby.

Then he heard a car arriving, and he strolled out to the

driveway to see who it was. The car screeched to a halt and Sunday Simmons jumped out.

At first he didn't recognize her. Her hair was uncombed, wild, and there were deep shadows under her eyes. Then he looked at the rest of her and remembered. There was no one else built like that!

'You're a bit early, love,' he said, and then noticing how her eyes couldn't quite focus, he quickly went over to her and took her arm. 'Hey, what's the matter?'

She leaned on him, not quite sure how she had ever found the house, feeling sick and tired. 'I think I'm going to throw up,' she muttered. He got her inside and over the downstairs toilet. He held her while she vomited.

What was it all about? Was she a drinker? Had she been on a bad drug trip?

She was wearing nothing under the thin sweater. She had probably had a bad scene with her boyfriend. But why come to him?

When he could see she was all right, he left her alone, went into the kitchen and told the maid to make tea and toast. He drank a big glass of apple juice, and took two spoonfuls of wheat germ and honey. He was on a health kick.

She didn't emerge for twenty minutes. She had washed her face and brushed her hair back.

He took her hand, led her into the breakfast-room and made her drink the hot sweet tea waiting there.

Neither of them spoke.

She leaned back in the chair and stared out of the glass doors at the wedding preparations.

He thought he had never seen a woman quite so beautiful.

'This is the best cup of tea I've had since I was in London,' she said at last. 'Can I have some more please?'

He poured her another cup. 'I always bring me own tea,' he replied in a funny Cockney accent. 'These bleeding Yanks got no idea when it comes to tea.'

She smiled softly.

The 'phone rang and she signalled wildly that she was not there.

It was Marshall. Charlie kept the conversation short and told him he would call back later. He turned to Sunday and said, 'Don't you think I should know what's going on?'

She nodded. 'I suppose you should, since I came and dumped myself on your doorstep. It's a long story and I feel pretty awful. What I'd really like to do is have a bath and a sleep. I came here because I didn't want to miss Carey's wedding. I don't want her to know about any of this, I don't want to spoil her day. You see, she was right all along, she warned me that . . .'

She stopped abruptly as Maggi came bouncing in, clad in a short towelling beach jacket, her red hair in bunches. 'Ooops, sorry, am I interrupting something?' said Maggi brightly. 'I thought I'd get up early and help.'

'That's all right, love.' Charlie was secretly choked. Maggi had never risen before ten yet. She was just bloody nosey.

'Maggi, this is Sunday Simmons.'

'Hello,' Maggi said, and sat down, grabbing a piece of toast.

'I expect your room's ready now,' Charlie said to Sunday. 'Y'know, love, it's really a nice surprise you were able to get here so early. Come on, I'll show you the way.' He led her upstairs. 'Take no notice of Maggi,' he said, 'she's an idiot. Have you got anything to wear for the wedding?'

Sunday shook her head. 'I don't even have shoes.'

'If you write down your sizes I'll send someone to Saks for an outfit.' He took her into a guest suite overlooking the garden.

'You've been really kind,' she said. 'I'll explain it all to you later, but please, promise me, don't tell Carey.'

'I've got nothing to tell her, have I? She'll be here at eleven, but I'll put her in the other side of the house, and if you stay here, I'll come for you before the wedding. O.K.?'

'Fine. Thanks again, Charlie. I just don't know how to thank you.'

I do—he thought—I know the ideal way. Bye, bye, Maggi, it was short and sweet.

Carey had a mild case of panic coupled with a bad attack of nerves. She arrived accompanied by her sister, a fat girl dressed entirely in pink. What a mistake to have brought Mary Jane before the others. She didn't understand, or even approve of the whole scene. To marry an older man was bad enough, but

243

a white one was worse. Carey's whole family presented a united front of ill-concealed disapproval.

She cornered Charlie, 'Listen, it's not that I usually turn on before lunch, but if you don't want a collapsed bride on your hands, please—just a little smoke.'

He grinned. 'What a marvellous idea, love, come along to my bedroom.'

'Let me just get rid of my sister and I'll be there.'

They sat on his bed, giggling a bit, and Carey said, 'Isn't this silly? Why should I be afraid of getting married?'

Charlie agreed, dragging on the joint and passing it to her.

When they came out Maggi was hovering. 'What have you two been up to?' she accused.

'Nothing that would interest you, my love,' Charlie replied, deciding that one couldn't make a bloody move in his own house without Maggi poking her nose in. He was half tempted to tell Carey about Sunday. After all, Carey was his friend, and surely his loyalties lay with her? But there was something about Sunday that inspired his confidence and he knew he wouldn't give her away.

The wedding went off beautifully. Carey made a stunning bride in a short gold brocade dress with flowers in her hair. Marshall was nervous and flustered. The place was thick with relatives from both sides, and although black and white made no difference to Carey and Marshall, both sets of relatives bristled with prejudice and resentment.

The ceremony itself was short and simple, and then there was champagne, a cold buffet, and a huge wedding cake inscribed '100 per cent at last!'

Charlie tried to keep an eye on Sunday, but shortly after Carey and Marshall departed for their honeymoon and the guests started to thin out, he couldn't find her. She had taken her car and gone.

51

Sunday hoped that no-one noticed her departure as she slipped out just before Carey and Marshall. She felt badly about Charlie Brick. He had been extremely understanding and kind, and maybe she owed him an explanation, but why involve him in her life? She had a decision to make, and only she could make it.

She was filled with anger, and disgusted with herself for being such a fool. Hadn't she learnt *anything* about men? She should have seen Claude Hussan for what he was at the very beginning. What kind of a man was it who broke into a hotel room and made love to a woman by way of introduction? And what kind of a woman was it who responded to an introduction of that sort?

'A frustrated one,' she muttered. 'And he knew it and just walked right in.'

She drove the car hard and fast, heading for Los Angeles and sanity.

Did Claude and his wife *really* think she would accept what had happened and continue with the film?

She wished she could have told Carey, but Carey had gone to Hawaii for a week, and she didn't want to spoil her honeymoon. Knowing Carey, she would have cancelled her trip and stayed to sort things out.

Actually there was nothing to sort out. Whatever happened, whatever harm it did her, Sunday had made up her mind not to finish the film.

Claude would lose too. He had gambled on the fact that her career meant more to her than her pride. She was an actress after all, and actresses *always* put their careers before all else, didn't they? Through all the hurt there was at least a slight sense of satisfaction that she could hurt him too. Her decision was to go home and wait. Claude had to make the first move. *He* was the one who had created the situation.

Of course there was the boy, Jean-Pierre. Still at her house.

She was quite willing to keep him, indeed she would do anything rather than give him back to Claude and his wife.

She entered the city on Sunset tired and hungry. She pulled the car into a drive-in and ordered a tuna sandwich and a glass of milk.

'Hey, Sunny, I can't believe it!' It was Branch Strong. He looked suntanned and brawny in T-shirt and jeans and was carrying four large milk-shake cartons balanced on top of one another. 'I thought you were still in the Springs. When did you get back? Why didn't you call?'

'I just got back. I'm on my way home now.'

'You drove? Alone? If you had asked I'd have come and fetched you.'

She smiled. 'Where are you going with all those milk shakes?'

He looked embarrassed. 'Well—er, these are for Max. He's got a craving for them right now, he's like an old lady. Hey, why don't you come back and see him. He'd like that.'

Branch knew perfectly well that Max would hate it, as at that very moment he was probably preparing himself for Branch's return by draping his naked body on the new fur bedspread he had bought. Max liked milk shakes followed by sex, and he didn't like varying the routine.

'I'm just grabbing a sandwich, then it's straight home. I'm really exhausted.'

Branch shrugged, disappointed yet relieved. 'Listen, I want to ask you to do me a *real* big favour. There's a première of "The Twelve Guns" tomorrow night. I only have a small part—but important—like it could mean a lot for me. It's a big première—everyone's going to be there—will you be my date?'

'I just got back—I don't know—I hate premières—I don't think so.'

His face fell. 'Hey, Sunday—like please. I need you there. It would be so good for me to walk in with you. In fact I told the studio you were my date. They gave me great seats.'

'How could you do that? You didn't even know I'd be here.'

He looked sheepish. 'I know. I figured I'd say you couldn't get away at the last minute. It was really kind of a stupid thing for me to do. Your name is advertised with the list of stars that are going. How about it? A helping hand, huh?'

'Oh, all right.' Let Claude see that she didn't give a damn. They made arrangements and parted.

Branch was elated. He ran whistling into Max Thorpe's house. Max, as expected, was reclining nude on the fur bedspread.

'Bad news,' Branch mumbled, placing the milk shakes carefully on a bedside table. 'I just ran into Sunday and she came back specially to go to the première with me. She saw all the ads and figured she should be here.'

'What?' Max said, going red in the face. 'But what about me? You promised the ticket was for *me*.'

'Yeah, I know that. But I had to tell the Studio I was taking a girl, and it was *your* idea I said Sunday as she was away. Well, now she's back.' Trying to hide a smirk, Branch unzipped his trousers and pulled off his T-shirt before joining Max on the fur bedspread.

Max waved him peevishly away. 'I don't want you tonight,' he said in a petulant voice. 'What about my violet dinner jacket? Brand new and wasted.'

Branch shrugged, quickly getting up and pulling on his clothes. 'Sorry, it's not my fault.' He was fed up with Max, bored with the whole faggoty scene.

He liked girls. How much longer before he could tell Max Thorpe to get stuffed?

Sunday was surprised, there were lights and music coming from her house. She glanced at her watch; it was nearly eleven. What was Katia up to? She had been hired because she seemed quiet and responsible.

She walked into her house, into a sea of strange faces, most of them Mexican, dancing to a James Brown record, colourfully dressed and noisy.

In the midst of the crowd she saw Katia pressed up against the wall by a young man, her face soft and smiling. She was wearing a blue dress that belonged to Sunday, and nearby, curled up in a corner, his knees tucked under his chin, was Jean-Pierre, his big eyes gravely watching.

'Hey, baby, who are you?' A boy grabbed Sunday's arm. 'Where did *you* spring from?'

Angrily, she snatched her arm away.

A perfect ending to the day!

She strode over, picked up Jean-Pierre, and turned on Katia. The girl's eyes had become big and frightened and she was stammering something about it being her birthday.

'Get everyone out of here right now,' Sunday said, and carrying Jean-Pierre, she marched into her bedroom.

All her clothes were spread out across the bed. A spilled bottle of perfume dripped from the bedside table.

'Are you all right?' she hugged the little boy.

He nodded shyly, burying his head on her shoulder.

She moved the clothes off the bed and put Jean-Pierre beneath the covers.

There were sounds of doors slamming and cars starting up.

Sunday brushed her hair back wearily and sighed. Would this day never end?

52

Herbert Lincoln Jefferson confronted Louella Crisp the day after Marge had told him about the deal—and the money Louella had to have. They had never met, although of course he had seen her through the window when he was spying on Marge. She had stringy breasts and short veined legs and rolls of fat around the belly of her otherwise skinny body.

He prepared himself carefully, showering, shaving, combing his straight dark-brown hair for a long time. He cleaned his fingernails, and had Marge polish his shoes, a job she had given up because of her recent triumphs. He wore a grey suit recently returned from the cleaners, and a sickly yellow sports shirt with a green wool tie.

He considered he looked immaculate, and admired himself for quite some time in the bathroom mirror.

Louella Crisp would soon see she was dealing with a man of substance, not a pathetic fool like Marge.

Louella in fact took one look at Herbert and decided that here was a mean sonofabitch. She didn't want to mess with him: She wanted to grab the money and run. Maybe she might even forget about the money. He had such evil little eyes, cold, empty and spiteful.

He sat down in her living-room and stared at her. 'I'm not Marge, you know,' he said at last. 'You've been taking advantage of Marge. I know what's been going on. I've seen the things you do in this house.'

'Never mind what you've seen,' Louella said quickly, making up her mind that she *would* get the two thousand dollars out of him. 'What about the things *I* know. Personal things about you, things my friends in the police department would be interested to hear about?'

His eyes stared at her, flat and expressionless. 'You're not talking to Marge. I'm not a fool. The money's for *you*. Two thousand dollars, and that's the end of the matter. I can get it for you, but I'll need your help.'

'In what way?' she asked suspiciously.

'In a way you'll like. In the way you make your money now.'

'What are you talking about?'

He reached into his jacket pocket and produced two glossy photos of Sunday Simmons which he had stolen from her house. Across one he had scrawled, 'Any time you call—Love, Sunday.'

He handed the pictures to Louella, who looked at them blankly. 'Who's this?'

'A friend of mine,' he said briskly. 'A very *close* friend of mine. In fact, we're so close that she'd do anything for me.' He paused meaningfully. 'Anything.'

53

When the last guests departed Charlie felt depressed. He had sent Maggi packing during the afternoon. She had started to say things like, 'All my friends say I should be an actress, what do you think?'

'I think you'd better go home,' he had replied.

Now he was alone again and miserable. So miserable in fact that on impulse he climbed into his new black Ferrari and started to drive to Los Angeles. He felt in need of company, a change of locale. He planned to check into the Beverly Hills Hotel and telephone Clay.

It was two in the morning when he arrived, and he thought better of disturbing Natalie. He called Thames Mason because he was lonely.

She dutifully got out of bed, came over, got into bed and consoled him. She told him all about her scene with Clay, laughing all the way. Then she finished by saying, 'Man, is that guy hung!'

Charlie immediately felt inadequate and sent her home, but not before she made him promise he would take her to the première of 'The Twelve Guns' the following night.

He wondered if she discussed what *he* was like in bed, and decided to ask Clay.

He slept fitfully and had a weird sexual dream involving himself, Natalie, Thames, Sunday, and his mother. He awoke feeling lousy, and went down to the pool.

It was too early for anyone else to be there, and he swam undisturbed. He had made up his mind to go back to London. There was no point in hanging around, going mad doing nothing. He decided to return and build a house, put down roots somewhere. It would keep him busy, and when the house was finished he would tell Lorna that he wanted the children every weekend. They would love it. He would even let them design their own quarters.

He phoned Clay, who was happy to come over for breakfast. On impulse he told him about Sunday.

Clay said, 'Well, I reckon she fancies you, and when you've finished I wouldn't say no to that one.'

'If she fancied me she'd have hung around, wouldn't she?'

'Women are funny creatures. She probably thought *you* didn't fancy *her*.'

Charlie shook his head. 'Your logic! How's Natalie feeling?'

'Fat. She'd love to see you. Why don't you have dinner with us tonight?'

'Can't. Taking Thames Mason to a première.'

Clay whistled. 'Now *there's* a raver!'

'Yes, you're telling me.'

'I didn't know you'd been there.'

'You don't know everywhere I've been.'

Later he dressed for the première in a new Doug Hayward dinner suit. He inspected himself in the mirror and was forced to admit that the rest had done him good. He was thin, in great shape, with a nice dark tan. He had abandoned the John Lennon specs and was back in his horn-rims. His black hair was just long enough to curl slightly over the back of his collar.

He drove the Ferrari to Thames's apartment.

She lived in typical Hollywood bachelor-girl style in an apartment building on the Strip. There were photos and stills of herself everywhere.

'I must photograph you,' he said, accepting a Scotch in a green plastic glass with 'I like you' printed on the bottom.

'Oh, I'd love that,' she cooed, 'I'm *very* photogenic. In fact I've been told I have *perfect* features. Maybe we could do a whole bit for one of the fan mags. You know—*you* photographing me and *them* photographing us.'

She looked spectacular in thigh-high silver boots and a silver body stocking with intriguing patches of material missing.

'I'll probably be going to London this week,' he confided.

She was not the least bit interested. 'Do you think my eyelashes look too thick?' she asked anxiously.

He peered at her. It was difficult to tell; her eyes were surrounded with silver shadow. 'I don't know, love, I'm not much good at make-up, but you look great.'

'Do I?' She twirled around in front of him. 'It should be a

fantastic première, *everyone* will be there, and everyone will notice me with you.'

He could hardly see how they could miss her, with him or not. A six-foot-two-inch redhead who looked like Thames Mason was hardly an everyday occurrence.

'Would it matter if I wasn't Charlie Brick? If I was just Joe Nobody, would you still want to go with me?'

She frowned. 'Who's Joe Nobody? I've never heard of him . . . Oh, I see,' she giggled, 'Trying to put me on, huh?'

'Come on, we'll be late.'

Outside her apartment, Thames surveyed the Ferrari with a slight sneer.

'Don't you have a Rolls and driver?' she asked in surprise.

Charlie was beginning to count to ten under his breath. Would he *never* learn? This was positively the last starlet.

54

Sunday hated scenes. She hated firing people, but Katia had to go. The next morning she paid her two weeks money in advance and told her to leave.

The girl was sullen about it, but her departure didn't seem to bother Jean-Pierre. He was so delighted to have Sunday back that he never left her side.

They went to the market and stocked up, for Katia had left a refrigerator full of cold chilli beans and rancid hotdogs.

'What have you been eating?' Sunday asked Jean-Pierre. He grinned and sat in the supermarket trolley, picking out blocks of ice-cream, apples, chocolate, cookies, all his favourite things.

Limbo was thin and jumpy. Sunday was furious with herself for having gone to Palm Springs and left them. It was Claude's fault. Everything was Claude's fault.

Branch 'phoned at lunchtime. 'What time shall I pick you up?' he inquired. 'I've got a limo.'

'Oh!' She had forgotten all about the première, and what was she to do with Jean-Pierre now? 'Look, Branch, I don't think I can make it. I had to fire my maid and I've got no sitter for Jean-Pierre.'

'You *have* to make it. You promised. *I'll* find you a sitter, don't worry about it, just make yourself real beautiful and I'll call you back.'

She was stuck. She didn't want to go, but how could she let Branch down?

For the première she decided to wear a filmy chiffon top over harem trousers tucked into satin boots. Her hair was loose, not quite concealing gold gypsy earrings. She looked very beautiful.

Branch was on time, bringing with him Esmé Mae, Max Thorpe's long-time maid. A fat placid lady, she made immediate friends with Jean-Pierre and fussed around Limbo.

Sunday departed quite happy with the arrangement. She left instructions where she would be and emphasised the importance of contacting her immediately if she were needed. In her mind was the vague thought that Claude might arrive to take Jean-Pierre away.

Branch wore a fringed leather white suit, and a big ten-gallon hat. He was laughing and pleased with himself. 'I may only have a small part in this here movie, but I'm sure as hell gonna get me noticed, walkin' in with you.'

She decided Branch was a typical good-looking hunk of Hollywood idiot. Sweet and nice, but dumb.

Suddenly she found herself thinking about Charlie Brick and how different he was. How warm and amusing and—yes attractive, in an off-beat way. She wished that she attracted men like that instead of all the bastards.

'How's Max?' she asked, making conversation.

'He's fine,' Branch replied with false enthusiasm. Max wasn't fine at all. He had been in a bitchy fury since Branch had told him that he couldn't take him to the première, and today they hadn't spoken at all.

Sunday sighed and leaned back in the limousine.

She wished that the evening were over.

55

Planning the operation had not been easy, and until Herbert read in the newspaper that Sunday Simmons was attending the première of 'The Twelve Guns', he had been uncertain how to achieve his purpose. When he read that she was to be there, everything fell into place, and he picked that night as *the* night.

His only worry was that she might not return from Palm Springs, but the newspapers said she would be at the première, so he just had to take a chance.

Louella had been getting impatient and making cracks, but she seemed satisfied when he gave her the date and told her to go ahead with arrangements.

Marge was sulking. Nobody would tell her what was going on. Louella simply stopped contacting her, and Herbert was rude and bad-tempered. What really upset Marge was the fact that Louella and Herbert kept meeting. She found her only solace in the local supermarket, and successfully gained ten pounds. Fortunately they gave credit.

Herbert got up early on the day of the première. There was much to do. The previous evening he had spent parked outside Sunday Simmons's house at the beach, and had been rewarded by her return home quite late in the evening.

He was delighted when all the people in the house left shortly afterwards. Her Mexican maid was a little bitch. He had telephoned several times during Sunday's absence, and when he gave her the pleasure of a few poetic utterances, she had hurled a stream of foreign abuse at him and hung up.

Marge said, 'You wanna have breakfast?'

He cast her a look of contempt, 'No.' Did the fat cow not realise that this was the last morning they would ever spend together? Of course she didn't! In fact, not even Louella knew of his plans for Marge.

He showered and put on a clean shirt and trousers. Then he went next door to see Louella.

'Is everything prepared?' he asked.

'Yes. Are you *sure* she'll do it?'

'You keep on asking me that,' He replied in an irritable voice. 'She *said* she'll do it. We have a *very special* friendship. I told you she will do anything for me.'

'Why doesn't she just give you the money, then? Why's she going to go through this?'

'Because she wants to,' He replied patiently. 'How many men will there be?'

'Fourteen guys at a hundred and fifty bucks apiece. They're all lined up hot and ready, so don't think you can pull a fake on us. They're going for a lot of money, so you had better produce the genuine goods.'

'She'll be here. Nine o'clock, I'll bring her in. She doesn't want conversation or anything like that, just a normal circle-of-friends evening, everything the same as usual. The men will take their turns exactly the same as with Marge, and then I'll take her home.'

Louella shook her head. 'I wouldn't have thought a movie star would have wanted to do this sort of thing.'

'Oh, she'll want to do it all right.' He narrowed his cold mean eyes. 'She's very good at it.'

Later that day he dressed in his chauffeur's uniform and went by bus to the car lot, where he had arranged to borrow a black Lincoln Continental. The car was perfect for his purpose, as it had belonged to a pop star and was fitted with black-tinted windows and various locking devices on the doors and windows which insured complete privacy. It had also been tuned to a very high degree and could go extremely fast.

The man at the car lot had advertised the car and was delighted when Herbert appeared and told him he worked for Charlie Brick. He had been happy to make an appointment for Herbert to borrow the car for an evening to get Mr Brick's approval.

Herbert was a convincing liar.

He collected the car and drove to the beach. There, at a deserted spot, he changed the licence plates and worked on the interior speakers for a while. Then he fixed the glass panel which separated the front seat from the back in such a way that it could only be opened from the driver's position. He also altered the interior mechanism so that all doors would lock automatically. Anyone getting into the back seat would be a prisoner, unable to get out until he released them.

Satisfied with his work, he drove to Sunday's house and waited.

Soon she would come out, and he could go in and get what he wanted.

And then the final steps.

56

Two huge revolving searchlights lit up the sky around the Cinerama Dome on Sunset where 'The Twelve Guns' was being premièred.

Police held back the hordes of oohing and aahing fans who spilled across the sidewalk, craning for a glimpse of their favourite stars.

A television unit was set up in the foyer with Jack Julip of the Jack Julip show doing quickie interviews with anyone who mattered.

Anxious cameramen milled around, flashes at the ready to catch the overflowing cleavage and long ripe legs being paraded before them.

Stu Waterman, head publicity man for Now Productions, disappeared into the men's room for the fifth time in twenty minutes to gulp another slug of whiskey from his very useful gold-plated present-to-himself hip-flask.

Things were not working out as planned. Carol Shipman, who had worked ass-naked for ten days on 'The Twelve Guns', had refused to arrive at the première in the buff on a horse—refused because she didn't think it dignified. Dignified indeed, coming from some little English hooker who showed her pussy to anyone who asked!

Stu was incensed. As an alternative, he had had to settle for Cindy Lawrence, a starlet with forty-two-inch boobs who had never appeared in anything.

Cindy wore a long flowing wig that covered nothing, and a lot of poster paint saying 'The Twelve Guns'. Stu helped get her on the horse at the back of the cinema, and she set off round to the front with her escort of five cowboys.

Stu dashed through the cinema, lining up the television cameras and lensmen.

He was just in time to see Cindy arrive. The horse, nervous from the screams of the crowds, immediately bolted, and Cindy fell off, breaking an arm and exposing a lot more than even *she* was supposed to.

Somehow, a blonde with a forty-two-inch bust, sprawled naked in an ungainly position on the sidewalk, did not have the impact that was originally intended.

Carol Shipman arrived in what appeared to be a nun's habit, wearing no makeup and her hair scraped back. Stu had to nudge his own photographer to take her picture. Jack Julip was not even interested.

'I thought I told you to look sexy?' Stu hissed.

She stared at him, not even bothering to reply.

He bit his lip angrily. Where were all the new stars? These little fuckers couldn't even bother to run a comb through their hair.

Angela Carter arrived, all red hair and white furs. The crowd pressed forward, the flashes started, Jack Julip grabbed her anxiously.

Stu sighed with relief and darted off to the back to see what was happening. His assistant—Mike—was helping a round-assed brunette up on to one of the horses.

'Who's that?' Stu hissed.

'I don't know,' Mike replied. 'She's with Brad Lamb and *he* won't get on a horse.'

'Well, get her off. The whole point of this gimmick is to have the *stars* arrive on the horses. I didn't set this up for a load of unknown cooze.'

Mike helped the girl off. She glared at Stu as he took another swig from his flask, and dashed back to the front.

Just then a white Bentley drew up and the chauffeur opened the door to let out Dindi Synde and her escort.

'Hello, Dindi, sweetheart.' Stu wrapped his arm around her. She was wearing little more than a pair of black leather shorts, a gold-studded bra and thigh-length boots. 'I've got a little stunt planned that you'd be just right for.'

'Name it, baby,' she giggled. 'You know I'll do anything.'

'You were right,' Charlie said irritably to Thames, 'I should have had a Rolls and chauffeur tonight.'

They had been stuck ten minutes in a line of traffic approaching the cinema.

Thames was studying her face in a giant-sized compact. 'We'd still be stuck here, chauffeur or not,' she remarked.

'We could get out and walk,' he suggested.

'With that crowd? Are you kidding? They'd mob me!'

She laughed briskly, shutting her compact, delighted with her appearance.

An official approached them, checking the pasted number on the windscreen of their car.

'Mr Brick?' he asked.

Charlie nodded.

'Mr Brick, sir. Please turn off at the next side-turning. We have arranged a quicker way for you to reach the cinema.'

'But I've got a driver meeting me at the front.'

'It's all been arranged, sir.'

Charlie shrugged. Anything was better than being stuck in traffic, which was one of his pet hates. He did as the man asked, and was shortly stopped by another official.

'Lookee at all those horses,' said Thames. 'I guess it's some kind of stunt.'

Mike hurried over, extending a nervously sweating hand. 'I'm Stu Waterman's assistant,' he said. 'Stu thought it would be nice for you and the lady'—he peered at Thames - ' to arrive on horses, or both on one horse if you like.'

'One horse would be fun,' Thames cooed.

Charlies laughed out loud. 'Not me, mate, the only time I ever got on a horse I was being paid, and I ended up flat on my backside.'

'I don't think there's any fee,' Mike said earnestly. He wished Stu would return. It wasn't fair sticking him round the back with the horses, which nobody seemed to want to ride.

'Oh, Charlie,' Thames cooed, 'it would be fun. Please let's do it.'

'Forget it,' he replied tersely.

'You would have an escort of five cowboys,' Mike said. 'It will be very effective. Everyone's doing it.'

'Yes, well I'm not,' Charlie said. 'But I'm not stopping you,' he added to Thames.

'I can't do it alone,' she said sulkily. She didn't want to miss the opportunity of arriving with Charlie.

Branch said, 'What a *wild* idea!'

The thought of drawing up to the cinema on a horse, with Sunday up there with him and an escort of five cowboys, appealed to him immensely.

Sunday was not so impressed. 'You go right ahead, Branch. I'll meet you in the lobby.'

'Hey, honey, what do you mean? You're with me. I'll hold you tight, won't let you go.'

'It's not that I'm frightened of falling off. I just—er—don't want to do it.'

Stu Waterman had been listening patiently. He took Sunday persuasively by the arm. 'Sweetheart, think of the publicity, think of the TV cameras, think of—'

She shook her arm free. 'I think it's a stupid stunt.'

Branch coughed in an embarrassed fashion. 'Hey, Stu, maybe I should do it alone, and Sunday can kinda come out and meet me.'

'I'm not doing that either,' she said quickly. She was sick and tired of being pushed into things.

'Now listen, baby,' Stu Waterman said, 'you made it on publicity and you're only just there, every little bit helps.'

'I'm sure it does, Mr Waterman—*you*.' She climbed back into the limo and said to Branch, 'I'll meet you inside.'

Torn between a desire to be seen arriving with Sunday or drawing up on a fine white stallion, Branch shuffled uneasily.

Stu solved the problem. 'Come on, boy,' he said, 'you'll make all the papers tomorrow—the Warren Beatty of the range!'

Herbert, having attended to his business at the beach, parked the limousine several blocks away from the Cinerama Dome, locked it, and headed on foot to join the crush of people milling about outside. He shoved his way through to the front, oblivious to all the insults hurled at him as he squeezed and groped his way forward.

In the front line he squashed between two elderly queens and a group of teeny boppers.

The queens were shaking their heads sadly and saying, 'Who is there to compare with Joan Crawford today?'

The teeny boppers were screaming 'There's Randy! It's *him!* Doesn't he look fan-*tas*-tic!!'

Herbert slid his hand onto the backside of one of the jumping girls. She didn't seem to notice. She was wearing very tight rolled-up blue jeans and a skinny knit sweater that ended around her ribs.

Herbert contemplated the fact that it was disgusting the way mothers let their daughters parade themselves. He squeezed her bottom ever so slightly, and she stopped jumping and looked around. She nudged a girlfriend, whispered something, and they both giggled.

Herbert stared ahead, noting with hardly a flutter the arrival of Angela Carter, who had once been the recipient of his letters, but who had never had the good fortune to meet him. That was to be Sunday Simmons's privilege—and tonight.

Charlie saw Sunday arrive while he was talking to Jack Julip.

She walked in alone, slightly hesitant. The camermen leapt forward. Jack was already ending the interview with Charlie, and nodding at an assistant to bring Sunday over next. He shook hands with Charlie, a clammy insincere shake.

Thames, who had been silently pushed to the sidelines, muttered, 'That guy's a bum, his show stinks and so does he.'

Out of the corner of his eye Charlie observed Sunday refusing to be interviewed. The look of amazement and shock that spread over Jack Julip's face was classic.

In his confusion Jack grabbed Thames, announcing, 'And this lovely young lady, accompanying Charlie Brick, is none other than rising star—' He left her to name herself.

'Thames Mason,' she preened and waved to the crowd. 'You're a doll, Jack I *looove* your show!' She then proceeded to bore with details of how she took off her clothes in her latest movie, all in the cause of art.

Charlie went over to Sunday. 'You owe me an explanation; not to mention,' he added jokingly, 'the money for the outfit I got you—hundreds of dollars worth of—.'

'Did you arrive on a horse?' she asked.

'No.'

They both laughed.

'In that case I'll pay you.'

'Who are you with?' he asked.

'Branch Strong. *He is* arriving on a horse any second.'

'If I had known, we could have done a swop. Thames was longing to get in the saddle.'

She smiled. 'I'm sorry about running off. I should explain, you were *very* kind and understanding.'

'How about later? Thames has a nude scene she can't wait to rehearse and I'm not in the mood.'

He was sorry as soon as he said it. She froze up immediately, giving him a cold little smile and saying, 'Sorry, but I'm busy. If you can tell me how much I owe you, I'll see you get a cheque tomorrow.'

'I don't want the money, I was joking.'

'But I owe it to you, I insist.'

An intrepid photographer was taking shots of them together, and as soon as her interview was over Thames came striding to join them.

'I guess we should wander on in,' she said, gripping Charlie's hand possessively glaring at Sunday.

'Plenty of time, love. Do you two know each other?'

Satisfied, Herbert watched Sunday Simmons arrive. She was safely in the cinema now, and everything was progressing smoothly. He checked his watch, and slowly started to ease out of the crowd.

57

Inside the theatre, people jostled for their seats. There was much neck-craning as positions were checked out. It was important to be sitting in the right place, not shoved to the side or the back or in the cheaper seats.

Charlie had good seats and Thames was delighted. Most premières she attended were with two-bit actors. She was usually given the tickets, which were invariably bad. The film companies wanted her at their premières for the publicity she might get posing in the foyer, but they were not prepared to give her good seats.

'Isn't Jack Julip just great?' She enthused, licking her lips and smiling at a wandering photographer who had managed to get inside.

Sunday and Branch sat a few rows back in aisle seats.

Branch was nervous and sick to his stomach. Two rows in front of him sat Maxwell Thorpe in his new violet dinner-jacket, and next to him was Oliver Ritz. In appearance, Oliver was frail and intense, darkly handsome. Like Branch, he had a small part in 'The Twelve Guns', but everyone knew he was a raving fag. Until that very week he had been openly living with a very famous male star.

Branch swallowed a lump in his throat. He liked Sunday very much, but not enough to wreck his whole future. If he had known that Maxwell would plan this revenge, there would have been no question who he would take to the première. Goddamn it, he *liked* living in a big Hollywood mansion. He *liked* being able to have a choice of an Excalibur or a Lincoln to drive. He *liked* walking into Cy Devore and ordering whatever he wanted.

Would it all still be available after tonight? Or was this Maxwell Thorpe's way of telling him he was out?

Sunday shut her eyes and wished the film would begin. She hated all the phoney ballyhoo, the gushing hellos from people who wouldn't even talk to her when her career crumbled flat, as well it might if Claude Hussan had his way.

She had already decided that she would not go with Branch

to the party afterwards. She would plead a splitting headache, and she didn't really care if he believed her or not. She was through being nice to people at cost to herself.

Branch meanwhile was wondering if he could redeem the situation with Max by getting rid of Sunday and taking Max to the party instead. He could make some excuse to Sunday and send her home with the chauffeur.

He had almost decided to edge his way over to Max and invite him, when the lights faded and the movie began.

Outside in the lobby, Stu Waterman was saying to Mike, 'I don't give a fuck what you do with the horses, just get 'em out of here!'

The television crews were removing their equipment. The photographers had already left. The crowds had trickled away, and the policemen gone.

Stu took a swig from his flask and swore with disgust when he found it empty. He needed a vacation, his ulcer was killing him. Working for actors was a lousy way to make a living.

Herbert sat in the car. His palms were sweating but he remained outwardly calm. It was most important to behave in a normal everyday manner.

He started the big limousine, which rolled slowly forward.

He glanced at his watch once more. 'The Twelve Guns' had been on for exactly one hour.

He drove the car to the cinema's parking-lot, and got out. Then he unlocked the trunk and removed a brown paper bag, which he placed on the back passenger seat. He locked the car carefully, and went into the theatre.

Charlie just couldn't believe that anyone could talk so much.

All through the movie, speaking out of the corner of her mouth like some bizarre Southern gangster, Thames kept up a running commentary.

'You see that guy—we were at drama school together; and that one—baby, what a swinger—living with two chicks and balling day and night . . . now she's got the worst body I've ever seen, where they ever found her I don't know—just look at those boobs, hangin' down like grandma's!!'

'*Will you be quiet,*' he hissed for the twentieth time.

Pouting, she paid attention to the screen for a minute, then, 'Pubic hair in *Westerns!* Whee! What next?'

'*I am telling you,*' Charlie said angrily, 'if you don't shut up I am going to leave you here to talk to yourself. *I can't stand it.*'

Thames chewed on a fingernail. Jack Julip had promised her a spot on his regular TV show if she could manage to come by his house later and discuss it. It was tempting. Much as she wanted to go to the party with Charlie, maybe a television show would be better exposure.

'Hey,' she said, 'look at that guy's ass, there's more bare ass in this movie than "Oh Calcutta!"'

Sunday was finding the film boring and distasteful. It was a strong combination of violence and sex, and apparently nothing else.

Branch was mesmerized. He had just appeared in close-up, and boy was he photogenic! Even the chicken-pox scar next to his mouth looked good. This was his best scene in the movie: four close-ups, ten lines.

Herbert strolled through the lobby. It was very quiet. He walked over to the box-office, where a girl sat silently filing her nails and thinking how much prettier she was than all the movie stars she had seen that evening.

'I have an urgent message for Miss Sunday Simmons,' Herbert said. 'Do you know where she's sitting?'

The girl inspected Herbert, ordinary and neat in his chauffeur's uniform. One had to be very careful nowadays with so many lunatics wandering about. She had a special security button by her foot which she was supposed to press if she were robbed or attacked or if any maniacs appeared. This man was certainly all right.

'I don't know where she's sitting.' She said. 'I did see her come in. Maybe the boy who took the tickets would know. In fact I'm sure he would, he always notices the celebrities.'

'Where can I find him?' He could not control a quick glance at his watch.

'Oh, he'll be standing at the back. The tall boy.'

A five-dollar tip and the tall usher immediately accompanied Herbert to where Sunday was sitting.

On screen Branch was slowly unbuttoning his shirt, his eyes staring at the camera.

The usher leaned across Branch and said in a loud stage-whisper, 'Miss Simmons, I'm sorry to disturb you, but your chauffeur is here. He says it's very urgent.'

'Urgent?' Sunday said in a startled voice.

On screen Branch was slowly unbuttoning his jeans, his eyes staring at the camera.

Sunday stood up and nudged Branch, who was apparently mesmerized by his image on the screen. He didn't budge, just gave her a hurried push as she squeezed to get past him.

The camera was moving in on his face, which now filled the whole screen. He wondered how Max felt *now*. He hardly even noticed Sunday leave.

Thames said, 'That guy sure is one hell of a piece of beefcake. I hear he's a faggot, isn't that a waste? I bet I could . . .'

Charlie got up. There was no reason on earth why he had to stay and put up with this. Let her call him all the names she wanted: he was going.

Once in the lobby Herbert took over. He brushed the usher aside who was searching in his pocket for a pen to get her autograph, and said quickly, 'Miss Simmons, we must hurry. It's the boy, he's had an accident. They sent me for you at once.'

Sunday went white. If Claude Hussan had laid one finger on that child . . .

'Is it bad?' she asked, the words sticking in her throat.

Herbert nodded gravely, rushing her through the foyer and out to the parking-lot.

Politely he held open the door of the car while she climbed in. Then he allowed himself a short sigh of relief.

So far so good.

She was in the trap.

58

Sunday sat back in the car and closed her eyes tightly. If anything had happened to Jean-Pierre because of her . . . it didn't bear thinking about.

She couldn't see a thing in the car. The chauffeur was blocked off by black glass, and the side windows were tinted in such a fashion that she was unable to see out of them. She groped for the button to release the glass between her and the chauffeur, but although she pressed it sharply several times, it didn't seem to work.

She leaned forward and tapped on the glass. The car glided smoothly on.

Slowly it dawned on her that perhaps this was Claude's idea of a joke.

In the driving seat Herbert permitted himself a fleeting smile of triumph. It had all been so easy. Masterly planning on his part, of course.

He heard her bang on the glass and his smile widened. He would not reveal too quickly who he was. Let her imagine things. It would do her good to worry a little. Women were much too secure nowadays, everything handed to them on a plate.

When *he* had finished with *Miss* Sunday Simmons, she would *know* who the *master* was.

The car slowed. A traffic light? As soon as it stopped she tried to open the door. It was locked tight. Then the car was off again.

She wasn't frightened. Nothing Claude could do would frighten her. It was the child she was concerned about. Was the idea to blackmail her to finish the film? She wouldn't put it past them. She wouldn't put anything past them.

Damn Branch for sitting in the cinema so entranced by his own image on the screen! He should have come with her. He shouldn't have let her leave by herself.

She sat back in the seat and composed herself to meet Claude.

Once in the lobby Charlie had second thoughts. Wasn't it kind of shitty to leave Thames on her own?

Well, a girl like Thames would not be on her own for long. Besides, it was her own bloody fault. The girl had driven him *mad* with her inane chatter.

As he walked towards his car he thought he saw Sunday getting into a black Lincoln. There was something vaguely familiar about the chauffeur. Wasn't it Herbert something-or-other whom Clay had loaned him?

He quickened his step. They had both agreed on the fact that it was a rotten film, so maybe she *would* have dinner with him after all.

Before he could reach the Lincoln it moved off in the opposite direction. He got in his Ferrari. Maybe he would just follow her for a bit, see where she was going. After all, he had nothing else to do.

Herbert switched on the speaker and spoke into a small hand microphone.

'We have the boy. He is quite safe and will remain so as long as you do everything we say.'

'Who *are* you?' Sunday asked angrily. 'Where is Mr Hussan?'

Herbert paused, momentarily taken aback by her anger. He had expected her to be cowed, frightened.

'We have the child,' He continued. 'His safety depends on your behaviour. *Mr* Hussan can't help you now. You are in our hands. You must be obedient and quiet, otherwise the child will end up the same way as the dog.'

'What dog?' She asked, a sinking feeling taking hold of her. She had heard the man's voice somewhere before.

'Look in the package on the right-hand corner of the seat'.

Abruptly interior lights went on. She looked around. God! it felt as though she were imprisoned in a black cell. The car sped forward and she could see nothing through the opaque black glass.

On the seat there was a brown paper bag. She touched it. It was damp. She reached inside, looked, felt, and screamed.

The package contained Limbo's head.

Marge Lincoln Jefferson stuffed another chocolate in her mouth. She was fed up. Ever since she had told Herbert about Louella wanting the money, she had been cast out by both of them.

Louella fobbed her off with excuses when she tried to see her. She found it impossible to get beyond the front door.

'What about the circle of friends?' Marge whined. 'When will the next evening be?'

'I can't say,' Louella had muttered hurriedly, and slammed the door in her face.

Herbert was no better. He had always been a difficult man to please, but now she could do nothing right, and he snapped and snarled at her the whole time.

She was reduced once more to just the television for company, and they were threatening to take that away, because Herbert had not made the last payment.

Marge sat and brooded. She knew they were up to something, for that morning Herbert had been surprisingly cheerful, and when he went out he had produced a large box of chocolates which he gave her. She had been amazed beyond words.

She had noticed activity at her neighbours'—Louella and her husband carrying packages and suitcases out to their station-wagon all day, loading up as if they were going on a trip.

Marge popped another chocolate in her mouth, and went to the window again. She had a good view of what was happening. If there was going to be another circle-of-friends evening, she planned to be in on it.

'Listen carefully,' Herbert said. They were nearing their destination and it was time to give instructions.

Sunday huddled on the back seat as far away from the grisly package as she could get. The fact that she could not see the owner of the flat grey voice seemed to make matters worse. She was frightened, but determined to try and remain as calm as possible.

'Who are you?' she asked again. 'What do you want?'

'Just listen,' Herbert insisted gruffly. 'If you listen and do as you are told, everything will be all right. If you *don't* do as I tell you, the boy will die like the dog.'

'How much do you want? I have money, I can get more. How much?'

He paused. It hadn't occurred to him that he could get money from her. The thought was appealing, but it was even more appealing to go ahead with his original plan.

'Money can't help the boy. We are going to a house. At this house you will do as you are told. You will not speak to anyone but me. *One* word in the wrong place and the child will die. At a signal from me there are people who will act, so don't try and get away with anything. Do you understand?'

'Yes, I understand.' She desperately tried to remember where she had heard his voice before. 'And what am I supposed to do?'

'Nothing that you haven't done before and enjoyed. You should have waited for me. If you had waited for me I wouldn't make you do this.'

'Waited for you? Do I *know* you?'

'Oh yes, you know me.'

It was like a continuation of the bad dream in Palm Springs. She felt sick and trapped. This must be Claude Hussan's doing, although how could he involve Jean-Pierre? And who was the madman driving the car? She knew his voice . . . who was he?

Charlie was getting bored. Following Sunday had been a ridiculous, childish thing to do. He was not even positive it was she in the car; he had only caught a glimpse. And where the hell were they going? Away from Beverly Hills and down into dreary little streets with rows and rows of shabby houses.

Twice he decided to stop and twice he changed his mind, because having come so far he might as well see where she was going. Of course he wouldn't let her see him; it would be too embarrassing to let her know he had followed her.

It occurred to him that he must fancy her. No, it was stronger than that. There was something about her . . . just something about her.

*

Esmé Mae peered once more at Jean-Pierre. He was fast asleep in bed, his long black lashes curling over innocent cheeks. Where was that little bit of a dog? She had looked for it everywhere. Its dinner was waiting, and Miss Simmons had said to be sure that the dog came in for its dinner.

Well, it must have run off up the beach somewhere, for Esmé Mae had shouted herself hoarse.

She pulled the covers up over Jean-Pierre and waddled into the kitchen for a good hot cup of coffee.

59

The car stopped.

The voice warned, 'Now just remember everything I've said. If you do as you're told, you'll be getting back in this car in a couple of hours. We'll collect the boy and I'll take you both home. If you *don't* co-operate—well, you know what to expect. The boy's life is in your hands.'

She waited silently for the voice to present himself. There was no point in trying to scream or run. If he had Jean-Pierre, she would just have to do as he said.

The door opened and she saw they were in a quiet street. Herbert's eyes avoided hers as he took her by the arm and helped her out of the car. She was almost sure she had never seen him before.

He walked her silently up the pathway to a small shabby house and rapped sharply on the door.

A woman answered it, small and brittle in a green satin dress with loads of fake jewelry.

They didn't speak to each other, but her eyes darted over Sunday inquisitively.

Herbert hurried her up creaking stairs into a bedroom, and quickly shut the door. He was breaking out in a sweat. His clothes felt too tight, his skin clammy. He longed for a shower.

He leant against the door. 'Take your clothes off,' he said, 'and put that on.' He nodded at a black robe lying on the bed.

She stared at him.

'Get your clothes *off*,' he snarled.

Slowly she bent and pulled her boots off first; then turning her back to him, she slipped off her trousers and chiffon top Underneath she wore flesh-coloured panties and bra. She put the robe over her head.

'Everything off,' Herbert stated. There was an uncomfortable tightness in his trousers.

'Tell Claude the joke's gone far enough,' she said weakly. 'I'll finish the goddamn film, I'll do it.' She started to cry.

'This is nothing to do with Claude—this is *me—me*. Don't you know who I am?'

'What do you want from me? What have I done?'

'Stop snivelling and take the rest of your clothes off. It shouldn't worry a whore to take her clothes off.'

Slowly she pulled the panties off under the robe. He took them from her and stuffed them in his pocket.

She fumbled with her bra and he said, 'Take the robe off. I want to see you naked.'

She wondered if he would kill her. He had such blank and evil eyes. She shivered uncontrollably. 'Who are you?' she asked. 'Why are you doing this to me?'

'*Take the robe off*,' he muttered. He felt stifled, enclosed. A vein throbbed in his throat. His eyes were glazed.

She lifted the robe over her head and faced him.

He stared at her, filled with hate. His eyes roamed shiftily over her naked body.

Then before it was too late, he commanded, 'Turn round and *don't look back*. If you look back the boy will die!'

She turned away from him, shutting her eyes in terror. Clenching her body in anticipation of what was to come.

He ripped open his pants, his hands clumsy in their haste, and with a low anguished groan he relieved his desire into her panties, which he snatched from his pocket.

He made no attempt to approach her. Let her wait, let her suffer a little in waiting for his touch.

She heard him fumbling with his clothes, and then the short

271

anguished groan. She caught her breath in disgust. She knew what he had done.

And *then* she knew who he was. It was the maniac who had written her all those obscene letters. It *had* to be! And the voice—now she was almost sure it was the same voice that had muttered obscenities to her over the 'phone.

Herbert felt strong again. Once more he was in control. He glanced guiltily at his watch. Louella would be waiting.

'Put the robe on and follow me,' he said.

Charlie parked on the other side of the street further down from the Lincoln.

He watched Sunday as she was hustled into the faded little house by the chauffeur.

It was all very odd. Why would she leave a première half-way through to come dashing down to this place? Perhaps this was where her family lived. But vaguely he remembered Carey telling him that she came from South America and that her parents were dead.

It was none of his business, of course, and she would probably be embarrassed and upset is she ever discovered he had followed her. Yet maybe he ought to stay around for five minutes. There was something not quite right.

He lit a cigarette, and wondered at his sudden hang-up with Sunday Simmons. She was only another actress. Beautiful of course, but just the sort he had sworn to stay away from. Mmm . . . there was definitely something different about her. He wanted to see her, to get to know her, to spend time together.

Of course she probably wouldn't want to know about him. She probably had every guy in Hollywood after her. Clay literally drooled whenever her name was mentioned.

He shrugged and decided to drive off, but he hesitated, because while he had been sitting thinking about her, nine men had gone into the house and there was another one arriving now.

What was it, a party? If so, where were the girls?

He decided to wait just a little bit longer.

Marge knew what it was all right. It was a circle-of-friends evening. She bit her pudgy nails and muttered under her breath.

Louella thought she was so smart-assed clever. *And* Herbert, the two of them plotting and planning to deprive her of her rights.

Well, they weren't as clever as all that. It was *her right* to attend *all* circle-of-friends meetings. She had paid, hadn't she? She was a member, wasn't she? She would *exercise* her rights and join in.

The only problem was that she didn't feel well. She had a nagging pain in her stomach, but she wasn't going to let *that* stop her. She found a bottle of brandy and took a few deep swigs. Then she popped a couple more chocolates in her mouth to take away the taste. Her head was throbbing and she felt dizzy from the alcohol.

To hell with Louella and Herbert. She was on her way.

Herbert whispered sharply to Sunday. They stood outside a closed door in the hallway of the house.

'Now remember, whore,' he said, 'not one word or the boy gets it. Just do as your told. I'll be watching you all the time.'

She shivered, cold in the nearly transparent black robe.

He opened the door and they walked in.

The room was lit by long black candles, and all around stood naked men, naked except for masks covering their faces.

The woman who had let her in approached them with arms outstretched. She was naked too, with stringy breasts hanging down. 'Welcome to the "circle of friends", my dear.'

Sunday shrank back as she tried to embrace her, and Herbert dug her sharply in the back.

Louella took her by the hand and led her over to what seemed like a board, covered with black velvet and propped against the wall. It was surrounded by black candles and reminded Sunday of a coffin.

The atmosphere was horribly weird—all the silent naked men in the flickering half-light, with Herbert hovering, still fully dressed.

'Divest yourself of your robe, my dear,' Louella said soothingly. 'Take off your clothes and you take off sin.'

Almost in a daze she allowed the robe to be pulled off, and

then Louella and a man assisted her on to the board, where she lay.

Louella murmured some kind of chant. The men repeated it after her.

She dipped into a pot of black cream and rubbed it on Sunday's nipples until they were black and greasy.

Shivering with disgust and horror, Sunday tensed her body, trying not to feel Louella's short stubby fingers. She attempted to clear her mind of all thoughts and become just a body. A body was all they wanted. If she could only disconnect her mind then it wouldn't matter. Nothing would matter. They could do what they wanted and not even touch her.

She lay very still. Whatever happened she had to be sure they wouldn't harm Jean-Pierre.

Louella was chanting again. They were all holding hands and walking slowly around her.

Masked faces and naked bodies were moving closer—closer . . .

60

The fat woman intrigued Charlie. She had emerged from next door, approached the front door of the house Sunday was in, changed her mind, peered in through a side window, gone back to the front door, changed her mind again, and now she was standing on a straggly bit of grass at the front seemingly indecisive about what to do.

Charlie got out of the car. He intended to stroll casually around the house and then leave. The whole thing was becoming ridiculous. Sunday probably had a very good reason for being where she was, and anyway it was none of his business. He only knew her slightly, and he had no right to be spying on her like this.

Marge staggered. She had a pain in her gut. It was so uncomfortable she could hardly breathe. She wanted to march into Louella's house and surprise them—but she had to wait a minute, catch her breath, let the pain subside. She could see nothing through the windows. They had pulled heavy drapes.

She knelt down on the grass, and suddenly to her surprise, she fell right over.

She lay there stupidly, hoping that she would soon feel better.

Charlie saw the fat woman fall, and realized that here was his chance to get into the house if he wanted to. He hurried over to her. 'Are you all right?' he asked. 'Here let me help you up.'

She looked at him with sick yellow eyes and decided he was a member of the circle of friends. 'Take me in with you,' she mumbled, 'I'm gonna get my rights.'

'Certainly,' he replied soothingly. The woman looked very sick indeed. He propped her up. God, she was a weight. 'Come on, dear,' he said, 'make an effort.'

She heaved herself up. 'That little bastard's not gonna get away with it,' she announced, weaving and swaying.

Together they reached the front door. 'I've gotta key,' she said. Louella had given it to her some time ago and forgotten to get it back.

Charlie opened the front door. Then it struck him that Sunday might not be pleased to see him. She would know he had followed her, and he would look like a fool.

Marge had a grip on his arm. 'Come on,' she mumbled, 'we'll surprise 'em' She dragged him over to a door and flung it open.

He could hardly see anything. The room was lit only by candles. Then his eyes accustomed themselves to the flickering gloom and he saw everything.

Marge began to yell. 'I've come for my rights. Don't think you can get rid of me you bastards . . .'

There was Sunday, so pale and beautiful, resting on a black board, surrounded by a circle of naked, masked people.

Herbert, the chauffeur, started to smack the fat woman viciously round the face.

Oh Christ! Charlie thought. It's some black-magic scene. She's involved in a weird fucking cult. Oh shit!

Marge fell in a heavy heap on the floor, groaning.

The naked men started running for their clothes, all piled in a corner.

A short nude woman pleaded with them. '*Wait*, everything will be fine. *Wait*. We'll get rid of her.' She indicated the heap that was Marge. 'It's my sister, she's drunk—*wait*.'

Nobody took any notice of her. The scene was confusion.

Charlie stood by the door. Nobody appeared to notice him. He shook his head in disbelief. He knew Hollywood was full of kooks, people ready to do anything for a kick, but he just had not figured Sunday as one of them.

She hadn't moved. She lay as if hypnotized, completely beautiful, completely blank.

He shrugged. There was nothing for him to hang around for, and yet he had a strange feeling that he should go to her, persuade her to come with him, get her out of this crazy scene.

Herbert looked around in panic. What had happened to his plans? *Why was Marge here*? He had given her the chocolates, hadn't he? If she had eaten them, she should have been dead by now. Dead and out of his life! Each chocolate had been carefully treated. He had used enough arsenic to kill an elephant.

Maybe she *was* dead. She was lying awfully still. It was time to get out. . . .

Sunday remained motionless. She had forced herself into a self-induced state of oblivion which a doctor would call severe shock. Perfectly still, she waited for the inevitable. The only important thing was that Jean-Pierre remain unharmed. She noticed the chaos around her as if from a great distance.

Just as Charlie decided that he would try to talk some sense into Sunday, Herbert grabbed her. He caught her roughly by the arm and commanded, '*Move!*' propelling her towards the door, towards Charlie.

The hell with it, Charlie thought, he had gone this far, why not all the way? He stepped forward, blocking their path. Before he could say anything, Herbert kicked him swiftly in the balls, and dragged Sunday out of the house.

For a brief moment she saw him, her eyes focused, recognized, and she began to scream as reality hit.

Charlie was doubled over in agony. He couldn't move. The

pain was intense. Now Sunday was screaming uncontrollably.

Louella heard the screams. She had pulled on an old dressing-gown and was darting around the room, trying to restore some kind of order. She ran to the window. Something was horribly wrong. Marge was too still on the floor. If Sunday Simmons had come of her own free will why was she screaming?

She remembered how this whole evening had come about. *It was because Herbert had murdered a girl.*

Charlie was trying to stand.

'You'd better stop him from taking her in that car,' Louella yelled at the few remaining men, struggling with trousers and jackets. 'He's mad. He'll kill her!'

Charlie was the only one to move. He made it to the front door in time to see Herbert shove Sunday in the back of the Lincoln. He reached the car just as it sped off.

The pain was lessening. He ran across the street to the Ferrari and threw himself in.

It was all so clear now. The man was Herbert Lincoln Jefferson, the chauffeur Phillipa had made the unbelievable accusations about. And he had laughed, told her not to be so silly.

And now the man had Sunday.

There was applause at the end of the movie. Branch was pleased, proud to have been a part of it. He looked around to receive Sunday's congratulations, and realised she had left.

Where *had* she gone? He vaguely remembered someone coming to fetch her in the middle of the film. He thought perhaps he should telephone to check that everything was all right, but just then Maxwell Thorpe walked by with his new young actor, and Branch leapt to his feet.

'I sent her home,' he whispered. 'I want to take *you* to the party.'

Maxwell smiled. 'You're a little late, my dear, but you may come with us if you wish.'

'Fine, Max, I'll do that,' Branch said eagerly. 'How did you like the film? How did you like *me*?'

He had forgotten all about Sunday.

*

'I know who you are,' Sunday said. She tried to make her voice sound calm and collected, although in fact she was terrified as she huddled, still naked, in the back of the car.

She wasn't sure if the speakers were on. She wasn't sure if he could hear her, but she was determined to appear in complete control. It was important, she sensed, with this madman, not to break down. 'Can you hear me?' she asked. 'I'm cold. Give me something to put on.'

There was silence.

'You wrote me the letters, didn't you?' she continued. 'Answer me. You wrote them, didn't you?'

There was no reply.

She bit her lip hard. Where were they going? What now? Was Jean-Pierre all right? And the biggest question of all—where had Charlie Brick appeared from?

Herbert drove wildly. He had to take her somewhere quiet.

He was thirteen-years-old and jerking off when his aunt walked in the room. She was much younger than his mother, and skinny, with pointed tits that she never bothered to conceal. She stood and looked at him, hands on skinny hips, and then she started to laugh. Her laughter went on and on as she pointed gleefully at his penis and said, 'You don't wanna waste all that on yourself, sonny.'

She slipped off her skimpy gown and made him lie down. Then she straddled him and moved herself up and down, up and down on top of him—in and out, up and down—laughing all the time.

Afterwards he stood under the shower for hours, scrubbing, scrubbing; but it was days before he could get rid of the smell of cheap perfume.

He left home, grew up, and there were whores, lots of them, but none of them could help. The only way he could do it was by himself.

Then he met Marge with the great wobbling breasts. She served him tuna fish on rye and a cold beer and ended up marrying him.

She reminded him of a picture he had been using in his fantasies. The picture was of a nude girl in thigh-length black boots, climbing on to a horse, one leg in the stirrup. When he managed to identify the girl in the picture with Marge he was able to perform, so well and often, that soon she became pregnant. She lost the first baby, and the second. After that he just couldn't do it any more.

He would have liked a baby, a little girl to play with and take for walks, but it was not to be. It was back to the pictures, and then the letters and the telephone calls. He found them satisfying enough, but every once in a while he wanted to try again, and before the hippie girl on Sunset there had been several whores, all of them beaten up in a frenzy of frustration and hate.

Now he had Sunday Simmons, the pinnacle of his desires. If he couldn't perform with her, there was no hope, and nobody else was going to have her. If he drove high enough into the hills, he could park the car safely, and she was in the back, naked and ready. If it worked they would go away together.

If it didn't work, well then, what was there to lose? A woman would never be satisfied if she wasn't getting it. She would never stay with him.

He knew a spot high above Hollywood where he could send the car whirling over the top. Both of them together.

It was the only way.

61

Charlie felt a sense of unreality. Things like this only happened in the movies. But he had *heard* her scream. He had *seen* her pushed naked into the car.

He felt a sense of exhilaration, as though very pleasantly stoned.

He got behind the Lincoln and stayed there. They were heading back to Hollywood.

It occurred to him that he should call the police. He had a

'phone in the car, conveniently placed near his right hand. But what could he say. How would it all sound?

'Hello, this is Charlie Brick. I'm following some madman who's got Sunday Simmons stripped off in the back of his car.'

'Oh yeah?' he could hear the reply. 'And I'm Mickey Mouse.'

But what if he *didn't* call the police? Eventually the Lincoln would stop, the nut would get out, and what then? Charlie was not renowned for his strength, and what if Herbert had a gun?

At the first opportunity he dialled the operator. It was difficult to remove his hand from the wheel for a minute, because the Lincoln was jumping lights, stop-signs, everything.

They were bolting up La Cienega heading for the Strip. 'I want to report a kidnapping,' he said, when he was put through. 'It's Sunday Simmons.'

'Oh yeah,' said the cop, 'and I'm Donald Duck!'

'I'm cold,' Sunday pleaded again. '*Please* stop. Give me something to put on then we can talk.' She paused. 'We can talk about your letters.'

There was still no reply. The car rushed maddeningly on. If only he would *say* something. She felt a rising sense of panic.

There seemed to be no air in the car. 'Stop, please stop,' she begged. 'I think I'm going to faint . . .'

They were nearly there.

Herbert licked his lips, which felt dry and cracked. He reached in his pocket for some lip-salve and felt the locket, the thin gold chain that had fallen off the neck of the girl he had murdered. He planned to give it to Sunday as a present. He stuffed it back in his pocket, found the lip-salve, and liberally applied it round his mouth.

He was unaware of the Ferrari close behind. He slowed down as the Lincoln twisted and turned higher and higher into the Hollywood Hills.

Nervously, his hand unzipped his pants and he stroked himself, steadily, stealthily, almost as if he were petting a snake.

It was nearly time. They were reaching the spot he had been seeking. It was off the road up a makeshift drive-way: There was a house, half built, jutting out over the peak.

280

He took the car to the edge, and stopped. Then he got out and opened the back door of the car.

Sunday stared at him in the dark. She could see his outline as he peered in at her. The only sound was of crickets chirping. She could smell grass and damp earth.

Herbert climbed in the car, leaving the door open. His hands fell upon her breasts like scavengers, the fingers twitching and kneading.

She shrank back as his lips fastened on one breast.

She started to struggle, to pull herself free.

He pinned her down. He was strong.

They fought silently. He prised open her legs. She clawed and raked at his face.

'Whore!' he muttered, and slapped her.

Then, as she felt him about to enter her, there was a sudden release of pressure and he was pulled off.

Charlie stopped the Ferrari when the other car turned off the road. He left it with a special red light flashing, and followed the path of the Lincoln by foot. To say he was nervous was putting it mildly.

He didn't have far to go before reaching the car. He could hear the wordless struggle, the grunts and groans. He didn't hesitate, and plunged straight in, grabbing Herbert by the back of his shirt, hauling him off.

Charlie had never been in a fight, but he followed his instincts, and when Herbert rushed him, he tripped him with his right leg and followed that up with a hefty kick to the crotch.

'That will pay you back for the one you gave me, mate,' he muttered. 'One good kick in the balls deserves another.'

Herbert rolled on the ground.

Charlie pulled Sunday out of the car. 'Let's move before he does,' he said, and taking her hand, they started to run back to the Ferrari.

'Just hold it right there, mister.' A cop stood by his car, his gun pointed straight at them.

62

A week later Charlie and Sunday sat on the big jet, side by side. They held hands, his protectively over hers.

They were the most publicised couple in the world. Beyond the endless headlines, speculation and rumours, people wondered what had *really* happened that night.

All of Hollywood had its own theory: 'They both belonged to this weird black-magic cult, and it got out of hand.' 'She was *always* at orgies.' 'He's a well-known pervert.'

Marge Lincoln Jefferson was found dead of a massive dose of poison.

Herbert Lincoln Jefferson was arrested, and charged first with attempted kidnapping and rape, and then, after the discovery of Marge, with murder.

Louella Crisp was tracked down with her mild little husband in Arizona and brought back for questioning. Later she was charged with being an accessory.

Carey and Marshall flew back to Los Angeles when they heard the news.

Sunday was under sedation in hospital. She was perfectly all right, but still suffering from shock.

Charlie had taken over. He dealt with the police and the press. 'She is not to be bothered with *anything*,' he informed Carey.

'Of course,' Carey agreed. 'But I sure have got a lot of questions to ask you . . .'

Claude Hussan arrived from Palm Springs to collect his son from the beach house. He came to see Carey at her office.

'I'm sorry, I'm cancelling Sunday's contract. We are recasting.'

'You're kidding?' Carey exclaimed. 'You must have read what happened to her, she's on every front page in the world.'

Claude shrugged. 'It's unlucky. *She* left the film. Anyhow, you may give her my regards and this message—just tell her the extra footage is useless and we won't be using it.'

Carey glared at him. 'If you're not using her, why would you use extra footage anyway?'

'Just give her the message.' His eyes lingered and again she felt their physical pull. 'Goodbye,' he said abruptly.

Carey was not sorry about his film, but she wondered how Sunday would feel. Why *had* she returned to Los Angeles.

After two days Sunday came out of hospital. Besieged by photographers and reporters, she fled to the comparative safety of Carey and Marshall's house. They protected her as best they could.

She had made many decisions in the past week. She told Carey she never intended to appear in another movie. In a way she felt responsible for the whole mess. Carey couldn't believe it. 'What will you do?' she asked.

'Whatever I do, it will be something private.'

It had been announced that Dindi Sydne was to replace Sunday in Claude Hussan's film.

Carey was surprised at the way Sunday took the news. She just smiled and said, 'I think he's got the right girl now.'

Something had happened between Claude and Sunday, but Carey did not feel it was the right time to pry.

Charlie visited Sunday every day, and sat and talked with her in the garden. He made her laugh, he made her happy. And when he asked her to come to London with him she accepted. She felt low, depressed, and only Charlie made her feel good. He said, 'No hang-ups, we'll see what happens . . .'

'I'm going to take you to Manchester,' Charlie said. 'It's a funny place, but I was born there. Serafina nipped in the hospital and had me between shows.'

Sunday squeezed his hand. 'I wish I could have met her, she sounds like such a grand old lady.'

'Yes, she would have liked you. Isn't it funny, love? Here we are, side by side, like we've known each other all our lives. What a lot of time we wasted.'

'Nothing's ever wasted in life, Charlie. You always learn something.'

'Yes,' he looked at her intently. 'I suppose you do.'

*

The jet was swooping in to land.

'Stay behind me like a Japanese housewife and leave the press to me,' Charlie said. 'I'll answer a few questions and tell them you're my secretary.'

She smiled softly. 'Now that would be a good job for me. I *can* type, you know.'

'Yes? Good God—hidden talents!'

They both laughed.

63

Cedric Homer peered into the driving mirror of the sleek silver Rolls Royce parked outside the arrival gate at London airport. He combed his straight dark brown hair. He was an ordinary-looking man, thin and sharp-featured. In his grey chauffeur's uniform he seemed to blend in with the car.

He finished combing his hair and stared rudely at a passing girl in a mini skirt.

'Little scrubbers!' he muttered. 'Going around flashing their bums at everyone.'

His eyes followed the girl out of sight, then he got out of the car and stood beside it.

He thought about the previous evening, which he had spent with his mother in the old flat they shared in Islington. It had been a good evening. They had looked through his collection of photos and cuttings. He had every item that had ever appeared about Sunday Simmons in the English papers and magazines. She was so beautiful, so lovely, even his mother agreed with him.

Then later that evening he had shut himself in his own room, and the evening had been even better . . .

A policeman strolled up to the car. 'This is a no-parking zone,' he said. 'You've been here fifteen minutes, you'd better move along.'

'My party will be here in a minute,' Cedric said. 'I'm meeting Charlie Brick.'

'Oh, Charlie Brick. That's all right then, I suppose. Coming in this morning, is he?'

Cedric nodded. It was good luck that his boss had picked him to be the driver to meet Charlie Brick at the airport. Charlie Brick knew Sunday Simmons. If he told Charlie, explained that he wanted to write a letter of admiration, then he was sure Charlie would give him her address.

Cedric hummed softly to himself . . .

ROCK STAR

Saturday, July 11, 1987
Los Angeles

It was a perfect, cloudless Los Angeles day. The Santa Ana winds had driven off the smog, and Saturday, the eleventh of July, dawned crisp and clean, settling into a seductively lazy heat.

Kris Phoenix awoke early. Unusual for him, but he had flown in from London the previous afternoon and gone straight to bed. Fourteen hours later he surfaced in his over-sized California King bed, in his over-sized palatial Bel Air mansion, and rolled over to find that his Los Angeles girlfriend, Cybil Wilde, had joined him sometime during the night. Fortunately for her, she had not tried to wake him. Sex was great, but woe betide anyone who came between Kris and his jet-lag.

Cybil slept on, her nineteen-year-old body smooth and naked. Long, honey-blonde hair fanning out around her wholesomely pretty face.

Cybil Wilde was a highly paid, extremely visible commercial model. Not quite Christie Brinkley, but on her way. Recently she had appeared on the cover of *Sports Illustrated* in a revealing one-piece swimsuit. Now the offers were pouring in, but Cybil never accepted anything without deferring to Kris's superior judgement. And he preferred having her at home – whether he was there or not.

He debated waking her – after all, it was several weeks since they'd seen each other. Then he remembered the concert tonight, and decided he could wait. Astrid, his London live-in, had not exactly let his motor idle. In fact, Astrid was a maniac in the sack, she never left him alone.

Astrid, the clothes designer. They'd met four years ago in Paris, when his manager hired her to design some leather pants for him, and she'd ended up feeling a lot more than the material. At twenty-eight, Astrid was nine years older than Cybil, but she had the requisite long blonde hair and knock-out body, plus she was Danish, and everyone knew about Scandinavian women.

He liked his women blonde and long-legged, with big bosoms and an amiable disposition. What more could any man ask?

Silently Kris stepped from bed, making his way into his black-mirrored bathroom. Fortunately he'd managed to stay sober on the flight from London. It was amazing the difference it made — he actually felt like a human being. And on close inspection in the mirror above his marble sink, he actually looked like one.

Kris Phoenix was thirty-eight years old. He had intense, ice-blue eyes, longish, dirty-blond hair subtly streaked by the sun (and if the sun wasn't around, an English hairdresser called Spud took care of it), and rakish good looks. Neither tall nor short, he hit a comfortable five feet ten inches — and since taking up weight training he was all dynamic body power and rippling muscles. Hardly Arnold Schwarzenegger — more Bruce Springsteen fused with Mick Jagger.

Kris Phoenix was a rock star. A very famous rock star indeed.

In fact, some said, Kris Phoenix was a rock legend.

All that talk never bothered him. As far as he was concerned he made music, sang songs and played a mean guitar. So did a lot of other guys. Kris reckoned he had a hold on reality. Just because he divided his life between two fantastic mansions, made millions of dollars a year, owned seven cars, and kept two beautiful live-in females, it didn't make him any different inside. He would always — deep down — be plain Chris Pierce from Maida Vale, London. There was no getting away from the fact that his mother once scrubbed other people's floors, and his stepfather drove a bus.

"Ohh . . . my . . . God! You . . . are . . . *sooo* . . . sexy!" Cybil barefooted her way into the bathroom, and it wasn't only her feet that lacked coverage. "I've really *missed* you, Kris!" she sighed, throwing her arms around him.

Suddenly, Astrid the maniac began to fade from his thoughts.

"You too, kiddo," he replied, kissing her warm, inviting lips.

She rubbed her full breasts against his bare chest, knowing full well what *that* would do to him.

One snag. Sex was *out* on the day of a performance. Only somebody should tell the massive hard-on growing in his pyjama pants.

Regretfully he pushed her away. "Leave it out, Cyb. Y'know the rules, and tonight's that goddamn private gig for Marcus Citroen."

Snaking her arms around his waist, she rocked him back towards her. "How about a private gig just for me?" she whispered in her best sexy voice. "After all, I *am* asking nicely. And I promise I'll be good." A meaningful pause. "*Very* good."

There was no way Kris would break his rule. And nobody – not even the gorgeous Cybil Wilde – could make him. On the day of a performance he was like a fighter entering the ring: he needed every ounce of his precious sexual energy. Not one drop got spilled until it was all over.

"Later," he promised, disengaging himself and moving purposefully towards the shower.

Cybil pulled a disappointed face.

"I said later, luv," he repeated, flashing his famous crooked grin as he stepped under the icy needles of water and grabbed a bar of lemon soap.

Lathering his chest he decided the shower felt good. Freezing water. Freezing out the old sexual urges. Making him feel alive and alert, ready for anything.

Anything except a private performance for Marcus son-of-a-bitch Citroen.

Coldly Kris reflected on how much he loathed the powerful record magnate.

And with dull resignation he realized there was nothing he could do about it.

Not yet, anyway.

*

Rafealla alighted from Marcus Citroen's private jet and entered Marcus Citroen's personal Mercedes stretch limousine waiting on the tarmac. She nodded curtly to the driver, and was relieved to see upon entering the limo that there was no welcoming committee to greet her.

Great, she thought, *no one to bother me until I reach the hotel*.

She was wrong. As soon as she settled back, the driver requested she pick up the car phone. "Mr Citroen on the line," he said reverently.

"Thanks." Her voice was flat. Marcus Citroen followed her every move. She couldn't go to the bathroom without his knowing about it.

"Hi, Marcus," she said listlessly.

"Mr Citroen will be with you in a moment," replied the velvet-toned voice of his ever-so-efficient secretary, Phoebe.

Rafealla waited. Marcus liked to keep people waiting, she had seen him do it countless times. "Builds character," he would say dryly – with just a hint of the European accent he had never quite managed to get rid of.

Nervously she leaned forward and asked the driver if he had a cigarette.

"I gave it up," the man said with an apologetic shrug. "Would you like me to stop and get you a pack?"

"No," she said, shaking her head vigorously. She too had given up the dreaded habit, although right now she was prepared to kill for the chance of one long deep drag on *anything*.

"Rafealla?" Marcus's voice. The slight accent. The oily thickness.

"Yes, Marcus."

"You're here."

Of course I am, you summoned me, didn't you? "Yes."

"Was your flight comfortable?"

"Very."

"Good, good." He cleared his throat. "I have booked you into a suite at L'Ermitage. I'll call you as soon as you get there."

Yes. Probably the moment I walk through the door. "Fine," she said coolly.

"Rafealla?"

"Yes."

"You won't regret your decision."

Ah, but I will, Marcus. I will.

He had given her no option, she thought, running a hand despairingly through her long, dark hair. With a deep sigh she slumped back against the plush leather seating.

Rafealla. She was known by just one name.

Rafealla.

When she sang, her voice evoked magic. Sultry nights and smoky nightclubs, for she did not sing of virgins and fresh young love, she ventured back to Billie Holliday territory and the blues. At twenty-seven years of age she knew plenty about the blues. More than she ever should.

Rafealla was an exotic beauty. Green-eyed, with sharply etched cheekbones, a wide, luscious mouth, and a deep olive complexion. Her dark hair swept in a curtain to her waist – straight and shining. She was slight of build, not voluptuous – but her body was still quite something in the oversized man's suit and thin silk top she wore.

Rafealla had risen to the heights from nowhere, it seemed. Eighteen months ago she was unheard of. Now she was a star. Burning bright. A meteor streaking her way to the top of every record chart in the world. And whereas she had imagined stardom would bring her freedom – exactly the opposite had happened. Stardom had brought her Marcus Citroen. And she hated him with a deep and burning passion.

*

"Bobby Mondella, do you have any idea how much you are loved?" crooned the affectionate tones of the pretty black woman perched on the edge of a large circular desk. Her name was Sara.

Bobby, sitting in a comfortable leather chair next to the desk, reached out to touch. "Tell me, girl, tell me good."

Bobby Mondella gave new meaning to the word "handsome". In his thirties, he was tall, well over six feet, with dark chocolate skin, curly jet-black hair, and a great body.

"I'll do better than tellin' you, honey," Sara said enthusiastically, grabbing a random pile of press clippings from the desk. "I'm gonna read you some of the reviews comin' in on *Mondella Alive*. We are talkin' *dy. . .na. . .mite!*"

Bobby reached for the dark glasses covering his unseeing eyes, took them off, put them on again. He made the same gesture about a hundred times a day. It was impossible for him to accept the fact that he would never see again.

"Yeahhh. *Dy. . .na. . .mite!*" Sara repeated excitedly.

"I know 'bout the reviews," Bobby said patiently. "The album's been number one on the soul charts for five weeks now."

"Six," Sara corrected matter-of-factly. "Six straight weeks, an' *still* goin' strong." She paused for breath. "Oh, sure, *Mister* Mondella. I know you've heard all about the *Billboard* rave, an' *Rollin' Stone*, not to mention the *L.A. Times*, *Blues an' Soul*, an'—"

"What's happenin'?" Bobby interrupted. "Whyn't you just get to the train station an' save me the trip?"

"What's happening," Sara said importantly, "is that all across the country, in this great land we call America—"

"Cut it, babe."

Ignoring him, she continued her speech. "In every little hick town – they are lovin' you, honey, but I mean *lovin'* you." She paused triumphantly, shuffling the stack of press clippings. "Want me to read you some of this stuff?"

"Sure," he said casually, not wishing to appear too eager, although hiding anything from Sara was almost impossible, she knew him too well.

"Ridgway, PA," she read crisply. " 'Bobby Mondella *is* King Soul. Buy *Mondella Alive* an *really* get down, for Bobby Mondella puts more meaning into a lyric than anyone out there.' " She paused, then said, "You like?"

"Not bad."

"Hey – listen to Mister Conceited!"

"Bring your cute ass over here, I wanna play basketball."

"Will you *stop*," she scolded. "Here's another one. The *Duluth Herald*. 'The return of Bobby M. makes for the finest soul album of the last decade. Since his unfortunate tragedy the Mondella magic is hotter than ever.'"

Sara's sweet voice droned on – heaping praise upon praise. Superlative after superlative.

Listening carefully, Bobby couldn't help being delighted by all the extravagant praise. It was good to be number one again. Real good. Especially since everyone had counted him out, said he was finished, written him off as a has-been.

Everyone.

Except Sara.

And Marcus Citroen. Damn him.

Bobby felt the hate envelop him like a noxious cloud. He loathed the man, and for good reason. But he had to admit that Marcus Citroen was the only one who had given him a chance to come back, and back he was – with a vengeance.

"Enough, Sara," he interrupted quietly. "I want to get some rest before tonight."

"I don't know why you agreed to do this dumb fund-raiser," she grumbled. "Marcus Citroen and his rich friends don't deserve to be entertained by the likes of you. Especially your first live appearance since the accident."

How come everyone – including Sara – referred to his loss of sight as an accident? It was no accident, goddammit. It was a crime. And one day he would find out who was responsible.

"It's for an interesting event," he said shortly.

"*Her* event," Sara sneered, taking his arm and guiding him towards the door of his bedroom.

Her event. Bobby hadn't seen *her* since it happened. Nor had he heard one word from the cold-hearted bitch.

Nova Citroen. Marcus Citroen's wife. The thought of being in her company excited and disgusted him. He wondered what she would do . . . say . . .

Oh Christ. Don't tell me I'm still hung up, he thought. *I can't be. I mustn't be . . .*

As if sensing his thoughts of another woman, Sara withdrew.

Her voice became shrill and businesslike. "The limo will be here at three o'clock. What time shall I wake you?"

"Make it one-thirty." His hand reached for her smooth cheek. "An' I'll have a bacon sandwich with all the trimmings. Okay?"

"I'm not your resident cook," she said stiffly.

"I know, baby. But nobody — like I mean *nobody* — makes a better bacon sandwich than you."

Letting out a deep sigh of resignation, she realized she would do anything for Bobby Mondella and he knew it. Whether he appreciated it or not was another matter.

Left alone, Bobby made his way over to the bed, took off his shirt, unzipped his pants, and lay down.

Nova Citroen. Now that he had started he couldn't stop thinking about her.

Removing his dark glasses, he realized with a dull feeling of hopelessness he would never be able to set eyes on her again.

*

Nova Citroen could not decide which important piece of jewellery to wear that night. The Harry Winston emeralds were inviting, so green and rich looking. A single huge stone surrounded with diamonds for her neck, matching earrings, outrageous ring, and a magnificent bracelet. But she had worn that set in February to the great annual Niven/Cohen/Moss Valentine party, and again to Irving and Mary's Oscar event. Twice in one year was enough, so she discarded the emeralds, moving on to the Cartier rubies.

Ah, such nice bright baubles, but a touch too jazzy for her requirements tonight.

Without hesitation she turned to the deep burgundy box which housed her new diamond necklace, bracelet, and earrings. No contest. She had known all along that the evening cried out for nothing less than dazzling diamonds to complement her upswept white-blonde hair, and the stylish Galanos dress she planned to wear. So appropriate for a simple summer evening by the sea.

Nova Citroen's idea of a simple summer evening by the sea and the rest of the world's might possibly differ. Nova and her husband, Marcus, lived part of the year on Novaroen, a magnificent twenty-five-acre estate, perched on the top of a high bluff overlooking the Pacific Ocean a few miles past Malibu. The estate boasted two separate mansions – one especially for guests – an Olympic-size swimming pool, three north-south tennis courts, a recording studio, a fully equipped gym, a luxurious movie theatre, stables for their expensive Arabian horses, and garage space for Marcus's collection of immaculately restored antique cars.

They called it their weekend hang-out. Only this particular weekend a little more than hanging out was taking place. Nova and Marcus Citroen were hosting a fund-raiser for Governor Jack Highland – *the* fund-raiser of the year. An exclusive black-tie affair for fifty couples, each of whom had paid a hundred thousand dollars per couple for the privilege of being there. It was called protecting their future. And a very select group they were too. Nova had been ruthless in her choice of whom she would allow to attend. Once word got out that it was an impossible ticket, everyone clamoured to part with their money. After all, those in the know felt that Governor Highland was a sure thing for the next President.

Nova was suitably pleased with her final guest list. Only the *crème de la crème*. The richest, the most powerful, the most talented, and the most famous. She had not wanted too much Hollywood – her desire was to attract the *real* power, with just a scattering of rare stardust. And she had succeeded. They were flying in from all over the world.

The evening she had planned for her guests was spectacular. A five-course open-air dinner catered by the ultra chic Lilliane's restaurant. Followed by a surprise concert, where three of the biggest recording stars in the world would appear. The legend – Kris Phoenix. The comeback – Bobby Mondella. And the rising star – Rafealla.

One night. Five million dollars raised for Governor Highland's forthcoming campaign, and that was *before* the silent auction and raffle, where anyone – for a thousand dollars a ticket – could win prizes ranging from a case of Cristal champagne to a Mercedes coupé.

Clasping the magnificent diamond necklace to her throat, she decided it was perfect for later, and carefully replaced it in its velvet-lined box. After all, she had a certain reputation to live up to. She was known for her fabulous jewellery collection.

Nova Citroen was an elegant-looking woman in her early forties, with lightly tanned skin, fine aquiline features, and mesmerizing violet eyes. Men got lost in Nova's eyes. They were her greatest asset. She was not beautiful, but seductively attractive, with a body slim to the point of anorexia. It suited her, enabling her to look wonderful in clothes.

"Excuse me, Mrs Citroen." Discreetly, Norton St John, her personal assistant, entered the room. "Mr Citroen would like to speak to you. He's on your private line."

"*Is* he?" For a moment she considered telling Norton to inform Marcus he could go to hell. It was a pleasurable idea, but one she thought better of. Marcus Citroen was her continuing ride to the top, and much as she detested him, she was aboard for the entire trip.

*

Speed liked money. Only one snag. Money didn't seem to like him. Every time he made a bundle — something happened. He'd win at the track and some big-boobed bimbo would take it all from him. He'd score in Vegas. Whammo! A showgirl or two would step into the picture and it was all over. When he worked legitimately, which wasn't a steady activity, his ex-wife's lawyer was on his case within hours of his first paycheck. What was it with him and his freakin' luck? He just couldn't figure it out.

And then, one day, a meeting came to pass with a dude named George Smith, and Speed finally *knew* his fortunes were about to make a drastic U-turn. There was a big job going down, and George Smith wanted him in, because, goddammit, Speed was the best freakin' driver in the whole of Southern California, and let nobody forget it.

There had been several meetings since the first one, and now today was D-Day, and Speed knew exactly what he had to do.

Dressing carefully in the grey chauffeur's uniform he had

hired from a Hollywood costumiers, he admired his reflection in the long hall mirror of his one-room apartment.

So he wasn't very tall. Big freakin' deal. Nor was Dustin Hoffman.

So the hairline was receding. Big freakin' deal. Mr Burt Reynolds had the same problem.

So he had the features of an inquisitive ferret. Was Al Pacino a matinée idol?

Speed creamed over the way he looked. As far as he was concerned he was a real ladykiller. And when he had the money to back up his imagined charm, he was a hotshot with women. All women except his ex-wife – a platinum blonde stripper with bazoombas to break a man's heart, and nagging to break a man's balls.

Speed thought the uniform looked pretty ritzy on him – he admired himself for quite a few minutes before turning to other matters at hand. There were things to do before the evening's big caper.

He nodded to himself knowingly. This was the big score he had been waiting for all his life, and there was no way he was going to blow it.

*

Vicki Foxe had a strong urge to kick the grinning jackass security chief in the balls. Men. Sex. That's all they ever thought about. Most of them, anyway. There *were* exceptions – few and far between, and those always turned out to be the ones who played hard to get.

For a moment Vicki allowed herself to think about Maxwell Sicily – now *he* was an exception. Of course, he'd crap in his pants if he ever thought she knew his true identity – but who the hell did he think he was dealing with anyway? Some dumb dingbat with big tits? Oh no. When Vicki Foxe got involved in a business caper, she *knew* what it was all about.

George Smith, my ass, she'd thought, when he first contacted her. And it didn't take her long to find out his real name. It never took Vicki long to find out anything.

"Are y'all wearin' a bra, sweetie?" The beefy man leered,

staring bug-eyed at her greatest assets.

Up yours, dickhead, she thought. *What a cretin!*

If he ever saw her at her best he would go into cardiac arrest without pausing to make a will. Right now, skilfully disguised as a maid, she looked her worst. Her bright red hair was scraped back in a bun. She wore little makeup on her face. And her truly sensational body (39D cup, small waist and accommodating hips) was mostly concealed beneath a drab maid's uniform.

"Don't be so nosey, Tom," she scolded, flirtatiously batting her eyelids at him, forgetting that she was not wearing the sweeping false lashes she usually favoured. "It's none of your business, big boy."

Tom was chief of security on the Citroens' vast ocean-side estate, and already – after Vicki had only worked there for six weeks – he was hot to do anything she might ask in exchange for a sexual favour or two.

"I'd sure like ta find out," he drooled.

"Well . . ." Suggestively licking her lips, she gave him a little body brush. "Whatcha doin' later?"

They both had a good laugh at that one. Later was the big concert . . . the giant event. Tom would be up to his eyebrows handling massive security arrangements.

"If only we could watch the concert together," Vicki sighed, deliberately popping a button on her uniform, and then another, and then – very slowly – another.

Tom almost choked on his coffee. "You've got great ti—' he began.

Somebody walked into the service kitchen and he shut up.

Vicki quickly turned away, doing up her buttons. She could hear Tom's heavy breathing all the way out the door. And when the time came to take care of him, it would be no problem. Absolutely no problem at all.

*

Across town, Maxwell Sicily reported for work at Lilliane's, the exclusive Beverly Hills restaurant. Maxwell Sicily was twenty-nine years old, five feet eleven, one hundred and forty pounds, and of Sicilian origin. His hair was patent-leather black and greased back. His eyes were brooding and close set. His nose was too long, and his mouth too thin. But the overall effect was of a certain cold handsomeness. He looked like the son of a mob boss.

He *was* the son of the infamous Carmine Sicily – one of the top drug king-pins in Miami.

Father and son did not speak. Maxwell had come to California to make it on his own. He'd certainly had the right training.

"Hiya, George," said Chloe, the pudgy woman supervisor who sat behind the desk at Lilliane's answering the phones and keeping a sharp eye on the waiters as they punched in.

Maxwell nodded. At work they knew him only as George Smith – a suitable pseudonym.

"Hot today, isn't it?" Chloe said, coquettishly fanning her drooping bosom with a copy of *People* magazine.

Maxwell ignored her, thought better of it and nodded a curt "Yes."

"I never got to ask you before," she said quickly, glad of an opportunity to chat with the handsome waiter whom she'd had her eye on ever since he started work there. "You're an actor, aren't you?" She gazed at him hopefully. "I'm right, huh? I can always spot 'em."

Maxwell repeated his nod. Thank God this was the last day he had to put up with this. Tomorrow he would be on a plane to Brazil with a king's ransom supplied courtesy of Mr and Mrs Marcus Citroen.

Maxwell Sicily couldn't wait.

Kris Phoenix 1965
London

Chris Pierce celebrated his sixteenth birthday three weeks after being expelled from school. He hit the streets with a vengeance, changing his name to Kris Phoenix because he wanted – more than anything else in the world – to be a rock star.

His entire family thought it was the dumbest thing they'd ever heard. Out of school and out of work, he was not the most popular member of the household. Both his older sisters called him a lazy layabout. His stepfather said he should get himself a job and throw away the third-hand guitar he'd been strumming since he was thirteen. And his brother, Brian – considered the prince of the family because he'd landed a job as a bank clerk the moment he'd left school four years earlier – said, "Come off it, deadbeat. You're never goin' to get anywhere with your lousy voice and stupid guitar. Pack it in, make mum happy for once."

Mum. Kris wondered why it always had to come back to mum. Everyone knew she ruled the family with her loud voice and sarcastic tongue, but she hardly ever gave him a hard time and it pissed them all off. Especially Brian, who liked to think of himself as her favourite.

The truth was, Avis Pierce was secretly pleased her youngest son showed signs of wanting to do something different. She had worked as a cleaner in other people's homes since she was fourteen, and was proud of the fact she'd done that *and* raised a family. Shortly after Kris was born his father was killed in an industrial accident, and for six years Avis had got by on her own. It was tough with four hungry kids to feed, but she'd managed, until eventually she met and married Horace Pierce, a bus driver, and a brave man to take on the responsibility of a woman with four children.

Kris had no memories of his real father. Just a faded snapshot of himself balanced on his dad's knee when he was a few months old. His father appeared to be quite a lad with his spiky hair and crooked grin.

"Ah, yes," Avis would often say, a faraway gleam in her eyes. "'E was a real caution – your old man. Give 'im a beer an' a smoke an' 'e was 'appy as a pig in muck. 'E was a wicked bugger!"

Avis had a way with words.

Kris wished he'd known the father he looked just like. He never seemed to be able to communicate with Horace – who spent most of his waking hours glued in front of the television.

While he was growing up, Kris spent a lot of time with his mum. When he was a kid she used to take him with her on her rounds. Mondays, Wednesdays, and Fridays she cleaned the Edwards' house on smart Hamilton Terrace. And Tuesdays and Thursdays, around the corner on Carlton Hill, she "did" for Mr Terry Terence, a show business agent.

The Edwards lived in a five-storey luxury house, with a permanent maid and butler. Avis was brought in to do the hard work, such as polishing floors, cleaning windows, and taking care of the laundry. Kris liked it best when the Edwards had one of their frequent dinner parties, and early the next morning he was sent around the living room and the library to empty all the ashtrays. At eight years of age, pocketing the cigarette butts and producing them at school made him quite popular with the other lads.

The Edwards had two daughters, snobbish little fair-haired girls. Kris developed a crush on both of them, but they never gave him the time of day.

Mr Terry Terence was his favourite. Avis liked him too. "A real gent," she was fond of saying.

"He's a pansy!" Horace used to sneer whenever his name came up.

It wasn't until Kris reached the ripe old age of ten that he found out what a pansy was.

Mr Terence was an interesting man. He had an autographed picture of Little Richard in a pewter frame on his desk, and a large poster of Johnnie Ray in his hallway.

"Who's Johnnie Ray?" Kris asked one day.

"Johnnie Ray is the best bloody singer in the whole bloody world!" Avis replied with gusto. "I saw 'im at the Palladium once. Nearly wet me pants, din't I."

Mr Terence thought that was most amusing. He gave Kris two Johnnie Ray singles, and threw in an Elvis Presley for good measure.

Kris listened to them on his sister's record player. He hated Johnnie Ray, was crazy for Elvis, and decided then and there – he was eleven years old – he would be a singer and learn to play the guitar.

Now, five years later, he was trying to do just that. Only it wasn't easy. In 1965 teenage boys with aspirations to rock and roll were everywhere. Ever since the giant success of the Beatles and the Rolling Stones every Young Turk in England fancied himself as a future international rock star. The only difference was that Kris was dedicated, and thought of nothing else. Not even girls.

"Ain't it about time yer got a leg over?" his best friend, Buzz Darke, asked one day. "I got two little darlin's lined up fer later. Whyn't yer come with?"

Buzz was always trying to drag him along on his girl finding missions. Kris preferred to practise his guitar in the dank and dusty back garage attached to the old house Buzz lived in with his divorced mother.

"I thought we were goin' to play tonight," Kris said accusingly. "You promised me."

"Not *every* night we can't," Buzz replied in exasperation. "Cor! I don't believe it! Ain't yer interested in crumpet?"

"It's more important getting our group together," Kris said stubbornly. "If all you want to do is chase scrubbers instead of practisin' – fat chance we got of ever gettin' anywhere."

"Balls! I need t'get me leg over!"

"I'll practise without you then."

"Good. An' *I'll* tell yer wotcha missed."

"I'm pantin' t'hear," Kris replied sarcastically.

At seventeen, a year older than Kris, Buzz Darke had developed a look all his own. He never wore anything that wasn't black. He never smiled. He was thin and agile as a snake, and had a bruised, satanic look. Girls loved him.

Kris loved him too, because they were soul-mates when it came to music. They could spend hours on end discussing the merits of the Rolling Stones as opposed to the Yardbirds. Or was Bob Dylan's latest album better than the Beatles? And who was the greatest soul singer in the world — Sam Cooke or Otis Redding?

Also, Buzz could play a mean guitar — not quite up to Kris's standard, but pretty impressive all the same.

Kris had decided long ago he couldn't be bothered with girls. He had his guitar, his singing, and his treasured import record collection. That was his life. Besides, he always came off like dunce of the year whenever he got anywhere near a female. At school he'd never been able to understand any of them, and once he'd even caught two of them discussing him. "That Chris Pierce is a weirdo," one had said. "Yeah," the other replied. "He's got 'orrible starey eyes. Wouldn't like to come across *'im* on a dark night!"

That overheard conversation, plus the sneering giggles of the two little Edwards girls over the years, put him off the female sex altogether. Anyway, what did they know about music? Exactly nothing.

Buzz had set up a rehearsal room in the garage of his house. There was a third-hand drum set he had cadged off an uncle, a large tape recorder Kris had found on a garbage dump and promptly repaired, their joint collection of records, and an ace stereo with giant speakers, a gift from Buzz's mum, Daphne — an emaciated-looking woman who wore too much makeup, constantly chain-smoked, and worked as a hostess in a Soho nightclub.

Kris liked Mrs Darke, although she didn't seem at all mumsy

with her stiletto heels and all-black outfits. In a funny sort of way she looked exactly like an older, female version of her son.

Sometimes, when Kris and Buzz were locked into their music, playing guitar riffs along with Chuck Berry – the great Chuck, who had taught them more than any music academy ever could – she would enter the garage and stand silently by the peeling paint of the old double doors. "Hmmm . . . not bad," she would say when they'd finished. "You boys are going to get somewhere one of these days."

Yeah, Kris thought, if only Buzz would give up on stupid girls and concentrate.

It annoyed him that his own mother hadn't heard him play in years – ever since he palled up with Buzz and moved all his stuff over to the garage. His family were relieved. "Thank God we don't have to put up with your bloody racket night after night," Brian had said. "You sound worse than the bloody cats around the dustbins."

Kris made up his mind there and then that if he ever made it, his brother would be the last person he'd invite to one of his concerts.

"Well, mate, see yer," Buzz said, throwing a tatty black scarf around his neck. "Sure yer don't want t'change yer mind?"

"Give 'em one from me," Kris said with as much enthusiasm as he could muster – and wondered exactly what he was missing, and why Buzz pursued it so relentlessly.

He didn't have to wonder for long. Soon he was lost in the magic of the music – playing along with his precious record collection – fighting Chuck Berry for a solo – shouting out the lyrics on a Little Richard track – marvelling at the Ray Charles mastery on *What'd I Say*.

Kris had taught himself everything he knew just by listening to the greats – starting off at eleven on an old acoustic guitar kept in the music room at school, and graduating to his own, third-hand electric model bought at thirteen with his savings from a paper round and a little help from his mum. Avis hadn't exactly encouraged him although, to be fair, she hadn't discouraged him either. It was the rest of his family who were a pain in the neck, always bitching and complaining about the noise.

Getting together with Buzz – two likely lads with the same dream – saved him. They shared the rock star vision, and were prepared to work hard to achieve it.

He was deep into a guitar lead on Buddy Holly's *That'll be the Day*, when he realized Mrs Darke was leaning against the garage door quietly watching him. "Don't stop," she said, smoke curling from her nostrils.

So he didn't, allowing the music to envelop him, feeling the beat, the heat, letting his instrument become a welcome part of him.

When he was finished along with the record, she clapped, scattering cigarette ash on the floor. 'You're not half bad,' she said, walking towards him.

"Thanks," he mumbled.

"And not bad looking either for a kid."

Was he hearing right? Nobody had ever told him *that* before. Oh, sure, he knew he wasn't ugly – just sort of ordinary looking – maybe weird if he listened to the girls at school.

"Tell me something? How come you're not out cattin' around with my Buzz?" she asked, squatting down on her haunches and flipping through some of the albums stacked against the wall.

"I'd sooner practise," he replied, trying not to stare at the thin line of flesh showing between her tight black skirt and form-fitting sweater.

She turned to look up at him, and to his embarrassment he felt a solid hard-on begin to grow in his pants.

"Don't you like girls?' she asked, staring at him intently.

"Uh . . . n-no . . . I mean . . . y-yeah," he stammered, wishing only for a locked loo and a *Playboy* magazine – for that was the only way he could deal with the urgent feeling in his pants.

"No?" she said, with an amused glint. "Or yes?"

He struggled to regain his composure. "Er, I like 'em okay," he managed, and repeated weakly, "I'd just sooner – y'know, like practise."

"Hmmm . . ." She licked her lips. They were thin like the

rest of her. And then, as if it was the most natural move in the world, she raised her arms and took off her sweater, revealing small, hard breasts, with large, purple nipples.

Kris actually heard himself gulp. The sound echoed across the dusty garage.

"You're sixteen," Mrs Darke said matter-of-factly. "And I'm thirty-two, luv. It'll be better for you to do it with me than some messy little teenager who'll get herself knocked up before you can turn around."

Reaching for the zipper on his jeans, she pulled it down slowly. Then she touched his cock, which he knew was just about ready to burst. Springing it loose from his Y-fronts she deftly rubbed the tip, and to his embarrassment he came all over her hand.

A blush suffused him from head to toe, but Mrs Darke didn't seem at all put out. "First time?" she asked sympathetically.

He nodded dumbly, too humiliated to speak.

"Don't worry," she continued. "You learned how to play the guitar pretty good. Now you'll learn how to make love to the ladies. Just lie back an' enjoy lesson number one. I'm the best teacher *you'll* ever have."

*

Having a secret thing with Buzz's mum was not exactly easy. Whereas, before, Kris was always badgering his friend to practise, now he couldn't wait to get Buzz out of the way.

"What's the *matter* with you?" Buzz asked irritably one day, after a long and not very good practice session. "This used t'be all yer wanted t'do, an' now 'alf the time yer screwin' up. We'll never get anybody innerested in us if yer carry on like this."

Kris shrugged. It was true. He *was* screwing up, but not on purpose. Somehow, for the time being, playing had lost its edge, and being with Daphne was a greater thrill.

"It's my bloody job," he muttered. "I hate it."

His mother had insisted he do something rather than just pick up unemployment cheques. "It's about time, lad," she'd announced grimly. So he'd found work as a window-cleaner, and it frightened the shit out of him every day when he had to ride on the precarious little platform hanging from the side of a multi-storey giant office tower.

"Do somethin' else then," suggested Buzz. He'd got himself a job as an attendant at an amusement park for the summer, and was enjoying every minute. "I can pull twenty birds a day if I want," he boasted. "An' right little darlin's, too."

The truth was Kris was undergoing a massive guilt trip. He'd discovered the joys of sex along with the culpability of sticking it to his best friend's mother. Plus his brother was getting married, which meant the atmosphere at home was chaotic, with Avis acting as if a *Royal* wedding was about to take place.

Brian's bride-to-be, Jennifer, was the daughter of an accountant. Brian was marrying up, and Avis let no one forget it as she nagged them all about how they were to dress and behave in front of Jennifer's family.

Kris was elected best man. His mother made him hire a suit. It was too tight and smelled faintly of stale sweat. One day, he thought to himself as he stood behind his brother in the church, he was going to buy suits that he only wore once and then gave away – maybe to Brian if the bugger was lucky.

The summer progressed.

Kris's affair with Mrs Darke progressed.

Buzz announced he was fed up with England and wanted to go abroad for a while, suggesting Spain. "It'll be a right giggle," he said. "Plenty of cheap booze, lotsa crumpet, an' I've 'eard we can get jobs playin' our guitars in the local restaurants an' bars. It beats stayin' here through the winter freezin' our balls off. Besides," he added with a knowing wink, "if yer don't get laid soon, yer balls are gonna *fall* off – without any help from the bleedin' winter thankyouverymuch."

Buzz still had no idea of the steamy affair going on in his own house.

Weighing up the possibilities, Kris decided it wasn't such a bad idea. He had just turned seventeen and nothing was happening. He hated his job. He hated the duplicity involved in seeing Daphne. He hated watching his mother arrive home every day, worn out, her hands red and chapped from cleaning other people's dirt. He hated listening to his sisters fight all the time. He hated the weekly Sunday visits from Brian and his uptight wife. And – worst of all – he was getting nowhere with his music.

"Okay, we'll do it," he decided.

"Fanfuckin'tastic!" yelled Buzz, quite elated for once.

Avis had a fit when he told her. "You're too young to go to one of them dirty foreign countries," she informed him. "They eat dogs an' drink filthy water in them disgusting places."

"Let 'im go," said Horace, an unusual ally, rousing himself from the telly. "It's about time 'e stood on 'is own two feet. 'E's old enough an' ugly enough."

Daphne Darke took the news calmly. She even helped pay for the second-hand bikes they bought, and gave them money for the ferry trip across the English Channel to Belgium.

Kris had a funny feeling he would never see her again.

Bobby Mondella 1966
New York

At sixteen years of age Bobby Mondella was a handsome if blubbery singing star (he weighed over two hundred pounds). "Sweet Little Bobby", as he was known, had made quite a few country and western hit records between the ages of eleven, when he started to sing professionally, and sixteen, when it was suddenly all over.

His voice broke, and before you could say "Two flop records in a row" "Sweet Little Bobby" was dropped by his record company, his manager, and all his so-called friends.

Mr Leon Rue, his guardian/manager in Nashville, relinquished both appointments, gave him a cheque for six thousand dollars plus twenty-five dollars in cash, and put him on a plane back to his Aunt Bertha in New York, from where he had plucked him five years previously.

"Sweet Little Bobby" didn't know what had happened. One day he was churning out best-selling records, the next he was on an airplane heading home, and he was so used to doing what he was told that it seemed the right thing. It wasn't until the plane landed at Kennedy Airport and there was no one to meet him, and no waiting limo, that slowly realization dawned. He'd been disposed of. Cleanly. Neatly. He was on his own. And the funny thing was, he didn't mind too much. No more pressures, no more non-stop work. He was free! And he was coming home to dear old Aunt Bertha.

Managing to find a cab, he got himself and his luggage (three suitcases filled with glittery stage and television outfits) into it, and set off for Aunt Bertha's house in Queens.

There was only one problem. Aunt Bertha had expired six months earlier, leaving behind six cats and a thirty-year-old daughter named Fanni, who was even fatter than Bobby.

Fanni's greeting was not friendly. "What *you* want, boy?" she screamed, standing on the doorstep, hands on ample hips, huge bosom quivering with indignation.

"I've come home," he said simply.

"You done *what*? This ain't your home no more," she yelled, attracting the attention of several neighbours, who leaned from their windows in rapt attention. Everyone within miles knew who "Sweet Little Bobby" was. Hadn't Bertha kept his picture in a frame on her window sill? Hadn't she always talked of him proudly – boasted about how she'd brought him up, ever since her sister died when he was only two years old?

Yes, indeed.

"Where's Aunt Bertha?" Bobby asked plaintively. He was beginning to feel tired and hungry – not to mention depressed, for he knew it was all over, and at sixteen that was a frightening thought, even if it did mean freedom.

"Don' give me none of that *where's Aunt Bertha* crap." Fanni mimicked his voice with mounting fury. "She done be ten foot under six months now, an' you don' even sen' no flowers. Big star my fat ass!"

Bobby felt the tears well up in his eyes. For five years he had been away from his aunt, recording, writing songs, performing. And all that time he had known that one day he would come home. Now that day was here and Fanni was telling him that Aunt Bertha was *dead*.

"Mr Rue would have t-told me," he stuttered. "I d-don't believe it."

"You callin' me a *liar*, cousin?" Fanni roared.

"Nobody told me," he repeated dully.

"Well, ain't *that* a good excuse." Sarcasm dripped from Fanni's wide, angry mouth. "I guess when you all are a *star*, little things like a *death* in the family are sure 'nuff kept from you."

By this time the cab driver, a gum-chewing Puerto Rican, had dumped all three of Bobby's suitcases on the doorstep and was getting impatient. He started doing knee bends and cracking his knuckles. "Ya wanna pay me?" he asked. "Or mebbe I wait around, have a meal, play some pool, huh?"

"This boy ain't stayin' here," Fanni said firmly, indicating Bobby. "You kin put his stuff right back in your cab."

The Puerto Rican grimaced. "Hey lady – I look like a porter? Ya wanna put his bags back in my cab? Sure. *You* put 'em there, mama."

"Don't you call *me* mama," Fanni cautioned, giving him a filthy look.

"Just pay me, lady," the cab driver said wearily.

Suddenly Bobby remembered his cheque. Six thousand dollars for five years' hard work. Pulling it from his pocket he handed it to Fanni. "This is for you if I can come home."

Fanni eyed the cheque, devoured the amount, held it up to the light as if it were a counterfeit bill, and then finally she said, "Inside, cousin. *I'll* take care of the cab fare."

Fanni lived with a man called Ernest Crystal. Ernest was large in every way. Six feet five inches in height, and a solid three hundred pounds. A former pro football player, Ernie did a little bit of this and a little bit of that. He had two ex-wives, and several children. Right now he was staying with Fanni and not doing much of anything.

Ernest took one look at the six-thousand-dollar cheque Fanni brandished in front of his eyes and his face lit up. "Woman, where you get this?"

"Sweet little Bobby's back."

"Holy mother! Don't you be tellin' me I finally stepped in *she . . . it!*"

Ernest and Fanni were married two weeks later, whereupon Ernest appointed Fanni and himself as Bobby's legal guardians. The first thing he did was drag Bobby around on a relentless tour of all the record companies. Only he was too late to make a killing. Nobody wanted to know about "Sweet Little Bobby" anymore. He was yesterday's news. A fat teenager with a baby face and cracked voice.

Aggravated, Ernest then set about hiring a lawyer to find out what had happened to the rest of Bobby's earnings from the five years he had spent with Mr Leon Rue. Six thousand bucks didn't seem right at all. And it wasn't. But Mr Leon Rue had covered himself with legal documents giving him most of everything Bobby earned right up until he cut him free. Plus he owned every song Bobby had ever written.

"Shyster honky bastard!" Ernest complained to Fanni. "Your mama musta bin some dumb woman. She jest signed the kid away. Now *we* got him back worth nothin'."

"We have ourselves six thousand dollars," Fanni said tartly.

"Pig swill," Ernest spat in disgust. "That honky cheater stolen hundreds an' thousan's of big bucks shoulda bin *mine*."

"Ours," Fanni corrected him, double chins quivering indignantly.

"Yeah, ours," Ernest agreed.

Bobby couldn't help overhearing their discussions. He had the little room next to the kitchen, and most of the day he just lay on the bed munching cookies and candies, thinking about how nice it was just to laze around doing nothing. The five years he'd spent with Mr Leon Rue was all work. Weekdays, weekends, and if he wasn't performing Mr Rue had him sitting at a table, writing. He had lost count of the number of songs he'd composed. No time to make friends or get to know anybody. A tutor taught him schoolwork three times a week. A hooker gave him his first sexual experience when he was fifteen – paid for and organized by Mr Rue. He hated every minute of it. The woman had hair like an oven-cleaning pad, and smelled of sour milk.

There were always lots of girls in the audience when he performed. They squealed and giggled, but he never got to meet any, and now it was over. The truth was he didn't care if he never sang or wrote another song again. He couldn't sing anyway, puberty had struck, and his voice was now an unfamiliar croak.

Mr Leon Rue had discovered Bobby the day after the boy's

eleventh birthday. Bobby was singing and playing the piano in a local talent contest, and he was good, having learned to do both at Aunt Bertha's weekly prayer meetings. The music came naturally to him and gave him enormous pleasure. It gave Aunt Bertha pleasure too. She encouraged her nephew, and boasted about his God-given talent and pure falsetto voice to all her friends. Bobby won the contest and fifteen dollars, while Mr Leon Rue won Aunt Bertha's confidence, and within weeks he had persuaded her to let him take over Bobby's career, become his legal guardian, and build him into a big singing star.

"It's for your own good, Bobby," Aunt Bertha whispered sadly when the time came to say goodbye. "This be the only way you'll ever get yourself a *real* chance."

Soon he was whisked off to Mr Rue's large house in Nashville, where he was put to work writing simple country and western ditties. He was used to gospel, but he soon learned what Mr Rue wanted by listening to countless country records — most of them with the same familiar theme.

Churning out hits was easy, even though it failed to inspire him.

*

Bobby's six thousand dollars did not last long. Ernest needed a new car, which took most of it. And Fanni needed new clothes, which took care of the rest of it. Aunt Bertha had left her only daughter the house and a small amount of money, but the time soon came when everyone had to get a job, including Bobby.

Fanni resumed her old position as book-keeper in an accounting firm, and Ernest began working as a magazine salesman.

"What *you* gonna do, boy?" Ernest demanded belligerently. "Can't sit 'round here on your fat ass livin' off your cousin all day long."

Conveniently he had forgotten Bobby's six-thousand-dollar contribution to the family's fortunes.

Bobby had no idea what he *could* do. The only thing he knew was music, and that part of his life was over. He was sixteen years old and finished, and yet there had to be a future for him. Scanning the job ads, he circled anything that looked remotely interesting and did not require a college degree.

Five interviews later he found he had been turned down for a variety of reasons. Too young, too inexperienced, too fat, too uneducated, and most of all – too black.

Of course, none of the people who interviewed him actually came out and gave their reasons, but he knew. Living in New York, he was wising up fast.

Finally, after several weeks of looking, he tagged three years onto his age and got a job in The Chainsaw, a vast Manhattan discotheque, as a men's room attendant.

The final humiliation. "Sweet Little Bobby" no longer existed.

Rafealla 1967
Paris

It was Rafealla Le Serre's seventh birthday, and as she skipped along the Paris street hand in hand with her best friend, Odile Ronet, she could feel her heart beating fast with excitement. Odile had celebrated *her* birthday ten days earlier, and she had received a bicycle – a fantastic, shiny red bicycle.

Rafealla desperately hoped she would be as lucky.

Mrs Macdee, her Scottish nanny, walking ahead with Odile's nanny, turned to scold the two little girls, but in an affectionate way. "Come along, do come along," she said briskly. "There won't be time to change into your pretty frocks if you don't hurry."

Rafealla giggled nervously, squeezing her friend's hand. Odile giggled too, and they whispered together about bikes and dolls and dresses and chocolate cake.

Nanny Macdee led the way as they turned briskly into the Avenue Foch, where Rafealla and Odile lived in neighbouring houses. The two little girls kissed each other on the cheek and ran up the steps to their respective homes.

"All this fuss! You're going to see each other in a minute," grumbled Nanny Macdee.

The front door was opened by a uniformed manservant. Rafealla rushed by him, racing up the grand staircase to her room, where her party dress was laid out on the bed, just waiting for her to climb into. *Oh, what a beautiful dress*, she thought, gazing at the pink organza creation with a full skirt and white satin sash. Throwing off her school uniform, she attempted to struggle into it.

"Dearie me, no," stated an out-of-breath Nanny Macdee as she entered the room. "We'll have a wash first, missy, won't we?"

Rafealla stifled a groan. Washing was so *boring*. She obliged anyway – arguing with Nanny just wasn't worth it.

Soon she was ready. Face washed. Hands scrubbed. Long dark hair brushed and ribboned. Pink dress in place on her lithe young body.

"*Now* we're ready," said Nanny Macdee, finally satisfied. "Come along, dear."

In the living room, Anna and Lucien, her parents, waited. Rafealla paused in the doorway so they could both see how pretty she looked. Then with a whoop of delight she ran straight towards her father, who swooped her into his arms, swinging her around and around as if she was a limp rag doll.

"Poppa! Poppa!" she shrieked happily.

"Happy birthday, my sweet little sugar-cake," he said in his wonderfully deep booming voice.

Wriggling free, she ran to her mother, who enclosed her in exotic fragrances as she hugged her close.

Out of the corner of her eye Rafealla spotted a pile of colourfully wrapped presents.

"Yes, they're for you," smiled her mother, gently releasing her. "You may open them now."

To her great consternation Rafealla couldn't see any package that looked big enough to conceal a bicycle. With grim determination she began tearing open the fancy paper wrappings, wondering if perhaps her precious bicycle was divided into pieces and scattered among the presents.

"Not so fast," admonished Nanny Macdee from the doorway.

"It's all right, she's so excited," excused Anna Le Serre, watching her daughter with warm amusement.

"Just like her mother when she gets presents," teased Lucien, putting his arm around his delicately beautiful wife, causing her to gaze up at him with open adoration.

Nanny Macdee averted her eyes. She had never worked for people who were quite so openly affectionate as the Le Serres. They acted like a honeymoon couple, always billing and cooing as if no one else existed.

Nanny Macdee had been in their employ since Rafealla was born, and she had decided long ago it was because of Mr Le Serre's background. He was ... different. Not only was he extremely famous – a great tenor who performed in the most prestigious opera houses in the world. He was also black – half Ethiopian, half American – and quite the most imposingly handsome man Nanny Macdee had ever set eyes on.

Anna Le Serre was the perfect foil for her giant of a husband – he was six feet five inches, and she was a bare five feet four. Her skin was alabaster white, and her hair raven-black. Combining English and French blood, she possessed a rare and gentle beauty and was fine-boned and slim. Once a promising ballerina, she had given up her career to marry Lucien, a career she now hoped her daughter would follow.

Rafealla had inherited the best of both her parents, with her smooth olive complexion, luxuriant, thick dark hair, long legs and budding beauty.

Her mouth down-turned with disappointment as she unwrapped the last of the presents and discovered no cleverly concealed bicycle.

The doorbell rang, and her school friends began to arrive for her afternoon tea-party. Breathlessly, Odile, in brown velvet with a white lace collar, asked to see her gifts. Her eyes commiserated with her friend when she realized a bicycle was not among them.

Tea was delicious. Cakes and scones and tiny little English tea sandwiches filled with cream cheese and cucumber, jam and chocolate spread. All of Rafealla's favourites. And then out came the cake – a huge confection of meringue and strawberries, with seven candles.

I'm seven, Rafealla thought in wonderment. *I'm almost grown up*.

Lucien picked her up and gave her a big kiss. "I love you,

sweet-cakes," he said in his big gruff voice. "You make my life so very pleasurable. And don't you *ever* forget it."

He then carried her into the front hall, where there was the biggest, the best, and the shiniest red bicycle she had ever seen.

With yells of joy she fell upon it. Her day was complete.

Later, when her friends had gone home – all except Odile, who as a special treat was to stay the night – Rafealla and Odile sat at Anna's feet as she prepared for an evening out. Both little girls found it fascinating to watch as she applied makeup, pinned her luxurious tresses on top of her head, and clipped on exquisite diamond and turquoise earrings and a matching necklace.

Rafealla knew for sure that her mother was extremely beautiful, and it made her very proud.

Nanny Macdee soon arrived to shoo the girls away. "Give your mama privacy, for goodness' sake!" she scolded.

They fled downstairs to the library, where Lucien was entertaining Odile's father, Henri – a prominent French politician. The two men were good friends as well as neighbours, and tonight they were attending an important political dinner together. Odile's mother, Isabella, was away visiting relatives in the country.

"What naughtiness have you two been up to?" Lucien demanded with a big smile.

The girls protested their innocence, and were each rewarded with a tall glass of forbidden Coca-Cola. Nanny Macdee would have a fit. No fizzy drinks, especially just before bedtime.

Anna entered the room, a vision in pale lilac chiffon. "I'm ready," she said apologetically. "I do hope I haven't kept you waiting."

The men told her how lovely she looked, and she accepted their compliments with grace and charm.

Rafealla felt happy inside – it had been a lovely birthday.

"We'd better get moving," Lucien announced. "We cannot be late." He stared intently at his daughter. "There's something different about you, my sweet little girl. Ah, yes, I know what it is," he added with a chuckle. "You look like you must be seven!"

Amid much laughter the three grown-ups moved towards the front door. Lucien flung it open, standing back to allow his wife to pass through first.

"Oh, dear!" Anna exclaimed. "I forgot something. You start the car, I won't be a minute."

"We're going in Henri's car," Lucien said with a sigh of impatience. "Hurry up."

Smiling at Odile's father she said, "You can't take Lucien's driving either, eh, Henri? I thought it was just me!" With that she hurried upstairs.

Rafealla stood on tiptoe to kiss her father, but even then she couldn't reach. Picking her up he whispered, "Sweet dreams, my baby girl."

"Poppa, I'm grown up now," she protested.

"Ah, well." He kissed her affectionately. "In that case, sweet dreams, my *big* girl."

And then he and Mr Ronet walked down the front steps and climbed into Mr Ronet's silver Mercedes.

The two little girls stood at the open door waving as Nanny Macdee came bustling up behind them with a cross expression. "You'll catch your death!" she complained. "And I'll be blamed. Now come along, upstairs. *Right now.*'

Obediently Rafealla turned away, ready to do as she was told. So did Odile.

"I should think so too," sniffed Nanny, not really as cross as she made out.

Anna was on her way downstairs, lilac chiffon flowing behind her as she rushed so as not to keep Lucien and Henri waiting. She had never looked more beautiful.

Together they all heard the roaring explosion. It came from the street. A blast so loud it sounded as if a bomb had landed on top of the house.

And then came the effect. Windows shattered, as the full force hit, and they were all thrown to the ground and showered with lethal shards of glass.

Rafealla saw her mother begin to fall down the stairs, and it was as if she were watching a slow-motion ballet.

As pieces of glass embedded themselves in her legs causing unbearable pain, she began to whimper.

"Poppa," she called out in frozen terror. "Oh, poppa! Save us! Please save us!"

Kris Phoenix 1968

After a late start, Kris discovered sex with an enthusiasm surpassing even his best friend's.

"Cor blimey!" Buzz exclaimed one day, as they lounged on the beach in Majorca. "You never bleedin' stop! At least I give it a breather once in a while."

Kris laughed. Two and a half years away from home, fending for himself, including a year and a half spent hitchhiking across Europe, had given him a new sense of confidence. He was not only sure he could be independent without scrounging handouts from his mum, but he was now secure in the knowledge that he could pull the birds with the best of them. He might not be tall, dark and traditionally handsome, but at nearly twenty he had his own style. Crooked good looks, dirty-blond hair, a wiry body, and a solid suntan.

"Best thing I ever did was draggin' yer out of England," Buzz remarked.

Kris rolled over on the hot sand. He had his eye on two giggling girls in bikinis standing by the edge of the water. "I'm not gonna argue with *that*, mate." He squinted at the girls. "Which one you want?"

Buzz looked surprised. "Am I gettin' first choice for a change?"

"Yeah, why not," Kris said generously.

"The one with the big tits," Buzz decided.

"Aw, c'mon. Do me a favour. Y'know you like 'em skinny."

"I feel like a handful today."

"Screw *you*."

The two friends laughed, while the girls – who knew they were being watched – pretended not to notice.

"*You* pull 'em, then," Kris said.

Buzz groaned. "I'm still recovering from that little Swedish raver last night. I can't bleedin' move, can I?"

Buzz had lost his eerie pallor, and was now a deep gypsy brown. He wore his black hair long and unkempt, and one gold stud earring decorated his right earlobe. He was so thin his ribs stuck out.

"Bloody hell!" Kris said, with mock annoyance. "Why have I always gotta do the pulling?" Leaping up, he swaggered across the sand towards the giggling girls. "'Ello, darlin's," he said confidently. "Speaka da English?"

They spoka da English all right. They were on vacation from Liverpool.

Taking a survey one day, both Kris and Buzz had decided that the easiest girls to have it off with were the English. A quick bit of the verbals and it was up, up and away. Second were the Scandinavians – Swedish, Danish and Finnish – easy pickings. The local Spanish señoritas were a no-no, while German and French girls were a pain in the backside. And Americans – impossible, unless you romanced them and got them pissed – which took time and money. Neither of which Buzz or Kris was inclined to do.

After a brief chat-up, Kris took the two giggling females over to meet Buzz, and before long it was Sangrias (a lethal combination of red wine, fruit and lemonade) all round, and playful gropings on the hot sand.

By sundown things were getting serious, and a romantic stroll along the beach led the way to a quiet wooded area, where after five minutes of concentrated foreplay it was time for the great moment.

Kris got off on that first plunge into a new girl. Every time he did it he thought of the two stuck-up little Edwards girls and the other girls at school who'd called him weird and wouldn't give him the time of day. When he jammed it into a new female he was doing it to all of them, and it felt good.

"Will I see you later?" his latest conquest asked, awkwardly hitching up the bottom half of her bikini.

"What hotel are you at?" Cleverly he avoided answering her question.

She told him and he nodded knowingly. "An' how long you stayin', luv?"

"Six more days," she said obligingly, adding hopefully, "Can I see you later?"

Ah, six days to avoid that particular beach and hotel, and then it would be safe again. "I wish I could, but I can't manage tonight," he said regretfully. "Whyn't I see you here tomorrow?"

And that was how it usually went. In and out and on to the next. Evenings were for work. A gig at a local restaurant playing the guitar and singing – and then usually a late night session at a club or discotheque where they got together with other musicians and really let rip. They were getting so hot on their guitars that they'd acquired quite a reputation, and any visiting players sought out the two English kids to jam with.

They had stayed in Majorca for nearly a year, sharing a one-room apartment. The weather was sensational, the booze cheap, and a continual stream of tourists kept the place interesting, not to mention hot and cold women on tap at all times. Before that they had travelled across Belgium, Germany, France and Italy – taking jobs along the way, and enjoying every moment of their new-found freedom.

The drag was they hadn't been discovered, and that bothered Kris more than it did Buzz, who seemed quite content to live his life in the sun without any of the hassles of England. Kris knew for sure that if they were ever going to put a group together and try to do something decent, it was not going to be in some Spanish holiday resort getting laid regularly. Eventually they were going to have to go home, whether Buzz liked it or not. England was where it was all happening, and he was anxious to be a part of it. New groups were springing to prominence all the time – he read the trades – a couple of weeks late but better than nothing. The *Musical Express* and the *Record Mirror* were full of success stories – Rod Stewart, the lead vocalist from the Jeff Beck Group, was making his mark, and groups like Blind Faith, Yes, and Led Zeppelin were leading the trends.

It was 1968, and ever since the advent of the Beatles and the Rolling Stones, England was hot. The swinging sixties all started in London, with fashion, movies, style, and most of all – music. London was definitely the place to be.

One day, after receiving a letter from his mother, Buzz said, "I think I'm gonna ask Daphne t'come an' stay with us fer a couple of weeks."

Buzz never called Daphne mum, he always referred to her by name.

"Why?" Kris blurted out, forgotten guilt creeping up on him.

Waving her letter in the air Buzz said, "She's given up 'er job, chucked out that new bloke she was livin' with, an' – I dunno – she sort of sounds on edge, y'know what I mean?"

"Where'll she sleep?" Kris asked. "There's no room here."

"She can have my bed, I'll kip on the floor. Yer don't *mind*, d'you?"

Christ! Did Buzz know? Impossible. Daphne had sworn him to secrecy – she would hardly confide in her son.

Forcing himself to sound casual he said, "I couldn't give a monkey's."

"Okay, I'll give 'er a ring then," Buzz decided. "I guess I can just about scrape up enough readies for 'er ticket."

Kris wondered if Daphne would expect him to resume service. He had no desire to do so. After all, he was no longer the innocent virgin she had initiated on her garage floor. It wasn't that he didn't like her, it was just that the guilt of giving one to his best friend's mother was too much to take.

Buzz went off to the local bar to call her, while Kris figured out what he was going to do.

He didn't have to figure too long or too hard. When Buzz returned he was pale beneath his tan.

"What's the matter?" Kris asked quickly.

Buzz sat on the edge of his bed, his thin face a mask of shock. "She topped 'erself, didn't she. Daphne's dead."

*

Returning to England for the funeral was the most depressing thing that had ever happened to Kris. It was October, and he had forgotten the icy cold, the afternoons when it was dark by four o'clock, the relentless drizzling rain, and the heavy traffic. Most of all he had forgotten what it was like to live at home with his two sisters – both unmarried – shrieking at each other all the time; his stepfather, Horace, the television zombie; and his mum, Avis – still cleaning other people's houses, and ruling the home front with her loud voice and bossy manner.

"Yer too skinny," she informed Kris sternly. "Why didn't yer write? I could box yer ears, y'little bastard!"

Both his sisters stared at him jealously. The younger of the two said, "It's all right for *some* people, ennit? Just laze about in the sun all day an' don't send mum no money. *I* pay for *my* room an' board."

"Don't get your knickers in a twist," Kris said quickly, "I'm not stayin'."

"Shame!" exclaimed his other sister, who had inherited her mother's sarcastic tongue. "Goin' off to *America* to be a *pop star*, are we?"

He couldn't stand his sisters, but his dislike for them paled in comparison to his relationship with his brother. Brian came over for Sunday tea trailing his wife, Jennifer, and two snotty-nosed kids. The two-year-old was the reason Brian had been forced to get married in the first place, and the baby, Kris figured out, was just to make *him* feel bad. Brian's smug face said it all. *I've got a job, a wife, and a family. What have you got, little brother?*

"It's about time you decided what you're going to do with yourself," Brian lectured him pompously. "Don't you think it's a bloody disgrace the way you're worrying ma?"

"Fuck you," Kris muttered, a low aside destined only for Brian's ears.

Unfortunately the two-year-old caught the rhythm and proceeded to chant, *"Fuckoo, fuckoo, fuckoo!"*

"You low-life scum," Brian said angrily. "Teaching my boy to swear. You're just a no-good layabout — whyn't you start behaving like a man, cut your hair and get a job?"

"Is that what you think being a man is all about?" Kris asked, with a derisive snort. "Short hair an' some lousy job?"

"*I* don't have to worry about it," Brian puffed self-righteously. "*You're* the one that looks like a bloody queer."

Kris started to laugh, which infuriated Brian even more.

Avis cracked the whip. "Will you two shut up?" she said, her loud voice booming across the table. "If yer wanter act like squabblers, go outside an' do it."

"Yes," chorused the sisters, livening up at the prospect of a possible fight.

"Another cuppa tea, luv," Horace requested, oblivious to the simmering hostilities around him. "I don't want ter miss the football on telly."

Kris knew he wasn't going to be able to take family life for long. He was used to his freedom now, and sleeping on the couch in the front parlour — because one of his sisters had taken over his old bedroom — was a real drag. He had only been home five days, and already it was time to move on. The problem was he had no money, and Buzz was no help. Ever since Daphne's funeral Buzz had refused to leave his house. He didn't want to practise, or go round the clubs. He didn't want to do anything.

Daphne had killed herself in the traditional way — stuffed her head in the oven and turned the gas on. Nobody knew why. "Poor dear. She got depressed a lot," a relative explained at the funeral. "Depression's a terrible burden to bear."

Buzz thought differently. "It's 'cos I left her alone," he said grimly. "We was always close, an' I deserted her."

Kris didn't know what to say. He still felt guilty — maybe it was *his* fault.

"C'mon," he told Buzz. "You can't just sit around bein' miserable. We gotta get somethin' goin' for us."

"What?" Buzz said stonily. "Fuckin' what?"

"I dunno," Kris replied in desperation. "But I'm goin' to figure *somethin'* out. You can bet on it."

*

With fifty pounds borrowed from his mother, and a temporary job washing windows again, Kris moved away from the family home dragging Buzz with him. Buzz couldn't stay in his house anyway, the lease was up and he had to get out. Daphne had left a few hundred pounds. Unfortunately the funeral and legal fees soon ate that up. Buzz gave all her possessions to relatives, and followed Kris to the squat he had found in nearby Kilburn. The squat, an abandoned derelict house, had been taken over by a bunch of hippies whose credo was LOVE AND PEACE. The place was a mess, but Buzz fitted right in to the indolent lifestyle – it suited him fine to do nothing all day, and then sit around at night playing his guitar by candlelight watched by a bunch of admiring long-haired girls.

It did not suit Kris. He had far more ambitious plans. With the money he'd borrowed, he bought himself a second-hand motor-scooter, enabling him to get up to the West End of London, where he began hanging out at all the rhythm and blues, rock, and all-night jazz clubs, hoping to get a chance to connect.

He soon found out he was not the only one. Before long he met a black guy called Rasta Stanley, a would-be drummer currently making time running errands for a record company. And Ollie Stoltz, a talented bassist straight out of a scholarship year at the Royal Academy of Music.

Triumphantly he told Buzz he thought he'd found their group.

"It's all horseshit," Buzz said, dragging heavily on a joint – his new favourite habit. "I'm not gettin' into any of that competitive crap."

"Right," agreed Flower, Buzz's current love, a sixteen-year-old runaway from Brighton with huge, limpid blue eyes, and fair hair which hung in a straight curtain to below her ass.

Kris felt the anger boil up inside him. This is what they had been striving for since school. The right combination. The dynamite group. And then . . . POW!! Rock stardom would be theirs, and there'd be no looking back. He could buy his mum a mink coat, and tell Brian to go shove it in his left ear.

Now this little frother with the dirty hair and big stoned eyes was telling Buzz what to do. He wasn't going to stand for it. No way.

"Flower, luv," he said calmly, "whyn't you go down to the corner shop an' buy yourself a packet of fags an' a box of Maltesers." He fished a precious pound note from the pocket of his jeans. "My treat."

This got Flower's attention. After smoking dope and screwing, normal cigarettes and chocolate were her main passions.

"Really, Kris?" she asked unsurely, as if he might whisk the pound note away as soon as she got up.

Pressing the money into the palm of her grubby little hand he said, "Yeah, only I want you to go right now. Okay?"

She looked at Buzz for approval. Laconically he nodded. Jumping off the old mattress where they lounged away most of the day, she smoothed down her crumpled blouse, added a miniskirt and floppy sandals, and scurried off.

Buzz drew deeply on the last of his joint, stubbed it out on the floor, and leaning back clasped both hands behind his head. "Go on then," he said. "Start pissing me off."

Kris knew how to play it. Turning away he said, "Hey, man. You wanna stay on your back all day gettin' laid an' stoned, *I* don't care."

"It suits me," Buzz said stubbornly.

"Good, 'cos I just wanted to be sure before I take off on my own."

"Whadderya mean – on your own?" Buzz asked suspiciously.

"If you think I'm goin' to sit around here watchin' *you* get bed-bugs, you're barmy. I'm settin' somethin' up with Ollie an' Rasta, an' there's another bloke – he plays guitar – does vocals. He can take your place." A meaningful pause. "I just wanted to be certain you didn't want in."

"Fuck!" Buzz grumbled. "*What* other bloke?"

"He's an okay guy, you'll like him. When, we get our first gig you'll come an' see us."

Buzz sat up. "Like hell I will."

"'Course, he's not quite as good as you, but with practice..."

"Sod it!" exclaimed Buzz, hauling himself off the bed, and throwing a dirty black shirt over stovepipe black jeans. "Yer won't quit until yer got me. Let's go."

A few days later they had their group. And a name. The Wild Ones. Two lead guitars – Kris and Buzz. A bassist and sometime keyboard player – Ollie Stoltz. A dynamite drummer – Rasta Stanley. And vocals shared between Kris and Buzz.

They were all set to fly with nowhere to go.

"Fuck!" snarled Buzz. "We'd better get our freakin' act together or die. I've *had* this being poor shit."

All of a sudden Buzz had ambition. Kris decided it was a good sign.

Bobby Mondella 1968

"You're a fat lazy sonofabitch, an' I don' wan' you livin' with us no more. So pack your bags an' git the hell *out*."

So spoke Ernest Crystal, all six feet five inches of him. He had never forgiven Bobby for not laying the golden egg.

"No way this boy goin' nowhere," cried Fanni, shaking chubby fists in his direction. "He *my* flesh, *my* blood, an' the only way he done go is if'n *I* say so."

"You arguing wit me, witch?" demanded Ernest, glowering ferociously.

"I'm jest sayin' what's right," retorted Fanni, refusing to back down. "An' don' you be callin' *me* no names, Ernest Crystal. You watch your damn mouth."

"I'll call you what I pleases, woman," steamed Ernest.

Standing between them, Bobby felt as if he hardly existed. Neither of them cared about him. They merely enjoyed using him as a prop for their never-ending fights. He had lived with them for two years, and throughout that period Ernest had tried to throw him out more than a dozen times, with Cousin Fanni always springing to his defence. She did not do it out of love — more a bitter desire never to let Ernest get the better of her.

"The day this'n boy goes, *you* go," she announced spitefully, glaring at Ernest.

Bobby hoped she knew what she was saying, because in one

week it was his eighteenth birthday – and as soon as that day came, he was out of there.

For two years now he had been working in the men's room at The Chainsaw discotheque, and he had learned plenty. Being locked up in Nashville all those years, being looked after by Mr Leon Rue, had taught him exactly nothing.

"You-all are *dumb*, boy," Ernest Crystal often said, and in the beginning he was right. "Sweet Little Bobby" was about as dumb as they came.

Working at The Chainsaw gave him the opportunity to see life as it really was, and he soon began to get a whole lot smarter – fast. The fact was, he had to. Surviving the rigours of The Chainsaw's men's room was like treading through a mine-field in lead boots. The last thing people came in for was a simple pee. They entered the men's room for many different purposes – the number one reason being to score drugs. Bobby cottoned on to that the first night he worked there when he tried to stop a major sale and nearly got fired for his trouble.

"Listen, kid," Nichols Kline, the manager, told him. "You clean up piss, you clean up shit, you stop any fights, an' you keep your mouth tightly zipped. *Don't* interfere with the customers, an' they won't interfere with you. Got it?"

Yes, he got it, especially when he heard about the last men's room attendant, who'd had his face carved up by an irate drug dealer claiming the attendant was ripping him off by selling his own stash.

"Keep clean an' you'll stay alive," a white waiter called Rocket Fabrizzi warned him. "They're hirin' kids now 'cos it's a tough pace. The guy before the last one had a heart attack an' dropped dead over the crapper. Oh, an' you'd better watch out for your ass. Don't get caught with your pants around your ankles."

Bobby didn't figure that one out for several weeks, until he had to fight off an overexcited old queen who kept on crooning, "I just *adoooore* chubbos, especially *black* ones. I'll give you three hundred dollars and a simply *delicious* time!"

And so he learned. They came in to –

Buy

Sell

Cruise

Talk about sex

Pop pills

Sniff cocaine

Have sex

Smoke a joint

Throw up

Shoot up

You name it, they did it.

At least once a night Bobby had to eject some drunken but willing female who was either sitting across a guy's lap in the one john with a door, or giving all and sundry a blow job.

Dull it wasn't.

Sordid it was.

However, it certainly afforded him a crash course in survival. He'd lied about his age to get the job – making himself three years older than he actually was. And once he had it, he was determined to stay, because working at The Chainsaw certainly wasn't ordinary.

The Chainsaw was the first of the really large discotheques – a vast two-storey emporium of flashing strobe lights, outrageously loud music (sometimes live groups, mostly records). It had hot-looking bartenders in black bell-bottom pants with skin tight white vests, and equally hot looking waitresses in leather mini-dresses.

The Chainsaw was what hip New Yorkers called a happening place. It catered to the rich, famous, and infamous – most of them notorious for never picking up a cheque. And to pay the bills it also catered to whoever looked beautiful enough or bizarre enough or outlandish enough to gain entry. In other words – no polyester crowd ever broke through the heavily guarded doors of The Chainsaw. And the word "tourist" was *never* mentioned.

"I gotta go to work," Bobby announced, squeezing past his cousin Fanni, who had now launched into a loud tirade about Ernest's disgusting bathroom habits.

They both ignored him as he left.

He was sweating as he walked towards the subway and he knew why. Anyone would sweat carrying around the extra weight he packed, and he'd finally decided to do something about it. A new waitress had started work at the club a few weeks earlier. Her name was Sharleen. She was black, about twenty-three, and she was gorgeous. Bobby was in love. The only problem was she had no idea he existed. Every time he tried to talk to her she gave him a blank look as if she'd never set eyes on him before.

On quiet nights he studied his reflection in the ornate mirror above the line of porcelain sinks in the men's room. When he was "Sweet Little Bobby" the chubbiness kind of suited him – it went nicely with his white sequinned stage suits and modified Afro. Now, at nearly eighteen, and growing taller every day, he looked like a huge blob. "Fat Big Bobby" could be his new title.

Living with Fanni was no help. The woman loved to cook. Grease was her middle name – even the once muscular Ernest was getting fatter by the minute.

Bobby knew he had to move on. If he stayed with Fanni and Ernest, he'd remain fat forever, and there was *no way* Sharleen would notice him.

He had his plans. Rocket, the waiter, had promised there might be a bed available in his basement apartment as his roommate was leaving. Bobby had said he'd take it, and handed over a month's rent in advance. Unfortunately, every time he asked what was happening, Rocket had a ready excuse. Finally Bobby insisted he move in on his birthday or get his money back. Rocket had promised everything would be worked out.

Arriving at the club, Bobby found the usual frantic staff activity. Friday night was the hottest night of the week. It was also the night the celebrities came out to play before taking off for long restful weekends.

Hurrying straight to his supply cupboard, he checked out boxes of Kleenex, soap, clean towels, packets of Durex, and bottles of cheap aftershave.

"Bobby," said Nichols Kline, the manager, appearing at his side.

"Yes, Mr Kline," Bobby replied alertly. He had this lingering fear that one of these night he would get fired, and would be unable to afford to move away from Fanni and Ernest.

"I'm puttin' you in charge of the private men's room tonight," Nichols Kline said. He was a tall, jumpy-looking man in his thirties, with a shock of abundant rust-coloured curls and a Captain Hook nose. He had the reputation of being a formidable stud, and was often to be found behind locked office doors with any female of his choice. "Seymour's out sick. Can you handle it?"

Jumping to attention, Bobby said, "Yes, *sir*."

The private men's room. Wow! He wondered what was wrong with Seymour, the usual attendant. He hadn't missed a night since Bobby worked there.

"Just take it easy, play it cool, an' let 'em do what they want," Nichols said, lustfully eyeing a passing waitress.

Oh God! He's checking out Sharleen, thought Bobby.

She sashayed by with a pert, "Good evening, Mr Kline," failing to notice Bobby.

"Famous people – y'know, like singers, film stars, society folk. Well . . . they're different," Nichols explained. "You gotta leave 'em alone, yet be right there if they want anything." He scratched inside his shirt, jangling a few gold chains. "Never stare. They don't like that. And *no autographs* – even if it's for your dying mother in Nebraska. Got it?"

"Yes, Mr Kline."

"Oh, an' if they do any drugs, just ignore it." Casually he added, "Of course, if they wanna score you can send 'em to me. *No* selling. One complaint, kid, an' you're *out*. I don't care *how* many years you've worked here."

"Yes, *sir*!"

For one brief second Bobby thought about telling Nichols he had once been a famous person himself. Minor league, of course, but he'd had his moments.

Common sense told him to forget it. Firstly Nichols would never believe him. And secondly, what did he have to gain by letting everyone know he was a has-been?

No. His secret was locked deep within him. Since leaving

Nashville and Mr Rue he had not sung one note or written one word. Music was his past. It had to stay that way.

The private men's room – or Seymour's Palace as it was known around the club – was a Deco fantasy of black granite floors, black marble washstands, shining urinals, and silver walls adorned with framed sepia photographs of Marilyn Monroe – caught at every stage of her career. Nichols handed Bobby a key to Seymour's famous locked cupboard, and there he found atomizers of expensive aftershaves and colognes, the finest hair brushes and combs, a half-filled bottle of Courvoisier, a glassine envelope containing a white illegal substance – probably cocaine – and an assortment of mixed pills.

Bobby shoved the cocaine and the pills to the back of the cupboard, took out what he needed as far as supplies were concerned, and locked up. He had never had much contact with Seymour, a short, dour black man in his fifties, who – the rest of the staff informed him – only enjoyed talking to his famous clientele.

After setting up, Bobby made his way down to the kitchen, where the staff had an early dinner before the club opened.

Rocket waved to him, so collecting a plate of pasta from an assistant chef he went to sit with his waiter friend.

Rocket was an aspiring actor from the school of method acting. He was of Italian origin, in his early twenties, with long, greasy hair, and darting, inquisitive eyes. "I hear you got lucky tonight," he said in his flat, nasal voice. "Upstairs doin' big time, huh?"

"That's right."

"Shame you didn't know about it earlier. If you'd known you could've come prepared." He dropped his tone to a low whisper. "You could've done us both a favour."

"I *am* prepared," Bobby said.

"Naw," Rocket explained, "you're not gettin' my drift. In the private john y'can *really* get a score goin'. They got big bucks, an' they ain't got nothin' to do with 'em but buy. Why d'ya think Seymour never socializes? The creep is a fartin' king up there. Makes a fortune." He looked furtively around before continuing. "Give me an hour – if I can get someone to cover for me I'll try t'get everything you're gonna need. Then we'll split your take — fifty-fifty."

Bobby didn't want to get into selling drugs. He was smart enough to know it only led to trouble. Besides, Nichols Kline had already warned him.

"No," he said, shaking his head. "Like it's too dangerous, man. I don't wanna risk my job."

"You'll risk your fartin' job if you *don't* give 'em what they want," Rocket said knowledgeably. "Hey — old Seymour's lasted a long time up there, right? He gives those famous fuckers pronto service, an' if you don't — believe me — you're *out*. They're *mean* rich motherfuckers."

Bobby thought about Seymour's locked cupboard. Maybe there was something in what Rocket had to say after all.

"C'mon, Bobby, we gotta make a killin'," Rocket pleaded, sensing a weakness. "Maybe we only got tonight — so let's go for it, huh?"

*

Working the private men's room was a different world. Bobby was used to a crowded, never-ending line of noisy sweat-soaked, hyper customers, who — if he was lucky — might leave anything from a ten-cent to a dollar tip. He was not used to a thin trickle of expensively clad movie stars, rock stars, sports stars, producers, clothes designers, investment bankers, occasional politicians, directors, and a mixed bag of other success stories.

Remembering Nichols Kline's words, he tried not to stare. But it was difficult when a fair amount of the faces were so very familiar. Most of them were in and out, some leaving no tip at all, while others threw down a ten or twenty as if it was nothing. Jefferson Lionacre, a famous black singing star, palmed him a hundred-dollar bill with a wink and an encouraging "Today the crapper — tomorrow the world."

Bobby wanted to shake his hand. What a title for a song! Only he wasn't writing anymore.

Why not? he asked himself. He had lost his sweet, childish voice, not his song-writing abilities. Why *shouldn't* he go back to composing — if only for his own enjoyment? And not the country and western stuff Mr Leon Rue had made him write – but soul, sweet *sweet* soul music. *His* kind of music.

Lately he'd been listening to a lot of James Brown and Aretha Franklin. The two of them certainly knew how to sell a song.

Hey – if he set his mind to it he could write soul. Fresh melodies were always churning around in his head. Wasn't it about time he did something about it?

Okay, first he was going to move out. Next he would write a song. Just for himself.

"Hey – *you* – fat boy."

His reverie was interrupted by a skinny, stoned rock and roll star wearing a tight lizard-skin jacket, orange pants, high-heeled boots and a spacy leer. "Where's Seymour?"

"He's not here tonight," Bobby replied, humiliated at being called "fat boy" although he knew it was true.

"Sheeit, I kin see *that*," the rocker said, posturing in front of the full-length mirror. "Where is the old bum?"

"Uh, I think he's out sick," Bobby replied, recognizing the rock and roller as Del Delgardo – lead singer with a group called The Nightmares.

The rocker pouted his thick lips and adjusted his bulging crotch. "Did he leave you my stuff?"

"What stuff?"

Narrowing his eyes, Delgardo said, "Don't give me dumb Sambo shit or your ass'll be on the auction block. You goddamn spades always stick together." His voice developed a whiny quality. "I want my stuff. It's paid for. And I want it fast."

For a moment Bobby thought about smashing the skinny asshole's face in. But it wouldn't achieve anything, he'd only get fired.

Taking a deep breath he thought about the glassine envelope in Seymour's locked cupboard. What did he do? Go for the hunch, or wait for this maniac to start screaming?

Going for the hunch he unlocked the cupboard, reached inside, took out the envelope and shoved it at the jerk. "Is this it?"

The rock and roller claimed what was his with a petulant snarl. "How come ya didn't ask me to get down on my fuckin' knees and *beg*?" He then proceeded to lay out thin lines on the black marble and snort an inordinate amount.

Bobby turned away. He'd only sampled drugs once. Two years of seeing what dope did to people was enough to warn him off forever.

"Join me," Del commanded, suddenly becoming friendly.

"No, thanks. It's not my scene."

"Do it!" the rock star insisted.

"I can't, I'll lose my job."

Del Delgardo reverted to his true self. "You'll lose it if you *don't*, you fat fuck."

Bobby wished someone would come in before he punched this jerk out. But the private men's room remained private.

"I said do it!" Del repeated threateningly.

Bobby wondered how the great Seymour would handle a situation like this. And then he was saved. A middle-aged man in a tuxedo walked in, attracting the rock star's attention.

"Hey, Marcus," Del greeted him. "You're just in time. Come on in an' join the fuckin' feast!"

To Bobby's surprise, the affluent-looking man walked over to the stoned singer as if they were the best of friends, patted him warmly on his lizard-clad shoulder, extracted a small gold straw from his inside pocket, and elegantly snorted a line of the addictive white substance.

Bobby heaved a sigh of relief. He was no longer needed. Crisis over. Discreetly he busied himself polishing the pristine marble sinks.

"My album's walkin' out the stores – fuckin' walkin'. Right, Marcus? Right?" demanded Del.

"Yes, indeed it is," replied the man, with a slight European accent.

"I'm fuckin' beatin' the *cock* out of Mick. Right?"

"We're making money. That's all that's important, isn't it?"

"Yeah," replied Del unsurely. The most important thing to him was outselling Mick Jagger and the Rolling Stones. Never mind the money.

"Shall we return to our ladies?" Marcus asked smoothly.

Greedily Del Delgardo snorted his last line of coke. "Yeah,

let's do that. Why not?" He took one final look at himself in the mirror, liked what he saw, and unsteadily accompanied the older man from the room.

As soon as they were gone, Rocket darted furtively through the door. "You know who that was?" he asked excitedly.

"Del Delgardo. What a creep."

"Not *him*. The other guy."

"Who was he?"

"Marcus Citroen. He owns Blue Cadillac Records. He's power, man, with a capital P. Here—" Rocket emptied out his pockets. "I got joints – pills – ammis – an' some sleepers. It's the best I can do for tonight. Let's hope Seymour stays away for a while."

"How much I gotta charge?" Bobby asked, not really wanting to become involved.

"Jeeze!" Rocket rolled his eyes. "Sometimes I wonder about you, Bobby. Where the hell you *bin* all your life?"

*

"I hear you met Marcus Citroen last night."

Sharleen was talking to him. She was actually acknowledging his existence!

"Yeah," Boby mumbled. He didn't know how to handle it. They were standing next to each other clocking in. It was the closest he'd ever been to her, and he hadn't realized she was so petite, like a little doll. And pretty! Oh, was she pretty.

"Listen." Sharleen leaned towards him speaking in an urgent whisper. "I can't get near any VIPs. I'm stuck downstairs with the junk skunks. So do me a *big* favour, if he comes in tonight give him this for me. *Please*." Pressing a cassette into his hand, she gazed at him pleadingly.

This was his golden opportunity. All he had to do was say, *Sure. Go out with me, and I'll pass him your tape.* Real flip and cool, exactly like Rocket would do.

Instead he just about managed a weak "Yes."

"Thanks, sweetie." Sharleen stood on tiptoe and kissed him on the cheek. "You're a nice guy."

And then she was gone, and he'd lost his chance. Damn!

Rocket appeared, grinning with anticipation. "Have I got us the works tonight! Primo, primo! Seymour's not back, is he?"

Secretly Bobby hoped he was. Catering to the big shots was too much like hard work – he preferred the hustle and craziness of downstairs. And selling dope wasn't to his liking either, although he had to admit he *could* use the money. After all, it wasn't as if he were out on the street pushing to kids. As Rocket pointed out – these people had plenty of money, nobody was *forcing* them to buy.

"You're back upstairs again tonight, Bobby," announced Nichols Kline, looming up behind them, causing Rocket to jump guiltily. "You're doing okay up there. No complaints."

"What's the matter with Seymour?" he ventured.

"Don't you worry about Seymour," Nichols replied lightly. "Just do your job, and stay out of everyone's way."

"Yeah," crowed Rocket as soon as Nichols walked off. "Do your job, an' stay *in* everyone's pocket!" He cackled hysterically.

It turned out to be another crazy night, and when anyone asked, Bobby supplied them with what they wanted, soon learning that money was of no great concern to the rich and famous, they seemed to enjoy throwing it around.

At closing time he looked for Rocket to pay him his share, but his waiter friend was nowhere to be found, and since he was in a hurry to get home, he left. Marcus Citroen hadn't shown up, and Sharleen's tape was still in his possession. He couldn't wait to hear it.

When he got home he played it on his portable tape machine – a souvenir from Nashville – and was mortified to discover she sounded terrible, straining to be heard above a far too loud backup group, her voice small and tinny.

So . . . Sharleen wanted to be a singer. Well, at least they had music in common, and Bobby knew – just by listening to her – he could help her sound a lot better.

With that comforting thought in mind he fell asleep, only to awake several hours later with agonizing cramps in his stomach.

"Oh . . . Jesus!" Moaning with acute pain he dragged himself out of bed and into the bathroom, where he promptly threw up.

Relief was not forthcoming. The unremitting pain persisted, tearing at his gut like a constant jagged edge.

Panic overcame him. Something bad was happening, and he didn't know what to do. Gathering all the strength he could muster he staggered into Fanni and Ernest's room, switching the light on and waking them both up.

"What you-all doin', boy?" yelled Fanni, launching herself into a sitting position, huge bosom escaping from a cheap pink nightgown.

"I'm sick," he gasped. "I got this terrible pain."

"What kinda pain?" Fanni asked suspiciously.

"He's drunk," muttered Ernest, pulling the covers over his head.

"The boy don't drink," retorted Fanni, always ready for a fight.

"That's what *you* think, woman," replied Ernest knowingly.

Bobby clutched his stomach. This was his punishment for selling dope. He'd known it was wrong. Why'd he let Rocket talk him into it?

He felt the sweat break out all over his body, followed by a spiralling sensation of serious pain. And then, with an enormous thud, he fell to the floor, unconscious to the world.

The last words he heard were Ernest saying, "*Shee...it!* I need my rest, woman. I don' expect these kinda goin's on in the middle of t'night. Do somethin' about it, witch. Throw him *outta* here! I can't stand lookin' at his fat, lazy, no-good ass one more day!"

Saturday, July 11, 1987
Los Angeles

Emerging from the shower, Kris found the delectable Cybil arranged across his bed, completely naked except for a blooming red rose placed strategically between her thighs.

"Wanna pick a flower, ya lucky man?" she drawled in a put-on street accent. "Twenny bucks for a trip to the Rose Parade, an' you don't even havta go to Pasadena!"

Why was she tempting him like this? Feeling the heat rise he was aggravated. Retreating back to the bathroom he said, "Do me a favour, luv, put your knickers on an' stop messin' about."

"Oh, *boy*, you'd better have some *good* things in store for me tomorrow," she threatened.

He closed the door. "I'm not coming out until you're dressed."

"You *veel* regret *zis* day," she said in a heavy foreign accent. "I *veel* 'ave my *beeg* revenge."

One thing about Cybil, there was never a dull moment. She was good-natured and fun, a natural-born joker. She was also fancied by every straight male in America, yet it was his bed she was sharing. He had exclusive rights to the gorgeous blonde body, the Miss America face, and the cascades of shining hair.

So why did he need Astrid – the mistress of his English mansion?

Insurance. While Astrid was on the scene he couldn't get too

He should know. His father had taught him at a very early age. Which is why he stuck to hookers.

Pay, and you know exactly what you are getting.

Pay, and you're the boss. No argument.

Women were inferior creatures. Keep them on their knees where they belong. Let them know who's in charge. Never take any of their garbage. Never.

He thought about Vicki Foxe for a moment. A lot was riding on her involvement. If she screwed up . . .

Stop! No negative thoughts. Vicki might be a woman, but she came highly recommended, and if he wasn't certain she could do her part he wouldn't have hired her. The same with Speed.

Usually Maxwell preferred to work alone. Who needed the headache of depending on other people? But this job was too big. He had to have help, and Speed and Vicki were it. Already Vicki's inside information had proved invaluable. She was good. He'd had no doubts really. She was a woman used to getting paid for her services, and therefore she knew how to deliver.

He wasn't so sure about Speed. The man was a weasel, crafty and devious. But when it came to driving he was supposed to be one of the best. And that's all he had to do. Be in the right place at the right time. And just drive. Maxwell felt sure everything was under control.

He was on his way to a fortune, and nobody was going to stop him.

*

The moment Rafealla entered her suite at L'Ermitage, Marcus Citroen was on the phone.

"Are you comfortable?" he asked.

"Yes, thank you."

"Do you have everything you need?"

"Yes, Marcus, I do."

"I'm going to try and come over."

"Please don't," she said quickly. "Not today. I'm tired and I have the concert to think about. I'll see you tonight."

He didn't sound too pleased. "Very well. I'll phone you in an hour."

She had an hour's grace. An hour to unpack, soak in a long hot tub, lie on the bed and chain-smoke while flicking the channels on American television.

She found herself on MTV. Rafealla, doing what she did best. Looking sultry and moody, her long dark hair a lush curtain framing an exquisite face. Her smoky voice evoking erotic thoughts in all who heard it.

Rafealla.

Sophisticated.

Worldly.

Knowledgeable.

Sensual.

What a phoney! She hadn't been to bed with anyone for a year.

Career first.

Life second.

Her choice.

Dear Marcus Citroen, make me a star and I will be yours.

Well, he had kept his part of the bargain, and now the day of reckoning was here.

She was surprised she'd managed to keep him waiting so long.

*

The girl behind the desk at the care hire company studied the papers Speed handed her with a blank stare as rhythmically her jaw decimated a piece of chewing gum.

"The grey Cadillac limousine," Speed repeated patiently. "I took it out last Saturday, and the weekend before that."

Without saying a word she picked up a pen, scrawled authorization on the hire form, reached for the phone and mumbled, "Dan, grey Caddy limo." Then she nodded at a side door. "Pick it up in the alley. How're you payin'?"

He fumbled for cash. She counted it out, handed him his copy of the papers, and automatically mumbled, "Have a nice day."

"I will," he replied with a quick wink, knowing she probably thought he looked pretty ritzy in his smart grey chauffeur's uniform with the jaunty peaked cap.

Could he help it if women loved him? Even his ex-wife wanted to give him a roll every time he visited her – which, he had to admit, wasn't often, on account of her residing in Las Vegas, a town he tried to stay away from, because every time he went back there he either got married or gambled away every last cent he possessed.

Jeeze! Tits and gambling. His two passions.

A mechanic brought the Cadillac around, and Speed climbed inside. He loved the smell of an expensive car. Once, he'd done a stint as private chauffeur to a rich Pasadena couple. The woman used to arrange for her maid to place a dozen white roses in the car every day. What an aroma! He'd fucked the maid, enjoyed the roses, and left after three months. Legitimate work was boring.

The Cadillac handled nicely. And so it should. On the two weekends he'd taken it out he'd given it plenty of tender loving care. Under the hood throbbed an engine hot to trot. When Speed tinkered with an engine, miracles happened. It wasn't that much different from handling a woman. A little delicate finger action, some rubbing and dipping and smearing on of lubricant. Searching for just the right spot to make that sucker purr.

Speed chuckled to himself. Today was going to be easy. All he had to do was be in the right spot at the right time. And then fly.

For ten grand he could manage that.

*

The smell of bacon woke him before Sara did, and Bobby Mondella lay on the bed lost in his own private world of darkness. Sometimes he got panic attacks, other times he was quiet and in complete control. Sara helped. She was always there for him, and suddenly he desired her with a force that surprised him.

He heard her walk into the room with that special step he would recognize anywhere.

"One bacon sandwich, one alarm call comin' up," she said cheerfully.

"Come over here, woman," he said, his voice thick with desire.

She didn't need asking twice. Sara knew everything Bobby wanted, sometimes before he knew it himself. Placing the tray on a table, she went to him willingly.

His arms reached up, pulling her onto the bed beside him.

She lay very still, her heart beating fast with the anticipation of what was to come, for Bobby Mondella was the greatest lover in the world.

Slowly he began to feel her body through the clothes she wore. Lightly his sensitive hands roamed across her large breasts, rounded stomach and child-bearing hips. His fingertips barely touched, but soon she was longing for him to rip her clothes off.

She moaned, a stifled sound, for Bobby liked her to remain passive until he indicated otherwise.

With maddening restraint his hands leisurely found their way inside her blouse. He undid the buttons one by one, opening the garment.

Her breasts strained to escape the confines of her bra. But he teased some more, playing with her swollen nipples through the material, tracing intricate patterns of intent.

"Please, Bobby, *please*," she had to beg.

"Be patient, momma," he crooned. "I'm gonna get there, all in good time. Just you be quiet."

"Oh, *God!*" Her face was flushed, he tortured her with the waiting, and yet it was sweet torture and she was addicted to every wonderful moment of it.

At last he snapped the clasp, allowing her breasts to burst free. She almost climaxed there and then, that's how good his touch was. But he didn't allow her to — ignoring her newly liberated bosom he moved down to her thighs, feeling the inner flesh, caressing, teasing, lifting her skirt inch by inch, pulling down her panties at a snail's pace.

"Bobby, you are drivin' me *crazy*," she managed to gasp.

"Honey baby, you don' know what crazy *is*."

And then he proceeded to show her with slow and sure expertise, bringing her to orgasm twice with his hands and tongue before finally consummating the sexual act.

As he thrust in and out, Sara sobbed with a mixture of relief and pleasure. She loved the man so much, and yet she still wasn't sure of his feelings for her. He needed her – oh yes, she was confident of that. But did he love her? He had never said so, although in moments of passion she told *him* all the time. In fact she was saying it now. "I love you Bobby Mondella. Love you, love you, love you. Oh, how I *loooove* you." And again she was climaxing, just for him, the man she loved, the man she wanted more than anything in the world.

His reply was no more than a long-drawn-out groan as he finally allowed himself release.

Immediately he withdrew, rolling across the bed, pulling a sheet over his nakedness as if he didn't want her to see him in any other state except arousal.

"Was it good for you, baby?" She couldn't stop herself from asking.

The fires were vanquished, he was back in control. "I'm hungry," he said, abruptly changing the subject. "Did I hear talk about a bacon sandwich?"

Dutifully she got off the bed, announcing, "It's cold, I'll make you another one."

"Cold is fine. Just hand it to me."

Without bothering to cover herself, she padded over to the table where she had left the tray, and took it to him. Normally she would have been self-conscious about displaying her body. She considered her legs too short, her ass too rounded, and her breasts too big, but with Bobby it didn't matter, he couldn't see her anyway. And if he could, he wouldn't want her, she was sure of that. Because, in his time, Bobby Mondella had been with the most beautiful women in the world – black and white.

Sara remembered the magazine stories, the scandals and the gossip. She also remembered the first time she saw him perform onstage back in 1980. She was eighteen years old and had just graduated from high school. Two girlfriends dragged her to a concert he was doing in Philadelphia. "He's the sexiest man *alive!*" they both assured her. "Wait'll you *see* him! This man is pure horn!"

And she'd had to agree they were right. When he walked out on that stage in finely cut black pants and a white silk shirt, fifty thousand women began to wet their pants while screaming their lungs out. Bobby Mondella exuded sex. He was a walking, living, breathing phallic symbol. And what a voice!

Sara became an immediate convert. She'd never dreamed that years later, soon after his terrible accident, she would be working for him as his personal assistant, and more.

"I'm gonna take another shower," Bobby said, finishing the sandwich in a couple of hungry bites. "Are my clothes ready?"

"Everything's set," she replied. "Your favourite black pants and white silk shirt."

"Thanks, babe." Yeah, they were his favourite clothes all right. His lucky outfit. Only his clothes hadn't been so lucky for him on that fateful night two years ago.

Oh, Jesus. Soon he would be in the presence of Nova Citroen. That seductive cold *bitch*.

He didn't know if he could take it.

Sara held his arm, assisting him to the bathroom.

He shook her hand away. "I know the lay-out," he said sharply. "You've got to stop takin' every step for me."

Sometimes he wanted help. Sometimes he couldn't stand it. Today he wanted to do everything on his own.

"I'll go get dressed," she said quickly, in that small, hurt voice he couldn't stand.

She was such a sweet kid, so warm and helpful. She'd brought him back from the brink, and he didn't know what he'd do without her. And yet, there were times she got on his nerves.

Lightening up, he said, "You mean you're still walkin' around bare-assed, girl? Shame on you! Somebody might see you."

Bobby's idea of a joke. Sara didn't find it very funny.

*

Nova Citroen prowled around her luxurious estate checking the details that had made her one of America's number one hostesses, and aggravating the hell out of everyone who worked for her. She had an eye for the smallest speck of dust, the slightest imperfection, everything had to be just so.

Concentrating on the guest house, she ordered a collection of silver frames to be repolished. Insisted there were fresh rolls of toilet tissue in every one of the seven bathrooms. Made a manservant change every light bulb, and personally rearranged nine vases of garden-picked flowers.

Finally she returned to her bedroom with her masseuse, hairdresser, manicurist, and a top makeup artist – an English girl called Tracy – the only one allowed to touch the precious Nova Citroen skin.

"This is all so boring," she informed her diligent entourage. "However, I enjoy raising money. And the Governor is *such* a *worthy* cause, don't you think?"

Little did any of them suspect that twenty years ago Nova Citroen had been one of the highest-paid call girls in her native Germany.

*

Vicki Foxe had a way of moving around that enabled her to go wherever she wanted. The uniform helped. The dreary brown and white maid's uniform that Mrs Citroen insisted every female employee wear.

The old broad probably doesn't want any competition, Vicki thought smugly. Man, without the uniform, and with all her makeup and shit in place, Vicki Foxe could give competition to any of those big fancy movie stars. Not that the new ones were so big and fancy anymore – mere shadows of what they used to be like in the good old days. Not that Vicki had been around then, but she knew. There were no Marilyn Monroes and Lana Turners today.

Vicki Foxe had arrived in Hollywood at sixteen, a runaway from Chicago, with sixty bucks in her pocket and two great assets – her incredibly large breasts.

The sixty dollars didn't get her very far at all, but the assets got her a job as a topless waitress and go-go dancer, and from there she graduated to nude modelling. Hooking came next, and by the time she was twenty-five she was scoring fairly big bucks, until she met a small-time hood who was married, generous, and wanted her all to himself. He set her up in an apartment on Ventura Boulevard and paid all the bills. She sat at home filing her nails, eating chocolates, and watching soap operas all day. Four years passed quickly, and then her boyfriend got himself arrested down on Florida on an armed robbery charge and was promptly sent to jail. Vicki, a little older, a little plumper, went back to hooking, but her heart wasn't in it, and when Maxwell Sicily – who had shared a jail cell with her former lover – contacted her, she was ready for a touch of excitement. At thirty she was all set for action. She was also undeniably attracted to Maxwell Sicily, so she accepted his plan without question. Now she was playing dress-up and loving every minute. After all, what was the whole scam anyway? Just taking from the rich and giving to Vicki and Maxwell. Nobody gave a shit when the rich got ripped off. So what? They had insurance and all that crap. Stealing from them was nothing, it wasn't like a real *bad* crime.

Entering Marcus Citroen's private study, she carried a feather duster lest she was stopped. Nobody bothered her, the rest of the staff were all too busy worrying about the evening's big event.

Vicki *never* worried, she just went for it and did what she had to do.

*

Marcus Citroen employed three personal secretaries – each one more loyal than the next. He made it a strict rule that they were not to fraternize out of office hours – the penalty for breaking that rule was immediate dismissal.

The three women (Marcus did not believe in male secretaries) vied with each other for their boss's attention. They told him absolutely everything that went on below boardroom level at Blue Cadillac Records, and therefore – between the three of them – he knew every piece of gossip, who was sleeping with whom, and other non-business-related facts which might not have reached him through normal channels. Keeping people at each other's throats was one of Marcus's specialities. He was the master at it. And knowing everything helped.

His three secretaries were all spinster-type women in their fifties. Marcus did not wish them to be bedded by anyone who might work for him. He demanded complete loyalty, and got it. They loathed each other. It suited him fine.

"Mr Hawkins is here," announced Phoebe, his senior secretary, on the intercom.

"Send him right in," said Marcus. Certain people he kept waiting. Hawkins Lamont was not one of them.

The man in white entered Marcus's spectacular office, which looked more like an antique-filled living room than the workplace of a record magnate. He went straight to the humidor on the ornate walnut desk, and selected a thick Havana cigar.

"You don't mind, do you?" the Hawk asked, confidently sitting himself down in a plush leather chair across the desk.

Amused, Marcus said, "Go ahead."

At fifty-nine Marcus Citroen radiated power. An inch under six feet tall, and forty pounds overweight, his impeccable English tailoring covered a multitude of flaws. Mostly bald, his head was egg-shaped and olive-hued, the same colour as his face. He had a thin upper lip, an obscenely thick lower one, a prominent nose, and mysteriously hooded eyes with indolent drooping lids. Originally from Beirut, he had lived in America for over forty years, and been a citizen for thirty. He was enormously rich, extremely powerful – and in the business he had chosen to excel in, universally feared. A somewhat different figure from the young man who had arrived in New York in 1948 aged twenty, with barely one hundred dollars to his name, but a heart already as hard as steel. Marcus Citroen had seen too much of life ever to change. He'd grown up in wartime Europe, and knew everything about the darker side of man's nature. He'd seen his wealthy father reduced to poverty. His beautiful mother become a whore, his brother the plaything to a group of perverts.

Marcus desired money. He desired power. And he came to America to seek both out.

He'd succeeded.

"Well," the Hawk said. "Kris Phoenix is delivered. Bobby Mondella will be there. Has Rafealla arrived?"

"She's here," Marcus confirmed. "At L'Ermitage." Fixing the Hawk with an intent stare, he leaned back, placed the tips of his elegantly manicured fingers together, and said, "And so the game begins, my friend."

The Hawk puffed on his cigar. He'd known Marcus for over fifteen years, and yet – deep down – he felt he didn't really know him at all. Nobody did. The man did not encourage intimate friendships, although the Hawk considered himself as close as anyone could get. He laughed dryly, almost nervously. "What game?" he asked, his curiosity aroused – for Marcus had been obsessive about the three stars being there – especially Rafealla.

Marcus' expression was inscrutable. "Any game I wish to play," he said slowly. "Any game at all."

Kris Phoenix 1970–1972

For two years The Wild Ones played their collective asses off with nothing to show for it except an increasingly appreciative cult audience and as many girls as they could manage. Which wasn't bad, but it certainly didn't mean as much as getting a manager, an agent, a recording contract, money, and maybe the smallest speck of recognition from an industry which chose to totally ignore them.

Whenever they could get a booking they appeared at clubs all around the suburbs of London. Small clubs, big barns, local hops, anywhere they could get a chance to be seen. Sometimes they landed a gig at a wedding or a birthday party. It was all experience. Only none of it paid the rent, so they continued with their daytime jobs. Kris packed window cleaning in, and along with Buzz got himself a stint as a lifeguard/attendant at a local indoor swimming baths. They were both strong swimmers, and the work was not unduly taxing, although the smell of chlorine and the hordes of screaming school kids drove the two of them crazy. Buzz made out with every fanciable female who ventured into the place – even though he was still living with Flower. Kris found he was becoming more choosy – just because they were under twenty-five and moved didn't mean he automatically had to get a leg over. They were never short of female company. Show a girl a guitar and the little darlings almost came on the spot.

Rasta Stanley, their black drummer, worked at a small radio station as a general gofer. It was a useful gig, enabling him to smuggle out all the new record albums, which Kris taped before Rasta smuggled them back in again.

Ollie Stoltz, bassist and keyboards, had a job in a library.

During their year together they'd become a tight-knit foursome. Kris was the driving force. Buzz, the moody one, with a bizarre, off-centre black humour. Rasta, the easygoing comedian. And Ollie, serious, studious, kind to animals and old ladies.

The Wild Ones. They had their own look. Kris – so alive and sexy, with his raunchy strut, shock of dirty-blond hair, and intense, ice-blue eyes.

Buzz – quite the opposite with his emaciated satanic demeanour.

Ollie – an innocent face, John Lennon glasses, shoulder-length brown curls and a cherub's smile.

Rasta – a ball of energy and cheeky good looks.

Girls loved them. Girls came to dance and stayed to stare.

When they were up on stage playing, everything fitted together nicely. Rasta on drums, Ollie handling bass and keyboards, Kris and Buzz exchanging guitar solos – swapping back and forth from lead to backup with swift, practised precision.

They covered every big hit, taking turns as vocalist, although it soon became obvious that Kris was the favourite when it came to singing. On guitar he was an original, doing anything he felt like, but on vocals he played it safe – a touch of Rod Stewart, a pinch of Mick Jagger, shades of American soul and a rock and roll swagger.

He could do a perfect *Jumping Jack Flash*, a moody *Gasoline Alley*, a hot and raunchy *Ain't Too Proud to Beg* and a touching *Your Song*.

"The trouble is," Buzz announced one day as they stood idly by the side of the steamy indoor swimming pool watching a bunch of kids being taught to swim, "we're not doin' anythin' *different*. Y'know what I mean?"

Kris knew exactly what he meant, only it wasn't his fault. The audience wanted to hear familiar songs, and that's *all* they wanted to hear.

"We should be writin' our own stuff," Buzz said reflectively. " 'Stead of churnin' out other people's hits. We gotta get Ollie t'come up with somethin' – he'd be good at it."

Kris nodded. He didn't feel like saying anything, but he'd been working on a few ideas of his own, and had several songs he was anxious to try out. He'd held back because he didn't want the others putting him down.

Buzz eyed a buxom brunette emerging from the girls' changing room. "Nice pair of bristols," he remarked casually. "I bet she's a right little raver."

"When have you ever seen a pair you *didn't* like?" Kris retorted.

"We gotta 'ave original material," Buzz repeated. "It's the only way we're goin' t'get bleedin' noticed."

"I know *that*," Kris replied. "As a matter of fact I—" He didn't finish his sentence, because out of the corner of his eye he noticed a swimmer in trouble. Without hesitation he made a racing dive into the pool, and headed for the struggling man, who was flailing around in the deep end in an advanced state of panic.

Manoeuvring himself behind the victim he grabbed him under the arms and began to swim to the side of the pool and safety.

Only it wasn't so easy. The man really thought it was all over, and with arms and legs thrashing in every direction he fought for survival, not realizing – in his panic – that Kris was trying to save him.

Together they sank beneath the water, whereupon the man suddenly changed tactics, clinging on to Kris for dear life, wrapping his legs around him in a death hold, dragging him to the bottom of the pool where they hovered in a state of battle as Kris desperately tried to free himself from the man's fierce grip of unadulterated fear.

Without the intervention of Buzz it might have been all over. Buzz didn't hesitate. He dived in like a Kamikaze pilot, prying the man off Kris with lethal force, grabbing him around the neck.

With a sudden wild burst the three of them surfaced, and between them Buzz and Kris managed to drag the man to the side of the pool, where helping hands hauled him out. Kris immediately went to work pumping water out of the poor old sod.

"Fuck!" exclaimed Buzz. "This gig deserves danger money."

"Really . . . you're both so brave!" cooed the brunette he had observed earlier, now in a wet bathing suit with very sympathetic nipples on red alert.

The victim gasped and tried to sit up. A group of school children burst into applause.

Kris peered at the man he had rescued. He looked familiar, even in his half-drowned state. "Mr Terence?" he asked tentatively.

"Oh . . . my . . . God. I owe you . . . my life," the man spluttered. "I had a cramp – an unimaginable pain. I couldn't move. I was—"

"Mr Terence?" Kris repeated, definitely recognizing him as the show business agent whose house his mother used to clean.

Terry Terence gazed up at the cocky-looking twenty-year-old with the bulging crotch and crooked grin. Maybe he'd died and gone to heaven. Ah . . . he'd always liked them young.

"Yes," he replied dreamily. "Do I know you?"

*

Mr Terry Terence no longer lived in his house on Carlton Hill. He had moved to a rather grand apartment on Abbey Road, quite near the famous Abbey Road studios where the Beatles made all their records.

Later that day, when Kris and Buzz turned up for tea, they were greeted by a lanky, effeminate-looking man with watery spaniel eyes and a low cultured voice. "Do come in," he said softly. "I'm Justin, Mr Terry's companion. He's resting right now, but his instructions were to wake him as soon as you arrived." Justin extended a limp, white hand. "My deepest thanks for your bravery. You know, Mr Terry suffered a heart attack six months ago, and the doctor advised him to take more exercise. He started walking, soon got bored with that. Then tennis – *much* too strenuous. Finally he settled on swimming – the perfect answer."

"Yeah, it was nearly the answer all right," joked Buzz morbidly, peering at an Andy Warhol poster of a series of soup cans.

"How's he feeling?" Kris asked, checking out the photo frames – searching for the old signed picture of Johnnie Ray he remembered from his childhood.

"Thankful to be alive," Justin said crisply. "Usually he swims at the Grosvenor House pool, but today, for some unknown reason, he decided to venture locally." Justin made a clucking sound. "Life! How blithely we tread the path of fate!"

Buzz threw Kris a look as much to say *Who is this wacko?*

"Maybe we should come back another day," Kris suggested. "Y'know, if he's restin' an' all."

"Not at all," Justin said quickly. "He'd be *most* upset. I'll wake him now." He hurried from the room.

"Talk about light on yer feet!" Buzz said.

Kris zeroed in on the old photo of Johnnie Ray – different frame, same picture. "Look at this," he said triumphantly, picking it up.

"Who is it?" demanded Buzz.

"Johnnie Ray."

"Who's 'e when 'e's at 'ome?"

"A big singer in the fifties. My mum loved him."

"Hey – get a load of *this*," Buzz said, picking up a picture of the Beatles. "The fab four themselves. *An'* they signed it – all of 'em."

"Really?"

"Yeah. This old fart must really know people."

"I told you, didn't I?"

Mr Terry Terence entered the room resplendent in black pyjamas worn under a scarlet dressing gown elaborately embroidered with gold, and matching slippers. He was a middle-aged man, rather plump, with bland features, a ruddy complexion, and a puff of dyed brown hair. He bore a passing resemblance to Liberace.

"Well, boys," he said. "How am I ever going to repay you?"

And that was how The Wild Ones acquired their first agent and manager.

*

Right from the beginning Mr Terry Terence had eyes for Buzz. He took one look at the moody, unsmiling twenty-one-year-old with the agile body, pale complexion and ragged black hair, and it was love at first sight. Although he was careful to conceal the way he felt, it soon became common knowledge and a great joke among the boys. That's what Mr Terry Terence called them once he took them in hand – the boys – *his* boys – he was going to mould them into stars – or so he said – and after a year of trailing around the clubs getting nowhere, they were only too happy to put themselves in his experienced hands.

First he attended a couple of their local gigs, after which he sat the four of them down in his office and told them exactly what they were doing wrong.

"You're a copycat group," he told them. "Bleating out other people's hits – any bunch of musicians can get together and do that."

"I told 'em," Buzz said in his best know-all voice.

Kris shot him a disgusted look. "It's what the kids *want* to hear," he said stubbornly. "We'd love to do original stuff."

Mr Terence sipped from a cup of strong black coffee. "Naturally. They're *used* to hearing familiar songs. Only you must understand, it's not going to get you anywhere. We have to have original material. Can any of you compose and write lyrics?"

Tentatively Ollie raised his hand. "I write music," he said. "Lousy on lyrics, but I'm quite into creating a melody."

Kris was surprised. It was the first *he'd* heard of it.

"Anyone else?" asked Mr Terence, anxious eyes lingering on Buzz as usual.

"Uh . . . yeah . . . I got some stuff," responded Buzz with an embarrassed shrug. " 'Course, it probably stinks – sod it – what the hell . . ." He trailed off.

Kris had always thought he and Buzz were pretty close – and now this revelation. Shit! He'd better make his own announcement soon or he'd be left out. "I've put together quite a bit of material," he said quickly.

Now it was Buzz's turn to look surprised. He raised a cynical eyebrow. "You 'ave?"

Rasta laughed, always one to break the tension. "Seems like you've *all* bin at it in secret. Someone should've told *me*, I'd 'ave given up wankin' an' done somethin' useful with me right hand!"

"It's never too late," said Mr Terence fussily, ignoring their ribald laughter. "The more original material the better."

"Right on," agreed Buzz.

"Next, we have to work on your image," Mr Terence continued, adjusting the knot on his old school tie.

"Why?" Kris demanded. "There's nothin' wrong with the way we look."

"There's nothing right with it either. On stage you resemble a raggle-taggle group of misfits. There has to be a sense of unity – a feeling you belong together."

"I'm not wearin' no stupid stage costume," Buzz warned. "I wear me black gear, an' that's that."

"You could *all* wear black," Mr Terence suggested, diplomatically, careful never to say anything that might offend his favourite.

"I'm better in red, man," argued Rasta. "I got enough black on me already thankyouverymuch."

"I have the answer," Mr Terence said triumphantly. "All-black outfits with red scarves." Naturally he had observed that Buzz usually wore a long, tatty scarf wound around his neck.

"I don't want some faggot outfit," Buzz said rudely. "I think we should go with whatever we got on at the time."

"The Beatles look good," Ollie observed.

"Bunch of wankers!" Buzz sneered.

Mr Terence inspected his nails, buffed to a pearly shine. "Next we have to talk about buying you decent equipment," he said. "And sending you out on tour, so you can acquire *real* experience."

"What about a recording contract?" Kris asked, getting down to the nitty-gritty.

"That's not something that just happens," Mr Terence replied testily. "It's a goal we have to work towards. If I sent you into a studio now you'd be laughed out of the room." Pausing, he took another sip of coffee. "First you'll develop original, fresh material, and if you can't do that, we'll buy you some. Then you'll go out on the road and learn *presentation* and *discipline*. It'll all be worthwhile. When *I* say you're ready to go into a recording studio, that's when we do it."

"What about our jobs?" Ollie inquired seriously. "How can we tour and still work?"

"You can't. That's obvious." Mr Terence was crisp and to the point. "I have decided not only to be your agent, but to manage you as well. As your agent I will receive ten per cent of your collective earnings. As your manager I shall require a further twenty-five per cent. And for that I take it upon myself to finance your climb to the top. I will purchase new equipment, a van for you to travel around the country in, clothes for you to wear on stage, and I will also advance you a reasonable living allowance."

"Wow!" exclaimed Rasta. "That's fuckin' fabulous!"

Kris shot him a warning look. "We'll have to think about it."

"Yeah, right," agreed Buzz, catching on that enthusiasm could only lead to getting screwed.

Mr Terence was perfectly calm. "Think away," he said. "You can let me know within a week."

"You'd be gettin' thirty-five per cent of us," Kris said unsurely, calculating aloud. "Isn't that a lot?"

"Thirty-five per cent of nothing," Mr Terence pointed out. "*And* risking a goodly amount of my own money, not to mention my valuable time. Take it or leave it." He sighed, as if he couldn't care less either way. "*I* think you have potential. Others might not."

A week later all four of them signed individual contracts tying them irrevocably to Mr Terry Terence for the next seven years. Kris had to have his mother sign for him as he was still a few days away from his twenty-first birthday.

Avis came to Mr Terence's office in her best yellow dress, a silly hat perched rakishly atop her greying hair. "I bought it for you, luv," she whispered to her son. "For luck. Two quid in Marks & Spencer."

Impulsively he hugged her. "Thanks, mum."

"Mrs Pierce! What a joy to see you after all these years," Mr Terence said, and in a low aside everyone in the office heard, "*Nobody* polishes silver the way *you* used to."

"Thank you, Mr T." Her voice was stiff and proper, unlike her usual raucous shout. She had never told anyone why she'd abruptly left Mr Terence's employ over nine years ago. He had accused her of stealing a pair of gold cufflinks, and when one of his gentleman friends turned up with them two days later he merely said, "Found 'em, dear," as if that was apology enough. She never went back.

Now here she was, in his office, signing important contracts on behalf of her Kris. She'd sooner have given him a black eye for his stinking mistrust.

After signing they went to the pub to celebrate, just mother and son. Mr Terence had wanted them to stay in the office and split a bottle of champagne, but Avis tugged on Kris's sleeve and hoarsely whispered, "I'd be more comfortable down the pub, lad." So the pub it was.

They sat there for two hours enjoying each other's company and a few beers. It was one of the best times Kris had ever spent with her. She only mentioned Brian four times.

"I'm goin' to buy you a mink stole, mum," he promised, as they walked out into the cold night air. "You deserve it."

She laughed – her wonderfully familiar, bawdy cackle. "Cor luv us! You an' who else – Prince bleedin' Philip?"

*

The Wild Ones toured for a full year, covering the country. They travelled across England, Wales, and Scotland. Up north, down south, across to Ireland and back again. And all the time squashed together in a cramped Volkswagen bus with their equipment piled high around them. They took turns to drive, and on one-night stands slept in the back of the bus smelling like a bunch of clapped-out camels. They even took turns having girls in the bus. One little raver in the front, and another on her knees in the back. Some of them were barely in their teens. "Baby groupies," Buzz christened them. "Straight off the bottle an' onto the rod!"

Once in a while Mr Terence came to see them. He made full note of the enthusiastic audience reaction, listened carefully to their new material, made his criticisms and general observations, then left.

"When are we coming to London?" Kris always asked.

"As soon as you're ready. I'll let you know" was Mr Terence's unswerving reply.

They were exhausted and burnt out. Where was the recognition Mr Terence had promised them? Where was their recording contract? Where was Fame, Fortune and the Good Life?

To say they were disillusioned and fed-up would be putting it mildly.

"We have seen the asshole of England," Kris observed solemnly, late one night as they sat in a roadside café outside Manchester, sharing a greasy plate of sausages and chips. "And it bleedin' stinks."

"Write a song about it," Buzz said, yawning. "Yer manage t'write about everything else."

"Oh, yeah, very pretty – *The Asshole of England* by Kris Phoenix. I can see it now – a big hit. It'll knock the Stones right off the charts!"

Rasta began beating drum rhythms on the table, while Ollie made fake *boom boom* sounds.

"*I met a girl an' 'er name was Sally. Kissed 'er on the cheek an' fucked her in the alley,*" sang Buzz. "*She looked so sweet, she looked so neat. An' I didn't know she lived in* – ALL TOGETHER NOW – LET'S BLOODY HEAR IT—"

"*THE ASSHOLE OF ENGLAND!*" They all screamed, hysterical with laughter.

"Enough of that," grumbled a fat counter-man in a filthy apron, looming over their table. "You're makin' too much noise."

"Sod it!" sneered Buzz. "Can't even have any fun anymore."

"What's fun?" Kris asked wearily.

"Gettin' your dick sucked in a bed instead of behind a bloody amplifier?" Rasta suggested.

"I dunno," Kris sighed. "I'm tired. I just wan' t'go back to London."

"Call the fag an' tell 'im," Buzz said. "It's about time 'e kept some of his bloody promises. If I 'ave to sleep with your hairy arse in me face one more night, I'm packin' it in."

"*You* call him," Kris countered. "*You're* his blue-eyed boy."

Adopting an exaggerated pose and mincing voice, Buzz said, "Hmmm, do you really think so, dear?"

"You'd make a horrible girl," Ollie remarked. "All white and pasty!"

"Yeah, but you'd like t'fuck me, wouldn'tcha?" Buzz joked. "You'd like ter give me one, wouldn'tcha, darlin'?"

"Not bloody likely," Ollie retorted indignantly.

"Aw, c'mon, admit it," Buzz taunted. "Don't be shy. We all know what goes on in them fancy *music* academies. I bet you've slipped it up an arse or two in yer time."

Ollie leaped to his feet, red-faced. "Don't even joke about it, you fucking wanker."

Buzz narrowed his eyes. "Hit a nerve, 'ave I?"

"Shut up, you two," Kris said, flicking a greasy chip in his friend's face.

"Yeah, shut up," agreed Rasta, grabbing a handful of chips and throwing them at Ollie and Buzz.

"'Ere we go!" yelled Buzz, reaching for a sausage, which he proceeded to tear into pieces and pelt across the table

Kris responded with a squirt of tomato ketchup, and Ollie followed with the mustard. Within seconds they were yelling and screaming – letting out the tension – embroiled in an enthusiastic and enjoyable food fight.

"That's about enough of that, you yobbos, ENOUGH!" commanded the fat counter-man, lumbering over.

Ignoring him, they continued their fun.

"Sling the buggers out, Bert," roared a heavy-set truck driver sitting nearby. "Fuckin' bunch of pansies with their long 'air. Chuck 'em out. Me an' my mates'll help yer."

Bert had no say in the matter. The truck driver and his friends were only too happy to join in the fight. The trouble was they weren't playing with food – fists were their weapons, and they launched into the unsuspecting boys with vicious gusto, taking them by surprise.

"Let's teach the fuckin' *girls* a lesson," shouted the heavy-set driver, encouraging his troops into battle.

"Aw ... *shit*," groaned Kris, as one of the bullies grabbed him by his long hair and attempted to frog-march him to the door. He twisted free, kicking the much bigger man sharply in the balls.

"Yer fuckin' scummy bastard!" roared the man, doubling over.

Kris took quick stock. Five burly truck drivers and four skinny would-be rock stars. The odds weren't good.

"Let's get the fuck outta here," he yelled.

But he was too late. The fight was on.

Bobby Mondella 1972

"Happy birthday, honey," Sharleen said with a captivating smile, placing a tempting chocolate cake in front of Bobby.

"Yeah, man," agreed Rocket, hovering nearby. "How about this bein' *our* year?"

"Ain't gonna fight with *those* sentiments," Bobby said – a new Bobby – a slimmed-down version of the former blimp. Bobby Mondella, at twenty-two, was tall, good-looking, and fit. Impossible to recognize as the fat boy who had been carried from Cousin Fanni's house four years ago and rushed by ambulance to the emergency room, where he nearly died.

*

The two ambulance attendants almost had hernias on account of having to lift the stretcher with Bobby on. He had a burst appendix, and the surgeon who operated told him that another hour and there would have been no chance of saving him. As it was he hovered on the danger list for several days.

"Cutting through your fat nearly cost you your life," the surgeon said bluntly when he came to remove the stitches. "You'd better get rid of the blubber or be prepared to check out early."

"Check out of the hospital?" Bobby asked innocently.

"No. Check out of life, young man."

Fanni came to visit a week after his operation. She brought *Playboy* magazine and three Hershey bars. *Jerk off and get fat.* The story of his life.

"Did you call The Chainsaw?" he asked anxiously.

"Why? Was I 'spose to?"

Groaning, he said, "I'll lose my job. You should've called."

"They'll understand."

They didn't. When Bobby returned four weeks later, and already twenty pounds lighter, Nichols Kline was unsympathetic. "Your job's taken, Mondella. Get lost," he'd said.

Bobby hung around outside waiting for either Sharleen or Rocket. She arrived first and was about to walk right past, when he grabbed her arm and reminded her who he was.

Eyes flashing angrily she said, "Where's my tape?"

"I've got it."

"Yeah? Exactly *where*, may I ask?"

"At home."

"Why didn't you give it to Marcus Citroen?"

"He never came in that night," Bobby explained. "And after that I was rushed to the hospital with a burst appendix. The truth is, I nearly died. I was real sick."

She couldn't have cared less. "I want my tape back," she said flatly.

Shifting uncomfortably, he said, "Y'know somethin'? I played it – I'm sure it's not the best you can do."

Indignantly she glared at him. "How would *you* know?"

"I used to be in the music business, when I was younger." Hesitating, he decided he had nothing to lose, and added, "I . . . uh . . . made some records, wrote a few songs."

"When you was *twelve*, sonny?" Her voice dripped sarcasm.

"I *was* very young – but it's true – I swear it."

She was getting bored. "*Sure*, honey."

"I'll write *you* a song," he volunteered.

"Oh, boy! I can't *wait*."

"Listen, don't fight it, I can help you sound much better on tape."

"Just bring it on back, sonny."

She was being stubborn, but he was sure that given half a

chance he could convince her. "When?" he asked.

"Tomorrow."

"I won't be around. Nichols fired me. Let me drop it by your place in the morning."

Biting her lower lip she thought for a moment, then said, "What the heck," and produced a dog-eared card with SHARLEEN – CHANTEUSE printed on it. She scribbled an address and thrust it at him. "Ten o'clock. Don't expect to stay."

"I won't," he said hastily, watching her walk swiftly through the back entrance of the club.

Another ten minutes and Rocket appeared. "Jeeze, Bobby! I never expected to see *you* again. Thought you'd scrammed with all the bread – yours *an'* mine."

"Thanks for being so trusting."

With a nonchalant shrug Rocket said, "Ain't the first time I bin ripped."

It was great to come across two people so thrilled to see him. Trusting they weren't. He repeated his hospital story, adding that he'd been fired. "Any suggestions?"

"Clooneys," Rocket said without hesitation. "They're hirin' bouncers. Get your ass over there pronto." He flipped a cigarette from his pocket. "Do I get my money?"

"I don't have it on me." The truth was, Ernest had stolen every penny while he was in the hospital.

"Hey, man, I guess I've waited four weeks, I'll wait another day," Rocket said. "You can bring it by in the mornin'." Scratching his head, he added, "Just make sure you deduct the advance on rent you paid me – I got myself a new roommate. You're out."

Great! Before he was even in. But he couldn't blame the guy. After all, there'd been no guarantee he'd reappear. "I can't make the morning," he said, thinking of his rendezvous with Sharleen.

Rocket shrugged. "Lunch-time then. I'll buy ya a hot dog an' split a beer." Snatching Sharleen's card from Bobby's hand, he took a pencil from behind his ear and scrawled an address on the blank side. "Tomorra," Rocket said. "Try Clooneys. Ya look like a bouncer. Tell 'em you're over twenny-five. They'll buy it."

Rocket was right. They bought it, and Bobby had a new job throwing people out of one of the hottest singles bars on the West Side.

When he got home he confronted Ernest about the missing money.

Ernest was furious. "You accusin' me, boy?" he demanded belligerently.

"I sure am," Bobby retorted. As he was shedding weight, so he was gaining in courage. It was about time he stood up to Ernest.

"Well, *I ain't* gonna take it," Ernest fumed. "No, sirree, I ain't gonna take no more of your goddamn *she . . . it.*"

"It wasn't my money," Bobby tried to explain. "I was only—"

"I'm not innerested in your bitchin' an' whinin'," Ernest interrupted, obese belly heaving with emotion. "You all's jest a weight 'round your good cousin's neck. That woman bin too damn good to you. Whyn't y'git *out*. An' do it *now*."

"If I had my money I would," Bobby retorted angrily. "You *took* the six thousand dollars I came here with. You spent it pretty good."

"*I* took it? You done got the goddamn *balls* to say I, Ernest Crystal, took somethin' wasn't his?" He started to yell. "Fuck you, boy. *Fuck you*."

Fanni arrived home, causing Ernest to shut up, and Bobby to go to his small room in the back. He made up his mind that if Rocket was prepared to wait for his money, he would take his first week's paycheck and get the hell out. The sooner the better.

The next morning, clad in his best pants and jacket, both now too big for him, he arrived on Sharleen's doorstep, tape in hand. She lived in a basement off Tenth Avenue. The steps down were littered with garbage, lewd graffiti were scrawled all over the door, and there was no doorbell.

He knocked tentatively. After a few minutes and no response, he knocked again. A large rat scuttled out of its corner hiding place and raced past him up the crumbling stone steps.

"Comin'," yelled a muffled voice, and eventually the door was flung open.

Standing there was Rocket, in grubby jockey shorts, with his lank hair all over the place. He had a disoriented look on his face. "Bobby," he said vaguely. "I thought you was goin' to be here later."

For a moment Bobby was startled. But then he realized what he'd done. He'd made the stupid mistake of going to Rocket's address instead of Sharleen's. Both addresses were scribbled on the same card.

"I s'pose you'd better c'min an' visit the palace," Rocket mumbled, adding a loud burp.

Bobby stepped inside chaos. Peeling brown walls, a linoleum-covered floor, old furniture scarred with cigarette burns, stacks of used Chinese take-away cartons, and piles of old newspapers and magazines.

"This is the tidy part," Rocket said with an unapologetic shrug. "You should see the bedroom, an' what passes for the bathroom."

"Hey, at least it's yours," Bobby said enviously.

"Yeah, I know, I know – it coulda bin yours too." Lazily he scratched his stomach. "That's the breaks, I guess. You'll find somewhere." Pausing, he contemplated a rusty hotplate on a table in the corner. "Wanna cuppa coffee?"

Bobby thought of Sharleen, probably impatiently waiting for him, wondering why he was late. "I can't stay," he said quickly. "I just came by to ask if y'can hold out a couple of weeks for your money."

Rocket threw him a quizzical look. "Y'know somethin'? You *really* got jumpin' balls." Lighting a match beneath a saucepan of water, he flipped a cigarette from an open packet of Lucky Strikes. "If you weren't such a fartin' babe in toyland, I'd be pissed. What's the problem?"

"It's like this—" Bobby began.

A woman entered the room. A woman wrapped in a bath towel and nothing else. She smiled sweetly. "Bobby," she greeted in a low, sing-song voice. "Are you early or am I late?"

It was Sharleen.

The shock of discovering that the love of his life was living with his best friend did not exactly boost Bobby's morale. It was an emotional trauma, and one he faced the only way he knew how – straight on.

They made an incongruous couple. Sharleen – the pretty black girl who wanted nothing more out of life than to be the new Diana Ross. And Rocket Fabrizzi – a would-be actor who saw himself as a sort of seventies Marlon Brando.

Over the course of the next four years the three of them forged a solid friendship – based on mutual trust and respect. They were all basically orphans. Sharleen had no family. Rocket had long ago disowned his. And Bobby left Fanni and Ernest's with no regret on their part, and rented a room that made his friends' basement look like the Plaza.

What they had was a loyal support group. Bobby took up music again – mainly because of Sharleen's encouragement. He wrote songs for her. He helped her with voice training, presentation and style. And he got himself a daytime job selling sheet music, while still working nights at Clooneys.

Sharleen nagged him to diet and work out, urging him to return to music full-time. Although she was a lousy housekeeper, she made him the best meatloaf he'd ever tasted.

Rocket was just Rocket. Always there, always up, always working on schemes to make an extra buck or two, in-between going out on auditions and coming home with a turn-down and an undefeated grin.

A week before Bobby's twenty-second birthday he heard of a loft in Greenwich Village – a sub-let. Quickly he figured out that if they all shared on the rent, they could move in and begin living like human beings. It didn't take much to persuade Sharleen and Rocket.

*

"Blow out the candles," Sharleen urged, her ebony skin glowing.

Bobby smiled at her. She was still the prettiest girl in the world, but she belonged to Rocket and he had long ago learned to accept that sad fact of life.

"Yes, go on, Bobby, make a wish," said his current girlfriend, an adorable little blonde who looked exactly like all the other adorable little blondes he'd dated over the past few years – for when Bobby finally lost all the excess weight, the girls *really* came running. Now Sharleen was always teasing him, calling him Mister Stud and other crazy nicknames.

Shutting his eyes he wished for many things. When he opened them, Sharleen was staring straight at him. "Did you wish for me to become a star? Did you, Bobby?" she asked urgently, licking her luscious lips.

"Yeah, yeah, yeah," Rocket jeered. "We're *all* gonna be stars. Just hang around another ten, twenty, thirty years. We should live that long."

A week later Rocket got a small role in a movie shooting in New York. Two weeks after that Sharleen auditioned for a Broadway show and succeeded in joining the chorus. And Bobby sold his first song.

"Honey," Sharleen said to Bobby, her big brown eyes gleaming with delight. "When you make a wish – you *really* make a wish. We're on our way!"

Rafealla 1972

Birthdays always made Rafealla sick. She hated them. Each time another year passed she felt the pain and hurt and loss all over again. And this year, her twelfth birthday, was especially bad as her mother, Anna, was thinking of getting married again, and Rafealla was outraged at the very idea.

Mother and daughter had argued back and forth interminably.

"It's not fair to poppa," Rafealla had screamed.

"Your father's been dead for nearly five years," Anna tried to explain. "He wouldn't want me to continue being on my own."

"Yes he *would!*" Rafealla shouted. "He would! He would!"

She loathed the man her mother was seeing. He was an English lord with a stupid stammer and stupid red hair and a stupid son and a stupid castle in the English countryside. His name was Cyrus, Lord Egerton, and he was hateful.

"Well, young lady," Anna had finally said, a sharp edge to her normal gentle voice, "whatever I decide to do is *my* decision. Fortunately I do not need your permission, although your approval would be nice."

"Never!" Rafealla screamed dramatically. "I'd sooner be dead!"

And she meant it.

Nanny Macdee had tried to calm her, but to no avail. Rafealla knew for sure that if her mother remarried it was a terrible thing to do to her poor dead father. And nobody could change her mind.

Poppa. Lucien. She thought of him often. The nightmare of his shocking death was forever with her.

How could she forget? She was right there when it happened, standing at the door of their house in Paris, waving, while her dear father was blown to pieces by a terrorist's bomb planted in Henri Ronet's car. They had meant to kill Henri Ronet. Lucien Le Serre's being in the car was just bad timing on his part.

The noise of the explosion had wiped out Rafealla's world. Shards of glass embedded in her legs caused temporary paralysis, and put a dismal end to her hopes of a future in the ballet. She was in the hospital for several months, enduring two operations. When she came out her mother had already packed up, sold the Paris house, and was all set to move to England. "We'll leave the memories behind," she'd said to her daughter. "We have to. It's the only way."

Mother might think that, but Rafealla knew it wasn't possible. She would *never* forget her wonderful poppa and all that he'd meant to her.

Right from the start she hated England. Cold, damp weather. Rainy streets. Strange food, and a language she didn't care to speak, even though she was bilingual and had grown up speaking both French and English.

Anna sent her to a strict private school where the girls taunted her because she was "different". They nicknamed her "gimp", as since the accident she walked with a slight limp. And sometimes they called her "darkie" on account of her olive-hued skin.

Nanny Macdee spoke to her mother, and suggested that a private tutor might be a better idea until Rafealla became more acclimatized to the English way of life. Anna agreed, and Rafealla did not return to school until she was eleven. By that time she had toughened up, and anyone who called her names paid for it.

Now it was her twelfth birthday, and the memories were

flooding around her, and Anna was planning on marrying again, and it was all so unfair . . .

Rafealla went to her mother's bathroom, opened the medicine cabinet, emptied out every bottle of pills she could find, and swallowed the lot.

Soon she would be with her father again, and that's all she really wanted.

Kris Phoenix 1973

While getting beaten up in a motorway café just outside of Manchester was hardly the highlight of their tour, it did enable The Wild Ones to get back to London and an anxious Mr Terence.

Buzz had a broken nose, which upset Mr Terence far more than any of the cuts, bruises and black eyes of the other three. Nevertheless, he had them all checked out by his own doctor, and everyone was shocked to discover Kris had two broken ribs.

"I told you I was in bloody agony," he informed anyone who would listen. "Bleedin' hell, talk about ignoring an injured person."

"Getting into fights is irresponsible and just not done," Mr Terence tut-tutted.

"Wasn't *our* fault," Ollie explained.

"Yeah," agreed Rasta. "These great big bruisers came right at us outta nowhere."

Mr Terence cancelled the rest of their tour, moved them into a small house he owned near Hampstead Heath, and informed them that a record company had shown interest in them and that soon they would be going into the recording studios to make their first single.

"Soon" took three months, but the great day finally came, and they were ready for it.

Mr Terence had put them together with a young producer, Sam Rozelle, and Sam was as enthusiastic as they were. He loved their material – especially the songs Kris and Buzz had written together – and he predicted great things ahead.

Kris didn't know what to believe anymore. He still felt good about the group – especially now they were doing their own songs, and not just belting out copies of other people's hits. But he was also wary. There were so many fine groups out there – so many singers, songwriters and guitarists. And so few hit records. How could they possibly stand a chance with all the competition?

Sam took him out for a beer the night before the recording session. They sat in a pub in Kilburn and discussed things. Sam was a quiet man in his early thirties with thinning hair and a conservative style. He was married, with two small children, and a wife who looked ten years older than him. He seemed perfectly happy and content, and Kris sometimes wondered if he hadn't strayed into the music business by mistake.

"Well, Kris." Sam raised his glass in a toast, glancing around the crowded pub. "Make the most of this. Anonymity is something you'll miss."

"Huh?"

"Going about your business unrecognized."

Kris snorted with laughter. "Oh, yeah, *sure*."

"Don't underestimate your future," Sam said very seriously. "I *know* what's going to happen. Believe me. I've seen it before."

Kris tried to make light of Sam's prediction. "Well, mate," he said with a cheery wink, "I bloody well hope so, it's about bleedin' time. We've been at it for long enough."

*

Back at the house, Buzz was sitting on a sofa sharing a joint with Flower and a couple of her girlfriends. Ollie was asleep, and Rasta out.

" 'Ere, sit yourself down an' join in the outrageous fun," Buzz deadpanned when Kris arrived home.

"Yeah, c'mon, Kris," urged Flower, her wide blue eyes as

stoned as ever. She had only just forgiven Buzz for giving her a nasty case of the crabs.

Kris checked out her girlfriends. Usually he stayed well away from Flower and her friends, but tonight he was on edge, he needed something or someone to calm him down and force him to relax.

One of the girls was out of the question – she looked no more than fourteen. The other had possibilities for a one-night stand. She was the Julie Christie type – only not as good looking. Her name was Willow. She was nineteen years old and worked as a sales assistant in a dress shop with Flower.

Sitting down next to her he started with the chat. It never took long – half an hour later she was in his bed. To his amazement he soon found out she was a virgin. This was a first – he'd never encountered a virgin before.

"You shoulda told me," he said, thrusting for entry.

"Why?" she whispered, shivering. "Would it have made any difference?"

He pondered that one. Would it? When Kris Phoenix wanted to get laid nothing stood in his way. "I dunno." Pausing, he said, "D'you want me to stop?"

"No," she answered quickly. "Get it over with."

Get it over with! Oh, that was charming, *really* romantic. He felt his hard-on deflate, and suddenly sleep seemed the most tempting item on the menu.

"Listen, luv," he said, disengaging himself. "I think you'd better go home."

Willow began to cry. "I've disappointed you, haven't I?" she asked tearfully.

This girl was certainly different. He was so used to the lower-echelon groupies out on the road, and the hard nuts he encountered in London – tough little cookies who had been around and around and then some. Yes, this one was definitely unusual. She had *feelings*.

"C'mon, don't cry," he said uncomfortably. "It's not your fault."

Tentatively she touched his limp penis and started a slow stroke. "Can we try again?" she asked timidly.

Who was he to say no?

Rising to the occasion he made another attempt, and this time it was all the way home with hardly a sound from her and a loud grunt of satisfaction from him. Exploring uncharted territory was quite a kick.

After the deed was done they lay companionably in each other's arms. Usually, when it was over, he couldn't wait for them to get dressed and get out. With Willow he didn't seem to mind. She fitted into his arms nicely, and she had a lovely firm pair of bristols.

With a sigh of satisfaction he drifted off to sleep, not waking until the morning, when he was quite surprised to find her still there. Lustfully eyeing her sleeping form, he quietly rolled on top, making a stealthy entry.

She awoke with a little gasp, followed by a little smile.

"Somebody forgot to go home," he teased, thrusting back and forth. In the daylight, with no makeup, she was prettier than he'd thought. He liked the fact that she wasn't a slag.

"I wanted to stay and wish you luck," she said timidly. "Buzz said today's the big day."

"Yeah." He nodded, tweaking an appealing nipple as he deftly manoeuvred her above him, and *really* got to work.

Cheeks flushed, breathing fast, she did everything he asked.

"Spread your legs," he commanded.

She did so, and immediately began to climax.

Joining her in the dance, he realized he'd never felt so good in his entire life.

Today was going to be a winner.

*

"I'm fed up with the friggin' faggot makin' goo-goo eyes at me," Buzz complained. "If 'e's not bleedin' careful I'm gonna belt 'im one. I mean it."

Kris looked up from the newspaper. "What happened?"

"I went round to 'is flat today — 'e said he had to talk to me."

Kris put the newspaper down. He was angry — he'd told Rasta, Ollie *and* Buzz that if there was any talking to be done *he'd* do it. They had to have a leader, and he'd thought it was understood he was it. "Why'd you do that?" he asked sharply.

"Fuck! I dunno. He said it was somethin' private."

"What was it?"

"A bunch of old cobblers 'bout the record comin' out soon, publicity crap, an' how he thinks I should dump Flower. Bad for me bleedin' image." He scowled. "*What* bleedin' image?"

Rubbing his chin Kris shrugged. "Beats me."

"Then the stupid old geezer puts 'is 'and on me knee. Cor blimey! He's lucky he's still walkin'."

"What did you do?"

"What *din't* I do?" Buzz ranted. "I told 'im straight. Mr T, I says – do I look like a friggin' queen?"

"Very subtle. I bet that went down like a ton of shit."

"'E got all red in the face an' nervous. 'Dear boy,' 'e says, 'how can you even think such a thing?'" Angrily Buzz flung himself into an armchair. "'Y'know somethin'? All I wan' outta life is to play great guitar an' get rich. Then I can tell 'em *all* to go get fucked."

"Not a bad idea," Kris responded mildly. "Only if you'd leave everything to me, you wouldn't have to put up with his bollocks, *I'd* deal with it."

"Right. You're on. Just keep the creep away from me an' Flower. She's bin my girlfriend for five years, an' I'm not gettin' rid of her for any old fairy. Okay?"

Kris decided he'd have to talk to Mr Terence. He might be financing their rise to nowhere, but he certainly didn't own them. And when their record came out and the money started rolling in, he'd be making plenty on his initial investment. Thirty-five percent of The Wild Ones was a pretty secure bet.

Kris was excited about their record, *Lonesome Morning* – words by him, music by Ollie. He couldn't wait for it to hit an unsuspecting public. The big time had to be just around the corner, and he was ready. Oh, was he ready!

*

Five weeks later a conversation took place.

"I'm pregnant," Willow said, her pale face flushed.

"You're what?" Kris demanded, sure he couldn't possibly have heard her correctly.

"Pregnant," she repeated, with tear-filled eyes. "And my father's going to kill me."

"Oh, *shit*," he said.

Bobby Mondella 1973

"Please, Bobby, *please*," Sharleen was pleading with him, "there's no *point* in your tellin' Rocket. He'll only get mad, and you know what he's like when he's mad. And it's not as if anything's going to *happen*. This is a business date, purely business. If Rocket were here I'd take him *with* me. But he's not, he's in California, and I wish I *was* with him, and since I'm *not*, there's no harm in this. Honestly! Now pass me that rhinestone earring and stop *fussing*."

Reluctantly Bobby reached for her earring, and watched her clip it into place. She looked radiantly pretty as usual, with her glowing black skin, fluff of jet curls, and large brown eyes. Tonight she was wearing a slinky dress sparkling with deep purple sequins. It plunged in front, dipped in back, and he knew she must have blown a week's salary on it.

"I could come with you," he suggested.

"Bobby, Bobby, don't you *trust* me? Rocket trusts me, and he's my *boyfriend*. If anyone should be concerned it should be *him*."

"He's not here, Sharleen," Bobby pointed out. "And he doesn't know."

Spraying Arpège liberally up and down her bare arms and across her cleavage, she said, "No. He's not here and he doesn't know. Maybe he's out with one of those cute-assed

Hollywood starlets. A nice little *white* girl with pink skin and blue eyes."

"You know he's not."

"*How* do I know?" she sighed petulantly. "He ran off to L.A. fast enough, didn't he?"

"He's working on a movie."

Standing up, she surveyed the finished product in the mirror with a critical eye. "*I'm* working too," she said firmly, inspecting her body profile. "This is a *work* date, and nothing else."

He could see there was no way to argue with her. If she thought a "work date" involved going to a man's apartment at twelve o'clock at night – alone – that was her problem.

"Help me find a cab, huh?" She dazzled him with her smile.

Escorting her to the street, he hailed a taxi and saw her safely into it. "Call me if you need me," he said sternly.

"I won't need you, silly." Her silky hand touched his cheek. "This is my big chance, Bobby. There's *no way* I'm going to blow it. Please be happy for me."

Watching the cab skid off down the street, he couldn't help wishing Rocket would get back soon. The responsibility of baby-sitting Sharleen was starting to get to him. Two nights ago she had come home from the theatre where she was still in the chorus, a triumphant expression lighting her face. "*Guess* who was in tonight?" she'd breathed excitedly. "Just start guessing because I want you to *know*."

"Stevie Wonder."

"Nope."

"Billy Dee Williams."

"Would I still be alive?"

"The great Miss Diana Ross?"

"Bobby. This is important. This is my *future*."

"Who?"

"Marcus Citroen." She savoured the sound of his name. "Blue Cadillac Records. *The* Mister Citroen himself. And he sat in the front row an' never took his eyes off me all night!"

"Maybe he's short-sighted."

"Bobby! Get serious. I had the stage manager deliver an envelope to his driver with my résumé and picture. Oh, Bobby!

He called me from his car before I left the theatre, and invited me to a party at his apartment on Saturday night. *And* he said when the other guests leave we'll talk about my career. Isn't it *fabulous?*"

"Are you *kidding?*"

"No. I am most certainly not. This is the break I've been wishing for all my life."

There had been no talking her out of it. When he'd tried, she'd merely snapped at him, changing the subject. Sharleen was ecstatic, and in a way he couldn't blame her. For eighteen months she'd stood by and watched both his and Rocket's careers begin to warm up, while nothing — except the chorus — happened for her. Rocket landed small roles in two movies, and then a Hollywood agent signed him, and within weeks he was on his way to Los Angeles to play the second male lead in an important film.

As for Bobby, his songs were in demand, *and* his musical arrangements, not to mention his piano backing. He was doing very nicely, and several of his songs had been in the top twenty, recorded by various artists. He'd given up both his outside jobs, and now spent his days composing.

Twice he'd managed to get Sharleen studio time, where she recorded demos of two of his songs. The songs sold, Sharleen didn't. At least she had the tapes to console her. But she wanted much more than that.

Hey — what was *he* worrying about? She wasn't *his* girlfriend, although he had spent the last five years wishing she was.

Falling asleep with the television on, he awoke in a cold sweat at four in the morning. He'd been having some kind of nightmare, but couldn't remember what it was about. His mouth felt like sandpaper, and he was hot and covered in perspiration. Getting out of bed he padded silently into the kitchen and poured himself a glass of water. The loft consisted of a large living space with two screened-off bedrooms — one at each end. Before going back to his area he decided to peek in on Sharleen, just to make sure she was safely home.

She wasn't. Her bed was undisturbed.

Goddamn it! What was he supposed to do now?

Go back to sleep and mind your own business, an inner voice warned him.

But he couldn't, and when Sharleen came in at five-thirty that morning he was pacing around the loft like a deranged father. "Where the hell have you been?" he demanded, too angry to notice her bedraggled appearance and shaken expression.

"Leave me alone," she said wearily, pushing past him and locking herself in the bathroom.

"Just you listen to me—" he began.

"Shut up!" she screamed from behind the closed door. "I don't have to answer to you or anyone. *Leave me the fuck alone!*"

He did just that, and early that morning went off to a recording session at Soul On Soul records – a small record company run by a female producer named Amerika Allen. She was using him quite often. Today they were recording one of his songs with Rufus T. Ram, a young soul singer.

Amerika greeted him warmly. She was a heavily built black woman of thirty-three, with an enormous bosom and a taste for flowing, African-style clothes. "Hiya, Bobby Boy."

He kissed her on the cheek. "Hey – Amerika – my favourite lady. You are lookin' *hot*!"

"Charm! The man is learnin' charm." Narrowing her eye she peered at him closely. "Thing is, Bobby, *you* all look like you had a *haaard* night. One of your little blonde chickies keep you up?"

"Nope."

Amerika grinned. She had the widest smile and the whitest teeth. "You can't fool *me*, man. I can *smeeell* a sleepless night."

He wasn't about to tell her about Sharleen. Twice he had brought Sharleen to the studio and Amerika had not been exactly enthusiastic. "Pretty chick. Small voice," she'd said dismissively.

"I wish you'd give her a chance," Bobby had pleaded.

"Honey – not *even* for you. I only deal with genuine talent."

"*C'mon*, Sharleen's got a great personality. She'd really come across on television."

"Sure, baby, she'll come across all right, but not at *this* record company."

End of story.

"You bin holding out on me, Bobby," Amerika said accusingly, putting a friendly arm around his shoulders as they walked into the studio.

"I have?"

"Yeah, baby. I've bin findin' out things."

"Like what?"

"I'll buy you lunch, an' then I can tell you all about it."

"Hey – tell me now – you got me curious."

"Be patient. Don't you want a free tuna fish sandwich?"

Rufus T. Ram was six feet four inches tall, skinny, with wild Afro hair, and a high-pitched, musical voice reminiscent of a young Smokey Robinson. He'd already had a couple of near hits with Soul On Soul.

The song Bobby had written and arranged was a slow, throbbing ballad, *Girl, I Want Your Body*. Rufus T. Ram sang it with a cheerful beat.

"Wrong!" announced Amerika after a couple of run-throughs. "C'mon, Rufus, baby, you gotta get *down*, get *dirty*. I wanna *hear* the hard-on in your voice."

Rufus T. Ram nodded as if he understood exactly what she was saying. The only trouble was – he didn't. The way he sang the song evoked images of a breezy walk in the park, a light musical stroll. It soon became clear that Rufus T. Ram and *Girl, I Want Your Body* did not fit.

Amerika called an early lunch break. "We gotta talk," she said to Bobby, guiding him from the studio with a firm grip on his arm.

He really wanted to call Sharleen, but Amerika was on the move, hurrying him down the street to a small Italian restaurant she favoured.

"I'm gonna treat you to more than tuna," she announced with a wide smile. "I think we both need a *beeeg* plate of nourishin' spaghetti an' meat balls to survive the afternoon."

He agreed. Now that he was thin he didn't mind indulging once in a while, and he liked Amerika, she had been good to him – ever since a musician friend had taken him to the Soul On Soul studios nine months ago and introduced them.

"I gotta tell you, Bobby, your song is the greatest," she said, ordering a bottle of red wine, then reaching for a hot bread roll. "Only problem is – Rufus T. Ram can't sing it."

"I know," he admitted.

"So." Sitting back, she surveyed the crowded restaurant. "What we gonna do?"

"Write him another song," Bobby suggested logically.

She looked surprised. "You can do that now?"

"Huh?"

"Well, c'mon, Mondella, I got a studio full of musicians. I need a steady line of product. Can we have another song an' full arrangement ready to go right after lunch?"

Disbelievingly, he said, "Are you *crazy*?"

She selected a thin brown cigarillo from her oversized bag, reached for the book matches on the table, and lit up. "I want *you* to record the song."

"Me?"

"You."

"Now I *know* you're crazy."

The waiter arrived with the wine and poured a small amount for Bobby to taste. He passed his glass to Amerika. She sipped and nodded a brisk okay. When the waiter left, she said, "Hmmm . . . 'Sweet Little Bobby', Honey, don't you think it's about time you jumped back to where you belong? On vinyl, baby. Makin' hits."

*

Sharleen was not in when he got home later that evening. She had left for the theatre. Scotch-taped to the refrigerator door was a scrawled note:

> SORRY!
> LOVE YA!
> DON'T TELL ROCKET!!!
> DON'T WAIT UP.
> S

Quickly he figured out her shorthand. "Sorry" meant she didn't want to discuss it. "Love ya" was her salve to keep him at her feet. "Don't tell Rocky" meant exactly that. And "Don't wait up" translated into "I'll be home very late".

Luckily *he* wasn't involved with her. This girl was out chasing ambition, and nothing was going to stop her.

Sharleen . . . Sometimes he wished he'd never set eyes on her, let alone joined up with her and Rocket to become the adventurous threesome.

Tonight even thoughts of Sharleen couldn't bring him down, he was too goddamn high on life. Today he had sung for the first time in seven years thanks to Amerika Allen. He, Bobby Mondella, had gotten up in that studio and sung the pants off Rufus T. Ram. Yeah. He had surprised everyone – including himself. He had a voice, and it was really something! Not the plaintive, high-pitched wail of "Sweet Little Bobby" but a low-down, raunchy throb. And if anyone could put real meaning into his lyrics – *he* could.

Amerika had been thrilled. "You got it, my man," she'd said, hugging and squeezing him. "You *sure have* got it! Some bitchin' voice!"

What a day! Amerika hitting him with his hidden past was quite a surprise. It was a secret he thought nobody would ever discover. He'd never even confided in Rocket and only mentioned it to Sharleen once, and she hadn't believed him, so he'd let it drop.

But Amerika knew. She'd done a touch of detective work and come up with an old 1963 album of his with a fat, smirking "Sweet Little Bobby" on the record sleeve.

"First time I set eyes on you I figured I'd seen you before," she said. "An' I got to thinkin' an' thinkin' an' *thinkin'*. *Still* couldn't remember where. Then one day, 'bout a week ago, I remembered. More than ten years back I was visiting Nashville with some friends, an' I saw this cute little fat boy on a TV show. 'What's this black boy doin' singin' country?' I remember thinkin'."

"So how come all these years later you figured out it was me?"

"Honey – you come walkin' in here claimin' no musical past.

Hadda be something' wrong somewhere. My bones told me you'd bin in music all your life. An' then this one mornin' I just woke up an' *knew* you was once 'Sweet Little Bobby'." She laughed triumphantly. "I got a memory like a camel stores water!"

"I don't get it. I look different. I sound different. How did you make the connection?"

"Your eyes haven't changed, baby. They just got a little older an' a *whole lot* wiser. An' now it's time for you to get back to work – doin' what *I know* you can do. An' better than Rufus T. Ram."

Amerika was very persuasive. She talked him into giving it a try, and it was almost as if he had all this stored-up vocal energy just waiting to burst through. And when he opened his mouth out came the voice – the *new* Bobby Mondella voice. And he was certain that finally he was on the road to where he wanted to go.

Right now he felt like celebrating. Putting Marvin Gaye and Tammi Terrell on the stereo, he went through his phone book and finally settled on a cute ball of blonde fluffiness who worked behind the cosmetics counter at Bonwit's. Since Sharleen was going to be out late he decided he might as well take advantage of the empty apartment.

The blonde arrived in a backless summer dress with four-inch stiletto heels. Soon the dress was history, but the shoes remained. He satisfied his newfound lust for living, and she squealed. "I guess it's true what they say about black men!"

Within fifteen minutes she was history. Picking up the phone he reached Rocket in L.A.

"Everythin' all right?" Rocket asked anxiously.

No. You'd better get your ass back here. Sharleen is shacking up with Marcus Citroen. And it ain't my problem.

"Sure. How's the movie goin'?"

"Couldn't be better. I'm like a piece of shit off the streets of New York, bringin' back good memories to every fat-butt exile out here."

"Sounds exciting."

"Yeah, I guess it is. There's some kinda love goddess 'round every corner, an' tits an' ass a man could kill for."

"So?"

Rocket made a disgusted sound in the back of his throat. "So nothin', man. With what I got stashed at home there's no way I'd blow it. Let me speak to her."

Shit! If he told Rocket the truth, Sharleen and he might break up. Which would leave the field clear for a certain Mr Bobby Mondella who had been waiting patiently in the background for five long years.

No. He couldn't do that. Not to Sharleen.

"She's uh ... getting back from the theatre late," he said vaguely. "One of her girlfriends is throwing a birthday party."

"Where?"

"I don't know. Somebody's house."

"What a kid, that Sharleen," Rocket said fondly. "Y'know what I'm gonna do? I think I'll surprise her with a trip out here. Get her to meet my agent an' that kinda jazz. She'd like that, wouldn't she?"

"You said you were coming back next week."

"The film's runnin' over. Besides, I told you – they like me here – they're buildin' up my part."

"Great."

"Yeah." He juggled the phone, reaching for a cigarette. "Hey – guess who I ran into last night?"

Bobby remembered Sharleen asking him the same question. "I'm no good at guessing games."

"This is *really* gonna blow your mind."

"Who?"

"Nichols Kline. Can y'believe it?"

"Our old boss? The manager from The Chainsaw?"

"Ya think there's *another* Nichols Kline around?"

The Chainsaw had closed down four years earlier, the result of a major drug bust.

"What's he doing in L.A.?" Bobby asked curiously.

"Pretty fine if you ask me. I ran into him at this rock and roll party at the beach. He had a redhead on one arm, a brunette on the other, and more gold chains than a street hustler could rip off in a week. He's a concert promoter now. Not bad, huh?"

"Did he remember you?"

"Do hookers take money? Of *course* he remembered me. I'm unforgettable, man. One of a kind. When they made me they threw away my mother!"

"All right, all right, so he remembered you," Bobby said, anxious to tell his news.

He was too late, Rocket was ready to go. "I gotta hit the sheets, man. Gotta get some sleep. We're shootin' downtown tomorra — it's just like bein' home — rats, dirt, maniacs roamin' the streets. My kinda town!"

"Hey—" Bobby said quickly. "I just wanted to tell you — I'm singin'."

"So are the fartin' birds. All day long. California. It's a whole different world. Listen, tell Shar to call me tomorra. Love ya both."

After the phone call Bobby still didn't feel like sleeping. He was up and speeding. Elated, restless, full of boundless energy. Sitting down at the used piano he'd bought with the first money he'd made as a songwriter, he played a few notes. And before long the notes became a tune, blending with the lyrics he made up as he went along.

He wrote a simple, soulful ditty full of his feelings for Sharleen.

The lady herself staggered home at five in the morning, glassy-eyed and obviously stoned.

"What the hell is going on?" he asked grimly, thinking, *I'm beginning to sound like a broken record.*

She was giggly and mellow, the pupils of her brown eyes dilated and starey. "Bobby, Bobby, Bobby," she sing-songed. "Handsome, handsome, Bobby boy!"

"Sharleen." He gripped her by the shoulders. "What are you on?"

Gazing at him blankly, she said, "On?"

"What did he give you?"

She started to giggle. "Ohhh . . . Bobby doesn't wanna know *that.* Bobby's a *good* lil' black boy. He don' wanna hear no *naughty* things!" Hiccoughing and swaying, she began to fall.

He caught her in his arms, swept her up, and carried her to the bed she shared with Rocket.

She stared up at him, a goofy smile on her swollen lips.

"You look terrible," he said sternly.

"Lil' ole me's got herself a recording contract," she sang. "I'm gonna be bigger than Diana Ross. A star, baby, a *star*. Ooooh, Bobby." Reaching for him, she locked her hands behind his neck, pulling him down towards her. "Wanna celebrate? Wanna kiss me? Wanna make love t'me? I know y' do. You've *always* wanted to, haven't you, baby?"

The opportunity was right there. Sharleen, inviting him to do what he *had* always dreamed of.

Two things stopped him. His best friend, and the fact she was so stoned she didn't know what day it was. When he and Sharleen got together – and he knew that one day fate would arrange it – it would be after she and Rocket were through, and whatever else, the lady had to know *exactly* what was happening.

He wanted Sharleen.

But only on his terms.

Saturday, July 11, 1987
Los Angeles

Cybil arrived home early from her photo session. She was fully made up, her blonde hair a thick mane of stylized curls. She seemed to have forgotten about their fight, and was full of good cheer.

"How was your randy photographer friend?" Kris asked sarcastically.

"Gay," Cybil laughed. "*Veree* randy and *veree* gay and *veree* careful. My God, Kris, with this AIDS scare, nobody's *doing* it anymore."

He didn't want to discuss AIDS. The very word panicked him. Somewhere he had heard that every time you got into bed with a new person you were also getting into bed with every one of their sexual partners for the past seven years. Jesus! That meant hundreds of people – maybe even thousands – all rolling around together swapping germs. Frightening! One of the reasons he stuck to Cybil in America, and Astrid in England. Playing musical beds was out.

"I'm going upstairs to change," Cybil said. "What time are we leaving?"

She obviously expected to go with him to Novaroen, although he couldn't recall inviting her. But what the hell, he wasn't in the mood for another fight. "The Hawk's comin' by in half an hour. Will you be ready?"

She grinned. "I'm a quick-change artist. Just watch me!"

*

The smell in the bus was stifling, and Maxwell Sicily was delighted when the vehicle turned off the Pacific Coast Highway and started up a steep incline to an open-space area where everyone was instructed to disembark.

The air was fresh and strong, a brisk ocean breeze tempering the afternoon heat. Glancing around he noticed security guards everywhere busily organizing the restaurant staff into groups, readying them to board the small shuttle buses which would take them up to the main estate.

As they climbed into the shuttles – eight at a time – a guard ticked their names off a lengthy list, while a uniformed woman holding a two-way radio relayed the checked-off names to some unseen person.

"This is worse than prison," joked one of the waiters.

"How would *you* know?" sneered another.

True, Maxwell thought. How would any of them know? The grim realities of prison life bore no relation to a glorious sunny day on a billionaire's estate overlooking the white-tipped waves of the Pacific.

"George!" The plaintive whine of Chloe, the plump woman who sat behind the desk at Lilliane's, wafted through the air. "Wait!"

Putting his head down, pretending not to notice the floppy cow bearing down on him, he mumbled his name to the guard as he jumped on the shuttle.

Chloe pushed her way through, managing to squeeze on beside him. "Phew!" she exclaimed. "What a journey. I'm tired before we even begin!"

Cheap perfume assailed his nostrils. Sweet and clinging. Hooker perfume. The kind the filthy whores the prison guards smuggled in for hefty compensation wore. Dirt bags, as they were known around the joint.

Chloe laid a pudgy hand over his. "You'll havta keep an eye on me today, George," she trilled coyly. "You watch out for me, an' I'll do the same for you. One thing's for sure, I'm not gonna miss the concert. I'll find us a nice place t'watch it. How would you like that?"

She shifted on her seat, leaning against him, enveloping him in her cheap stink.

He didn't say a word. Chloe was just another minor irritation to dispose of when the time came.

*

Two representatives from Blue Cadillac Records and an abrasive young publicity woman arrived at L'Ermitage ready to escort Rafealla to Novaroen and the evening concert.

She kept them waiting in the lobby for forty-five minutes, causing all three of them to break out in a nervous sweat.

At last she appeared, wearing baggy khaki pants and a loose shirt, her long dark hair tied back. A bellboy trotted behind her carrying a plastic hanging bag containing her outfit for the concert — a simple black dress.

She had requested neither a makeup artist nor a hairdresser.

"This one's gotta be weird," Trudie, the publicity girl, had said. "I never *heard* of a female artist who didn't want the whole she-bang."

The two record executives fawned all over Rafealla, while Trudie stood back and took stock. Who needed makeup and hair when they looked like this? Rafealla was startlingly beautiful, more so than her publicity photos, which did not do her justice at all. The reverse was usually true. Gorgeous, glamorous photographs always seemed to belong to very ordinary-looking women. Rafealla was certainly the exception.

"We'll do a sound check as soon as we arrive," one of the record executives said, helping her into the limo. "Then you'll have at least a couple of hours to relax before the show."

"Fine," she said quietly.

Not the talkative type, Trudie noted.

"You'll be on after Bobby Mondella, and before Kris Phoenix," the executive said.

Rafealla did not reply. *Bobby and Kris*. Two names from her past. *Kris and Bobby . . .*

Sadly, only one of them would remember her.

*

Speed was running early. He had the uniform. He had the car. And he had several hours to kill.

No big deal. There was a new Sylvester Stallone movie just waiting for his attention. Or maybe he should catch up on *Beverly Hills Cop II*. Speed loved going to the movies. He always bought popcorn, candy and Coca-Cola. And when he sat down in that darkened theatre, with those larger-than-life images flickering on the screen, he *became* the character he was watching. Shoot! He was tougher than Clint, hornier than Warren, fairer than Redford, and funnier than Chevy.

Speed often thought he'd missed his vocation. He should have been an actor. No, not an actor. A movie star. Yeah. For sure.

With a snort of resignation he realized there was no way he could go to the movies today. Too much of a risk. How could he possibly leave the Caddy limo? What if it was stolen?

Reluctantly he knew that whatever he was going to do, he was going to have to do it from the car.

He headed for Westwood, picked up some Kentucky Fried Chicken, stopped to buy *Penthouse* and *Playboy*, and set off towards the beach.

*

The limousine driver was a brother. A brother with a script and a mouthful of ideas.

"Shut him up," Bobby muttered to Sara. "I don't need this."

"Driver," Sara interrupted politely. "Mr Mondella is very tired. He'd appreciate silence."

"Silence!" the driver exclaimed excitedly. "I wrote a song called *Silence* once. Maybe I should sing it for y'all!"

"No!" Sara said hastily, vowing never to use this limo company again. The least they could do was check out their drivers and not send out would-be screenwriter-singer-song-writers.

"I understand," the man said in a hurt voice, sounding like he didn't understand at all. "I'm cool."

"I'm sure you are," Sara said. But just to make sure, she found the button to raise the glass partition and hurriedly pressed it.

*

Nova Citroen's white-blonde hair was swept up in an elaborate, twisted chignon. Her fingernails and toenails gleamed with slick, crimson polish. Her body tingled – the result of a vigorous massage – and her makeup was porcelain perfect.

She was ready hours too early, but that's the way she liked it. Slipping on a plain blue silk shirt and matching slacks, she thought about the three superstar singers due to arrive at Novaroen shortly. A glimmer of a smile brought back the memories.

Kris Phoenix. What a randy bad boy *he* was.

Bobby Mondella. Ah . . . Bobby . . .

And Rafealla. Her smile faded. The bitch Marcus wanted to fuck.

Nova decided to greet them all personally.

*

One of the things Vicki Foxe enjoyed as she play-acted at being a maid was the downstairs gossip. Boy! What scandal and rumour. It made the *Enquirer* seem positively tame!

Everyone loathed Nova Citroen. The Iron Cunt was her nickname. "She makes Imelda Marcos look like a pussy," was the general opinion of her loyal staff.

Marcus Citroen was regarded with a sort of grudging admiration. "At least he says please an' thank you once in a while," was Bertha the chief cook's, opinion.

Talk was rife of the Citroens' bizarre sexual practices. "There's handcuffs in his bedside drawer," revealed one maid.

"And a closet full of kinky outfits," said another.

Vicki had personally found a concealed cupboard with whips and chains and all the paraphernalia of sexual perversions. She couldn't care less. Her years as a professional had taught her many things, and one of them was never to be surprised. The thought of either Nova or Marcus Citroen trussed up and ready for action amused her. Sado-masochism wasn't her kick. But each to his own. Vicki Foxe never judged anyone.

She often wondered what turned Maxwell Sicily on. He certainly hadn't given any hint. Most men, faced with her lethal charms, started drooling on the count of three. Maxwell had stayed cold as an ice-pick. That kind of disinterest intrigued her. Where was he going after tonight? What did he have planned? Was there another woman in his life?

So far he'd only paid her a quarter of the money she was supposed to get. The deal was he would contact her twenty-four hours after the caper and tell her where she could pick up the rest.

"Yeah? An' what makes you think I'm gonna trust you?" she'd asked suspiciously.

"We do it my way. Are you in or out?" he'd replied icily, without so much as a moment's pause.

She admired a man who didn't waver. "I'm in," she'd said, and set about finding out exactly who George Smith *really* was. Not so difficult. Vicki had her ways.

"I've been lookin' for you." Tom, the chief of security, startled her as he came up behind her in the front hall of the main house.

She held her shoulders a touch straighter and thrust her bosom forward, straining the limits of her drab uniform. "And you've found me," she answered sassily. "What's up?"

He edged close to her, his bad breath offending her nostrils. "How about you an' me watchin' the concert together like you suggested?" he asked with a knowing leer.

"Don't be silly," she said guilelessly. "You're working, and so am I. It's not possible." Softening her voice she added, "Much as I'd love to."

His eyes dropped to her breasts, big balloons just straining for his touch. Tom knew when a tootsie wanted him, and this broad had been giving him the eye for weeks. Now he'd finally figured out a good time to get her to himself. "I got a place for us to see it," he said.

Looking surprised she cooed, "*Oooh*, Tom, you're so smart! How exciting!"

"It will be, honey," he said, managing to brush against her. "Just keep everything hot."

With one deft movement her hand slid across the telling bulge in his pants. "It'll take a *real* man to cool *me* down," she whispered. "See ya later, big boy!"

*

Marcus curbed his desire to visit Rafealla at her hotel. He had to be so careful. The girl reminded him of a horse he'd once owned, a magnificent Arabian filly which allowed nobody close.

Marcus had tamed the excitable, exquisite animal. It had taken him many months of discipline and extreme patience.

He planned to do the same with Rafealla. Only this time he was running out of patience.

Kris Phoenix 1975

The baby was whining – some might say it was crying, but Kris knew a whine when he heard it.

He wasn't good with babies, couldn't quite get the hang of them. And he knew for a fact that it wasn't *his* job to be watching over some smelly little sod with a nappy full of crap, even if it *was* his.

Putting down his pen, he picked up a newspaper. Writing songs was a kick, but only when he could concentrate, and who could concentrate with a whimpering baby making distracting background noises?

Willow was going to have to give up her job, there was no other answer. They'd just have to manage without her salary. Screw it. He needed peace and quiet to create, and he sure as hell wasn't getting it at home.

Home was a basement flat in Kilburn – was he ever going to get out of there? It had a tiny, dark bedroom, matching bathroom, a cramped kitchen, and a dreary living room, which led out to a seven-foot patch of weeds, where they kept two rusting deck-chairs and the baby's pram – a rather fancy gift from Willow's uptight parents.

Kris thought for a moment of Willow's formidable mummy and daddy. Mr Wigh, a bank manager in Esher, and his neurotic wife, a raging snob with delusions of grandeur.

No wonder Willow had run away from home twice before she was sixteen, finally moving out on her nineteenth birthday to attend secretarial college in Hampstead. Her parents sent her such a paltry allowance she was forced to get a part-time job working in a dress shop with Flower. Flower, of course, introduced her to Kris. Before he could turn around she was pregnant, and he – suburban schmuck that he was – married the girl.

Kris Phoenix – rock star. Forget it. Let's all give a big hand to Kris Phoenix, husband, father, jerk of the year.

He threw the newspaper down in disgust, not even bothering to study the naked page three girl with tits you could balance a mug of beer on.

"Shit!" he said aloud, and the baby shifted from a whine to a hearty wail.

Nothing was going right for him, not one damn thing. Eighteen months ago The Wild Ones had cut their first record, *Lonesome Morning*, and everyone had been so high on it. Kris hadn't doubted that success and all that went with it was just around the corner.

Lonesome Morning descended on an uninterested public, and got no radio play. "How can people buy it if they've never heard it?" he'd demanded of anyone who would listen.

"You're not on any of the play lists," Sam Rozelle told him regretfully.

"So tell the fucking record company to *get* it on. That's their job, isn't it?"

"Everyone's doing their best," Sam replied, not looking him in the eye.

Kris suspected otherwise. He went into six record stores, and not only were they completely unaware of the record's existence, but after searching, found they didn't even have it in stock.

"There's somethin' funny going on," he complained to Mr Terence, who took absolutely no notice.

"Nonsense!" Mr Terence said. "The time isn't right for you. You all need more experience." And he promptly sent them back on the road. Back to the one-night stands, greasy roadside cafés, groupie slags, and sleeping in the back of the clapped-out Volkswagen bus.

Back to square one. Do not pass Go. Do not collect a fucking thing.

In London, Willow's pregnancy progressed. Flower relayed news bulletins when she arrived to visit Buzz.

"Her father's furious."

"Her mother's having a nervous breakdown."

"Willow moved home last week."

And finally: "Her old man's making her have an abortion."

"What?" Kris shouted, the blood draining from his face. "No fucking bank prick's gettin' rid of *my* baby." And before anyone could stop him, he was on a train.

He turned up at Willow's parents' house in the middle of the night. A frightened au-pair let him in and immediately shouted for Mr Wigh, who came downstairs and attempted to throw him out. Mrs Wigh appeared next, and feigned a fainting fit. And then Willow, scrubbed and clean, with just the hint of a tiny belly beneath her robe.

"I'm gonna marry you," Kris blurted.

"No you're not," stormed Mr Wigh.

"Just watch us, mate," retorted Kris. And he took her back to Leeds, where they got married in the local registry office with Buzz as best man, a stoned Flower, Ollie, Rasta and an assortment of teenage groupies in attendance.

The wedding ceremony took less than ten minutes, and after it was over they all went to a local café and got well and truly pissed.

In the heat of the moment it was an exciting time. After that it was downhill on a fast sled. What was an aspiring rock star supposed to do with a wife, let alone a pregnant one?

Mr Terence went ape-shit when he found out, ranting and raving, threatening to tear up their contract, swearing them all to secrecy. "Nobody is to know about this. Absolutely no one," he said severely. "And if anyone finds out – deny it. Do you hear me? It never happened, she's just a girlfriend."

Apparently, in their quest to become rock stars, girlfriends were acceptable, wives were not.

Willow agreed she wouldn't wear a wedding ring. Not that Kris had bought her one. Who had the money?

When Mr Terence calmed down, he took the situation in hand, finding them the furnished flat in Kilburn, and advancing Kris the cash to pay for it. "I'll deduct this from your song-writing royalties," he'd said testily.

"What royalties? I haven't *had* any bleedin' songs published yet – only *Lonesome Morning*, an' that's dead in the fuckin' water," Kris replied.

"Didn't I tell you?" Mr Terence said vaguely. "Del Delgardo and the Nightmares heard it, liked the song, and cut their own version. It'll be out in America next week."

"No, you didn't tell me," Kris was furious. He felt betrayed.

Lonesome Morning, the Del Delgardo and the Nightmares cover, was a smash, reaching number three in the States, and a healthy number two in England.

Proud as he was of the song, Kris would sooner the hit belonged to The Wild Ones. Still, after he got over his initial anger, it was a satisfying feeling for both him and Ollie – who had written the music to his lyrics. It would have been nice if Mr Terence had asked their permission before handing their song over to someone else, but at least it was a hit.

The most annoying thing of all was that when they performed the song on stage everyone thought they were covering Del Delgardo and the Nightmares' smash single, even though Kris announced that they could go out and buy The Wild Ones' original recording. Big deal. Nobody did. Or maybe they just couldn't find it.

With Willow installed in the flat, Kris at least had somewhere to go on the one weekend a month he managed to get back to London. It made a pleasant change from being constantly on the road. Willow could cook, and she cared about him. She was pretty, clean and loving. What more could any man ask?

She was also getting bigger every day, her stomach swelling like a large ripe watermelon preparing to burst.

Naturally he had to introduce her to his family. Mum acted okay, but his two sisters carried on alarmingly, telling her every embarrassing story they could think of about him. Brother Brian sneered derisively. "How did *you* get to marry the daughter of a bank manager?" He was impressed, in spite of himself.

"Just a big cock, I guess," Kris replied nonchalantly. "Shame it doesn't run in the family."

"You're no good at anything you do," Brian hissed with a baleful glare. "Why don't you pack this stupid singing lark in, and get yourself a proper job with a future?"

"Why don't *you* shove it up your arse?" Family. He tried to stay away from them.

When Willow gave birth he was on stage in Glasgow playing to an audience of appreciative, squealing girls. The Wild Ones had quite a following in spite of no record deal, no publicity agent, and no-hope venues.

Avis took Willow to the hospital in a taxi. She phoned the uptight Wighs, who drove down from Esher the following morning. By the time Kris arrived from Scotland he was the father of a seven-pound-six-ounce baby boy. Willow sat in her hospital bed surrounded by a loud-mouthed Avis, a stoned Flower, and a tight-lipped Mr and Mrs Wigh. The perfect group. From that moment on he felt completely trapped.

They named the baby Peter (after Willow's grandfather), John (after Kris's father) and Buddy (a respectful gesture to the late Buddy Holly – one of Kris's personal heroes). Somehow Peter John Buddy never got called any of those names. Bo was his nickname. Baby Bo.

He'd been with them for fourteen months, and in that time The Wild Ones split up – temporarily. Rasta went on a tour of Europe with a German rock and roll band who made him an offer he didn't want to refuse. Buzz took off with Flower to Ibiza, where he got a job as a waiter and resident guitarist in a local restaurant. And Ollie concentrated on composing new songs, while Kris settled down to supplying the lyrics.

They sold a few of their songs, causing Mr Terence to grab a hefty percentage. But their best compositions they saved for the re-forming of The Wild Ones.

Mr Terence was furious with the group for splitting up, but as they straggled off the road he could see they were all burnt out and needed to do other things for a while, so he didn't put up too hard a fight.

"When we get back together," Kris informed him, "We're goin' to do it properly. No more screwin' around. An' if *you* can't do it for us, we'll find someone who can."

"Let us not forget that we have a contract," Mr Terence said waspishly. "A *legal* contract."

"Fuck the contract an' fuck *you*," Kris fumed. "You sold us down the river with *Lonesome Morning*, and it *ain't* happenin' again."

"How *dare* you! I've supported you boys through thick and thin. Given you money, a roof over your heads, looked after your personal problems. I've—"

Kris held up a commanding hand, stopping the fussy Mr Terence in his tracks. "I know all that," he said. "An' believe me – we're grateful. But we're *not* goin' to waste any more days bustin' our arses in deadbeat cities performin' to crummy audiences who don't know shit from chocolate. We want the big time."

Kris had made that little speech three months ago, and he meant every word of it. He was twenty-six years old, getting up there. The dreaded thirty was only four years away and he was determined to make it before then. The Wild Ones were good and he knew it. God! He wanted success so much he could taste it in the back of his throat every morning when he got up, and every evening when he went to sleep.

The baby's crying increased. Gingerly he picked the infant up, cradling it awkwardly. Holding the baby reminded him that since giving birth, Willow did not like to make love. She just lay there, a stone slab with all the enthusiasm of a deceased fish.

Miraculously Bo stopped crying, and gurgled happily, Kris carried his son over to the table, laying him on a clean towel. Removing the baby's nappy he stared down at the Phoenix crown jewels. It certainly looked as if Baby Bo had a major inheritance coming his way.

Kris grinned, just as a steady stream of pee hit him straight in the left eye.

★

"I don't know," Willow said, a worried frown creasing her brow. "What about germs, and the water, and all that heat?"

Kris had just suggested a welcome family holiday in Ibiza with Buzz and Flower, and she was moaning about germs and heat. She was lucky he was even considering taking her and the baby. The smart thing would be to leave them behind while he talked Buzz into rejoining the group. The time had come for The Wild Ones to get back together. He'd already contacted Rasta, who was raring to go. And Ollie waited impatiently on red alert. They had a stash of dynamite songs, and Kris had no doubts that this time around it was all going to happen. All he needed was Buzz.

He had not, as yet, given the good news to Mr Terence. He wanted to be sure of Buzz first, and he knew the best way to hook the lazy layabout was to tell him face-to-face.

The holiday idea seemed perfect. There were cheap flights to Ibiza, and Buzz had said they could stay with him and Flower anytime they wanted. Kris had thought Willow would be delighted. No such luck.

"C'mon, luv," he wheedled. "It'll be fun."

"For *you*," she said, with a toss of her head. "*I'll* be looking after the baby the whole time."

"We'll share."

"You say that now, but I *know* you."

"No, you don't." He grabbed her playfully around the waist. Lately he was feeling randy all the time. Maybe it was because Willow tried to limit their sexual adventures to once a week, which was about six times too little for him. Before he was married he'd had sex every day. Wasn't marriage supposed to improve things?

Sliding his hand up, he cupped her right breast.

She tried to wriggle free, but his grip on her waist was firm. "Stop it, Kris," she scolded.

"Why? We're a respectable old married couple," he said, hand diving beneath her blouse, burrowing under her bra like a mole.

"I said stop it," she repeated, her voice developing an annoying whiny quality. "It's the middle of the afternoon."

He was on a mission and had no intention of coming back to

earth until mission accomplished. Pulling her reluctant hand down to his hard-on he said. "Feel this. I don't care *what* the fucking time is."

"Don't swear."

"Why?"

"It's coarse."

"So am I. You didn't marry the bleedin' Prince of Wales, y'know."

Roughly he pulled her blouse open and unhooked her bra, as she stood motionless in the centre of the room like a martyr about to be sacrificed.

He didn't care. He was beyond caring. He was too busy deciding whether to suck on one of her deliciously inviting tits, or go for the goal in one.

The boobs triumphed. It was more fun for him if she enjoyed it too, and he'd noticed she was never averse to a certain amount of stroking and caressing in that area.

And so they both stood there, Kris carefully working her up to the great moment.

Finally she gave in, sinking to the floor with a small moan of acceptance.

Pulling her panties down he zeroed in for the home run. It was quick but ultimately satisfying.

"We're going to Ibiza," he said firmly. "Pack your bags an' count on it. Okay, luv?"

Rafealla 1975

"Remember when you tried to kill yourself?" Odile Ronet asked matter-of-factly. Like Rafealla she was bilingual, and spoke perfect English without a trace of her French accent.

"Remember when *you* tried to do *yourself* in?" Rafealla retorted sharply.

'Hmmm . . .' Odile replied with a reflective shrug. "Neither of us did much of a job, did we?"

"Thank goodness!" exclaimed Rafealla.

"It certainly would have been a waste," stated Odile, admiring her slim figure in the full-length mirror.

Odile was visiting from Paris. Since she and Rafealla had been living in different countries they had spent nearly every summer together, usually dividing their time between their two families. Odile's mother, Isabella, had also remarried.

"Yes," agreed Rafealla, standing beside her best friend so they could compare reflections.

Two fifteen-year-old girls on the threshold of adventure. Both long-legged and coltish. Both attractive promises of things to come. But there the resemblance ended. Rafealla was dark, Odile fair. Rafealla's looks were strikingly unusual. Odile had a simple prettiness.

Best friends and not a secret between them. They shared

more than friendship, they shared a tragedy that would never go away.

"My breasts are bigger than yours," Odile announced, sticking her chest out to get the best effect.

"No they're not." protested Rafealla vehemently.

"They certainly are."

"Certainly *not*."

"See." Odile raised her sweater, exposing firm, small breasts without the hindrance of a bra.

"Ha!" exclaimed Rafealla, opening her shirt. "Look at these."

"Fabulous!" exclaimed a male voice from the doorway. "Utterly fabulous!"

"Rupert – you little shit," she screamed, pulling her shirt closed, while just as quickly Odile dragged her sweater down. "I've told you never to come into my room without knocking. *Never!*"

"The door was ajar," Rupert Egerton, son and heir of Cyrus, Lord Egerton – the newspaper magnate – pointed out.

"So what?" yelled Rafealla furiously. "So bloody what?"

"Hmmm ... And what are you two doing anyway, comparing each other's thingies? Couple of lesbos, I bet."

"Fuck off, Egerton."

"I will not." Rupert sat himself down on the edge of the bed. "I'm bored."

At nineteen, Rupert was an amiable, younger mirror-image of his father, and his grandfather, and his great-grandfather before him. Ancient portraits decorated the halls of Egerton Castle. There was no mistaking Rupert's heritage. He was tall and gangly, with a shock of bright-red hair, hundreds of freckles on parchment-white skin, and pointed patrician features. The only thing he hadn't inherited was the Egerton family stammer.

When Rafealla's mother, Anna, had married Rupert's father, Cyrus, Rafealla had thought she would die. For one whole year she'd refused to acknowledge Rupert's existence – until one day, while out riding in the grounds of Egerton Castle, Rupert had sneaked up behind her on his horse, startled her, and made her mount rear into the air, causing her to be thrown to the muddy ground. "I hate you!" she'd yelled. "You stupid, freckly dumb *boy*!"

"And the same goes for me, missy," he'd yelled back. "You're a stuck-up, conceited wog brat. I wish you'd never come here."

Rafealla had burst into tears. She was thirteen and he was a big bully of seventeen. It had never occurred to her that he didn't want her around either.

After that little incident they began to talk to each other, grudgingly at first, but soon they found they had certain things in common – like riding, and jazz records, and a hatred of Cook's pot pies. One night they sat together in the empty ballroom and began to speak about their outrage and hurt at losing a parent. Rupert's mother had drowned in a boating accident when he was seven – exactly the same age as Rafealla when she lost her father to a terrorist's bomb.

Suddenly they were close, and from that moment on Rafealla loved her stepbrother as if he was the real thing. Of course, like the real thing, he could be an absolute pain, and today was one of those days.

"Rupert," Rafealla said briskly, "I don't *care* if you're bored, I really don't. Odile and I hardly ever see each other, so will you kindly go and be bored elsewhere."

"Yes," Odile agreed. "Why don't you run away and read the *National Geographic*?"

"Nobody reads that anymore. Not when you can see human, white – well, almost white – bosoms at home."

"Fuck off, Egerton," Rafealla repeated, with a finger gesture to match the phrase.

"Hmm ... just when I thought I might treat you two young ladies to a night on the town in London," he said casually, getting up and wandering towards the door. "Of course – if you want me to leave ..." He trailed off, waiting for their response.

"Really?" asked Rafealla suspiciously. She wouldn't put it past him to dangle the carrot and then withdraw it at the last moment.

"I don't offer idle invitations," he said, quite affronted.

"Yes you do," Rafealla contradicted him.

"I most certainly do not."

"Children!" interrupted Odile. "Let us not waste precious time arguing. A night in London sounds divine. The answer is yes, Rupert. Yes, Yes. *Yes.*"

*

Rafealla loved going to London, although it was usually during the day with her mother. They always lunched at Harrods, shopped around Knightsbridge, and then devoured a delicious tea at Fortnum and Mason. Sometimes Lord Egerton drove in to meet them, and they dined at his favourite restaurant, Wheeler's, in Old Compton Street, where Rafealla always ordered the crab salad.

Once or twice she had played truant from school, taken the train and visited London with a girlfriend. They'd walked up and down the King's Road admiring the fashion parade of punks – with their purple and green spiked hair, bizarre makeup, and outlandish dress. And Sloane Rangers – the properly brought-up daughters of well-bred and affluent parents – clad in twin-sets, pearls, and sensible Gucci shoes.

After watching the fashion parade they'd spend hours looking through the record albums in W. H. Smith before going home.

Rupert's London was different altogether. He took them to San Lorenzo, an Italian restaurant in fashionable Beauchamp Place, where he seemed to know almost everyone.

Mara, the warm proprietress, chucked him lovingly under the chin. "You like 'em young, Rupert, huh?" she asked with a wicked twinkle.

"This is my *sister*, Mara," he said reproachfully. "Rafealla, say hello to the great Mara. She runs this place with an iron fist. We're all terrified of her."

Shyly Rafealla shook hands.

"Your *sister*, Egerton," said a tall young man with a sly smile. "Since when did *you* have a sister?"

"Since my father remarried," Rupert replied. "Rafealla – meet Eddie Mafair – he's a pain in the backside and rolling in filthy lucre. And Eddie – this is Odile Ronet. Hands off. One day I'm going to marry this girl."

Rafealla and Odile exchanged amazed glances.

"Didn't I tell you?" Rupert said casually, winking at Odile. "Must have slipped my mind – thought I did."

They dined on mushroom salad and fresh pasta with shrimp, followed by a wonderful creamy dessert concoction called zabaglione. Rafealla spotted two Hollywood movie stars, a world-renowned tennis player, several English actors, and Del Delgardo – lead singer with the Nightmares.

"I think I'm dreaming!" she whispered to Odile. "Isn't Del Delgardo *gorgeous*?"

"Ugly," replied Odile with a pantomimed shudder. "Those teeth!"

"Who cares about his teeth. Everything else is perfect!"

"How do *you* know?"

"I can dream, can't I?"

Pulling a face, Odile said, "He's old. He must be at least thirty."

"That's not old."

"One foot in the grave, my dear."

Sometimes even best friends got on one's nerves. Rafealla shot Odile a dirty look.

After dinner Eddie Mafair reappeared and hovered by their table. "We're all going to Annabel's," he said. "Why don't you come with us?"

"Can we?" Rafealla and Odile questioned in unison, turning hopefully to Rupert.

"I don't know." He shook his head vaguely. "I suppose I should drive you girls home."

"Why?" Rafealla asked anxiously. She thought Eddie most attractive, and could imagine nothing better than spending the rest of the evening with him. "My mother and your father are away this weekend. There's nobody waiting up for us."

"True," he said.

"Well?" the two girls demanded.

"All right," he decided. "But you'll both have to chip in on the bill, I'm not made of bloody money."

Annabel's presented a world Rafealla hadn't seen before. It was a sophisticated nightclub, with music courtesy of the Beatles, David Bowie, Aretha Franklin, Jefferson Lionacre, Gary Glitter, Olivia Newton-John, Del Delgardo and the Nightmares — a mixed group — whose records blared forth from loudspeakers stationed above an overpacked dance floor.

"Ohhh! I love discotheques," Odile exclaimed, with a delighted smile. "I've been to Le Club in Paris, you know. My mother took me there for my fifteenth birthday."

Rupert raised his eyebrows as if he'd only just realized how young they were. "For God's sake," he hissed. "If anyone asks, you're both eighteen."

"Yes, Rupert," Odile said obediently.

"And *I'm* twenty-one," he added, a trifle sheepishly.

Rafealla nodded, her eyes darting all over the place. "How old is Eddie?" she asked innocently.

"Too old for you," he snapped.

They joined Eddie Mafair and a group of his friends. The girls at the table all resembled the Sloane Rangers Rafealla had spotted strolling in Knightsbridge and the King's Road. She was glad she'd chosen to wear a short black skirt and white turtleneck sweater — at least she looked different, and certainly older than fifteen.

"How about some champers?" Eddie offered, already filling her glass with the fizzy liquid.

She decided he liked her too, and felt a shiver of excitement. Rupert was seated further down the table with Odile next to him, so she was safe. Tentatively she took a sip. It tasted wonderful.

"Drink up. That's my girl," encouraged Eddie, staring straight into her eyes.

She studied his face. He had sharply handsome features, sallow cheeks and light brown hair worn appealingly long. His clothes were a casual blue blazer, white shirt, dark pants, and a blue and red striped tie. She imagined he was only a year or so older than Rupert.

"I say, Eddie," brayed the Sloane Ranger sitting on his other side. "Let's trip the light."

"You'll have to excuse me, Fiona. I promised this one to Rafealla."

Fiona pouted, not prettily. "Drat! I simply adore The Who."

Rafealla stifled a giggle. She couldn't imagine Fiona adoring anything other than a walk in the country with a panting labrador sniffing at her crotch.

"What are you laughing at?" asked Eddie.

"Nothing."

He took her by the hand and stood up. "Shall we?"

"I simply adore The Who," she mimicked wickedly.

"Now, now," he chided, with an amused smile.

They danced the night away. Slow ones, fast ones, sambas, even a waltz! Until at one-thirty in the morning a rather irritable Rupert insisted he drive them home.

"I want to see you again," Eddie Mafair whispered in her ear as they were leaving. "Very, very soon. I'll give you a ring."

She nodded, knowing full well her mother would object strongly if an older, sophisticated man like Eddie rang her for a date. She was allowed to go to the cinema with a mixed group and that was about it. To her chagrin she'd only been kissed once, and it was no big deal. The boy in question was one of the gardener's assistants. Reasonably good-looking, he had a black front tooth and missing finger, which quite spoiled the effect.

Odile was dying to find out everything, but managed to control herself until they got home and Rupert went off to his room.

"Well!" she exclaimed. "Tell me all! And don't leave *anything* out."

Rafealla realized there was not that much to tell. After all, the only thing they'd done was dance. "He wants to phone me," she said lamely.

"Of course he does," Odile enthused. "*And* he probably wants to make mad, passionate love to you."

"*I* don't know."

"You must *know*."

"How?"

Odile rolled her eyes. "You had all those slow dances with

him . . ." She hesitated, then rushed on. "Was he . . . you know . . . stiff?"

"What a question!"

"Well, *was* he?"

Rafaella felt a fit of the giggles coming on. She was sure she was blushing, even though Odile was her best friend and they told each other everything.

"Yes," she said at last. "He was stiff as a sergeant on drill parade!"

"Good Lord!" said Odile, collapsing with laughter. "And will you go out with him when he phones?"

"Yes," Rafaella replied defiantly. "Why shouldn't I?"

Bobby Mondella 1975

"No," Bobby said.

"You're one stubborn son of a bitch," Sharleen replied, dragging nervously on her cigarette. "Why not?"

"We've been over it a hundred times," he said flatly. "You know how I feel. I got loyalty – an' it belongs to Amerika Allen."

"Goddamn!" Viciously Sharleen stubbed her cigarette into an ornate lead-crystal ashtray. "Blue Cadillac and Marcus can do so much more for you. Why don't you listen?"

"Because you're wrong," he replied calmly. "Soul On Soul have been very good to me."

"They haven't taken you to number one on the crossover charts," she said, reaching out and selecting another cigarette from a fancy silver box on an expensive mahogany coffee table. "What do you have to say about *that*?"

"You know something?" he said mildly. "You're gonna ruin your voice if you keep on smoking those things."

"Don't wanna talk about it, huh?" she jeered. "Don't wanna admit that Soul on Soul is a little fish in a large pond, an' Blue Cadillac with Marcus Citroen is the goddamn *shark*."

"Oh yeah, he's a shark all right," Bobby said quietly.

"You've never even met him," she said accusingly. "Don't assume power equals bad."

He stared at her. In two and a half years she had changed considerably. No longer the wide-eyed, enthusiastic girl he'd first met, she was now a twenty-nine-year-old, polished, sleek woman. Pretty — yes. Vulnerable — no. Loving — yes. But only when it could get her somewhere or something she wanted.

He was still her friend. He still loved her, but he wasn't sure he liked her anymore.

"I spoke to Rocket yesterday," he said, changing the subject.

"*That* bastard!" she snapped.

When had Rocket become *that bastard*? The day she dumped him. Or the day he married Roman Vanders, a black actress ten years his senior?

"I guess you don't want to hear how he is."

"Bobby." She leaned towards him persuasively, close enough so he could study her perfect makeup, and observe the unhappiness in her big brown eyes. "All I want is for you to be part of the Blue Cadillac family. It's right for you. I *know* it is. And think how great it will be when you and I can work together. I'd really love to cut an album with you."

"I'll ask Amerika. Maybe she'll have you over to the studio an' we'll do somethin' for Soul On Soul."

Sharleen's expression grew stony. "That's impossible."

"Why?"

"Don't be ridiculous." She got up from the couch and walked over to the french windows of her Park Avenue apartment. Marcus Citroen paid the rent. Marcus Citroen owned every inch of Sharleen.

Throwing the windows open she strolled outside onto the terrace. A panoramic view of the New York skyline greeted her.

"Come outside, Bobby," she called. "Come and see what you're missing."

The only thing he was missing was a woman in his life, and Sharleen no longer fit the bill.

Following her outside he had to admit the view was impressive. But what kind of woman sold herself for a view and a couple of hit records?

Oh yes, Marcus had kept his promise. Sharleen was a rising

star, and she loved it. Privately Bobby thought the stuff she was recording was pop crap. While Sharleen had never possessed the greatest voice in the world, she'd always had soul and feeling. Now she sounded as if she was singing by numbers. It didn't appear to be important. The public loved her, and along with Marcus Citroen they had made her what she was today.

He grew restless standing on her terrace. "I gotta split," he said, pulling up the collar of his jacket.

"Can't you stay for dinner?" she asked, a note of disappointment creeping into her voice.

"I never planned on it. I'm meeting Amerika."

"Of course." She swept back into the apartment. He walked behind her. Suddenly she turned on him. "Are you sleeping with her?"

"That's none of your business, lady," he replied with a sharp edge to his voice.

"Obviously she has *some* hold over you. Why else would you turn down the best offer of your life?"

"A little thing called loyalty. L-O-Y-A-L-T-Y. Remember that word – you may need it someday."

Later he met with Rocket and his wife, Roman, at a restaurant in the Village famous for its Southern fried chicken and black-eye peas.

Rocket looked good. Fame as a New York method-style actor suited him. He was still short, dark and moody, but now he had confidence and style, and he was successful enough to pick and choose his roles. He was in demand, and he loved every moment of it.

Roman was a serious-looking black woman who had a fine reputation as a character actress. The two of them had met on location in Georgia. Bobby still suspected that Rocket had married her on the rebound from Sharleen.

He remembered the night of the break-up with a sour taste in his mouth. Sharleen had been seeing Marcus Citroen for weeks, arriving home in the early hours stoned and uncommunicative. Bobby didn't know what to do. Finally he'd weakened and called Rocket in L.A., telling him there was a problem.

"I've got two more days dubbing and I'm back," Rocket had said confidently. "No problem."

He was back all right. In time to greet Sharleen as she staggered home at six in the morning.

They screamed at each other for two hours, made love for another two, and later, when Rocket and Bobby strolled down to the corner deli to pick up some cold cuts and potato salad for lunch, Rocket confided that everything was great, Sharleen was sorry, and they were just as much in love as ever.

Somebody forgot to tell Sharleen. When they arrived home with the food, she was packed and gone – courtesy of Marcus Citroen, who had sent his chauffeured car for her. Rocket had sworn he'd never forgive her.

Amerika joined them at the restaurant for coffee. She was full of enthusiasm about Bobby's new single, which was creeping steadily up the black music charts.

"It'd be sensational if it crossed over," he said casually, thinking of what Sharleen had said.

Amerika shook her head. "The most difficult task in the world. You can count the black artists who cross over on one hand."

"Stevie Wonder."

"Dionne Warwick," chimed in Roman.

"Johnny Mathis," said Rocket.

"We are talkin' *mainstream* singers here," Amerika said. "Bobby Mondella is pure soul. He has a hard-core black audience. They love him. Surely that's enough, isn't it?"

For once Bobby thought that maybe it wasn't.

*

"Lookit – boy. How come we don' never see you? Don' git no word at all. What you think this kinda behaviour gonna do to your fine cousin, Fanni? You got a short memory or *what*? That woman done plenty for you when you was nuttin'. Now you big time an' we don't git t'hear no word. What you gotta say 'bout *that*, boy?"

The blustering voice on the other end of the telephone was unmistakably Ernest Crystal.

"Don't call me boy," Bobby said ominously, wondering how Ernest had managed to track him down after almost seven years of silence. "What the hell do you want?"

"What I want? *What I want?*" Ernest's voice reached a falsetto level of outraged insincerity. "You-all have *family*, boy. Relatives who *care* 'bout you."

Sure. When he left Fanni and Ernest's, he'd attempted to keep in touch. But neither of them had shown any interest, and eventually he'd stopped calling.

"How'd you get my number?" he asked resignedly.

"Your record company done tole me – once I tole *them* I was your dear *uncle*."

"My what?" Bobby spluttered.

"A relative is a relative, boy."

"Didn't you hear me the first time?" Bobby said, his words measured. "Do not call me boy."

"Jest habit, I guess." Ernest cleared his throat, getting ready for the pitch. "Listen t'me. *We* was the ones who done took you in when Mister Leon Rue set you loose on the streets of New York City wit nowhere t'go. *We* was the ones done gave you a bed, an' food, an' a roof over your head. *We* looked after your ass when you was sick, *an'* never asked for nuttin' in return."

Conveniently Ernest seemed to have forgotten about the six-thousand-dollar cheque Bobby had arrived with, plus a healthy piece of his pay from The Chainsaw every week.

"Cut to the chase," Bobby said abruptly, having no desire to listen to Ernest's whining. If they needed money he was prepared to give them some. He wasn't rich, but he could certainly afford it, and Fanni *was* his only living relative.

"You talk tough, bo – uh – Bobby. You don' sound like that sweet, fat kiddy we once knew an' loved."

"He died," Bobby said dryly. "How much?"

"Did I say *one damn word* 'bout money!" Ernest yelled indignantly.

"How much, goddammit?"

"Well . . ." Ernest hesitated. "Since you bein' gentleman 'nuff to ask . . . Fanni bin feelin' bad. She can't work no more. She done gain a pound or two, an' she bin havin' trouble wit her heart."

"Has she seen a doctor? They could put her on a diet, you know."

Ernest rolled his eyes. "She don' have no truck wit them doctors. They jest take your money an' laugh you in the face." He paused, waiting for the right moment to strike. The trouble was, he didn't know how much to ask for. Best to go for high, he decided. "We could sure use ... say ... uh ... twenny thousan'."

Bobby laughed.

"Or fifteen," Ernest added sheepishly. "Wit all the bills we got to pay ..." He trailed off, waiting for a reaction.

Bobby couldn't believe the nerve of the man. Twenty thousand dollars! Fifteen! He should tell the son of a bitch to take a hike. "I'll send Fanni a cheque for three thousand. And you can tell her it would have been nice if she'd taken the time to call me herself."

"Three thousan'!" bitched Ernest. "You-all mus' be makin' *plenty*. An' you're tellin' me all y'kin spare is three thousand—"

"You don't want it, just say so," said Bobby, cutting him off.

"Aw, I guess we'll take it, we'll take it," Ernest whined, an unsatisfied man, but three thousand was better than nothing.

Bobby put down the phone, and for one lousy moment flashed-back on life with the Crystals. Their constant fights. The insults he'd endured. His pokey back room behind the kitchen – freezing in the winter and hotter than a sauna in the summer. Food. Greasy, plentiful ribs and potatoes and fried chicken. Pies and cakes, cookies and candies. Was it any wonder he'd remained a fat piece of blubber while living with them?

It was true though – Fanni *had* taken him in, and defended him many times against the bullying Ernest.

He went to his desk and wrote out a cheque before he changed his mind. Then he addressed an envelope to Fanni and scrawled a short note telling her to call him and maybe they'd get together.

Needless to say he never heard a word in return, although his cheque was cashed quickly enough.

Sharleen was silent for several months too. He was used to not hearing from her – she only called when she needed something, and since he'd turned down Marcus Citroen's offer to join Blue Cadillac he was obviously not on her wanted list. He got on with his life, writing songs, recording, doing quite nicely, dating a variety of girls and having a good time. Until one summer night, round about midnight, the buzzer sounded on his apartment door and wouldn't quit.

He was alone, watching a late-night movie on television.

"Who is it?" he called out before opening up.

The answer was incomprehensible. Instantly he knew it was Sharleen.

Throwing open the door, he was just in time to catch her as she fell into his arms – a beaten, bleeding wreck.

Kris Phoenix 1975

"It's bloody hot here," Kris complained.

"Don't knock it," Buzz replied, a sardonic grin lightening his debauched features. "The booze is cheap. It's friggin' dope paradise. An' the crumpet runs around with nothin' between them an' a cold!"

Kris could see it was going to take quite a speech to get Buzz back to rainy London and work. He had to admit his friend looked great with his gypsy tan, long hair, and single gold hoop earring. In England Buzz was always whiter than washing powder, managing to resemble a walking corpse. Here, at least, his malevolent looks came with a healthy tan, and he didn't appear to be five days away from death, although he was still frighteningly skinny.

"Sounds like your cup of tea, all right," Kris remarked casually.

"I can tell yer, it beats the piss out of spendin' me days an' most of me nights in that stinkin' Volkswagen, with Rasta's smelly feet in me face, and Ollie *fartin'* the bleedin' night away."

Lounging on faded beach chairs, they both laughed. Flower brought out cans of beer. At twenty-three she was still the perennial hippie. Flowing hair and flowing clothes. Spacey eyes and an angelic smile. Kris figured she and Buzz had been together a long time – almost eight years. He half expected them to get married and be done with it. "Are you two ever goin' to make it legal?" he couldn't help asking.

"Wot? 'Ave you gone friggin' barmy?" Buzz retorted while Flower just smiled dreamily.

Yeah, Kris decided, Buzz certainly had the right idea. Why get married if you didn't have to? Willow had caught him in a trap, and he knew it.

They'd arrived in Ibiza a few hours before, after a bumpy flight. Willow complained all the way.

Buzz met them in an open jeep wearing nothing but the smallest black briefs and a welcoming leer. Throwing their luggage in the back seat he said, "Blimey! You're the two unhealthiest lookin' humans *I've* ever seen!"

"Thanks," Kris replied. "You always *did* know how to make a person feel good."

"It's me charm," Buzz said with an evil wink, reaching for Peter John Buddy, who was clutched tightly in Willow's arms. "Let's see the baby, then."

"No!" exclaimed Willow sharply, holding on with a sudden show of strength.

Buzz did not back off. He continued to try and pry Bo from her protective grasp.

"Stop it!" she shouted, a touch hysterically, turning to Kris for support.

"C'mon, let Buzz hold him," Kris urged. "He's his godfather. He's entitled."

Willow glared at her husband, reluctantly allowing Buzz to take Baby Bo for a second or two.

"'Ello, mate," Buzz said, peering down at the child.

"That's enough," announced Willow crisply, snatching her precious bundle back.

Kris had only met his wife's mother a couple of times, and not under the best of circumstances, but he was beginning to realize with growing dread that Willow was just like the snobbish Mrs Wigh.

Buzz drove like a maniac, the battered jeep careening along old cobbled streets at full speed, his foot jammed down hard on the gas.

Petrified, Willow sat silently in the back, squeezed in next to their luggage, with the baby bouncing around on her knee. "Can't you slow down?" she pleaded a couple of times, but neither of them heard her as the jeep sped along the increasingly bumpy roads towards its destination.

Their holiday home was a run-down, dusty villa by the sea, and they were not the only occupants. Along with Buzz and Flower lived Inga, a blonde, strapping Swedish girl, plus Klaus, a bearded German man who spoke no English, and twenty-year-old American twins, both female, named Chick and Chickie.

"Why didn't you tell me there were other people living here?" Willow hissed angrily.

"How was *I* supposed to know?" Kris replied, dreading what would happen when she found out what was *really* going on. Buzz had filled him in as soon as they arrived and Willow and Bo were safely deposited in a damp bedroom with a sea view and an old mattress on the floor.

"It's free sex," Buzz confided with a knowing wink. "You want it – it's yours."

Buzz always *had* liked the hippie lifestyle, and Flower obviously raised no objections.

Kris knew he was in for trouble – one way or the other.

*

"You've got a lovely body," Chickie whispered in his ear.

"Smooth skin," murmured Chick.

"When are we gonna get it on?" they asked in unison, a chorus of hope.

Kris knew he was developing a hard-on, no need to check it out. Christ! Where was Willow when he needed her?

Shifting on the hot sand, he rolled onto his stomach and glanced furtively around. Buzz was lying nearby wedged between Swedish Inga and delicate Flower. What a picture postcard *that* made, since both girls wore only the bottom halves of their bikinis. Inga's huge knockers made an interesting contrast with Flower's small buds.

Willow and the baby were nowhere in sight.

"Well?" teased Chick and Chickie, running their fingers up and down his spine.

This was torture! All he really wanted to do was turn over and ram it into each of them one after the other. He was so horny it hurt.

Well, who wouldn't be? They'd stayed on the island for over two weeks, and Willow was consumed with anger about the sleeping arrangements, the half-naked house-guests, the food, and anything else she could think of.

"I won't tell wifey," Chick whispered, bending over to reach his ear, which she proceeded to nibble, her bare boobs brushing tantalizingly against his back.

Chickie followed suit. "Nor will I."

It was more than any man could reasonably take. "I'm goin' for a swim," he said weakly, getting up and making a wild dash for the sea.

Plunging in, the shock of the cold water abated some of his excitement. Not enough. Especially when Chick and Chickie, full of giggles, bosoms jiggling, ran down the sand to join him.

Jesus! What was he supposed to do? They'd been coming on to him ever since he'd arrived. And while on the one hand he liked the idea of making it with the dynamic duo, on the other he *was* a married man, and his old-fashioned values urged him to stay true – even if Willow continued to deprive him.

Chick swam towards him, with Chickie in close pursuit. The two of them wore very determined expressions.

The answer lay with his wife. *Willow, my love*, he thought grimly, *you are just going to have to put out, or else.*

With that he dodged the randy twins, swam ashore, and hot-footed it up the beach towards the villa.

"Where are you goin'?" called out Buzz.

He didn't stop. Whatever Willow was doing, she was going to have to drop everything and give him what he wanted. He was her husband. He had his rights.

The villa was peaceful and quiet, which meant Baby Bo was asleep. Perfect. Maybe she was taking a siesta too, and he could be all the way to paradise before she even realized what was happening.

Treading quietly he entered their room. Bo was asleep in his carry cot, a thin muslin cover protecting him from any marauding bugs or mosquitoes. The kid looked great, suntanned and healthy. *He even looks a little bit like me*, Kris thought proudly. Yeah. Willow might have trapped him, but it was all worth it when he saw his son.

The wife's probably in the kitchen, he decided – she'd spent most of their holiday hunched over the sink washing anything she could get her hands on. You couldn't even take off a pair of jeans without her grabbing them.

No, she wasn't in the kitchen, nor the big dusty living room. He wouldn't put it past her to be snooping through Buzz and Flower's room – she had an insatiable desire to know everything about everyone. "Nosey little cow, isn't she?" Avis had said when she'd caught her going through their bathroom cabinet one Sunday lunch with the family.

She wasn't in Buzz and Flower's room. Chick and Chickie's was also empty. And as Inga slept on the couch, that left only Klaus, and his door was closed.

Kris knocked, and getting no response he pushed it open.

Spread-eagled on the bed, naked from the waist down, lay Willow. A pillow covered her face, but he would recognize that uptight, suburban pussy anywhere.

Kneeling between her thighs, his bearded face embedded in fairyland, was Klaus, the German.

Rafealla 1976

To Rafealla's consternation and eventual disappointment, Eddie Mafair did not bother to call her. And it wasn't until almost a year later that she bumped into him at the rather elaborate wedding of the daughter of one of her mother's friends. He was the best man, and heading in the direction of being extremely drunk.

"Hello," she said sulkily, when he didn't acknowledge her as he attempted to stagger past her table at the reception.

Glancing at her vaguely he said, "You're going to have to remind me, sweetheart. I'm pissed."

"You certainly are," she replied coldly, aching all over with the desire to be in his arms once more, even if it was only on the crowded dance floor of Annabel's.

Peering closely at her he said, "Suzanna?"

"No."

"Diana?"

"*No.*"

"A clue?"

"Rafealla."

Her name obviously meant nothing to him either. "Nice to see you," he slurred, and was off.

So much for mutual attraction. She had thought he liked her. In fact she'd been positive, and made up a million excuses why he hadn't called. Now it was quite obvious he didn't remember her.

Still . . . she wasn't going to let it get her down. After all, she was sixteen now, no longer the stupid fifteen-year-old who had fallen for his casual charm. There had been several close encounters over the last year. Stefan, the twenty-two-year-old male nurse whom she'd sat next to at the movies and secretly dated for several weeks until he tried to go too far. Jimmy, a young American college student who took her dancing and taught her the fine art of giving what he called a "blow job" because she refused to do anything else of a sexual nature. And Marcel, a young French waiter who worked in a local restaurant. He took her for long walks in the woods and kissed and caressed her breasts for hours on end, bringing her great pleasure. Until in return — after many weeks of pleading — she finally gave him the special "blow job" Jimmy had taught her, and marvelled at his ecstasy and gratefulness.

She wanted to do the same for Eddie. It gave her a gratifying sense of power, and did not interfere with her virginity, which she planned to hang on to until marriage. Odile and she had discussed it many times, and decided that everything else was allowed, but going all the way was definitely out. Too risky for one thing. Unnecessary for another. Boys were perfectly satisfied with the alternative.

The wedding was a riotous affair, a mixture of young friends of the bride and groom, and the older contingent of relatives and close family friends. Rafealla knew quite a few people, and found herself on the dance floor with a variety of enthusiastic would-be suitors. Occasionally she glimpsed Eddie. He seemed to be attached to a sinewy blonde in a mini-dress who was almost as drunk as he was.

Rafealla stared at him. She was not used to being ignored. With her long dark hair, exotic features and slim figure, she usually received more than her fair share of attention. How *dare* Eddie Mafair not even remember her.

The band began playing Beatles songs — a request from the bride. *Yellow Submarine, Eleanor Rigby, She Loves You.*

Eddie was crotch to crotch with his blonde on the dance floor.

Feeling the urge to do something to make him notice her, Rafealla brazenly approached the bandleader. "Do you know *Yesterday?*" she asked.

"We certainly do."

"Can I sing it?"

"Can you?" the bandleader asked with a quizzical look.

"Of course I can," she replied, full of bravado.

"All right, darling, show us." He handed her the microphone.

Oh boy! What had she done to herself! She loved singing, but only in the privacy of the shower with that wonderful echo making every note sound good. Oh wow! How was she ever going to pull *this* one off.

"*Yesterday,*" her voice wavered, "*all my troubles seemed so far away.*" Everyone was looking at her. She had to make this good. "*I believed that love was here to stay. Oh, I believed in yesterday.*"

She had it! Sounding good. Getting everyone's attention, including her mother's, who was staring at her, probably really annoyed that she was making an exhibition of herself.

Her voice was pleasantly low, an older sound than her years. She sought out Eddie Mafair with her eyes, and finally — yes — she had his attention. *Now* he'd remember her.

When it was over there was applause and a lot of "*I* didn't know you could sing." And finally there was Eddie, who said. "Where have *you* been hiding all my life?"

Before she could reply her mother appeared, ruining everything with news of their imminent departure. At least he now knew she existed. That was something.

Two weeks later she left for France, and a summer vacation with Odile. Arriving at Nice airport and rushing outside to find her friend, she felt a surge of excitement, for standing no more than three feet away was Eddie Mafair, arguing in fluent French with an irate cab driver.

Just along the kerb a waving Odile emerged from her stepfather's chauffeur-driven Mercedes.

Rafealla stood transfixed.

Odile yelled, "Kid! Over here."

Eddie stalked away from his cab and marched into the airport without noticing her.

Odile ran over. 'What's the *matter* with you?" she scolded. "Are you deaf?"

"No,' Rafealla replied dreamily, hugging her friend. "Just in love!"

*

Odile's mother had married into show business. Her husband was Claudio Franconini, an aged Italian crooner with an enormous European following. He had been a star for many years, and revelled in his success. Marrying the widow of the prominent politician Henri Ronet was another plus in his life. Claudio adored the spotlight.

Odile had always considered him to be a bore. And on the occasions Rafealla had met him before, she was forced to agree.

"He *still* colours his bald spot with boot-polish," Odile confided with a wild giggle. "And he *still* thinks that every woman should fall at his feet with delight. Nothing changes."

"I don't know how your mother stands it," Rafealla commented.

With a Gallic shrug Odile said, "She doesn't mind. They're good together. Mama is very patient, as you well know."

Claudio greeted Rafealla warmly, kissing her on both cheeks and saying, "Welcome, welcome. What a joy to see you again, my dear. Our humble home is yours."

Their humble home was a magnificent gated château in the hills above Cannes. Guards were on permanent duty. Ten servants looked after the guests. And there was a party every other day. Claudio loved entertaining.

"We'll make our own fun," Odile promised. "We don't have to hang around her with the old fogies."

Rafealla wondered what Eddie Mafair was doing at the airport. Probably on holiday. Too bad he'd left.

The weather in the South of France was glorious. After a rather dreary English summer, Rafealla was delighted to lie in the sun doing absolutely nothing. She found it entertaining to observe Claudio Franconini and his constant stream of guests.

Odile and she staked out their corner of the pool and watched the famous come and go. There was a Greek shipowner and his fiery mistress. An American gangster with his very proper English wife. A financier with two girls not much older than they were. A black female singer and her lover.

"This is what I call entertainment!" Rafealla said. "Is it always like this?"

"Yes," Odile assured her. "Last year we had dozens of movie stars, a President's widow, oh . . . all sorts of strange people. You should've come."

"I wanted to. But as you know, my dear mother always considered I was too young to enjoy the *wicked* pleasures of the South of France until now."

"I guess sixteen signals wicked pleasures are okay. Right?"

"I bloody well hope so!"

When they got bored sitting beside the pool, the chauffeur dropped them off in nearby Juan-Les-Pins, where they wandered around the colourful shops and open pavement cafés. Sometimes they water-skied from the beach. Male attention was not lacking, for they made an alluring if very young combination. Odile – so blonde and innocently pretty. And Rafealla, dark and mysterious. They were the perfect foil for each other as they stalked the beaches in minuscule bikinis, attracting an avid following of admirers.

Odile struck up more than a friendship with a Norwegian law student, and Rafealla found herself practising the fine art of the blow job with an extremely handsome Swiss medical student. She met him on the beach every evening, and they had a perfectly delightful time. This all had to take place before ten o'clock, when the chauffeured Mercedes would arrive to collect the girls and transport them back to the Franconini luxury château high in the hills.

"I feel like Cinderella," Rafealla joked. "You know – it's as if we're leading a double life or something."

"We are," Odile said grimly. "My mother will kill us if she ever finds out what we get up to."

"Mine too."

A pause, and then Odile added, "Surely *they* were young

once? They must have done all these things."

"And more," agreed Rafealla, although she could hardly imagine her mother ever doing anything as rude as giving a man a blow job. Come to think of it, she couldn't even imagine her mother making love, and yet it was patently obvious she had – at least once.

Rafealla's medical student decided it was time she went one step further. "Trust me, I'm a doctor – well almost," he said. "I want to give *you* pleasure too."

She had never allowed anyone below the belt. Too intimate, too sticky, too embarrassing.

The lure of the white sand, the balmy nights, and the seductive lapping of the sea finally got to her. Besides, he was very good looking, and a medical man. Pushing Eddie Mafair to the back of her mind, she allowed him to embark on a short exploration of uncharted territory.

Removing her jeans and the bottom half of her bikini, he began gently touching her with his fingers. She had to admit it *did* feel good, especially when his fingers moved in a strangely soothing circular motion. Automatically she spread her legs, gasping at new-found sensations which suddenly and unexpectedly culminated in a rush of pure pleasure.

"Your first orgasm," he said matter-of-factly.

Her heart was pounding. This was something else. This was great.

"Now let me just put it there," he continued, working his way on top of her. "Nothing can happen now."

She felt pressure, and warning signals fired off in her head. "No," she said, quickly shoving him away.

"Yes," he insisted, moving back on top.

"No!" she snapped.

"Do you plan to stay a virgin forever?" he asked nastily.

Absolutely not, she said silently. *Only until I can have Eddie Mafair. And I will. Oh yes, I will.*

*

One morning Rafealla got up very early, before everyone else, and went down to the pool to swim lengths. She was bronzed to perfection, her long limbs oiled and gleaming, her stomach flat and faintly muscled.

"You have a beautiful body, my dear," said a thick male voice with a slight accent.

She turned and encountered Marcus Citroen, a record magnate who had arrived the night before from New York with his ultra-chic wife.

Rafealla grinned – she didn't know what else to do. There was nothing worse than trying to avoid the lecherous leers of dirty old men. "Thanks," she said, and dived in the inviting pool, hoping he would be gone when she surfaced.

To her surprise, when she came up for air, Marcus Citroen was in the pool, close to her.

"Look at this," he said cheerfully, as if he'd spotted some unique form of starfish.

Without thinking she peered below the clear blue water.

Marcus Citroen was taking risks. The man was stark naked, with a full erection.

Bobby Mondella 1976

It took months of patient handling to nurse Sharleen back to health. Her bruises and cuts healed first, but her pride took a whole lot longer.

"What happened?" Bobby demanded. "Who did this to you? Is it Marcus Citroen, 'cos if it is I'll kill the white son of a bitch."

"No, no," she said, panic-sticken. "It wasn't him. You mustn't get involved."

"I *am* involved. Now you've gotta tell me what went on."

"No way, Bobby. I can't."

There was no use pushing her, but gradually, over the next few weeks, he heard her story.

At first, she told him, Marcus Citroen was a gentleman. Oh yes, he persuaded her to join him in cocaine parties, and expected sex. But in return he gave her a lucrative contract with Blue Cadillac, a lavish apartment, and gradually began to build her into a star.

"I'm not naive," she confided tearfully. "I've been around the block an' then back again. But everything that was happening was so good. And I thought I could handle Marcus and his crazy demands."

His demands turned out to be watching her have sex with other girls. And more and more drugs.

"He liked me stoned," she admitted. "That way he could control me."

Stardom arrived, and vainly Sharleen attempted to cut back on Marcus and his perverted ideas. One night she completely rebelled, and refused to go to bed with a man and two other women. Marcus beat her up, and that was when she fled to Bobby.

"I hope I can stay here," she said simply.

She'd been stupid, but she'd learned a harsh lesson. His heart went out to her. "For as long as you like," he said. And concentrated on getting her better.

The trick was to be there for her every minute, supporting her, encouraging her to take a drug cure, watching over her at all times.

After a lot of persuasion she entered a private clinic under an assumed name, emerging weeks later looking like the Sharleen he used to know.

"How're you feelin'?" he asked.

"Great."

"*Really* great?"

"You gotta know it."

"I'm real proud of you, baby. You know that, don't you?"

Smiling wanly she said, "Thanks. Now tell me, where do I go from here?"

He didn't hesitate. "I've spoken to Amerika. Soul On Soul wants you. I've already written two songs we can record together. How about that?"

"Really?" Her smile lit up the room.

"It's done, baby. Sharleen an' Bobby. We're gonna be a team."

It wasn't done at all. Blue Cadillac Records refused to release her from the contract she'd signed, and they also refused to give her songs to record. In other words she was left in limbo, unable to do anything at all.

Bobby was outraged. "I'm going to see this Citroen character," he said angrily. "They can't do this to you. No way."

"Oh, yes," she said softly. "Marcus can do anything he damn well pleases."

Over the months Bobby discovered she was right. Blue Cadillac had her under an exclusive, unbreakable contract, and there wasn't a thing anyone could do, not even the hot-shot lawyer Bobby hired at his own considerable expense.

Sharleen, whose star had once shone so brightly, now had to sit back and watch other female singers get the attention that was once hers.

After a few months Bobby realized that if something didn't happen soon, she was going to revert to her old ways. He'd already caught her drunk a couple of times, and he could see she was restless and getting ready to move on. Their relationship was strictly platonic, even though she was living in his apartment. He wanted to make a move, but somehow – because they had been friends for so long – it wasn't so easy. At this particular time in her life he had no desire to put any more pressure on her. Whatever was going to happen would take place naturally or not at all.

Amerika Allen said to him one day, "What is it with you an' that girl? You've all but stopped working since she's around. You can't talk about anything else except her. To tell you the truth, I reckon you should get on with your *own* life, and let Sharleen do the same."

Amerika was right and he knew it. Too bad. While Sharleen was with him he couldn't change.

Rocket called several times from Europe, where he was filming. "How is she?" he always asked.

"Fine," Bobby replied evenly, wanting to say – *What do you care? She's no longer your concern. You're married now. You're out of the picture.*

Without Sharleen knowing, he tried to call Marcus Citroen on more than one occasion. All he got was – "Mr Citroen's in a meeting." "Mr Citroen's out of the country." "Mr Citroen's unavailable."

One morning he awoke to find Sharleen staring into the medicine cabinet sizing up the pill collection. "What are you doing? Planning your death scene?" he joked.

"Yes," she said, deadly serious.

Screw Marcus Citroen. He'd had enough.

Dressing hurriedly, he looked up the address of Blue Cadillac Records and took a cab over there.

He arrived at a minute past nine, and the receptionist — an attractive black girl with multicoloured fingernails, was just settling herself behind the front desk.

"Hello, gorgeous," he said, turning on the charm.

She looked up, her wide red lips breaking into a welcoming smile. "Bobby Mondella!" she exclaimed. "What a nice way to start my day!"

He wasn't used to being recognized, but this couldn't be better.

"I *looove Dream Baby*," she gushed. "It's a *sensational* cut."

"Thanks," he said modestly. "Glad you approve."

"I wish you were with our company," she said, fluttering extra-long eyelashes. "An' then maybe you'd get the attention you deserve."

Shrugging, he said, "Who knows?" Then, casually leaning across her desk he asked, "Is Marcus in yet?"

"Mr Citroen is always in his office from seven-thirty on," she replied, all of a sudden very businesslike. "Are you his first appointment?"

"Sure am," he said easily.

She glanced down at a large red appointment book, tapping the page with extended fingernails. "His secretaries don't get in until nine-thirty. There's no notation of your name here."

"That's because we made the date late last night."

"*Oooh.*" Her eyes gleamed. "I bet you were at the Stevie Wonder party. Am I right?"

"Sure was."

"Lucky *you.*"

"Yeah . . . well . . . I'll just go on in. Where's his office?"

"Down the hall, last door on the right. You can't miss it, there's a solid gold record on the door."

"Cute."

"I'll buzz and tell him you're on the way."

"Don't bother. He's probably forgotten. I want to see his face when he realizes *I* remembered."

The receptionist giggled and patted her teased hair. "Keep on makin' those records!"

"Only if *you* keep on buyin' 'em."

Striding down the hall he tried to decide exactly what he was going to say. What would make a man like Marcus Citroen set Sharleen free?

He remembered their one and only encounter many years ago. The men's room in The Chainsaw. He was the attendant and Marcus Citroen was the customer, snorting cocaine with Del Delgardo. Jeeze! That seemed like lifetimes ago.

The door with the gold record attached to the centre faced him. The record was larger than the real thing, and boldly printed on the label was – MARCUS CITROEN – HITMAKER – BLUE CADILLAC RECORDS. Very subtle.

Without knocking, he opened the door and walked right in.

Marcus sat behind his oversized desk, speaking on the phone. He indicated that Bobby should take a seat. There was not a flicker of surprise anywhere on his impassive face.

Bobby didn't want to sit down, only there seemed to be no alternative. What else could he do? Snatch the phone from the man and start berating him?

No way. This had to be a civilized meeting. It had to make sense, and above all, he had to walk out of there with some kind of a solution for Sharleen.

Marcus was obviously talking to someone in London, for he made references to various English events, and ended the conversation by saying, "I'll be in on the Concorde next week, I expect everything to be worked out by then. Oh . . ." His eyes, behind steely shades, settled on Bobby. "And you can tell the motherfuckers that if it's not, someone will be floating in the Thames. And, I can assure you, it won't be me."

He hung up.

Bobby cleared his throat, ready to do battle for Sharleen.

Marcus stared at him, put the tips of his fingers together, and continued to stare.

Bobby cleared his throat again. Fuck it. This son of a bitch wasn't going to intimidate him. "You don't know me," he said gruffly. "I've come to see you about Sharleen."

Marcus nodded.

There was something wrong here somewhere. Why wasn't

the great Marcus Citroen screaming for his secretary? Why wasn't he telling him to get the hell out?

Bobby pressed on while he had the opportunity. "Uh ... Sharleen's very unhappy ... suicidal in fact. And I think you know why."

Marcus plucked a cigar from a carved box on his desk, reached for a silver table lighter in the shape of a Cadillac, and lit up. Still he didn't say anything.

What kind of game was this man playing? Bobby's voice rose with anger. "The bottom line is, either you let her out of her contract, or I'm gonna see your name in headlines over every tabloid rag in the country, with *details* of what you made her do."

"Good morning, Mr Mondella," Marcus said smoothly, the oily thickness in his tone as sweet as syrup. "I've been expecting your visit for quite some time. What took you so long?"

Was this his day for being recognized or what? And exactly *why* had Marcus Citroen been waiting for him to show up?

"I want you to tear up her contract," Bobby said, feeling a surge of anger overpower him.

"There *is* an easy answer to all this nonsense," Marcus said calmly. "And if you think about it, you'll find it's the only sensible way."

"What's that?" Bobby asked grimly.

"Why, *you*, of course. *You're* the answer."

"I don't get it."

Marcus drew deeply on his cigar, blowing a steady stream of smoke towards the ceiling. "Ah, but you will. Once I explain, you'll understand perfectly." And he proceeded to do just that, while Bobby listened intently.

Marcus Citroen's solution was simple. Blue Cadillac Records wanted Bobby Mondella. Blue Cadillac Records were prepared to offer him an excellent deal, plus they would buy him out of his Soul On Soul contract. Blue Cadillac Records were also prepared to build Bobby Mondella into a big star, and they had the connections and clout to do so.

The deal included Sharleen. Once Bobby signed on the dotted line, her career would automatically be reactivated, and in no time at all they would guide her back to the top – where she rightfully belonged. An album of duets with Bobby was in her future, plus a possible movie for the two of them – depending on how everything went.

"I don't believe this!" Bobby said vehemently. "It's blackmail."

"I would have thought you might jump at an opportunity to get away from a second-rate outfit like Soul On Soul," Marcus said, puffing on his cigar. "They've done nothing for you except squander your talents."

"Hey – listen. They gave me my first chance. They believed in me."

"Ah . . . loyalty. I do admire it. But you must realize *I* believe in you too, Mr Mondella – or may I call you Bobby?" Marcus rubbed the bridge of his nose, raising his sinister tinted glasses to do so. "I've had my eye on you for quite some time. In my estimation, with your song-writing abilities, your looks and talent, you can be the biggest black star in the country. You can be number one. And, with Blue Cadillac to guide you—" He paused, allowing his words to sink in. "There is nothing you cannot achieve."

Bobby was filled with mixed emotions. It wasn't exactly discouraging to hear Marcus Citroen's plans for him – if it wasn't a trap. And yet, he knew he was being manipulated, and that didn't sit well with him at all. Besides, he couldn't imagine anything worse than being in a man like Marcus Citroen's control. And how could he leave Soul On Soul and Amerika after all they had done for him?

Soul On Soul is holding you back, an inner voice warned him. *Amerika Allen says your records can't cross over, and you know damn well they can.*

Yes. He knew it all right. Much as he loathed Marcus Citroen, Blue Cadillac were big enough to do it for him.

Besides, if he wanted to help Sharleen, he had no choice, did he? The decision was out of his hands.

Saturday, July 11, 1987
Los Angeles

The ride down Sunset was long and boring, but Kris didn't mind. The limo was well stocked with every kind of alcoholic beverage, plus a VCR, a stack of tapes, and an excellent sound system including a compact disc player with a selection of the latest discs.

He put on Motown's Twenty-Five Number One Hits from Twenty-Five Years, and would have settled back to enjoy The Temptations, The Four Tops, and Marvin Gaye – if Cybil hadn't decided to be the life and soul of the party, and burst forth with a running commentary on her day.

The Hawk seemed interested enough. He leaned forward in the seat facing her, looking immaculate in a white silk dinner jacket, with his perfect tan and ultra-white capped teeth. Tombstone teeth, Kris thought, all the better to gobble you up with.

The Hawk was not a handsome man, but he certainly made the best of what he had. He was married, with a wife who lived permanently in Buenos Aires and only came to Los Angeles once a year. Every six weeks the Hawk got on a plane and visited her for a long weekend. A rather strange arrangement, but one that seemed to work, for they had been together for fifteen years.

It did not prevent the Hawk from being a player. He had a

stable of luscious girlfriends – none of them a day over twenty-two. Although rumour had it that he merely liked to be seen with them – nothing else.

"So . . ." Cybil continued excitedly. "Jerry doesn't take any shit from anyone – well maybe from Mick, but that's about it. Anyway – she looked this guy straight in the eye – like a real confrontation stare, y'know what I mean? And then she said in that crazed drawl of hers – 'Honey, the screwin' you'd get ain't *nothin'* compared to the screwin' you'd get!'"

The Hawk laughed. He was amused by Cybil's inside gossip about the world of modelling.

Frankly, Kris didn't want to know. Glancing at his watch he asked irritably, "Are we nearly there?"

"Relax," the Hawk said. "Sit back. Enjoy yourself. It's a beautiful day."

When wasn't it a beautiful day in sunny California?

Fuck it. He wasn't happy about this gig, and nothing was going to improve his mood.

*

"Name?" barked a fierce-looking guard as Maxwell Sicily got off the shuttle bus.

"George Smith."

The guard adjusted his opaque sunglasses, and checked out a long list. "Okay," he said at last. "Wear this." And he handed Maxwell Sicily a badge with Lilliane's, GEORGE SMITH, and a number printed on it.

Organized, Maxwell thought, but they would have been better off doing their homework.

"Name?" the guard asked Chloe.

"I'm management. I don't need a badge," she objected, with a haughty toss of her frazzled hair.

"*Every*one gotta have one," the guard said grimly. "Otherwise, lady, *you* ain't goin' nowhere."

"Hah!" she said. "And who's going to stop me?"

"Lady, *I* am. Them's the rules."

Maxwell took the opportunity to move swiftly away, joining a group of waiters busy receiving instructions on where they were and were not allowed to go.

"No cameras. No recording equipment. And no trespassing other than your allocated area," snapped the latest guard.

"What if we wanna take a piss?" asked one of the waiters.

"There's facilities."

"Oooh, and do *you* come with us, to hold our ... uh ... hand?"

The security guard did not crack a smile.

Maxwell followed the group to the back of one of the two main houses on the estate, where a makeshift open-air kitchen had been set up under a large tent. Chefs were busy organizing their equipment, while the waiters were being given a variety of jobs to do.

He got in line, and was instructed to help set out silverware. Grabbing a few boxes he followed a tall woman supervisor who was shouting out orders as she led the way down a narrow pathway to an enormous sunken area, where there were lots of round tables waiting for decoration, and a curved stage that looked like it was balanced right at the edge of the cliff.

By nightfall, with the fairy lights twinkling in the trees, the backdrop of clear sky, and the faint rush of the ocean, the effect was going to be spectacular.

A shame to ruin such a splendid evening, Maxwell reflected grimly. But they deserved it.

All of them.

*

The attention always made Rafealla faintly uneasy. People jumping at her every command. Didn't they realize she was just like everyone else? Or were stars supposed to be different?

She hadn't been a star long enough to quite get the hang of it. Maybe she should be more demanding, behave like a bitch, have hysterics and scream a lot. But that wasn't her style.

"Do you always do your own hair and makeup?" Trudie, the publicity girl, asked curiously.

'It's easier if I do it myself," Rafealla replied, as the limousine turned onto the Pacific Coast Highway. She wished she could tell it to stop. She wanted to get out and run on the beach, or just sit on the sand watching the endlessly fascinating ocean.

For the last few months she hadn't been able to do anything without being recognized. It was an outrageous invasion of privacy, and she didn't enjoy it one bit. And yet she'd wanted it desperately, had craved fame with relentless dedication.

"If I had a chance to have professionals get *me* together, I'd jump at it," Trudie admitted, reaching for an M & M candy set out in a small glass dish.

"I'm sure Rafealla knows what she wants," said one of the record executives, shooting her a warning glare. Rule one – never criticize anything a celebrity does.

"Uh, you know something – it's disturbing," Rafealla said, feeling she had to explain herself. "Having a stranger paw at your face. I don't like it."

"With a face like yours you don't need it," Trudie observed grudgingly. "Me – they'd have to pile it on with a trowel and then some!"

Rafealla smiled faintly, and wished she was somewhere else.

*

Speed had no intenton of hitting on the Mexican broad in the tight red pants and halter top, but she was coming on to him with such force he'd have to be dead to resist her.

She sashayed past the parked limousine several times, wriggling her big ass and jiggling her tits, before finally saying, "Hiya, handsome. It'sa too hotta day to be sittin' in a car."

It was hot all right. He'd found a nice quiet side street off San Vincente. Residential. Nobody to bother him. First he'd eaten his chicken, then he'd studied both *Playboy* and *Penthouse* cover to cover.

Oh yes, it was hot. And when Miss Mexico tottered by on stiletto heels, he couldn't help but notice her, and she *certainly* noticed him. Well, he had this magic with women, didn't he? Sort of a Burt Reynolds magnetism without the looks.

Not that his looks were anything to complain about. Somebody had once told him he resembled Roy Scheider on speed.

He didn't do drugs. Well, only sometimes. A few uppers, downers. A snort if he was feeling flush.

He wouldn't mind a snort today, *and* a piece of fine Mexican ass. *Playboy* and *Penthouse* had gotten his engine revving.

Furtively sneaking a look at his watch he realized there was still time.

Miss Mexico hovered near the window, waiting for a go signal.

Speed knew he was irresistible to women. He also knew this one was a hooker – although what she was doing plying her trade in this respectable area in the middle of the afternoon was beyond him.

"How much?" he asked, trying to make up his mind whether to proceed or not.

"Beeg good time or leetle good time?" the woman leered, suggestively fingering one of her nipples.

"Head."

"What?"

"Suckee."

"Ah." She put a finger to her lips, touching it reverently with her tongue. "Twenny dollar."

"Forget it."

"Fifteen." Her nipple hardened beneath her touch.

Speed let out an anticipatory grunt. He'd always been a sucker for big bosoms. "Get in the back," he said gruffly, springing the locks.

"You no disappointed."

Quickly he got out of the car, glancing up and down the street. It was deserted. Ready to rhumba he joined her on the back seat.

"Money," she said, holding out her hand, palm up.

Struggling in his back pocket he came up with three fives, shoving them in her eager hand.

"Vice," she said, dropping the Mexican accent and miraculously producing a police badge. "You're under arrest, buster."

*

And so the limousine carrying Bobby Mondella arrived at checkpoint number one on the vast ocean-side estate. A guard spoke to the driver, and then peered inside.

"What's happening?" Bobby asked. This is what he hated more than anything, having to ask about every little thing.

Sara laid a reassuring hand on his arm. "Just a security check."

"What for?"

"I don't know. I guess they have to be careful at an event like this."

"Sure," Bobby said acidly. "Someone might try to blow Marcus Citroen's ass sky high – an' not a moment too soon."

"Bobby! Don't talk like that."

What did Sara know? Exactly nothing. She had no idea how evil a man like Marcus Citroen could be.

The car moved smoothly off, up a steep incline and along a narrow private road which would eventually lead the way to Novaroen.

Bobby took a deep, strangled breath, and remembered Nova Citroen. The bitch of all time.

*

I'm not a fucking maid, Vicki Foxe wanted to say to the bossy housekeeper who seriously thought she was Joan Crawford reincarnated. However, she could not say that, because – right now – she *was* a maid, or at least playing a role. So instead she said, "Yes, Mrs Ivors, as soon as I've finished cleaning the silver champagne goblets for the guest house."

"Mrs Citroen needs attention *now*," the Ivors woman snapped, scarlet lips and heavy eyebrows a fond tribute to *Mommy Dearest*. "Those goblets should have been polished days ago. I don't know what you girls do with your time."

Vicki didn't say a word. Thank God this was the last day she would have to put up with this unbelievable crap.

"Go to Mrs Citroen. Now," instructed Mrs Ivors. "And when she's finished with you, come right back here. I don't want to find you cosying with the guards. You're much too familiar with them. We'll have to have a talk about attitude if you're to continue in this job."

How Vicki longed to say – *Get stuffed, you silly old cow. You can shove this crappy job right up your drawers – and watch out for moths.* Smiling serenely she said, "Yes, Mrs Ivors. I'll be right back, as soon as Madame lets me."

Madame! What a great touch! Even Mrs Ivors shut up.

Vicki made her way upstairs to the master suite, humming softly to herself. Within hours it would be all over. And not a moment too soon.

*

"Good afternoon, Mr Citroen."

"Nice day, Mr Citroen,"

"Delighted to see you again, Mr Citroen."

Minions. All of them. Worker ants. The guards. The gardeners, the staff, the security. The place was a hive of activity. If he'd had his way they would never have thrown open their home for such an event.

"It's not our home," Nova had reminded him scornfully when he'd voiced his objections. "Merely a weekend shack. And if *I* want to have the party here, *this* is where it will be."

Sometimes she challenged his authority, not too often. Nova knew exactly how far she could go. Only as far as he'd allow her to. If she stepped beyond the bounds he punished her.

Nobody took the punishment the way Nova did. Nobody . . .

As far as Marcus was concerned it made their relationship perfect.

For a moment he thought about Rafealla. So young . . . so spirited . . .

It had been a very long time since he'd been forced to wait for a woman. But Rafealla was going to be worth it. Of that he was sure.

*

Nova Citroen glanced up as the maid entered after knocking discreetly. "What took you so long?" she asked irritably.

"Mrs Ivors only just told me you needed someone—"

"Yes, I do," Nova interrupted rudely. "Get down and find my ring. I think it rolled under the bed."

How Vicki yearned to say – *Find it yourself, you spoilt bitch*.

Dutifully she assumed the position and scanned the dusty underneath of Mr and Mrs Citroen's custom-made bed. She spotted the ring immediately. A huge solitaire diamond.

What would happen if she slipped it casually down her cleavage and claimed she couldn't find it? It was a thought. But too risky on today of all days.

"Here we are, Mrs Citroen," she said brightly, scooping it up.

Nova took the ring and slipped it back on her finger.

The maid was staring at her. Nova hated scrutiny. She was perfect from a distance, but up close sometimes the cool perfection cracked. "You can go now," she snapped. Stupid bovine creature. Take your eyes *off* me. God! She was getting too thin, that was why her ring had fallen off. As one grew older svelte turned into scrawny, and when rings started slipping off one's fingers it was time to do something about it.

"Thank you, Mrs Citroen." Vicki bobbed a curtsy, another perfect touch. She was almost beginning to enjoy this!

As soon as the girl left, Nova resumed her agitated pacing. She twisted the magnificent diamond on her finger, and thought about its history. Marcus had bought it for her. A blood present between the two of them, and only she knew why.

Kris Phoenix 1977

The noise was a deafening roar. A cacophony of excited sound.

"KRIS! KRIS! KRIS!"

"BUZZ! BUZZ! BUZZ!"

One of the roadies had told him there wasn't a dry seat in the house when they were finished, just like it was when the Beatles were performing.

They moved together, the four of them, The Wild Ones, surrounded by their people. A makeup girl, a hair stylist, Mr Terence, a couple of bodyguards, and the ever-present Flower.

Buzz swigged from a bottle of scotch, shoving it towards Kris, who drank his share before passing it on to Ollie and Rasta.

"WE WANT THE WILD ONES!" chanted the crowd. "WE WANT THE WILD ONES!"

"Yeah," muttered Kris. "An' you're gonna get 'em."

As they neared the side of the stage Flower passed Buzz a joint. Taking a couple of deep hits, he automatically handed it on to Kris, who did the same.

Mr Terence pretended not to notice.

Kris held up the roach, waving it at Ollie and Rasta. "Anyone?"

"Naw," said Rasta. 'I'm high enough, man."

"Let's go get 'em then!" shouted Kris, adjusting his guitar.

"Let's go rock the shit outta 'em!"

"We're goin' in for the kill!" yelled Buzz.

And the four of them ran frantically on stage as the screaming reached high fever pitch.

"KRIS. WE LOVE YOU!"

"BUZZ! BUZZ! BUZZ!"

"KRIIIIIIIIIS!"

It had been that way from the beginning of the incredible relaunch of their stalled careers. Within a fast eighteen months they had become media superstars. Roaring a path to fame and glory with nothing and no one to stop them.

The Wild Ones. White hot and ready to play. Sexy. Talented. Four likely contenders in the rock and roll sweepstakes.

While Ollie and Rasta were considered cute, and definitely necessary to the over-all picture, it was Kris and Buzz who culled the major attention.

Kris Phoenix. How the little teenyboppers loved him. They went crazy for his irreverent looks, his spiky, dirty-blond hair, his ice-blue eyes, and his wiry body. They *especially* liked his wiry body.

Buzz attracted the slightly older fans. Suntan long gone, he was back to his usual whiter than white pallor. And with his long, raggedy black hair, oblique unsmiling expression, and skinny snake hips, he had a certain satanic quality parents feared and loathed. Therefore rebellious teenagers worshipped and adored him.

Kris Phoenix and Buzz Darke. Two new English heroes for the seventies – a triumph over punk music, which was all the rage – with groups like The Sex Pistols, The Jam and The Damned getting most of the attention.

The Wild Ones were no way punk influenced. All four of them hated the tuneless mindless music of the "fuck you" generation of punk musicians. The Wild Ones took their influence from a combination of early rhythm and blues, Buddy Holly, Chuck Berry, Sam Cooke and Otis Redding. They threw in a little of the Rolling Stones drive, the melodies of the Beatles, the guts of Joe Cocker's vocals, and the pure guitar genius of Eric Clapton.

What emerged was a very distinctive sound, especially as they only performed their own compositions.

In eighteen months they'd made it. Quickly enough for some of the music press to label them an overnight success.

"Overnight bleedin' success, my arse!" sneered Buzz. "What about the friggin', sloggin' years nobody would friggin' look at us? What about explorin' England in a friggin' Volkswagen?"

True words. But now they were stars. In England. They hadn't cracked America yet. They hadn't tried.

Flash! Photographers captured that initial crazy moment as they launched into their first hit record – *Dirty Miss Mary*. Kris had written the lyrics to go with the melody Buzz created. It was a quirky tune, reminiscent in a way of the Beatles' *Eleanor Rigby*.

Kris and Buzz sang it together, sharing the centre microphone for effect – working off each other – singing the hell out of the sardonic lyrics.

Kris felt the adrenalin pumping through his system – charging him up – making him razor-sharp and ready for anything. Christ! There was no feeling in the world like performing for an appreciative, yelling, stamping, screaming audience of fans. Hell, no.

And yet it had almost never happened. Buzz hadn't wanted to leave Ibiza, where he sat around stoned all day with naked girls to satisfy his every need. It had taken a great deal of not-so-gentle persuasion. In fact, they'd almost come to blows, with Kris calling him every name he could think of. Well, he had to have *someone* to vent his frustration on. Once he'd packed Willow and the baby back to England, he took it all out on Buzz. They fought for five long weeks, arguing back and forth until finally Buzz gave in. "Fuck it!" he'd said bitterly. "I can see I'm never goin' t'get any peace again if I don't do it."

"Bloody right," Kris agreed.

Since Willow left he'd been to bed with Inga, the strapping Swede, both Chickie *and* Chick, and a variety of other females. Oh yes, and he'd taken part in his first orgy, which didn't thrill him one little bit. "Too messy," he'd informed Flower when she invited him to attend another one.

"Don't be so silly!" she'd chided lightly. "It's fun!"

His idea of fun was not squirming around on the floor with a bunch of sweaty, maybe disease-ridden strangers. Buzz and Flower got off on it at least twice a week. Kris couldn't understand why.

Catching goody-goody Willow with Klaus, the German, was a real downer. He couldn't remember having felt such rage over anything. After discovering the two of them, he'd dragged her out of the room, slapped her stupid face, and told her to get packed. Then he'd booked a flight for her and the baby, driven them to the airport, and put them on the next plane to London.

Willow cried. "Please come too," she'd begged.

"I'll be back when I feel like it," he'd said without emotion.

"I'm sorry," she whimpered.

Was she sorry she'd been caught? Or sorry she'd done it? He didn't know and he didn't care. He felt betrayed. But he wasn't going to let it ruin his life.

Working on Buzz to come back kept him sane. And sleeping around restored his ego. By the time they arrived in London he'd decided to forgive Willow for the sake of their baby. After all, they were even now.

He was too late. She'd gone. Fled home to mummy and daddy in Esher, taking Baby Bo with her. Divorce papers awaited him.

He didn't waste time worrying about it. But he did get hold of a lawyer to make sure he could visit his son regularly.

From then on it was all work. Once they'd rehearsed the new material, they went out on the road to try it out. The old, familiar Volkswagen van transported them up north.

"Bloody hell!" Buzz grumbled. "Is this what I bleedin' dragged meself back for?"

Audience reaction was great. Mr Terence came up for the concert when they reached Scotland. He liked what he saw so much he arranged for a well-known booking agent to fly in and see them the next day.

Within a week they had signed on to open for Del Delgardo and the Nightmares, the big American group who were due to do a two-week tour of England.

Night after night they stole the show from Mr Delgardo and his Nightmares, causing major friction, and a rapid pay-off after only one week. Kris couldn't care less. Del Delgardo was a prick. Besides, a scout from Force Records had seen them and signed them to make an album of their original material. The power of positive thinking obviously worked. Kris had instinctively known that this time it was all going to come together.

Force Records put a strong P.R. push behind them when they released the first single from the album. There were interviews, photo sessions, promotional appearances, and radio shows. When *Dirty Miss Mary* began to climb the English charts, they got on *Top of the Pops* – the record plugger's dream television show. Within weeks *Dirty Miss Mary* went to number one. The Wild Ones were a hit!

Kris often thought about his mother's face when he told her. She'd gone quite pale and clutched the sleeve of his shirt. "Does number one mean it's selling more than anyfing else?"

"Yes."

"More than Johnnie Ray?"

"Ma, Johnnie Ray was a long time ago."

She'd beamed. "I'm proud of yer, lad. We all are."

And they all were, except Brian, who still treated him like his snotty-nosed kid brother. "You'd better save your money," Brian had said airily. "It won't last."

It had lasted long enough to give them two more hit singles and a successful album. Now they were on the last leg of a sold-out European tour. Next stop – London. After that Kris planned to sit down and discuss how they were going to conquer America.

America was the world.

And he wanted it.

Rafealla 1977

Mother decided finishing school was in order. Preferably Switzerland. And she finally settled on L'Evier, an exclusive, expensive all-girls school nestled deep in the lush green countryside.

"Why finishing school?" Rafealla complained. "I'm nearly seventeen. I'm too *old* for school."

"One year, and then we'll send you to a suitable American college. You're looking forward to that, aren't you?"

"If I survive a year in Switzerland," Rafealla groaned.

Touching her lightly on the cheek her mother smiled. "You'll survive, my darling, you're just like your father."

It pleased Rafealla when Anna spoke of her father. She cherished every mention of him – after all, she was so young when Lucien died, and her memories were vivid and very precious.

She often wondered how different her life would have been were he still alive. No England. No castle in the country. No stepfather. No Rupert.

Ah ... Rupert. He truly was like the brother she'd never had, and she loved him very much. Right now he was travelling across America with a backpack and the daughter of an earl. Everyone hoped they would marry. Everyone except Rafealla – in her mind she was saving him for Odile.

L'Evier turned out to be a strict prison, with lights-out at ten, and a formidable headmistress. Rafealla took classes in English literature, languages, cooking, singing, social graces, and history of the arts.

She hated every minute. What kind of life was she preparing for? She had no desire to marry some rich titled man and live in luxury giving great charity.

Phoning Odile in Paris she complained bitterly. "This is a real crock."

"Leave," Odile said simply. "My design college is the greatest. Ask your mother if you can come here with me. You don't learn much, but the male talent is *vrroooooom!*"

"She'd never let me. Not after I made the mistake of telling her about that New York flasher in the South of France."

"Stupid old Marcus Citroen. He does it to everyone – including the maids. You should *never* have told your mother."

"I know. Now she thinks you're all a bunch of perverts!"

"How crazy. Maybe I'll have mama telephone her and beg for your freedom."

"Would you?"

"Why not?"

Isabella Ronet and Lady Egerton had a long chat, the result of which was that Rafealla stayed in Switzerland. Both mothers decided that the two girls – although lifelong best friends – were not always the best influence on each other.

So Rafealla slogged it out at L'Evier, loathing it more and more as each day passed, only enjoying her singing classes and choir practice. She had a strong, deep voice, a talent obviously inherited from her father.

Some of the girls at school were unbearable little snobs who ostracized her because her skin was darker than theirs.

"Touch of the tar brush, dear?" Fenella Stephenson, one of the ringleaders, asked one day as they stepped out of the communal showers.

"Sorry?" said Rafealla, reaching for a towel and tying it across her chest.

"I thought they had a policy here," Fenella sneered. "No *blacks* allowed."

Rafealla felt a rush of colour sting her cheeks. Fenella was unpleasantly plump. "Funny," she said, keeping her voice nice and even. "And *I* thought it was *fatties* they didn't allow in."

The ensuing fight would have thrilled any voyeur of young girls. They went at each other with no thought of modesty as their towels fell off and they rolled on the cold stone floor.

"Black bitch!" Fenella yelled.

"Fat white tub of lard!" Rafealla retorted, as they kicked and thrashed, pulling at each other's hair.

A crowd of enthusiastic girls gathered, cheering them on with pithy comments. Nothing like a good fight to break up the monotony.

"What *is* this fiasco?" demanded the piercing voice of the principal as she pushed her way through to reach the scene of the crime.

Quickly Rafealla grabbed her towel. "Sorry, ma'am," she said, in spite of a split lip and a threatening black eye. "I slipped on the tiles, and Fenella was helping me up."

"Is this true, Fenella?" thundered the principal, not believing a word of it.

"Yes, ma'am," said Fenella, struggling to cover herself, obviously relieved at Rafealla's discretion.

"Golly!" said Rafealla, innocently widening her eyes. "You should *do* something about these slippery tiles. Wouldn't it be awful if somebody *sued* the school one of these days?"

The principal glared at her, pursing thin lips. She hadn't liked Rafealla from the moment she'd arrived. She reminded her of another girl quite a few years earlier, a girl called Lucky Saint – or Santangelo as it turned out. A gangster's daughter of all things, and a troublemaker from the beginning. Because of Lucky they'd had to have extra locks fitted on all the windows to curb any nocturnal wanderings.

Yes. Rafealla had that same dangerous quality. She'd probably end up getting expelled just like Lucky – in spite of being Lord Egerton's stepdaughter.

As it turned out Rafealla lasted the term, gaining top grades in languages and English literature, and great praise from her singing teacher. She also became good friends with Fenella, and organized a diet for her that really worked. After their unfortunate introduction, they found they had mutual acquaintances, and that they lived quite near each other in the English countryside. With prejudice out of the way, they got along extremely well, although no one could ever replace Odile as Rafealla's best friend.

When vacation time rolled around, Fenella invited her to spend a weekend in Oxfordshire at her family's estate. Her father was a property tycoon, and her mother a society butterball. Rafealla had to control her laughter when she met Lady Stephenson. The woman was outrageous, dressed in more frills and flounces than a drag queen!

On Saturday night Lady Stephenson had an invitation-only fancy dress ball for five hundred of her most intimate friends.

"Mummy does this twice a year," Fenella disclosed. "She says she sees everyone in a different light when they're wearing costumes."

Rafealla dressed up as a Chicago gangster in one of Fenella's brother's suits which was several sizes too large for her, a black shirt, bold white tie, and beige fedora – under which she stuffed her long dark hair. With no makeup she looked like a beautiful, fierce young man.

When Eddie Mafair appeared – in costume as a pirate – she knew, with a deep sigh, he was never going to recognize her.

On the contrary. One look and he was by her side.

"What a bore these things are," he muttered. "How about you and me taking off early?"

She could hardly believe her luck. "Yes," she said quickly.

Glancing around, he said, "Meet me here in an hour. I suppose I must be sociable. Bloody boring way to spend an evening."

A cryptic exchange to say the least. No *Nice to see you again*, or *How have you been?*

With difficulty she managed to get through the next hour, checking her watch every ten minutes. It seemed like an eternity. At the allotted time she was ready and waiting.

Eddie Mafair appeared twenty minutes late, unapologetic and flushed. Taking her arm he guided her outside to an open sports car parked on the edge of the driveway. Hopping around to the driver's side he failed to open the passenger door for her.

Opening it herself, she climbed inside, wondering if she should have warned Fenella of her adventure. Wouldn't they worry when they couldn't find her at the end of the party?

What the heck! She was past caring. She had thought about Eddie Mafair for almost three years and now the great moment was here. Nothing was going to spoil it.

Casually turning the ignition with one hand and reaching for a cigarette with the other, he said, "Eton or Harrow?"

'Sorry?'

"Which *school* do you go to?"

"Oh. L'Evier in Switzerland."

Pulling the car to a sudden halt he said in a surprised voice, "Isn't that a *girl's* school?"

"Of course it is." With a gesture she pulled off the fedora, and her long hair tumbled loose.

"Jesus Christ!" he said.

"What?"

Choking on his cigarette, he managed, "Nothing, nothing."

"You *do* know who I am, don't you?" she asked suspiciously.

Quite indignantly, his choking fit abated, he said, "I most certainly do."

"Rafealla," she reminded.

"I know," he said testily.

Eddie Mafair was a strange one. The sooner she gave him a blow job and got him under her spell, the better.

*

Two hours later they lay naked under tangled sheets in Eddie Mafair's mews house in Chelsea.

An hour to get there, driving at breakneck speed. A glass of neat vodka, and Billy Joel on the stereo repeatedly singing *Just the Way You Are*. And then sex. No kisses. No lingering build-up. No caresses. Just straight to it.

Inexperienced as she was, Rafealla soon realized something was wrong as he jabbed away with a soft penis. Eddie Mafair had what Odile crudely described as "two inches of cock and dynamic fingers!" Only he didn't have dynamic fingers.

Far from being dismayed, Rafealla knew she had to help him

over his unfortunate hurdle. Instinctively she said what he wanted to hear. "I'm a virgin. I've never been to bed with a man before."

Well, the virgin part was accurate. And she'd never actually been *in* bed with a man. The beach – yes. The woods – yes. And many other places. But never bed.

"You're so ... manly," she breathed. "I love being with you."

And that did the trick. Eddie Mafair performed like he hadn't performed in a long time. And Rafealla let all thoughts of saving herself for a husband drift by the wayside. All she could think about was Eddie. She loved him. It was as simple as that.

Bobby Mondella 1977

"Black," Nova Citroen said. "Silk."

The tailor nodded.

"And white. All white. Very clinging."

"I understand."

"A dozen shirts. A dozen pair of pants. No colours."

"Yes, Mrs Citroen."

"Oh, and he dresses to the left."

The tailor didn't miss a beat. "Yes, Mrs Citroen."

A flick of her elegant wrist dismissed him.

When he was gone she paced around the living room of the Century City penthouse with views stretching all the way to Catalina. Picking up a cigarette, she didn't light it, merely held it thoughtfully between her manicured fingers.

Today was the day.

She had waited long enough.

*

Bobby, sweat dripping from his body, begged for mercy. "Enough," he pleaded.

"More curls," his personal exercise instructor insisted. "Those arms need it."

"*Nothing* else needs it," Bobby gasped, dropping the weights and flopping on his back.

"Tomorrow," said his instructor, a short man with formidable muscles and torturous smile.

"Can't wait!"

So . . . Bobby thought. *This is what it's like to be number one.* Hell – he'd had more fun when he was fat and a men's room attendant.

Life, at the moment, was nothing but work. And not the real thing – preparation – back-breaking, gut-busting, getting-ready preparation.

His daily grind included dancing, voice practice, movement, and weight training for the ultimate body.

Then there were publicity photos to do, hair stylists to see, nutritionists to consult, and daily jogging for hours on end.

And then, of course, there was Nova.

Nova Citroen.

What an incredible woman!

Closing his eyes, he thought about the past year.

He'd shaken hands with the devil, and his whole world changed overnight.

*

Amerika wasn't pleased when she heard about Bobby's defection. She was angry and hurt – and above all incredulous. "How can you do this to yourself?" she asked, her lower lip quivering with emotion. "Don't you have any black pride? Marcus Citroen is a *killer*. He'll own you, exploit you, then drop you."

"No way," Bobby argued.

"What makes you think *you're* so different?" she spat, her voice shaking. "And how can you walk out on *me*?"

"Blue Cadillac are willing to pay you a lot of compensation."

Her eyes flashed. "They'd *better*."

He didn't know what else to say. Light conversation was out of the question, and he couldn't explain about Sharleen.

"I suppose it has something to do with that tramp," Amerika said icily, reading his mind.

Springing to her defence, he said, "C'mon. Don't call Sharleen names just 'cos you're mad at *me*."

"Hey – Bobby," Amerika jeered. "Why don't you admit she's got your balls in her pocket, and be done with it?"

He'd shown her the courtesy of telling her himself. Now he walked out with a clear conscience.

Sharleen bubbled with joy when he gave her the news. "*Oooh*, Bobby, Bobby, Bobby! You're wonderful! The best!" She hugged him tight. "An' it'll be good for you too, honey. Just wait. If Marcus says he'll make you number one – well, baby, he's gonna do it."

"I just want to be certain you'll be all right," he said, full of concern.

Kissing his cheek she murmured, "I've learned my lesson. I won't make a mistake again." A pause. "Do I get my apartment back?"

"Who cares? It's better you stay here where I can watch out for you."

"You're right," she agreed demurely.

A week later came the bombshell. Blue Cadillac wanted him in L.A. where he would undergo intensive training for major stardom.

He burst into Marcus's office. "What is this shit? I don't wanna go to L.A."

"Insurance," Marcus said mildly.

"For what?"

"For both of us. Like a world-class fighter you have to train to be at peak performance level. In September of next year we present you to your public at the Hollywood Bowl. Bobby Mondella. In concert. A three-night sold-out engagement. Rave reviews. A television special. All *you* have to do is deliver."

Marcus Citroen seemed to have it all planned out. He wanted Bobby to drop out of sight, and reappear like the brightest meteor in the sky.

"Your album will hit in the stores that same week. A single from it will already be a smash," Marcus assured him.

"What album?" Bobby asked, perplexed.

"The one you're going to write and record in L.A. You have a year to do it. And a magnificent penthouse apartment in Century City ready for your arrival."

"How about Sharleen?"

"She stays here."

"Why?"

"Because she wants to."

"And if she doesn't?"

Marcus did not waver. "Nobody's stopping her from doing anything she cares to do."

"You mean if I persuade her to come with me, you won't object?"

"Absolutely not."

The choice was Sharleen's and she wouldn't budge. She had a new single to record, a video to make, and a hundred and one interviews. Her career was back on track and she was happy.

"Be careful," Bobby warned. "Stay away from Marcus Citroen."

Indignantly she said, "You really think I'd ever get involved with him in a personal way again? Are you nuts? After what I went through." Dancing around the apartment she added, quite sternly, "Now, Bobby. I want you to take off an' stop worrying about me. Think about yourself for a change. Promise?"

There was no point in fighting it. Deep down he knew the best thing was to get away. Sharleen was becoming an obsession, and now that he'd helped her straighten her life out there *should* be space between them. Only then could he put their relationship in proper perspective.

Los Angeles was a revelation. The wide, clean streets. Sunshine and palm trees. Friendly people and a kind of laid-back ambience he wasn't used to after the frenetic activity of New York.

Walking into the apartment Blue Cadillac had rented for him, he couldn't believe it was his. After all, he hadn't done anything to deserve it. But he would. Their confidence in him was going to pay off.

The months spent recording an album with a top producer and great musicians in a first-class studio were the most exciting of his life. There was no watching the clock because studio time was so expensive, just an easy, relaxed atmosphere – with plenty of good-natured banter, and a certain amount of pharmaceuticals passed around. Usually Bobby didn't approve of drugs, but recording late into the night it made sense to get a little high – keep the energy level really up.

The album material he had written worked. The songs, arrangements, everything, came together perfectly.

In New York, Marcus decided to combine the talents of Bobby and Sharleen in a duet. Bobby wrote a song called *Baby – I Care About You*. And Sharleen arrived in L.A. to record it with him.

She looked spectacular, glowing with success. Accompanying her was a female bodyguard who never left her side.

"Don't I get to see you alone?" he joked.

"Why, honey," she replied, affecting a heavy Southern drawl. "You're so *biiig* an' *baaad* an' *haaan'some*. I don't think I'd trust myself alone with you at *all*!"

She stayed three days, gave an impeccable performance – her vocals weren't great, but what she lacked in voice she made up for with sensational style – and flew back to New York.

And then Bobby met Nova Citroen. The kind of woman he had never encountered before.

Nova Citroen travelled in a chauffeured Rolls-Royce, wore only the most expensive designer clothes and real jewellery, and smelled of big bucks. Bobby was dazzled.

She arrived at his apartment one afternoon, unannounced, with an executive from Blue Cadillac Records who jumped nervously at her every command.

"I'm Mrs Citroen," she said, a slight accent colouring her speech. "I hope you're comfortable in this apartment. I chose it from several. I meant to visit you before, but I have only recently returned from Europe."

"*You* found me this apartment?" he asked, surprised.

She smiled faintly. "The apartment, the body expert, the nutritionist – all of them. I hope they're doing a good job. Hmmm . . ." She narrowed her quite amazing violet eyes, allowing them to sweep over him from head to toe. "Yes. I can see they're doing an *extremely* good job, Mr Mondella – or may I call you Bobby?"

In spite of his nine-year crush on Sharleen, he was not exactly inexperienced when it came to women. They hit on him all the time, and he knew how to handle any situation.

This one was different. This one was a lady. She was also Marcus Citroen's wife, and therefore untouchable.

In spite of that he found her powerfully attractive.

"Yeah, please do," he said, meeting her direct gaze with one of his own.

"Thank you." Amusement glinted in those mesmerizing eyes.

The executive from Blue Cadillac Records said, "Mrs Citroen was anxious to meet you, Bobby. Word has it everyone loves the album material in New York. Are you nearly finished?"

"Two more tracks to go."

"Perhaps I can come to the studio," she said. "I always enjoy watching the creative process."

He enjoyed watching her, with her drawn-back white-blonde hair and slim figure. Nova Citroen represented class with a great big capital C.

"It gets kinda rough in the studio," he said.

"Really?" Holding him a tight captive with her eyes, she allowed too long a pause before saying, "Well, Bobby, if things get *too* rough I'll just have to leave, won't I?"

She turned up on two successive nights, each time with a different male escort. She stayed fifteen minutes in the recording booth watching him intently through the glass, and left before he took a break.

It was annoying. He wanted to talk to her, find out more about the mysterious Mrs Citroen. For she was mysterious – nobody seemed to know much about her, except that she moved in high society, and had been married to Marcus for a long time.

She vanished after that, and did not reappear until six weeks before his Hollywood Bowl debut.

By this time his duet with Sharleen was number one on the soul charts, and steadily climbing the mainstream list. Things were going as planned.

He couldn't help being in a nervous sweat, even though he'd never looked and sounded better in his life. The Hollywood

Bowl concert was make-or-break time. He knew he could perform on record, but a stage performance was a whole other deal.

No one could say he wasn't prepared. He was at fighting weight and raring to go.

Nova arrived at his apartment one morning – again unannounced, and this time alone. She wore a white silk suit, green blouse, and crocodile accessories. "What are you planning to wear?" she asked coolly, as if they had just paused in the middle of a conversation.

"Huh?"

"At the Bowl."

"Uh . . . the stylist has a selection of leather suits for me."

"Leather?" She raised an elegant eyebrow.

"It's sexy." He laughed, sending himself up. "Or so they tell me."

"It's sweaty."

He challenged her. "It's what I'm wearing."

A faint smile. "I don't think so."

*

Bobby stretched, and slowly sat up. The workouts were hard, but the rewards were worth it. In fact, the entire year had been quite something. And now Nova Citroen was in his living room instructing her own personal tailor to measure him for size.

He would wear whatever she wanted. Instinctively he knew her choice would be the right one.

The tailor entered the mirrored workout room armed with a tape measure and a determined expression. "Mrs Citroen knows exactly what you want," he said, busily unrolling the measure.

"Yeah, an' I know exactly what *she* wants," Bobby muttered under his breath.

Kris Phoenix 1977

The cavernous dressing room was filled with people all milling around a long wooden trestle table piled high with cans of beer, paper cups, dishes of crisps, and several plates of stale sandwiches. Hardly luxury, but The Wild Ones were finishing their first tour and had not yet learned to make demands.

Buzz had his own bottle of scotch, given to him by an admirer. He sat in a corner swigging blissfully.

"He'll get drunk," Mr Terence fussed.

"No way," argued Kris. "It'll improve his voice."

Mr Terence raised a disbelieving eyebrow. "Go and talk to that girl over there. She's from the *Evening News*. Say something witty." He mopped his forehead with a polka-dot handkerchief.

"Shit!" muttered Kris. He hated this socializing bit before a concert. Why did he have to make nice to reporters and other assorted hangers-on, when all he wanted to do was concentrate on the performance ahead of him? He'd tried to explain to Mr Terence on numerous occasions, but Mr Terence insisted that the press were too important to shut out. How come everyone expected *him* to do it, and not the rest of the band?

"Kris!" The girl from the *Evening News* had lank hair, buck teeth and an upmarket accent. "*Do* tell me how it feels to be number one?"

'Bloody marvellous," he replied.

"Super!" She jotted something down in a loose-leaf notebook. "And *do* tell me, when the critics knock your music, does it upset you *terribly*?"

"I didn't realize we were bein' knocked," he said, helping himself to a soggy potato crisp.

"There's a review of your Manchester concert in the current issue of *New Musical Express*. Let me see . . ." Cocking her head on one side, she sucked on her pencil. "I think it said something like, Kris Phoenix sounds like a cross between a sore throat and a foghorn in a bad storm."

"Charming!"

Pencil poised, buck teeth facing him like a firing squad, she said, "Any other comment?"

"Fuck 'em. It's not the bleedin' critics who are buying our records."

Scribbling furiously, she agreed with an enthusiastic "Quite. I like your attitude."

He wandered off, looking for mum and the rest of his family. They were all supposed to be here tonight, the lot of them – including dear old brother Brian. He'd given Avis backstage passes and told her exactly where to go, but he couldn't spot any of them.

Rasta rushed over. "You see those two little darlin's over there," he said, pointing out two girls hovering on the edge of the crowd. "How about one for you an' one for me – I'll book 'em in now, while I can. If Buzz spots 'em, it's all over."

Kris glanced across the room, checking out two very attractive but extremely young females. "Juveniles," he said dismissively.

"Leave it out," Rasta complained. "I bet they're at least sixteen. That's old enough."

"I like 'em over twenty, and smart," Kris said firmly. No more Willows in *his* life. For the last year he'd bedded a variety of girls, scrupulously steering clear of teenagers, or any girl who didn't look like she knew what she was doing. His opening line was always, "Are you takin' precautions or shall I?"

It got the ball rolling nicely, in more ways than one.

Willow was behaving like a right cow. When he was nothing

she'd been only too happy to agree to a quickie divorce. But as soon as he started to make it, she was there with a sharp lawyer and a suitcase full of demands. Bitch! What had *she* done to deserve any of his hard-earned money? He didn't mind supporting Bo, but Willow's demands were ridiculous. Even his lawyer agreed. It wasn't as if he were making a fortune. Everything he earned – except the publishing – had to be split four ways, and that was after Mr Terence had taken his fat thirty-five per cent. And then there were all the expenses – including travel, roadies, a sound man, lighting, publicity, clothes, a secretary, bodyguards, et cetera, and finally, the dreaded tax.

As a matter of fact he was almost as broke as he'd ever been.

Every day he realized more and more that if they wanted to score big – America was the place.

Tonight Mr Terence had promised that several hot-shots from American recording companies would be in the audience. *Okay, we're gonna show 'em what we can do*, Kris decided. *We're gonna really rock 'n' roll!*

"Christopher!" shrieked a fat butterball of a woman in a flounced lavender dress. "Your music sends me!"

"Kris," he corrected, backing away from her over-zealous approach.

"Ah . . . but short for Christopher, dear boy. Am I right?"

Who the fuck was this weird old bird? "No," he said, looking round for someone to rescue him.

"We're having a little thingy at Annabel's later. Simply marvellous fun. Can you join us?"

Annabel's. He'd heard of it. The poshest nightclub in London, where all the chinless wonders and their birds hung out. Royalty, too.

Annabel's. Yeah! But not with this apparition, who was old enough to be his mother.

"Can't make it, luv," he said, trying to sound regretful. "Sorry. Gotta take me mum out."

"Shame!" brayed the fat lady. "Fenella is *dying* to meet you."

"Well, she'll just have to wait, won't she?" Edging away he

bumped into a red-faced Mr Terence. "What did she say?" Mr Terence hissed anxiously.

"Who?"

"Lady Stephenson."

"Is *that* who she is when she's at home."

"Well?"

"Wanted me to join her at Annabel's, didn't she."

"Just you?"

"I dunno."

Mr Terence did a nervous jig. The Wild Ones making it so quickly and with such strength had left him out of his depth. He wasn't quite sure how to deal with it. Too much was happening too fast. Half the offers he received on their behalf he didn't even tell them about. America was begging for attention, and yet he'd done nothing, because, knowing Kris and his raging ambition, they'd run off to the States and never return. A contract was no real protection once those beady-eyed Yank lawyers got their hands on it.

Mr Terence was in a turmoil. Snatching a quick peak at Buzz, lounging happily in a quiet corner swigging from his bottle of scotch, calmed him down. Buzz would hate America and the gaudy razzamatazz that went with it. In fact, he was doing Buzz a favour keeping all the lucrative offers to himself.

"C'mon." Ollie grabbed Kris by the arm. "Let's get out of here. This circus is no good before a show. We should be tuning up."

Ollie, the perfectionist. So straight and serious. He'd found himself a red-headed girlfriend who played the cello and hated what she termed "the pop business".

"Right," agreed Kris. "Let's grab the others an' find a quiet corner backstage."

"I'll round up Rasta, Buzz is all yours," Ollie said.

"You got it."

Lady Stephenson grabbed his arm as he walked by. "Kris, dear," she said, as if they were old and intimate friends. "*Do* say hello to my daughter, Fenella, and her friend, Raffi."

He was face to face with the two baby girls Rasta had fancied earlier. "Hello," he said, hardly noticing them.

"Now, Kris, dear," Lady Stephenson continued, double chins wobbling above lavender and lace frills. "If you *can* get away later, *do* join us. You might find it to be rather an interesting group. Quite a few American music people who I'm sure you must know. The Dorfmans, Marcus Citroen. Oh, and Sharleen — the famous" — she lowered her voice — "black singer."

"Maybe," Kris said. Now he was *really* interested in going, but he had promised his mum and the family a night on the town, and he couldn't dump them.

"Cheers!" gushed Lady Stephenson. "Don't forget. Annabel's. I'll leave word at the door."

*

The concert was a blast. Finally London — and the fans loved them.

What a raw sense of power! What a roller-coaster high!

Kris knew there were a lot of important people out there watching them live for the first time, and he really let rip — straining his gravelly voice to the limit, performing virtuoso guitar solos, taking turns with Buzz, who was full of piss and sardonic strut.

The crowd yelled, cheering and stamping their approval. The usual chants rose above the yelling and clapping.

"KRISSSS . . . WE . . . LOVE . . . YOU!"

"BUZZZZ . . . WE . . . LOVE . . . YOU!"

Kris leaped across the stage, his energy level at an all-time peak. He wore high-top sneakers, skin-tight faded jeans, and a tee-shirt with THE WILD ONES '77 emblazoned across the front.

Buzz weaved back and forth, picking at his guitar with talented fingers, face impassive, body clad in black footless tights, with a mangy long black shirt hanging loose.

"'Ere," Rasta had said when faced with them before the show. "Wot you two doin' then? 'Aving a who's-got-the-biggest-cock contest?" He'd fallen about at his own rather accurate observation.

Mr Terence had wanted them to wear matching blue gabardine jumpsuits. "You know where you can shove *that* idea," Kris told him. He ran the group now as far as what they played, how they played it, and certainly what they wore.

"Why the frig we payin' Mr T bleedin' thirty-five per cent?" Buzz bitched. "Whyn't we dump 'im?"

The thought *had* occurred to Kris. But he knew there was bound to be a big legal hassle, and their timing wasn't right. Also, they owed Mr Terence *something*. After all, he was the one who'd bankrolled them when they had nothing – even though he was deducting every penny of his initial investment from their earnings, on top of his hefty percentages. No wonder they were still broke.

The money was rolling in, but not in *their* direction.

There was a rumour backstage that Princess Anne was somewhere in the audience. The blinding lights left no room for searching the rows of eager faces, although Kris had noticed at all their gigs that the rows in front never contained the swooners and the screamers:

"That's because they're comps," Ollie had explained.

"Wot's that?" asked Buzz.

"Complimentary. Free seats for the managers, theatre owners, promoters, record execs, and all their friends."

Kris decided that when he had enough clout, comps would be moved to the middle of the venue, and only the real fans would be allowed up front.

Triumphantly they launched into their last song. A fast-driving rocker written by Kris and Ollie entitled *Skinny Little Slider*.

It brought the house down. The audience were on their feet, yelling and clamouring for more.

They did two more choruses of *Skinny Little Slider*, and then they were off, running from the stage, sweat-soaked and ecstatic.

"Fuck me!" screamed Rasta. "This is better 'n sex any day!"

"Bloody right!" agreed Kris.

Who needed one woman when there were sixty thousand lusting after your body?

*

"You looked like a bunch of tatty layabouts," brother Brian said, shovelling spaghetti into his mouth. "Can't you afford decent outfits?"

Jennifer, his wife agreed. "Oh, yes. Matching outfits would be ever so nice, wouldn't they? The Beatles always appeared so smart ..." She trailed off, silenced by the look Kris gave her.

He sat with his mum, Horace, his two sisters and their boyfriends, Brian and Jennifer, in Trattoria Terrazza, an Italian restaurant in Soho.

What a group! What a letdown! Why he had arranged a family outing on a night like this was beyond him. Christ! This was the downer of all times, and he'd *asked* for it. *Set* it up. While everybody else went off to parties and celebrations.

He'd done it for his mum, really. Avis, so proud. The matriarch of the family with her loud voice and work-worn hands.

She was beaming with pride, ignoring Brian for once. "I never thought I'd see the day," she said, craftily snagging a half-eaten roll, wrapping it in a tissue, and sliding it in her bag.

"Mum!" Kris objected. "I can buy you all the bread you want."

"Not like this, lad. Nice an' fresh. It'll go down a treat in the morning' with a bit of marge, a dab of jam, an' a nice cuppa tea." She smiled contentedly.

"Take one for me," Horace said irritably. "Streuth! I've got an 'orrible 'eadache after all that noise."

"Me too," agreed Brian. "Give me Barry Manilow any day." He threw his younger brother a smug look. "No offence, Kris. But even *you* have to admit that it's a bloody awful racket you make up there."

The evening went from bad to worse as Brian got into his stride, complaining about everything. Horace joined in, and his two sisters stared at him as if they'd never really noticed him before. Meanwhile Avis went on a food-stealing binge the likes of which he'd never seen. After the bread rolls she laid claim to a slice of veal Jennifer left over, almost an entire salad, and a large piece of chocolate rum cake.

"Ma," he pleaded. "Let 'em pack the stuff up for you. I'm payin' for it, y'know."

"That's all right, dear," she said cheerfully, having a wonderful time. "It's better this way. Don't want to embarrass you, do I?"

Oh, sure. She had a bag full of food wrapped in a few soggy tissues, and she didn't want to embarrass him. Great! At least she was happy.

A girl at another table recognized him and scurried over asking for an autograph.

"She probably thinks you're Rod Stewart," sneered Brian.

"Thanks," Kris snapped, and called for the bill.

*

By the time he reached Annabel's he was well gone. Once the family were dispatched into the night, he'd stopped by Rasta's party, held at a rowdy pub in Brixton. Several beers and a few vodkas later he arrived at the exclusive Berkeley Square establishment, his only claim to respectability being the chauffeured Daimler he'd hired for the night.

"I'm sorry, sir,' the doorman said, with frosty politeness. "This is a membership-only club."

"Yeah." Kris swayed slightly, cleverly concealing a burp. "The thing is, I'm joinin' Lady Stephenson. How's that for gettin' me in?"

"You'd better speak to them downstairs," the doorman said regally, indicating that Kris should descend the open stairway.

"Bloody basement," Kris muttered, holding onto the side for support.

Downstairs, inside the entrance to the club, a manager in evening dress greeted him. "Sir?"

"Uh . . . Kris Phoenix; that's me. I'm s'pose to be joinin' uh . . . Lady Stephenson."

"Ah, yes, sir. Mr Phoenix from The Wild Ones. Lady Stephenson is expecting you."

"Yeah?"

"Yes, sir." Lowering his voice the manager added discreetly, "We do have a dress code, Mr Phoenix. If you follow me I'm sure we can put that right."

"A what code?"

"Dress, sir. Jacket and ties for the gentlemen. Suitable attire for the ladies."

"You're kiddin'?"

"This way, sir."

The manager ushered him into a side room where he offered him a white shirt, blue jacket, and red tie.

"I feel like a bleedin' Union Jack!" Kris joked, putting the outfit on.

"We'll turn a blind eye to your bottom half, sir," said the manager, with a benevolent smile. "Perhaps you can sign my daughter's autograph book. She's quite a fan."

Ego was slowly being restored. Kris took the autograph book with a flourish. "Certainly mate. An' what's the little darlin's name?"

Rafealla 1977

Lady Stephenson, Fenella's mother, was the most amazing woman. She knew everyone and was invited to everything. Film premières, the best parties, restaurant openings, art galleries. If there was a gala occasion, it was a safe bet that Lady Stephenson, in her frills and flounces, would be there.

Fenella did not often accompany her, but when she heard The Wild Ones were doing a one-night concert in London, and that her mother – as usual – was invited, she telephoned Rafealla and said enthusiastically, "I'm going to ask mummy if we can go too. Are you on?"

"You bet!" Rafealla replied. Both she and Fenella were crazy about The Wild Ones. At finishing school they'd played *Dirty Miss Mary* whenever they could. Fenella quite fancied the black drummer, and Rafealla thought Buzz Darke the most interesting, with his sinister looks and "I Don't Give a Damn" attitude.

They set off for the concert full of great expectations. Rafealla was relieved to get out of the house. It was three weeks since she'd slept with Eddie Mafair, and she had not heard one word from him since. She couldn't believe it. What a *bastard*!

"Why don't you phone *him*?" Fenella suggested helpfully.

Phone him! Ha! She'd sooner die. He had her number, she'd scrawled it in his phone book herself.

He was a jerk anyway. After sex he'd fallen asleep, surfaced three hours later, and summoned a cab to spirit her back to the country. The cheapskate didn't even offer to pay for the taxi, so she'd had to borrow the money from the Stephenson's butler. Men! What a bunch of insensitive creeps.

And yet . . . she loved him. In spite of the fact that going all the way with Eddie Mafair had not been as physically fulfilling as the playful necking sessions she'd indulged in with her other boyfriends. It didn't matter. She *still* loved him.

So what? He obviously couldn't give a damn about her.

In her head she went through the excuses he might come up with.

Too busy at work.

What did he actually do? She had no idea.

Sick.

Did that mean his dialling finger automatically stopped functioning?

On vacation.

Well, he would have mentioned *something* about going away, wouldn't he?

It was not a happy time for her. But he *would* phone. If she just sat it out and waited patiently, she knew he would.

The venue for The Wild Ones' concert was crazy time. Lady Stephenson had special stickers attached to her car, and parking attendants waved her chauffeur-driven Rolls through the unruly crowd to a VIP roped-off parking area.

"Come along, everyone," she trilled. "Let's go backstage and have a drink."

"Divine, darling," said Pierce, her faithful walker, who did double duty as her interior designer. Lord Stephenson only made rare forays into his rambunctious wife's social activities. He infinitely preferred the quiet life.

The backstage party was an experience. Lady Stephenson and Pierce vanished into the mêlée of people, while Rafealla and Fenella stood at the entrance taking it all in. Rock and roll was a whole new world.

"Wow!" Fenella breathed. "Don't stare, but that's him. *That's* the drummer. And I think he's looking over here!"

'Hmm . . . whatever happened to 'black bastard'?" Rafealla

asked coolly, checking out the cheeky-looking drummer.

"Oh, God! Don't bring *that* up," Fenella groaned. "You can't imagine how embarrassed I am. How could I ever have said that?"

"What's his name?"

"Who?"

"The guy on the drums, idiot."

"Rasta. Sounds interesting, huh?"

"Yeah, your mother would find it *veree* interesting if she knew you fancied him."

"Girls!" The piercing voice of Lady Stephenson filled the air, rising above the clamour, followed by a frilled and flounced wave. "Over here!"

They edged their way towards the makeshift bar, where Pierce supplied them with two paper cups filled with flat Coca-Cola.

Another exciting evening, Rafealla thought. *Why hasn't Eddie Mafair phoned me? Why?*

"Isn't this *fun*?" Lady Stephenson shrilled.

*

> *She's a bank clerk's daughter*
> *An' y'know what I mean*
> *Y'see when I met her she was barely eighteen*
> *So I took her to my bed*
> *An' I gave her some . . .*
> LOVIN'
> YEAH!
> LOVIN'
> YEAH!
> *Y'know what I mean*
> *Oh yeah, y'know what I mean*

Screams rang through the air as Kris and Buzz gave it their all – sharing the microphone with a certain vagabond intimacy. Two talented likely lads on the make.

> *She's a bank clerk's daughter*
> *So pretty an' sweet*

Innocent as an angel with exceptionally small feet
Long yellow hair an' big blue eyes
An' I gave her some . . .
LOVIN'
YEAH!
LOVIN'
YEAH!
Y'know what I mean
Oh yeah, y'know what I mean

Every girl in the audience knew what they meant. The excitement factor ran high.

Rafealla found herself swept away by the sheer energy of their performance. Buzz Darke and Kris Phoenix made a formidable combination – whether they were singing or playing brilliant guitar riffs together, or merely running and jumping around, they both had pure animal magnetism. The whole group was great. It was an exciting concert.

Afterwards, at Annabel's, where they were joined by several Americans in the music business, plus Sharleen – the famous recording star – there was much discussion about exactly how good The Wild Ones were.

"*I* think they're the new Rolling Stones," announced Lady Stephenson knowledgeably – she liked to keep up with what she termed "the youth culture".

"No!" Pierce disagreed. "They're much sexier. And Kris Phoenix doesn't scream and make faces like that awful Mick Jagger."

"Mick Jagger's adorable," insisted Lady Stephenson, fluttering a quiver of fake lashes as she ordered champagne from an attentive waiter. "I will not listen to a word against him."

To her horror, Rafealla discovered that one of the Americans in their party was Marcus Citroen – her very own flasher from the South of France. He did not appear to remember their brief encounter, and merely nodded when introduced, turning his full attenton on the startlingly pretty singer Sharleen, who appeared to be his date.

Stifling a giggle she whsipered the story to Fenella, who shook with silent laughter.

Being in Annabel's reminded her of Eddie Mafair, and the night they first met.

I'm nearly eighteen, she thought despairingly. *My life is ahead of me. I have to forget about Eddie, he's just a creep.*

Lady Stephenson was a wow on the dance floor, twirling and twisting until her chubby cheeks were red with exertion. Pierce made a suitable consort in his Doug Hayward suit.

"Haven't we met before, young lady?" Marcus Citroen asked Rafealla, as soon as Sharleen went to the ladies' room.

"I don't think so," she replied shortly, wishing he would go away, for she would never be able to erase the mental picture of Marcus Citroen, naked, with an erection, in the Franconinis' swimming pool. As it was she had merely swum away, climbed out of the water, and vanished into the house, making sure their paths never crossed again.

"What do you do?" he asked.

"I'm a student," she mumbled.

"A student," he repeated her words, staring straight at her. "A very unusual and beautiful student, if I may say so. I'm sure I've seen you somewhere before."

She returned his stare, saying nothing, refusing to look away, challenging his intent scrutiny.

"If I can ever help you in any way, please call me," he said, handing her his engraved card. "I mean it."

Accepting it reluctantly, she stuffed it in her purse, and hurriedly turned to speak to Fenella – sitting down after a hectic session on the dance floor.

"Guess who's here?" Fenella whispered excitedly.

"The Queen Mum."

"Very funny."

"Who?"

"I don't think I'll tell you now."

"*Who?*"

"You're not going to like it."

"Will you stop playing games, and *tell* me."

Before Fenella uttered his name, she knew.

"Eddie Mafair," said Fenella.

Oh no! Her stomach knotted up. "Alone?" she asked wanly.

"He's with Fiona Ripley-Hedges. She looks like the back end of a bus, but her father owns most of London, and we all *know* how attractive *that* must be. Especially since there's a rumour going around that Eddie's broke."

*

By the time Kris Phoenix made his entrance, Rafealla was ready for him. She was ready for anyone actually, having surreptitiously drained every glass of alcholic beverage in sight.

As soon as he sat down she was on to him, wasting no time in forcing the rock star to pay attention and notice her. "I loved your concert," she said. "You were fantastic."

"Thanks, luv."

"I honestly mean it."

"Great."

"Before I saw you I used to think Buzz was the star of the group, but now . . ."

"That's nice."

He wasn't interested, dammit. He only had eyes for the record moguls and Sharleen. Especially Sharleen.

Without a doubt he regarded her as just another boring fan. Well, she would show *him* – Mister Star – Mister Who-Did-He-Think-He-Was.

Marcus Citroen had his attention now, but it kept wandering towards Sharleen. Helplessly Rafealla watched the eye-play between Kris and the pretty singer. Sharleen was coming on to him. Licking full red lips, touching fluffy hair, eating him up with those big brown eyes.

Rafealla stood up. She had youth on her side, that had to count for something. "Can we dance?" she asked aggressively.

"Uh," Kris glanced around, hoping she was talking to someone else. The kid was a looker, but just a kid, and he'd had that scene.

No escape was in view, so getting to his feet he staggered a bit and followed her onto the packed dance floor, where she pulled him into a close clinch, grinding her body into his. He immediately got a hard-on. Some men couldn't get it up when they were drunk. He was just the opposite – all that booze went straight to the old bone.

Rafealla experienced a moment of power. Young as she was, she already realized the sexual hold she had over men.

Screw you, Eddie Mafair. I can have anyone I want.

And then she saw him, dancing nearby, with horse-faced Fiona held tightly in his arms. He was laughing at something and didn't even notice her.

Determinedly she moved closer to Kris Phoenix, as inexplicably her eyes filled with tears.

Bobby Mondella 1977

"Drink?"

"Pernod"

"I don't think I have any of that, Mrs Citroen."

"Yes you do. Look in the cupboard under the bar, you'll find it's fully stocked."

He was the occupant of the apartment, and *she* was telling him where to find things.

Goddammit, this woman was too sure of herself by far.

"Maybe you can fix it yourself. I'm gonna shower an' put clothes on," he said, feeling at a disadvantage because she was fully dressed and he was still clad in his workout clothes – shorts and a cut-off tee-shirt.

She raised an elegant eyebrow, unused to being told to do things for herself. "Fine," she said coolly. "And can I make something for you while I'm playing barman? Or should that be maid?" she added sarcastically.

"Orange juice."

"My, oh, my. We *are* on a health kick."

"Your idea."

A slight smile. "In that case, one drink a night *is* allowed."

"Scotch."

"How about champagne?"

"I don't have—"

"Ah, but you do," she interrupted. "So why don't you go shower and simply leave everything to me." A glimmer of a smile. "I'm very capable when I have to be."

Walking into the bedroom, he was aware of a distinct feeling of anticipation. The tailor had left, and they were all alone in the apartment. Mrs Citroen was not staying around for her health. The lady was hot for action, and if that's what she wanted . . .

No! an inner voice warned him. *This is dangerous territory. The lady is the boss's wife.*

Yeah? he answered himself. *So what?* He was just about ready for a touch of danger.

Stripping off his sweaty clothes he entered the bathroom, turned on the shower, and stepped under the invigorating needles of spray.

Mrs Citroen. With her ice-queen looks and cool demeanour. The same Mrs Citroen whose husband had played games with Sharleen, nearly finishing her off. What did the lady want from him?

C'mon, Bobby – you know what she wants.

He almost laughed aloud. Yeah, he knew what she wanted, and if she was very patient . . . yeah, *really* patient. Then maybe, only maybe, mind you . . .

Naked, except for a black lace G-string and spike-heeled shoes, Nova got into the shower behind him, carrying an open bottle of Cristal. She nuzzled the cold bottle against his back. "I never really welcomed you to Blue Cadillac properly, did I?" she murmured, in her husky voice.

He'd known she was going to come on to him, but not this strong. And not this soon. She was not a patient woman.

"Don't turn around," she commanded, placing the bottle on the tile floor. "Just relax."

Sure. He could certainly relax with a naked, married woman cosying up behind him, running talented and expensive fingers along his spine. He thought about what to say, but it was too late for words. With great confidence she was reaching for his balls, cupping them delicately, applying just the right amount of tingling pressure before falling to her knees.

"Now!" she said urgently. "Turn around *now!*"

He did as she asked, plunging deep inside that elegant mouth, ready and waiting to taste and tease him with feathery jabs of her tongue and a low animal groaning sound.

Eat your heart out, Marcus, he thought. *I'm getting my own back for Sharleen.*

He surrendered to sensation. There was really nothing else he could do, except lean back and enjoy it.

Saturday, July 11, 1987
Los Angeles

The security checks aggravated Kris. "What is this shit?" he demanded. "Don't they know who I am?"

"Of course they do," the Hawk said soothingly. "They're merely following orders. You can't be too careful with the amount of terrorists around today."

"Yeah," Kris replied sarcastically. "We really look like a terrorist group, don't we? Y'know, in the limo an' all. Just ridin' on up to rip the bleedin' place to pieces."

"Have you been to Novaroen before?" the Hawk asked, quickly changing the subject.

"Once," Kris replied vaguely.

"You didn't tell *me* that," squealed Cybil. "One of the girls did a shoot here for that perfume Nova Citroen was pushing, and *she* says the place is amazing."

"It is," the Hawk assured her. "They have two houses, all decorated in different styles. The main house is Colonial. The guest house is—"

"Christ! Not again!" bitched Kris as the limousine stopped for a third security check.

"Lighten up," Cybil said, laughing gaily. "This is an adventure. *I'm* really enjoying it!"

He stared at his Californian girlfriend, all bright eyes, glossy hair, and whiter-than-white teeth. It didn't take much to make *her* happy, did it?

Sometimes she got on his nerves.

*

It was amazing how inefficient security became once the guards were sure everyone was doing something.

Maxwell Sicily surveyed the scene. The workers were all in place, name-tagged and running here, there and everywhere like an army of robots. Access between the makeshift tented kitchen and the open-air dining area was no problem. Now that there were over a hundred catering personnel busying themselves on the premises, a party atmosphere prevailed. Waiters and busboys were whistling and cracking jokes. The chefs were slicing and pounding as they prepared gourmet delights. The dessert cooks were hard at work creating creamy concoctions. And an army of barmen were unpacking crates of the finest champagnes and wines, plus a dizzying assortment of other beverages.

Maxwell picked his moment before slipping quietly away. He knew exactly where he was going. Thanks to Vicki Foxe he was aware of every inch of Novaroen.

*

Alighting from her limousine, Rafealla took a deep breath. The sea air was invigorating. If only the circumstances were different she might be enjoying herself.

"Here comes the greeting committee," warned Trudie, as a dapper man, with owl-like glasses and a pleasant smile, stepped forward.

"Welcome to Novaroen," he said, in a clipped English accent. "I'm Norton St John. Personal assistant to Mrs Citroen. Please allow me to escort you to your suite."   .

"He makes the joint sound like a hotel," Trudie said, in a low aside.

"Rafealla would like to do a sound check immediately," announced one of the record executives. "Are the musicians ready?"

"I believe they're planning a run-through with Mr Bobby Mondella," Norton St John replied. "However, since each artist is only performing two songs, it shouldn't take long."

"Rafaella wants to do her sound check *now*," said the executive testily. "You *do* know that Mr Citroen has given strict instructions for Rafaella to have everything—"

"Forget it," she interrupted quickly. "I can wait. In fact, if Bobby doesn't mind, maybe I'll watch him."

"Certainly, Miss Rafaella." Norton shot the bad-tempered executive a triumphant look. "I will show you to your suite first, and then I will ask Mr Mondella's representative. If everything seems to be all right, I shall return for you immediately."

*

"Shit!" exclaimed Speed for the tenth time. "I'm tellin' ya, the broad set me up. She wiggled her fat ass in my face an' demanded money. So I gave her a few bucks – just t'get *rid* of her. Big deal. Ya only gotta *look* at the witch t'know I wouldn't touch her with somebody *else's* hot rod! Shit!"

A bored detective burped in his face.

"I gotta warn ya – I know people," Speed said, rapidly changing tactics. "I got solid connections. My lawyer'll make fartheads outta all of ya with this dirt-bag bust."

"Don't threaten," said the detective mildly, "or I'll knock your yella molars outta the backa your dumb head."

"Huh?" demanded Speed, snapping to attention. He had lovely teeth. His incisors were a bit too pointed – but yellow? No way.

"I don't believe this crapola!" he said indignantly. "I'm just an honest citizen who's bin set up, an' I wanna call my lawyer. You got no right t'hold me."

The detective burped a second time, leaving no doubt in anyone's mind that he loved garlic. "Fuck!" he said mournfully. "I *hate* these Mickey Mouse arrests."

*

Bobby could smell the sea as Sara led him down a winding pathway. He could hear noise and bustle, the sounds of clinking cutlery and glasses being placed on tables.

God! Since the loss of his sight he depended so much on

smell, and feel, and sound and taste. He knew everything that was going on around him, he just couldn't see it.

"What does it look like?" he asked, yearning for information.

"Beautiful!" Sara replied. "We're balanced on top of the world."

Very descriptive. What the hell did she think he was going to get out of that? Maybe he should employ a person who was only there to be his eyes. A soothing voice to give him an account of every little detail without him having to ask.

"Sara," he said simply, "what colour is the sky? Can you see the sea? Are there clouds? Is the grass green? *Tell* me, goddammit, I need to know."

Nobody could imagine what it was like. A world of darkness, with no way out.

Sara stopped walking. He felt her tension. And then a soft, insistent hand touched his arm, and the familiar scent of danger wafted through the air.

"Hello, Bobby," said the unmistakable voice of Nova Citroen. "How very nice to see you again."

*

"Everything going okay?" Vicki Foxe asked, creeping up behind Tom and treating him to a little back rub with her massive bosom.

"You're not supposed to come in here," Tom said sternly. "This is security headquarters."

"Don't be silly," scolded Vicki. "You sound like a spy movie! Who do you think cleans in here? Anyway, I've brought you a nice, cold beer and a roast beef sandwich. You must be starving."

"I am," he admitted, his eyes automatically fixing on her outsize attributes, swivelling away from the bank of television monitors covering every key location on the estate.

"I knew you had to be a hungry boy," she purred, taking the sandwich from the plate and feeding him a bite.

"You're some damn hot woman," he said, consecutively chewing and feasting his eyes.

"And you're some *big* man." Innuendo was thick in the air.

"How would *you* know?" he asked, a red flush suffusing his bull neck.

"A girl can — well," she giggled, "sorta *tell*."

His attention was all hers as Maxwell Sicily appeared on Monitor Three. He didn't see a thing as furtively he darted a nifty hand up her skirt.

Parting her legs she allowed him a quick feel of warm thigh before squeaking with feigned indignation and slapping his hand away. "*Bad* big boy."

"Ya love it."

"Maybe. Maybe not," she responded tartly.

"When am I gonna find out?" He was almost panting with anticipation.

Licking her lips, she promised, "Tonight, if you're *real* lucky."

Out of the corner of her eye she watched Maxwell Sicily disappear from the monitor.

Timing perfect.

Mission accomplished.

"See you later, Tommy, baby, when you're not quite so busy. We'll have a *very* good time." Blowing him a juicy kiss she undulated out of the room.

*

Nova Citroen stared at Bobby Mandella. Three years and he still looked exactly the same.

The body. Tall, powerful, sexy.

The face. Strong, handsome, ebony-carved perfection.

His eyes were covered by dark glasses. She had no idea what was hidden beneath them.

"How are you?" she asked.

He felt the rage seethe up inside him as this woman — this bitch — casually inquired after his health.

Where had Nova Citroen been when he needed her? Where the hell was she then?

"Fine," he said, remembering every inch of her pampered

body. The smell of her special scent. The raw hunger of their lovemaking. "I'm glad you could come," she said.

Hey – lady. I didn't have a choice. I had to face you.

"C'mon, Sara, let's move it," he said impatiently.

"Yes." Nova withdrew her hand from his arm and looked directly at Sara. "The musicians are waiting for Mr Mondella. Be sure to let my people know if he needs anything."

"Hey – Mrs C. If I need anything you'll be the first to get the message," he said roughly. "'Cos I *sure* know I can depend on you . . . anytime . . . anywhere . . ."   His sarcasm was not lost on either woman.

Feeling uncomfortable, Sara began to move off, guiding Bobby away from trouble.

Nova watched them as they walked away. She wondered if he was sleeping with the pretty black girl. If he was – what a waste. Bobby Mondella deserved a woman – in bed and out. He might be blind, but he was still all man.

Nova felt the thrill of stalking the forbidden, and shuddered with anticipation.

*

As Marcus Citroen sat in his spacious study overlooking the ocean, a cigar in one hand, a Chivas Regal on the rocks in the other, he was savouring the moment. The peace before the storm.

The wheels were in motion, and there was no going back.

For anyone.

Kris Phoenix 1979

For nearly two years Kris had been having an on/off affair with Sharleen. Not easy when an ocean separated them, and she was a big star in America and The Wild Ones hadn't cracked it yet. Not easy when her main man was Marcus Citroen – the record tycoon – and if Marcus found out, Sharleen assured him, Kris would have both legs broken and a face full of smashed teeth. Charming! Nothing like living a dangerous life.

"Whyn't you get the fucker t'sign us to a record deal?" he suggested one day as they lazed on the big bed in her Dorchester hotel suite.

Sharleen rolled over on her stomach and smiled lazily. "Are you shittin' me, man? One mention of your name an' he'll suspect for sure. Marcus has an antenna for these things."

Sliding his hand beneath her stomach and down towards her furry warmth, he asked wryly, "How many of *these things* have there bin?"

Giggling huskily, she said, "Let's put it this way, honey – what Mr C don't know ain't gonna burn his balls!"

"Mebbe it'll burn mine," he retorted.

She laughed. "Oh, *suuure*! I just *know* when I ain't around you got it wrapped in cotton an' outta action."

"Shit! Somebody told you!"

They both fell about laughing, secure in the knowledge that

what they had together was great sex. And neither of them made any other demands. Sharleen turned him on with a vengeance. She was devastatingly pretty, a big star, and old enough to know what she was doing without bitching about a commitment. Every time he climbed into bed with her he couldn't believe his luck.

How had they met? He vaguely remembered meeting her in Annabel's the night of their first big London gig. Sharleen, all eyes and teeth and come-on looks. But somehow he'd ended up with yet another enthusiastic groupie – making it in the back of his car, with the chauffeur driving slowly around Berkeley Square, sneaking surreptitious looks in the rear view mirror.

He'd seen Sharleen again a few nights later at a Queen concert. This time she was without Marcus Citroen, who had flown back to New York. She was wearing a startling red dress and a wide smile.

He was with Buzz and Flower and a group of hangers-on, and she'd invited them all back to her hotel, where she'd plied them with food, booze, and the finest Colombian Gold grass, until eventually she'd taken Kris to one side and said, "Get rid of the entourage an' let's *really* party."

He didn't need asking twice.

Now they got together every time she came to London. And she flew in whenever she could. She was a favourite of Prince Charles, and always obliged if he asked her to appear at one of his favourite charity events. Her records in England automatically went to number one, and the public adored her. This time she was visiting for a television appearance on the popular *Top of the Pops*.

Kris had decided to use his connection. Mr Terence was getting nowhere with the Americans. Frankly, Kris suspected that when it came to the States, old man Terence didn't know his ass from a hole in the ground. It was time for some long overdue action. Maybe dumping Mr Terence was the first move. He'd been thinking about it on and off. Timing was everything.

There was no doubt that Marcus Citroen and Blue Cadillac Records would be a great label for The Wild Ones. They were among the best, along with Atlantic, Capitol and Warners. Kris only wanted the best. He'd turned down several offers from half-assed companies who wouldn't guarantee shit on advertising and promotion. Without the right launch behind them they were nowhere.

Sharleen didn't seem inclined to help, and he could understand why. He'd been toying with the idea of flying to New York himself.

"Forget it," Buzz had said dismissively when he'd mentioned it to him. "Doin' things ourselves is strictly amateur night. *You* know that better than anyone."

Buzz was perfectly happy with their present situation. They were big stars in England. Europe too. Buzz's attitude was "Who needs the bleedin' Yanks? We're makin' it here. What's the panic?"

Kris wanted America. He wanted it so bad it made his teeth ache whenever he thought about it.

Every Sunday he visited his son at his in-laws' house in Esher. Bo was a strapping three-and-a-half-year-old. A nice-looking kid, but Willow and her uptight parents were making the boy into a wimp. He could see all the signs.

"I want to take him out on my own," he informed his ex-wife.

"No," she said stubbornly. "I can't allow that."

"A court'll bleedin' allow it," he argued hotly.

"Take me to court then," she replied, red-cheeked and self-righteous. "We'll *see* what a judge will allow."

He couldn't be bothered. It wasn't worth the public hassle. Maybe when the kid was older.

Groupies were knee deep. He couldn't move without falling over them. They gathered outside the tiny house he'd bought in a quiet side street near Hampstead Heath. They phoned at all hours of the day and night, forcing him to change his number every two weeks. They followed him along the street whenever he ventured out, and sent him passionate hand-written notes chock-full of all the lustful things they would like to do to him.

Buzz and Rasta revelled in the attention.

Kris and Ollie hated it.

Ollie was on the verge of getting married to his cellist girl-friend.

"Do it!" Kris urged.

"Are you friggin' *mad*?" exploded Buzz.

"Not *another* wife to hide," groaned Mr Terence.

Ollie did it on a summer's day in the English countryside, with only close family and friends present. The news hit the press two days later and caused a cyclone. The Wild Ones belonged to the female population of England. This was a hostile act, and the screaming teenyboppers were furious. Ollie, in his own quiet way, was very popular.

Hate mail rained down on Ollie's new wife and her un-assuming, middle-class family.

Within a week Ollie made a momentous decision. He resigned from the group.

They were all shocked – except Kris, who calmly accepted the fact that Ollie considered a life more important than rock stardom.

Ten days after Ollie's defection they were auditioning for a new keyboard and bass player. Inadvertently that's how Doktor Head entered their lives, and America became more than just a possibility.

Rafealla 1979

"C'mere, *bitch*."

"Eddie. You're drunk. Leave me alone."

"I said *come here*. You *do it*. NOW!"

He was shouting, his eyes angry slits, his mouth slack and mean, as he sprawled on the chintz-covered couch in his mother's sitting room, a full glass of vodka balanced precariously in one hand.

Warily Rafealla approached the couch. She hated Eddie when he was drunk. He turned into an appalling, rough animal, and she had no idea how to handle him.

As soon as she was within reach he grabbed her wrist, spitefully digging his nails into her soft flesh.

"Hello, whore," he mumbled, with a sick grin. "Wadderya goin' t'do for me today?"

"Eddie." She could hear the pleading tone in her voice, and loathed herself for it. "Why don't we go to bed? It's late, and your mother will be home soon. You don't want her to see you like this, do you?"

He laughed. An empty laugh, full of venom. "Fuck both of you cunts. I don't give a damn what either of you whores think of me."

"Please, Eddie," she whispered. "Don't talk like that—"

Abruptly he yanked her down on top of him, roughly pushing her skirt up, and tearing at her panties.

"Open your legs," he commanded coldly.

"No, Eddie. Not like this. *No.*"

Her objections only served to excite him, and pinning her down he managed to free himself from the confines of his trousers and thrust towards her.

She struggled for a moment, finally going limp, allowing him to jab away until he lost his erection and pushed her to the floor in disgust. Then he started to cry. As usual she felt sorry for him, and with difficulty managed to help him from the couch, guide him along the corridor to their room, and dump him on the bed, where he promptly fell asleep.

Throwing a blanket over him, she hurried back to the living room and tidied up. Just in time, for Lady Elizabetta Mafair made a noisy entrance with her beau of the moment, an ex-Member of Parliament, with several chins and a penchant for discipline.

"Oh!" exclaimed Lady Elizabetta, hardly concealing her annoyance. "You're still up."

"I'm just off to bed," Rafealla said quickly.

"No hurry, dear," said the ex-politician, helping himself to a large glass of brandy.

"She's tired," Lady Elizabetta insisted. "Let her go."

"Yes, I'm very tired," Rafealla replied. "Please excuse me."

Walking rapidly from the room, she knew that everything was her own fault. With a sigh she thought about the events of the past two years, and realized with a feeling of deep despair that she had nobody to blame but herself.

*

The day Eddie Mafair announced his engagement to Fiona Ripley-Hedges in The Times *was the day Rafealla found out for sure she was pregnant.*

After her initial shock and horror, it occurred to her that she was carrying Eddie Mafair's baby, and that therefore they were irrevocably joined, and nothing and nobody could ever change that.

For several days she nursed her secret to herself, not even confiding in Odile or Fenella. Until eventually she went to her mother and confessed everything.

Anna was horrified. "You're barely eighteen," she said, appalled. "A mere child. Who is this Eddie Mafair? What kind of despicable man takes advantage of a child?"

"I'm not a child," Rafealla stated firmly. "And he didn't take advantage of me. I love Eddie, and I want to marry him."

Anna was even more horrified. "Marriage! At your age. I cannot say yes."

"Mama. Eighteen is old enough. In some countries girls get married at thirteen."

"Uncivilized countries."

"Ah, but you don't seem to understand. I will not have an abortion. So . . . you see . . . marriage is the only answer."

There was never any doubt in her mind what she wanted. Marriage. Eddie would marry her – should marry her. And they'd live happily ever after.

Anna, and Rafealla's stepfather, Lord Egerton, met with Eddie's widowed mother, Lady Elizabetta Mafair. She was a formidable-looking woman in her late fifties. Once a great beauty, with a scandalous divorce behind her, she was still fiercely attractive, with dyed raven hair, scarlet lips, and piercing dagger eyes. "I can't tell Eddie what to do," she said unpleasantly. "He's over twenty-one, and already engaged to some other girl."

"But you can influence him, can't you?" said Cyrus, a man used to getting his own way, and determined to do so now.

Lady Elizabetta reached for a cigarette, leaning forward so Cyrus could light it for her. The swell of her breasts fell into view.

Anna looked away. It offended her the way this woman was flirting with her husband.

"Perhaps," Lady Elizabetta said casually, drawing smoke deeply into her lungs.

"I've done a touch of investigating," Cyrus said, getting up and pacing around the room. "It seems that your son has gambled his inheritance away, and does not stand to gain another penny until you – please excuse me for saying this – pass away. Fortunately," he added, with a dry laugh, "you appear to be extremely healthy to me."

"I am," Lady Elizabetta said. "Unfortunately for poor Eddie. Although I understand this girl he's engaged to comes from a wealthy family."

"*I gather that is the main attraction.*"

"*Hmm, you seem to know all the answers., Lord Egerton. I wonder why our paths never crossed before?*"

"*Well, you see,*" Cyrus said wryly, "*when you were coming out as debutante of the year—*"

"*Please don't say what year,*" she interrupted, *with a tightly controlled smile.*

"*I wouldn't dream of doing so,*" he replied, *being charming, because Anna wanted him to settle this matter, and whatever Anna wanted he would do.* "*As I was saying,*" he continued. "*When you were being honoured I was just a copy boy — running errands on Fleet Street.*"

"*How you've risen,*" Lady Elizabetta mocked, *blowing a stream of smoke in his face.*

"*It took me many years of hard work.*"

"*I'm sure it did.*"

Anna rose from the couch. "*Let's get to the point,*" she said forcefully.

Cyrus glanced at her in surprise. It was unlike his darling Anna to assert herself. And then he realized she was jealous, and it pleased him, puffed him up.

"*The point is money,*" he said, taking an authoritative tone. "*If Eddie is willing to marry our daughter, I will settle an immediate million-pound trust fund on their unborn baby. Plus I will give Eddie a worthwhile job, and a bonus payment of two hundred and fifty thousand pounds a year for the next five years.*"

"*Generous,*" remarked Lady Elizabetta. "*Your daughter must really love him.*"

"*She does,*" said Anna. "*That's the only reason he was able to take advantage of such a very young and innocent girl.*"

Lady Elizabetta raised a sardonic eyebrow. "*We're living in the seventies, Lady Egerton. I doubt if Eddie took advantage of anyone. From what I read about girls today, quite the reverse is probably true.*"

A faint blush of anger suffused Anna's pale cheeks. "*Nonesense!*" she said vehemently.

"*Ladies,*" interrupted Cyrus. "*Shall we get to the reason for this meeting? A marriage between our daughter and your son. Let us not waste any more time. Is it arrangeable or not?*"

*

The wedding between Rafealla Le Serre Egerton and Eddie Mafair was a glittering social affair. Rafealla wore a stunning white satin Norman Hartnell wedding gown, and Eddie looked very handsome in his dark morning suit.

The bride's mother was clad in pale blue, and the groom's mother favoured attention-getting scarlet.

As bridesmaids, Odile and Fenella were pretty in pink. And Rupert was best man.

The ceremony took place in church, and the reception was held in the ballroom of the Grosvenor House Hotel on Park Lane, where Eddie had booked a suite for their honeymoon night, before their flight to Acapulco the next day.

Rafealla was incredibly nervous. She'd hardly spent any time with Eddie alone while the wedding was being hurriedly planned. Two dinners with her mother and stepfather present. Tea with Lady Elizabetta. And one lunch with Eddie at San Lorenzo, where he'd drunk too much wine and failed to tell her he loved her.

Hardly the perfect beginning, but they had their whole lives ahead of them, and things could only get better.

The wedding passed in a blur of faces. So many people, and only a few she knew. By the end of the day her cheeks were aching from smiling so much.

Eddie behaved impeccably. He didn't drink, and was polite to everyone. How handsome he looked in his morning suit. With a shiver of pleasure Rafealla knew she had made the right choice.

*

Eddie mumbled in his sleep, but didn't wake. Fortunately. For Rafealla was too exhausted to deal with any more of his vile behaviour tonight. She brushed her long hair and thought about their baby – Jonathan, or Jon Jon as everyone called him.

Their baby . . . The only reason she and Eddie were together. The only reason she could never leave him.

Soon Jonathan would be two years old. And he looked exactly like Kris Phoenix.

Bobby Mondella 1979

"They want you for a cover on People. Do you realize what that means?"

"The week in England is a sell-out. The tickets have only been on sale three hours."

"Can you make the July the fourth weekend in Washington? The President's wife requested you personally."

Stardom.

How sweet it is.

Bobby Mondella lived in Los Angeles, in a Hancock Park mansion with eleven bedrooms, eleven matching bathrooms, several huge entertaining rooms, and a lush, landscaped garden.

He lived alone, apart from six servants and two fierce Alsatians.

Outside the house there was a dark green Rolls-Royce, a white Porsche, and a 1959 vintage pink Thunderbird.

Whenever Rocket Fabrizzi was in town he stayed with Bobby. Rocket was also a star, a movie star. But since his divorce from the serious Roman Vanders, he shunned possessions, preferring to live out of a couple of suitcases and bed down in friends' spare rooms.

"Wadderya need all this garbage for?" he often asked Bobby. "You're not married. You have no kids. I don't get it."

"Why not?" Bobby replied. "I can afford it. I like havin' stuff. It's a kick."

Rocket shook his head. "I guess we've come a long way from Greenwich Village," he said, with a bitter twist of longing.

"The further the better," Bobby responded sharply.

Bobby Mondella, just as Marcus Citroen had predicted, was a superstar. He was Stevie Wonder with more sex appeal. Michael Jackson with balls. Teddy Pendergrass with a mainstream connection. He was that rare happening – a black star who crossed right on over to white America and was immediately accepted. In the two years since his debut concert at the Hollywood Bowl he'd had two smash albums, and seven hit singles culled from them – an unheard-of accomplishment, as most artists were lucky if they got one or two hits off an album.

He'd received six Grammy awards. Another unheard-of achievement in such a short period of time.

"You're the greatest!" everyone told him. It was a soothing mantra.

Rocket never told him any such thing, and when he jokingly complained, his friend laughed. "I'll cut a deal with ya," Rocket said easily. "You don't buzz me 'bout bein' the new Marlon, an' I'll never give ya any of that 'you're wonderful' crap. 'Cos, Bobby, ya gotta remember where we're both comin' from, an' never – like I mean *never* – get caught up in the bullshit. It don't mean nothin', man, an' it ain't gonna last."

Once every six weeks, Nova Citroen flew into town. She and Marcus owned a Bel Air estate and had recently purchased a huge piece of property at the beach. Nova came in to meet with architects and designers. Marcus usually stayed in New York – he was not overly fond of Los Angeles.

Nova had rented a small house in the Malibu colony under an assumed name. Having embarked on an affair with Bobby, she was quite strict about absolute secrecy. During her brief visits they usually got together for several hours of unadulterated lust. She was a very sensual woman, with extremely sophisticated sexual tastes. Bobby tried to discourage her overt kinkiness.

"Wouldn't you like to have me and another woman together?" she often teased. "I can arrange it very easily, you know. Most men would kill for such an opportunity."

"No way," he replied. "You're enough for me."

Usually she smiled and called him her "suburban lover".

"Don't you wish!" he boasted jokingly. "I'm a star, baby. I can have any woman I want."

"Never forget," she said quietly, "Marcus makes stars, and he can break them. For instance—" She paused meaningfully. "If he ever found out about us . . ."

She never had to say any more than that.

Sometimes he thought he was crazy for continuing the affair. But there was something about her that had him hooked. He needed Nova. This classy, rich woman with the hungry body and cool personality. And it was no longer a grudge fuck against Marcus. It was much more. She was so different from all the other women he'd had, the females who gathered around a star, anxious for any crumb of affection.

When Nova wasn't in town he forced himself to date other women. Currently he was seeing a bubble-blonde actress who couldn't pronounce her *th*'s properly, and was considered adorably cute. And a forty-year-old black feminist.

Rocket was dating no one. "Sometimes I like t'save it, man," he explained, when Bobby tried to fix him up. "Y'know – put it all into a performance."

Privately Bobby thought Rocket still had a case on Sharleen. Well, he was too late. Sharleen had just announced her engagement to a well-known clothes designer in New York. Bobby wondered how Marcus Citroen felt about *that*. The rumour was that she and Marcus continued to be an unspoken item. Bobby had lost touch with her a long time ago. He'd realized life was too short to live it for someone else.

Rocket wandered into the bedroom as Bobby finished dressing. They'd been invited to a party for the opening of Nichols Kline's new discotheque in Beverly Hills, and neither could resist the temptation of seeing their former boss from The Chainsaw.

Nichols had done very well for himself. He was the biggest

concert promoter on the West Coast, and he'd started Nichols Hit City, his own extremely successful record company. Now he was opening Nichols as an ego trip.

Bobby wore an immaculate white suit, while Rocket looked suitably scruffy in creased chinos and a workshirt.

"The odd couple," Nichols said, greeting them both at the entrance of his new club with overly familiar hugs.

Settling them at his own table, where there was champagne, caviar and plenty of pretty women on tap, he gripped Bobby by the arm. "I gotta talk to you, it's important," he said, nose twitching with the smell of money. "Hear me out, Bobby baby, 'cos this'll make us *both* billionaires. You can count on it, my man. Have I got a deal for you! Infuckin'*credible*!"

Kris Phoenix 1979

Doktor Head was a flamboyant character. In his mid-thirties, he was six feet four inches tall and portly, with wild, shoulder-length, flaming red hair, an out-of-control beard, permanently bloodshot eyes, and a crazed facial tic which gave one the impression that every few minutes he was winking obscenely.

An American citizen, he had lived and worked in England for ten years, originally coming over with Nellie and the Knockers, an all-girl group whom he had managed for three rambunctious years. When Nellie decided to become a nun and the group disbanded, he'd taken over the career of Michael Hollywood, a young solo artist. Under Doktor Head's management, Michael Hollywood became very big very quickly – and for several years the unlikely combination of the laid-back young singer and his outrageous manager flourished.

Michael Hollywood wa killed in a plane crash in 1974, at the peak of his career. Doktor Head never forgave himself for not being on the plane. He went on a four-year rampage of drugs and booze, and when he walked into the audition hall for The Wild Ones, with his new discovery – a female keyboard player whom he'd named Fingers – he'd been straight for exactly five weeks.

Kris, grabbing a can of Coca-Cola from a machine in the

back, noticed the odd duo first. Thinking that Doktor Head was the one preparing to audition, he figured he'd do him a favour and tell him to forget it.

"Hello, mate," he said casually.

Doktor Head fixed him with alarmingly bloodshot eyes. "Where can I take a piss?" he demanded.

Kris was tired. It had been a long day, and not one of the people who'd auditioned were up to par. "I dunno," he said irritably.

"In that case," Doktor Head replied grandly, with an unpreventable wink, "I'll give this plant the gift of life." And with that, he unzipped, and proceeded to deliver a steady stream of urine to a wilting fern in a large clay pot.

Fingers, a tomboyish American girl in faded blue jeans and a sweatshirt, yawned. She had obviously witnessed Doktor Head's eccentricities before.

"Go ahead," Kris said sarcastically. "Take a slash wherever y'want. Don't mind me."

"Thank you," Doktor Head replied, zipping up with a satisfied expression.

"Listen – I may as well tell you now," Kris continued. "Don't bother to stick around for the audition. You're too old, an' even if you're the greatest keyboard player in the world, y'aint got the look we need."

"I'm so glad you told me that," Doktor Head said gravely.

"Yeah, well, at least y'got a piss outta it!" Kris joked, and wandered back to the others, who were busily watching an acned youth do a major kill on *Dirty Miss Mary*.

Half an hour later Fingers jumped up on the stage ready to show them what she could do. She sat down at the piano and immediately began to rock and roll.

"Hold it!" Buzz yelled. "What the frig – it's a bleedin' girl, ennit?"

Mr Terence came to life. When Buzz spoke, he jumped. "We're not auditioning females, dear," he said tartly.

Fingers made a rude gesture and began to play the hell out of *Skinny Little Slider*.

Her talent was formidable – a fact Mr Terence ignored.

"Enough!" he shouted, going red in the face. "We don't have time to waste. Get out of here."

"Wait a minute, hold on," Kris began. "She's good—"

"Leave it out," sneered Buzz. "That's all we need – a fuckin' *girl*."

Kris hadn't really thought about it, but why not – if she was sensational?

Doktor Head strolled into the picture, waving his arms in the air. "If you want her you'll have to act fast," he said with studied authority. "She doesn't come cheap, but she'll be worth it to you."

"Who the hell are *you*?" demanded Mr Terence, bristling because he sensed competition.

"Her manager," Doktor Head replied, gesturing for Fingers to cease her frantic pounding. Fixing Kris with bloodshot eyes he handed him his business card. "Call me," he said. "Soon."

They auditioned for another three days, and not one applicant sparked any excitement. Kris kept on thinking of Fingers, with her tomboyish looks and fast talent. He got the lowdown on Doktor Head, and was impressed with his background. Michael Hollywood and Nellie and the Knockers had both been big at one time.

Without telling the others he called Doktor Head, who calmly informed him he'd changed his mind. The Wild Ones were not the right group for Fingers.

Kris was perplexed. "Are you crazy?" he asked in amazement.

"So I've been told," replied Doktor Head. "But then crazy is merely a state of mind, isn't it?"

They met for a drink in a Hampstead pub. Kris got plastered, while Doktor Head drank only warm milk, which stuck disconcertingly to his beard. He gave a long discourse on the pursuit of real stardom in the rock world, and the perils of booze and drugs in general. "I survived the sixties," he noted with satisfaction. "A lot of people in rock 'n' roll didn't." He then proceeded to relate the story of how he had acquired the name Doktor Head. It seemed that at one time he was famous for giving young ladies haircuts, specializing in a certain part of their lower anatomy. "Wonderful days," he sighed reverently. "Ah ... the sixties ..."

"So what's Fingers gonna do?" Kris asked, avoiding eye contact with the barmaid, who wanted more than an autograph.

"There's a new group — The Mission. I'm thinking of managing them. If I do, Fingers will join them. She's only eighteen, you know. She has a big future."

Laughing disbelievingly, Kris said, "So like there's this unknown *new* group, an' you reckon she'll have a better future with *them*? Come on, man — where are *you* at? We're friggin' huge."

"In England."

"An' Germany."

"Holland too, no doubt."

"Yeah, an' bleedin' Finland, *an'* Denmark."

"Congratulations," Doktor Head said dryly. "And if you stay with Terry Terence, that's about as far as you'll go. You should have conquered America years ago."

Kris swigged his beer. "Tell me about it," he said glumly. "America ain't that easy."

"Especially when you've got a manager who sells you short."

"What?"

"Terry Terrence fucked you over."

"No way. He's always done his best for us."

"Really?"

"Yeah."

"Remember *Lonesome Morning*?"

"How could I ever forget it. Our first recording."

"And a big hit for Del Delgardo."

Kris grimaced. "Distribution. He had it. We didn't."

"Not at all. Your great manager sold out on you. The American record company didn't want your version on the market. A deal was made. You got shafted."

Kris felt the anger begin to build. "How do you know?"

"Everyone in the industry knew. Ask around. Ask your producer at the time — what was his name? Sam something?"

"Yeah. Sam Rozelle."

"That's right. Call him. He'll tell you the truth. He wasn't happy about it, I can assure you."

They closed the pub, went back to Kris's house, and talked until four in the morning.

The next day Kris went to see Sam Rozelle and learned the truth for himself. Terry Terence *had* sold them out on what could have been their first big hit. "He just didn't have enough faith in you," Sam said, too embarrassed to look Kris in the eye. "When Marcus Citroen said jump, he did so. I'm sure he regrets it now."

"He'll regret it all right," Kris said grimly.

Without hesitation he called a meeting, summoning Buzz and Rasta to his house. There he told them the truth, and that it was time to get rid of Mr Terence.

"The old geezer's done okay for us," Buzz argued. "It don't seem fair." He quite liked the fact that Mr Terence hero-worshipped him and treated him like a god.

"He's screwin' up our chances of makin' it in America," Kris pointed out. "We need someone who knows what it's all about over there."

"Who?" asked Rasta, casually lighting up a joint.

"Yeah, who?" Buzz joined in.

"Doktor Head," Kris announced with confidence.

"Fuck me!" exclaimed Buzz. 'An' who's 'e when 'e's at 'ome?"

"We gotta trust him," Kris said urgently. "He's where we want to go. Believe me. I know when something smells good."

*

After a long-drawn-out battle, Doktor Head took over the management of The Wild Ones, Fingers joined the group, and Mr Terence – unhappy with the financial settlement suggested – instigated a heavy lawsuit.

Kris didn't care. He was positive they were making the right move, and within weeks Doktor Head had an American record deal for them with Nichols Hit City, a hot new company. The deal met all their requirements.

The night before leaving for New York to meet with pro-ducers and writers, Kris went over to his mother's flat.

Horace was slumped in front of the television watching *Charlie's Angels*. His sisters were out, and Avis sat in the kitchen drinking endless cups of strong, sugary tea. Smiling wanly at her youngest son, she imparted a few words of useless advice. She looked tired, and older than her fifty-one years.

Kris handed her a thousand pounds in crisp new ten-pound notes. He had planned the gesture for weeks.

She pushed it away, saying, "I don't want your money, luv. Keep it, you'll need it."

Her words aggravated him. Why would he need it when he was on his way to making a fortune? Didn't she have any faith in him?

"Go on, take it," he insisted. "There's goin' t'be plenty more where that came from."

"Well . . ." She hesitated, thinking it over. "Maybe Brian could use a little help . . ."

Fuck Brian! "It's for *you*, ma," he said pointedly.

"I'll put it away for a rainy day," she decided at last, shuffling the money into a neat pile.

At least she'd accepted something from him. For a year now he'd been begging her to give up work. Avis didn't want to know. "I can't let my people down," she'd explained. He'd wanted to say – *Ma – you clean their bloody bogs, you don't perform frigging brain surgery*. But he'd refrained from doing so. She had her reasons. He respected that.

"So . . . I guess I'll see you in a few months," he said, kissing her on the cheek, anxious to get out of there before his sisters came home. He hated goodbyes.

"America," Avis said with a sigh. "I stepped out with a Yank once. He was ever so nice. 'E 'ad lovely shiny fingernails."

"Sounds like a real winner."

"I fink 'e liked me too. Asked me to go an' live in Nebraska." She gulped her tea. "Where's that?"

He had no desire to listen to Avis's true confessions.

"I'll have t'let you know, ma. Hang about – I'll be in touch."

And so he said goodbye to England with no regrets. Christ! He was twenty-nine. No time to waste. His future was America. And he was more than ready to ride the wave.

Rafealla 1979

"I'd like to get a job," Rafealla said one day. "It'll help us out, and I'd enjoy meeting new people."

"What the hell do you think *you* can do?" Eddie sneered derisively. "And who will look after the baby? If you're thinking of my mother – forget it. She's not the maternal type. Take it from me, I *really* know."

"Eddie," Rafealla said, very quietly. "I'm going crazy, stuck in this flat every day with only your mother to talk to. There's an art gallery in Duke Street. The owner has a notice in the window for someone to work there. I know about paintings. I can easily do it."

"No."

"What do you mean – no?"

"You happen to be my wife – *your* choice, I might remind you. And no wife of mine is going to take a job."

"I want to," she said stubbornly.

"Too bad," he replied.

She stared at her husband. His eyes were too small, his cheeks sallow. Why had she once thought him so handsome?

Oh, God! What a trap she was caught in. Married to a man she didn't love. Stuck in an apartment with his loathsome mother because he'd lost all the money her stepfather had given him at the gaming tables and they'd been forced to leave his mews house in a hurry. Eddie loved to gamble. It seemed to be his one and only true passion.

She was too ashamed to tell her mother. She even coloured her stories to Odile and Fenella, telling them that married life was great, and that they were only living with Lady Elizabetta while they looked for a house of their own.

Lies. All lies. Married life was abominable, and had been ever since the first night they spent together in their suite at the Grosvenor House Hotel after their lavish wedding party.

*

"I feel so wonderful. This is like a marvellous dream, isn't it, Eddie?" Rafealla floated around their honeymoon suite in a white lace peignoir, her long hair loose, a smile on her lips.

Eddie had already summoned room service, and when it arrived he managed to consume three neat vodkas before getting undressed.

Rafealla climbed into bed and waited for her husband. Legal sex. She could hardly contain herself!

Eddie stripped down to his shorts. He had a strangely hairless body, with a thin white scar running from below his breastbone to his navel.

"How did you get that?" she asked curiously.

"One of these days, when you're a big girl, I'll tell you."

She reached up her arms for him. Ignoring the gesture he grabbed a nearby newspaper.

"Eddie," she murmured softly. "It's our wedding night."

Carefully putting the newspaper down he stared at her with a cold expression. "Does that mean you want another fucking? Didn't the first one get me in enough trouble?"

For a moment his words did not sink in. And then she could only imagine he must be joking. "Don't be so nasty," she said.

"Nasty, my sweet?" His tone was pure acid. "Is that what you consider being nasty?"

"Eddie, I—"

Without warning he pounced on top of her, pinning her hands above her head, tearing her nightdress, exposing her breasts.

With studied cruelty he bent down and bit one of her nipples.

She screamed with pain.

"Now that's nasty," he said, with a bitter laugh. "Isn't it, darling?"

For a moment she lay there, too stunned to respond. And then with a supreme effort she brought her knee up, catching him firmly between the legs.

Swearing angrily, he rolled across the bed clutching his balls. "You little cow."

"I thought we were playing nasty," she said innocently.

"One of these days I'll really show you how to play. You'd better watch out, bitch."

Not the ideal start for any relationship.

Their honeymoon in Acapulco was a disaster. The surroundings were beautiful, but that was about it. Eddie drank all day and gambled all night, while Rafealla consoled herself with the thought that once the baby was born he would change.

Back in London things worsened, and by the time they moved into Lady Elizabetta's flat she had grown to hate her husband, and yet she had no idea how she could escape.

*

"Jon Jon doesn't look like Eddie, does he?" Odile said, bouncing her godson on her knee. "And he doesn't resemble you either. Who *does* he look like? Your mother? No. Your father? Hardly . . ." She giggled. "Probably some sailor you forgot to mention, right?"

"The entire merchant navy, actually," Rafealla replied casually, her heart beating fast.

Fortunately nobody knew of her one-night stand in the back of a chauffeured car with Kris Phoenix. Not even Fenella. She'd been so ashamed of her rash behaviour that she'd confided in no one. And quite honestly, when she discovered she was pregnant, it had never occurred to her that Kris Phoenix might be responsible.

Looking at Jon Jon now, there was no doubt in her mind. He looked exactly like the famous rock star. Same eyes, same nose, same stubborn little mouth. He even had the same spiky hair.

God! What a bizarre twist of fate.

Odile glanced around the stuffy living room. "When are you

moving out of here and getting your own place?" she asked. "Isn't it terribly awkward living with his mother?"

Rafealla shrugged. "Not too bad. It won't be long now. We look at houses every week."

"I hope you find something soon."

"So do I."

"You're too thin," Odile said, her eyes suddenly very concerned and knowing. "Are you *sure* everything's all right?"

Rafealla stood up and smoothed down her blue cashmere dress. If only Odile could see the bruises covering most of her body, she would know that everything was certainly not all right. "Of course it is. I couldn't be happier."

"Good," said Odile, also rising. "Whoops! I think dear little Jon Jon just peed on me. Do you want to change him or something?"

Rafealla took the baby into her arms, and hugged him tightly. She was glad he wasn't Eddie's. And one of these days she would tell the world.

Bobby Mondella 1979

The throb of Aretha Franklin filled the discotheque. Aretha singing *Respect*. Nobody did it better.

The dance floor was packed with couples in various stages of getting it on. Smoke filled the air, and champagne flowed freely.

"Some place, huh?" sighed Nichols, glancing proudly around his glitter palace of Art Deco and twirling mirrored lights. "Some classy joint, huh?"

"Yeah," Bobby agreed.

"Beats the fuckin' Chainsaw any day," boasted Nichols.

Bobby drained his champagne glass and nodded. He was still thinking about Nichols Kline's ridiculous offer. Well ... jeeze ... it had to be ridiculous. If he said yes to it, Nichols was offering him the earth and the sky, *plus* the moon and the stars. It was – as Nichols had said – Infuckin'*credible*.

Of course, he'd said no. *Had* to say no. After all, he had a contract with Blue Cadillac.

"No problem." Nichols had seemed unperturbed when he'd turned him down. "My backers in the record company and the club, they're good guys – businessmen. They'll buy you out of Blue Cadillac. All you gotta do is give me the word."

"I'll think it over."

He'd left it at that.

Now Nichols was playing Mr Genial Host, catering to their every need, including trying to push a succession of available bimbos onto them.

"The guy was a creep way back, an' he's *still* a creep," Rocket muttered irritably. "Exit time is comin' up. Wadderya say, Bobby?"

"Sure. Whenever you're ready."

But they were too late. A TV camera crew was upon them, with Nichols saying, "C'mon guys, do me this little favour for old times. Say the place is the hottest club you've ever been in. Okay?"

Nichols was sweating profusely in a pink ruffled shirt and brown leather pants, worn with a selection of solid gold chains clinking around his neck. His once rust-coloured curls were dyed a dull auburn, and straightened. His once Captain Hook nose had been straightened too. He was forty-seven years old and still a stud, although he had swapped a different girl a night for a faded English bottle-blonde, with a dull Cockeny accent and floppy tits.

"This is Pammy," was his proud introduction. "We're engaged to be engaged."

Pammy Booser was a would-be photographer, former nude model (T and A only, dear, no bush shots), and all-round loser. She came on to every male in sight the minute Nichols's back was turned – just as long as she thought they could do her some good.

Nichols liked her because he imagined he had found himself a classy English broad with brains. She called herself a writer, but all she had ever written was a pornographic piece on male prostitutes (she'd sampled three) for a cheapo girlie magazine. In her time she'd been into girls, guys, all together please, bondage, water sports, S and M, and now she'd decided to write a book about it. The only problem was she couldn't write, so she latched onto Nichols to pay the bills.

Tonight she was having difficulty making up her mind whether to hit on Rocket or Bobby. She vacillated, finally centring her attention on Rocket, because in the long run a movie star was better pickings than a rock star.

While Bobby was being interviewed she whispered in Rocket's ear, "I'm not Nichols's private property, y'know."

As if he cared. Her grating, whiny voice was enough to put anyone off. And she was no chicken – this one had been around the track and then some.

"Back off," he warned in a low voice. "I'm not into used goods."

"Charmin'!" she snapped.

He squashed her with a look, exchanging eye signals with Bobby that it was certainly time to beat it.

The television interviewer zeroed in on him the moment Bobby was through. "Please!" she begged. "Just one comment – you don't know what a coup it'll be for me to get you on the programme."

She was black and pretty, just his style. He acquiesced.

Grinning, Bobby headed for the men's room, where he was surprised to discover Seymour. Good old Seymour. King of the VIP men's room when The Chainsaw was at its peak. "Hey – how're y'doin', man," he greeted him with genuine pleasure.

Seymour, well into his sixties now, bobbed his head respectfully. "'Evenin', Mr Mondella. Anythin' I kin do for you – just say – just say, sir. I'm here for you."

The old man didn't remember him. And indeed – why should he? They'd hardly ever spoken – Seymour was once the King upstairs, and Bobby had just been the fat boy catering to the masses down below. He liked the fact that Nichols had hired Seymour all these years later. It indicated a certain loyalty.

After relieving himself, he slipped the old man a hundred-dollar bill, remembering how Jefferson Lionacre had once done the same thing, handing him the money when he was at a particularly low point in his life. He'd never forget that night, and Jefferson Lionacre's encouraging words – "Today the crapper – tomorrow the world." How right the famous singer had been.

"Thank you kindly, Mr Mondella," said Seymour, bowing and scraping a touch too much.

Outside the men's room lurked Pammy Booser, trying to appear casual. "Bobby," she greeted him cheerfully, as if they

were old and dear friends. "Why don't you an' I take off somewhere for a private nightcap, just the two of us?"

What a cheap and obvious bimbo she was. "How about
Nichols?" he asked, curious to hear what she'd say.

"Him," she spat scornfully. "He can get along without me
for one night." Throwing Bobby a coy, come-hither look, she
added, "Or longer . . . depending."

Women! This was a *real* douche bag.

"I was just thinkin' about loyalty," he said. "Nichols has it,
why don't you learn it?"

When he got back to the table, Rocket – true to style – had
vanished with the television interviewer.

"He says he'll call you tomorrow," Nichols guffawed. "What
an operator!"

"He always was," agreed Bobby.

"Yeah, remember him and Sharleen? Look what happened to
her," Nichols said, plunging into an ice cream sundae with
double chocolate sauce. "Y'know somethin'? The Chainsaw was
like a breedin' ground for raw talent. You – Rocket – Sharleen
– me. What a team!"

Bobby nodded, although he could hardly remember them as
one big happy team.

"I guess I inspired everyone to get their act together," Nichols
bragged, with a sigh of satisfaction.

"You fired *me*," Bobby reminded him.

"Naw."

"Sure you did. Short memory, Nichols?"

"Naw. Whatever I did was for the best. Look at you today."

"Thanks a lot."

"Sharleen's the one I remember," Nichols said, lasciviously
licking his lips. "Now she was one *juicy* piece of ass. Man, I'll
never forget givin' her the jism for three solid hours."

Bobby went cold. "What?"

"I screwed that sexy piece for longer than I ever did any
broad before. Holy shit! My pecker needed a fire hydrant to
cool it down!"

"When?" Bobby asked, quite sure the creep had to be lying.

"When? How do I know? Back when she first came to work

for me." Shovelling more ice cream into his mouth, he added, "She was always an ambitious little lady, that one. I knew she'd make it." Ice cream dribbled from his lower lip. "Now I can't even get her on the phone. I wanted her to fly out for tonight, make it a proper reunion."

The thought of Sharleen with Nichols Kline turned his stomach. He had no wish to hear any more. "Listen," he said, getting up. "Tonight was uh . . . interesting. But right now I gotta date with my pillow. I'm recording tomorrow."

Nichols looked dismayed. "You're leavin'? So early? The place hasn't even started to jump yet."

"It'll have to jump without me."

Abandoning his sundae, Nichols rose also, grabbing Bobby's right hand in both of his. "Baby, you're a real friend. I appreciate you comin' by tonight. An' don't be a stranger. Wendy!" He signalled a tall waitress in a skin-tight silver lamé catsuit. "Go to the front desk an' bring me Mr Mondella's membership card. Number one. Make *sure* it's number one."

"I gotta go," Bobby said.

"Yeah. One minute. Where's my Pammy? She'll want to say good night." Stopping another waitress he said, "Where's Miss Booser?"

False eyelashes fluttered. "I don't know, Mr Kline."

"Find out, an' get her for me."

"Yes, Mr Kline."

"Bobby." Nichols leaned towards him, confidentially lowering his voice to a hoarse whisper. "Think about my offer. It's the greatest. *We're* the greatest. What a combination we'd be!"

"Sure," Bobby said dully. He'd had it with the noise and the smoke, and most of all Nichols's stinking revelations.

Pammy appeared, fake smile in place, lipstick smudged. Nichols would never know she'd been giving the disc jockey head in the store room while he took his ten-minute break. "Bye," she said, with an affected wave.

Nichols pinched her cheek. "What a girl!"

Out of there, in the limo, home and bed. Smokey Robinson on the stereo, and a glass of scotch by his side.

Bobby tossed and turned, unable to sleep. It had been a disturbing evening. Too many memories. Too many old times.

Eventually he had to get up and take a comfortingly warm shower. Only then did he feel better.

Finally he fell asleep.

Saturday, July 11, 1987
Los Angeles

"I'm not doin' press," Kris said stubbornly. "No way, José. You can take the reporters an' shove 'em up your ass."

"Thank you *so* much, Mr Phoenix," Norton St John replied politely. "And if *only* I had the room, I'd be more than happy to oblige."

Kris couldn't help cracking a grin – after all, he was dealing with a fellow Englishman, and he'd always had a soft spot for the gay brigade. Not that he'd ever been tempted to join them, but most of them were witty and well informed, and knew a hell of a lot more about what was going on in the world than the civilian population. Also they loved his records. He even had a gay fan club based in Denmark.

"Look," he said, trying to explain. "Talkin' to reporters wasn't part of the deal. Tell 'im, Hawk."

The Hawk nodded. "Whatever you want, Kris," he said smoothly, pausing for a moment before adding, "Although with the release of the new album, and the film talks talking place right now, it wouldn't be a *bad* move. This *is* such a prestigious event. And I'm sure that Rafealla and Bobby Mondella will be speaking to the press."

"They certainly will," Norton St John said confidently, in spite of the fact he had not received a yes from either of them. His demeanour was cool and collected, although what exactly was he supposed to say to a select group of press and television interviewers when he couldn't come up with one star willing to answer their questions?

"*I'll* meet them," Cybil suggested brightly. "They love me. I don't mean to sound immodest, but ever since the *Sports Illustrated* cover, they're all over me."

"No!" Kris said, picking at a bunch of grapes.

"Why?" pouted Cybil.

"'Cos *I've* decided t'do it. I'll give 'em five minutes." He turned to the Hawk. "An' set some ground rules. I'm not gonna answer any questions about The Wild Ones, Buzz, Doktor Head, or her." He jerked his head in Cybil's direction.

"Why not me?" she demanded hotly.

"My fans don't like it."

"How ridiculous!"

"An' all those assholes jerkin' off over your picture probably don't like it either. Single is sexy. I learned that one a long time ago." Swooping a whole bunch of grapes from the dish, he crushed them into his mouth. "Saw this in a French movie once," he explained between chews. "It's the only way to eat 'em."

The Hawk tried not to look offended at his star's lack of etiquette. Rock stars. They were all the same. Street kids with money to burn and the manners of pigs.

Norton St John heaved a hidden sigh of relief. "May I suggest we get it over and done with. The press are all assembled."

"Okay. You come too, Hawk. Cybil, plant your ass here. I mean it."

She wanted to argue, it was written all over her pretty face. Californian golden girls were always supposed to get their own way. This just wasn't fair.

*

Maxwell Sicily, ever watchful, fell back into position without anyone noticing he had been missing for over twenty minutes.

Chloe found him shortly after. "Quick," she said, tugging anxiously at his sleeve. "Bobby Mondella's rehearsing, come and watch."

"I'm working," he said, shaking her hand off.

"That's all right. *I* say you can take a ten-minute break."

The woman was a pest. She'd better stop bothering him, for there was no way he was going to allow her to screw up his plans.

"I'd better tell you something," he said shortly. "I'm married."

Without hesitation she jumped in with, "An' I bet your wife don't understand you."

"Yes, she does," he answered quickly.

Disappointment crossed her puffy face, but it didn't stop her. "I can't spot a wedding ring," she said accusingly.

Anger flickered behind his blank eyes. "Neither of us believe in useless symbols."

"I bet you don't believe in weddin' certificates either. On your fact sheet – the one you filled out when you came to work at Lilliane's – you said you was single. What is it? One of them hippie marriages?"

She was asking to be broken in pieces. "I guess you could call it that."

Chloe grimaced, all crooked teeth and a crafty expression. "Well, George, let *me* tell *you* somethin'. As long as it's not legal you're fair game." Once more she grabbed hold of his arm. "Come on, we're gonna see Bobby Mondella rehearse. An' *that's* an order from management."

*

"He's something, isn't he?" Trudie sighed, watching Bobby Mondella, as his powerful, haunting voice filled the air.

"Yes," murmured Rafealla, "he really is."

"I guess this is his first appearance in public since the accident."

Rafealla nodded.

"Do you know him?" Trudie ventured.

"Uh . . . I used to."

What kind of a reply was that? Either you knew someone or you didn't. "Well . . ." Trudie said. "I never saw one of his concerts before, but I've heard he had the horniest act going. I expect he'll have to change that now."

Rafealla didn't bother to reply. She was too caught up with the joy of seeing him again. He looked wonderful. Thank God – above all else – Bobby Mondella was a survivor.

*

Speed couldn't believe it. His luck he had to pick a street where the Mexican house-man of some rich couple who were away jiving in Europe, had set the place up as a brothel, with three under-age illegal aliens doing duty as flavours of the month. What a break! The street was crawling with vice, busting asses. They wanted it all. The house-man. The girls. Even the clients. He made it in the third category.

Finally, after hours of dumb questions, they allowed him to call a lawyer. He knew this one guy – a shyster, charged a month of steak dinners – but he was fast.

"Get me the fuck outta here," he pleaded on the phone. "Like yesterday."

"I'm in the middle of a family reunion," the lawyer said testily, wondering how a weasel-shit client like Speed had managed to obtain his home phone number.

"I don't give a piss if you're jerkin' off the President! Get me outta here!" screamed Speed. "I'll pay double – treble. Just *do* it!"

*

> *An' there's heat*
> *An' there's woman*
> *An' then . . . baby . . . there's you*

Bobby sang the song with as little effort as possible – saving himself for the real thing later on – just going through the motions to make sure the excellent musicians hired for the evening had his arrangement down pat, and everything sounded right. Sara had told him Rafealla wanted to watch him rehearse. "That's okay," he'd said. He had to face people sometime, and tonight was as good a time as any.

He felt strong and fit. Ready for anything.

· Successfully he'd passed test number one. A confrontation with Nova. Short. Not so sweet.

Sara hadn't commented. She'd just led him quickly away when he'd told her to. He wished she *had* said something. A bitchy remark would be better than her long-suffering silence.

These thoughts went through his mind as he automatically sang the lyrics.

Was Nova standing out there watching him?

Stop thinking about her, man.

Was Marcus around? Was the son of a bitch watching too?

He blew the lyric, touched his dark glasses, and tried to concentrate on the music alone. It wasn't as easy as he made it seem.

*

Vicki mingled, enjoying the frantic activity and general hubbub. Working as a maid at Novaroen was dull stuff up until today. If she breathed very deeply she could smell freedom. Wow! The first thing she was going to do was pile on the makeup, get dressed up in her fanciest outfit, and go out and get laid.

Bobby Mondella was rehearsing. What a voice! What a guy! Now she wouldn't mind a piece of *that*.

Grinning to herself, she spotted Maxwell Sicily with some blowsy red-headed broad clinging to his arm.

That stopped her in her tracks. Maxwell hadn't mentioned anyone else being involved. Dammit! Why was she feeling sharp stabs of jealousy?

*

"I'm going to change," Nova Citroen said to her husband. "Our guests will be arriving soon. May I suggest you do the same."

Marcus stared penetratingly at his wife. She was still an extremely attractive woman, no doubt about it. Even in her forties she had lost none of her seductive allure. The same allure that first attracted him to her all those years ago in Hamburg.

If only the world knew what the elegant Mrs Citroen was when he initially set eyes on her. A whore. A *putain*. Highly paid and highly skilled. A mistress of her art.

The first time he went to bed with her was almost a religious experience. She allowed him the freedom of mind and body women had always denied him. She encouraged him to live out his fantasies with an abandon he had not thought himself capable of. She coaxed him further than he had ever been before. And he loved every moment of her relentless discipline.

When she returned to visit him the next day, she manoeuvred a delicate switch of roles. Somehow she psyched into exactly what he needed, and this time *he* became the pain master, and she took what he handed out with exactly the right degree of controlled anguish.

A week in her company and he'd thought that would be it. But upon returning to America, he found he couldn't get her out of his mind. Nobody had ever satisfied him the way Nova did.

Of course, she was not called Nova then. Her hair was dark. Her nose was hardly the fine patrician shape it was today. And she was heavier, quite comely in fact.

He'd brought her to Paris, where he set her up in a secluded apartment and one by one exposed her to beauty experts in every field.

At the same time he hired a language teacher, and an elderly English woman who was most discreet and specialized in etiquette. He also engaged several other experts on everything from paintings to wine.

The one thing he could not teach her about was sex. When it came to pleasing him, her instinct was always right.

He married her exactly eighteen months after their first encounter. By that time she was a lady.

Just what he had always desired. A lady in the drawing room and a whore in the bedroom. He had the best of both worlds.

Now he wanted Rafealla. And whatever Marcus Citroen wanted, he got. Always.

Kris Phoenix 1981

"'Ere," said Buzz in a slurred voice. "There's more 'igh–class pussy lyin' around in the other room than *I've* ever seen. An' askin' for it. Bleedin' *beggin'*. Wot we gonna do, mate?" he asked gloomily. "I only got one cock."

"Yeah," replied Kris, staring at Buzz's reflection in the mirror of the luxury hotel bathroom in Chicago. "And I'm surprised y'can still get it up, the amount of blow you're doin'."

Buzz laughed, a crazed, satanic laugh, touching his forehead with a gesture of deference. "I forgot, din't I? I'm in the presence of Mister friggin' Clean. Smokes a *joint* an' freaks out."

"I don't get off on drugs," Kris said wearily. "How many times d'you want me to say I'm sorry for not rollin' around like some piss-assed zombie? Screw it, man. Sometimes you get on my fuckin' nerves. All you wan' to do is get stoned an' laid."

Buzz made a face. "'Ave you come up with any better ideas?"

"Yeah. Take some time out to rehearse. The other night in Boston, you played like some sloppy kid auditioning for his first gig."

"Crap!"

"Think about it."

"Bull*shit*. We just got the best friggin' review of our lives in friggin' *Newsweek*. The Yanks love our Limey asses. We're friggin' *superstars* here. Just wot you wanted, huh?" As if to bait Kris, he took a small packet of cocaine from the pocket of his leather jacket and laid out several lines of the loose white powder. Then he rolled a hundred-dollar bill and snorted each thin, powdered strip with greedy satisfaction.

Kris turned away. He knew what was happening to Buzz. He didn't have to watch.

Worldwide fame.

American fame.

Success.

Adulation.

Yeah, they had it all now. Everything he'd always dreamed of. And it was a kick. If you wanted to spend your life joined at the hip to three other people – plus Doktor Head and an ever-growing entourage.

The Wild Ones.

Super Group.

With an appeal somewhere between the Beatles – long broken up. And the Rolling Stones – still rocking when they felt like it.

The Wild Ones.

They covered every base.

Kris Phoenix. Raunchy rocker, with a charismatic stage presence, a wild throaty voice, and a magic touch on his guitar.

Buzz Darke. He inspired a cult following. The Americans loved his devilish looks and brilliant guitar work.

Rasta Stanely. Black. Funny. Sexy.

And Fingers. A tough little female with a genuine rock and roll talent.

We couldn't have put it together any better, Kris thought. *We're the mix everyone was waiting for*.

Buzz flipped up the collar of his leather jacket, pushing his way to the bathroom door. "I'm joinin' the party," he said. "Whyn't you do the same? It's wot it's all about, ennit?"

Yeah. Maybe, Kris thought.

When they'd first hit it in America, he'd gone crazy, just like the rest of them. He'd laid his way from New York to Los Angeles with absolutely no problem at all. Amazing groupies.

The supercunts, as Doktor Head endearingly christened them. Luscious lovelies with nothing on their mind except climbing into bed with a rock star. In the sack they name-dropped as much as they could.

Well ... when I was in San Francisco with Mick ...

Keith was the greatest. I'm telling you – that man could party 'til he dropped ...

David is the most brilliant human being I ever met ...

Buzz and Rasta completely freaked. They couldn't get enough. But after the initial thrill of having more or less any girl he wanted, Kris grew bored, preferring to hang out with the roadies, drinking beer and watching sports on TV. American television blew his mind. So many stations to choose from, and twenty-four-hour action. Horace would have a heart attack. In England the three channels shut down before midnight with a stern newscaster daring you to argue.

Goodnight.

Sleep tight.

Fuck that for a lark!

He'd seen Sharleen a couple of times when they'd first arrived in America, but she wasn't the same on home ground and told him she didn't think they should get together anymore. Fine with him.

Lighting a cigarette he leaned on the marble sink. It was time to rejoin the party, only he had no desire to do so.

A walk would be nice.

Impossible. Riff-raff groupies staked every hotel they stayed at, waiting to pounce with their blank, starey eyes, quivering lips and voracious appetites. They would do anything to get near one of the stars of a successful group, and invariably did. The bouncers, equipment drivers and roadies had many a bawdy tale to tell of teenage girls willing to perform whatever was required – and all for a mere backstage pass.

Buzz and Rasta had worked out a crafty system for picking the girls they fancied out of the audience. During the course of their performance they were able to give a series of hand signals to a roadie standing at the side of the stage, pinpointing the females of their choice. He, in turn, contacted a second roadie sitting in the audience. By the time the show was over, the chosen girls were assembled in a room waiting for the stars to take their pick. The leftovers were divided among the crew. And the girls seemed perfectly satisfied. They were thrilled to have been noticed in the first place.

Kris had no desire to go along with that kind of soul-less action. Random sex had lost its thrill. How about a relationship for a change? Someone who cared about Kris Phoenix the person – not the rock and roll image. The super god in black leather with a red-hot guitar between his legs. Jesus – that's what he needed, someone who really cared.

America.

It was theirs.

And he wasn't fulfilled or satisfied or any of the things he knew he should be.

Rasta banged on the door. "Are you bleedin' comin' out or wot? Mikki's goin' spare. She says you promised 'er tonight's the night."

Michelle Hanley-Bogart of New York City. A former deb of the year, an heiress with monied parents and a penchant for rock stars. She was twenty-three, exceptionally pretty, and self-titled queen of the groupies. According to Mikki she had been collecting notches on her Gucci belt since the tender age of thirteen. "Honey," she was fond of saying in her up-town gravelly voice, "you ain't a star until Mikki *says* you are."

Whispers informed him that Michelle Hanley-Bogart made no false claims to fame. She'd been to bed with all the greats, and was never proved wrong. Once in Mikki's bed and there was no limit.

Buzz wanted a crack, but since she'd joined the entourage in Philadelphia she had eyes only for Kris.

Pretty as she was, infamous as she was, he found himself holding back. On this – their second tour of America – he did not have jet-lag, he had groupie-lag.

Mikki waited patiently, endearing herself to the rest of the group and the roadies by picking out the best girls, the best restaurants, and the best places to have fun in as they trekked through city after city. Mikki would have made a sensational tour-manager – she knew it all.

Buzz was insulted she hadn't chosen him. She'd share a joint, but nothing else. "I'm waiting for Kris," she'd say simply, when pressed. It had become the tour joke. When was Kris going to get a leg over?

He'd promised her it would happen in Chicago. Now he felt like a reluctant bridegroom.

"Wot the fuck you *doin'* in there?" demanded Rasta.

"A tribal marriage dance," Kris replied dourly, and re-entered the real world.

The party was going strong. The Temptations blasted forth from the stereo. Wine, beer and champagne flowed. There were plenty of couples in advanced stages of necking, and joints being passed back and forth like dime store candy. Buzz seemed to be buried beneath two busty blondes. Flower was safely stashed in London, but even if she were present she wouldn't object, as group sex was her hobby.

Mikki stood serenly next to the stereo, wearing a turquoise mini-dress with patterned stockings and black patent-leather pumps. Her straight blonde hair was parted in the middle and held back with a neat barrette. The word "virgin" came to mind. Mikki looked like she'd never done it in her life.

Kris grinned. He couldn't help liking her. She had a terrific personality, always up, always fun. If she hadn't slept with a virtual *Who's Who* of the rock world, he could quite fancy a steady relationship.

"Hello – star," she said, her knowing voice arguing with her pretty image.

Why didn't he just close his eyes and think of England? Not such a great hardship.

Rafealla 1981

Escape had been on Rafealla's mind for many months. The only reason she'd stayed around so long was because of Jon Jon, now a robust four-year-old. Life was a series of dangerous skirmishes. She had to be on her guard at all times, ready to deflect Eddie's vicious temper tantrums and bouts of cruelty. She kept an old Turkish dagger in its tooled leather case under the bed – one of the few souvenirs she had of her father. Once, she had taken it out and threatened him. The beatings had to stop. It seemed a suitable way to warn him.

"You wouldn't dare use that thing," he'd jeered.

"Just try me," she'd said grimly, her eyes explosive pinpoints of trouble.

The beatings stopped. The verbal abuse, and the gambling, did not.

Lady Elizabetta obviously knew what was going on – but said nothing. They had moved from her apartment into a Chelsea service flat, and she visited every few weeks to see her grandchild and criticize. Anna, Rafealla's own mother, suspected all was not well, but Rafealla refused to break and tell the truth. She had too much pride. After all, the marriage had been *her* idea, and to admit defeat was humiliating – even to her own family.

Odile guessed. "Eddie's not perfect," Rafealla admitted reluctantly. "We're working things out."

The truth was that Eddie Mafair was a sadistic, gambling drunk, and Rafealla had finally faced up to the fact that things were never going to change. She had given him over four years of her life. It was enough.

Leaving him was going to be no simple task. He depended on Lord Egerton's money to support his gambling habit. And even though he had never availed himself of the job Lord Egerton had offered him, it suited him to know the opportunity was always available.

No, Eddie would not take kindly to her departure. He professed to love his son, although she had never seen any proof of it. He ignored Jon Jon, bitterly complaining when the child made too much noise or messed up the apartment.

Rafealla didn't mind. *He's not your son*, she thought triumphantly. What a lucky twist of fate *that* was.

Their sex life was almost non-existent. It had been that from the beginning. When they *did* sleep together, it was merely a physical release – and as far as Rafealla was concerned, not a very satisfactory one. At first she had tried to talk to him, attempted to make some sense out of their relationship.

"It's what *you* wanted," was all he would say. "You forced it on both of us, so don't whine – because it's too late."

True. But she was older and wiser now. Her life was ahead of her, and four years was enough of a chance to give anyone.

Odile and Rafealla's stepbrother, Rupert, shocked everyone with news of a quickie marriage in Rio de Janeiro. Odile phoned with the good tidings.

"It's wonderful!" Rafealla exclaimed, genuinely thrilled. "How come you didn't *tell* anyone? Mama will go crazy, and so will your mother. You know how they both *love* big weddings."

"Exactly what we wished to avoid," giggled Odile. "I'm *sooo* happy! We want you to come and visit us, and bring Jon Jon."

"I'd love to," Rafealla said quietly, thinking this might be exactly the opportunity she'd been waiting for. Rupert had been living in South America for two years, working on a mammoth engineering project.

Brazil. On the phone he spoke about it glowingly.

Brazil.

It could be the pefect escape.

*

"How long will you be away?" Eddie asked churlishly.

Forever. "Three weeks."

"That's far too much time," he said, swigging a third after-dinner brandy.

"It's a great distance," Rafealla replied carefully. "I can't just go there then turn around and come right back."

"And who's supposed to look after me while you're away?"

"You'll manage."

"I know I'll manage," he said petulantly. "But why should I? That's what I married *you* for."

"Thanks," she said, and did not regret her decision one little bit.

She packed carefully, taking only her very favourite things. It wouldn't do to make him suspicious.

As she was filling the last suitcase he came into the bedroom and stared at her. "You're taking a hell of a lot of stuff for three weeks," he said accusingly.

The fumes of his breath hit her in the face. She almost gagged. In an even voice she said, "I'm leaving you, Eddie, I'm never coming back."

For one split second he took her seriously, and then he began to laugh. He was quite convinced she couldn't live without him – he'd told her so on many occasions.

"I couldn't get rid of you if I tried," he said, with immodest confidence. "When you tricked me into marrying you it was a life sentence, wasn't it, sweetheart?"

You wish. "Yes," she said dully.

"C'mere."

Automatically she backed away.

His tone was threatening. "I . . . *said* . . . come . . . here."

"Eddie, I'm tired—"

"Oh, it's 'Eddie I'm tired' now, is it? I can remember when you never stopped complaining because we *didn't* make love as much as you wanted."

"It's just that—"

"It's just that what, sweetheart?" He grabbed her around the waist and pressed his lips down hard on hers.

She wanted to scream. All the times she'd yearned for his attention. All the lonely nights and frustrating encounters that started off hopefully and ended in drunken bouts of cruelty.

Now he seemed in control. He was not quite drunk enough to cramp his style, and she could feel his erection pressing insistently against her thigh, and his hands creeping under her sweater.

Oh, Eddie, once you were my dream lover . . .

What happened?

In spite of herself she began to respond to his practised touch. Her physical needs swept away their cloudy past, and she opened up to pure, unbridled passion as he made love to her like he hadn't made love to her before.

With perfect precision he brought them to mutual orgasm, kissing her on the mouth as it happened, murmuring words – unspoken before – of great love and tenderness.

"Eddie . . ." She gasped his name, filled with confusion and guilt. Could it be that after all this time she had finally touched him? And now they could live happily ever after?

No . . . Absolutely not. Pure fairy-tale time. But she fell asleep full of doubts, wondering if leaving was the right thing to do.

In the morning he woke her with gentle kisses and clean breath. He made love to her again, bringing her to new heights of dizzying sensation.

"What's going on?" she asked wonderingly.

"I simply realized how much I'm going to miss you," he said, kissing her face. "Hurry home, sweetheart."

Jon Jon was staying at her mother's. She had arranged to meet them both at the airport. Her mother knew nothing of her plan to stay in South America, nobody did. It wasn't too late to change her mind . . .

Eddie insisted on driving her to the airport. He organized the luggage and porters, then escorted her to the VIP lounge, where he procceded to play with Jon Jon, making the child scream with delight.

Anna smiled. She was relieved to witness such a happy family group. Sometimes she wasn't so sure that all was well with her headstrong daughter's marriage, but today her doubts were firmly put to rest.

When their flight was called, Eddie drew Rafealla over to a quiet corner. "I never learned to express my positive feelings," he said, staring intently into her eyes. "However, somehow, with you going away, everything's fallen into position, and I *know* I'm going to make it better for you. Trust me, sweetheart. Come home soon. I miss you and little Jon already."

By the time she was on the plane, strapped in and ready for take-off, she was a nervous wreck. What was she *doing*? Running off half way around the world to escape from what? It seemed too good to be true, but in a miraculously short period of time Eddie honestly appeared to have changed.

So, the voice of reason told her, *go for three weeks and come back.*

But I want to be with him now, another voice cried.

Forget it, see what happens, cautioned the sensible voice.

The large jet taxied down the runway.

Too late now, kid.

*

Three hours later they were still on the plane, which never left the runway, due to some kind of technical difficulty. The passengers were hot and impatient, and every half-hour they were promised an imminent take-off. Jon Jon was restless, flushed with excitement and tired.

Rafealla summoned a stewardess. "Can you tell me exactly what is happening?" she asked.

The stewardess shrugged. "I wish I could. Every half-hour they inform us it will be *another* half-hour. We know as much as you."

Eventually an official announcement was made. The plane was not going anywhere, and the passengers were offered alternatives. Everyone disembarked.

Rafealla found a helpful ground clerk, and inquired if she could take the same flight the following day.

"Certainly," he said, wishing she would take a flight into his life. This was some great-looking female.

"Keep my luggage and book us on it," she said, hurrying for a cab, with Jon Jon running happily beside her, his short little legs doing double time to keep up.

*

After dropping Jon Jon back at her mother's house – a mere twenty minutes from the airport – she borrowed her stepfather's Aston Martin, and drove in high spirits to the Chelsea flat she shared with Eddie. By the time she arrived it was early evening and already dark. She'd had all day to think things over and felt good about getting another chance to be with her husband before her vacation. Because that's what she'd decided it was going to be. A vacation. A break. And in three weeks they would both be ready to start their marriage afresh.

Placing her key in the lock she heard the muted sounds of Manhattan Transfer – one of her favourite groups. As she entered the apartment the record changed to Lou Reed's *Take a Walk on the Wild Side*.

Funny, Eddie never played records. He never lit candles either, and the living room was alive with small black votive candles in stylish Art Deco holders.

She immediately knew he had someone there, and her stomach turned.

Resolutely she marched towards the bedroom, determined to confront the woman face to face.

Just get out. What are you pushing it for?

Why should I?

Because he isn't worth it.

She burst into the bedroom, and felt sick.

The woman wasn't a woman. The woman was a man with silky pale hair, a boyish face and a hairless, naked body.

"Excuse *me*," the creature said tartly. "Might we have a touch of privacy?"

Eddie did not say one word.

Bobby Mondella 1981

Bobby Mondella arrived at the wedding of Nichols Kline to Pammy Booser in a metallic gold Mercedes limousine, with tinted, bullet-proof windows, and three personal bodyguards in close attendance.

Hey — he'd figured it out. When you're a star — go for it. Live the life. His public expected it — indeed, they loved it. And so did he.

He wore a black shark-skin suit, with a Russian-style silk shirt, and a long, masculine-cut sable coat thrown casually over his shoulders. Accompanying him was Zella Raven, a six-foot black performance artist with a *Playboy* centrefold body, and a marine crew-cut. Zella wore thin strips of rubber and thigh-high boots.

The photographers and television crews went crazy as their feet hit the ground outside the private Pacific Palisades home where the wedding was to take place. They paused — in perfect synch — to allow exactly eight seconds of frantic picture-taking. Then they were on the move, flanked by bodyguards, the crowd of star-watchers cheering hoarsely.

That's why Bobby liked taking Zella to public events. She had the routine down pat, never put a foot wrong. She had the right image, and it *really* steamed up Nova when he was seen out with her. The claws emerged with a vengeance.

Nova Citroen. The woman had him under her spell. But he was gradually breaking away, and he'd finally decided that if she didn't want to go for some kind of commitment, it was over. He was a *star*, for crissakes. A superstar. Not the fledgling, uncertain twenty-seven-year-old she had first come on to. It was about time she realized that.

Bobby Mondella. Sex symbol. Thirty-one. Rich. Handsome. Powerful.

Yeah – powerful. Because with great fame came the power to do whatever you damned well pleased. He said "Jump" and people jumped. He told a joke – and everyone broke up. He demanded pizza at four in the morning and there it was. He pointed out a woman – any woman – and she was usually obtainable.

Hey – hey – hey – he could have anything and anyone he wanted. Except Nova. She might share his bed on occasion, but she belonged to Marcus Citroen, and up until now she had exhibited no signs of moving on.

Bobby knew it was because as far as she was concerned they *both* belonged to Marcus. She was married to the man, and he was under contract to him.

A breakable contract. He had been meeting with Nichols Kline's lawyers for months trying to work out a way to go. After all, Nichols Hit City were offering him a better deal than he'd ever had with Blue Cadillac. With Blue Cadillac he was the singer they'd discovered and made into something. With Nichols Hit City he had no history – he was a world-famous superstar, and the contract they were tempting him with reflected that.

"There's no contract can't be broken," said Arnie Torterelli, one of Nichols's business associates. "You want out of Blue Cadillac – you got it. Leave everything to our lawyers. They'll spring you. No fuckin' problem."

Now the day was drawing near, and Bobby was ready to fly. All he had to do was hope Nova would fly with him.

*

The turnout for Nichols Kline's marriage to Pammy Booser

was eclectic – a mixed group of guests ranging from bank presidents and captains of industry to rock stars, well-endowed starlets, and representatives of life in the Hollywood fast lane. Neither marital candidate appeared to have any family. Nichols's best man was a long-time old friend of his from Miami, Carmine Sicily, a stooped, gaunt man in his late fifties, with sinister slit eyes and grey hair. Bobby remembered seeing him in The Chainsaw with Nichols all those years ago. He had the sort of face it wasn't easy to forget.

"Get your eyes on that dude," Zella whispered to Bobby as they watched Nichols and Carmine make the walk to take up their position in front of the Justice of the Peace who was to perform the non-religious marriage ceremony in the garden of Arnie Torterelli's house. "He's a *major* Miami drug king. And I mean Mister Big."

Bobby nodded, although he didn't believe her. Zella liked to think she knew everything about everybody. Sometimes she was wrong.

Looks-wise Zella Raven was sensational. Conversation-wise she did not grab his attention. In his entire life there had only been two women he'd seriously wanted. Sharleen and now Nova.

Unfortunately he'd never been more than friends with Sharleen, and although Nova and he were lovers, up until now she remained elusive, running the relationship on her terms.

No more. The choice would soon be hers.

Pammy Booser appeared on the arm of Arnie Torterelli. She tottered on stiletto heels, her white lace dress a Fredericks-of-Hollywood dream come true. Behind her trailed a gaggle of over-age girls-about-town – all with their eyes open for the main chance.

"No style," muttered Zella. Sometimes she was right on.

Pammy Booser and Nichols Kline were pronounced man and wife, and the wedding party progressed.

Married for the first time at nearly fifty, Nichols proceeded to get well and truly drunk. The many guests had now taken over the tented reception area of Arnie Torterelli's large house. Seated at round tables, they dined on lobster cocktail, and veal in a rich cream sauce. Bobby found himself at the top table, with Arnie's large wife on one side and Zella on the other. Beside Zella sat Arnie himself, and then Pammy, with a proud and flushed Nichols next to her. Her maid-of-honour, a fading beauty with stoned eyes and slack lips, kept Nichols's other side warm, while the sinister-looking Carmine Sicily patted her on the knee with less than fatherly intent. Rounding out the table of twelve was a sexy female singer with enormous breasts and a voice to match, her manager husband, and Kris Phoenix, star of Nichols Hit City's premier recording group, The Wild Ones. He was with a girl called Mikki.

Zella was more than pleased to be seated beside Kris Phoenix, but she couldn't wait to inform Bobby that Mikki was an infamous super-groupie. "I'm real surprised she hasn't given *you* a whirl," Zella drawled.

"Maybe tonight I'll get lucky," Bobby commented dryly, motioning for the waiter to refill his glass of bourbon.

"Over my dead tits an' ass, baby!" joked Zella, threateningly.

After dinner there was dancing. And in between there were speeches. Arnie made a lengthy speech, followed by his wife, and then Carmine Sicily – whose ponderous voice nearly sent everyone to sleep. Pammy stood up next – cloying insincerity at its very best. And finally Nichols – a drunk, sentimental, and genuinely happy man. "To my lovely bride," he said, raising his glass in a final toast.

Both Bobby and Kris Phoenix observed Pammy surreptitiously grope Carmine Sicily under the table. They caught each other watching and laughed.

Kris leaned across and shook Bobby's hand. "S'good t'meet you, mate. I'm a fan."

Bobby smiled. "Hey – that's fine t'know, because it's mutual. I really like your songs, in fact I wish I'd written some of them myself."

Pleased and flattered, Kris said, "Yeah? Which ones?"

"*Skinny Little Slider* is a big favourite. Oh yeah, and *Lonesome Mornin'*. I'm into those words, man. Shades of early Otis Redding."

"I wish," Kris said ruefully.

"No – I mean it."

Kris couldn't hide his delight. This was the kind of recognition he really appreciated. "Yeah?"

"You got it, man, you got the talent."

"That's somethin', comin' from you."

As soon as Zella and Mikki went off to find the ladies' room, Kris moved over next to Bobby. Soon they were talking in earnest, about writing and songs, early influences and the magic of the late, great Sam Cooke and other legends. By the time the girls returned they were too interested in each other to stop.

"Wonderful!" sighed Zella, turning her attention to Arnie, who, if he could shake his plump wife, would be hers forever.

Mikki spotted Del Delgardo across the room, and sidled over.

Pammy hit the dance area with Carmine. His bony hands dug into not-so-firm flesh beneath tight white lace.

Nichols danced with every one of Pammy's sad-sack girl-friends, including her maid-of-honour, who whispered in his ear that if he was ever lonely, unhappy, or merely horny, he should call her, as she had the perfect cure for such maladies.

Looking around, Bobby decided if he ever got married it would be a strictly private affair. Then again, who needed marriage anyway?

"You ever bin' married?" he asked Kris.

Kris grinned. "Once, mate. Once was enough. Y'can take it, an' shove it. *That's* what *I* think of the whole bleedin' institution."

Bobby laughed. "Right on!"

They cemented their newfound friendship with a conspiratorial wink in each other's direction.

Kris Phoenix 1981

To everyone's great surprise Michelle Hanley-Bogart became a
fixture in Kris's life. It happened after Chicago. And by the
time the tour reached New York City, where The Wild Ones
were due to play two sold-out performances in Madison Square
Garden, they were inseparable.

"Jesus Christ!" Buzz complained jealously. "She's a friggin'
slag. She's gotta bead on everyone's friggin' dick except the
Pope. An' if 'e sang, she'd 'ave 'im too!"

"Very funny," Kris replied. "You're just pissed because she
doesn't want to know about you."

"Yeah. Fuckin' her must be like doin' it with the rock 'n' roll
hall of friggin' fame. You're welcome, mate. She could suck the
chrome right off the bumper of a 1958 Cadillac!"

In New York Mikki introduced Kris to her disparate circle of
friends. They included a tall gay clothes designer of international
repute, a wild-eyed cabaret singer with spider eyelashes who
snorted cocaine for breakfast, a decadent European princess who
lent her name to a line of expensive cosmetics, and China Wal-
lineska – Mikki's best friend – a short girl with a wiry mass of
frizzy hair and generous curves. China was an artist, and lived
untidily in a Greenwich Village loft.

"She gives great parties," Mikki informed Kris. "And if she
likes you – she'll paint you."

"What makes you think I'd fancy being painted?" he asked warily.

"Because it's an honour," Mikki replied, adding casually, "China's quite famous, you know. Kind of an Andy Warhol for the eighties."

Madison Square Garden was the thrill of a lifetime. Their latest single, *Dirty Bits*, was number one, and the album of the same name was just entering the stores in huge amounts. Nichols Hit City were doing the job. Kris couldn't help being pleased with their distribution and sales, but deep down he wished The Wild Ones were with one of the giants. Blue Cadillac for instance.

When he mentioned his thoughts to Doktor Head, the man laughed. "You can't get any higher than number one," he said. "What's the difference?"

"*I* think it's the difference between driving a Ferrari or a Ford," Mikki joined in. "They both get you there, but only one gets you there in style."

"Yeah, that's it," Kris agreed. "Exactly what I was tryin' to say."

Doktor Head glared at Mikki. He'd had enough trouble with her when, at the tender age of sixteen, she'd attached herself to Michael Hollywood. They'd had five months together, breaking up a few weeks before his death.

At sixteen she'd been a pain. At twenty-four she was impossible. There was nothing worse than a rich groupie with connections.

"I know Marcus Citroen, the President of Blue Cadillac, very well," she said, as if reading his thoughts. "Why don't I set up a meeting?"

"No," Doktor Head replied, vehemently. "Any setting up I can do myself."

"Hey, listen, if she *knows* Marcus Citroen—" Kris began. "As a matter of fact I met him myself once."

"Forget it," Doktor Head snapped, grimacing wildly. "You think I just came over on the banana boat? I can get to Marcus anytime I want. Right now we're with Hit City. Our record's number one, and we are staying *right* where we are." He glared at Mikki, who glared back. "And another thing, don't forget you promised to show your ugly face at Nichols's wedding tomorrow. I've booked you on a Pan Am flight first thing in the morning."

"Mikki too?"

"Considering you're joined at the hip," he said sarcastically, "would I do anything else?"

"How about Buzz?"

"He won't go."

"Why not?"

"Ask *him*."

"Are you coming?"

"It's a twenty-four-hour trip. Do you really need me to hold your hand, or can I stay here and take care of business?"

"You can go fly a fuckin' kite for all I care."

*

On the plane Mikki started. She had been leading up to it for some time.

"How come you let your manager tell you what to do?"

Kris shrugged. "It's what a manager's for, ennit?"

"A manager is supposed to do what *you* want him to do."

"It's not just me. There's the rest of the group."

"Oh, yes, I forgot," she said sneeringly. "Everything you make has to be split four ways. *Very* smart."

"It's only fair."

"To whom? *You're* the main talent."

"We're a group."

"Listen to what I'm saying, Kris. *You're* the star. *You* write the best songs. *You* sing them. Really it should be Kris Phoenix and the Wild Ones."

He grinned, liking the thought, but knowing they'd all freak. "Sure, Buzz would *really* love that. It'd go down a treat."

Mikki wasn't about to quit. "Remember Diana Ross? Originally she was just a Supreme. Teddy Pendergrass was one of Harold Melvin's Bluenotes. Rod Stewart was a Small Face, and David Ruffin a Temptation. You want me to go on? Or are you getting the message?"

Yes. He was getting the message – loud and clear. And quite

frankly, by the time they reached L.A., he realized she did have a point. Kris Phoenix and the Wild Ones. It sounded good, and maybe he deserved it. After all, he *was* the one doing most of the work, *and* receiving the bulk of the fan mail. Buzz was out of it most of the time, too stoned to take anything seriously. Rasta played his drums with no great outstanding talent. Fingers was good, excellent in fact – but they weren't screaming and yelling for Fingers. The truth of the matter was Mikki happened to be right. And when they got back to New York he was going to insist that his name preceded The Wild Ones.

"If they don't like it you can always leave and become a solo artist," Mikki suggested slyly.

He'd never thought of that before . . .

*

At Nichols Kline's wedding, Bobby Mondella fired Kris with enthusiasm. The guy was the greatest, they had so much in common, and although their styles were completely different it would be a real blast to try something together one of these days.

"Where's your base?" Kris asked.

"Here in L.A.," Bobby replied. "I've got me a little shack over in Hancock Park. Maybe you and your lady would like to drop by later."

"We'd love it," Kris replied, looking around for Mikki, who appeared to be on the missing list.

"She's talkin' to Del Delgardo," Zella offered. "Shall I get her for you?"

Del Delgardo. The enemy. Del Delgardo, who'd dumped the Nightmares quite some time ago and was now a big solo artist. Fucking poxy-faced wanker. Kris felt the burn. After Willow, he'd promised himself he would never get jealous over any woman again.

Too late. Mikki had him. She was addictive.

He wondered if Del Delgardo was part of her past, or maybe she had him in mind for her future. Goddamn!

Zella unwound her rangy body from the chair. "I'll tell her we're splitting."

"Don't bother," he said quickly. He had no intention of chasing. "If she wants to come she will."

"Yeah, but how's she gonna know we're leaving?" Zella asked logically.

"She'll know," he said, rising, just as Pammy Booser Kline grabbed him from behind.

"Kris Phoenix," she slurred, rubbing herself against him. "One dance for the bride, huh, baby?"

"I don't do this sort of dancin', luv."

"One dance," she insisted, giving him no further chance to get out of it as she dragged him towards the dance floor, where she ground her crotch against his and whispered suggestively in his ear.

He tried to distance himself, but she was having none of it. "I've always fancied you, didja know that?"

"Leave it out, darlin'," he said firmly. "You only just got married, or did you forget?"

What a slag! A few whirls and he made his escape, said goodbye to Nichols, and found Mikki back at their table where she belonged. "Having a good time?" he asked casually, waiting to see if she volunteered any information.

"Not bad," she replied, hugging his arm. "Zella tells me we're going over to Bobby's."

Why did he have to get involved with a girl who had once whiled away the years as groupie numero uno to the entire rock world?

Just lucky, I guess, he thought grimly.

*

Bobby Mondella's house was a revelation. Kris was impressed.

"You mean people really live like this?" he asked, after a tour of the mansion.

"Remind me never to take you home to mommy and daddy," Mikki murmured, with a secret smile.

"Yeah, man," Bobby replied. "It's the rock star dream come true. You gotta get yourself the house, an' the pool, an' the cars. The whole bit. You can't miss out."

"I still live in England," Kris reflected glumly. "By the time

I've paid taxes, livin' expenses, and slipped a few bob to my family, I'm broke."

"You've gotta be kidding."

"Don't forget, what I make gets shared with the guys and Fingers. An' what with road costs, lawyers, my ex-wife, my kid, accountants, our manager ..." He trailed off. "Life's a bitch—"

"And then you die!" chorused Mikki, Zella and Bobby, breaking up.

They spent the rest of the night listening to soul and blues records while sharing a joint or two. Sam Cooke and Otis Redding, Chuck Berry and Jackie Wilson. All the old-time greats. Kris couldn't remember when he'd had a better time.

"I'm pleased to see you can relax," Mikki said during the limo drive back to the hotel.

"Who, me?" He laughed. "I'm always bleedin' relaxed."

"No you're not," she chided gently. "You spend your whole time worrying about something. It's either Buzz, or your son, where your record is on the charts, concert dates, back-up musicians—"

"Whoa! You makin' me sound like a neurotic nut."

"Well, you are."

"No I'm not."

"Yes you are."

"Mikki, luv?"

"Yes, Kris?"

"Whyn't you just shut up, an' get down on your knees where you belong."

She began to giggle. "I like a man with nothing on his mind but sex!"

"On your knees."

"What about the driver?"

"*Fuck* the driver. He can find his own blow job later!"

In the morning they had to leave the hotel at nine to fly back to New York in time for a limo ride to Philadelphia and a late concert. At exactly ten to nine Mikki dropped her bombshell. "I'm not coming," she said, wrinkling her pretty nose.

"What are you talkin' about?" he demanded angrily.

She wouldn't look him in the eye. "I've got business to do," she said vaguely.

"*What* fucking business?"

"Like family stuff. Trusts, investments. I really should take care of it while I'm out here."

He threw her a disgusted look. "I don't believe this crap."

Smoothing down her skirt, she said, "I'll meet you in Washington."

He knew she was staying for Del Delgardo. This made him determined not to mention his name. Why give her the satisfaction? "Suit yourself," he said, switching to don't-care tactics.

Women. Fuck 'em. He could live without their shit.

He returned to New York alone; performed in Philadelphia; partied with buxom twins; caught Buzz shooting heroin; told Doktor Head from now on it was going to be Kris Phoenix and the Wild Ones; ended the American tour in Washington – where Mikki never showed; and flew back to England.

Another change was in the works, he could feel it coming on.

Rafealla 1981

Within six months Rafealla was as settled in Rio de Janeiro as if she had lived there forever. "I *love* this place," she told Odile. "Love it, love it, *love* it! I *never* want to leave."

Odile smiled wisely. She was pregnant with her first baby, and quite content and happy herself. "*Never* is a strong statement. I'll tell you something – if it wasn't for the dreadful poverty all around us, *I* wouldn't want to leave here either."

Rafealla nodded. It was true. Such an affluent society, living in such an exquisite city, ringed with the most appalling slums she had ever seen. They were called *favelas*. Muddy hillsides packed with ramshackle tin huts. Slum dwellings that housed generations of families living side by side in rat-infested hovels.

"I know," she agreed. "It's shocking."

"But not our problem," sighed Odile. "So we mustn't let it bother us."

"I guess," Rafealla said unsurely, although deep down she felt there must be *something* they could do.

When they first arrived in Rio, she and Jon Jon lived with Odile and Rupert in their comfortable house, but after six weeks she felt they were imposing, and began to look for an apartment of her own. By this time she had phoned her mother in England and told her she was staying, and was instructing her lawyers to begin divorce proceedings against Eddie:

Anna was more than relieved. "I sensed all was not well, my darling," she'd said sympathetically. "But why run so far? Couldn't you have just moved back to the country with us?"

Rafealla decided it was too complicated to start explaining that she needed the distance, the breathing space. For once in her life she wished to be completely independent.

Money was no problem. At age twenty-five she was to inherit a large trust fund from her father, and even though she was only twenty-one it was not difficult for her lawyers in England to arrange for an adequate advance.

She found a modern, sunny apartment with a magnificent sea view near Copacabana beach, and she and Jon Jon, plus a stern English nanny Anna sent over, moved in.

Free at last! She hadn't heard a word from Eddie, and was not surprised. What could he say? Getting caught in the act was hardly conducive to a long, meaningful discussion about their future together.

"What actually happened?" Odile kept on begging for information.

Rafealla merely shrugged. "I don't know and I don't care. I never want to set eyes on Eddie again."

"Hmmm . . ." Odile said. "You'll have to let him visit Jon Jon."

Rafealla knew she would have to do no such thing. "We'll see," she said mysteriously.

She did not reveal the discovery of her husband's homosexuality to anyone. It was her secret, and as long as he caused her no trouble it would remain that way. For six months his silence had been constant. Their divorce was proceeding without any problems.

In Rio, she met a lot of new friends. At first she hung out with Odile and Rupert's affluent group of young marrieds, fending off the advances of all the eligible bachelors Odile regularly produced. But she soon grew bored, and got herself a job in an art gallery – the same sort of job she had wanted in London. This led to her meeting a different mix of people – artists, designers, and art collectors. She found most of them interesting, in fact she even went out on a few dates. However, once a man wanted more than conversation, it was over.

The owner of the gallery, a soignée divorcee in her forties, suggested she try older men. "You'll enjoy yourself *so* much more, my dear. A mature man *knows* how to treat a woman."

Reluctantly she allowed herself to be fixed up with Jorge Maraco, a man old enough to be her father, and found him comfortable to be with. He didn't jump on her at the end of the evening – which made a refreshing change. His conversation was interesting. And in his own rather staid way he was reasonably attractive.

On their second date she discovered he was a billionaire industrialist whose wife of eighteen years had tragically committed suicide four years earlier.

"I'm sorry," she said quietly. "It must have been a terrible ordeal."

Six weeks later he announced that he wanted to marry her. "The time has come for me to start my life afresh," he said gravely. "And you – Rafealla, my darling – are the woman for me."

Her refusal startled him – he was a man used to always getting his own way. Determinedly he began to pursue her in earnest, showering her with expensive gifts – all of which she returned – and dozens of red roses daily, giving the apartment a delightfully festive appearance.

"What *is* going on?" Odile asked, anxious for a full report. "He's a *very* important man, you know."

"And a very nice one," Rafealla replied truthfully. "Only not for me."

"Too old, I guess. I hear he has a daughter our age."

"Age doesn't matter."

"Sure it does."

A week later, Odile gave birth to her first baby, a ten-pound girl with blue eyes and no hair. Rafealla rushed to the hospital. Rupert needed her support. He was a nervous wreck, especially when they took the baby home and discovered that the young local girl they had hired to look after it didn't have any experience.

"What are we going to do?" wailed Odile.

"No problem," Rafealla said calmly. "Jon Jon's nanny will come and work for you, and I'll take your girl. After all, Jon is at nursery school most of the day – so he doesn't really need a proper nanny anymore."

A very sensible solution. Everyone was happy, except Jorge, who kept on asking Rafealla to find out who this strange girl was she'd brought into her home to look after Jon Jon, with no experience and no references.

"She's okay," Rafealla insisted. "Her aunt works for Rupert's partner."

"That's not good enough," he scolded sternly.

The girl's name was Juana. Small, slight and quiet, she worked hard, cleaning the apartment as well as taking care of Jon Jon, who took to her immediately. All week she lived in, and at weekends she went home, returning early Monday morning. As far as Rafealla was concerned it was the perfect arrangement. She loved being alone at the weekends with her son. It was fun to take him to the beach, swim, and play games.

Jorge Maraco hovered on the sidelines of her life, waiting patiently to be more than just a charming escort. She met his daughter, Cristina, and many of his friends. She spent time at his magnificent, heavily guarded mansion – for Jorge had a morbid fear of kidnappers. Being with him was safe and unthreatening. He could protect her from the world, and maybe she *would* marry him when her divorce was final. Why not?

So far she had not slept with him, and he didn't push. If nothing else he was a patient man, prepared to wait.

Both Odile and Rupert were fiercely against it. "He's much too old for you," they both said. "Are you mad? You don't need his money. What's the big attraction?"

Ha! Big attraction. She'd had *that* with Eddie, and look where it got her.

One Monday morning Juana didn't show up. By Wednesday Rafealla was worried, for she had no idea how to contact the girl, she only knew that her family lived in the notorious *favela*.

"You're lucky she's gone," Jorge said, in an *I-told-you-so* voice. "What did she steal?"

"Nothing," Rafealla replied hotly. "Don't be so quick to judge."

"You, my dear, do not understand," he said pompously. "Stealing is a way of existence for the slum people. It means nothing to them."

"How would *you* know?"

"Because I have lived next to these peasants all my life."

"Then it's a shame you haven't done anything with all your money and all your power to help them. I think the contrast between the very rich and the very poor in this country is disgusting."

"Oh, do you, young lady? And I suppose you think you know exactly what you are talking about."

"I know what I see."

"Perhaps you only see what you want to."

Soon they were embroiled in a fierce argument, with Jorge finally stalking from her apartment.

She made Jon Jon dinner, bathed him, and tucked him safely into bed, her little spiky-haired boy with the bright blue eyes. He was her life, her future. And whatever she did had to be the very best for him.

For a moment her mind drifted back to that cold London night four years ago. Kris Phoenix, brash and cocky – a typical rock star without a care in the world except himself. A ride around Berkeley Square in a chauffeured car. Hot, sticky, fast sex, and everything changed . . .

Perhaps marrying Jorge Maraco wasn't such a brilliant idea. Maybe she should try having a life first.

The doorbell rang, and thinking it was probably Jorge returning to apologize she did not bother to check the peep-hole.

Upon opening the door, she came face to face with the best-looking male she had ever seen. He was Brazilian, about her age, with long, black curly hair, green eyes, and a mouth she wanted to touch. He wore blue jeans, a workshirt and sneakers. With a jolt she realized their outfits were matching.

For a moment there was silence as they both checked each

other out. He was obviously as struck by her looks as she was with his. Instinctively she touched her hair, tied back in a ponytail.

"Uh . . . are *you* Mrs Le Serre?" he asked at last.

Recovering her composure, she nodded. Mrs Mafair was a name she'd dropped as fast as she could.

He smiled. White, even teeth. A devastating smile.

Once she had thought Eddie handsome. He was nothing compared to this man.

"Can I help you?" she asked, trying not to stare.

"I'm Juana's brother."

"Who?"

"Juana. Your girl. She work for you."

"Oh, Juana," she said, sounding like an idiot.

"Maybe you are wondering why she hasn't come in this week."

"Is she sick?"

"Food poisoning."

"How awful."

"Shrimp. She eat the shrimp and swell up like a basketball."

They were having this perfectly simple conversation about Juana and her problem, but really they were having a completely different conversation as their eyes met and spoke their own secret language.

Rafealla felt uncomfortably warm. Her eyes darted down to his jeans and quickly observed that he felt as hot as she did.

"Would you like a cold drink?" she asked quickly.

"Maybe a beer," he replied. "Before I go to work."

"What do you do?"

"I'm a musician."

"How interesting. What instrument do you play?"

"Many things. Guitar, drums, flute, and I sing."

She grinned. "Multi-talented, huh?"

He grinned back. "If you say so."

"I'll get your beer," she said, wondering why her heart was pounding so fast. "Please come in."

He followed her into the apartment, looked around and gave a low whistle. "Nice."

"I like it," she said, going to the fridge. "Is American beer okay?"

Nodding, he walked over to the counter that separated the kitchen from the living room.

Clumsily she pulled the ring on the can, and before she could prevent it, the beer frothed over the top. They both reached for a nearby box of Kleenex, and felt the burn as their hands touched. Hastily she pulled away, pouring the golden liquid into a glass which she passed to him.

"I tell you something, you're not like I expected," he said, sipping his drink.

"What did you expect?"

"Juana, she always talk about the grand English lady she work for. I imagine you older. Another thing – you don't look English to me."

"A quarter. My mother is half English and half French, and my father was half American and half Ethiopian. He died when I was seven. We lived in Paris, and then London."

Why was she telling a complete stranger her life history?

Gazing at her with disconcertingly direct green eyes, he said, "Juana will be back next Monday. Fine for you?"

She nodded, remarking, "Your English is perfect."

"Not bad. I taught myself."

"Was it difficult?"

Shrugging, he said, "Sometimes. But nothing good come easy. Right?" Finishing his beer he walked towards the door. "So I say goodbye, Mrs Le Serre."

"Goodbye," she said, breathlessly flustered.

When he'd left the apartment she realized she didn't even know his name.

*

"God!" exclaimed Odile. "What a fuss! *Why* do we have to go to this funny little nightclub? It's not one of the in places, you know."

"Don't be such a snob," Rafealla replied. "I've heard it's great."

"From whom?" Rupert inquired. "Not Jorge, I bet."

"She's put Jorge on hold, thank goodness," said Odile. "Her

apartment looks like a florist's shop. The poor man is obviously distraught."

"Oh, it's the poor man now, is it?" Rafealla said tartly. "Make up your mind. Last week you thought he was the worst thing that ever happened to me."

"He *is* one of the richest men in South America," Rupert remarked.

"So *what?*" Rafealla replied defiantly. "I'm fed up with you two. One minute he's right for me, the next he's wrong. And you've both said I don't need his stupid money."

"True," said Odile.

"Very true," agreed Rupert.

"Can we go now?" Rafealla asked impatiently.

With a touch of clever detective work she had found out Juana's brother's name – it was Luiz Oliveira – *and* where he worked, a club called Pussy Satin. Further inquiries revealed that it was a tourist joint, featuring nude dancers and gambling in the back room. Hardly a place she could take Jorge to, which is why she had conned Odile and Rupert into going with her.

The Pussy Satin club lived up to its name. Gaudy and noisy, it was a beehive of frantic activity. Colourfully dressed hostesses were scattered around the place in scanty, body-hugging clothes. There was a long, crowded bar, and up on a small stage a combo of musicians played lively samba music. On the dance floor, sweating, happy bodies swayed to the beat.

"Good God!" exclaimed Rupert. "Some dive!"

"Hiya, honey," greeted a comely woman in red ruffles and a turban, her tanned plump midriff temptingly exposed. "Wanna table?"

"I suppose so," Rupert replied gruffly.

"For three," added Odile, trying to avoid the eye of a fat man who leaned against the bar winking suggestively at her.

The woman in red ruffles passed them over to a young, undersized waiter. He led them to a table at the front, demanded an exorbitant cover charge, and asked Rupert if he required a hostess.

"Certainly not!" Rupert snapped, quite affronted.

The waiter shrugged. What did he care as long as they tipped well? "Champagne?" he asked automatically.

"No," said Rupert.

"Yes," said Odile. She turned to her husband with a winning smile. "Let's enjoy it now we're here. At least it's different. I'm so fed up with all those boring business dinners we have to go to."

"All right," said Rupert, relenting. "Bring us a bottle of Dom Perignon."

"House champagne only," the waiter said stoically.

"Bring it anyway," Odile said.

Casually Rafealla glanced beyond the milling bodies on the dance floor to check out the musicians. There were five of them, and none of them was Luiz. Concealing a sharp stab of disappointment she turned to Odile. "I told you it was different," she said, trying to sound cheerful.

"You don't have to convince *me*," Odile replied enthusiastically. "I adore the place. It's got such atmosphere, and the music is wonderful."

"Wanna dance, handsome?" A frizzy-haired hostess in a blue fish-net dress approached their table, her flashing eyes settling on Rupert.

He pursed his lips. "No thank you."

"Go *on*. Live dangerously," laughed Odile.

"Yes. Do it!" encouraged Rafealla. "I can remember when you used to be *fun*. Now you're becoming like a boring old fart!"

"Thanks a *lot*, little sister."

"Go for it," urged Odile.

"I dare you!" added Rafealla.

"Right!" Rupert said, jumping up. "You asked for it, you two nags."

The woman in blue fish-net beamed, revealing a single gold front tooth in a sea of crooked white ones. "C'mon, honey-pie," she tempted, wiggling her fat bottom. "Let us go *shake* it *out!*"

Without further hesitation Rupert hit the dance floor, his English manners loosening up considerably as the samba beat enveloped him.

"Come on," giggled Odile, leaping to her feet. "We'd better join them before he gets into trouble!"

Unable to resist the sensuous rhythm, Rafealla rose also, and began to dance. It didn't matter that she had no partner, the music was companion enough, the melodious Brazilian beat soon sweeping over her.

Several glasses of champagne later the three of them were feeling no pain. Rupert was methodically dancing with each and every hostess at five bucks a throw, while Odile and Rafealla warded off the amorous attentions of several stray men who hovered near their table. When Madame Red Ruffles announced it was cabaret time, they were reluctant to settle down.

"This is the best bloody night I've had in years," Rupert raved. "We've got to bring *everyone* here."

Rafealla collapsed in her chair, fanning herself with the drinks menu. When she looked up Luiz was sitting on a stool at the side of the stage tuning his guitar.

"An' now — ladies an' gennelman," said Madame Red Ruffles. "We are delighted to welcome MISS TOP OF PUSSY SATIN — the wunnerful EVE."

A tall, over-made-up woman, in a spangly outfit, descended from a suspended bird-cage. She was clad in silver from head to toe, including a cloche hat and very high-heeled shoes.

While Luiz picked out a soulful rendition of *The Girl from Ipanema* on his guitar, Eve, very slowly, began to take it all off. She started with her hat, from which she shook a mane of dyed silver hair, ending up in nothing but high heels, a minute G-string, and sparkling pasties covering each large breast.

"What an *amazing* piece of crumpet!" breathed Rupert admiringly.

"Do shut *up*," scolded Odile. "They're probably silicone."

Eve paused, striking a wide-legged pose, suggestively fingering the two pasties concealing her nipples from an expectant audience. And then, with a sudden flourish, she removed the stuck-on devices, exposing darkly swollen nipples.

Rupert gulped, nearly choking on his drink.

"Typical!" Odile snorted.

Eve smirked knowingly, flicking a hidden catch, allowing her G-string to fall away.

Total nudity for several seconds, then the stage went black.

When the lights came on again Eve was gone, but Luiz remained, singing of lost love and balmy nights in an appealingly husky voice.

Rafealla's heart went out to him. He looked so handsome, and his voice was so terrific, but who cared? Everyone was recovering from Eve – the big horse. He deserved better than this.

Over the next few weeks she went back to the Pussy Satin quite a few times, dragging into service anyone who would go with her. Although she never got a chance to speak to Luiz, he was well aware of her presence. Their eyes conducted a private, intimate conversation, of which they were both excruciatingly aware. Seeing him made her happy and sad, crazy and calm. She was almost in love with a man she'd hardly spoken to. Oh God! It could never work out, they came from two different worlds. And yet . . .

Jorge continued to pursue her hotly. He was determined they would be together, and she found it difficult deflecting his insistent attention, but right now she wasn't ready to make any lasting decisions.

Odile and Rupert were going on a trip to England with their new baby to show her off to the grandparents. Rafealla and Jon Jon were supposed to accompany them, but at the last minute she declined, finally allowing Jon Jon to go without her.

That night she hired a car and chauffeur, and went to the Pussy Satin alone. Her heart was bouncing around like a ping-pong ball, but instinctively she knew he would never make the first move, and it had to be done.

By this time they knew her in the club, and gave her a front table. Nervously she ordered champagne and waited.

As soon as he was finished on stage he slid into the empty chair beside her. "It seems you like it here," he said. "I am sorry you do."

"Why?" she challenged.

"Because it is no place for you. You don't belong with these people."

"God! You're not a snob too, are you? Rupert is bad enough."

"Who is Rupert?"

"My brother."

"A smart man."

"Bullshit!"

Fixing her with an intense look he said, "What do you want from me?"

"Take me home and we'll talk."

"Seriously."

"Yes, we can talk seriously if you like."

"Don't play with me, English lady."

"I'm *not* English," she said furiously. "Do I *look* English?"

Softening, he said, "You look beautiful." With a deep sigh of regret he added, "Too beautiful, too rich. And whatever we may both feel, we should not be together. I know these things."

Persuasively she gave it her all. "Take me home, Luiz. Please – take me home *now*."

*

Antonio Carlos Jobim on the stereo, more champagne, the apartment lit only by the glow of the street lamps.

Just kissing was a trip she'd never experienced before. His lips so cool, his tongue so hot. They stood up against each other in the dark apartment exploring – tasting, indulging in long, lingering soul kisses.

He was in no hurry and neither was she. They'd waited since the first moment they'd met, and now the time was here and there was no rush.

Running his hands through her long hair he softly murmured her name, "Rafealla, ah . . . Rafealla."

"Luiz," she whispered back, feeling the soft, fine curls at the base of his neck. "Ah . . . Luiz."

Slowly his hands moved down to her shoulders, and tantalizingly played with the thin straps of her dress, pushing them up and down.

She wanted him to pull the damn dress off. She wanted to feel his hands on her skin. She just wanted him . . .

Slowly, at last, he peeled the top of her dress down, caressing her breasts, gently at first, his fingertips barely brushing her nipples, until finally his touch grew stronger and soon he replaced his fingers with his mouth.

Sighing with pleasure she reached towards his hardness, releasing him, murmuring his name.

Together they sank to the floor. Cosmic twins, alike in every way. Somehow she knew exactly what would please him, while he anticipated her every need.

They were together. As far as she was concerned it was all that mattered.

*

In the morning he was gone. She waited for him to come to her apartment or call. He didn't. She went to the Pussy Satin, only to be told he no longer worked there. Meanwhile Juana had packed up and left with no explanation or goodbye.

One night and it was over.

Luiz was gone, and she had no way of ever finding him again.

Bobby Mondella 1981

"You're making the biggest mistake of your life," Marcus Citroen said. His voice on the phone was tempered steel, but it didn't frighten Bobby — nothing frightened a superstar. Goddammit! He was too big to be touched by anyone or anything. Right now he was merely angry that Marcus had him trapped. He didn't need this. The dumb lawyers were supposed to have handled everything without him getting involved.

"Hey," he said calmly. "It's my mistake, an' if I wanna make it, I guess I can."

"You're screwing me, Bobby. I want you to be fully aware of that."

I'm screwing your wife, just like you screwed Sharleen for all those years.

"Yeah, well, life goes on. I'm sorry you're not happy, Marcus, but business is business."

"You have a lesson to learn, Bobby." Marcus sounded ominous. "And believe me, you'll learn it with Hit City — the hard way. You have no idea what you're getting into with those people." He put the phone down, leaving a sharp dialling tone in Bobby's ear.

Who the fuck did the dude think he was? Some asshole businessman, that's all. While he, Bobby Mondella, was a star, and let no one forget it.

Whistling quietly to himself he checked out his image in the mirror. Nova was on her way over, confrontation time was here, and he wanted to be sure he looked his very best. She'd never been to his house before, and the fact that she'd agreed to meet him on his own territory was a coup.

Mrs Citroen was coming to tea, and everything had to be just right.

Taking another sip of bourbon, he decided to change from the all-white outfit he had on to an all-black one. She preferred him in black, said it gave him a sleeker look.

Sleek, hell. Nobody could beat Bobby Mondella when it came to looking sleek. He was the biggest superstar soul singer in the world, and soon he would be moving on. Nichols Kline had so many great plans – number one being a movie in which he would star.

Hey – Bobby Mondella – movie star. Yeah! He could go for that.

The new deal and getting away from Blue Cadillac had taken some working out. Fortunately Arnie Torterelli's lawyers were that rare combination – street smart and college educated. They'd handled everything, and Bobby was delighted. Moving to Nichols Hit City was about the best decision he'd ever made.

More bourbon soothed his throat. Lately he'd taken to waking up with it, and keeping a glass nearby at all times. Booze did not affect him, just kept him nicely mellowed out, because the pressures of superstardom were unbelievable.

Hey – he didn't do drugs – just cocaine once in a while before a show. So what was wrong with drinking – as long as he never took it too far?

The all-black outfit suited him admirably. He glanced at his solid gold Rolex. Nova should be arriving any minute. She knew the score, all he needed was an answer.

*

"You look tired, Bobby."

"I do?"

"Yes, you do."

Is that all she had to say — *You look tired, Bobby.* How about *Your house is sensational* or *I'm thrilled with the news* or even *Yes, I've made my decision — I'm leaving Marcus.*

"I guess it's all the hard work I've bin' doin'," he replied.

"Maybe even all the alcohol you're consuming."

She could talk. She drank champagne by the bucket.

It had been six weeks since he'd seen her. She was elegant as ever in a beige suit with her usual crocodile accessories and striking gold jewellery. Her white-blonde hair was pulled back into a neat chignon.

Mrs Citroen did not have matching collar and cuffs. Between her classy legs there was a patch of thick, black hair, overgrown and dense, and sexy as hell. The contrast was a real turn-on.

"How was your trip?" he asked, changing the subject.

"The Orient is always fascinating," she replied, reaching for a cigarette.

"So I've heard."

Gazing directly into his eyes she said, "You're a fool, you know."

He leaned towards her, lighting her cigarette. "Why's that?"

"Because you left Blue Cadillac without asking me. You did something extremely stupid."

She talked to him as if he were a child. It burned the hell out of him. "Tell me what you think's so stupid?"

"Leaving Marcus."

"*Fuck* Marcus," he exploded. "I don't give a shit about him, and neither should you. He's screwed around on you since the day you married him. You've told me about the games he plays with you, and his sick carryings on. Maybe *you* can forgive and forget, but lady, *I* certainly can't."

Drawing strongly on her cigarette she said, "I've managed to live with it."

"Yeah, well maybe *you* can. Let me repeat myself — *I* can't. So I've done something about it. I've gotten out. An' now I want you to come with me. Don't you understand, woman, I'm giving you a chance to escape."

Shaking her head ruefully she said, "Bobby, when we started

this affair, that's *all* it was – an affair. Somehow it grew into something more. But never did I say I would leave Marcus."

"You didn't have to say it. Just *do* it. I've got everything you'll ever need, baby. We can have a great life together."

"Don't you understand? Marcus won't allow me to go."

"What kinda crap is that? I'll get a tough lawyer on the case – I know just the right guy. You won't have to deal with a thing."

Stubbing out her barely used cigarette she sighed deeply. "You don't know Marcus at all, do you?"

"What's to know?"

Her tone was very measured. "If I ever left him he'd kill me. And whoever was responsible for my leaving would be dead meat too. Just remember what I'm saying, Bobby. Marcus Citroen would have us both killed."

Saturday, July 11, 1987
Los Angeles

The four subjects the press wished to discuss were The Wild Ones, Buzz, Doktor Head and Cybil. Kris blanked them nicely. He hadn't been in the business for so many years without learning a thing or two. With a cheeky grin he could joke them out of anything. "Cybil, who's she?" he asked, jollying them along when they inquired if he had any marriage plans. Skilfully he turned the question-and-answer session around, directing it towards his soon-to-be-released new album *Long-Legged Blondes*.

"Is the title track about Cybil Wilde?" demanded an English woman reporter, with scraggly hair and bad teeth.

Kris knew her – Cyndi Lou Planter. She was always digging for the dirt – her weekly page in a national British newspaper brought frustrated bitchery to new heights.

"C'mon, Cyndi, luv," he said good-naturedly, hoping to endear himself to her by remembering the old bag's name. "You know me – I never favour anyone. The song's dedicated to every long-legged blonde I ever fancied."

"*That* certainly covers a lot of ground," Cyndi Loui Planter said, with a knowing smirk. "Aren't you at an age when you should start thinking about settling down? What about marriage?"

Screw the stupid cow. What did age have to do with anything?

"I reckon I got a few years left in me yet," he joked.

"You're nearly forty," Cyndi Lou persisted. "How long can you continue to jump around on stage? There's nothing worse than an ageing rocker, is there? You said so yourself in an interview we did three days before your thirtieth birthday."

"I'm *just* thirty-eight," he snapped back. "That's hardly senile. An' I'm in the best shape I've ever bin in."

"What about Buzz? Do you miss him?"

"Excuse me," he said, smothering a strong desire to bash her face in. Spotting Jeannie Wolfe from *Entertainment Tonight*, he thanked the press, and walked over to do the TV spot. Television was a lot fairer than the written word. At least on television you could defend yourself. He could just imagine Cyndi Lou Planter's opening paragraph when she wrote her piece. *Ageing rocker Kris Phoenix, who reluctantly admits to being nearly forty, has no intention of marrying his long-legged blonde Cybil Wilde. The ageing Romeo prefers to play the field, even though he's over the hill.*

"Tell me, Kris?" Jeannie asked. "Is *Long-Legged Blondes* a summary of your love life?"

Bloody Albert! What was it with him and his love life? That's all they wanted to know about lately.

"The music comes first, Jeannie," he said sincerely. "It always has an' it always will."

Yeah, now he was *really* telling it like it was. He'd fooled around plenty, but there'd never been a woman who was more important than his music.

A sad fact of life. Sometimes he wished there had been.

*

As soon as Maxwell Sicily could shake off the clinging Chloe he did so, leaving her with the excuse that he had to take a leak. The woman was a pest.

Time was passing, and there was a lot to think about. With the help of Vicki Foxe he knew the layout of Novaroen backwards. Ten days ago Vicki had got him onto the estate on the pretext that he was a plant specialist. She had the head of security hot for her, and the guy didn't even question when she'd told him Mrs Citroen had specially requested her plant doctor from Beverly Hills to have full access to the grounds.

He'd spent over an hour finding his way around. Fortunately there were no problems. In this business you could never be too sure of anything.

*

When she had finished watching Bobby rehearse, Rafaella went for a walk, accompanied by Trudie, and the two Blue Cadillac executives, who didn't seem prepared to let her out of their sight. They were probably working under Marcus's strict instructions.

She had wanted to stay and talk to Bobby, but his manager — a pretty black woman — had said a polite but firm no, Bobby did not wish to speak to anyone.

At least he was alive, looking great and sounding sensational. Seeing him was enough for now.

They tried to lure her into the press room to meet with the media. Now it was her turn to say no.

"Mr Citroen will expect you to," one of the executives said, rather edgily.

"Then let him ask me himself," she replied defiantly.

After her walk, she did her sound check, then went back to her room and relaxed.

One entire house had been turned over to the three stars and their entourages. The guest house was balanced on the side of a cliff, with breathtaking views of the ocean spread out below. It was away from the main mansion and the frantic activity taking place all round. There were brightly coloured golf carts to transport them to and from the centre of activities should they wish to be part of the action.

"I've never seen anything to match this set-up," Trudie exclaimed. "I can't believe people really live like this."

Rafaella quite liked the publicity girl, but right now she wanted to be alone with her thoughts. "I'm going to rest," she said. "If you can let me know an hour before I'm on, that'll be perfect."

"Sure," Trudie said. "When you need me, I can be buzzed in

the fun room. I always fancied playing Pac Man!" Opening the door, she was just about to leave, when she spotted Marcus Citroen coming up the stairs. Darting back she said, "The Big Boss is on his way. Do you want me to go or stay?"

"Marcus Citroen?"

"Yup."

Rafealla's face clouded over. "Can you stay? Please?"

"You got it."

*

Patience had never been one of Speed's virtues. Pacing the holding cell, waiting for his lawyer, he almost began climbing walls.

If he blew this one . . . Jeeze! It didn't bear thinking about. His name would be mud-slime in the business. Who would hire a douche-bag driver who never even showed up for his own job?

Nobody, that's who. Reliability was the key to success, and if he didn't break out of this shit-palace soon, his reliability was about as hot as an Eskimo's ass.

Sugarbush would love this. Sugarbush, his ex-wife – the ball-breaking Las Vegas tootsie roll, with knockers to send a man to heaven and back. She got off on watching him fail. This one would *really* be a crowd-pleaser.

"Listen, I gotta make another call," he yelled, rattling the rusty bars of the holding cell.

Everyone ignored him.

So what else was new?

*

"You *should* meet with the press," Sara insisted. "They're here, and they're on your side."

"What makes you think that?" Bobby asked moodily.

"I don't think – I *know*. You're a survivor. You're right back at the top where you belong. Everybody loves a winner. Now go for it."

"Hey babe, I'm just not sure . . ."

"*Trust* me, Bobby."

"It's not you I'm worried about."

"*Pleeaasse*."

"I don't want anyone feelin' sorry for me," he warned.

"Sorry for you!" she shrieked. "Are you a crazy man? You're tall, you're handsome, you're singing better than you ever did before. Honey – you are right up there."

"Well . . ."

She picked up the phone. "Mr St John. Bobby Mondella is ready to meet the press. Can we do it right now before he changes his mind?"

*

"Who's the fat ding-bat?"

"Get away from me," Maxwell hissed.

"Who *is* she?" Vicki fumed.

"Get the fuck away from me. Anybody could be watching."

"Not until I know who she is, and if she's in on it."

"She's not in on anything," he said, his eyes darting furtively around. "She works at Lilliane's."

"So what?"

"So she likes me."

"Can't you dump her?"

'That's what I'm trying to do."

Vicki chewed on her lower lip, automatically thrusting her breasts forward as far as her confining maid's uniform would allow. "Shall I deal with her?"

His voice was a deadly whisper. "Just get back to doing what you're *supposed* to be doing, and don't bother me again."

"There's nothin' wrong with a maid talkin' to a waiter."

"Get lost before you blow it."

Reluctantly she moved away. There was zilch going on between Maxwell and her, but she certainly wasn't going to stand by while some other bitch invaded what could be her future territory. After all, she was putting a lot on the line for Maxwell Sicily.

Walking away she came face to face with Tom, her own special security guard.

"What are you doing down here?" he asked.

Suggestively licking her lips she lightly touched his arm. "Lookin' for you, sugar."

He was pleased. A woman hadn't paid this much attention to him in years. "Well," he said happily, "you've found me."

"Later, I'm *really* gonna find you," she said, with a promising nudge.

Taking a risk he patted her on the ass. "Who were you talking to?"

"When?"

"Just now."

"Was I talkin' to someone?" she asked innocently.

"A man."

"Oh, him. Some wop waiter needing directions."

"Where to?"

"The men's room." She laughed aloud. "Do I look like an information booth?"

"You look good enough to eat," he said, his eyes bulging.

"Keep the thought." She winked. "I'll catch ya later, lover."

*

"Welcome to Novaroen, my dear," Marcus Citroen said, taking Rafealla's hand in a courtly, old-world gesture and kissing it. With a dismissive wave in Trudie's direction, he said coldly, "You can go."

"Marcus, this is Trudie," Rafealla said quickly. "She works for you."

"Publicity." Trudie held out a hand to introduce herself – yet again – for she had met the great boss on countless occasions, although he never remembered her. "I handled Del Delgardo's last tour."

"Did you?" His interest was at zero level.

"I heard you were very pleased."

"I'm sure I was. You're still working for me, aren't you," he stated flatly.

"Trudie wants me to go to the press room," Rafealla announced, jumping up. "We were just on our way."

"Uh . . . yes," agreed Trudie, catching on quickly. "I know

her sales are going great, but publicity never hurt anyone. Right, Mr Citroen?"

With an effort he concealed his aggravation. "I wish to talk to Rafealla now. She can go to the press room later."

"No can do," Trudie contradicted gamely, quite enjoying a chance to put Marcus Citroen in the back seat for once. "Governor Highland is giving a press conference at five o'clock." She consulted her watch. "Which allows us twenty-five minutes of fun and games before he takes over – just enough time to answer every question you've answered eight hundred thousand times before, huh, Rafealla? But these things have to be done. That's the great old world of show biz."

Happily Rafealla played along, gathering her purse, glancing in the mirror to check her hair and makeup.

Marcus was furious, hiding his anger because there was no way he was going to give the loud-mouthed publicity girl tales to tell.

"I'll see you later," he said tightly. "Do you have everything you need?"

"Thank you, Marcus, yes," Rafealla replied. And without further hesitation she left with Trudie.

Marcus Citroen waited a few moments, his eyes scanning the room. He must be crazy, wasting his time pursuing this girl. What was the matter with him? He was Marcus Citroen. He could have any woman he wanted.

And yet . . . there was something about her. Something about the tilt of her head and the sway of her body that he simply had to possess.

Did the girl really think she was going to avoid him forever? Did she imagine he was a complete fool?

Ah . . . extreme youth . . . Rafealla had so much to learn. And he would teach her.

Yes. Eventually he *would* teach her.

Kris Phoenix 1983

For two years it had been Kris Phoenix and the Wild Ones.

For two years it had been war between Kris and Buzz.

For two years the group had continued to grow and soar, with Kris at the helm.

Tensions simmered. Egos raged. Vicious fights and arguments were a daily occurrence.

Doktor Head had just about managed to keep it all together. With difficulty. Everybody wanted to take off on their own, but – as he'd patiently pointed out – they were The Wild Ones. One of the biggest rock groups in the world. And to break up would be sheer lunacy.

To add madness to madness, Buzz had recently taken up with the infamous Mikki – Michelle Hanley-Bogart – who had only just ricocheted out of a stormy on/off two-year liaison with Del Delgardo.

Kris still carried a slight grudge about the way she'd treated *him*. Having her hanging around with Buzz wasn't the ideal situation.

Flower had finally been put out to pasture. An ageing child of the sixties, she wasn't happy about being given the boot after fifteen years of togetherness with Buzz. Within weeks she proclaimed herself an expert on The Wild Ones and the early days, and proceeded to write a book about them. When it was finished, excerpts were headlined in a four-page story in a tabloid English newspaper. They were all dragged through the mud, especially Buzz and Kris, whom she labelled drunken, drugged sex fiends with nothing on their minds except groupies, orgies, and dope.

Kris read it with mounting anger. It was true about Buzz, but how had *he* managed to get in on the act? First of all he hardly ever doped. Groupies were out. And he'd only attended one orgy – and that was at Flower's invitation – had hated it, and left immediately.

No. He was not at all like the crazed egomaniac Flower portrayed. Music was his main passion. He was a serious musician, and more and more people who knew what they were talking about acknowledged that fact. His guitar work was almost as acclaimed as Eric Clapton's, and along with the young and very accomplished Eddie Van Halen he was becoming a guitar legend – much to Buzz's fury. Buzz was brilliant, but sloppy. His work had a blurred edge, although sometimes – not often – he could take off into genius, playing a solo so wild and so perfect, nobody could match him.

Unfortunately his talent was not consistent. Heroin ruled his life. He seemed to like it that way, in spite of everyone's efforts to wean him off the insidious killer drug.

Mikki was no help. Her stint with Del Delgardo had turned her into a doper herself. At twenty-five she looked years older, a brash, over-made-up woman of the world. Before taking up with Buzz she'd tried another shot at Kris. He'd brushed her off so fast it made Concorde seem slow. Somehow he knew she was only with Buzz in a pathetic attempt to annoy him. It was working, but not for the reasons she had in mind. Addictive as she'd been, it was a short-term addiction, and when she ran off with Del Delgardo he'd soon forgotten her.

Mostly he went out with an assortment of girls – usually models or actresses, because they looked good, loved the publicity involved, and like him, had no need of any heavy involvements, for they had their "careers" to think of. Occasionally one came along who wanted more. Then it was *Wham Bam Thank You Ma'am* time. In and out and on to the next.

He was getting slightly paranoid about herpes – the latest sexual disease doing the rounds. Unlike the rest of the group he was lucky enough never to have caught anything, and he certainly didn't plan to start now. Ladies of his choice were asked to submit to a quick visit to his doctor. Most of them agreed, and the ones who didn't lost out.

"You're a fuckin' chauvinist pig," Fingers informed him one day, as they all sat around in the studio.

"Isn't everyone?" he asked, feigning surprise.

"Well y'can count *me* in," Rasta laughed.

"You – you're just a slag," Fingers said, in her very direct way. "If it can't run fast enough, you'll fuck it."

Buzz surfaced. "I thought that's what chicks was for."

Fingers threw a glass of beer in his face.

Another normal day in the studio, where constant bickering was a way of life.

In spite of massive American success, The Wild Ones still lived in Europe, and all owned homes in England, registered under company names – as they were tax exiles, and only allowed to spend a certain amount of time a year there. Kris had purchased a large apartment in Grosvenor Square. When his mother saw it she almost fainted. Upon recovering, the first thing she said was, "It's luverly, son. When can the others come over?"

The others meant Horace, his two sisters and their respective husbands – plus brother Brian, and his lot. Family never went away, it just got bigger.

"I'll arrange it," he'd said, with no intention of doing so.

As long as Avis was happy he had no particular interest in the rest of them. He sent over lavish presents – colour televisions, a washing machine, a dishwasher, even a car. He'd offered to buy his mum a house in the country, but she'd declined, saying, "I like me little flat, with all me friends nearby. It suits me nicely, lad."

At least he'd persuaded her to give up work and accept a monthly sum of money from him. He suspected most of it went in Brian's direction.

So what? He could afford it. Brian was still the world's worst jerk – a fussy, bitter man, with never a good word to say about anyone or anything. Instead of being proud of his younger brother, he was pathologically jealous – belittling Kris and his career at every opportunity. Finally it got so bad that Kris was forced to tell Avis to keep Brian away from him. She wasn't pleased, but she'd done as he asked, and he hadn't had the pleasure of his brother's company in over eighteen months. What a joy!

Apart from the Grosvenor Square flat he had a small farmhouse in the South of France, just outside Saint-Tropez. It was a good place to get away from everything, an enjoyable retreat where he could write with no interruptions, although the more famous he became, the more difficult it was to cut himself off.

Once a week, he took out his son, Bo, who now lived with Willow and her new husband – a chinless-wonder stockbroker – in a large house just outside London. Because of his limited time in England, it was not an ideal arrangement. His weekly outings with Bo were inconsistent to say the least, and Willow was being a real bitch, labelling him an uncaring father, when she knew there wasn't a damn thing he could do about it because of his tax situation. She would have made a perfect wife for Brian – two miserable human beings together.

Bo suffered. He was turning out to be a real sissy. At eight, he was frightened of everything, whined a lot, and ate too much. The kid was a right little pain in the neck. When Kris tried to talk to Willow, she laughed in his face. "Hah! The caring father. Where were *you* when he was growing up? Sleeping with slags, and making money." He'd written a song called *Making Money*, for the new album, and another called *Does Your Mother Know You're Pregnant*? They were both secretly dedicated to Willow. She wouldn't even allow him to take the kid away with him to France for a few weeks. His lawyer had been working on it, but now, with Flower's choice revelations in the newspapers, it didn't seem likely.

*

The Wild Ones were making a video in Paris. They had taken over one entire floor of a hotel and Doktor Head was going crazy trying to keep everyone on speaking terms.

Buzz had his own press conference, with Mikki by his side. The two of them, in dusty black outfits, paraded in front of the press announcing their future plans. "I won't be stayin' with the group much longer," Buzz said, attempting to control a continual sniff with the back of his hand.

This caused much excitement, especially when the news reached the others. Kris and Buzz had their usual confrontation, with Mikki standing defiantly by and Doktor Head acting as mediator.

"If you wanted to leave, why didn't you have the balls to tell me before shoutin' it out to the world and its bleedin' mother?" Kris demanded.

"So he's tellin' you now," Mikki said, glaring at him fiercely.

"Yeah, man," Buzz agreed, all stoned, bloodshot eyes and snake hips, his dirty black hair pulled back into a scruffy ponytail. "I'm tellin' yer now."

"Thanks a lot," Kris said sarcastically. "The Wild Ones are breakin' up after fourteen years together, and you're lettin' me know as an afterthought. *Very* nice."

"The Wild Ones don't have to break up if Buzz decides to do other projects as well," Doktor Head said, still trying to keep the peace.

"Aw, *shit*, leave it out," Kris said disgustedly. "It's over, man. Me and Buzz started the group, an' if he wants to go, it's all right with me." Shaking his head he added, "I'm tired of pickin' up after him anyway. Mikki, baby, he's all yours."

"Wait a minute," Doktor Head said quickly. "The new album comes out in a few weeks. We have four live shows to do in Australia next month, and there's the video we have to finish. Oh yes, and another album commitment to Nichols Hit City. He can't walk."

"He can do what he wants," Mikki said grandly. "Del Delgardo did when he left the Nightmares."

"I don't give a fuck about Del Delgardo," Doktor Head said, getting forceful. "Buzz has commitments, and if he doesn't care to keep them, he'll get the ass sued off him. Is that what he wants?"

"I'll finish the friggin' video;" Buzz mumbled. "An' the Australian dates, but that's it. After Australia I'm gone. Use someone else on the album. I don't give a frig."

"You can work everything out with me," Mikki said, very business-like, shooting Kris a spiteful look. "*I'm* his new manager."

After that, Kris and Buzz went out of their way to ignore each other. For years Kris had been trying to save his friend from himself. It was no good. Buzz was on a path to destruction, and now he had the perfect partner.

Early one evening Doktor Head arrived at the hotel with a pretty Danish girl. He introduced her to Kris as Astrid. "She makes the best leather pants in the world," he said. "You'll love her work – especially the way *you* jump around on stage. I'm going next door, I'll be back in a minute."

Kris was used to male designers, and Astrid looked too young to know what she was doing anyway. Lounging on the sofa, he said, "I don't need anything, luv. But hang about, we'll have dinner."

"No, thank you," she replied, with only the trace of an accent. "I have another engagement."

He was surprised. "No thank you" was a phrase he *never* heard. "Break it," he said, testing her.

She smiled. "I can't. It's with my fiancé, and I don't think he'd understand."

A turn-down! A genuine turn-down! This was interesting.

"Maybe I *will* have some pants made," he said lazily. "What d'you suggest?"

She was pretty in the way that only Scandinavian girls can be. Clear-skinned, with a smattering of light freckles. Wide grey eyes. A snub nose, and long, straight flaxen hair.

He noticed, beneath the pale blue tracksuit she had on, promising breasts, a small waist, and exceptionally long legs. Not bad. Not bad at all.

Approaching the back of the sofa, she asked, "Do you like leather?"

He gave her a shot of the Phoenix intense blue-eyed gaze, and said, "Only if it's *very* soft, luv. Know what I mean?"

She knew what he meant all right, but she chose to ignore his double entendre. Opening her sizeable purse, she produced a swatch of different colours. "The pale beige is nice. This particular leather is very comfortable to wear."

Fingering the material he wondered if she'd agree to a quick medical check.

"Maybe the orange," she pressed. "Or is it too hot for you?"

Was she, in her own not-so-subtle way, coming on to him?

"Nothin's too hot for me, darlin'," he said, grabbing her – and tumbling her over the top of the sofa. Scandinavian lips were hot lips, everyone knew that. Grabbing a tit he tried to kiss her.

"What are you *doing*?" she yelled indignantly, pushing him off and standing up. "How *dare* you! I'm not one of your groupies." Snatching up her swatch of materials, cheeks red with genuine anger, she stalked to the door, opened it and slammed out.

Kris felt like a fool. When Doktor Head reappeared he said, "What was *she* all about?"

"Who?" Doktor Head asked vaguely.

"The Danish bit."

"Oh, Astrid. She's the greatest. You'll be very pleased."

"With *what*?"

"The pants she designs for you. When Michael Hollywood was alive she made all his stuff. He swore by her."

"You mean she really makes things?"

"Yes." Doktor Head began to laugh. "You didn't come on to her, did you?"

"Why would I do that?" Kris asked sarcastically. "You parade her in here – a blonde with a body – an' then you piss off. What was I *supposed* to do, play chess?"

"Berk! You were *supposed* to order some pants."

He did. He ordered in every colour of the soft leather she'd shown him. And he sent her twelve dozen yellow roses along with a pair of trousers he wanted copied.

An assistant delivered the finished goods in three days with a hefty bill. Twelve pairs of perfect leather pants.

Before he could decide what to do about Astrid, he was summoned to London. His son had been in a car accident, and was in the hospital. They didn't think he would live.

Rafealla 1983

After her divorce from Eddie Mafair was final, Rafealla still refused to marry Jorge, but she did — eventually — move in with him. The pressures of being a young and beautiful girl in a big city with a small child to look after finally got to her. She didn't need his money, but she did need his protection. Besides, it suited her. After Luiz, she had decided there was no future with anyone else. The most painful thing of all was that she'd never heard from him again. Two years of silence. What was it with her and men? Did she turn them off to such an extent that after they slept with her, they never wanted to see her again?'

Jorge didn't feel that way. Jorge couldn't get enough.

Odile was disapproving. "If you're sleeping with him anyway, why don't you get married?"

"Because I don't ever want to be tied to a man again," she explained. "I need to be free."

"Why?"

With a shrug she said, "Who knows? Just to ride the rainbow without anyone stopping me."

"You're crazy." Odile shook her head.

"I know," Rafealla replied, perfectly happy.

She had taken up singing again, and that pleased her. Twice a week her voice coach, a stout Viennese woman, arrived at Jorge's mansion to put her through a vigorous routine. She loved the discipline and the pleasure. Singing was her joy. Having given up her job in the art gallery, she now spent the rest of her days shopping, going to the beach, lunching with Odile, and playing with Jon Jon – a sturdy six-year-old with a tough, stubborn streak. In the evening there were numerous parties and social events to attend with Jorge. He enjoyed entertaining, and was a gracious host.

"You're only twenty-three," Odile said to her after one of Jorge's dinner parties. "Why are you mixing with all these old people? You'd better watch out or you'll turn into one of them."

"I happen to enjoy their company. There's nothing wrong with being older, you know. I'm learning a lot."

"Like what?"

She sighed. "Odile. Get on with your own life and leave me alone."

"*My* life is going back to England soon," Odile replied, determined to get her point across. "I'm worried about you. You're just drifting along. You and Jon Jon should come with us. This place is fabulous for a few years, but surely you miss Europe?"

Yes. She did miss London and Paris and the South of France and her mother and stepfather and their big house in the country, and the horses she used to love to ride. But how could she leave Rio? If she left there was no way she would ever see Luiz again. While she stayed there was always a chance . . .

*

Carnival took place in February, and the entire city went crazy, getting ready for the few days of frantic pleasure with overwhelming zeal. Carnival time in Rio was the culmination of months of preparation. There were amazing flower-bedecked floats for the incredible parade, out-of-this-world costumes, and a glut of wild parties. For once the poor felt rich and the rich felt richer, and out on the streets there was a wild tangle of semi-clothed cariocas, handsome young men, fat mamas, sparkling transvestites, hustlers, pimps, con-men, hookers, tourists, and a general assortment of outrageous characters. The streets were alive with the samba beat, the sweet smell of flowers, and a swaying, singing, celebrating mass of people.

Parties were an everyday affair, starting early and going on all day and all night. Odile and Rupert threw a fancy-dress farewell celebration the night before the big parade. In two weeks they were moving back to England. The thought depressed Rafealla, for they were her family, and she knew she was going to miss them terribly. It couldn't be helped, she would just have to learn to manage without them.

For the party she dressed as Nefertiti, the Egyptian queen, and Jorge, with much persuasion, dressed up as a Roman general. They took little Jon Jon, clad as a Yankee baseball hero. He had the greatest time, and didn't want to go home. When they finally persuaded him into the chauffeur-drive Mercedes, he fell asleep across both their knees.

This was her family, she suddenly realized. Why wait any longer? She would marry Jorge and give Jon Jon a real father.

*

"Congratulations, darling!"

"*Wonderful* news!"

"How wise of you to wait. Now you're really sure."

"When is the wedding?"

Jorge had wasted no time in presenting her with the most magnificent solitaire diamond ring. The moment she'd said yes, he'd produced it from the safe, proudly telling her he'd bought it the day she moved in. Now she wore it to the big parade, where she was safely cloistered in a special box overlooking the route, with a dozen or so of Jorge's friends and business acquaintances who had flown in especially for the evening of festivities. Special boxes were erected to watch the parade, enabling the rich to see and be seen without ever really becoming involved.

Looking around, she was quite surprised to spot Marcus Citroen, the American record magnate, with his wife, Nova, an elegant, cold woman. She hadn't seen him since that fateful night in London at Annabel's, which he obviously didn't remember, for when they were introduced by one of Jorge's friends he showed not a flicker of recognition.

That's twice he hasn't remembered me, she thought, her mind quickly darting back to their first encounter at Odile's step-father's house in the South of France when he'd flashed her in the swimming pool.

He was a dirty old man then, and nothing had changed. As they were introduced his hooded eyes lasciviously stripped off the gypsy outfit she wore, checking out every inch of her body.

When Odile arrived she didn't wait for an introduction. "Mr Citroen," she exclaimed, winking at Rafealla with a certain amount of wickedness. "I bet you don't remember *me*."

Turning, he acknowledged Odile's blonde prettiness with a perfunctory nod. "You'll have to assist my memory, my dear."

"Isabella and Claudio Franconini's daughter, Odile. You came to stay at our château in France one summer. Don't worry if you've forgotten, it was a long time ago."

"Indeed I do remember. What a pleasure to see you again. Tell me, are your parents well?"

"Very well." Unable to resist, gamely stifling a giggle, she added, "And surely you remember my best friend, Rafealla? She was staying with us at the time."

Rafealla could have kicked her grinning sister-in-law.

Fortunately Jorge appeared at that moment, putting a pos-sessive arm around her shoulders as he said, "So Marcus, you've met my soon-to-be-bride, the most beautiful woman in Rio."

"Child bride," murmured Marcus, gazing at her reflectively, with a *haven't I seen you somewhere before* look in his eyes.

Rafealla shifted uncomfortably. There was something about Marcus Citroen that filled her with dread.

*

The gaiety and wildness of the night excited everyone. It was impossible not to get caught up in the delirious goings on. Carnival fever was catching – what with the noise and the smells and the insistent music. Pulsating bodies and decadent faces were everywhere. A heavy sexual feeling pervaded the air as Rio forgot about the rest of the world and surrendered to Carnival.

Odile was in an adventurous mood. Several glasses of champagne always made her a little crazy, and combined with the heady atmosphere of the evening, an earlier fight with Rupert, and the fact that she would soon be leaving Rio, she was ready to do the forbidden.

The forbidden was leaving the rarefied atmosphere of the box where the rich people experienced Carnival without getting too close.

"Why don't we skip out of here?" she whispered. "I can't stand being confined like this."

"No," Rafealla whispered back. "Jorge said it's dangerous."

"Please! Now you're beginning to sound like him. What happened to the girl who wanted to be free? This is a holiday — a festival. Let's go have fun for ten minutes. Nobody'll miss us, they'll think we're in the loo."

To dance in the streets was a tempting prospect. Being a spectator wasn't the same as participating. Why the hell shouldn't they?

Sneaking from the box they hit the street like two naughty schoolgirls, falling in with a swaying group of half-naked bodies, snaking along the side of the parade, giggling with the sheer energy and exhilaration of it all.

"We'll just go a couple of blocks and then back," Odile promised.

"Sure," Rafealla laughed, as a masked stranger grabbed her arm, propelling her along.

The crowds were dense and unruly. It took only moments for the two girls to get separated and lose sight of each other, but neither really cared, they were having too enjoyable a time. The music was loud and sensual. Inhibitions were left behind as they joined the swaying, laughing throng.

It wasn't until Rafealla began to lose her breath that she realized they should go back. When she looked around for Odile, she couldn't find her.

"Damn!" she muttered, knowing there was no way she could return without her, Rupert would be furious.

Now she tried to ignore the samba beat and the oscillating mass of bodies as her eyes began to search for Odile. An impossible task. Should she turn around? Continue forward?

Oh God! What to do?

A creature in an orange satin bikini, a trailing ruffled skirt, and exaggerated makeup pounced upon her. "Dahling!" the creature shrieked in a distinctly male voice, even though it had jutting breasts. "Dahling! Dahling! Dahling!"

Breaking away she tripped and almost fell. The creature pursued her.

"Go away!" she yelled.

"Be...ooo...tiful! *Sooo* be...oo...tiful."

She didn't feel beautiful, she felt nervous. Suddenly all of Jorge's warnings came back to her.

The Carnival is dangerous ...

Murders ...

Assaults ...

Pickpockets everywhere ...

The thieves wait all year for these few days ...

And most chilling of all – *Lepers walk the streets during Carnival ...*

With a sudden shiver she twisted the huge diamond on her finger so it didn't show, clenching her hand shut.

The creature waved gaily and danced off. Was she being paranoid? How could anything happen to her with all these people around? Resolutely she pressed on, furious with Odile for getting lost, and just as furious with herself for allowing it to happen.

An hour later she had no idea where she was. All she could do was wander the crowded streets like a zombie, hot, tired, despairing. If only she could get a cab, she would throw herself in it and go home. Odile had probably found her way back to the box ages ago, and Jorge – no doubt – had bodyguards combing the city for her. She felt like a fool as all around her the big street party went on, getting louder and wilder and more out of control.

Men were hitting on her from all sides, she was hearing everything from obscenely suggestive whispers to outright, bold come-ons.

Hands reached out to touch as she hurried by.

Stay calm, she told herself. *Don't panic.*

Two men slammed into her, pushing her up against a wall as their rough hands roamed her body.

"Leave me alone," she shouted, bringing her knee up and kicking out as hard as she could.

Right on target. One of the men howled with pain as the other snatched the gold beads from around her neck and dragged off her gold hoop earrings.

The man she had kicked suddenly went crazy, his ugly face contorted with rage. "Amerikain feelth!" he roared, just before smashing her in the face with his beringed fist.

She slid to the ground, unconscious.

[illegible faded text at top of page]

Bobby Mondella 1983

"Hiya, Bobby."

"Hey, Sharleen baby, you are lookin' great!"

His words were strictly automatic. She looked terrible, overweight with bloated features.

Touching her hair she laughed self-consciously. "Never bullshit a bullshitter. I *know* what I look like – an' Diana Ross it ain't. I gotta lose a pound or two."

"Hey – she's nothin' but a skinny little thing," he joked, trying to warm her up. "I like a woman with some *flesh* on her bones."

"I heard you just like women – period."

"That's my lifestyle, baby."

"I also heard you like one special woman a *whole* lot. An' honey, I am here to tell you, it ain't exactly peachy for your health."

They faced each other in his suite at the Helmsley Palace Hotel in New York. Sharleen had called and asked if she could come over. He hadn't seen her for two years, and since she was an old friend he'd said yes. Usually it wasn't that easy to get an audience with Bobby Mondella.

"How about some champagne?" he asked, cradling his glass of bourbon – the constant soothing companion.

"Why not?" she said, throwing off her fur coat.

With a gesture he summoned one of his bodyguards lurking at the back of the large living room.

"Champagne for Sharleen."

An impassive nod.

"And I'll have another bourbon."

"Bobby, Bobby, Bobby," she sing-songed. "You *really* made it, didn't you?"

"That's kind of an *old* story," he remarked. There was nothing he hated more than being reminded of his humble beginnings. Nichols was always trying to pull that garbage, until one day he'd told him if he ever mentioned The Chainsaw and how he was a men's room attendant one more time, he would seriously think about switching record companies again.

"You don't wanna discuss old times?" she asked, smoothing her dress down over generous curves.

"I don't get off on that. Do you?"

"When I'm feelin' blue I can get a real kick goin' back over it. Y'know, thinkin' 'bout how I'd change things, maybe do it differently."

The bodyguard handed her a glass of champagne and she began to sip the cold bubbly liquid. Bobby noticed her hand was shaking. Ever so slightly, but it was still a shake. He'd heard her marriage had broken up and she was still involved with drugs.

Funny, once Sharleen had been the most important person in the world to him, and he would have done anything for her. Now she was just another face from his past – and who needed to be reminded?

"So . . ." he said, hoping she wouldn't stay too long. "And what can I do for you, pretty lady?"

Glancing at the two bodyguards stationed at the back of the room she said, "Can we talk . . . privately?"

He gestured to the guards. "Come back in ten minutes."

The two burly men left.

"Wow!" she exclaimed sarcastically. "Ten whole minutes. I'm honoured."

Ignoring her sarcasm he said, "Gotta get a lot done before I fly back to L.A."

Glancing around the luxurious suite she said, "They're sure travellin' you in style."

"Better than Blue Cadillac ever did."

"Blue Cadillac made you the star you are today."

"I could have done it without them," he replied evenly.

"You really think that, huh? I guess you're forgetting that after strugglin' with Soul On Soul for all those years, you were still just another black singer. Marcus Citroen put you where you are today. He *made* you. Surely you gotta admit that?"

"What is this?" he asked restlessly. "A pitch to get me back with Blue Cadillac?"

"No, honey. It's a pitch to get you to stop leanin' on Marcus's wife. He doesn't like it an', Bobby, I'm warnin' you, you'd better quit, otherwise you're in real trouble."

Was she serious? How dare she come to him with this. "Still keepin' the old man warm at night, huh?" he asked with a mirthless laugh. "You haven't had a hit in two years. I would've thought he'd dumped you by now. But I guess he figures he can still use you to run his dirty errands, huh?"

Carefully she placed her glass of champagne on the table, and reached for her fur coat. "I knew you'd be too stubborn to listen."

"You can tell your fine friend Mr C,' Bobby said angrily, "to take his warnings an' choke on 'em. You can tell your motherfuckin' *friend* to dance at his own funeral. Because I DON'T CARE. One of these days Nova's goin' to leave him. An' when she does, I'll be waitin'. An' all the threats in the world ain't gonna change *that*. So, woman, shift out of here with your man's messages. I don't like bein' threatened. Especially by you."

Brown eyes flashing angrily she said, "Thank you, Bobby. What a Prince! Only thing is – Marcus never sent me, I came on my own, because once, a very long time ago, we were friends, an' I felt I owed you. But, honey, you are one changed person, an' I don't like what I see."

"Shove some more coke up your nose an' tell me what you don't like," he said harshly.

"Hey, man, last night I shoved it all over your girlfriend's pussy while Marcus eyeballed me licking it off. How does *that* grab you?"

"You're a *lying* bitch!"

"No, I'm not. I may be a doper, but baby, I don't make things up. Nova plays games with people. It's her kick. You'd better remember that's all you are to her – another kick. A big black stud she can control. So don't go gettin' no ideas 'bout how she loves you – 'cos, baby, you are on the *wrong* track. She'll *never* leave Marcus, you can bet on it. Only I'm here to tell you – you're pissin' him off, man. So I've warned you, an' that's all I can do."

She slammed her way from the suite.

Goddamn her! Why was she coming to him with her filthy lies?

Maybe Marcus forced her to do it. Yes. That was it. Marcus wanted to make Nova look bad, and what better way than to say she was rolling on the bed making out with Nova.

Angrily he picked up the phone and called Nova on her private line.

"Hello." She sounded guarded.

"It's me," he said.

Her voice was brisk and to the point. "I can't talk now. My dressmaker is here."

"One question."

A testy "Yes?"

"What did you do last night?"

"I told you yesterday. We had a business dinner at Le Cirque."

"Who with?"

"Several people."

"Was Sharleen one of them?"

A pause. "I think so."

"You *think* so. Either she was there or she wasn't."

"Yes, she was there."

Was she licking your pussy while Marcus watched? He didn't believe it. Not for a moment.

"Why?" Nova asked curiously.

"Hey – it's not important. I'll see you at our usual place."

"Five o'clock?"

"You got it."

Hanging up the phone he wondered how he could ever have doubted her. Sure Sharleen was there. Why not? She was still a Blue Cadillac star – even if a slightly tarnished one.

As soon as the moment was right, Nova had promised she was going to leave Marcus. "Don't force me into a corner," she'd said. "You have to let me do it my way."

True, he was still waiting after giving her an ultimatum two years ago, but what choice did he have other than giving her up, and he couldn't do that.

They still saw each other as often as possible. In Los Angeles they met at the secret beach house, and in New York at a small apartment he'd rented under an assumed name in a discreet building off Madison Avenue.

Arriving at the apartment ten minutes before five, he was there before her. Time to fix himself a drink, and put on some music. Today he chose Teddy Pendergrass.

Nova appeared promptly at five o'clock, wearing a belted mink coat, dark glasses and a headscarf.

"I wish you wouldn't call me at home," was her opening line. "Staff gossip, you know. I can't trust anyone."

He hadn't seen her in six weeks – her greeting could have been warmer.

Walking into the bedroom she started unbelting her coat, throwing it onto the bed. And then she began unzipping her dress.

They did have a very sexual relationship. But was that all it was – sex?

"Hey – hold it a minute," he said.

"I have exactly one hour," she replied crisply.

Sharleen's words taunted him – *That's all you are to her – another kick. A big black stud she can control.* "How's the move going?" he asked.

Stepping out of her dress, she said, "What move?"

"Your move out of Marcus's life an' into mine," he said tightly.

"I'm working on it."

"You're always workin' on it, babe. The thing is I can't understand why it's takin' you so long. It's not like you have kids to think about."

"Ah, but we do have property, and I want to make sure I walk away with my fair share."

"*I* can give you everything you'll ever need. How many times do I have to tell you that?"

Reaching towards him she fiddled with his belt, softening her tone. "Let's go to bed, Bobby, I've missed you."

He moved away from her. "Nova, I'm not in the mood."

She laughed disbelievingly. "You're *always* in the mood."

How come she sounded so sure of herself? Was he that easy? "I am?" he asked coldly.

Confidently she tugged at his belt. "You certainly are."

Drawing even further away from her he said, "Today I want to talk."

About to argue, she changed her mind and sat down on the side of the bed, primly crossing her legs clad in stockings and a lace garter belt. "Go ahead," she said in a resigned voice.

"I think," his words were measured, "that you're givin' me the run-around."

She tapped her long, scarlet nails on the side of the bed. "Really?"

"Yes, really. Because I can't see why it's takin' you all this time to leave Marcus."

"Hmmm . . ."

"What's *that* supposed to mean?"

"It means," she said with a slight pause, "I'll do it when I can."

Switching the subject, all the better to catch her off-guard, he said, "Were you in bed with Sharleen last night? Was Marcus watchin' the two of you?"

The look of guilty surprise which swept across her face told him everything he needed to know.

"Aw, shit," he said wearily. "You never had any intention of leavin' him, did you?"

Recovering her composure she said, "There are things I do with Marcus that mean nothing. Last night was one of them." She paused. "With you, it's different."

Bitterly he said, "Sure."

"I told you once, and you refused to listen to me. If I ever left Marcus he'd have us both killed. He can do it, you know. He can arrange anything."

This was all getting too much. "Nova, put your clothes on an' go home. I've just about had it with you."

For once in her life she looked vulnerable, the veneer of sophistication stripped away. "I was only protecting us, Bobby."

"Yeah, I bet."

"One day perhaps you'll understand."

"Goodbye, baby, goodbye."

Kris Phoenix 1983

For three weeks Kris kept a hospital vigil while his son lay in a deep coma. Willow and he put their differences aside and sat by the child's bedside day and night, until one afternoon — miraculously — Bo's eyes fluttered open and he said, "Hello, dad."

Willow burst into tears. Kris put his arms around her, cradling her sadness and joy with a great deal of tenderness. It had taken a near-tragedy for them both to realize how unimportant it was to bicker and fight over minor things, when all that really mattered was their son's well-being.

"You can take him away with you to France," Willow offered. "Twice a year if you like. I'm sure he'd love to spend his holidays with you."

"And I'll try to visit him more," Kris promised.

"He adores seeing you," she admitted. "He's very proud of his famous dad."

They were okay together, but their families remained a pain, fussing around full of unwanted advice. Avis insisted the accident was the fault of Willow's mother with whom the boy had been staying at the time.

"How *dare* that dreadful woman accuse me," Mrs Wigh screamed when she heard what was being said.

"Who's that old bat calling a dreadful woman?" yelled Avis.

It became the battle of the grandmothers.

Kris couldn't hang around to watch – Bo was out of the hospital in time for him to take off to do the Australian concerts. The Wild Ones' last stand. Buzz hadn't changed his mind about leaving, and in a way it was a relief. Working with him was like working next to a pressure cooker – any moment he could blow.

Doktor Head had negotiated some kind of record-breaking deal for them to appear down under. It was a fitting finale to fourteen years of madness.

Their opening concert in Melbourne almost caused riots. The fans were out in force, blocking the streets, charging the Festival Hall where they were due to appear, holding aloft banners proclaiming—

WE LOVE YOU KRIS!
THE WILD ONES FOREVER
BUZZ BUZZ BUZZ!

Locked in their suites at the Rockman Regency Hotel, they gave interviews and partied with the local so-called in group.

Buzz and Mikki declined any invitations. Instead they contacted their friendly neighbourhood drug dealer, and spent all their time in a vague stupor.

On stage Kris found himself covering up for Buzz more and more. He was glad it would soon be over.

After two days in Melbourne they flew to Sydney, where it was more of the same.

Kris complained hotly, "I've come half way round the bleedin' world, an' all I've seen of Australia is the inside of a hotel room."

Doktor Head suggested they try to disguise him, and then maybe he could be taken on a short sightseeing trip.

With the help of the daughter of their Australian tour promoter, they dressed him up as a girl, replete with long blond wig, granny glasses and a dirndl skirt.

"You're the ugliest bird I've ever seen," choked Doktor Head, spluttering with laughter. "I wouldn't want to cut *your* hair!"

"Get fucked. You're just jealous," Kris said, smearing on a liberal amount of bright red lipstick.

"Yeah, especially of the hairy legs. Nice touch, that."

The disguise worked, and he got to see Sydney – a beautiful city. In the morning they took a water-taxi round the harbour, admiring the modern architecture of the all-white Opera House. Then the taxi dropped them off in Watsons Bay, where they lunched at Doyles – an open-air restaurant situated next to the water, with delicious seafood and a friendly ambience.

"This is more like it," Kris said, sitting back and enjoying the freedom for a change.

"Give us a kiss, darlin'," joked Doktor Head. "You're looking better every minute!"

That night, their concert at the Horden Pavilion was another riotous success. Afterwards, Kris was tracked backstage by a beautiful – if somewhat older – French ex-movie star, who was travelling the world compiling a book of photographs. She wore a gold sequin dress, and clutched a Nikon camera close to her voluptuous cleavage. "I weel photograph you, no?" she asked him, after her manager had inveigled a yes out of him.

"Sure," he agreed. "Only not here, luv. You'd better come back to the hotel. There's a party."

There was always a party. It was the rock 'n' roll life. Booze, girls, drugs, food, music. Everything on tap. If you want something – just ask. For a star nothing is too much trouble.

The French ex-movie star took a few photographs. She had once been a great beauty – a world-class sex symbol. Kris could remember seeing her in movies when he was a kid. At thirteen he'd really lusted after those huge tits. They still looked in pretty good nick to him, although she had to be close to his mother's age.

After a while she asked, "Can we be more – how you say – preevit?"

"Private," he corrected.

"No?"

"Yeah, okay."

They went to his suite, where she took a roll of film of him lounging on the couch. Then she asked if he would mind re-moving his shirt.

She was beginning to get him going. He kept on thinking of this one film he'd seen her in where she'd played a slave girl, and she'd had this little pearl in her navel, and oh shit . . . here came the old trouser puppet, alert and ready to play *you show me yours and I'll show you mine*.

She was no slouch in the noticing-what-was-going-on de-partment. Putting down her camera she undulated towards him, placed her arms around his neck, and planted the biggest, wettest kiss he had ever experienced on his hardly unwilling lips.

They indulged in erotic tongue play for a few moments, until he decided enough was enough and slid his hands between flesh and gold sequins, peeling the top of her dress down and flipping as much of her breasts as he could over the top of a tight corselette.

She had the biggest nipples he'd ever seen atop her mag-nificent bosom. Large, ripe, peaked cherries. He couldn't decide what to do first — unzip himself and get some well-needed freedom; try to figure out how to ooze her out of the corselette contraption; or place those delectable cherries right into his mouth where they belonged.

Before he could make up his mind, it was all over. There was a wild, familiar throb in his pants, and to his eternal humiliation Kris Phoenix, rock star supreme, came in his pants. "Je. . .sus!" he exclaimed. "I don't believe it!"

The French ex-movie star smiled comfortingly, as if this mishap was an everyday occurrence — and around her it probably was.

"Now we do eet properly," she said, reaching behind her back to deal with hooks and eyes and God knows what else was keeping the gold dress up. "We go in zee bedroom, no?"

"Yes," he mumbled, feeling about fourteen. What a berk! He'd better make up for it or his reputation was shot to hell.

"I'll be right back, darlin'. Don't go away," he said, diving into the bathroom, stripping off his clothes and throwing himself under a quick shower.

Once, when he was a teenager, he'd sent away for some kind

of erection cream he'd seen advertised in a nudie magazine. It was called Stiff Stuff, and the instructions were to rub it on your cock just before making love. It promised hours of uninterrupted pleasure. He'd been over at this girl's house ready for action. Her parents were out, and they'd started to neck. When the time was right, he'd run into the bathroom, pulled out his tube of Stiff Stuff and rubbed it on. Two seconds later he came all over the bathroom floor. Wonderful!

In a funny way this reminded him of that night.

When he returned she was lying across the rumpled bed, the top sheet carefully arranged as if she were preparing for a pin-up session. Her breasts were covered, but one leg emerged from the sheet in a delicate pose.

He was naked, everything on show, and why not – he certainly had nothing to hide.

"Beeeg!" she exclaimed admiringly, which of course made him even bigger.

Without further ado he jumped on top of her, pulling the sheet away, exposing prime, French ex-movie star skin.

Stripped of gold sequins she was pleasantly rounded, completely unlike his usual bed companions, whom he liked long and lean – although large breasts were generally an essential part of the package.

Making love to her was all flesh and pulsating sensuality. After Daphne Darke – Buzz's mum – she was his second older woman, and he wasn't complaining. It was a bit like pigging out on a lusciously rich ice cream sundae. You wouldn't want to do it all the time, but oh boy, was it good while it lasted!

*

Arriving back in New York, to do a week of promotion on the new album, the shit really hit. Buzz was arrested at the airport for possession of heroin. Fingers publicly declared herself a lesbian. And Rasta was slapped with two paternity suits – both by white girls.

It was the end of The Wild Ones. The end of an era.

Kris didn't regret it one bit.

Rafealla 1983

Drifting in and out of consciousness Rafealla was vaguely aware of the sound of voices. Murmurs from another world. Her eyelids fluttered, and she made a half-hearted attempt to open her eyes. It wasn't possible. She couldn't do it. Why should she?

"Why should I?" she mumbled. And then she groaned, for there was a sharp, stabbing pain on her left cheek. Instinctively her hand reached up and felt a soggy bandage. With a supreme effort she opened her eyes.

A woman dressed in white peered down at her.

She couldn't remember a thing. Where was she? What happened? Why wasn't she at home in bed?

"Have I been in a car accident?" she asked, very slowly. Her lips were dry and her voice sounded more like a frog's croak.

"You were robbed and beaten," a male voice said. A disturbingly familiar male voice.

Luiz! Was it Luiz! Quickly she tried to sit up, but the room took off, an alarming kaleidoscope of flashing colours. Sinking back down she asked. "Where am I?"

"In a bar. The back room. Some people carried you in here for safety."

She was drifting. "Luiz? Is that you?" she whispered. "Luiz . . ."

*

The next time she woke up it was in a hospital, all pristine white with the smell of antiseptic in the air. Once again she was completely disoriented. She lay with her eyes wide open trying to figure out what had happened.

"Thank God you're all right, my darling," Jorge said, looming over her. "It was a nightmare." He clutched her hand. "We were so desperately worried."

Gradually it all began to come back. Carnival. Carnival. Carnival. Ah . . . And she and Odile out on the street, laughing, dancing . . .

"Odile," she mumbled anxiously. "What happened to her?"

"She's fine," Jorge assured her. "Repentant, naturally, but much better once you were found."

"Found? Where was I?"

"On the street where those animals left you."

"On the street . . ." she repeated vaguely, becoming aware of a pounding, relentless headache, and a painful throb down one side of her face. Automatically her hand reached up and touched the bandages covering her cheek. "I thought I was in a bar."

"A bar? What are you talking about?"

"They carried me into the bar . . . for safety."

He bent to kiss her. "Darling, you're still groggy – understandably so. You were found on the street by some American tourists. They brought you straight here."

Closing her eyes she thought – *Luiz. What about Luiz?* Was it a dream? Had she just imagined his voice?

"You're badly bruised," Jorge continued, matter-of-factly. "And your face is cut – nothing that a touch of plastic surgery can't take care of when the time comes. My own personal physician will visit you later. Meanwhile, the doctors here feel you should stay in the hospital for a few days of observation, just in case."

She tried to nod, couldn't quite make it, and drifted back into a deep sleep.

*

"Good morning, Miss Le Serre." So spoke a crisp nurse in a

virgin white uniform. "You slept through the night. I am sure you are feeling better this morning."

She might be sure, but Rafealla felt like she had the world's worst hangover. However, as soon as she opened her eyes she was functioning, which was an improvement.

"I want to go home," she said groggily.

"We'll see," replied the nurse, with an officious toss of her head.

An hour later Rafealla had her way. Jorge and Odile came to fetch her, and soon she was settled in her own bed, with Jon Jon playing happily nearby.

Odile sat with her, while Jorge – having plied her with dozens of pink roses – went off to his office.

"Sorry," Odile said, in a small voice.

"Don't be silly. It was just as much my fault. I wanted to hit the streets, you didn't force me."

"How's your face?"

"I'll live – it's just a scratch. The creep who bashed me apparently had a pinky ring which cut my cheek open. Jorge is talking plastic surgery, but I rather like the idea of a small scar. It's mysterious, don't you think?"

"Certainly *not*. Who wants to be reminded? You could have been killed."

"For what? A pair of earrings and a necklace? You know, they really were a couple of inept jerks – they didn't even look at my fingers." She held up her hand, staring at the huge ring Jorge had presented her with. "My diamond is intact."

"That's good."

"It doesn't really matter, does it? Jorge could buy me dozens of these and not even feel the pinch."

"Lucky you. A far better situation than Eddie Mafair sponging off your family and throwing it all away on gambling."

"I guess."

Odile, curled up on the end of the bed, hugged her knees and said, "Well, we'll soon be off, and I've made Rupert promise me faithfully that we'll come back for your wedding. Have you decided on a date yet?"

Rafealla shook her head. "Jorge and I will discuss it. Naturally, as soon as we decide, you'll be the first to know. Isn't it always that way?"

Odile smiled. "I hope so. I'd hate to be left out."

*

Two weeks later the drama of the Carnival was forgotten. Only the scar on her cheek reminded Rafealla that during one moment of violence, her life might have been over. It made her think very carefully about her future, and what she really wanted. Her one great achievement was giving birth to Jon Jon. No big deal, millions of women had babies every day. Was she just going to marry a rich man and settle into a life of safe, secure luxury? For Jorge continued to press about a date for their wedding, even though she had told him she thought they should wait.

No. She had to try and achieve something on her own before committing herself to marriage again.

Every day she woke up with a renewed sense of determination and vigour, until one day it came to her. What was she good at? What did she honestly love to do?

"Jorge," she said, very quietly. "I've decided I'm going to try a career as a singer."

He was barely awake. "I beg your pardon?"

"A singer," she repeated slowly. "As in entertainer."

He struggled to sit up. "Are you feeling all right?"

"Perfectly fine."

Deciding to humour her, he said, "If it amuses you, my darling, you can do whatever you wish."

She frowned. "I wasn't asking your permission."

"I realize that. I was merely giving you my blessing."

Sometimes Jorge turned into that rare commodity, an understanding man. It hadn't always been that way – he had mellowed as the years passed.

The months that followed were exciting. Now that she'd made up her mind to do something, there was no way she could be swayed. A singing career was the perfect choice – in a way it brought her closer to her father. He'd been one of the most famous operatic tenors in the world, and maybe she'd inherited some of his talent, although opera wasn't her style – she was drawn more towards the soft, lilting sounds of samba, infused with a mellow jazz influence.

Her father had been an avid collector of blues and jazz records – his particular favourites were Billie Holliday, Dinah Washington and Sarah Vaughn. Rafealla had inherited his collection, and had always been attracted to the rich, melancholy sounds of their voices. She didn't care for the heavy-metal, rock or punk influences of today, finding them too hard-edged. The Brazilian flavour, combined with soothing jazz and blues, suited her nicely. And it also fitted her low, smoky voice to perfection.

Jorge wanted to help her, but she'd told him up front she did not require his assistance. If she was going to achieve anything it had to be on her own or not at all, so reluctantly he stood back, allowing her to do things her way.

At twenty-three, Rafealla embarked on a career. She was determined to succeed.

Bobby Mondella 1983

They were sitting around in Nichols Kline's Century City penthouse office, when Bobby reached over and poured himself another bourbon.

"You're drinkin' too much," Nichols said bluntly. He was the only one who dared talk that way. Everyone else kissed ass.

"Gee. Sue me," Bobby said sarcastically.

"Take a look in the mirror," Nichols insisted. "You got sleepin' bags under your bloodshot eyes a boy scout group could camp out in."

"Very funny, man."

"*And* you're gettin' a gut."

"Tough shit. Nobody said I had t'be perfect."

Nichols leaned back in his custom-made leather chair. "For the Leibovitz photo session you've got to be. The cover of *Rolling Stone* still means plenty."

"Big fuckin' deal. I don't need it," Bobby replied confidently.

Bobby Mondella, Nichols decided, was beginning to believe his own publicity. "A cover on *Rolling Stone* you always need, and don't you forget it."

"Yeah, where's it written?" Bobby challenged.

"In small print. On your ass."

"You're turnin' into a comedian, Nichols."

"An' you're turnin' into an asshole."

It occurred to Bobby that he didn't have to take this kind of disrespectful shit, not from anyone. It was bad enough that Nova was still giving him the run-around – why should he let Nichols get away with talking down to him?

"Hey—" he said threateningly. "You want me to split from Hit City – keep on needlin' me an' you got it, man. I can walk into Warners, Motown, any place I want. They'd get down on their fuckin' *knees* to have me."

"Really?" Nichols asked snidely.

"You'd better believe it."

"You can't walk, Bobby," Nichols said, his tone hardening. "You belong to Hit City. You can't walk anywhere." He paused, allowing his words to sink in. "Which reminds me – Carmine's comin' to town for his goddaughter's twenty-first birthday party and he's requested you sing."

Bobby frowned. "What are you talkin' about?"

"Sing. Entertain. Make nice to his friends."

"Are you shittin' me? I gave up weddin's and bar mitzvahs a long time ago."

"This is a favour. A very personal favour for Carmine. He owns most of the company, you know. So I suggest you take it seriously."

Bobby walked to the window and stared out at the view. He could see the apartment building he used to live in. The same apartment where Nova first came on to him. "Why's that?" he asked, not really interested in Nichols's reply, because he had no intention of singing at anyone's twenty-first birthday.

Nichols pressed his fingers together, forming a dome. "Have you ever studied your contract? Like I mean looked into the small print? I'm sure you're aware that when Hit City bought you out of Blue Cadillac you signed yourself into a new deal – right?"

Bobby nodded.

"A dynamite deal with everything you ever wanted, huh?"

"What is this – rerun time?"

"No. Just a reminder. Hit City is owned by Arnie Torterelli,

Carmine Sicily, and a syndicate of investors. I have a piece of
the action – naturally."

"So, what the fuck are you gettin' at, Nichols? Don't be shy.
Spit it out."

"Check your contract. If Carmine or Arnie don't want you
to work for ten years, there's not a damn thing you can do
about it. Because *this* contract is unbreakable. There's *no* gettin'
out, unless we say so." A meaningful pause. "If I was you, I
wouldn't make Carmine mad. Keep things nice an' smooth,
know what I mean, Bobby?"

He didn't answer. Instead he studied Nichols Kline, sitting
behind his desk so full of his own importance, and tried to
decide whether the jerk-off was actually *threatening* him.

No. He was too big to be threatened by anyone.

"The party is next Saturday," Nichols said mildly. "How
about it?"

*

It started with one simple twenty-first birthday party. A favour.
For Carmine Siciliy. He did it, why not? It was better than
getting into a hassle.

And then there was Arnie Torterelli's parents' wedding anniversary in Florida. They made it very easy for him. A private
jet, the whole bit.

A week in Las Vegas at the Mirage Hotel he fought against.
"I'm not a Vegas performer," he said. "Get Lionel Ritchie or
Jefferson Lionacre."

"They want *you*," Nichols insisted. "They'll pay whatever
we ask." And then the ominous words, "It's a favour for
Carmine. He's promised you'll do it, you can't let him down."

Bobby felt like he was living two lives. On one hand he was
this enormous superstar. And on the other – every time the
word "favour" was whispered, he was expected to jump.

Nichols Kline had turned out to be right. His contract was
unbreakable. Professionally he was completely in their hands.
When he consulted a sharp, independent lawyer, the man said,
"There's only one way you can break *this* contract. Kill yourself."

Very funny.

He raged at himself for having been so stupid. Money and artistic control had led him into the biggest trap of his life. The favour trap. He was their pet superstar, wheeled out for weddings, birthdays and anniversaries.

He hadn't seen Nova in months and he missed her. Not that she cared — if she had she would have contacted him. When he'd told her goodbye at their last meeting she'd obviously taken him at his word. For compensation he moved Zella Raven into his house. Zella, the amazon. It was better than sleeping with a different girl every night. It was better than being alone.

Hey — he was a star — what did anything matter? As long as he had lots of money to throw around, an entourage of "yes" people, plenty of booze and the more than occasional snort of cocaine — what did *anything* matter?

Bobby Mondella was a superstar. That was the bottom line. And the bottom line was all that counted.

Saturday, July 11, 1987
Los Angeles

"I don't know why I couldn't go to the press conference with you," Cybil complained. "You know, Kris, sometimes you act like you're ashamed of me."

"Don't be daft."

"It's true. You never include me in anything that's important to you."

"Sure I do."

"Like what?" she demanded belligerently.

"The Song for Food gig. I took you with me."

"Big deal. The world was at that."

"It was a very special session."

"I know. So special that I got completely left out. I was hanging around like some kind of—" she gulped, hardly able to say the word – "groupie."

"C'mon, luv." He touched her hair. "Nobody would mistake *you* for a groupie."

She had been saving the next bit of information, knowing it would aggravate him. "Well, Del Delgardo did."

"Did what?"

"Thought I was a groupie. I was *so* humiliated."

She'd aroused his interest. "When?"

"At the Song for Food recording session."

"What did the bastard do?"

"He came on . . . you know."

She was just trying to get him going. Why was he falling for it? "You're probably imagining it," he said dismissing her accusation.

"Kris," she replied in a hurt voice. "I *do* know a come-on when I see one. He asked me back to his house for a party, like I was just some cheap little bimbo standing around waiting for him to notice me. When I told him I was with you, he laughed."

"Laughed, did he?"

"Don't you *care*?"

"I've got more important things on my mind right now."

"Like what?"

"Like gettin' this bleedin' gig over an' done with, an' gettin' the hell out of here."

*

As the start of the evening's gala drew closer, things were heating up. The chefs were busily preparing hundreds of tantalizing appetizers for the early part of the event, and screaming at any waiter they could catch. The tables were set with pale pink cloths, fine silverware, and an assortment of glasses. Waiters and busboys were diligently placing the centrepiece flower arrangements, decorated with pale lilac long-stemmed candles.

Soon the guests would be arriving, and gathering on the tented tennis course, where they would sip cocktails and nibble on fine hors d'oeuvres before sitting down to dinner.

"You!" One of the chefs caught Maxwell's attention with an authoritative snap of his fingers. "Take this tray over to the guest house for Bobby Mondella. Make it quick."

"Where's the guest house?" Maxwell asked blankly, although he knew perfectly well.

"Ask someone else," yelled the chef. "Can't you see I'm busy?"

Maxwell took the tray. On it was a covered dish, under which was a plain omelette, with an accompanying order of crisp french fries. Balancing it on one hand he headed in the wrong direction. A uniformed guard stopped him. "Where are you going?"

"Delivering an order for Bobby Mondella."

The guard said, "Wait a minute," and consulted a special map. "The big guest house. Take one of those golf carts over there. Follow the main path all the way past the swimming pool and you can't miss it."

"Thanks," said Maxwell, thinking that a golf cart in his possession was exactly what he needed. Placing the tray on the passenger seat, he got behind the wheel. This was probably going to be the last errand he would ever have to run.

*

Trudie was dying to ask Rafealla what the deal was, only she didn't quite dare. It wasn't like they were girlfriends or anything. Rafealla was the star, and Trudie merely publicity. They had common ground – only it didn't include the true scam on Marcus Citroen.

Trudie would give anything to know the real story. She'd worked at Blue Cadillac for five years and heard *the* most outrageous stories about her boss. Maybe Rafealla could enlighten her.

"Uh . . . how long have you known Marcus Citroen?" she asked on the ride back from the press room. It was worth a shot.

Rafealla blanked her with a look, ignoring the question, asking instead, "Are you pleased with how everything went in there?" talking about the press conference.

"Considering you weren't prepared, I thought you were brilliant," Trudie replied. "Especially the way you handled that English bitch – Cyndi Lou whatshername."

"Thank you. I've come up against her before. There's no point in answering her questions, she's already decided what she's going to write."

"One of the guys was telling me she gave Kris Phoenix a hard time. Do you know him?"

An innocent enough questions. Did she know him? No, she didn't know him at all. But she did have his son. God! What a secret to live with. *Her* secret, for she had never told another soul. She wondered if they would come face to face tonight, and shivered. "I'm hungry," she said. "Do you think we can get something to eat before the concert?"

Rafealla had a disconcerting habit of not answering direct questions. Trudie was becoming quite used to it. "In this place? Are you kidding me? I think we can get anything we damn well please."

*

"What the fuck took ya so long?" Speed demanded, a nervous tic dominating the left side of his face.

The lawyer stared at him coldly. Clients like this he could do without. His fee would most certainly be exorbitant.

"I got here as soon as I could."

"Don't jerk me around, ya took ya freakin' time."

"I'm here. You're out. That's good enough, isn't it?"

"Fuckin' lawyers," Speed mumbled under his breath as they both left the police station.

*

He'd rehearsed. He'd run the gauntlet of the press, and now he just wanted to take it easy before performing.

"Sara, babe," he said. "I'd just like to be on my own for a while. Do you mind?"

"Not at all," she said brightly, although of course she did. It hurt her when he shut himself away. She was happy to be in his company twenty-four hours a day. Why couldn't he feel the same?

"Shall I come back in an hour?" she asked.

"Yeah, that'll be fine."

"Maybe I should wait until your omelette arrives."

"I can handle it."

"There's a small table next to the door with a bowl of flowers on it. If you walk over, be careful—"

"I *said* I can handle it," he interrupted, aggravated by her fussing.

"I know, I know."

"Then get the hell out." His tone was joking, but she knew him well enough to exit fast.

He felt her absence by the silence. People didn't have to speak when they were in a room with him, he always knew they were there by the sound of their breathing.

Getting up, he made a tour of the room, leading with his hands. Once, Sara had suggested he use a white stick. "Never!" he'd told her vehemently, also rejecting the idea of a seeing-eye dog. Not that he disliked animals, it was just that he had to be responsible for his own safety, there could be no props to hang onto.

A knock on the door heralded the arrival of the food he'd ordered.

"Come in," he said, groping his way to the couch.

Her perfume reached him first, the rich, sensual, unmistakable Nova Citroen musk.

He'd known instinctively that once he'd got rid of Sara, she would come.

"Hello, Nova," he said quietly.

*

"What's you name, honey?"

The sudden influx of able-bodied men to Novaroen had Vicki in hot demand. For weeks all she'd seen were Mexican gardeners, a few gay house-men, plus Tom and his merry band of security heavies. Now the place was crawling with out-of-work actors, male models and the like, all doing double duty as waiters. And a good-looking bunch they were too. The barmen weren't bad either.

Vicki decided if a girl wasn't working she could have a real peachy time.

"Don't you worry 'bout *my* name, sailor," she said sassily, fixing the waiter who was coming on to her with a flirtatious look. He had a yellow cowlick of hair and a body that would have fitted nicely into Chippendales. "Just get on with what *you're* supposed to be doing."

"Talkin' of gettin' it on,'" he winked suggestively.

"Forget it," she replied, shortly.

"You can't blame a guy for tryin'."

Maybe she didn't look as bad as she thought. Tom certainly had the idea she was Marilyn Monroe back in business.

Moving right along she walked back towards the main house, where Mrs Ivors – the Joan Crawford housekeeper – waited impatiently.

"Go over to the guest house," Mrs Ivors ordered. "And stay there until further notice. If any of the celebrity guests need anything at all, see they get it. I may as well warn you, Mrs Citroen will fire anyone who is caught not doing their job tonight. That is official. Do you understand?"

Vicki bobbed her head. "Yes, *ma'am*. I'll make sure I do my job *real* good!"

*

Marcus Citroen could be the most charming man in the world when he wanted to be – smooth, knowledgeable, a man of taste and money. Most women found him attractive, even though he was not good looking in the conventional sense. With his bald, egg-shaped head, dark-hued skin, and hooded eyes, he had the look of a Middle Eastern potentate. Power was his main attraction. It radiated from him drawing people toward him like a magnet – especially women. And Marcus was used to women being available at his command. Like Sharleen, who'd needed him to guide her career. From the very beginning she'd understood the game. And he'd made her a star. It wasn't as if he'd used her and not done as he'd promised.

Rafealla was something else. She was an obsessive challenge, and he looked forward to breaking her in.

Nova had *always* understood the game. Far better than anyone else. In her own peculiar way, Nova was the female equivalent of him – which was why they were irrevocably tied together – sexually and otherwise.

As far as Marcus was concerned, most women were dispensable. When they played their role correctly he kept them around. When they didn't, he discarded them without a second thought.

Over the years Nova had come close, very close. But she'd always known when to draw the line.

Tonight was a testing time. He wanted to see if she had learned her lesson.

He had to make absolutely sure.

Kris Phoenix 1984

They were shooting the third video from his first solo album, *Erotic*, in the grounds of Novaroen, Marcus Citroen's extravagent beach estate.

"Bloody hell!" Kris exclaimed. "This is some place!"

Doktor Head nodded his agreement.

"I wouldn't mind movin' in," Kris joked.

"Put in an offer."

"Ha ha!"

A trio of girls in extremely brief bikinis paraded past. They were extras, hired for background. Once Kris would have had them, one by one, but not now he was older and wiser and living in a world where AIDS was the killer everyone feared.

He sat back in his canvas chair with his name stencilled on it and merely watched.

"Hi, Kris," one of them said boldly, with a cute little wave.

"Hello, darlin'," he replied, even though he had no idea who she was.

"Watch out," Doktor Head muttered. "Here comes the lady of the house. Make nice, she runs the show."

Kris stood up. He had heard plenty about the alluring Mrs Citroen, and was interested in meeting her.

She walked briskly over, cool in linen slacks and a silk shirt.

her white-blonde hair a startling constrast to her lightly tanned skin.

"Mr Phoenix," she said graciously. "What a pleasure to meet you. And belated congratulations on joining Blue Cadillac. I've just returned from Europe. Now that I'm back, I'd love to give a dinner for you."

"Sounds great."

"Tuesday?" she questioned.

"That's good for me."

Doktor Head arose also, a fierce sight with his wild mass of flaming red hair and messy beard. "Madame," he said politely. "I'm Doktor Head. The manager."

She raised a cynical eyebrow. "Doktor . . . *Head?*"

"A strange name, I know. Bestowed on me many moons ago. But fitting, I can assure you."

Kris had never seen Doktor Head grovel before, and he tried not to laugh.

Nova didn't seem to find him particularly amusing. Dismissing him with a perfunctory nod, she turned back to Kris. "Where are you staying?"

"The Westwood Marquis."

"I'll send a car for you. Seven-thirty on Tuesday. Casual. Will you have a young lady with you, or shall I arrange a selection?"

It sounded as if she were talking about a box of chocolates! "I'll be alone," he said.

She smiled. "In that case I'll put together an interesting group. Seven-thirty. Don't forget. Oh, and please enjoy yourself today – if there is anything you need, anything at all, don't hesitate to ask."

She strolled over to talk to the director – a young hot-shot who knocked off videos in between making hugely successful feature films.

"And what exactly am I? Chopped liver?" demanded Doktor Head, twitching and winking overtime. "Why didn't you tell her to invite *me?*"

"Because I hardly reckoned it was your kind of deal."

"Oh, and I suppose it's yours?"

"I *can* go to a dinner party without you comin' along to hold my hand, can't I? It was bad enough when I had the whole mob to think about."

The second assistant hurried over. "Mr Phoenix, we're ready for you now."

In just over a year he'd made it on his own. Thank God he'd listened when Mikki told him all that time ago to tag his name onto the front of The Wild Ones. When they split, everyone knew who he was, there was no great identity crisis. The other three had not been so lucky. Buzz was deported from America, and stormed back to England with Mikki in tow, where he'd eventually formed a new group called Mania. They'd disbanded after six months, and Buzz occasionally did gigs on his own.

Rasta was keeping a low profile while he fought his two paternity suits.

And Fingers had become a sort of underground cult figure.

The main problems had been sorting out the legal hassles involved with breaking up a successful group. Kris had taken Doktor Head's advice and hired the best lawyers to look after his interests. Meanwhile, he'd gone to his house in France, with Bo, and an au-pair girl.

It was a soothing transition period. After all, he'd been twelve years on the road on and off, with hardly a break. During that time The Wild Ones had become public property, and their lives reflected that. Not to have any commitments was sheer bliss.

While Bo was staying with him they spent all their time together, swimming, going out on the powerful Riva he'd bought, snorkelling, and water skiing – which they both learned to do together. At the end of three weeks he felt a lot closer to his son, and more at peace with himself because of it. Then, like a fool, he shattered everything by inviting his mum to come for a visit.

"Can I bring Brian and 'is family?" she pleaded. The brothers were talking again since Bo's accident.

"Why?"

"It's all right fer you, lad. You've got everyfing. Brian 'asn't. Brian packed in 'is job, 'e *needs* a holiday."

Some holiday. Brian arrived, more pompous than ever, complete with Jennifer – who had turned into the stereotype of a nagging wife – and their two whining kids. He wasted no time in launching straight into his pitch. "I've left the bank as you already know," he said imperiously. "And I've been thinking, now that you're on your own, you need new management."

"I'm stickin' with Doktor Head."

"No, no. You should have *new* representation. I've already decided to help you out."

"What are you *talkin'* about?"

"*I'll* be your manager," Brian announced magnanimously.

Kris doubled over laughing. "You?" he exploded with mirth. "Fuck me!"

"Naturally," Brian said, ignoring his brother's outburst. "it's a sacrifice on my part. But I decided blood is blood. Who can run your affairs better than me?"

"Jesus Christ! You've really flipped, haven't you?"

"Obviously I'll need to learn a thing or two about the music business. But working in a bank for the last nine years, I certainly know how to deal with people."

"Leave it out, mate. I'll bust a gut laughin' if you keep this up."

Brian was affronted because Kris didn't jump at his offer. He complained to Avis, who in turn complained to her younger son. "If yer can't give yer own bruvver a job, I don't know what," she said huffily.

They accepted his hospitality for two weeks, and then returned to England. Not a moment too soon as far as he was concerned. He later heard from one of his sisters that Brian was claiming Kris had *asked* him to leave his job to come and work for him, and then changed his mind. Now he was the family villain. Charming!

Finally, when he got rid of everyone and was alone, he started to write, composing the words and music for several new songs.

Things were going well, so well that he wanted to share it with someone. One day he thought of Astrid, tracked her down and called her in Paris. "You still engaged?" he asked.

"Yes," she replied.

"I need some pants."

"I'll mail them to you. What colour?"

"No good. I've put on a pound or two. I'll have to get a fitting."

"Really?"

"No kidding. I'm in the South of France, can you fly down?"

A long thoughtful pause. "Okay."

"I'll send you a ticket. Bring a bikini."

"I can't stay."

"Bring a bikini anyway. You've got time for a swim, haven't you?"

She arrived for a day and spent the summer. They'd been together ever since. Right now she was in London keeping the Grosvenor Square flat warm, and overseeing the renovations to the country house he'd bought.

Astrid was a calming influence. It was nice to have someone to confide in and share things with. She was also a right little raver in bed – once he finally got her there.

The break-up of The Wild Ones made world-wide headlines and caused a lot of heartbreak for their legions of fans. Kris refused to give interviews or talk about it, and when intrepid reporters turned up on his doorstep in France they were turned away.

One weekend Doktor Head arrived with news of a solo deal he was negotiating with Blue Cadillac.

"I don't want to get caught into anything long-term," Kris warned. "Just make it for one album an' I'll see if I'm happy."

He was happy. *Erotic* was his first album with Blue Cadillac, and it was a smash. Not only a huge commercial success, but critically acclaimed also.

Yes, Kris Phoenix was extremely happy indeed.

*

Nova Citroen's dinner party took place at her Bel Air house, an enormous mansion with startling views and an army of servants to attend to the sixteen guests' every need. Marcus was not in residence.

"He's in London," Nova explained, when Kris arrived. "Business, as usual."

She introduced him around to a group that included two movie stars, a writer, a couple of important producers, *the* personal manager, Hawkins Lamont, and several gorgeous, apparently unattached blondes. When Nova Citroen said she'd arrange a selection, she' *knew* what she was talking about.

One of the blondes, clad in a short leather dress, slinked over to him. "Hi," she said with a welcoming smile. "Didn't we meet at Allan Carr's last week?"

"I was in London last week," he replied, wondering if the pushed-up tits were silicone or real.

"Shame! Think of the fun we could've had!"

The leather dress – appealing as it was – put him off. It reminded him of Astrid, waiting patiently in London. They'd promised each other there would be no screwing around. It just wasn't fair any more with all the diseases lurking about. Not that any of Nova's guests looked disease-ridden, but that was the whole point – with AIDS you couldn't notice a thing. Having sex with strangers nowadays was like playing Russian roulette.

Two handsome waiters served drinks while Nova flitted among her guests. Kris found himself making conversation with a man he had grown up watching on the movie screen. The man, once a matinée idol, now had yellowing teeth, grey hair, and a large paunch, but he was pleasant enough – especially when he started to carry on about how much he liked Kris's music.

Funny, Kris had never considered he appealed to old people too.

Hang about, a little voice warned him. '*What's old? You're bleedin' thirty-five.*

Christ! Thirty-five. He was getting up there. A nerve-wracking thought. In his mind he'd always imagined that when he reached forty he would quit. But forty was creeping closer every day, and he had no intention of going anywhere. Look at

Mick Jagger – over forty and still prancing about like a teenager. And Rod Stewart – he had to be around the dreaded Four O mark, not to mention Paul McCartney, Pete Townsend, and a whole slew of ageing rockers.

"I think I need another drink," he said, grabbing a glass of champagne from a moving waiter.

Nova took him discreetly to one side before they went into the dining room for dinner. "I've put Hawkins Lamont on your right – he's the most fascinating man, and certainly the right manager for you. Unfortunately he's not taking on any new clients right now. But I felt you should meet him. Tell me, who would you like on your other side?"

"You," he said, without thinking.

The shadow of a smile. "I was hoping you'd say that."

Rafealla 1984

I fall in love too easily
I fall in love too fast,
I fall in love too terribly hard
For love to ever last.

As Rafealla sang the poignant Sammy Cahn and Julie Styne song, there was rapt silence in Julio's, the small, discreet supper club she had begun to call her second home. Originally booked to appear once a week, she was now performing nightly, singing her particular blend of popular American classics set to a throbbing jazz/samba beat.

Clad in a simple white dress, her long hair loose around her exotically beautiful face, she sang of undefined yearnings and intoxicating passion. Her voice, low and smoky – filled with bittersweet sensuality.

After only a year of performing professionally, Rafealla was a hit. She had an appeal that struck home immediately, and whether she was singing in Portuguese – which she'd learned – or her native English, the Brazilians loved her.

Recently she'd been offered a recording contract, and a permanent singing spot on a popular television show. She could hardly believe it, everything seemed to have happened so fast.

Although Jorge gamely tried to pretend, he was not happy.

He'd lost his would-be bride to a career, and it did not sit well with him. A month ago she'd moved out of his mansion, taking Jon Jon with her. "I can wait," he'd said bravely. "You'll come back."

Rafealla had shaken her head as she kissed him sadly. "It was never meant to be. You'll find someone who loves you more than I ever can."

She left behind her huge diamond ring, plus all the other gifts he'd lavished upon her. And once again she was by herself.

Jon Jon accepted the move without complaint. Now nearly seven, he combined the best physical qualities of both parents. Tall for his age, he had Rafealla's deep olive skin and high cheekbones, along with Kris Phoenix's intense blue eyes and spiky blond hair.

"You're such a good-looking kid," she told him every day, accompanied by a big hug. "How did I ever get so lucky?"

"'Cos you got *me, me, me!*" he yelled happily.

Yes. She had Jon Jon. And a career. And an agent/manager – Tinto Reuben – who looked after her well. Life was pretty good.

Once a week her mother phoned from England. "When are you coming to visit, dear?"

"Soon," Rafealla replied dutifully.

They had the same conversation every time. Rafealla didn't want to go home. Going back would only remind her of Eddie Mafair, and God forbid he should try to see Jon Jon, although up until now he'd made no attempt. Odile had bumped into him at Annabel's one night, and apparently he hadn't asked after either of them. Great! She couldn't be happier. Hopefully she would never have to set eyes on him again.

Her manager was waiting when she finished her set. Tinto Reuben was a short, jolly man of fifty, with chubby cheeks and a chipmunk grin. He had been recommended by her singing coach, and they'd hit it off at once. Tinto was married with seven children. He'd once been a singer himself, and understood the business thoroughly. No big-time agent, he was well respected and liked, with a middle-of-the-road client list. Rafealla, he knew, was on the verge of making it in a big way. When she first came to him the beautiful young girl had everything except experience. Now, a year later, she was ready for anything.

"What's up, Tinto?" she asked, lighting a cigarette as she sat down.

"You smoke too much," he scolded.

"I've got to have *one* bad habit," she laughed. "It's a hangover from my school days when smoking was the most decadent pursuit around."

Tinto smiled. He had good news. "Next week there's a very special song festival in São Paulo. You are invited to appear."

Her face lit up. "I am?"

"It's an honour."

"Why me?"

"You're becoming popular, my dear."

"I love it!"

"Wait. This is only the beginning."

*

São Paulo was a lovely city. Flying in at noon, Rafealla gazed out of the window of the aeroplane absorbing the panoramic view spread out below.

"You've never been here before?" Tinto asked.

"I've always wanted to."

"My wife was born here. She tried to come with us – not so easy with seven children to look after, eh?"

"Plus one of mine."

"She loves having Jon Jon to stay. Maria is mother earth." He beamed, a contented man.

After checking into the hotel they were due to go over to the rehearsal hall and meet Rafealla's back-up musicians. She preferred the minimum of help. Just guitar and keyboard, sometimes a touch of percussion. Originally she'd asked if she could bring the musicians she usually worked with, but Tinto thought the cost too prohibitive to fly them in for one night's performance.

The weather was hot and sultry. Arranging her long hair in a thick braid, she put on loose cotton pants and a sizes-too-big tee-shirt. Tinto was clad in his usual pale pink suit – he had several of them – and a brown shirt that strained across his protruding stomach.

"Tell you what," Rafealla said as they entered the rehearsal hall. "You give up eating and I'll stop smoking."

"You have a deal!"

"When?"

"When what?"

"*When* are you going to start dieting?"

"After Christmas."

"That's eight months away!"

Innocently he said, "Really?"

Shaking her head she couldn't help smiling.

Tinto introduced her to several of the organizers of the festival. She made polite chat about nothing much at all, until a svelte woman dressed in red, said, "Ah, here come your back-up musicians – Carlos Pinafida on the piano, and Luiz Oliveira, guitar. Luiz is a very talented young man. He has a wonderful style. Later in the concert he will be performing his own composition – *English Girl*. He's very popular locally."

And so Rafealla came face to face with Luiz once more. Three years after their last encounter.

Holding her breath she stared straight at him.

He stared back.

The air was charged with electricity.

Bobby Mondella 1984

The success trip. He'd climbed to the top of the mountain, taken a deep breath and found the air stank. Why wasn't it cool and clear and pleasant? How come everything was such a fuck-up?

Bobby Mondella stared at his photographic image on the cover of *Rolling Stone* and wondered why it didn't thrill him. *You're a handsome son of a bitch*, he told himself dispassionately, reaching for a drink.

Zella Raven floated into the room, a black superwoman in leopard-print leather. Zella enjoyed the high life. Zella snorted coke for breakfast and finished the day with a touch of free-basing. In the back of his mind he knew he had to get rid of her, she was dragging him down.

Once . . . long ago . . . he'd been anti-drugs. He, more than anyone, had seen how they destroyed people. Now he let it go on all around him, and he wasn't averse to joining in occasionally, because drugs gave him even more power and strength – and fuck it – when he was high he owned the whole *world*, and *nothing* and *no one* could bring him down. Including Nova.

Ah . . . Nova. His obsession. How come he had everything, and everything wasn't enough, because he would give every-thing just to possess the one woman he couldn't have? It didn't make sense.

When he was drunk or stoned-it didn't even matter.

He knew one thing. *Rolling Stone* was correct when they said he couldn't write any more. The songs stopped coming one day – just like that.

No inspiration. No drive. *No shit?*

Hey – *Rolling Stone* wrote that Bobby Mondella was not the talent he once was. What did he care? He'd reached the top and it was a long fall down.

Zella liked to party. Every night they hit a new club or restaurant. They *owned* Las Vegas, where he regularly appeared – a favour for Carmine, his best friend Carmine – or was it Arnie? – good old Arnie.

"How come y'alls lookin' like you're dead in the water?" Zella asked, fluffing out a wild Afro wig which perched atop her head like a frothy cake. "An' you're not even dressed."

"Why should I be dressed? We're not goin' anywhere."

"*Sure* we are, sugar. You-all forgotten? It's Arnie's big party at the beach."

Another party. Another lousy time. And everyone would probably have read the put-down piece in *Rolling Stone* which he chose to ignore because who gave a shit? Fuck it! What did he care? They'd only remember seeing his picture on the cover. Another cover. More fame. And he was a handsome son of a bitch. . . .

Yeah . . . Mister Soul Superstar was a handsome son of a bitch . . .

And so fuckin' what?

*

Women always came on to him. It was a fact. They smiled and tried to act normal, but Zella had captured it like it was when she'd said, "Honey, they are creamin' their scanty lace panties what*ever* damn stuff they're talkin'."

Sex symbol.

Black sex symbol.

A double hit.

"The storms were quite devastating," said a beautiful woman

with a diamond the size of an acorn on her finger. "But we'd never sell."

"You wouldn't, huh?" commented Bobby, swaying on his feet.

"Never," she replied, gazing at him steadfastly. "Malibu is the best."

Was she hot for him? Was she steaming?

Oh yeah, he could tell.

"Bobby, darling!" Greetings from Poppy Soloman, the ebullient wife of a studio head. "How *nice* to see you again. Thank you, thank *you* for appearing at my charity. Everyone was thrilled."

Did she want him? Was she ready?

A simple yes would do it.

He watched Zella, taking off across the room. Ever since landing the villainess role in a Rambo-type film she was Miss Movie Star – playing the role on screen and off, and loving every minute.

At least someone was happy.

"Hey, man – long time, how're ya doin'?"

He turned to face his old friend Rocket. The same old scruffy Rocket, with his long, greasy hair and beat-up clothes. The same Rocket who last year had been nominated for an Oscar – honouring his fine performance in a stark movie about corruption in politics.

Bobby was pleased to see him. They'd lost touch, and hadn't run into each other for a long while. With genuine cameraderie they exchanged hugs.

The beautiful woman with the diamond, and the wife of the studio head, waited anxiously to be introduced to the moody actor who was not known for his social graces. Since Bobby couldn't remember either of their names, he didn't bother. Instead, he grabbed a fresh drink, and walked outside with Rocket to the pool area.

"Will ya look at this," Rocket said, exasperated, throwing his arms wide. "Whadda they need a pool for when they have a whole ocean?"

"Hey, man." Bobby shrugged. "That's show biz – if ya got it – put out."

Rocket wrinkled his face in disgust. "One hell of a philosophy. Whyn't they jam some of their big bucks back where they belong – with the people?" Taking a crumpled joint from his picket he lit up.

"What are you doin' in L.A. anyway?" Bobby asked. "I thought you hated it."

"Another movie. It's a true story about a Hollywood cocaine freak who snorts his life way. This guy has the world by the balls an' screws everything up. Real powerful stuff."

"You get off on those kind of roles, huh?"

"A lot of people out here are goin' to identify with this one." He dragged on the roach, passing it to Bobby, who declined. "I forgot, this ain't your thing, is it?"

"I'll take some blow if you got it."

Rocket raised a cynical eyebrow. "I wouldn't touch that poison for a million big ones."

Why did Rocket always make him feel like a loser? He was more famous than his actor friend would ever be. Or was he?

"Didja see me on the cover of *Rollin' Stone*?" he found himself asking.

"Why d'you do that stuff?" Rocket said, his voice full of contempt. "You're bendin' over an' beggin' for the screwin' they're gonna give yuh. It don't make no sense to set yourself up for it. Y'should do what *I* do. Nothin'. No press. No shit, Nada."

Before he had a chance to defend himself, Zella was upon them. She was all over Rocket like a sinuous, gleaming snake.

Bobby left them to it. He'd had it with Rocket and his superior attitude. Who the fuck did the prick think he was anyway?

Finding a group snorting cocaine in a bathroom, he joined them.

It didn't matter. Nothing really mattered. Being a star meant never having to explain anything to anyone.

Kris Phoenix 1985

Bedding Mrs Citroen might not have been the greatest idea in the world, but he'd done it – once – and there was no going back.

When Kris reflected on it – which wasn't often – he realized it had not been his fault. After all, what was a guy supposed to do when faced with the wife of his new boss wearing nothing but stilettos and an icy smile? *Sorry, no thank you* wouldn't have seemed polite – especially when she'd just given a dinner in his honour, and sat him next to one of the most sought-after personal managers in the music business.

Once was enough, thank you. Kris knew a balls-breaker when he saw one.

Mrs Citroen. She didn't give up easily. She called him. Sent him presents via chauffeured Rolls-Royce. Tried to pressure him.

He didn't weaken. No way. In fact, what he did do, just to prevent any future complications, was tell Astrid as soon as he got back to England. She was cool, broke some furniture and chipped one of his teeth, but basically she took it well.

This had all taken place a year ago, and a lot had happened in that year. The big news was that he'd been forced to get rid of Doktor Head. It was a move he hadn't been happy making, but it was inevitable once Doktor Head started drinking again – for when he drank he became an uncontrollable maniac, and Kris wanted none of it. As far as his career was concerned he had a killer instinct, refusing to allow anyone to fuck it up. He gave Doktor Head several chances and then fired him. Fortunately they had no contract. Theirs was a handshake arrangement — unethical, but that's the way they'd both wanted it.

Two days after the firing, Kris called Hawkins Lamont. "I need someone to take me higher," he'd said.

"Come into my office and we'll talk."

They met. They talked. They both had the same desire. To make Kris Phoenix into the biggest rock star in the world.

A deal was set.

"You'll move to America," the Hawk had said. "If we intend to make you into an international star you have to be based in the States."

"Astrid'll hate that."

"Don't bring her. Leave her in England. It's better for your image if you're unattached and available."

An excellent solution. Astrid loved the English countryside — she'd be quite happy pottering about there. And he'd spend plenty of time visiting because of Bo.

"Sold!" he'd said.

Six weeks later he said sold again when he purchased a vast house in Bel Air.

True to his word, the Hawk set about making Kris Phoenix into a major superstar. He renegotiated Doktor Head's deal with Blue Cadillac. He put Kris in the hands of one of the hottest and most prestigious PR companies on the West Coast. He suggested a theme for the new album. And he planned a special tour across fifteen key cities to set America alight.

"We have to forget The Wild Ones ever existed, and start afresh," he'd announced, with all the enthusiasm of a great general going into battle. "From now on it's Kris Phoenix all the way. Go home, sit down, and write the best songs you've ever written. The theme is family. Don't forget — family and roots and relationships."

Kris flew back to England, holed up at his country estate, shut off the phones and went to work — emerging, seven weeks later, with twelve gritty, truthful songs full of everything the Hawk had asked for.

The new album was called *Gettin' Down*. The tour was called simply KRIS PHOENIX '85. Both broke every existing record.

The Hawk had done as he'd promised. Within one year Kris Phoenix was the hottest name to hit the rock world since Bruce Springsteen.

Rafealla 1985

There were moments when Rafealla couldn't keep her hands off Luiz, and fortunately he seemed to feel the same way. Bumping into him by chance made her determined never to be apart from him again. A year had passed and she had her wish.

At first they were both uncomfortable to see each other. After the initial shock, they were stiffly polite.

"I didn't know you sang," he'd said.

"And I didn't know you lived in São Paulo," she'd retorted accusingly, longing to say – *Why did you disappear? How come I never heard from you? How dare you treat me like that!*

They'd rehearsed with all the warm interaction of a suspicious Siamese cat and a fierce Doberman.

"What's the matter, Rafealla?" Tinto had asked. "Do you two know each other?"

"Yes," she'd snapped, at the same time as Luiz said a sharp "No."

"Ah . . ." Tinto had sighed wisely, and known exactly what was going on.

Finally, music brought them together. The caressing, insinuating strum of his guitar melded perfectly with her low, sensual voice. By the time they did the concert, they still weren't friendly, but they were in tune.

The next morning, shortly before she and Tinto were due to leave their hotel for the airport, Luiz turned up.

"I think we must talk," he'd said.

"A little late for that," she'd replied.

Tinto had rolled his eyes and handed over her ticket. Rafealla was all work and no play. It wasn't natural. "Yes, talk," he'd encouraged them, nodding understandingly. "Catch the later plane."

When he'd said that, he hadn't meant two weeks later. But that's the way it was. And when she returned, she was glowing – as only a woman in love can.

Luiz, she had discovered, was a very intense and complex young man. His original disappearance was not because he didn't like her, it was due to the fact that he liked her too much. "I had nothing to offer you," he explained simply. "We would not have been happy."

"Yes, we would," she argued.

"No," he insisted. "I had to leave the city. For if I hadn't, the temptation would have trapped me."

So he'd had his reasons. Pride and such-like. And in São Paulo his career progressed, and when they met again he felt ready to accept the challenge of a relationship.

Within weeks of her return to Rio, he followed her, for Tinto had promised he could get them work together. It was an easy promise to keep. They had a magic between them that the public loved. Luiz settled into her apartment and her life as if it were destined, and they were inseparable. Soon, thanks to the success they enjoyed, he was able to afford his own place. Once again Rafealla gave up her independence, and along with Jon Jon moved in with him.

They made a beautiful trio. Rafealla and Luiz – both so dark, with their matching green eyes and jet hair. And Jon Jon – blond and tanned with his shining, innocent baby-blues.

Now, for the first time in her life, Rafealla truly knew what happiness was. She had a career she loved. A man she adored. And Jon Jon.

Odile phoned often. She was insistent. "You *have* to come

home for a visit soon," she said firmly. "Or your mother will have a positive cow!"

"Yes, soon," Rafealla promised, not meaning it at all. For one thing she had no intention of ever letting Luiz out of her sight again, and for another – the thought of him meeting her family was hardly one she relished. Not that they were snobs, the very opposite – but Luiz came from the *favela*, and it would be difficult for him to understand her beginnings, he would feel intimidated and out of place visiting her stepfather's enormous country estate. Meanwhile she sent home her records and press clippings – first censoring the ones that mentioned she and Luiz were living together. Even though she was twenty-five, she knew her mother would be shocked. Especially because of Jon Jon.

They lived an idyllic existence. Working together, playing on the white sandy beaches, enjoying their leisure time and work equally. Luiz was terrific with Jon Jon, just like the father he'd never had.

Their singing success was particularly rewarding. Not only were they both doing something they loved, they were also getting paid for it – and handsomely so. In Latin America they were fast becoming famous, and had enjoyed several hit records.

Tinto sat back like a proud father as he watched and helped their careers grow. When he'd first taken Rafealla on he hadn't planned on handling her as a double act. But she and Luiz were perfect together. Their love shone through everything they did.

"I think we might get married," Rafealla confided to Tinto one day. "Only don't tell Luiz, he doesn't know!"

"My lips reveal nothing."

"Good. Keep it that way."

To celebrate Luiz's latest composition hitting number one – a song they'd recorded together and their third consecutive hit – Tinto threw a big party. Rafealla sat back, allowing Luiz to bask in the limelight and enjoy most of the attention. He was so handsome and exhilarated. He deserved this success.

Proudly she watched him circulate, charming press and guests alike. He never mentioned marriage, but lately it had been on her mind a lot. Oh, sure, she was happy just being with him, only marriage was a more permanent commitment, and since she never wanted to be apart from him again, it seemed like a good idea. Determined not to be the instigator, she'd begun to long for him to ask her. But he remained silent on the subject, obviously quite content with things they way they were.

Other women threw themselves at him. During the course of the party Rafealla noticed several females coming on strong. Luiz had a way of deflecting their advances without hurting their feelings. He was studiously polite and well-mannered, which of course made him all the more interesting. Nothing turned women on more than a man they couldn't get through to. Especially when that man was talented, young, and extraordinarily handsome.

Rafealla couldn't hold back. In the car on their way home she hugged him warmly. "I've got a fantastic idea,' she said.

"What?"

"A sensational idea."

He smiled – white, even teeth, and emerald green eyes she couldn't resist. "Tell me, my carioca," he encouraged, his hand lingering on her knee.

"Let's get married."

A silence. Too long a silence. A *dangerous* silence.

Before he even spoke she knew something was wrong.

He hesitated, and then falteringly said, "I was going to tell you."

She could hardly breathe. "Yes?"

"Uh ... how I say this? He paused again, and then, very slowly, "Rafealla, you know I love you ... But, this is the thing. I am already married."

Bobby Mondella 1985

The crowd at Rio airport to greet Bobby Mondella was gratifyingly large. It took several bodyguards and security police to get him through safely. In the Rolls-Royce sent to meet him he sat back with a satisfied sigh. "Y'see, they still love me," he said.

Nichols Kline, momentarily unnerved by the massive crowds and roaring fans, said, "Sure. This is a foreign country. They're a year behind."

"You're a real downer son of a bitch," Bobby responded angrily. "One record doesn't make number one, an' in your book I'm finished."

"Your last *three* singles," Pammy corrected, with a toss of her dyed hair.

Bobby couldn't stand the phoney bitch. How come Nichols put up with her? She'd laid every one of his friends, and treated him like dirt. But Nichols hung in there, thinking he'd found himself some kind of English princess instead of dumb cunt of the year.

Bobby ignored her. He'd grown expert at pretending she didn't exist. God! He needed a drink. "How far is the hotel?" he asked brusquely.

"Do I look like a fuckin' tour guide?" Nichols snapped. "Ask the driver."

They were all tired after the long journey from Los Angeles.

Hey — Bobby didn't give a damn — he hadn't asked Nichols to come, especially with Miss Congeniality in tow. Nichols had insisted on making the trip. Carlos Baptista, the Brazilian concert promoter, had been begging him to visit for years, and with Bobby due to do three concerts at the Maracana stadium, he'd grabbed the opportunity — with a little persuasion from Pammy.

Bobby half wished Zella was with him, at least he'd have an ally. And then again he was relieved she wasn't. Zella was crazy — certifiably so. She'd freaked out on the set of her latest movie and beaten up two petrified makeup men before being subdued, and ultimately carted off to the Betty Ford Center for a spell of drying out.

Zella was bad news, she dragged him down with her. It wasn't her fault, the woman just couldn't resist causing trouble.

He'd visited her at the clinic before leaving. With a weary smile she'd said, "Hey — superstar — maybe *you* should be in here with me, huh?"

Why the hell should he be? Yeah — he drank. Sure — he did cocaine. But he could control it. He knew *exactly* what he was doing. And anytime he wanted to stop, no problem.

Deep down he was well aware of what he really wanted. To dump Nichols Hit City and get back to his roots. Nine months ago he'd run into Amerika Allen at the Grammy Awards. She'd done pretty well over the years. Soul On Soul was second only to Motown with the cream of black recording artists.

He was pitted against one of her people for Best R & B Vocal performance, an award he'd won several times. Her star got it. A fresh-faced kid with long, corn-rowed hair and a toothy grin, full of enthusiasm and sass.

Bobby applauded along with the rest of the audience. It was the first year since 1977 he'd won nothing, and it hurt.

On the way home he made his driver go into Tower Records on Sunset and buy the kid's record. Back at his house he played it. Some monster hit, with synthesizers and a mesmerizing African beat. It sounded new and exciting.

Then he put on *his* last record. The same old thing. Hot, throbbing, sensual soul. Maybe it wasn't enough anymore.

He'd been using a producer Arnie Torterelli had thrust upon him instead of doing it himself. Another favour. It was time to make some changes.

Insisting on a new producer, he'd said, "I'm tryin' out somethin' different."

Something different hadn't worked. As Pammy so kindly pointed out, his last three singles had failed to hit the number one spot, although the album from which they were pulled had achieved fairly respectable sales.

Respectable didn't cut it. Where were the regular number ones? Where were the album mega-sales he was used to? He was a superstar, for crissake, there was no coming down from that.

Bobby Mondella was on a slide, and he didn't like it one little bit. He especially didn't like it when he had to hear about it from Nichols's moron wife.

He knew what the problem was – he'd been pushing himself too hard, appearing here, there and everywhere, making too many records without concentrating on the content. Bobby Mondella was overexposed. He needed to lay back and return to the people who really cared. Nichols Hit City was money-oriented, that's all they took notice of – making the buck, and pushing, pushing, pushing. They were worse than Blue Cadillac in that respect.

Soul On Soul were interested in quality and style and nurturing the performer. Amerika was an inspiration to work with, and yet he'd dumped on her, had walked when she could have used the support. It was to her credit that she'd behaved so cordially when they ran into each other.

He'd made up his mind that on this Rio trip he was going to tell Nichols he wanted out. If he offered Hit City some kind of over-ride deal where they still continued to get a piece of his future, he was sure they'd let him go. He'd had enough weddings and Vegas stints and doing goddamn favours. He needed time to straighten out and get back into the flow of writing and performing music he had a genuine feeling for. With Zella out of the way he could do it.

The Copacabana Palace was a swank, glitzy hotel overlooking

the ocean, and the famous white-sand Copacabana Beach. Bobby was installed in a magnificent suite on the top floor, where there was champagne on ice, a huge basket of fresh fruit, and several elaborate flower arrangements in both the bedroom and living room.

First he reached for a drink, then he glanced at the attached cards. *Carlos and Chara Baptista welcome you to Rio . . . With the compliments of Carlos Baptista and his staff . . .* And so on.

That night there was a dinner planned for him to meet the concert promoter. To Nichols and Pammy's fury he cancelled out, climbed into bed with a bottle of bourbon and a plate of room service chicken, and watched television. New rule – he was sick of doing what everyone else wanted. No more favours. In future he was going to do exactly what *he* wanted, and if they didn't like it – fuck 'em.

Maybe he'd even try to lay of the booze and drugs for a while. Not that he couldn't stop anytime . . . anytime at all.

Carlos Baptista phoned. The man was polite and concerned, not pissed off like Nichols had been. "We are so sorry you cannot attend our dinner for you. Is there anything you need?"

"I guess I'm just tired," Bobby explained. "The flight an' everything."

"Carlos understands perfectly. Maybe a young woman to massage away the tensions . . ."

"I'm not into arranged sex."

"I didn't mean to insult you."

"Hey, man. No insult. Everything's cool."

Idly he flicked the channels on the television, stopping to watch a young couple singing together. They were fresh and innovative, the girl exotically beautiful, and the man darkly handsome. Their Brazilian blend of samba and jazz was soothing and yet up-beat and very sensuous.

With a burst of interest he sat up. Could this be the inspiration he was looking for? Soul with a mix of samba and jazz. *His* kind of soul done *their* way?

Suddenly he was high. This was it. He knew this was the sound he'd been looking for.

As the credits rolled at the end of the show he searched for their names.

Rafealla and Luiz. Reaching for a pad he scrawled them down.

Rafealla and Luiz, he thought, *you may just have hit pay dirt. Oh, yeah, baby. Oh, yeah!*

*

Rio was his salvation. Rio, with its laid-back ambience, and wonderfully friendly people. His three concerts at the Maracana stadium were a smash, and he revelled in the adulation. The South Americans certainly still loved Bobby Mondella.

After much thought, and to Nichols's great consternation, he told him he'd decided to stay in Rio for a while.

"You can't do that," Nichols objected harshly. "We got commitments to fulfil."

"Cancel 'em."

"Are you *insane*?"

"I like it here. This place is good for me. I'm not drinking. I'm relaxing. And oh yeah – I'm stayin'."

Nichols was furious. The muscle in his cheek twitched as he attempted to remain in control. "For how long?"

"For however long I feel like."

"I'm tellin' you – no can do, Bobby. You have a contract."

"*Fuck* the contract, an' *fuck* you. I've had it with bein' manoeuvred into position every time I breathe. You know something? I've worked for people since I was twelve years old, and now I've decided to do nothin' for however long it takes to get my head straight. We had a contract, so I'll give you a piece of whatever I decide to do in the future, but right now I want out. You got it?"

"You'll regret this," Pammy suddenly shrieked, joining in.

"Shut up, you dumb broad," yelled Nichols, taking his frustrations out on her.

The result was a very flustered Nichols with a sulking wife forced to return to L.A. without Bobby.

Six months had passed, and in spite of numerous threats and angry phone calls Bobby was happy. He'd arranged for his business manager to sell his Hancock Park mansion and all his possessions. He'd told Zella it was over – she wasn't surprised. And he'd started afresh.

For a while stardom had caught him in its trap and sent him spinning out of control. Now he was back on the ground and he liked it. He had a nice apartment in the Chopin building, next to the Copacabana Palace. A variety of girlfriends – nobody special. And most important of all, he was drug free, and hardly drinking at all.

Leisure, he discovered, was very pleasant. And because he didn't *have* to write, the songs began to flow, and his creative juices went into over-drive.

Shortly after seeing Rafealla and Luiz on television, he'd arranged a meeting. Over the following months they became his good friends as well as his musical collaborators, and although they were unable to record together because of his battle with Nichols Hit City, occasionally they snuck in a performance somewhere or other just for the pure enjoyment of it.

The moment he thought his life was settled, Nova reappeared. Two years of silence, and one day she phoned on his private line as if they'd been together all along. "I'm at the airport. I must see you," she said urgently.

"Come right over," he replied calmly.

His heart didn't give him a choice.

*

Just like old times she walked back into his life. Cool, classy Nova Citroen. The Ice Queen to those who didn't know her. The love of his life.

Like a replay he opened his door to a woman he hardly recognized, and she almost fell at his feet. Sharleen – all those years ago – a beaten wreck, and now Nova in the same condition, her face puffed and swollen. She was wrapped in a mink coat, dark glasses covered her eyes, and she was shaking.

"Jesus Christ!" he exclaimed. "What happened to you?"

As if he didn't know. Marcus Citroen.

"Bobby." Even her voice was shaking. "Oh, Bobby! I got on a plane and came straight to you. I didn't know where else to go."

They'd had a long relationship, and not once during the times they were together had she ever shown any vulnerability. Nova was always on top of things.

He opened up his arms and she walked right into his embrace. "C'mon, baby," he comforted. "It's okay, I'm here for you. Everything's gonna be fine." It was as if they'd never been apart.

She began to sob, long-drawn-out cries of pure anguish. "I never thought I'd find you . . . it wasn't easy . . . *God*, Bobby . . . I hate him, I've always hated him . . ."

He led her into his apartment, removed her mink coat, settled her on the couch, and poured her a large glass of brandy.

"Calm down, baby," he said soothingly. "Just take it easy, an' tell me everything."

Slowly she recovered her composure, and removed her dark glasses. Her eyes were swollen slits, the skin black and blue.

"That son-of-a-bitch sadistic bastard!" he said angrily.

"I've left him." Her voice was hardly more than a whisper. "And now he'll try to destroy me."

"Destroy you! Are you *crazy*? *He's* the one in big trouble. Look at yourself, for crissake. Look at what he's done to you."

"You don't understand," she said despairingly. "He *can* destroy me. And I know Marcus. He will."

"How's that?" he asked, humouring her.

"He's going to tell the world the truth about me."

"And what's the truth?"

Lowering her eyes she said, "That when he found me I was a whore."

He looked at her disbelievingly. "Come *on*—"

"It's true." Her voice was bitter. "The Mrs Citroen everyone knows – the *elegant* Mrs Marcus Citroen – was once a highly paid, highly skilled whore in Germany. Marcus . . . discovered me. He . . . changed me. He moulded me into the woman he wanted, and then, when I was exactly the way he desired, he married me."

Bobby's throat was dry. For the first time in months he needed a drink. "Nova," he said, "there's no way I believe this."

"Why not? She gazed at him dispassionately. "It's true. Does it disgust you? Are you sorry we had an affair?"

Shaking his head, he didn't know *what* he felt. For years he'd begged Nova to leave Marcus, and now this.

"There's more," she said. "I need to tell you everything, Bobby, because I have to know how you feel." She paused, and gave a brittle laugh. "Whatever you think, I'll understand. All I want from you is the truth."

Taking a deep breath he said, "C'mon, babe, you're building it way out of proportion."

"Like *hell* I am," she shot back, staring at him defiantly. "Bobby, I'm half black."

"What?"

She touched her white-blonde hair. "Oh, you'd never guess it, would you? No one could ever tell. When Marcus sent me to Paris to be worked over, he had my skin bleached along with my hair. Not that I was ever noticeably dark. My mother was white. My father was a black GI she had a drunken one-night-stand with. Unfortunately she waited too long for an abortion, and the result was me."

"*Je. . .sus!*"

"So you see," she continued in a flat voice, "I am not the woman you imagined me to be. I'm a half-black whore from Germany. Not the ritzy lady who appears on the front pages of *Women's Wear Daily*, and gives the best parties in town. I'm a fraud, Bobby, and Marcus is going to expose me because I've dared to leave him."

*

He cancelled all his arrangements and summoned a doctor to check Nova over. The man glared at Bobby with accusation written all over his face.

"I didn't do it," Bobby explained quickly. "She's runnin' from her husband."

"What's her name?" the doctor asked, filling out a prescription for sleeping pills.

"Margaret," Bobby lied. "Margaret Smith."

"She needs rest. There's no internal damage. Cold compresses on the eyes, and plenty of liquids." A pause. "I really should report it. This woman has been badly beaten."

"Come on, doc. She's had enough trouble."

Another accusatory look. "Very well."

Gradually Bobby pieced together the story. One of Marcus's friendly visits to a whorehouse in Paris. He liked to watch his wife with hookers. She obliged. It was part of their agreement. Later he invited two of the girls back to their apartment. For once Nova objected. But Marcus insisted. The girls were street tarts, they stole clothes and jewellery. Nova said she'd had enough. Marcus said she'd take whatever he handed her. They fought, and he beat her with a golf club, then walked out. As soon as he was gone she'd grabbed a few things, taken a taxi to the airport and boarded the next plane to Rio. Marcus had no idea where she'd run to.

"How come you finally did it?" he asked.

"It was time," she replied simply.

Now she was in his apartment and he didn't know how he felt anymore. He needed a while to work out his true feelings. Hell! She couldn't expect to walk back into his life and find nothing changed, could she?

On top of everything else he got a surprise phone call from Carmine Sicily. "We want you to go back to work, Bobby," Carmine said pleasantly. "We want you on a plane to L.A. this week. I *mean* this week, otherwise you might never go on a trip anywhere ever again. Do we understand each other?"

"I'm not comin' back, Carmine. Don't try to push me. Talk to my lawyers."

"You're playing fuck-you games with the wrong people," Carmine said mildly. "It's my sister's birthday next Tuesday. She likes you, Bobby. She thinks you're handsome. Be there. Be smart."

He didn't mention the phone call to Nova. Screw Carmine Sicily and his threats. They couldn't touch him, they were all talk.

For days Nova lay in the centre of his bed watching television. Her bruises began to fade. He cooked her scrambled eggs and soup, and brought her magazines. The one thing he couldn't do was make love to her. He needed time.

She waited, patiently. She said nothing. It was her way of testing him, and he knew it.

Nova baby, he wanted to say. *I don't give a damn about your past, it doesn't matter to me. What I do care about is the hold Marcus has had on you all this time. How come you didn't break out when I gave you the chance two years ago? What made you keep on doing the things he forced you to do?*

Why, baby?

Why?

The *why* stood between them like a brick wall.

He had to get out of the apartment for a while, go for a walk, grab a beer, anything.

"Hey – will you be okay?" he asked solicitously. "I'll be back in an hour."

She nodded.

He left, and went straight over to Luiz and Rafealla's. They were delighted to see him.

"We've missed you," Rafealla said. "Where have you been?"

He shrugged. "Nowhere. I've got a friend stayin' with me from the States."

"A lady friend?" Rafealla asked playfully.

"Yeah."

"Anything serious?"

Making light of it, he said, "Let's put it this way – I'm not gettin' married."

He didn't stay long, he was too restless. He couldn't help thinking of Nova lying in his bed, waiting for him to make a move, to show her his support.

So she was a whore once upon a time. Did it really matter?

No. But what she did with Marcus mattered.

They had to talk. Decisively he headed home.

The apartment was dark when he let himself in, the flicker of the television from the bedroom providing the only light. The sound on the TV was loud, too loud.

He knew something was wrong a moment too late, for as soon as he sensed danger, he was grabbed from behind, his arms twisted in an immovable lock, and the struggle began.

Bobby was strong, six feet two inches of powerful muscle. But there was more than one man behind him – two, maybe three. He could hear them grunting, smell their lousy breath.

Thoughts flashed through his head. Nova. Was she all right? If they'd hurt her he'd fucking kill them.

They were trying to propel him forward – kicking, thrashing. A heavy object crashed down on his head, his skull exploded, lights flashed. So it was true – you did see stars.

Jesus, blood was trickling down his face, and so was something else. He could smell liquor.

What the fuck did they want? They were half dragging him now, across the thick pile carpet, over towards the balcony.

Terror swept over him.

They were going to throw him over the fucking balcony.

They were going to kill him.

Jesus!

JESUS!

He screamed, but it was too late. He was falling . . . falling in space . . . falling . . .

It was all over.

Saturday, July 11, 1987
Los Angeles

The parade of Rolls-Royces, Mercedes, chauffeur-driven limousines, and other expensive automobiles arriving at the Citroen beach estate was impressive. Each car was stopped at the point of entry while the occupants were identified and checked off a master list. Then a numbered sticker was attached to the windshield, and the driver was allowed to take his party up to the main house, where they were dropped off. After that the chauffeur drove the car back to an allocated parking lot five minutes away. When the guests were ready to leave, their car would be summoned by number.

Several parking valets were in charge of this operation, making sure that everything ran smoothly and there were no traffic jams.

The guests then went through a second security procedure as they entered the reception hall of the main house. Their names were double-checked on another list, and then they were escorted outside to the tented tennis court area, where the party really began.

Hawkins Lamont circulated in his immaculate dinner suit with the white silk jacket – specially tailored for him in Hong Kong. Cybil Wilde was by his side, not really dressed for the occasion, but it didn't matter. Cybil was so stunningly pretty that nobody noticed what she was wearing. Hawkins had no objections to squiring her for the cocktail hour — she made a delightful accessory.

"Take her out there, for crissakes," Kris had grumbled. "She's gettin' on my nerves."

Hawkins obliged. That was what a personal manager was for, wasn't it? To take care of all the things the star couldn't be bothered to deal with himself. Including girlfriends.

With a wry smile Hawkins wondered if perhaps Kris might like him to make love to her too. He would not oblige on that score. Hawkins liked to be seen with pretty girls. He even liked to watch them play together. But he didn't care to take them to bed. He'd lost interest in sex when he discovered business. Money, it turned out, was the greatest satisfaction of all.

"This is *fantastic!*" Cybil enthused. "Have you *seen* who's here! I think I've spotted my favourite Italian movie star."

"Yes, it's quite a group," agreed Hawkins. "Leave it to Nova and they turn out in force."

"Did these people *really* pay one hundred thousand dollars a couple?" Cybil gasped.

"It's only money," Hawkins replied sensibly. "They can afford it. And if the Governor ever makes it to the White House, he'll owe them all a seat at his dinner table."

"Wow! I'd love to meet him. Then he can owe *me* a seat too!"

"I'm sure Governor Highland wouldn't mind meeting you," Hawkins replied, knowing full well the Governor would adore to be introduced to a luscious California blonde who was just his type — breathing. "Come." He offered his arm. "Let us go and find the gentleman."

*

Alone at last, Kris brooded about Cyndi Lou Planter, the moon-faced English journalist, and her dumb questions. Why did he let reporters bother him? Why did he waste his time burdening himself with negative thoughts?

Kris Phoenix was at the top. Naturally everyone wanted to drag him down. It was only human nature . . .

*

Maxwell Sicily passed among the illustrious guests, his tray held aloft, bearing small squares of pizza covered in smoked salmon and golden caviar – the chic L.A. snack. Bejewelled fingers grabbed. Thick hairy wrists wrapped with ten-thousand-dollar watches propelled bony hands in the right direction.

He hadn't even gotten half-way round before his tray was empty. With a purposeful step he returned to the supply bar and picked up a fresh load of hors d'oeuvres. This time he was given tiny crab-cakes with a dipping sauce.

"How delicious!" exclaimed a fat woman in a pink satin ballgown, grabbing two. She stuffed one in her mouth, dipping the second one in the red, zesty sauce. Maxwell observed a splodge of the stuff fall upon her ample bosom as the crab-cake vanished into her mouth. Too bad.

He moved away, listening to fragments of conversation, checking out the lavish jewellery. Why did party guests treat waiters as if they didn't exist? Hands grabbed, eyes rarely met, and a thank you was out of the question. Fucking rich parasites.

Fortunately he didn't have to do this for a living. Thank God he was smarter than everyone at this party put together.

Maxwell Sicily was one of life's winners. By the end of the night he was going to be richer than all of them.

*

Marcus Citroen's voice on the phone was commanding. "Rafealla?"

"Yes, Marcus."

"I wish to see you after the concert."

"Surely you'll be busy with your guests?"

"Kris Phoenix will appear after you. And then there'll be speeches and the auction. We'll have plenty of time. When you finish, you will return to your room. Get rid of the publicity girl and anyone else hanging around. I will see you then. Alone. Do you understand?"

A feeling of dread swept over her. But there was a price, and she had promised to pay it. "Yes, Marcus."

*

Racing down San Vicente towards the beach, Speed glanced at the clock on the dashboard. He was running late. Jeeze! His freakin' luck.

He put his foot down hard, and the sleek limousine surged forward, overtaking a yellow Porsche with a blonde driving. He slowed down just long enough to check her out in his rear-view mirror.

Hot! A blonde in a Porsche. His kind of babe!

He hit the accelerator again, and the big limo sped down the highway.

If only I could make it with a fox the way I make it with a car, Speed daydreamed, any broad would be in freakin' sex heaven! Take Sugarbush, his ex-wife. That barracuda didn't break balls, she crushed them in a blender and drank 'em for freakin' breakfast!

Sugarbush. What a flashy cooze-machine *she* was, with her zoomer tits and bright red hair – pussy hair too, because she dyed it down there. Every guy who eyeballed her – and they all did – tried to give her a roll.

The trouble was – she let 'em. Which is why he'd dumped her one steamy Vegas night with ten thousand winnings in his pocket and a stacked blonde on each arm.

Unfortunately the bucks didn't last, nor did the blondes.

Thinking of his ex always jerked his blood pressure way up. Sugarbush was something else – she gave *hookers* a bad name.

Jamming his foot down, he shot through an amber light.

A police vehicle swept out of a side street, settled in behind him, and began to flash its lights.

Holy shit! What was this? Rent-a-cop city? They were freakin' *every*where.

Reluctantly he pulled over to the side.

*

Bobby Mondella paced around the room. He had a headache, a throbbing, skull-shattering ache driving him crazy. Damn Nova Citroen. Damn her! She thought she could walk back into his life as if everything was still the same. As if Rio had never happened.

Well, she was wrong. He was no longer her own personal sex-machine. As far as he was concerned, he couldn't care less if he never spoke to her again.

*

Vicki made sure they were each settled in their rooms, the three celebrities. Big deal. A famous person was no different from anyone else. They went to the bathroom, didn't they? Just like the masses.

Vicki was not awe-struck by any means. She'd had a few famous ones in her time. Well, not exactly *world-wide* famous — more like an L.A. disc jockey with pimples on his ass and a rubber fetish. Also a very rich Hollywood realtor who claimed to know absolutely everybody. Oh yeah, and she'd once had a Senator from the East who was staying at a local Holiday Inn. At least he'd *said* he was a Senator. He'd made her get down on her knees and pledge allegiance to the flag, and then he'd made her pledge allegiance to something he obviously considered far more important.

Men! What a bunch! And yet she had to admit she loved 'em — they were so goddamn *easy*! Tom was the perfect example. She'd had *his* balls in an uproar with just one glance.

She looked around, making sure nobody was observing her as she slid into the unoccupied guest suite. Opening the closet, she checked that everything was in position — the empty Vuitton bag she had placed there yesterday, and Maxwell's small holdall, pushed out of sight. Everything was in place.

With a quick glance in the mirror, she made a few adjustments to her personal appearance. Oh, was she going to be happy to shed the godawful maid's uniform she'd been forced to wear for six long weeks.

Quickly she undid a few buttons, hiked the skirt shorter, fluffed out her hair, and applied a liberal amount of jammy red lipstick.

"That's better, sweetie-bird," she murmured to herself.

It was almost show time, the props were all in place and she couldn't wait.

*

Marcus Citroen caught the eye of his wife as she moved graciously among her guests. An impressive woman, Nova Citroen. Elegant, assured, the perfect partner. He'd made the right choice when he'd picked her, although it had meant taking a very calculated risk, and it could have backfired – badly.

In all their years of marriage there had only been one dangerous period, a time he preferred to forget. But he had dealt with it, just as he'd dealt with everything else in his life. Expertly.

Marcus Citroen knew exactly when to be ruthless. Nobody crossed him. Nobody dared.

Kris Phoenix 1986

The girl on the television commercial had big blue eyes, a wide smile complete with all-American teeth, a pert nose, cascades of pale honey-gold hair, and a sensational body.

"I want to meet her," Kris Phoenix said. "Find out who she is."

That didn't take much doing. She was Cybil Wilde – a hot new model, with a Christie Brinkley/Cheryl Tiegs future.

She was in New York. Kris was in L.A.

"Fly her in," Kris said.

She said "Thank you, but no thank you."

"I want her for the cover of my new album," Kris said.

He was told she was very expensive. Three times the price of an ordinary model.

"Fuck it. Pay her," Kris said.

A photo shoot was arranged, and Cybil Wilde flew into L.A. Kris made sure there was a limousine to meet her at the airport, filled with white roses. And a note from him asking her to join him for dinner. He also made sure the record company paid.

She had her mother phone him to make an excuse. Her mother! It turned out she was a California girl who'd migrated to New York, and her family still lived quite comfortably in Encino.

Kris decided he wanted her before they even met. Astrid was

settled in England – she hated America and what she referred to as the rock and roll circus. He was perfectly happy with Astrid, but he needed a woman in America, and from the moment he spotted Cybil in her TV commercial – which incidentally was for yoghurt – he knew she was the right girl.

One of his minions was put in charge of compiling a dossier on her. The night before the photo shoot he sat in bed and studied it.

> *The Cybil Wilde Fact Sheet*
> AGE: 18
> HEIGHT: 5′ 9″
> MEASUREMENTS: 36, 22, 36
> HAIR COLOUR: Honey-blonde
> WEIGHT: 120 pounds
> EYE COLOUR: Cornflower blue

She'd attended local high school, gone steady with the boy next door, kept two dogs and a pony, and been an A-plus student. When she was sixteen her boyfriend entered a photograph he'd taken of her in a "model of the year" magazine contest. She won a trip to New York and an introduction to one of the best model agencies in town. A year of training. A year of learning on the job. And then she hit it. Along the way she'd broken up with her boyfriend and dated a variety of men. Nothing serious.

Kris decided he would be her first something serious.

*

Antonio was a famous photographer. Italian by birth, American by choice, he practised his craft with impeccable style. He'd recently had a book of his work published – a weighty tome of portraits entitled *Antonio – The Face*. On the cover was a glorious shot of glamorous television star Silver Anderson in a dramatic pose. The book lay casually in the dressing room, awaiting inspection.

Cybil arrived at the studio first. Scrubbed and shining she could easily be mistaken for a teenage cheerleader.

"Hmmm . . ." Antonio inspected her, hands on hips, a critical look in his beady eyes. "Antonio think *mebbe* the raw material okay."

Cybil twinkled – she'd been warned what a pain in the ass the temperamental little photographer could be. "Only maybe?" she asked nicely.

"Fernando!" – Antonio snapped his fingers for the hairdresser. "José!" – another snap to summon the makeup artist. "Paulette!" – the stylist came running. "What we do weeth thees plain leetle creature?" The three of them waited for Antonio to answer himself. Which he did. "We make her *bellissima*, no?"

"Yes," they dutifully chorussed.

"*Bene, Bene*," Antonio said, with a satisfied clap of his hands. "Go to work. Make the child dee*vine*. *Pronto!*"

Kris arrived a couple of hours later, by which time Cybil was certainly divine, although closeted out of sight with Fernando, José and Paulette.

"How're you doin', mate?" Kris asked, casually putting an arm around the diminutive photographer's shoulders.

"Kreees," purred Antonio, becoming quite skittish. "How *sexy* you are. I *looove* your leetle tight ass!"

Antonio had photographed Kris for his last two album covers, and the two of them had a playfully wary relationship.

The famous Phoenix grin. "Yeah, well, *you're* not gettin' any."

Antonio pursed his lips. "You have no idea what you miss, dear boy."

"Let's just keep it that way, mate."

"As you weesh," Antonio said, lascivious eyes roaming over his favourite rock star, who stood before him in jeans and a sleeveless black tee-shirt with GOLDS GYM emblazoned on the front. "You seem to be so ... hmm ... how I say it?" A meaningful pause. "*Strong.*"

"Yeah, well, I've bin' workin' out, haven't I? It's my new thing. Good for the old muscles, huh?" He flexed an arm, just to get the randy little photographer going.

"*Bene!*" exclaimed Antonio admiringly. "*Sooo* athletic."

"All the better to beat you up with if you ever lay a finger in my direction," Kris joked. "Not that you ever would, of course." Plucking an apple from a nearby bowl he crunched into it. "Is the girl here yet?"

Antonio sighed. "We *try* to make her into sometheeng."

Spud, Kris's English hairdresser – brought over for every important photo session – whistled as Cybil emerged from the dressing room flanked by Fernando, José and Paulette.

Looking sensational in a cutaway yellow swimsuit, with her hair styled into a wild mane and a startling makeup on her face, she smiled.

The all-American teeth attracted Kris like a flash of lightning. *All the better to eat you up with!*

"Hello, darlin'," he said. "How do you feel about moving to L.A.?"

*

Cybil was no pushover. He had to work on her. He had to turn on the charm. He even had to follow her back to New York.

"I don't like rock stars," she announced.

"What kind of stupid remark is that? You might just as well say you don't like policemen or kids or any sort of group. What's a rock star, anyway?"

"A guy who thinks he can get anything he wants just by winking."

"I winked. I didn't get *you*, did I?"

Gradually he won her over, and within several weeks convinced her that life in his Bel Air mansion was exactly what she wanted.

She came to stay. Georgeous Cybil – with the hair and the teeth and the body. It was fun having her around – she was a real upper, full of enthusiasm and high spirits.

What with Astrid – no slouch in the looks stakes herself – stashed safely in England, and Cybil, the lady of his Bel Air mansion, he felt pretty settled. Not bad for a working boy who started out with zilch.

Kris Phoenix. Rock superstar.

He'd been on his own for three and a half years. Long enough to have had three smash solo albums – each one breaking records and outselling the last. First there was his debut album *Erotic* in

1984, followed by 1985's *Gettin' Down*, and later in the year *Busted!*, a real breakthrough, putting him up there with the best-selling albums of all time. And now *Poor Little Bitch Girl*, which he was just putting the finishing touches to. One of the finishing touches was having the luscious Cybil Wilde on the album sleeve. She was an asset, no doubt about *that*.

He didn't love her.

He didn't love Astrid either.

He was thirty-seven, would soon be thirty-eight, and he had no idea what being in love was all about. Oh, he'd been in lust many times, but love – no – he'd never had that insane, urgent longing to spend the rest of his life with one woman.

And yet he knew it existed. He could write about it, think about it. Probably it was something that was never going to happen to him. He had his music, his guitar, his creativity. It was enough. Or was it? Sometimes at night he'd lie awake and think of all the things he'd achieved, and it was those times he wished he had someone to *really* share it with. Often he thought he might have quite fancied having more kids. Bo had a step-sister – courtesy of Willow and her stockbroker husband. What could have been if he hadn't discovered Willow cheating on him?

No – that wouldn't have worked either.

Deep down, he had to admit he missed Buzz. They'd grown up together, shared each other's lives – including the back of that horrible Volkswagen for months on end. Buzz had been closer to him than a brother could ever be. They'd had some good old times together. One of his favourite memories was their early sessions in the dusty garage – with only Buddy Holly and Otis Redding for company. And with a great deal of nostalgia he remembered travelling through Europe screwing everything that moved – and even a few who didn't!

Finally success, and all that came with it. After that things began to change.

Not only did he miss Buzz as his closest friend, he missed performing on stage with him. God! They'd had some great times, writing their songs, hanging out, just being together.

Now it was all over. Their past was gone. Recently Buzz – who'd formed another new group, his fourth since The Wild Ones split – had been interviewed for *Rolling Stone*. *Kris Phoenix is a wanker*, he'd said. *All he ever wanted was the money and fame. Look at him now, with his big mansions and Hollywood lifestyle. He's success crazy. As far as I'm concerned his music is bubble gum pop shit. The wanker sold out.*

When Kris first read it he'd been angry and then hurt. The Hawk had advised him to take no notice. "Everyone knows Buzz Darke is a burned-out junkie and just about finished," he'd said. "Ignore it. Don't dignify his jealousy of your success with any comment at all."

So he hadn't. But it still hurt.

Occasionally he saw Rasta – the same good-natured joker. Rasta had weathered his bad publicity, married a pretty German actress, and bought a song-publishing company which kept him busy.

"Don't you miss being up on stage?" Kris often asked.

Rasta always came out with the same stock reply. "When you've had the best, why go for seconds?"

Rasta was right. Kris realized how lucky he was to have made it twice. No wonder Buzz was bitter – every group he'd put together had turned out to be a dismal failure. Mainly because the majority of the time he was so stoned he had no idea what he was doing. Plus he couldn't get back into America due to his drug bust. Strangely enough he was still with Mikki – his partner in crime. Whenever Kris read about their public antics he felt sorry for both of them. A couple of losers.

Shortly after Cybil moved in, he persuaded Willow to let Bo make his first trip to America. She said no at first, having returned to her usual mean-spirited self six months after their son's accident was history, but Kris was insistent. The boy was twelve, hardly a little kid anymore.

Bo arrived, very much the proper English schoolboy with a posh accent to go with his neat appearance. Willow was doing a great job of squeezing out any individuality the kid might possess. Kris remembered himself at the same age – a right little tearaway, guitar crazy with the rock star dream.

"Well, son, how's it going?" he asked, strangely uncomfortable.

"Fine, thank you, sir," Bo replied stiffly.

Sir! What was this *sir* shit? Three years ago they'd shared a wonderful time together at his house in the South of France. They'd swum and snorkelled and done all the good father-and-son things. Then Willow had insisted on enrolling Bo in a strict naval academy, and look at the little wanker now.

"Don't call me sir," he said tightly. "Don't call *anyone* sir."

"Yes, si . . . er . . . dad."

The visit was not a success. Bo was uncomfortable and ill at ease, especially with Cybil. When she was around he withdrew completely, and Kris could not get through to him, however hard he tried. When the boy finally left, he blamed himself for their lack of communication.

"Don't worry," Cybil said comfortingly. "When *I* was thirteen I didn't even *speak* to my parents. They were like the enemy, y'know?"

"Yeah, but at least they were together. I never get to see Bo. An' that's the way Willow likes it. The only contact she wants me to have with him is to make sure I pay the bleedin' bills!"

"Poor baby." Nineteen-year-old Cybil wrapped her golden curves around him, making him feel a lot better. Cybil was good at that. So was Astrid.

His two blondes . . . Fortunately they didn't know about each other, although he realized it was only a matter of time.

One day he might have to make a choice.

Rafealla 1986

"Mama! You look marvellous! Oh, and the house is so festive with the Christmas tree and the decorations – I remember every single one."

Anna Le Serre Egerton smiled as her beautiful daughter ran around the house, followed by Jon Jon, who, at nine, was quite the best-looking boy she'd ever seen. "It's a shame you weren't here for Christmas," she scolded. "I don't understand why you couldn't have managed it."

"Mama," Rafealla explained patiently. "I told you a hundred times, we were working. There was a New Year's Eve booking that was impossible to cancel."

"Yes, dear. However—"

"It's January the fourth," Rafealla interrupted gently but firmly. "And we're here. Let's not have an inquest on why we missed Christmas. We'll celebrate our Christmas now, won't we?" She rushed over to the big leather bag she'd carried on the plane. "Look," she said, pulling out several gift-wrapped packages. "Peace offerings!"

"Yeah, yeah! Presents, gramma," encouraged Jon Jon. "Shall we *all* open presents, gramma?"

"What makes you think you got any, kid?" Rafealla said sternly, ruffling his spiky hair.

"Aw, come on, mom." He grinned, squirming away from her touch.

"Get lost, small stuff. We'll open presents later. *If* there are any for you. Which I seriously doubt."

"Would you like to explore outside, Jon Jon?" suggested Anna. "We have horses and dogs—"

"Fierce dogs?" he asked hopefully.

"Not exactly fierce," she replied. Then, noting his disappointed face, she added matter-of-factly, "They'll kill a burglar, of course. Maul him to death."

Rafealla laughed. "Mama! What kind of talk is *that*?"

"Small boy talk, dear."

One of the stable lads was summoned, and an excited Jon Jon was taken off on a tour of the grounds.

Rafealla embraced her mother. "It is *sooo* good to be home," she sighed. "You just don't know."

"Indeed I do," replied Anna. "I've been looking forward to this moment for five years. Do you realize that's how long it is since I've seen you?"

"I know. I plead guilty."

"Well, dear, and what exactly is your excuse?"

"What's *yours*? You could have visited *us*, you know."

Anna lowered her eyes. "I didn't want to worry you, not until I could tell you f ce to face."

Rafealla felt panic. "What?" she insisted. "You're not sick are you? *Tell* me."

"I will when you give me the chance. Cyrus had a mild stroke shortly after you left. Nothing serious, but the doctors felt he shouldn't make any long journeys."

"Why didn't Rupert tell me?" Rafealla demanded.

"Because he didn't know," Anna replied patiently. "When he and Odile came back, I made them promise *not* to tell you."

"Oh, God, mama. Why?"

"He's fine. Really he is," Anna reassured her. "You'll see."

Cyrus, her stepfather, was not as fine as Anna seemed to imagine. For one thing he had a limp and difficulty with his speech, and for another he'd aged twenty years.

Rafealla was consumed with guilt – and then anger, for she

should have been informed. While Cyrus was not her father, and could never have replaced Lucien in her heart, he'd been an excellent and caring substitute, and she loved him.

Thank God she'd finally come home. It was only for two weeks, but that was better than nothing.

Luiz hadn't come with her. They'd debated for months about whether he should, and in the end they'd both decided it was best for him to stay in Rio putting the finishing touches to their second album. He wanted to do some remixing, and make sure everything was perfect.

It hadn't been an easy year. When Luiz first blurted out the news that he was married, Rafealla felt her safe new world collapse. The one person she loved and depended on had been lying to her all along.

"I didn't lie," he'd stated vehemently.

"Of course you did. We've been living a lie."

"No, Rafealla." A Brazilian shrug. "You never asked me."

"Screw *you*, buster," She'd shouted, exploding with fury. "What do you think this *is*? A game? A joke? Well, it might be to you, but *I* don't find it very funny."

She'd taken Jon Jon, and two hurriedly packed suitcases, and descended on Tinto, Maria, and their seven children.

Tinto was philosophical. "Have you asked him to whom he's married? Have you found out when this took place and why? Does he love the woman? And if so, *why* is he with you?"

Good questions, every one of them. And she had a right to know. Storming back, she confronted him.

Calmly Luiz explained things. Being born in the *favela* did not give one much hope for the future. Observing his brothers and sisters he realized he was caught in a trap, and there was hardly any chance of getting out. At fourteen he was roaming the streets with the rest of his friends, occasionally robbing a rich tourist, or stealing from one of the big hotels. At sixteen he was sleeping with the tourists – in the long run it was more lucrative than robbing them.

"One day I met a woman," he shrugged noncommittally. "An older woman. She offered me an escape."

"And you took it?"

"Yes, I took it." His handsome features darkened. "And so would you if you'd had my life. I was eighteen years old and she was fifty-seven. A Brazilian woman, not rich, not poor. She took me out of the *favela*. She bought me clothes, paid for my music lessons, and made sure I learned good English."

Rafaella felt a wave of nausea sweep over her. "Where is she now?"

"In a nursing home. She's been in this place for several years. Now it is *my* turn to take care of *her*. I won't divorce her, she does not deserve that. She's dying, Rafaella. When she goes I am free. Until then . . ."

There was nothing she could do about it, except try to understand and reluctantly admire his loyalty. She moved back in with him, much to Tinto's relief, for their career as a singing duo was really taking off.

When the American soul superstar Bobby Mondella came into town and asked to meet them, Tinto was in heaven. Especially when they all hit it off so well and became friends. Tinto immediately imagined a glowing future in America.

Rafaella loved Bobby. He was like a big brother – the other side of Rupert, who was so very English. Bobby represented the black side of her, and she could listen to his tales of Hollywood and New York and life in the fast lane forever. She sensed he was a troubled man finally coming to peace with himself. His music was sensational, and she was thrilled he enjoyed performing with them.

When the accident happened she was as shocked as everyone else. She and Luiz rushed to the hospital as soon as they heard, but they were not allowed to see him – nobody was. Armed men guarded his hospital room, and one night he was secretly flown back to America.

The headlines screamed the news:

SUPERSTAR IN DRUNKEN FALL!
BOBBY MONDELLA – BLIND DRUNK!

Rafaella couldn't understand it. Bobby hardly drank anymore, and he never went out onto his terrace, claiming a bad case of vertigo. She also wondered about the woman he'd said was staying with him. Where was *she* when it happened?

Combing the newspapers, Rafealla could find no mention of her. The stories merely stated that Bobby was drunk and alone when the accident took place.

Several times she and Luiz tried to contact him in America, but all they received in reply was a form letter – *Bobby Mondella thanks you for your good wishes* . . . et cetera.

Eventually they stopped trying.

*

"Isn't it odd," Odile said, after an enormous turkey dinner, "that Eddie Mafair has never tried to get in touch with you." They were sitting on the bed in Rafealla's room, just like old times.

"Why should he?" Rafealla replied defensively. "We *are* divorced, you know."

"Really?" Odile said sarcastically. "I had *no* idea."

"Shove it, missy."

"No, *you* shove it, *star*."

Rafealla giggled. "I'm glad you realize I'm famous."

"Sure. In bloody South America," Odile said good naturedly. "Nobody's heard of you here, so don't start getting bigheaded."

"They will," Rafealla said confidently.

"Yes, and then I bet Eddie Mafair will come running. He'll probably sell his story to the *News of the World* – 'My Life with Rafealla'. What a hoot!"

"You're obsessed with Eddie."

"Merely curious. I know you too well, and there's more to the Eddie Mafair story than you're telling. For instance, how come he's never tried to see Jon Jon? He's his father. It's not normal." She clapped a hand to her mouth. "Holy shit! I've got it! After all this time I've got it!"

"Got what?" Rafealla asked warily.

"You must think I'm the world's biggest idiot!"

"Only some of the time," Rafealla commented dryly, reaching for a cigarette even though she'd promised Luiz she would give it up.

"Eddie," Odile half-whispered, "is not Jon Jon's father, is he?"

Rafealla felt the blush of truth suffuse her face. She fixed Odile with a steely glare. "Don't *ever* say such a thing."

"It's true, isn't it?" Odile persisted. "I *know* it's true. You don't have to confirm or deny, because *I know*. Your expression gives you away." She shook her head in amazement. "Jon Jon doesn't even *look* like Eddie. I can't imagine why I didn't guess before."

"If you say one word of this to another living soul, I will *never* speak to you again," Rafealla warned her fiercely.

Odile's blue eyes were serious for once. She took her friend's hand in hers. "We're almost blood sisters, aren't we?" she asked earnestly. "You can tell me anything and your secret is mine."

In a way it was tremendously therapeutic to confide in Odile. After all these years of holding everything in she let it all pour out. The hot, sticky night in the back of a limo with Kris Phoenix. Eddie's lies and beatings, and finally her brutal discovery of his homosexuality. For good measure she even told Odile about Luiz's marriage.

Odile listened quietly, and when Rafealla was through she hugged her close. "You should have trusted me before," she said. "I might not have been able to do anything, but I could've helped you beat the stuffing out of that bastard Eddie."

"It's not his fault. I forced him into a marriage he didn't want."

"Listen to yourself. You're always making excuses for people. You've got to stop it, and toughen up."

"Is that an order?"

"You bet. Now I'm telling you, don't go rushing into anything with this Luiz character."

"He's not a character, Odile," she corrected. "He's a warm and caring man, and I love him very much."

Odile raised a cynical eyebrow. "Don't forget, I've seen his picture on the album cover. He's a good-looking, probably horny as hell, *married* man. So watch out – don't go falling into any more traps."

Rafealla laughed. "You'll have to meet him."

"I intend to. Rupert is getting his orders. No South of France this summer. We're coming to Rio – I can't *wait* to see you in action!"

Two weeks with her family was enough. They were wonderful, but smothering. Her mother still treated her as if she were a scatty teenager, and Rupert drove her crazy with his teasing.

She was used to her independence – besides, she missed Luiz desperately. And at the end of the fortnight, Jon Jon was anxious to get back to his friends.

Leaving Heathrow Airport was a wrench. Once they were on the way it was easy.

*

"Marcus Citroen is *very* interested," Tinto said excitedly, pacing around his office.

"Who?" Rafealla asked coolly, although she knew exactly who Marcus Citroen was – how could she ever forget?

"Marcus Citroen owns Blue Cadillac Records in America," Tinto said, practically jumping with joy. "Blue Cadillac is one of the big fish."

"I thought it was a car," she said uninterestedly.

Luiz glanced at her quizzically.

"He's coming into town for Carnival. He does so every year," Tinto continued.

"How nice," she murmured.

"And he wishes to meet you."

"We'll meet him," Luiz decided. "It is time we began to think of the American market."

Tinto cleared his throat and shifted uncomfortably. "I don't know how to say this, so I will come straight out with it. Rafealla is the one he wishes to meet. Blue Cadillac are not interested in a duo."

"Well, then, I'm not their girl," she said staunchly. "They'll just have to search elsewhere."

"Rafealla—" Tinto began.

"End of story," she said, imperiously tossing back her long hair.

Tinto turned to Luiz for support. Luiz merely shrugged.

"Is that all the business for the day?" she asked briskly. "For if it is, we're going swimming. Want to take the day off and come with us, Tinto?"

The disappointed manager shook his head.

Hand in hand they left his office, strolling along the street to Luiz's red sports car, a present from her to him on his recent twenty-sixth birthday.

People turned to scrutinize them. They were local celebrities. To the man and the woman in the street they represented youth and glamour.

A secretary on her lunch break timidly asked Luiz for his autograph, thrusting a magazine at him with his picture inside.

He smiled and requested her name.

Rafealla watched the girl blush, and the way she gazed at Luiz as if he were a king. "That female wants your body," she murmured teasingly as they walked away.

"Ah, but it is taken, my carioca."

"Don't I know it!"

Somehow they didn't go swimming. They went home and spent a lazy afternoon in bed making love. Jon Jon was away for the weekend, so Friday night drifted pleasantly into Saturday morning without any disturbances.

Rafealla awoke early and thought she would surprise him. Cooking was not her forte, but she could manage a delicious concoction of scrambled eggs, tomato and bacon. Wearing nothing but an oversized tee-shirt, her hair braided, she set to work in the kitchen, singing softly to herself.

Luiz slept naked. He walked into the kitchen without benefit of clothes, his body bronzed and hard, his black hair tousled.

"I think I love you," she said, staring pointedly between his legs.

Responding appropriately, he embraced her from behind, his hands exploring under her tee-shirt.

Soon the scrambled eggs were history. Who needed food when they had each other?

Bobby Mondella 1986

"Mr Mondella?"

The voice came from far away.

"Mr Mondella, are you listening to me?"

What kind of a dumb remark was that? He couldn't do anything else but listen. He was lying in a hospital bed bandaged from head to toe, trussed up like a chicken waiting to be roasted. Even his eyes were covered. They'd given him morphine, but he could still feel the throbbing, unremitting pain.

"Mr Mondella," the doctor said in a serious voice. "Can you see me?"

"I will when they take the goddamn bandages off," he mumbled.

"They are off," the doctor said. "You can't see me, can you? CAN YOU . . . CAN YOU . . . CAN YOU . . .

*

He sat up in bed with a jolt, the sweat pouring off him. Recurring nightmare number one. Jesus Christ, he couldn't even sleep without reliving the horror of that fateful night one year ago.

I'm blind, he thought hopelessly. I'm fucking blind. And nobody gives a damn.

With a shaking hand he reached for the bottle of bourbon,

kept beside his bed at all times. The table lamp went flying, crashing to the floor with a dull thud.

"Shit!" he screamed, full of pent-up frustration.

The girl he'd hired a week ago came running into the room. Her name was Sara, and she had a sweet voice. Better than the others he'd employed. There'd been a procession of personal assistants – none of them stayed long and they'd all driven him crazy. Before Sara he'd had a man look after him. A brother who'd ripped off his clothes and brought women to the house in the middle of the night so he could hear them making love. Son of a bitch.

"Are you all right, Mr Mondella?" Sara asked anxiously.

"Yeah, I'm fine."

No, baby, I am not fine. My life is totally fucked up and what I really want to do is end the whole fucking ball game. Because, hey – I don't think I can take it much longer.

"Get back to bed," he said roughly.

"No problem. I'm awake," she replied in a soothing voice. "Let me clear up this mess."

He could smell her. A womanly musk mixed with a light scent. The last female assistant he'd had – an ex-nurse – smelled of disinfectant and disdain.

"Don't worry about the mess," he said. "Just get me another bottle."

"It's the middle of the night, Mr Mondella," she said pointedly.

More frustration burst forth. "So fuckin' what? Do you think it makes any difference to me?"

She held her ground. "I'm sure it doesn't. But a good night's sleep is what you really need."

Christ! Now he had a do-gooder. This one was going to try and get him off the booze and out into the real world. No, thank you very much.

He wondered what she looked like. Juicy. Succulent. He could tell by the way she moved around the room. And young. Twenty-five she'd told him when he'd hired her.

Inexplicably he felt horny. It hadn't happened in a long time. The only woman he allowed to see him in his current state were paid call girls brought to the house late at night by his driver.

Leave her alone, he warned himself. *Do not ruin a good thing. She works for you.*

It didn't matter. Nothing mattered.

"Sara," he said, warming up his tone.

"Yes, Mr Mondella?" She sounded wary.

"Hey – babe, you can call me Bobby, you mustn't be shy. I don't like things to be too formal."

"Okay."

"Sara?"

"Yes."

"Come sit on the bed. Talk to me. Tell me about yourself."

"I'm not dressed," she said primly. ·

He laughed bitterly. "Baby, it's not exactly like I can *see* you, is it?"

"Mr Mondella, it's very late."

"I told you to call me Bobby," he snapped.

"Okay," she said soothingly.

His voice was a command. "Come sit."

"I don't think so."

"What the fuck d'you mean by that?" he exploded.

Taking a deep breath, she said, "I'll get you another bottle of bourbon, Mr Mondella. I work for you as an assistant. Please let's not forget that."

He heard her leave the room. Bitch! Once she would have been begging on her knees to have a star like Bobby Mondella. Well, screw her. Who did she think she was? Tomorrow he would fire her.

Sara hurried from his bedroom and looked behind the bar in the living room. She was flushed and breathing fast. There were cases of bourbon stacked high – the man was drinking himself into a stupor and nobody seemed to care. The only people allowed to enter the house were his doctor, driver and business manager. She didn't trust any of them. Why didn't his doctor stop him from drinking? How come the driver was able to sign cheques and was probably ripping him off? And why wasn't the business manager advising him properly? All his money was

being channelled into a variety of investments, which he didn't
even have a lawyer check over. For a start he should get out of
the large house he was renting and into a smaller place. The
money was going out every week and nothing was coming in
except occasional song-writer's royalties.

Sara was shocked at what was going on. She'd only been
working there a week, but she could smell a rip-off a mile away.

Sara Johnston was a smart girl. Born and raised in Phila
delphia, she'd graduated from high school at eighteen and gone
straight into a business management course. From there she'd
started work at her father's accountancy firm, specializing in
show business clients. She'd handled the accounts of a lady soul
singer, two managers, and a singing trio. The ins and outs of
show business intrigued her, and she found the music end of it
particularly interesting. Sara would love to have tried a singing
career herself – unfortunately she had no voice. She had also
thought about becoming a model, but she was too short and far
too curvy.

Working for her father was merely a stepping stone to more
exciting things. When she heard – through inside connections –
that Bobby Mondella was looking for a personal assistant, she
flew out to California the next day for an interview. First she
saw his business manager – Nils Holmer, a swarthy white man
with shifty eyes. Next she was ushered in to see Bobby, and she
was shocked by his appearance. He sat in a chair by the window,
overweight and unshaven. His hair was too long, and his general
appearance uncared for. Wrap-around, dense black sunglasses
covered his eyes.

She remembered her first sight of Bobby Mondella in the
flesh. Philadelphia, 1979, on stage. She was eighteen years old
and she'd thought he was the most gorgeous hunk she'd ever
seen in her entire life.

Now this angry man sitting next to the window stirred her
with a feeling of great compassion.

"Why'd you want this job, girl?" he'd asked harshly.

"Because I need the money," she'd lied.

"Hell, that's a good 'nuff reason to sit around with a blind
man. Hire her, Nils."

She'd started work ten days later, and after one week in his company she vowed that she, Sara Johnston, was going to bring this wreck of a man back to life.

*

"What d'you look like?"

"I beg your pardon?"

"You speak English, girl. It's a simple 'nuff question."

Another week had passed and she was still in his employ, in spite of rejecting his advances that one night.

"Uh, I have shoulder-length black hair."

"Let me feel it."

"I'll make you a bargain."

There was a weary tone to his voice. "What's that, babe?"

"Allow me to arrange for a barber to come to the house and cut *your* hair, and you can feel away."

He laughed cynically. "Cute."

"Is it a deal?"

"Why would I want my hair cut, huh? I don't get to show it to anybody."

"*I* look at you all day."

"You're paid to do it."

"So I am," she said, with a faint hint of sarcasm.

This girl pissed him off. She was feisty, not scared of losing her job. Sara, with the sweet voice, was a tough little cookie.

"Okay, we got ourselves a deal. Come here."

She walked over to him and stood by his chair. He reached up and felt her thick, curly hair, breathing deeply as her light scent invaded his nostrils, and – oh no, here came that old familiar feeling. This girl was turning him on again. What *was* it with her?

Before she had a chance to realize what was happening, he dropped his hands to where her breasts should be, and got himself a surprise. This girl was stacked. This lady was more than a handful, she was something else.

"Don't!" She jerked away angrily.

"Come back here *now*," he commanded.

"No way."

"Hey, baby," he said harshly. "Do you want this job or not?"

"Have you ever heard of sexual harassment, *Mr* Mondella?"

"Aw, get out. Send my driver in."

His driver had long Rastafarian locks, and a permanent sneer. Nothing would give her more pleasure than to fire him.

He spent five minutes with Bobby, left, and returned half an hour later accompanied by an ugly black woman in a tight dress emphasizing her huge bosom.

"Hooker time," the driver said, with a knowing leer. "An' they don't even havta be pretty."

Sara found it sheer torture thinking of Bobby with the whore. She wanted to murder the sleazy driver, but she managed — with difficulty — to keep her cool. "How often does he have them over?" she asked, trying to sound casual.

"Not often," the man replied, picking his teeth with a packet of book matches. "The dude can't get it up no more." A wink. "Not like us *normal* studs."

In the bedroom, Bobby struggled with his feelings of sexual inadequacy. His driver was right. Bobby Mondella couldn't do it anymore. What was the goddam point? What was the point of anything? He'd been to the top, and now, with some cheap prostitute slobbering all over him, he'd hit the bottom.

Bobby Mondella. The star who fell from grace. Literally. Only he hadn't fallen, he'd been thrown from that balcony in Rio. Doused in booze, and tossed from the terrace of his tenth-floor apartment. Jesus! They'd intended to murder him, and yet he'd survived to tell the tale — which nobody believed. "You were drunk," everyone — including the police — said. "You were alone." They all agreed. "You fell."

And no amount of argument on his part could convince them otherwise.

Well, fuck 'em all. *He* knew it was no accident. If an awning hadn't broken his fall he would have been dead. Someone had tried to have him killed. Only he couldn't put a name to the person who arranged it.

What did it matter? He was finished anyway. They'd achieved their objective.

Nova had apparently vanished from the Rio apartment long before the police arrived, leaving no trace. Bitch. Fucking bitch. He'd heard she was back with Marcus like nothing happened. She'd certainly never tried to contact him. Not even when he lay in the hospital with nearly every bone in his body broken.

The bones healed. His eyes didn't. He was blind, and nobody could tell him why. It wasn't clinical – psychological, they said.

Psychological, ha! What the fuck did all those fancy-assed doctors know? If he could see – he would. It was as simple as that.

Nichols Kline took care of everything. Guards in the hospital to keep away the press. A private flight to L.A. Nichols even organized the rented house, hired the private nurses and security guards he'd had for the first six months, and arranged for Nils Holmer to have power of attorney and take care of Bobby's money.

The money deal wasn't so great. It was all spend, spend, spend, with nothing coming in. He'd never been good at financial matters, always leaving it to accountants and business managers. Now Nils kept on telling him he was almost broke. And Nichols vanished out of his life forever.

"I don't understand it," he said, when Nils came by with more bad news. "You've gotta know I was one of the biggest-earning stars in the goddamn *country*. Where the fuck has it all gone?"

"Taxes, expenses, bills, and bad investments. Plus you lived a pretty extravagant lifestyle."

"Jesus Christ! *You* were supposed to be lookin' after the investments. What happened?"

Nils looked affronted. "I only make 'em. I can't guarantee 'em. It's the financial climate, Bobby. There's no way I can control that."

"Are you tryin' to tell me I've lost everything?"

Nils shrugged. "You've got enough left to get by on. Move out of this house, get a smaller place. I have to leave the country for a while – I'll have someone else in the office take care of things for you."

Bobby knew he was being shafted. So fucking what? There

wasn't any place left to go. He was finished. Why prolong the agony?

That night he overdosed. Took every goddamn pill he could lay his hands on.

Sara found him at three o'clock in the morning. He was unconscious on the bathroom floor, with spilled bottles of pills all around him.

From that moment on she took charge. Sara Johnston was a very determined young lady, and she knew – without a doubt – she was going to bring Bobby Mondella right back to the top where he belonged.

Kris Phoenix 1987

"Marcus Citroen would like you to appear at his wife's fund-raiser for Governor Jack Highland in July."

So spoke Hawkins Lamont, resplendent in tennis whites, with his impeccable George Hamilton suntan. The two of them sat in the garden room of the Polo Lounge eating lunch.

"Screw Marcus Citroen," Kris replied, chewing on a bread roll.

The Hawk raised a quizzical eyebrow. "What's *that* supposed to mean?"

Kris stared at his manager. "It means Kris Phoenix don't jump for anyone."

The Hawk waved at an acquaintance across the room, sipped his fresh grapefruit juice, and said, "Has Marcus done something I should know about?"

"The whole bleedin' record industry knows about it," Kris responded sharply.

"In that case," the Hawk replied smoothly, "perhaps you can enlighten *me*."

"Come on, man," Kris said roughly. "Don't give me that 'you got no idea what's goin' on' shit."

"What *is* going on?"

"Sharleen."

"Ah." The Hawk shook his head sadly. "A most unfortunate incident."

"Jesus!" Kris exclaimed. "I don't *believe* you people. A woman kills herself, fuckin' *kills* herself, an' you call it an *incident*."

"I didn't realize you knew Sharleen," the Hawk said.

"Yes. I knew her. It was a long time ago, but we kept in touch here an' there."

"She was a drug addict."

"She was a poor bitch who got herself fucked over by the record industry, an' *especially* by your friend – Marcus Citroen."

"*My* friend – *your* boss."

The waitress placed a Neil McCarthy salad in front of Hawkins and a juicy hamburger for Kris.

Kris waited for her to leave before saying, "I don't have a *boss*. I work for myself, an' my record company gets rich off me – just like you do, Hawk."

"We get rich off each other," the Hawk pointed out coldly. Rock stars. Ungrateful, uneducated, unappreciative egomaniacs.

"Anyway," Kris said flatly, "everyone knows she did it because of Marcus. It's not exactly a secret."

"Supposition."

"What?"

"The good old rumour-go-round. As far as I'm aware, Marcus was always very generous to Sharleen. He kept her under contract long after she stopped making hits."

"He sucked the juice out of her. An' when she was dry he cut her loose an' left her with nothing."

"Nonsense."

"Yeah, well, you've got your opinions an' I've got mine, an' there's *no* way I'm doin' a fund-raiser for him. No bleedin' way."

*

"Do you love me?" Cybil demanded, raising her golden curls from the task at hand.

He wished she wouldn't ask him that. What was he supposed

to say? *Yeah – when I've got a hard-on I love ya t'death. An' when I don't – well – it's only rock'n' roll, ain't it?*

Maybe he wasn't capable of loving anyone. Perhaps catching Willow in bed with that German prick all those years ago had done him in as far as women were concerned. Not to mention ten thousand groupies along the way.

He knew one thing. Women. You couldn't trust 'em.

"Go for it, baby, don't stop," he said, pushing Cybil's glorious mane of hair back into place.

One

Two

Three

JOLT!

Later there was American football on TV and a catered dinner for two from Trader Vic's. Cybil watched the football with him, daintily gnawing on a spare-rib as she sat cross-legged on the bed wearing nothing but a man-sized sweatshirt.

At midnight the phone rang. Usually he let the service deal with all calls, but this time he picked it up. The first thing he heard was the faint crackle of long-distance, and then a desperate plea. "Kris, Kris, is that you? Uh . . . this is Mikki, remember me? Look, I don't want to bother you, I really don't. But . . . Kris . . . you've got to help Buzz . . . you've got to help him . . . *Please*. We're desperate."

*

British Airways' six o'clock evening flight got him into London's Heathrow Airport at noon the next day. BA's Mike Baverstock met him at the plane and whisked him through passport control and customs with no problem. There was a time when they always used to stop him and search for drugs. But that was back in the bad old days when The Wild Ones first ran riot and he wasn't considered a respectable elder statesman of rock.

He hadn't warned Astrid of his imminent arrival. Better to surprise her, keep her on edge.

A chauffeured Rolls took him straight to his country mansion. Astrid was out with the dogs. He unpacked his one carry-on bag and made a few calls. Mikki had promised to get Buzz over to the house that evening. He wondered if he'd come. He'd bleedin' better.

"Dinner for four, luv. An' I fancy a roast," he informed Astrid, when she entered the house.

"Kris! What are you doing here?" she shrieked as his two Alsatians jumped all over him. "God! I bet I look awful!"

Astrid's idea of awful was jeans and a sweater with no makeup, her long flaxen hair in a ponytail. She looked pretty good to him, and refreshingly healthy.

"I live here. Remember?"

Throwing her arms around him she said, "How could I ever forget? Welcome home."

They spent the rest of the afternoon in bed. He felt like a sailor with a wife in every port. Only fortunately they weren't wives, and there were only two ports.

Astrid had never met Buzz, and as the evening approached she became more than apprehensive.

"Stay cool," Kris warned. "He's likely to insult you *an'* me. That's his way. The thing is, I don't mind – I just want to see him back on his feet. Understand?"

She'd read plenty about the notorious Buzz Darke. "He's not going to smash up our dining room, is he?" she asked nervously.

"Don't worry. All you gotta do is take Mikki off somewhere after dinner. I want to be alone with him."

"What's Mikki like?"

"Listen, I haven't seen either of them in four years. She used to be just another rich groupie out on a slumming trip. Get the picture?"

Astrid nodded. She wasn't looking forward to the evening ahead.

"Let's just hope she gets him here," Kris said. "She sounded pretty frantic on the phone. I told her to pretend she bumped into me on the street an' I insisted they come for dinner."

"So," Astrid said. "You flew all the way back here just to help a friend. That's if he even turns up."

"Don't go makin' a big deal out of it. I owe him. We're mates – or at least we were."

She shook her head. "You're unbelievable!"

"Listen, luv, it could've bin *me*. *I* was the lucky one. If things were reversed I reckon he'd do the same thing."

Buzz and Mikki arrived two and a half hours late, just when Kris was beginning to give up. They came in a taxi, with no money between the two of them, looking like a couple of tramps: Kris paid.

Buzz walked around the house. "Fuckin' rollin' in it, ain'tcha?" he sneered, adding sardonically, "Can yer spare a few bob while yer at it?"

His appearance was devastating. Whitish grey skin drawn tightly over bony features. Sunken dead eyes. Badly dyed black hair curling over the collar of a decrepit leather jacket, and long, skinny legs encased in jeans with well-worn snake-skin boots rounding out the ensemble. A joint seemed to have affixed itself permanently to his mouth, and he dragged on it without benefit of hands.

Mikki had turned into a plump, untidy woman with frizzed yellowish hair. She was not yet thirty, but her lined skin and weary eyes made her seem ten years older. She had on a stained green sweater, and baggy khaki pants.

Kris remembered the pretty Mikki he'd once known, and wondered where she'd gone.

Both of them headed straight for the booze. Buzz favoured straight vodka, while Mikki settled for red wine which she immediately spilled down the front of her sweater. It didn't seem to bother her.

"Well," Kris said, pouring himself an Old Kentucky. "It's great to see you two."

"Congratulate us," Buzz said, throwing himself into a chair. "We got married this morning. She's not just fat, y'know, she's pregnant. Fucking stupid cow."

"You're kiddin?"

Mikki nodded. "It's true, Kris. We suddenly became respectable in our old age."

"Shit! Let's break open the champagne."

"Shit!" Buzz mimicked. "It's not like yer can't afford it."

The evening dragged along, with Buzz making crack after

crack about selling out and recording crap and going for commerciality above all else. Halfway through the meal he vanished into the bathroom and didn't come back for twenty minutes.

"You've got to find him a job, Kris," Mikki pleaded, when he was gone. "*You* know how good he can be. He's sensational, and all he can get is backing work on the occasional lousy session. It's criminal. And I'm frightened he's going to do something . . ." Lowering her red-rimmed eyes she whispered, "Y'know, like Sharleen . . ."

"Jesus, Mikki. I can't get him shit while he's strung out."

She gulped her wine, talking too fast, pressing out of desperation. "He's coming off dope. Honestly. All he needs is a chance."

Kris had heard that The Orange Dragons, Blue Cadillac's hot new group, were due to do six concerts in England next month and were looking for an opening act. Put Buzz together with a good keyboard player and backing – and if he was on top of it, he'd be perfect for the gig.

"Why don't I see what I can do," he said. "Only you've got to promise me you'll make sure he dries out."

"Oh, yes, Kris. I can promise that. Honestly. You can trust me."

"Someone from Blue Cadillac Records will be in touch. I'm goin' to give you a cheque – get him in a fucking clinic to clean up, and *don't* tell him I had anything to do with it. Okay?"

Later, on the phone long distance, he said, "Hawk, I want you to arrange something for me."

"What?"

He told the Hawk exactly what needed doing.

An hour later he got a call back. "It will all be taken care of."

"That's great. I'm pleased."

"One thing, Kris."

"Yeah?"

"Marcus Citroen's fund-raiser. He *can* depend on you, can't he?"

Rafealla 1987

Coolly Rafealla stared at the man sitting behind the ornate antique desk. Marcus Citroen. He'd held her future in his hands and he'd delivered. How strangely fate had intertwined their lives over the years.

"Well, my dear," Marcus said triumphantly, "I told you I could do it for you, and now, I am delighted to inform you that your single, *Perfume Nights,* will be number one next week in *six* different countries, including the only two that really matter – England and America."

Standing up, she walked over to the window and gazed out. Marcus Citroen's London office overlooked Hyde Park. It was a crisp February day, and the wind was blowing. People were huddled up in overcoats and scarves as they scurried by.

Sometimes, on days like this, she really missed Rio. But what had she actually given up?

Nothing . . . Nothing . . .

*

Carnival came and went. Marcus Citroen came and went. Much to Tinto's chagrin, Rafealla refused to meet with him. "You're very foolish," he scolded. "He could make you into a big international star."

"And what about Luiz?" she responded tartly. "We're a team. We do things together or not at all."

"Ah, but, Rafealla, maybe you should think of your future."

Stubbornly she stood her ground. "Luiz is my future."

Tinto shrugged. "Perhaps, perhaps not." He didn't know how to tell her that while she was in England, Luiz had been seen out with the very rich Vivienne Riccardo – or, as she was known by her adoring public, the queen of the television soaps.

"You can stuff your negativity," Rafealla said gaily. "And plan on a wedding."

Tinto couldn't conceal his surprise. "When?"

"Soon."

"How soon?"

"You'll be the first to know."

Luiz had been a little quiet since she'd returned from England. She had thought the new album was all finished, but most nights he spent at the studio. "I'll come with you," she suggested.

"You'll be bored," he replied. "It's all technical details."

"I'm bored staying at home," she protested mildly.

Playfully he kissed her. "Ah, my spoiled little English carioca is bored. Just be patient, my darling. Luiz is working for both of us."

"I am not English. I am not spoiled. And hurry up with all this work."

She knew the album was important to him. He'd produced it, and written four of the songs. Naturally he was concerned about every detail. When it was finally out in the stores he could relax.

She was anxious to ask him about his wife again. The old woman dying in a nursing home somewhere. But it seemed like such a crass thing to do, so she remained silent, waiting until he chose to speak of it. It must be painful enough for him – why should she add to his burden?

One night he failed to come home at all. She reached out upon waking, and he wasn't there. "Luiz?" she called out. Then she got up and padded around the apartment. Jon Jon had already left for school, and Constanza – their daily maid – was cleaning the kitchen floor.

"Meester no here," said the surly Constanza.

"He must have slept at the studio," Rafealla explained, wondering why she felt the need to make excuses to the maid.

*There was no reply when she rang the studio. Feeling foolish, she
phoned Tinto at home. "Luiz is missing," she said half jokingly.
"Have you any idea where he might be?"*

*Tinto wanted to say, "Try Vivienne Riccardo's satin sheets." The
whole town was talking about Luiz's blatant affair with the glamorous
older actress, and yet no one dared tell Rafealla — including him. He
hesitated. "Er . . . I don't know——" he began.*

*"Give me the telephone," commanded his wife, Maria, snatching
the instrument from him. "Rafealla, dear," she said firmly, "we meet
today for lunch. We talk. There are things you should know."*

Tinto groaned.

*Before they could meet, before they could talk, the news hit the air-
waves. Luiz Oliveira and Vivienne Riccardo were secretly married
that morning.*

*

"I love London," Rafealla murmured.

Marcus rose from his desk and stood next to her. "Is that all
you have to say? I have just told you your record will be number
one across the world. Don't you understand what that means?"

Turning to look at him she said, "Does it mean I'm a star?"

"Yes."

"Famous?"

"Yes."

"Rich?"

"Eventually. With me to guide you."

With me to guide you. It was not the first time he had said
those words to her. Not the first time . . .

*

"I want to meet with Marcus Citroen, Tinto."

"You're too late. He's returned to America."

"Call him."

"With all due respect, Raffi, he probably won't even remember his
former interest."

She raised an eyebrow and said mockingly, "What an agent! Such
enthusiasm!"

"I can try."

"Do it."

Marcus Citroen did remember her. He suggested she fly to America and cut a demo record. Tinto was ecstatic.

"Forget it," Rafealla said. "Ask him to come back here."

"Don't be silly," Tinto argued. "It is obvious to me you have no idea how important this man is."

"Yes, I do know. Ask him anyway." Instinct told her Marcus Citroen would do as she wished.

A week of silence. Then Phoebe, Mr Citroen's personal secretary, called to inform Tinto that Mr Citroen did indeed have further business in Rio, and would be returning in ten days' time.

Rafealla merely nodded when a jubilant Tinto told her. He was full of plans, deciding how to approach the great man, and what strategy they would employ to get the best deal.

"No," Rafealla said evenly. "I want to see him alone."

Tinto shook his head, puzzled. Rafealla was a strange and wonderful girl — and he didn't understand her at all. When Luiz married Vivienne Riccardo, he — along with Maria and everyone else — had expected her to go to pieces — explode — have hysterics — do something. No. Not Rafealla. She was calm as could be. A shrug. A philosophical "Luiz must do what he has to do." And that was that.

Privately she told Tinto she would never work with Luiz again, and to cancel all their bookings.

"But what about the new album?" he'd asked worriedly. "Surely you will do promotional appearances?"

A flat "No." And then she'd requested the meeting with Marcus Citroen.

Now it was arranged, and she was saying she didn't want him to come. Peculiar girl. He didn't argue. Rafealla had her own way of doing things.

They met in his suite at the Copacabana Palace Hotel, Marcus Citroen and Rafealla Le Serre. She was even more exotically beautiful than he remembered. He was even more of a dirty old man than she had thought, with his licentious hooded eyes and dissipated expression.

"Well, my dear, it seem our paths cross again," he said. "You grow more beautiful each time."

She stared straight at him, her brilliant green eyes challenging and direct. She knew exactly what she wanted from Marcus Citroen. She also knew exactly what he wanted from her.

For a moment she thought of Luiz. He could burn in hell for all she cared. He was the last man she would ever allow to hurt her again.

Dear, sweet, wonderful Luiz. Bastard. Basta! He had lied to her from day one. A private detective found out the truth because she had to know.

Luiz Oliveira. Not his real name. Try Lupe Veira. A child of the favela – his one true statement. He was thirty-two years old, not twenty-six as he'd claimed.

Luiz Oliveira alias Lupe Veira. A convicted thief and male prostitute. Married twice before the lucky Vivienne Riccardo. The first time to Juana – the girl who'd worked for her and who he'd claimed was his sister. The second to a very old woman in São Paulo, who'd died after six weeks of marriage – leaving him her fortune. Her grown children immediately contested the will, and after many months of legalities he'd ended up with a paltry pay-off settlement. A month later he'd re-entered Rafealla's life.

By chance? Or had he planned it?

She didn't know and she didn't care. Men were users. Now she was going to join the club.

"Marcus," she said coolly. "I can call you Marcus, can't I?"

He rubbed his thumb and forefinger together, gazing at her with lustful dedication. "Certainly, my dear."

"You know what I think?"

"What?" Sweat beaded his bald head. This girl had everything he required. A strong, earthy sexuality, combined with a certain aloofness, and that wonderful milk chocolate skin. In a way she reminded him of Nova when he'd first set eyes on her. She had that same exotic quality he craved.

Of course, this girl was different, she already had breeding and class. And she was talented.

Rafealla stared directly at him. "Let's not play games, Marcus. I'll be very straight with you."

"Yes?"

Briefly she thought of Luiz again, and Eddie Mafair. The two loves of her life. Two phoneys. Two lousy sons of bitches.

"*Marcus,*" *she said strongly.* "*I want your power. You want my body. Why don't we see if we can cut a deal?*"

*

"So," Marcus said, snaking his arm slowly around her shoulders. "I kept my part of the bargain. Now, my dear, I think it is time for you to deliver."

Deftly she moved out of his grasp. "Not yet, Marcus. I have to see it all work."

"You wouldn't try to back out, would you?"

"No."

Rafealla was playing with him. Perhaps she didn't realize she was playing with the greatest game expert of all time. But perversely, Marcus rather enjoyed her independent attitude. It was quite a change to come across a woman who expected him to wait. A true diversion. She obviously had no idea of his real power. He would have to teach her, and he looked forward to the lesson.

"You'll appear at my wife's fund-raiser in July," he decided, with a faint smile. "We'll consummate our relationship then. *And,* my dear, I'm sure you'll find it will be a long and fulfilling one." He paused, adding meaningfully, "For both of us."

Bobby Mondella 1987

The first time they made love was the most exciting day of Sara Johnston's life. She hadn't come to work for Bobby Mondella with the sole purpose of climbing into bed with him — but when the opportunity arose, who was she to say no? The man might be blind, but in her book that didn't make him any less of a man. She'd brought him back from the brink. Nurtured him, cared for him. Moved him out of the big, expensive mansion he could no longer afford, and into a small, cosy place in Nichols Canyon. She'd got rid of his business manager — slightly too late, as the man had already stolen most of his money. And with enormous pleasure she fired his driver, and changed his doctor.

"You're some bossy, woman," Bobby grumbled, as she set about getting him back into shape. "Where you comin' from with all this attitude?"

"Heaven," she replied dryly. "Or hell. Depends which way you look at it."

"Hell!" he complained when she forced him to start swimming and exercising and using his body again.

"Heaven!" he crooned, the first time they made love, and he found everything to be in working order, just as it was before the accident.

What a lover he was! Sara felt weak just thinking about the hours they spent in bed together.

Bobby Mondella. Once she had him in good physical shape she set about getting his brain in gear. "You planning on sitting around doin' nothing for the rest of your life?" she challenged.

"Yeah," he replied defiantly.

"No way, man."

"You're a pushy little thing."

"An' you love it. Because I'm gonna push you all the way back to the top – whether you wanna go there or not."

"Get lost, woman."

"Don't go givin' me none of your lip, man."

He'd refused to see anyone since the accident. Sara opened the doors and invited some musicians he'd worked with in the past over to the house. At first he was angry – it was almost as if he was ashamed to face anyone. And then gradually he'd relaxed when he found no one was judging him or feeling sorry. He'd ended up having a good time, and in bed that night he'd showed her his appreciation.

The next day he sat down at the piano and began composing and singing again.

It was a magic moment for Sara. She'd spent months getting him to this point. "You're going to make an album," she told him. "We'll call it *Mondella Alive*, an' it'll be the best thing you've ever done."

He didn't argue. He started writing new songs, arranging them, spending every waking moment on creating something both beautiful and powerful.

When he'd compiled enough rough material, Sara took it around to a few of the big record companies, starting off with Soul On Soul, where Amerika Allen politely said they weren't interested. Reaction after that was not friendly. Doors were closed in her face.

"Bobby Mondella? No way. His time is over."

"Bobby Mondella? I thought he was *dead*."

"*That* drunken bum. You must be putting us on!"

One day she got a call from Marcus Citroen, the president of Blue Cadillac Records. "I understand you have new Bobby

Mondella material," he said. "Is it good?"

She hesitated — Bobby had told her under no circumstances was she to go to Blue Cadillac. But what the heck — this was their only chance. "It's not just good, Mr Citroen. It's sensational," she said, with every ounce of enthusiasm she possessed.

"I'd like to hear it."

Within six weeks Bobby was in the recording studio with a fat new contract.

Marcus Citroen was giving him the chance to come back.

*

"I'm sorry," the specialist said gravely. "There is nothing I can tell you. The cause of Mr Mondella's sight loss is a complete unknown. There is no physical reason. No deterioration or damage to the optical nerve. The cornea and retina are in perfect condition." The doctor shrugged hopelessly. "This is just one of those medical mysteries one day we hope to be able to solve."

Sara nodded — they'd heard it all before. She took Bobby's arm and they left the office. According to the many doctors and eye specialists they'd visited, Bobby's loss of sight was caused by a traumatic situation and therefore there was no treatment. His blindness was unexplainable. They had been told everything from psychosomatic to perhaps he should see a psychiatrist.

"I'm learnin' to live with it, stay cool," he said, squeezing her hand. "Hey, mama, I'm workin' again. I feel good. Things aren't that bad."

He never let on to Sara how muuch it hurt inside to know he could never see again. The pain was his, and he had to bear it in silence, although sometimes, in the middle of the night, he lay awake for hours just thinking about things. Why? Why had this happened to him? And who was responsible?

Marcus Citroen was giving him the opportunity to shine again. Was he doing it because of guilt?

Hell, no, that piranha had no conscience.

So maybe Nichols and his band of business associates was responsible . . .

Shit. He shouldn't even think about it, because it was something he'd never know.

The same week *Mondella Alive* came out, Sharleen committed suicide. She slit her wrists and bled to death in her New York apartment.

Bobby mourned long into the night. He'd loved that woman once, and wished he'd been kinder to her the last time she'd visited him in New York.

Too late now. She'd written him after his tragedy, a sweet note asking if she could come and see him. He'd never replied, because he hadn't wanted her to view him as a victim.

Now she was gone. Poor, pretty Sharleen.

A day later he contacted Rocket Fabrizzi – another friend he'd rejected. Rocket was in L.A. making a movie. He came over and they talked the night away, reliving every good old memory.

"I'm glad t'see you're back, man," Rocket said warmly when he left. "Let's stay in touch. You an' I – we'll always remember Sharleen the way she was."

Early reports on his album were excellent. As a favour Rocket directed a promotional video to help it take off. Sara was by Bobby's side at all times, urging him on.

When Marcus Citroen phoned to say he wanted Bobby Mondella to appear at his wife's fund-raiser, Sara's initial reaction was a short, sharp no. She knew some things about Bobby's affair with Nova – he'd told her bits and pieces, but not the whole story by any means.

When she informed Bobby of Marcus Citroen's request, he hesitated for only a moment, and then – to her surprise – said, "Yeah, I'll do it."

Privately he thought it was time he laid some ghosts of the past to rest. And maybe – just maybe – he could find out the real truth about that fateful night in Rio.

"Really?" Sara glared at him disapprovingly.

With an affirmative nod he said, "Sure. You can tell Marcus Citroen I'll definitely be there."

Saturday, July 11, 1987
The Dinner

"Can I see you?" Governor Highland asked in a low voice.

"Huh?" Cybil widened her big blue eyes. "You *are* seeing me."

Leaning closer he murmured, "You know what I mean."

She thought about what Hawkins had said — one day this man might be in the White House. Quite an exhilarating prospect. Then she thought about Kris. He'd been two-timing her with some Danish floozy in London.

"Do you mean lunch?" she asked.

"Dinner," he corrected.

"Okay," she said, with a shiver of excitement. "Where and when?"

Governor Highland smiled. He had sharp, pointed teeth. *Attack-dog teeth*, she thought, suppressing a wild giggle.

"I'm married, you know." He was agreeably honest. "Therefore I have to be very discreet."

"That's all right," she replied. "I'm living with someone — I have to be just as careful as you."

"Write down your phone number," he said, surreptitiously handing her a packet of book matches and a pen. "My aide will contact you."

It was an unfortunate choice of word. Grim realization dawned on Cybil. Governor Highland was probably putting it about all over the place – politicians were known to be a randy bunch, especially the married ones. Too risky, as Kris would say.

Quickly she scribbled the wrong number.

More attack-dog teeth as Governor Highland pocketed the information with a true politician's smile.

*

"Dinner is served." Several maître d's made the announcement, causing a procession of richly clad and bejewelled guests to begin the walk down towards the dining area. Leading the way was a strip of thick red carpet covering the winding path.

Maxwell Sicily took a wooden tooth-pick from his pocket and dug it into his gums as he watched them move out. How come his father wasn't among them? The great Carmine Sicily. The great pig. Carmine had tried hard enough to insinuate himself into high society. He'd bought large chunks of a variety of high-profile companies, even gaining controlling interest in a bank. But Maxwell knew the way things were – he was smarter than his old man any day. The big shots might come to Carmine when they needed a favour – only they would never think of mixing with him socially. To them he was nothing but a rich gangster.

Maxwell had to make sure *his* life was different. In South America a new identity awaited him. He would have money *and* respect.

Unlike his father, *he* would have everything.

*

Nova Citroen moved among her guests, assured and in control. She knew Marcus was watching her. Damn him. Let him watch away. There was nothing more he could do to her. He'd taken her to the very depths and then dragged her right up to the top again.

He'd done the same to Bobby Mondella.

Ah . . . Bobby. For a moment she thought about her former lover with a feeling of nostalgia. At least he was alive. By all rights he should be dead.

She twisted the huge solitaire diamond ring on her finger. A blood present – from her dear husband, and she had accepted it, and kept her silence. After all, deep down, a whore was always a whore.

Memories of Rio returned . . . the nightmare lingered.

Touching her magnificent diamond necklace she turned to speak to Governor Highland, seated on her right. "I do hope you're enjoying yourself," she said pleasantly.

"Nova, dear, when a man is in your company *everything* is a treat. You are truly the most gracious hostess of all. I cannot begin to tell you how much Mary and I appreciate this evening."

"It's nothing, Jack" she murmured modestly. "I adore entertaining. And doing something for you is always a pleasure."

Gazing into her eyes he said a very sincere, "Thank you Nova. Thank you so very much. You'll never regret the support you've given us."

*

Restlessly pacing around her tastefully appointed guest suite, dreading the fact that soon she was going to have to confront Marcus Citroen, Rafealla decided to talk to Bobby, because tonight was the perfect opportunity, and why should she allow him to blank her out of his life? Once they'd been close friends – was that friendship supposed to end because of his unfortunate accident?

"Trudie," she said, "I'm going to see Bobby Mondella."

"Right now?" Trudie asked, doubtfully. "Well, I guess if you're dressed and ready to go on, we can stand at the side of the stage."

"I don't mean watch him perform. I want to visit him now."

"That's not a good idea at all," Trudie said firmly, wondering what this was all about. "Bobby is on first, and I'm sure he'll be getting ready even as we speak."

"What room is he in?"

"Uh . . . seriously, Rafealla. The guests are eating dinner.

You should be getting dressed, and Bobby is probably already on his way down there."

"What room is he in?" she repeated stubbornly.

Trudie shook her head. "I don't know. This isn't a hotel, there are no numbers on the doors. And there's enough doors to house three families!"

"Don't worry about it, I'll be right back."

"Rafealla—" Trudie wailed.

"Five minutes. I promise."

Stepping into the hall she looked around. There were several doors, obviously all leading into guest suites like hers. She knocked on the first one, and a masculine voice called, "Come in."

Tentatively she did so.

Lounging on a couch, flicking the channels on a large-screen TV, was Kris Phoenix.

A silent moment while their eyes met. Oh, no! She hadn't seen him since that memorable night in his limousine ten years ago. Oh, no! For a moment she almost panicked.

"Hi," she mumbled, feeling like a stupid fan.

"Hello, luv," he said, without a flicker of ever having met her before. "Nice of you to come by an' say hello. I like your music, you're doin' all right, girl. Keep it goin'."

*

"Ooooh, Tom. I thought I'd never find you," Vicki cooed softly, creeping up behind him in the security control room. "I should've guessed you'd be here."

"Where else would I be?" he asked, a trifle pompously, indicating the bank of TV monitors surrounding him. "I get to see every single thing from this seat."

"So you do," she said in an admiring tone. "What a clever system. Did *you* set it up?"

"It's all based on my suggestions," he boasted, turning to ogle her cleavage in the partly unbuttoned uniform. She'd been cosying up to him for a while now – it was obvious she couldn't resist him.

He felt Mr Stiffy stir in his pants. Mavis, his wife of twenty-five years, had named it Mr Stiffy on their honeymoon. Unfortunately, over the years, it had not exactly lived up to its name, but this red-hot, not-so-little number certainly had its full attention.

"*I* think you're brilliant," she sighed, wondering to herself if she wasn't going just the tiniest bit too far.

"You do?"

"*Oooh*, sugar-pie, I do!"

He was just about to get up and grab her, when the door opened and one of his guards walked in.

"What is it, Sturgon?" Tom snapped, caught at the pass.

The guard was no idiot. He took one look at Vicki, hovering in the corner, and another look at Tom, red-faced and ready for action, and quickly said, "Just reporting in, boss. No problems. Everybody's in position."

"Good, good," Tom blustered. "Get back to checkpoint one an' stay there."

"Don't you need me to man the screens with you?"

"It's not necessary. I'll contact you later."

Sturgon favoured Vicki with a long, lustful leer. He wouldn't mind a crack at her himself. Some people had all the luck. "Okay, boss," he said, with a smart-aleck salute. "I'll see you later."

Tom grunted. He didn't like the way Sturgon eyeballed Vicki. She deserved more respect than that.

*

Standing at the side of the stage, Bobby smelled money. It was all around him. Along with the light outdoor breeze there was a subtle mix of heady perfumes and expensive aftershaves. Above that, the rich aroma of two-hundred-dollar cigars filled the air.

Sara had one hand firmly on his arm. "How do you feel?" she whispered anxiously.

It was the fourth time she'd asked him. "Will you quit," he muttered angrily. "You're really starting to piss me off. Get lost. Go watch the show someplace else."

"Bobby . . ."

He could hear the hurt in her voice and didn't care. The main thing was to get this show over and done with. Sara by his side would only bug him.

"I said get lost," he repeated harshly. "I need to be left alone right now."

"Sure," she said, hurt and angry at the same time. "I'll go and enjoy the party."

"Do that."

"I will," she replied defiantly. Not that he gave a damn. Since she'd left him alone earlier he'd been in a foul mood. It was confusing being with Bobby. One minute she was his lover, the next merely an employee. What did he *really* feel about her? Did he care at all? Sometimes she doubted it.

One of the musicians had already been elected to escort him on stage, so there was no reason for her to hang around. Norton St John had invited her to join the press table and she decided she would. With a firm step she left Bobby standing alone.

*

Rafealla wanted to laugh. Kris Phoenix had known who she was all right. New hot recording star – Rafealla. And that's *all* he'd known.

Ha! She must have *really* left a lasting impression that night so long ago in London. He'd had no idea they'd ever met, let alone made love together – if that was the right way to describe their one-time encounter.

It was funny really – since achieving fame she'd been nervous about running into him, quite sure he would remember the silly little girl he'd taken advantage of and make fun of her.

No such attitude. Just a friendly grin and words of encouragement.

Wouldn't it blow his mind if he knew the truth!

Backing out of his room, she hurriedly returned to Trudie, who urged her to get changed as they had to make their way down to the performance area. Slowly she put on the simple black dress she'd chosen to wear. It made her crazy, because she couldn't help thinking about Marcus taking it off her later. Why had she ever agreed to go to bed with such a vile man?

They'd cut a deal, hadn't they? And he'd kept his side of the bargain. He'd made her famous, and after Luiz's betrayal that's all she'd wanted. Fame. Because her one big desire was to get back at Luiz – and fame was the only way to do it. Luiz had always been so ambitious. America was his dream – he'd talked about it all the time.

Now *she* had it and *he* didn't. Too bad. She knew he must be wishing he'd stayed with her.

Smoothing the black dress over her slim body, she decided it was perfect for tonight. Thinking about Luiz still upset her. He'd hurt her badly – devastated her, in fact. But one thing she was sure of. No more love entanglements. Sleeping with Marcus Citroen was better than falling in love any day.

*

Maxwell Sicily walked away from the open-air dinner with authority, carrying a full tray.

"Where do you think you're going?" A burly guard stopped him at one of the exit points.

Maxwell indicated his badge and the tray. "A snack for Kris Phoenix. I'm taking it over to the guest house."

"You got authority?"

"Yeah," Maxwell said sarcastically. "The chef stopped everything and wrote me a note. Jeez! You guys take this crap seriously, don't you?"

With an angry wave the guard passed him through.

Security. Forget it. These guys knew nothing. Fortunately for him.

*

Kris dressed for his appearance in white pants, Reeboks, a black tee-shirt and pink Armani jacket. With his longish hair spiked and streaked, intense ice-blue eyes, athletic body and deep suntan – he looked exactly like the rock superstar dream.

Okay, so he was thirty-eight years old. Big deal. He still had it. The old bones hadn't given up on him yet. Kris Phoenix was the *hottest*.

Norton St John arrived to escort him to the stage. He'd sent

Cybil off with Hawkins again. Let her enjoy the evening – it was better than having her hanging around driving him nuts.

*

"Have you seen George Smith anywhere?" Pudgy Chloe grabbed hold of a passing waiter.

"Who?" he asked, balancing a tray of coffee cups.

"George Smith," Chloe repeated impatiently. "He's a waiter, about your height, dark haired an' good looking."

"We're all good lookin'," he smirked.

"Yeah, well, he's *really* handsome," retorted Chloe irritably. "If you see him, tell him I'm looking for him."

The waiter peered at her identification badge – Chloe Bragg – Supervisor – Lilliane's. "Listen," he said, "I'm only temporary. D'you think you can use your influence an' get me on permanent?"

"Find George Smith for me, an' we'll see."

He nodded. "I'll keep my eyes open."

"Thanks," she said, stationing herself at the high-traffic area between the kitchen and the dining area. Waiters and busboys were buzzing back and forth, but no sign of George Smith, damn him.

Chloe was deeply disappointed.

*

Much to his disgust the highway patrol cop gave Speed a ticket. Racing along the Pacific Coast Highway he growled to himself, sounding like a Doberman pinscher. He was late. It didn't matter. He'd make it. He always did.

Saturday, July 11, 1987
The Concert

And so it began.

Bobby Mondella took the stage with confidence. Fuck it. He wasn't going to let the fact that he couldn't see stand in his way. Once he was out there, in position, he went for it, falling into the rhythm of a live performance as if he'd never been away.

The audience were receptive, rising to their feet to welcome him back.

Nova was out there watching him, and for once it didn't matter. He'd faced his past, and that's all she was now – his past.

*

Maxwell Sicily rode the golf cart to the guest house. There was one black guard roaming around outside, the same guard he'd seen when he'd delivered Bobby Mondella's food earlier.

"Here we go again," Maxwell said, with a friendly wave.

"What's happening down there?" the guard asked, wishing he was part of the real action.

"Bobby Mondella is just about to go on."

"Yeah? Really?"

"It's a shame you're missing it."

The guard pulled a disgusted face. "Tell me about it. My wife'll kill me. She thinks I'm gonna come home with a full report."

"Sneak down and take a look," Maxwell encouraged "Nobody'll miss you."

"I wouldn't mind," the guard said longingly.

"Do it! Who's to know?"

The guard laughed. "Tom. Our chief. He checks us out every twenty minutes."

Maxwell nodded knowingly, hoisted his tray, and said, "I'd love to help you, but I've got work to do. I'm supposed to clean this place up while they're performing."

"Good luck."

Maxwell entered the guest house. It was deserted, just as he'd known it would be. The stars and their entourages were all down at the dinner.

Placing the tray in the kitchen, he hurried upstairs. Vicki had told him exactly which guest suite would be unoccupied. He found it, opened the closet, and located his holdall pushed out of sight in the back. From it he took a rolled black garbage bag, a cache of tools, and a small snub-nosed revolver, just in case.

Prepared, he hurried downstairs and slipped out of the kitchen door. Then he sprinted across a vast lawn until he reached the far side of the main house. Entry was no problem – earlier Vicki had fixed the catch on the sliding glass windows to Marcus Citroen's study.

Letting himself in, he stood quietly for a moment, taking stock. The room was exactly as Vicki had described it, which meant safe number one was located behind the Matisse hanging tastefully in the centre of the wall. He would take care of that one on the way out. Right now his mind was on the real money. Nova Citroen's bedroom safe.

*

The applause was deafening. It swept over Bobby like sweet nectar as he was led off stage. Performing live had been a challenge hanging over his head. Could he do it?

Yeah, man, he could do it.

For a moment the deadly heat of revenge left him and he was free. "Sara?" he called out, but she wasn't around – he'd sent her away.

"You were wonderful!" a female voice breathed.

He reached out. "Who's this?"

She took his hand. "Rafaella. Remember me? Your friend from Rio."

"Oh, Jesus! Raffi. This is great!"

"*You* were great."

They hugged.

"I'm mad at you," she scolded.

"Hey – baby – don't be mad – you gotta understand what happened. Things were out of my control. I—"

"Rafaella." Hands were pulling at her. "You're on."

"Bobby, don't go away," she commanded sternly. "We'll talk. We'll catch up."

"I ain't movin' from here, babe. You can depend on that."

Kissing him, she whispered, "Welcome back, superstar. I *do* love you."

He gave her a little push. "Kill 'em, baby, go give 'em hell!"

*

Vicki had her timing down pat. She knew exactly when to distract Tom. She knew exactly how. When Vicki Foxe exposed her two greatest assets, grown men crumbled, and Tom was no exception.

She led him to the magic moment carefully. Timing was everything, and if she didn't get it right the first time there were no second chances. Manoeuvring him into position, she slowly undid the buttons on her uniform – one by one.

"Holy mother!" Tom groaned, bursting at the seams. He'd never seen anything like her before. This woman was stacked and *then* some.

"Wanna suck on the candy, big man?" she tempted him, giving him no choice as she thrust an upstanding nipple into his mouth.

He was lost in heaven, while behind him, on television monitor five, Maxwell Sicily went to work breaking and entering Nova Citroen's safe.

*

Rafealla felt great. There was nothing like an audience to give you a buzz, and she was thrilled Bobby Mondella was standing at the side of the stage waiting for her.

What could Marcus do if she turned up with Bobby? Kill her? Ha! She'd make him wait. She'd make him wait forever.

A wave of relief enveloped her. That's what she'd do – MAKE HIM WAIT FOREVER! Why hadn't she thought of it before?

Fame was already hers – he couldn't take it away, and if he did – well, to be quite truthful, fame was a drag anyway – who needed it?

She was a survivor. She'd survived Eddie Mafair, and Luiz and his lies. Now she'd survive Marcus Citroen.

In the long run survival was the only thing that really mattered.

*

"I'm glad t'see you're out an' about," Kris said happily, clapping Bobby on the shoulder as they both waited at the side of the stage. "I've bin meanin' t'get hold of you – I thought it might be a giggle if we recorded somethin' together. Remember? We always threatened we would."

"Yeah, we did, didn't we?" Bobby replied, reaching out to touch the brash English singer, whom he'd always liked.

"You do know I tried to call you a few times—" Kris said. "After all that shit you went through I figured you might like to hear a friendly voice."

"Sara told me," Bobby replied. "But, uh, I guess I never felt like talkin' to anyone."

"I can understand that. Only now you're around, let's do it, huh? We gotta make ourselves a record for *us* – y'know – like give all the proceeds to one of them charities. That'd *really* piss Marcus off. How about it?"

"Hey – anythin' that'd piss Marcus off, you can count me in."

"An' you know somethin'? We'll get *her* to do it, too," Kris said, warming to his theme.

"Who?" Bobby asked.

"Rafealla. She's got an interesting sound. I like her voice – plenty of style. Whadderya think?"

"Sounds good to me. I love that girl."

Rafealla finished her second song, followed by rapturous applause. She ran off the stage elated and glowing.

Winking at her, Kris said, "You were great, darlin', really great."

She smiled at him. God! It was like looking at an older version of Jon Jon. Quite spooky.

"Hang about," he said. "Bobby an' I – we got a proposition for you. The three of us'll split a bottle of champagne up at the house when I'm through. Okay?"

Why not face Marcus with Bobby *and* Kris. Perfect! She nodded. "Terrific."

Blondes were his scene, but this girl was something else. *And* she could sing. "I'm countin' on it, luv," he said, with a crooked grin. Clenching his fist in the air, he yelled, "Okay, let's get this bleedin' show on the road. In and *out*." And with that he raced on stage. Mister Energy. Mister Strut. Still full of piss and vinegar and raw, exciting talent.

The sophisticated audience went wild as he launched into *Long-Legged Blondes*. Blasé they might be, but they knew a superstar when they saw one.

*

The moment Rafealla left the stage, Marcus excused himself from his two dinner partners and slipped away.

Nova saw him leave. Her expression tightened. She didn't care how many whores and starlets he had, but this girl Rafealla represented a threat. She was too young and beautiful by far, and Nova didn't like it one little bit.

*

Maxwell Sicily worked quickly and methodically, well aware that time was at a premium and it was essential he moved fast. The months of planning paid off. Thanks to Vicki he knew the exact makes and locations of both safes. In prison they'd nicknamed him the Cracker, because it was a well-known fact that he could break open anything in record time.

True to his reputation, he had Nova's big safe ajar within seven minutes. With satisfaction he noted it was stocked as if he were in the world's most expensive jewellery store.

Without hesitation he began filling the large plastic garbage bag with jewels, tipping them out of their boxes indiscriminately, until the sack was almost half full.

What a cache! More than he'd thought. Enough to set him up for a long, long time. Enough to buy him freedom from the goddamn system.

Shutting the safe, he hurried from her bedroom, careful to duck beneath the laser beam alarm across her door so as not to trip it. Vicki had been most thorough in her description of the alarm system throughout the house.

Outside, two lone guards paraded up and down. Maxwell could make out their shadows through the window. Normally this house was full of staff, but tonight they had gathered on the grassy knolls surrounding the outdoor dining area and the open-air stage to watch the concert. The dogs – usually running wild in the grounds – were locked up because of the influx of people.

He had known this would be the perfect night.

Returning to Marcus's study he began his work there.

Ten more minutes and he'd be finished.

Ten more minutes and he'd be rich.

*

"How do I nail him, Hawkie?" Cybil asked, squirming with pleasure as Kris finished his performance to tumultuous applause.

"I beg your pardon?" the Hawk asked, wishing she wouldn't call him Hawkie.

"Well, I know he's got a girlfriend in England," Cybil said matter-of-factly. "And I guess he must like her – a bit. But she's old, you know, almost thirty."

"God forbid!" the Hawk murmured sardonically. "When's the funeral?"

Cybil giggled. "*You* know what I mean. I want him to marry me. How can I get him to do that?"

"Force and torture."

Dazzling everyone around her with a wide smile, she said, "You're so *silly*, Hawkie, really you are!"

*

Tom was at the point of no return. Vicki had him straddled against the circular counter, his back to the bank of television monitors, his pants and undershorts twisted around his ankles. She was on her knees, squashing his erect penis between her magnificent breasts, and every time he felt he was about to climax she sensed it, and backed away, cooing, "Be patient, big boy. We've waited so long, let's not *rush* it."

He was mesmerized by her thrusting, heaving, heavy tits. Nothing else mattered. Nothing in the whole wide world.

*

As soon as Kris came off stage he took control. He was good at that. After all, he'd been the driving force behind The Wild Ones for all those years — he knew how to get his own way.

"We'll take the golf cart back to the house, just the three of us," he decided, grabbing Bobby by one arm and Rafealla by the other. "Let's have some fun for a change."

"Mr Phoenix," Norton St John said in his best concerned voice, "I have a table for you all to sit at while the speeches take place. And then there's the auction, and I *know* Mrs Citroen wishes to introduce you to some of her more important guests. The Governor and his wife certainly want to thank you personally. And there is a French princess who has particularly requested an introduction."

"Must be the same little raver who's bin tryin' to give me one for the last six months," Kris said with a wink. "I think I'll pass. Whaddaya say — Bobby? Raf?"

"I pass," said Bobby solemnly.

"Me too!" agreed Rafealla, enjoying herself for the first time in ages.

"Really—" objected Norton St John, now surrounded by an anxious Trudie and the two matching record executives.

"We're okay," Rafealla assured everyone, helping Kris assist

Bobby onto the golf cart. "Go listen to the speeches, we'll see you all later."

"It looks like we're not needed, boys," commented Trudie dryly, wishing she were in Rafealla's position.

"Everyone aboard," yelled Kris. "Let's hit it!"

The electric golf cart jerked into action, while a worried Norton said, "Are you sure you know the way?"

"We'll find it, that's if we don't drive over the cliff first," joked Kris cheerily.

*

Marcus paced around Rafealla's room. He had instructed her to come straight back when she'd finished performing. Where was she? This was not good enough. Rafealla was going too far – she was testing his patience.

The first thing he would do, he decided, was to teach her a lesson. An unforgettable lesson, as only he knew how.

*

A flat tyre. No. This couldn't be happening. No freakin' way.

Speed zigzagged the large limousine over to the hard shoulder of the road and climbed out, cursing to himself.

Yes. It was a flat tyre all right. What the a for ass was going on? Did her majesty, the ditz – his ex-wife – have a doll made up in his image? Was she even now sticking pins in it and chanting little "I'll get you" songs. Je . . . *sus!*

Springing the trunk he searched for the spare.

There wasn't one.

Saturday, July 11, 1987
The Scam

Maxwell stuffed everything from Marcus Citroen's safe into the bag. There were deeds and letters, photographs and other papers. He decided he would study them at his leisure – it would be interesting to see what he discovered.

There were also a lot of single, unset stones – diamonds, sapphires, rubies and emeralds – plus several expensive watches, men's gold jewellery, and wads of cash.

Maxwell licked his lips. His mouth was dry. Glancing quickly at the television camera mounted on the ceiling he realized how foolish rich people were. They spent fortunes on security, and yet, if the person in charge was busy elsewhere, it all meant nothing.

Vicki was certainly keeping Tom the moron busy. She deserved a bonus.

Quietly shutting the safe, he signalled her, V for victory – playing directly to camera.

Now she would allow him two minutes to exit the room, and then she was in the clear. A job well done.

*

The Governor was speaking. Governor Jack Highland.

Nova watched him, but she wasn't really listening, she was thinking about Marcus with that little tramp. How dare he pick *her* fund-raiser for *his* tryst. How dare he!

Governor Highland was an attractive man. He had the look. Honest, sincere, boyish – the Kennedy look.

Ah . . . a man like Jack Highland could change the world, and she, Nova Citroen, was helping to put him in position. Great power marked out his future. Everyone who mattered said so.

Watch out, Marcus, she thought, the day might come when I have someone even more influential than you to turn to.

*

"Jesus H. Didja get a load of all those stuffed shirts?" Kris asked, as the golf cart careened down a twisting path.

"I think we're going in the wrong direction," Rafealla pointed out.

"Hey – they clapped pretty fine," Bobby yelled, gripping the side of the cart for dear life.

"You betcha, baby," Kris shouted gleefully. "I'd clap pretty fine too if I'd paid a hundred thousand big ones for fuck all."

Pretending to be indignant, Rafealla said, "Thanks a lot!"

"Nothin' personal," Kris replied with a grin. "But c'mon sweetheart, let's face it, it's only rock 'n' roll, ain't it? No big deal."

*

Tom let out an anguished groan. "I can't hold it any longer," he gasped.

Vicki had been doing a slow countdown in her head. Ten more seconds and she was free and clear. Maxwell was long gone from the TV monitor.

With a little sigh she pulled her left tit out of his mouth, gasping dramatically, "This isn't right, you're a married man. I don't know what came over me."

"Huh?" Tom said stupidly, staring in disbelief as she struggled into the top half of her dress, covering acres of paradise.

"It's just that deep down I'm a religious girl," she explained.

His erect penis drooped miserably.

Tears brimmed from her eyes. "What we were about to do is a sin. You're *married*, Tom."

As if he didn't know.

She finished buttoning her dress, gazing at him tearfully. "I'm sorry. I know you must hate me. Oh, I'm so *sorrreeee*, Tom."

Not half as sorry as he was. He had an ache in his groin the like of which he couldn't recall.

"Just suck me off an' we can pretend it never happened," he said hopefully.

She looked at him in horror. "What kind of girl do you think I am?"

"A prick-tease," he muttered angrily, full of frustration. "A first class blue-baller!"

★

Now came the tricky part. He'd cleaned out the safes, but Maxwell knew that getting the contents and himself off the estate was not going to be easy.

The black plastic sack was heavy as he carried it across the lawn to the comparative safety of the guest house. He slid through the kitchen door and headed straight upstairs to the unoccupied suite.

Just as he was about to enter, a harsh voice called out, "You!"

"Yes?" He turned around slowly, only to face Marcus Citroen. Jesus Christ! Marcus was supposed to be watching the performers and listening to the speeches along with everyone else.

"What are you doing?" Marcus asked.

"Cleaning up, sir," he replied, without taking a beat.

"Cleaning up what?"

"Ashtrays, drinks, food. They want this house spotless before the artists return. Mrs Citroen's orders." He indicated his badge. "I'm with Lilliane's, sir. George Smith at your service."

"Okay, okay." Marcus waved him away impatiently, changed his mind and said, "You can do this room now."

"Certainly, sir."

Maxwell walked into Rafealla's suite, lugging the black sack with him, while Marcus stood back and watched.

Picking up an ashtray he dropped the contents into the sack. And then he gathered the dirty dishes and glasses, adding them too. With a polite nod he said, "That's all, sir."

Marcus was busy lighting a cigar. He didn't reply.

For the first time Maxwell felt that everything was not going according to plan. He was never supposed to come face to face with Marcus Citroen. What was the man doing in the guest house anyway?

No time to think about it. Into the unoccupied suite. Straight to the closet where Vicki had hidden an expensive Vuitton bag. Working fast, he transferred everything into it – leaving out the dirty dishes. Then he locked it, pocketing the key, and stuffed it into the garbage bag, along with his holdall.

Now for the next move. If he dared to make it with Marcus Citroen so close by.

Goddammit. He had no choice.

*

"So I think the three of us could get together on something really great," Kris said enthusiastically, pulling the golf cart to a jerky halt outside the guest house. "I mean, we're all so different, with such diverse styles. An' I'll get Buzz involved too. Y'know he's doing' all right now since he came off drugs. Like it'd be a real challenge to blow everyone away. Know what I mean?"

"I'm willin' to try," Bobby said. "In fact maybe I can write us somethin'."

"If it's for a suitable charity, and considering we're all with Blue Cadillac anyway, I don't see what can stop us," Rafealla joined in.

"*You* can name the charity, luv," Kris said, helping her down, and then taking Bobby's arm. "Starvin' kids. Ethiopia. The homeless. Whatever."

His eyes were just like Jon Jon's, blue and intense. "Let me think," she said, hoping that the tingly feeling she had was just her imagination.

Kris decided she was one of the most beautiful girls he'd ever seen. Californian blondes paled in comparison. He wondered if she had a steady boyfriend.

Companionably they all walked into the house, the guard nodding them on their way.

"Any of our mob here yet?" Kris asked, as they passed.

"Only a waiter from Lilliane's. Oh, and Mr Citroen arrived a while ago."

"I can't stand that son of a bitch," Kris muttered. "He treats everyone an' everything like shit." He turned to Bobby and Rafealla. "What's he here for anyway? It's not like Mister Big to come slumming with the talent, is it?"

Rafealla said nothing.

*

Vicki exited as fast as she could – no good prolonging the old fart's anger. *Put your pecker away and shut up*, she wanted to say.

But she didn't. Instead she hurried out of there, leaving a very unhappy Tom buttoning his fly.

*

Chloe was seething. George Smith had done a pretty good job of avoiding her, and she didn't like it one bit. Didn't he realize she had clout at Lilliane's? Didn't he realize she could get him *fired*?

He'd snuck off somewhere to watch the concert without her, and her feelings were hurt. She'd tried to be friendly, nice, but he'd rejected her, and she was determined to do something about it. Chloe didn't take kindly to being turned down.

"One of my waiters is missing," she informed a uniformed guard standing near the entrance to the dining area. "He's about five foot ten, dark hair, not bad looking. Perhaps you've seen him. George Smith is his name."

To her surprise the guard responded, "Yeah, I think I know who you mean. Sounds like the one who took a tray over to the guest house an' never came back. I guess they needed him over there."

"The guest house?"

"Yes, ma'am. That's where all the celebs are holed up."

Her mouth tightened. What was George doing at the guest

house? "Thank you," she said brusquely.

"A pleasure, ma'am. Any time."

*

They commandeered the living room – Kris, Rafealla and Bobby, talking and joking, making plans to do something *they* could enjoy *and* control for a change.

"I hate bleedin' record bosses, agents an' managers," Kris said with feeling. "They're just a bunch of untalented wankers on for the ride."

"You got it," agreed Bobby, wishing Sara was with him. "They don't give a shit about quality, only sales."

"Hey – hey – hey – sales ain't bad," admitted Kris, walking to the bar. "I can get off on selling a few million here an' there."

Rafealla laughed. She felt quite carefree, considering Marcus was in the house, and bound to appear at any moment. "Do me a favour," she said quickly.

"Only if it means takin' me clothes off," Kris joked, fixing himself a rum and coke.

"I don't want to be alone with Marcus."

"Nobody wants to be alone with Marcus," Bobby said, fiddling with his dark glasses.

"I mean it," she said urgently. "Promise you won't leave me?"

Kris stared at her. She had the greenest eyes he'd ever seen, and the most incredible, smooth olive skin. The rest of her wasn't bad either. Maybe he'd give up blondes forever. It was a thought, because this girl was something else. And in the short period of time they'd been together, he felt connected to her in some strange and special way. It was weird. "Are you married or anything?" he couldn't stop himself from asking, feeling like a right berk.

"Hey," Bobby said light-heartedly. "Stop hittin' on our partner. Don't you answer him, Raf. This old stud considers himself a real ladykiller. I don't want you goin' anyway *near* him. Got it?"

*

Chloe set off towards the guest house with a determined expression. Not only had George Smith let her down, but he was slacking off on the job, an even greater crime. If she wanted to get him fired she could – and unless he gave her good reason not to, that's exactly what she intended to do.

*

With a snort of anger Marcus marched from Rafealla's room. He'd waited long enough. She would pay dearly for her behaviour.

Along the corridor, Maxwell Sicily hung back, willing Marcus Citroen to get the hell out of his way.

The next part of his plan should go smoothly, only it had to take place while everyone was occupied with the speeches and the auction. He was supposed to leave the guest house, still dressed in his waiter's uniform, carrying the sack of garbage. The guard would wave him on his way, and he would take the golf cart to a prearranged meeting spot near the swimming pool, where Vicki would be waiting with an evening suit for him to change into. Once changed, carrying the Vuitton bag, he would stroll down to the parking area as if he were an early departing guest, climb casually into his limousine – which Speed would have in the right place at the right time – and take off.

Easy.

If all went according to plan. And there was no reason why it shouldn't. All he needed was for Marcus Citroen to get the hell out of his way.

Saturday, July 11, 1987
The Confrontation

Marcus Citroen threw open the door of the living room and discovered Kris Phoenix, Bobby Mondella and Rafealla – *his* Rafealla – sitting around enjoying themselves.

His expression registered pure rage as he attempted to keep control.

"How ya doin', Marcus?" Kris asked cockily, raising his glass in salute. "Slummin' tonight, are we?"

Marcus ignored the spikey-haired rock star. He suspected Nova had slept with him, although she denied it. Marcus only tolerated her indiscretions up to a point. It was fortunate for Kris she hadn't become involved – as she had with Bobby Mondella. The black cocksucker was lucky to be alive, and doubly lucky to have been given his career back. Marcus considered himself a fair man. He didn't hold a grudge forever.

"Rafealla," he said sharply. "We had a meeting. Did you forget?"

Kris watched the eye play between them. Rafealla had a trapped look, while Marcus exhibited a malevolent predatory glare. No wonder she didn't want to be left alone with him – the horny old guy was just about ready to eat her alive.

"Come," Marcus said, holding out his arm. "I do not appreciate being kept waiting."

Her voice didn't waver. "I'm busy right now, Marcus."

His mouth tightened into a thin line, while his hooded eyes clouded with anger. "We have business to discuss. Let's go."

"I'm quite happy here," she said bravely.

"Rafealla." His voice was ice. "I want you to come upstairs with me *now*. That's an order."

"An order!" Kris tried to make a joke of it. "I didn't know we were back in bleedin' school!"

Marcus turned to glare at him, just as Maxwell Sicily hurried past the open door.

*

Huffing and puffing, Chloe arrived at the front of the guest house the same time as Maxwell walked outside.

"Oh," she said, quivering with indignation. "*This* is where you've been hiding, is it?"

She stood between him and the golf cart, a solid lump.

"Mrs Citroen told me to come here and clean the place up," he said, wishing the fat cow would drop dead.

"Mrs Citroen told you, did she?" demanded Chloe sharply. "And since when did Mrs Citroen tell *my* waiters what to do?"

He shrugged, attempting to dodge past her. "We're all working here tonight, aren't we? I was just trying to help out."

Chloe knew plenty about waiters, and the one thing they never did was volunteer their services for nothing. There was something suspicious going on, Chloe knew it – she had a sixth sense about such things. George Smith was a strange one. Handsome, she had to admit, but not honest, and certainly not a gentleman. She didn't like the way he'd treated her at all. Leading her on, and then running off and deserting her.

Automatically her eyes dropped to the bulging garbage bag he was carrying. "What's in there?" she asked suspiciously. Some waiters had a very lucrative sideline removing whole sides of beef, chickens and the best fillet steaks via the old garbage sack trick.

No! A voice screamed in his head. The goddamn cunt was going to put him away with her interfering. Why couldn't anything ever go right for him?

Out of the corner of his eye he noticed the guard strolling towards them.

Was this how he got caught?

Fuck! No!

Without saying another word, he shoved past her.

"Stop!" she shouted, and then as if she knew she was on to a sure thing, "Stop, thief!"

At the word "thief", the guard quickened his pace. "What's going on here?"

"This waiter is removing property that's not his," Chloe yelled in a shrill voice. "I demand that you stop him."

Maxwell had one foot on the golf cart. He wasn't going to blow this set up. Winking conspiratorially at the guard he said, "The old broad's crazy. She's probably on the rag."

"Hold it a sec," the guard said. "Let's clear this up before you go anywhere. Step down."

Outwardly calm, Maxwell did as he was asked. His mind was racing. What he really wanted to do was take out his piece, jam it into the dumb bitch's mouth, and blow the fucking cunt away. That would teach her to stay out of Maxwell Sicily's business.

The guard approached Chloe. "What's the problem, ma'am?"

Flashing her identification badge, she said, "I have reason to believe this man is removing property that does not belong to him."

"Horse*shit*," Maxwell muttered.

"We can soon clear this up," the guard said, coming to a logical conclusion. The last thing he wanted was any trouble. "Open the sack, make the lady happy."

"I resent his," Maxwell said bitterly. "I resent being falsely accused by this frustrated fucking *bitch!*"

As he spoke he edged back towards the front door.

"Let's not get excited," the guard said, still trying to smooth things over.

"Did you *hear* what he called me?" screeched Chloe. "Did you *hear* his language? You're fired, George Smith. You are *fired* from Lilliane's right now. Guard! Make him open that sack!"

"Open it," the guard said wearily. How come everyone else got to see a sensational concert, and all he got was a whining restaurant supervisor and a thieving waiter — because, come to think of it, the sack did look kind of bulky.

"All right," Maxwell said, bending down as if to do as he was asked.

Chloe glared. She had him now. They were probably going to discover every ashtray and ornament in the place. She hoped the Citroens would be willing to prosecute, and send the petty thief to jail where he belonged. She'd always known there was something strange about George Smith.

With the element of surprise working in his favour, Maxwell swung the heavy sack up in the air, catching the unprepared guard in the stomach and knocking him off balance. Chloe began to yell and scream.

Quickly Maxwell backed into the house, slamming and locking the front door behind him.

*

Nova fidgeted in her seat. The speeches were finished — a great success — and now the auction was going well, but Marcus had not returned, and she was seething. On tonight of all nights she wished to reap the adulation that came with being one of the most sought-after and elegant hostesses in America. She wanted to share this triumph with her husband.

But no, it was not to be. Marcus Citroen was too busy making love to his latest conquest.

Why *should* she let him get away with it unchallenged? Standing up abruptly, she excused herself. Marcus was going to get a visit from her, whether he liked it or not.

*

With a roar of frustrated fury Maxwell hurled himself into the living room, waving his gun threateningly in the air. The black garbage sack skittered across the floor ahead of him.

"Get your hands up, motherfuckers," he screamed. "This is a hostage situation and you're fucking *it!*"

Saturday, July 11, 1987
The Conclusion

Four hours had passed. Four of the longest hours of Maxwell Sicily's life.

He'd always tried to be low-key, stay away from the spotlight, keep out of other people's business and hope they would afford him the same courtesy.

It wasn't easy being Carmine Sicily's son. No, it wasn't easy at all. In school it was like he'd had a neon sign over his head proclaiming the fact. Decent kids stayed away from him, while the scum couldn't do enough favours.

He grew up confused. Carmine was a larger-than-life figure to have as a role-model. Everybody loved Carmine Sicily. Every low-life who ever breathed.

His mother, Rose, didn't count. She died when he was fourteen, leaving him alone with Carmine and a parade of whores.

He had his first woman the day after his mother's funeral. Carmine forced her onto him – pushing the girl into his room with the words, "She'll cheer you up, an' if she don't, forget about hangin' around *me* with your miserable face."

The girl was twenty-two and experienced. She milked him like a cow, holding his penis in one hand, rubbing between her legs with the other.

He hated it. He hated her. He hated his father.

When he was sixteen he took a gun from Carmine's closet and robbed a liquor store. His father's fury knew no bounds. He was beaten for a week.

When he was eighteen, he fucked Carmine's nineteen-year-old girlfriend, stole twenty-six thousand dollars in cash and a black Lincoln from the house, and took off.

Carmine had him tracked down and brought back. This time he was locked in the cellar for three weeks with only bread and water for sustenance.

At twenty-two he shot and nearly killed a bank guard during the course of a violent robbery.

"I give up," Carmine said. "Let him rot in jail. He's not *my* son."

And so he spent the next seven years in prison without a word from his father.

When he got out he headed for California, and it wasn't long before he decided what his next job would be. Reading a magazine one day, he found out all about Nova and Marcus Citroen and their fabulous wealth. Then he saw the newspaper piece about their forthcoming fund-raiser for Governor Highland. The two articles jelled in his head. It was too good an opportunity to miss.

Now here he was. Fucked.

And outside the house there were police, and people and TV cameras and press.

He was FUCKED.

"Can I please have a drink of water?" Rafealla asked wearily. Like the others she was bound hand and foot, lying on the floor in the corner.

Maxwell had forced them to tie each other up shortly after he broke in. Wild-eyed, he'd brandished his gun in the air threatening to shoot every one of them if they didn't comply with his wishes.

He'd sent Rafealla upstairs to fetch sheets. "If you're not back in two minutes I'll put a bullet through his head," he'd warned, nodding at Bobby.

Shaking, she'd raced through the bedrooms, dragging sheets from the beds.

When she'd brought them downstairs, he'd made Kris and Marcus tear them into strips and tie first Bobby, then Rafaella. Next, he'd had Marcus truss Kris up, and finally he'd done the honours to the furious record magnate himself.

Marcus had tried to reason with him. "Be sensible," he'd said. "You'll never get away with this. *Never*. So why don't you be smart, and walk away *now*, before you do something you'll really regret?"

Walk away. That was a joke. He couldn't walk away. He was trapped. All his life he'd been trapped.

Marcus Citroen reminded him of Carmine. A fat cat. A man who thought money could buy him anything.

"How much if I walk?" he'd asked, seeing what price Marcus would put on his life.

"Ten thousand dollars. Cash," Marcus had replied, with all the confidence of a man able to buy himself out of any situation. "And you have my word. I'll make absolutely certain you're set free."

Sure. And Mother Teresa will get a job in a go-go parlour. Marcus Citroen insulted his intelligence, just like Carmine. Two rich pigs.

Maxwell had laughed in his face, whereupon Marcus Citroen doubled his offer, then tripled it. But by that time Maxwell wasn't listening.

Once his hostages were tied up he'd felt better. Leaving them for a moment he'd scanned the house, making sure every window was secured from the inside, and pushing the bolts and chains on the two outside doors.

Soon the police would arrive.

He wasn't wrong.

*

All Rafaella could think about was Jon Jon. If anything happened to her, how would her little boy survive? He was ten years old. What would he do without her? Who would teach him about life, and how to treat women, and the difference between right and wrong?

Who would comfort him when he was sad? Laugh with him when he was happy? Scold him when he was naughty?

She was his mother, *goddammit*, and she was determined to get out of this alive.

*

Locked into a world of blackness Bobby struggled with a terrible feeling of inadequacy. There was nothing he could do – he was tied up, helpless, he couldn't even see what was happening.

He, Bobby Mondella, was a prisoner in every way.

*

On the other hand Kris felt pretty damn strong. When Marcus was tying him up he'd managed to loosen the bonds as they were going on. Strips of sheet weren't going to hold *him* back when the moment came to take this psycho out. And the guy *was* a psycho – Kris knew he was right – you only had to look at the creep with his flat, starey eyes, and edgy, unsure movements.

Hey – Andy Warhol had said it pretty good – everyone can be famous for fifteen minutes –and that's what this asshole wanted. To hit the headlines, sell his story, have a book written about him, maybe even a mini-series.

Right now he was on the verge. He had three of the biggest recording stars in the world and a billionaire record tycoon wrapped up as hostages. But hey – Kris could figure out what the freak was thinking. If he let them go, what then? One headline, and that was it, he'd fade into obscurity without a trace. The only way he was going to hit it big was if he did something major – like kill them all.

With a shudder, Kris managed to roll towards Rafealla. "You okay?" he whispered.

She nodded.

"Hang in there, kid," he said comfortingly. "Because we're gonna get out of this. An' that's one thing you'll learn about me, I'm *never* wrong."

*

Gathered outside the house there was a virtual army of people. The police, along with the SWAT team, had cordoned off a large area. Behind them were the TV crews, reporters and photographers. Most of the important guests had fled the scene, but Governor Highland had remained, giving Nova Citroen comfort, and maintaining a suitably heroic image with the press.

Maxwell, in his phone negotiations with Police Captain Lynch, had insisted the media were allowed onto the estate, figuring he was safer that way. His demands were simple. A helicopter to take him and his hostages to a quiet location, where an unmarked car would be waiting for him to make his getaway. "When I'm certain I'm safe, I'll release the hostages," he'd promised.

"Sure," Captain Lynch had muttered under his breath.

This conversation had taken place during the second hour of the siege – once the police captain took charge, and telephone contact began. "Who are you? What's your name?" was the first question he'd asked.

"George Smith," Maxwell lied.

"No way, pal. We had George Smith checked out. He's only been around for the last couple of months. How about telling us your *real* name, and saving us all a lot of trouble?"

Maxwell felt the frustration build. Just who exactly did they think they were dealing with? Did they imagine he was as stupid as they were?

"If I don't get what I want," he'd said, slowly and precisely, "I will shoot the hostages, one by one. Do we understand each other?"

*

Sara's eyes were red-rimmed. She'd tried to stay on top of it, but finally she'd broken. She couldn't bear to think of Bobby and what he must be suffering.

Trudie tried to comfort her. "He's going to be fine," she said. "They all are."

Sara knew it could go either way. Of course it was possible they'd walk free without a scratch. On the other hand something terrible could happen. She remembered the jewellery store incident on Rodeo Drive in 1986. For many hours the police had insisted the hostages, trapped in Van Cleef & Arpel, were okay. It turned out one was killed within minutes of being taken captive, and more died later in a hail of gunfire.

With a choked-back sob she realized just how much she loved Bobby Mondella. He had become her life, and it wasn't healthy, because if she were truthful with herself, she had to admit he didn't give a damn about her. Sure, he made love to her, and was nice when he felt like it. But he wasn't *in* love with her, and she might as well face up to it.

If he gets out of this I'm going to leave him, she thought. *He's a success again – the man doesn't need me, he'll be a lot happier without me.*

That decided, she said a silent prayer for his safety.

*

Maxwell held the glass of water to Rafealla's lips.

She sipped it slowly, and asked his name. Somewhere she had read that in a hostage situation it was important to develop a connection with the person holding you prisoner.

"What the fuck has my name got to do with anything?" he said angrily.

"I'd like to be able to call you something," she ventured.

"I know what you can call him," snarled Marcus, unbowed by his captivity. "You can call him a dumb sonofabitch."

This comment incited Maxwell. He turned on Marcus and said threateningly, "Nobody calls Maxwell Sicily dumb."

"There's your answer," Marcus said with a triumphant snort.

"For Christ sake, shut up," Kris hissed, flexing his muscles beneath the loose bindings, and trying to decide if he could grab the psycho now. One lunge and it would be all over.

But what if his bindings didn't break? What if the creep had time to turn his gun on him and blow Kris Phoenix away? There was something very unsettling about a gun being pointed in your direction.

Christ! His mum in England must be going crazy. The newspapers had probably called her already. Poor old Avis. She was never short of a bit of excitement with him for a son. And how about Willow and Bo? Willow would somehow make out it was all his fault. And as for Bo – who knew how the kid would react?

Maybe I've been a lousy father, he thought. *If I get out of this I'll try to be better, spend more time with him.*

If I get out . . .

*

Cybil rested her honey-blonde head on Governor Highland's sympathetic shoulder. "I'm so *tired*," she moaned.

They were sitting in the main house along with Hawkins, Nova and a slew of other-people.

"Maybe you should take a nap," he suggested. "Nova, is there a spare bedroom Cybil can lie down in?"

Nova signalled to her assistant. "Norton, take care of it."

Norton St John escorted Cybil and a concerned Governor Highland upstairs to a spare bedroom.

"Thank you," the Governor said, dismissing Norton with a wave of his hand. "I'll see she settles down."

Cybil sat on the side of the bed, brushing a weary hand through her mane of hair. "This is so awful," she sighed.

"I know," he agreed, sitting down beside her.

"Poor Kris."

"I'm sure he'll be all right."

"I hope so."

"Cybil."

"Yes."

"You're a very lovely young lady."

"Thank you."

Clumsily he began to kiss her. She fell back on the bed, too exhausted to resist. All she could think of was that one day Governor Highland might be President, and wasn't it funny that every man – be it rock star or future President – was exactly the same. Sex crazy. And who was she to object?

*

Impatiently Maxwell picked up the phone. "I've waited long enough," he said with cold intent. "If the helicopter isn't here in fifteen minutes, I'm shooting a hostage."

"Come now, let's think about this. Don't be foolish," the Captain reasoned. "It'll be here."

"Don't fuck with me," Maxwell warned, his voice rising. "You've been giving me shit for over an hour. Either it arrives within fifteen minutes, or I'm taking one of them out. This is no idle threat. Am I getting through to you?"

"Yes," the captain said, humouring him. "I promise you the helicopter is on its way." He wanted to add – *so is your father*, because they had discovered "George Smith's" true identity by lifting his fingerprints off his locker at Lilliane's and running them through the main computer.

Some discovery. Maxwell Sicily. Only son and heir of the infamous Carmine Sicily. And Carmine had been tracked down to a suite at the Beverly Wilshire Hotel, where he was staying on a business trip.

At first Carmine didn't want to know. "My son? I don't have a son." But when the situation was made clear to him, and he found out who was involved, he said, "I'll be there. Don't do anything until I arrive. This can be cleared up in seconds."

Yes, he'd clear it up all right, Carmine decided – he'd put a hit out on his own son, and get him out of his life forever. The boy was no good, never had been. How dare he embarrass him like this with such important and influential people. Carmine was deeply humiliated. What had he done to deserve a son like Maxwell?

*

"You still okay, luv?" Kris moved closer to Rafealla, whispering in her ear. "The berk won't do anything. Trust me." They'd all heard Maxwell's furious threats to shoot one of them, and he wanted to reassure her.

Her voice sounded shaky. "I don't know, Kris. This is like a nightmare, and I keep on expecting to wake up."

"I know, babe. But don't worry, the guy's a loser, he's all talk an' no balls – you can see it just by looking at him."

Trying to sound brave she murmured, "I hope you're right,

for all our sakes." Reaching over, she touched Bobby's shoulder.

"Hey-Bobby, I'd give you a runnin' commentary," Kris said in a low voice, "but it's boring. We'll be out of here soon."

Bobby grunted.

Maxwell was pacing up and down the room agitatedly, trying to decide what to do next. Everything had been going so smoothly until that cow from the restaurant had gotten in his way. He wished he had her in here with him now. Oh, yes. He'd show her a thing or two. He'd jam his gun in her mouth and blow her head off.

Surprising everyone, Marcus spoke up in a harsh, loud voice, his lingering accent guttural with intensity. "Why don't you shoot the nigger," he urged. "Shoot the coon and throw him out of here. Then perhaps we can get this charade over and done with."

"You motherfucking *son of a bitch*," Bobby said, reacting immediately, and rolling toward the sound of Marcus's voice.

"Oh, Christ!" groaned Kris, sensing trouble.

"You're filth, Marcus," Rafaella cried out. "You are the lowest slime."

"And what do you think *you* are?" Marcus snarled in return. "You're one of them too. I should have had you thrown over that balcony in Rio along with your friend, you black cunt."

The truth at last. Enraged beyond belief, Bobby kicked out toward the sound of Marcus' voice – feeling the thud of his heel connect with something hard.

He caught Marcus on the side of his jaw. And with a snort of agony, Marcus retaliated by lifting his hands, still bound together, and smashing them down like a lethal club on Bobby's head, rendering him unconscious. Meanwhile Kris was struggling to free himself.

Watching this scene, Maxwell felt like he was losing control. He raised the hand-gun threateningly, and fired a warning shot in the air.

Kris lunged toward him, tripping on the ties that bound his ankles together.

Caught off balance, Maxwell fired wildly, hitting Marcus in the stomach with a stray bullet.

"Oh my *God!*" screamed Rafealla, watching in horror as blood pumped forth from a gaping hole.

"Help me," moaned Marcus, clutching his stomach in vain. He looked toward Rafealla, then desperately his eyes. sought out Kris. "I beg you . . . help me . . . stop the blood. I'll give you anything." His voice began to fade. "All . . . the . . . money . . . you . . . could . . . ever want. Anything . . ."

At that moment the sound of the helicopter hovering above arrested their attention.

With icy calm, Maxwell said, "We're leaving now. And I don't expect any more trouble."

*

The noise of the helicopter drowned out the sound of gunfire. Captain Lynch had no idea what had taken place when he next spoke to Maxwell.

"It's time to evacuate," he said. "The helicopter is here."

"Get everyone away from the house," Maxwell instructed. "Just leave one television camera in place. Is that understood?"

"Yes," Captain Lynch replied.

"Do it!" Maxwell insisted. "I'm watching you."

And your daddy is watching you, you little bastard. He's right here ready to surprise the ass off you. "It'll be done."

"We're coming out in five minutes," Maxwell warned. "And if anything goes wrong – anything at all – I'll shoot them all. Do you understand?"

"You're making yourself very clear."

"Good."

Maxwell turned to confront his hostages, a sorry-looking bunch. Amazing how you could cut the mighty down to size. Walking over to Rafealla he untied her and said, "Go upstairs and bring down a blanket."

There was blood everywhere Marcus was slumped on the floor, ominously silent. "I think he's dead," she whispered, staring at Marcus in shock.

"So what?" Maxwell said callously. "The same thing can

happen to you if you don't follow my instructions. Go upstairs *now*, get a blanket, and come right down. If you don't — *he* gets it next." He waved his gun at Kris.

"Big fuckin' man with a gun pointed at my head, ain'tcha?" Kris jeered. "I'd like t'see what'd happen if it was just the two of us."

Maxwell ignored him. He wasn't about to be drawn into a confrontation. Kris Phoenix was nothing. They were all nothing. And if he killed one of them, he might as well do away with them all. It didn't make any difference.

But not now, not until they'd finished being useful. At this moment they were his only protection.

*

Captain Lynch had his sharp-shooters in place. He also had Carmine Sicily standing in the shadows behind him. The helicopter waited in the middle of the vast lawn at the front of the house. At the controls was a trained member of the SWAT unit.

The press had been cleared, moved far back on the estate, all except one television camera crew.

Nova Citroen hovered in the background with Hawkins by her side. She'd changed into a warm brown jumpsuit, boots, and a loose mink coat. She was surprisingly calm.

The Hawk said, "When they come out, the captain is going to tell this Maxwell character to drop his weapon and surrender."

"What makes the captain think he'll comply?"

"Because at that stage of the game he'll be vulnerable, out in the open. And then his father will step forward and reason with him."

"He can still shoot his hostages."

"No," the Hawk said sharply. "They'll have him under such strict surveillance that if his hand even tightens near the trigger, they'll take him out. One bullet through the head."

"It's dark."

"They have special equipment."

She wondered how Marcus was taking his captivity. Not well. If the police didn't kill his captor, he would certainly see it was taken care of. Marcus Citroen insisted on being in control at all times.

*

"This is how we're going to do it," Maxwell said. "Listen carefully, because any mistakes can mean the end of your life." Contemptuously he kicked Marcus, rolling him on his side, until the dead man came to rest in a pool of his own blood. "Like him."

Lying on the floor, still bound, Bobby heard the words as he drifted back into consciousness. Opening his eyes he saw a blurry haze. Gradually the haze sharpened, and came into focus.

He blinked once, twice, hardly believing what was happening. He could see! Goddammit, HE COULD SEE!

The doctors had said it could happen, just like that, anytime, anywhere. A conversion reaction could take place, they'd said, brought on by a traumatic situation. Jesus Christ! He could see, and he couldn't tell anyone because he was well aware of the danger they were all in.

"We'll walk outside under the blanket," Maxwell said. "You'll be in front, and I'll be behind with a gun in your backs. The police won't know who is where. Do you get it?"

"Very smart," Kris jeered.

"Yes, very smart," Maxwell agreed. "Because they'll have marksmen out there ready to pick me off, and this way they can't take the risk of making a mistake."

Slowly Bobby looked around, taking in the scene. On the floor, nearby, were his dark glasses. Surreptitiously he groped for them with his hands still tied. He got them on without anyone noticing.

"I'm going to untie your feet," Maxwell announced. "I'm sure I don't have to keep on repeating that what happened to Marcus Citroen can happen to any one of you."

Bobby groaned, to let them know he was conscious.

"Are you all right?" Rafealla asked anxiously.

If she only knew! "Yeah," he muttered. "I'm fine."

"Good," said Maxwell sarcastically. "It's nice to know everyone is well."

*

"Here they come," said Captain Lynch, with a grunt of anticipation as slowly the front door swung open. "Carmine, get ready."

Carmine Sicily stepped up next to the police captain. He was ready all right.

Nova Citroen shuddered. She had an ominous feeling of doom.

The Hawk put his arm around her, patting her mink-clad shoulder comfortingly. "It'll soon be over," he said. "Don't worry."

"Jesus Christ!" exclaimed Captain Lynch, as the blanketed group of figures shuffled from the house "*Shit!*"

"What's the matter?" asked Carmine.

"They're under a fucking blanket. We can't see who's who." Grabbing his walkie-talkie he barked out a command. "No firing. Hold all gunfire."

*

Under the blanket it was hot and uncomfortable. Rafealla was positioned in front of Maxwell, his gun jammed into the small of her back. Every step she took, she feared it might go off by mistake.

Kris was next to her. Maxwell had tied them together around the waist, making it difficult to walk. Bobby brought up the rear, tethered loosely to Maxwell.

"Any bullets an' you're the ones that get it, my friends," Maxwell boasted. "One false move from any of you, and I'll blow her in half – so don't even think about it."

Slowly they trundled towards the helicopter, every step an ordeal.

The night was silent, except for the sounds of nature. Waves crashing on the beach far below, crickets chirping, and the sway of the palm trees in the night breeze. There was a bright moon in the sky.

"Maxwell." Suddenly a voice boomed through the bullhorn, breaking the silence. "This is your father, Carmine. I want you to quit what you're doing *now*. Release your hostages, an' give yourself up. That's an order."

Maxwell stopped stock-still, frozen in shock. What the fuck was Carmine doing here? What the fuck was that cocksucker interfering for? Wasn't it enough that he'd had to grow up in his shadow, always Carmine Sicily's son, Carmine Sicily's boy. He hated his father with a passion. "What are you doing here?" he screamed hysterically.

Instinctively both Kris and Bobby knew this was their moment, and as if operating on thought telepathy they acted as one. Kris knocked the gun from Maxwell's hand with a vicious turn of his body, while Bobby kneed him in the back with every bit of force he could muster.

Maxwell fell to the ground, dragging all of them down with him.

"Get the lights on." Captain Lynch yelled the order, as he raced toward the scene, accompanied by several of his officers, guns drawn.

Floodlights lit up the area.

It was over.

It was all over.

Epilogue

At Marcus Citroen's funeral there was a bizarre combination of rock and rollers, high society, the movers and shakers of show business, and the powerful world of real money.

They came from all over to pay their respects, the most popular mode of transport being private plane.

The line of limousines at the burial ground was impressive, and later, at Novaroen, a party atmosphere prevailed.

Nova went through the motions. She made an impressive grieving widow.

Hawkins Lamont – the Hawk – delivered the eulogy. He was going to miss his friend and mentor.

Marcus had remembered him in his will. The Hawk inherited Marcus's prized collection of antique cars, two solid gold Cartier watches, and an assortment of Tiffany cuff-links. The Hawk appreciated the gesture, but above all else he was a deal-maker, and owning a collection of old cars did not appeal to him. He sold them, and with the proceeds bought himself a white Ferrari, a black Maserati, and a weekend apartment in London.

Three months after the funeral he divorced his wife. A few weeks after that he and Nova Citroen were married in a secret ceremony in Mexico City.

They returned to New York triumphant, the latest "power"

couple. Together they ran Blue-Cadillac Records, expanding into televison and movies.

Nova Citroen maintained her reputation as one of the most elegant hostesses in America. And the Hawk continued to guide the careers of the cream of the superstars.

Together they made a formidable combination.

*

By the time Speed fixed the flat tyre on the hired limousine, and got himself and the car up to the Novaroen estate on that fateful July night, he was too late. The hostage situation was in progress, and everyone was going crazy.

He'd grabbed hold of a parking attendant, demanding hoarsely, "What's going on?"

"There's a guy up there gone wacko. He's grabbin' people, tying' 'em up an' demandin' money."

"Who is he?"

"Some waiter from that fancy restaurant. George somethin' or other."

"George Smith?"

"Yeah, that's the dude's name."

Speed had gotten out of there fast. Gunning the limousine, he'd raced back to Hollywood, cleared out of his apartment, dumped the limo outside the rental place, and taken the next plane to Vegas. There, he'd thrown himself upon his ex-wife's mercy, begging her to alibi him, lest George Smith pointed the cops in his direction.

She'd obliged. Reluctantly. It had cost him.

He stayed with her for three months. They'd fought every day, but he'd been forced to admit she had the best pair of bazoombas in captivity. Unfortunately she also had a lethal dose of the clap – contracted from a lounge singer with bad teeth and no talent. Naturally, Speed, with his luck, picked it up too.

He left in a fury, drifting back to Hollywood and his old haunts.

One night he met a man in a bar. There was a big job going down and this dude had heard he was the best freakin' driver on the West Coast . . .

*

Chloe remained at Lilliane's, quite the restaurant celebrity. If it wasn't for Chloe and her diligent eye, Maxwell Sicily might have got away with the robbery of the year. She revelled in the attention.

It never crossed her mind that if she hadn't interfered, Marcus Citroen would be alive today.

*

Cybil Wilde and Kris Phoenix broke up, whereupon Cybil embarked on what was supposed to be a top-secret, extremely discreet affair with Governor Highland.

One late summer weekend they played together on a mutual friend's yacht in Acapulco – where, unbeknownst to them, they were photographed by a lone paparazzi operating with a powerful long-distance lens.

The resultant pictures made headline news, damaging Governor Highland's spotless reputation beyond redemption, and catapulting Cybil into a starring role in her first movie.

*

Vicki Foxe made the best of a bad job. She fled Novaroen during the height of the hostage situation, hitching a ride into town with one of the party guests – an old and shaky lawyer, who believed every word of her hastily made up story about a fight with Mrs Ivors, the dragon-lady housekeeper.

"Do you need a job, my dear?" he'd asked.

"Yes," Vicki had nodded.

She'd stayed long enough to share her sexual favours, and steal his precious and valuable stamp collection, which she sold for three thousand dollars to a pawnshop. It was worth over a hundred thousand.

Then she ticketed herself to Amarillo, Texas, where she set herself up in an apartment doling out submission and discipline.

Business was good.

*

Maxwell Sicily did not fare so well. In prison, awaiting trial for the murder of Marcus Citroen, he mysteriously passed away in his sleep one night. There was no official investigation.

The tentacles of Carmine Sicily's power stretched far and wide.

*

Sara Johnston and Bobby Mondella planned a quiet wedding ceremony in her home town of Philadelphia. Both of them couldn't be happier.

It had taken him some time to win her over, but he'd done it. After the night at Novaroen so much had happened. Firstly, the shock of recovering his sight had sent Bobby into a tailspin. At first he hadn't known how to handle it, everything seemed so strange.

Seeing Sara – a woman he had virtually shared his life with for the last eighteen months – was the biggest shock of all. He'd imagined her to be darker, shorter, plumper, plainer. Instead she was dazzlingly pretty – reminding him in a way of a young Sharleen.

Before he had a chance to tell her how much she meant to him, she took off, leaving him a short note on which she had written, *You don't need me anymore, so I'll say goodbye. It was great, Bobby, and I'll always love you. But now you've got your life back. Enjoy it. Sara.*

It took him two months to find her, and when he did, he told her in no uncertain terms, they would never be apart again.

She acquiesced. After all, she loved him, it was as simple as that.

*

Kris Phoenix and Rafealla went their separate ways.

After breaking up with Cybil, Kris returned to England and told Astrid it was over. They'd been together four years, which was long enough. He bought her a house in the country and allowed her to keep the dogs. They parted friends.

Then he sought out Buzz – still off drugs and well on the way to recovery, and suggested they did something together, just the two of them.

"Yeah, I'd like that," Buzz said.

"Yeah, I rather thought you would," Kris replied, adding with a wink, "Ya always fancied workin' with a superstar, didn't you?"

"You're *still* full of it, you old wanker," Buzz replied, with a wicked grin.

"Yeah, an' you wouldn't have it any other way. Right?"

"Right, mate."

The years disappeared as they broke up laughing and spontaneously hugged each other.

*

Rafealla returned to England, collected Jon Jon from her mother's, and the two of them settled down in the small house she'd bought near Regent's Park.

It was good to be back in England after all the years she'd spent abroad. And it was certainly nice to be an established recording artist without the threat of Marcus Citroen hanging over her head. Of course she regretted his death, it was a terrible thing to have happened, but life went on.

*

Kris Phoenix and Rafealla made the trip to Philadelphia for Bobby Mondella's wedding. They arrived separately, neither aware of the other's presence.

Rocket Fabrizzi was best man, and although Bobby and Sara had tried to keep the wedding quiet, there was a huge turnout of fans and press.

Rafealla hadn't seen Kris Phoenix since their shared ordeal. She glanced across the aisle, and there he was, cocky as ever, with that ridiculous spiked hair and those intense blue eyes — Jon Jon's eyes.

Tentatively she waved.

He waved back.

She smiled.

He smiled back.

Oh God! Not again. For the third time in her life she felt that old familiar tingle of anticipation.

She'd struck out twice, that didn't mean she had to stop playing, did it?

Kris was on his feet, heading in her direction. Soon he was beside her.

"Anyone sittin' here?" he asked, indicating the half-empty pew.

"No."

"Mind if I join you?"

"I think I'd like that."

They watched Bobby hurry down the aisle, Rocket beside him.

"He looks nervous," Kris remarked jauntily. "Poor sod."

"He probably is."

"Yeah, well, it's a big step."

"It certainly is."

"Have *you* ever taken it?"

"Once."

"Me too. I'm divorced now."

"So am I."

Music began to play, indicating the arrival of the bride.

Sara wore white, and a big smile.

Bobby turned to look at her as she walked down the aisle. He thought she was the prettiest girl he'd ever seen.

"Romantic, huh?" whispered Kris.

Rafealla nodded. She was frightened to look him in the eye, because once she fell into those two intense pools of blue she might be lost forever.

Maybe she should risk it. What was that old superstition? Third time lucky, or something like that.

"Hey, Raf." He leaned towards her, speaking in a low, intimate voice.

"Yes."

"There's something I've bin meaning' to tell you."

"Yes?" she repeated.

Their eyes met, and it was memorable.

"Uh . . . I just want you to know this."

"What?"

"Did I ever mention that after I met you I gave up blondes forever?"

Gazing at him solemnly she said, "No. You never told me that."

He winked. "It's true." And with perfect timing he took her hand in his, squeezing it gently. "C'mon, we'd better watch a wedding, see how it's done. It might come in useful one of these days." A cheeky grin. "Right?"

She grinned back. Kris Phoenix was an adventure waiting to be experienced, and this time she was old enough to enjoy it. "Right," she agreed.

"After all—" he began.

Catching his rhythm she joined in, and together they completed his favourite expression — "It's only rock 'n' roll!"

A special interview
with Jackie Collins

Why does Hollywood still fascinate us?

Because Hollywood is a magic name – a name that conjures up glamour, great romance, mystery, the movies and scandal. All the subjects I cover in *Hollywood Wives*, *Hollywood Husbands* and *Rock Star!*

What is it like to live in Hollywood?

Living in Hollywood is a double-edged sword. I love it! I can either play the game and go to all the big, glitzy parties filled with superstars, studs, movers and shakers. Or I can just stay home and write about them. Believe me, in my books you are getting the *real* truth, not the front page of some supermarket rag.

Where do you do your best observing of the Hollywood scene?

I have many places I like to go to observe the Hollywood scene. Everywhere from the ritziest and most "in" restaurant, to a wonderful little hideaway coffee shop in Hollywood where I once came across a major superstar with somebody else's wife!

What's different about today's Hollywood parties compared to those of, say, five years ago?

I think Hollywood parties are certainly calmer today, because of the fear of disease. Sexually, things have slowed down, and a lot more marriages are taking place. But the parties are still extravagant and exciting. Recently I attended a wild party in Malibu where I recognized every single guest as being a character straight out of *Hollywood Husbands*.

Do Hollywood acquaintances still confide in you, even though they know you write such "inside" novels?

Since I wrote my first book, *The World is full of Married Men* in 1968, people have been confiding in me. I'm like a free psychiatrist. Sit down with Jackie and tell her everything! My books reflect the truth about relationships — especially in Hollywood. And yes, the Hollywood husbands couldn't *wait* to spill the beans. And I loved writing about them — secrets and all!

What is it like to go on an author tour?

Author tours are fun, because I get to meet the general public who read my books, and they are so nice and supportive — in fact, they almost know my characters better than I do!

Lucky Santangelo from my book *Lucky* is a big favourite with women. A lot of them would like to emulate her crazy life-style — not to mention meet the men in her life! Men like her too. And they love Montana Grey from *Hollywood Wives* and Jade Johnson from *Hollywood Husbands*. I enjoy writing strong, beautiful, sexy females. I also enjoy writing incredibly attractive male characters with a terrific sense of humour.

On an author tour I am constantly asked about Gino Santangelo from *Chances* and *Lucky* — I follow his life from the age of 13 to when he is 72! And believe me, at 72 he is still going strong, and quite irresistible to women. Right now NBC is preparing a television mini-series of *Chances* and *Lucky*. Now I'm continuing the saga of the Santangelo family in a third novel about them entitled *Lady Boss*.

Who are your favourite male characters in your books?

Well , I have to say I really love Buddy Hudson from *Hollywood Wives*. He starts out as a hustler and ends up as a Hollywood Prince! I think Buddy has a lot going for him. Apart from being great looking and street-smart, he has a vulnerable streak that really appeals to women. I know – because I receive a lot of letters from women asking where they can meet him!

Lenny Golden in *Lucky* is another of my favourites. He's smart, funny, a true man of the eighties.

And for old-fashioned glamour and charm, try Nico Constantine in *The Bitch*. A fascinating gigolo.

And Charlie Brick in *Sinners* is another charmer. He's an English movie star with plenty of women and an ache to find the right one.

Some of my favourite male characters are in *Hollywood Husbands*. Jack Python, the talk-show host. I think Jack has it all – style, money, power and intelligence. And Wes Money, the barman with a heart of gold and an amiable, very very sexy disposition. What more can any woman ask?

Can you tell us about Rock Star?

Rock Star is about three famous singers and their climb to the top.

First there is Kris Phoenix, a raunchy, wild English rock star with spiky hair and a crooked grin. Kris has a preference for gorgeous blondes and plenty of trouble.

Then there is Bobby Mondella, a black superstar soul singer who becomes involved with the mob.

And finally, Rafealla, a girl with mixed blood, plenty of money and outrageous style.

Rafealla comes between Kris and Bobby with a vengeance, and so the story starts, leading to a startling and shattering conclusion.

I must say I find the world of music just as fascinating as Hollywood. It has all the elements – glamour, sex, great power and huge fortunes. It's not just about sex, drugs and rock 'n' roll – it is also a world full of hopes and dreams, drop-dead ambition and ruthless power.

I hope, when you read *Rock Star*, you will learn a lot more than you thought you already knew. *Rock Star* exposes the music business the way *Hollywood Wives* exposed Hollywood.

I write because I love telling stories, and I enjoy revealing the *real* truth behind the headlines.

So . . . Happy Reading!

Jackie Collins

Jackie Collins
The World is full of Married Men £5.99

*Only fools let a little thing like marriage get in the way of their careers
. . . especially someone else's . . .*

David Cooper cheats on his wife. She doesn't – and that suits him
fine. Until Claudia appears and David wants out of his marriage.

But Claudia has different ideas – different dreams: to be a model, an
actress, a star. And she'll do anything to make it. Just name a price . . .

The World is full of Married Men is a devastating exposure of the cut
throat media business – the phoney promises and the very real power
of the casting couch.

'You'll enjoy every shocking page' EVENING STANDARD

The World is full of Divorced Women £6.99

*One rule for men, another for their wives – is it any wonder that the
world is full of divorced women?*

In New York, Cleo James finds her husband in bed with her best
friend . . . and knows it's time to move on. In London, Muffin, the
hottest model in town, finds her man wants more than even she is
prepared to give . . .

On the surface, they have everything. But theirs is a world in which
love counts for nothing and sex is the only weapon.

Fidelity is strictly a no-go area – when *The World is full of Divorced
Women* . . .

'A high-voltage novel of the glittering superstar scene by Jackie
Collins who knows it best' BOOKSELLERS

The Stud £5.99

At a private club like Hobo, *there's no such thing as an impossible fantasy . . .*

Come to the nightspot where the beautiful people hang out, and meet

Tony Blake – your host and guide – and anything you want him to be . . .

Fontaine Khaled – jet-setting beauty – her face is her fortune and men are her weakness;

Alexandra – her nubile step-daughter, determined to sample everything the big city has to offer.

Like no book before or since, *The Stud* gets to grips with the debauched and decadent life-styles of society's high flyers. You won't believe your eyes . . .

'Sexual athletics among the in-crowd' THE SUNDAY TIMES

The Bitch £5.99

She's a woman who's never short of a man. And they call her the bitch . . .

Fontaine Khaled has an Arab millionaire among her yesterdays and hard-gambling Nico for all her tomorrows. Which only leaves the problem of choosing a man for today . . .

From London to Las Vegas, Hollywood to Athens – she calls the shots from her plush limos and black satin sheets. She is The Bitch and she is in control. And that could never change – could it?

The Bitch is the sizzling sequel to *The Stud*.

'Casinos, swimming pools, orgies, race horses, gangsters, sex-in-the-shower – it's all there!' THE OBSERVER

Chances £6.99

From the casinos of Las Vegas to the streets of New York, chances was the name of the game . . . and everybody took them.

Gino Santangelo – a boy from the New York slums carves himself a crime empire that takes him all the way to the top.

His daughter, Lucky, proves herself to be as deadly as her father. Sensual and provocative, she is too much like him not to make a bid for his empire . . .

Chances spins through six decades like a giant roulette wheel, where the high stakes are on big money, dangerous sex and irresistible power.

'Ferociously entertaining . . . an outrageously uninhibited saga of sex and ambition' SUNDAY EXPRESS

Lucky £6.99

Like father, like daughter, winning runs in the family . . .

Daughter of one of the world's richest and most powerful men, wildly beautiful Lucky Santangelo is set on continuing the family tradition . . .

Sex and the rich fruits of crime are her aphrodisiacs. Power is the ultimate thrill – power over the Santangelo empire, power over the men of her choice.

Moving in the fast lane from Las Vegas to New York, Beverly Hills to a Greek island paradise, *Lucky* takes up where *Chances* left off. Winning is all that matters – and luck has nothing to do with it . . .

'If you take *Lucky* to the beach for sun bathing company, you may still be lying there reading when the moon comes up' COSMOPOLITAN

Lady Boss £6.99

She's ruthless, wild and dangerous.

She's beaautiful, smart, and powerful.

She's Lucky Santangelo and she's back!

Brn into a top crime family in *Chances*.

Married three times in *Lucky*.

Now – in *Lady Boss* Lucky Santangelo takes on Hollywood, and there's no stopping her. What Lucky Santangelo wants she gets.

She's The Lady Boss. And *Lady Boss* is the ultimate Hollywood power trip.

Sinners £6.99

In the hard-hitting world of Hollywood, sinning and winning are one and the same . . .

Sunday Simmons and Charlie Brick came to Hollywood to make a movie. They live off their looks and rely on their agents. Today they're stars, so why worry about tomorrow?

They've got money, success and adoring fans. Fans like Herbert Lincoln Jefferson, a Hollywood chauffeur with perverse sexual fantasies – whose biggest dream is meeting Sunday Simmons . . .

Sinners peels away the glittering façade of Tinseltown like never before.

'Scandalously sexy . . . a racy tale of two celebrities in Hollywood's celluloid-and-sex race' NEWS OF THE WORLD

Hollywood Wives £6.99

*Loving, spending, succeeding – no one does it better than the
Hollywood wives . . .*

They're a privileged breed – glamorous, beautiful and very, very
tough. When life is this fast, there are no guarantees. Status is
everything – and that's only as high as the box office of your
husband's last movie . . .

Elaine Conti – wife of a fading star, who'll do anything to put his
    career back into orbit;

Angel Hudson – a breathtakingly beautiful starlet with a wildly
    ambitious stud for a husband;

Montana Grey – gorgeous renegade, she'll stop at nothing to make it
    in the male-dominated world on the other side of the camera.

Hollywood Wives is a scorching blockbuster that exposes the glittering
world of Beverly Hills as never before – and races to a
chilling and unexpected climax . . .

'Miss Collins at her raunchy best' NEW YORK TIMES

Hollywood Husbands £6.99

They're sexy, successful and shameless. But the past has a habit of catching up with everybody – even Hollywood husbands . . .

In a small American town, a young girl is beaten by her husband, raped by his friends and left for dead. Years later, the Hollywood Husbands may be the ones to feel the heat of her burning revenge.

Mannon Cable – macho superstar;

Howard Soloman – star maker, star breaker;

Jack Python – the hottest talk-show host in town.

The Hollywood husbands have everything – until one woman draws them into a terrifying game where the only prize is survival . . .

Hollywood Husbands is the follow-up to the six-million selling *Hollywood Wives*. Be warned – the heat is on once again!

'Her characters are as racy as Ferraris. Her plots fast-moving as Porsches . . . *Hollywood Husbands* is like a box of chocolates. You feel a bit guilty but, God, you enjoy it'
JEAN ROOK, DAILY EXPRESS

The Love Killers £5.99

Powerful men, beautiful women and exquisite revenge . . .

Beth, Lara and Rio – three exotic women with a common cause and vengeance in their hearts.

They're out to avenge a murder and they'll go to any lengths. Their targets: the heirs of the Bassalino crime family. Their weapon: sex. The result: a bloodbath of sexual mayhem through the lethal corridors of organised crime.

Three beautiful women set out to prove that when it comes to revenge, the female is far deadlier than the male – especially when they're *Love Killers* . . .

'Sensational, bitter, completely compulsive' SHE

Lovers and Gamblers £6.99

When success takes a hold of your life, it can be tough keeping a grip on your sanity . . .

From London to New York, Hollywood to Rio, meet the lovers who gambled with the highest stakes imaginable.

Al King – soul superstar and legendary stud;

Dallas – a smouldering beauty with big ambitions and a secret past.

Theirs is a story that will shock you. For *Lovers and Gamblers* everywhere . . .

'Erotic . . . glitter and glamour . . . a beauty queen and a rock superstar . . . Riots, bomb scares, orgies and drug trips . . . High powered fiction . . . a real blockbuster' THE STANDARD

involved with Cybil. And vice versa. Kris had a natural-born aversion to marriage. The very word sent cold chills up his spine. To him being married equalled being trapped. He had sampled it once, and had no intention of getting caught a second time.

Dressed in jeans and a casual shirt he peered into the bedroom. Cybil was gone, only her perfume lingered. *Eau de Horny Blonde*, he thought with a ribald laugh.

Downstairs his live-in Scottish couple busied themselves with domestic tasks, jumping to attention when they saw him.

"Welcome back, Mr Phoenix," said the plump and motherly Mable. "Why don't I make you a nice cup of tea?"

Nodding, he wandered outside to inspect his property. Immediately his two golden labradors came bounding over to greet him. Bending down he petted them for a good ten minutes.

His Bel Air mansion stood on two acres of impeccably kept grounds. Flowing lawns, sumptuous flower beds, lemon and orange trees, brilliant bougainvillaea, and the obligatory Hollywood swimming pool and tennis court. Not bad for an English lad who was chucked out of school at fifteen without two pennies to rub together.

Several Mexican gardeners toiled diligently. He gave them a cheery wave. Being back in Los Angeles was a kick. The weather appealed to him. Having grown up in England with constant rain and fog, he appreciated warmth and sunshine. Besides, he enjoyed cultivating a healthy tan.

Cybil came running out of the house in a minuscule bikini. The gardeners stopped work and stared. The dogs barked. Flashing Kris a winning smile she dived gracefully into the pool.

Was there no end to her desire to turn him on? Tomorrow she would pay for her teasing, oh how she would pay!

"Coming?" she called innocently, surfacing with a lethal crawl.

"Naw. I'm gonna work out."

He made his way into the luxurious pool house where there was a fully equipped gym. He'd been working with a body trainer and weights for almost two years and the difference was amazing. Whereas before he'd been wiry and naturally athletic, never a slouch when it came to moving around on stage, now he was in incredible shape – fitter than he'd ever been. Thirty-eight was the age when some rock stars began to think about winding down – not Kris – he had a new energy – a steely strength. Whatever he was doing it worked for him – plus he was performing better than ever.

Twenty minutes of punishment and he was ready for a swim. The pool was empty. Cybil had moved on to other activities.

Churning up and down for thirty lengths he emerged fit and refreshed.

Waiting poolside was his manager, Hawkins Lamont – an American usually known as the Hawk.

The Hawk was fashionably dressed in white duck pants, a white polo shirt, white loafers and a pale beige crocodile Gucci belt. A tall man in his forties with a George Hamilton tan, the Hawk radiated an air of supreme confidence. And so he should, he was one of the most successful and sought-after managers in the business, with a stable of first-class talent. Kris had been with him for three years, ever since leaving his former manager – the notorious Doktor Head.

"You seem to be in excellent shape," the Hawk said, settling himself at a patio table under a yellow striped umbrella.

Kris nodded. "I feel great – I mean we're talkin' *really* great."

And he meant it, only too aware of the fact that he couldn't have made that claim a few years ago.

The Hawk smiled. A Hollywood smile made entirely of porcelain. "I just came over to convey a personal message. Marcus Citroen is delighted you've agreed to appear at his wife's function tonight."

Wrapping a towel around his waist Kris sat down. "I didn't have much choice, did I?" he said dryly.

"You made the *right* choice," the Hawk replied pointedly. "Tonight is special. Marcus wanted the three hottest recording stars in the business, and he got them. I wouldn't have been pleased to see your place taken by Springsteen, would *you*?"

Kris stared at Mabel walking across the lawn bearing a tray with tea and toast for him, and a lead crystal glass of Perrier decorated with a slice of lime for his guest. "As long as I'm in an' out," he said dourly.

"We agreed on that. You're appearing last, *after* Bobby Mondella and Rafealla. That was one of my conditions to Marcus, the star spot or nothing."

"Sure," Kris said listlessly. He hated the whole deal.

"Is Cybil coming with you?" the Hawk asked smoothly.

"I dunno. Haven't asked her."

"It's going to be quite an evening."

"Yeah, but I'm not stayin', am I?"

"You might change your mind."

"Naw."

The Hawk took one sip of Perrier and rose. "I'll check with you later. The limo will be here at three-thirty. I'd like to plan on leaving at the latest by four."

After the Hawk had departed, Cybil reappeared. Luckily she had dressed, although her ensemble left little to the imagination. A skimpy tank-top under which she very obviously wore no bra. Crotch-hugging shorts, and white ankle socks worn with nifty Reeboks. She looked like an over-developed cheerleader.

"Where are *you* off to?" he asked.

"Didn't I tell you?" she said, wide-eyed. "I've got a shoot with a *vereee* randy photographer. He'll probably want to ravish my girlish body – what shall I do?"

"Make 'im wear a condom!"

She frowned. "Kris! That's not funny. You wouldn't like it if I *did* sleep with him, would you?"

"I'll tell you something, luv. You wouldn't be around to tell the tale."

"No?" she said challengingly.

"Nope. You'd be out, kiddo. Bags packed an' on the door-step."

Cybil was unamused. Suddenly she was all grown up. "You're such a chauvinist. I suppose you think I don't know about that Danish hooker you keep in London."

There it was, out in the open. It was the first time in the months they'd been living together she'd ever dared to mention Astrid.

"Listen carefully," he said calmly. "I never pretended I was perfect. The only thing is — I *do* expect you to be."

"You're an asshole!" she blurted out. "All my friends keep on telling me what a two-timing rat you are. Why *should* I put up with it?"

"Nobody's tying you to the bedpost, are they?"

"I hate you, Kris Phoenix. One of these days I won't be around when you get back, then you'll *really* be sorry."

She flounced off.

He sighed deeply. It wasn't going to be a good day.

*

Maxwell Sicily — alias George Smith — piled into the first of the special buses hired to transport the waiters and entire catering staff of Lilliane's to the rambling Novaroen estate in preparation for the most exclusive party of the year. The chefs, waiters, and busboys talked excitedly among themselves. This was one event nobody wanted to miss. The press had been headlining it for weeks, it was the hottest ticket around. Fifty couples at one hundred thousand dollars per couple was some shot.

Maxwell settled back in a window seat, staring out as the convoy of buses set off along Sunset — a winding, twisting route which would take them all the way to the Pacific Coast Highway, where there would be a further twenty-five-minute drive along the scenic coastal road.

Humming softly to himself he tried to blank out the conversations going on all around. Snatches reached him anyway, mostly about money, because everyone was anxious to get a load of the people who could afford to pay such an unbelievable price for one evening's entertainment.

"I wanna see Rafealla sing," said a young busboy to nobody in particular. "She's the greatest."

"Nah. Give me Whitney Houston any day," argued an assistant chef. "Now there's a *real* sexy broad."

"So what? They all fuck," sniffed a skinny waiter with eyeglasses and a permanent sneer.

Yes, Maxwell thought, it's true. They all fuck, and they all lie, and they all spend your money and run out on you.